ULYSSES Abridged

~ A Shorter Journey through
James Joyce's Masterpiece ~

Chapbook Press

Schuler Books
2660 28th Street SE
Grand Rapids, MI 49512
(616) 942-7330
www.schulerbooks.com

Ulysses Abridged - A Shorter Journey through James Joyce's Masterpiece

ISBN 13: 9781957169248

Library of Congress Control Number: 2022918394

Printed in the United States by Chapbook Press.

ULYSSES Abridged
~ A Shorter Journey through James Joyce's Masterpiece ~
The original Joyce ULYSSES redacted by Michael James Fallon, 2022

*

redaction, *n.* **1** the preparation of another person's writings for publication; redacting; revising; editing. **2** a redacted form or version of a work; edition

----

ULYSSES by James Joyce was excerpted in The Little Review in 1918-20, at which time publication of the book was banned, the work excoriated by authorities for being prurient and obscene. The writings were first copyrighted in 1914; the novel published in book form in 1922 by Sylvia Beach, proprietor of the Paris bookstore Shakespeare and Company. **The Paris Bookseller** tells the story of Ms. Beach, her association with Joyce, and how – through her legendary bookstore – she became the first person to publish James Joyce's ULYSSES in its entirety in 1922.

ULYSSES, Copyright, 1934, by The Modern Library, Inc.. *Random House* is the publisher of *The Modern Library.* Works by James Joyce published before 1923 are in the public domain. Joyce's ULYSSES, atop a list of this century's greatest English-language novels, is a public domain work that can be published in the United States.

ULYSSES was published in 1934 upon "The Monumental Decision of the United States District Court Rendered December 6, 1933, by Hon. John M. Woolsey Lifting the Ban on ULYSSES: "The new deal in the Law of Letters is here. Judge Woolsey has exonerated *Ulysses* of the charge of obscenity, handing down an opinion that bids fair to become a major event in the history of the struggle for free expression. Joyce's masterpiece, for the circulation of which people have been branded criminals in the past, may now freely enter this country."
-- Morris L. Ernst, *New York, 1933*

Text formatted and cover design by Ron Nicholas
Book advisement by Gary Eberle
Published by Michael Fallon and Schuler Books/ Chapbook Press
Publishing coordination by Pierre Camy, Schuler Books

MICHAEL JAMES FALLON was born in Toledo, Ohio. He attended St. John's Jesuit High School; received his BA from the University of Notre Dame; Teaching and Administrative Credentials from San Jose State University; his MA from the University of San Francisco. Michael and family reside in Santa Clara, California. He is a Lecturer Emeritus from San Jose State University, College of Sociology and Interdisciplinary Social Sciences.

Michael is author of *The Definitive St. Patrick's Day Festivity* (1998) and co-author of *Kevin Moore's Hail Mary Pass* (2015). Michael is co-author with Martin Tolich, Otago University, New Zealand, of "The virtue of teaching public sociology in the neoliberal university" (2022) in which he cites Mary Robinson, former President of Ireland.

Michael values living in the San Francisco Bay Area which is a hub of Celtic activities, featuring the United Irish Cultural Center, the Irish Literary and Historical Society, The Irish Herald newspaper, AmeriCeltic Network, the Scottish Games, and numerous Irish pubs! As are many Irish, he is a lover of horse racing and relishes the racing references in *Ulysses!*

Michael has thrice visited Ireland, though knowing little of James Joyce on his first two visits, recalling only that he read Joyce's *The Portrait of the Artist as a Young Man* in high school, and posing for a photo beside Joyce's statue on O'Connell Street. While he first took up reading ULYSSES during Christmas week 2004, he became seriously engaged with reading, comprehending, and condensing the novel in 2013 upon his participation in a week of Bloomsday festivities while staying at All Hallows College, Dublin. Michael completed this **ULYSSES Abridged ~ A Shorter Journey through James Joyce's Masterpiece** prior to Bloomsday 2022, the Centenary Year of the first publication of the novel in Paris, France. With celebrations of Joyce's birth February 2, 1882; his death on January 13, 1941; and of Bloomsday every June 16; Michael believes Joyce's classic, *Ulysses,* will stand the test of time.

CONTENTS

Preface and Foreword by this editor

The Episodes. Neither Joyce nor the Publisher provided a Table of Contents. Joyce did not identify the 18 chapters or episodes of his novel per se. The episodes are recognized by their parallel to books of Homer's *The Odyssey*, and further by the CAPITALIZATION of the first line. The episodes are listed here as those titles of *The Odyssey* and without page numbers. Perhaps Joyce relished the reader's hunt for episode beginnings!

I

II

III

PREFACE

One frayed, faded newspaper clipping and two equally frayed and aged
letters were tucked inside the cover of the tainted cloth-bound copy of
James Joyce's **ULYSSES** which I inherited on the death of my grandfather
Thomas Fallon a.k.a. "Grandpa with the pipe." The first typewritten letter,
on Arthur Williams & Co. Cotton Goods letterhead dated April 3, 1934,
read in part:

"Dear Tom: I am sending you today this book by James Joyce, called
Ulysses, that I spoke to you about couple (sic) of weeks ago…. Now read
the paper by the judge at the beginning, admitting the book to the U.S.
Then you will find the book itself a bit hard to read, but as I found, it was
only after reading carefully that I found entertainment in it and a great
deal of the latter then…. Scene is laid in Dublin, Ireland, and if you know
or can interpret some of the Irish words, you will secure that much more
enjoyment…. With best regards, I am, Very truly yours, Arthur Williams"

The torn, sepia-toned Toledo Blade news clipping with a photo of
James Joyce, round glasses, eye-patch, mustache, pinstripe shirt
and bowtie, announced in part:

JAMES JOYCE'S ULYSSES
AMERICAN EDITION. 768 pages. Random House.

January 25, 1934.   Ass'n. price, $3.50

"The complete and unabridged text, with an introductory note by the author,
a foreword by Morris Ernest, and a reprint of the historic decision by Judge
John M. Woolsey whereby the Federal ban on this book was removed once
and for all."

" 'Ulysses' will immortalize its author with the same certainty that
'Gargantua' immortalized Rabelais." -- **New York Times.**

"To my mind, **ONE OF THE MOST SIGNIFICANT AND
BEAUTIFUL BOOKS OF OUR TIME."** -- Gilbert Seldes, in **The
Nation.**

"I doubt if I have ever read anything to equal it." -- **Arnold Bennett.**

"In the last pages of the book, Joyce soars to such rhapsodies of beauty as
have probably never been equaled in English prose fiction." -- Edmund
Wilson, in **The New Republic.**

The third insert, a handwritten, fountain-penned letter with the slanted cursive of a female hand, detailed the following:

Dear Tom: I'm returning Ulysses with only 200 pages read. Had long looked for a copy after hearing interesting comments and surely appreciate your thinking of me. However -- the disjointed style of writing gets me down and my mind wanders in spite of anything I can do. Have gone back to it no less than two dozen times so it's no use, this in spite of occasional breathtaking passages, sentences or mere words. Surely James Joyce is a master of artistic license. Should love to hear Mr. Morris give a review of it…. Thanking you again, I am, Sincerely, Irene Gutuilge

[Actually, "Morris L. Ernest" appears to be a lawyer for free speech, censorship and publishing, whose Foreword is not an overview or critique, but a simple statement as excerpted: "Joyce's masterpiece, for the circulation of which people have been branded criminals in the past, may now freely enter this country…. The *Ulysses* case marks a turning point…. Writers need no longer seek refuge in euphemisms. They may now describe basic human functions without fear of the law."]

I was intrigued. Relishing all things Irish, I determined that at some point in time I must read this book. I vaguely recalled that our senior high school class had read James Joyce's *A Portrait of the Artist as a Young Man,* but that is as far as my knowledge of James Joyce extended. Now coincidental as I think back, in 1997 I compiled a *Definitive St. Patrick's Day Festivity Book* which offered a party game matching Irish Authors to their most celebrated work. This reinforced my desire, my necessity, to read *Ulysses.*

My first effort reading *Ulysses* is memorable – Christmas week in Maui 2004. I struggled (as had Irene Gutuilge) to follow along, so in the vast space of oceanfront lawn, I took to reading it out loud, appreciating the sound of words, the flow of sentences, and the conjuring up of concepts to which I could relate – by virtue of my visits to Dublin, and circumstances in my contemporary life. Though lacking context which limited my comprehension and appreciation, I was now able to say at the very least: yes, I have read *Ulysses.*

As to comprehension, Episode 3 - Proteus **begins**: "INELUCTABLE MODALITY OF THE VISIBLE: AT LEAST THAT IF NO more, thought through my eyes… Limit of the diaphane in. Why in? Diaphane, adiaphane. If you can put your five fingers through it, it is a gate, if not a door. Shut your eyes and see… Five, six: the *nacheinander*. Exactly: and that is the ineluctable modality of the audible. Open your eyes. No. Jesus!" -- At this point one scholar states the book often **ends** for the casual reader! And be forewarned: Episode 9 – Scylla and Charybdis also is a difficult read.

In time, spurred by colleagues at my university and by Irish friends of literature, I deemed the time had come to read again *Ulysses* for understanding, AND in doing so, to formulate an annotated, condensed version of this classic despite the warning of my dramatist friend that "Joyce scholars will be horrified!" I wanted to produce a rendition that (despite Episode 3!) people would persevere through without turning away. To this end, I did what any college student would do – seek out the widely available study guides (there were multiple copies available) to which I owe a debt of gratitude in aiding this undertaking! Three additional websites further guided my editing. I encourage reading the succinct Rosenbach summary as it integrates not just the plot but the themes and motifs as well: http://www.sparknotes.com/lit/ulysses/themes/ https://rosenbach.org/collection/james-joyces-ulysses/ https://rosenbach.org/ulysses-plot-summary/

While other academic analyses deserve respect, my need was not detailed analysis, but general understanding. It was further suggested that I read Laurence Sterne's *The Life and Opinions of Tristram Shandy* (1759-67), with a similar stream of consciousness, which survey further convinced me to take on such a task. [Note that popular contemporary author James Patterson is quoted as saying *Tristram Shandy* was the book that changed his life as a yearling writer: "How could this author seem so much braver than the rest, and how was he able to break every writing rule ever made? And why was the story so much more fun because of it?" One wonders if Joyce had also read Sterne and felt the same?]

Then by coincidence, I was gifted The Great Courses The Irish Identity - Independence, History, and Literature taught by Professor Marc C. Conner, Washington and Lee University. This outstanding course included five lectures on Joyce, three specific to *Ulysses,* from which I gleaned valuable insight.

Still nagged by the need for scholastic understanding, I purchased The Great Courses <u>Joyce's *Ulysses*</u> taught by Professor James A. W. Heffernan, Dartmouth College. Listening to Heffernan's lectures chapter by chapter and sourcing the guidebook, I was able to better distinguish the essential elements of the story, themes, motifs and symbolism. To Emeritus Professor Heffernan I am equally indebted.

Salient to this notion of re-reading and rendering the novel digestible, I discovered that the storybook day of June 16 (1904) was celebrated as "Bloomsday" not only in Dublin, Ireland, but in several major cities around the world. This further inspired me to resurrect Leopold Bloom's journey throughout that day and night, and raised in me the desire to experience Bloomsday in Dublin. As fate would have it, faith 'n' begorrah, a graduating student of mine pursuing a Religious Studies degree at All Hallows College, Dublin, knowing of my Joycean fantasy, extended an invitation to stay with her during June of 2013, during which time we participated in a string of Bloomsday events. The reality of such a book as envisioned took hold; *Ulysses* was for me now in the context of place and time. (Concomitantly, this adventure presented a new dynamic -- to expand beyond a condensation of *Ulysses* and incorporate actual experiences of Bloomsday. Upon short deliberation however, that is a story for another Wednesday.)

Award winning author Colum McCann, when asked about 'time travel' answered that he'd like to "wander in the streets re-created by James Joyce in *Ulysses*." He adds that "one of the feats of the greatest novel of the 20th century is that its superimposition of a real world on an imagined one renders the gulf between the two invisible... I'd be happy to meet the other imagined people of my life: my great-grandfather, for one, who is most likely slumbering in a pub on the south side. I'd pull up a bar stool and explain to him that I had already met him in a novel that not only obliterated the line between literature and life but obliterated time as well. The day would affirm that the imagined is at least as powerful as the real." -- This perfectly sums up what I hoped to experience for myself and others in the reading of *Ulysses*.

In a New York Times column, February 13, 2022, titled: "D.C. and Joyce – Both Incomprehensible," Maureen Dowd states: "On this centenary of James Joyce's colossus, we can borrow a thought from W. B. Yeats' poem 'The Fascination of What's Difficult.' Is *Ulysses* hard because it's great, or do people assume it's great because it's hard?" Meanwhile, Colm Toibin, Irish writer, affirms: "For the ordinary reader … It is a challenge and then, for those who have read the book, a matter of pride." If reading an abridgement does not equate to the pride of running a marathon, running a half-marathon is nonetheless a feat.

This abridgement strives to offer the reader a happy medium of text, understanding, and a vicarious experience of place and time, perhaps too, a parallel to matters in one's own life.

Initially concerned about copyright, on a most fortuitous note, faith 'n' begorrah, while visiting the Joyce Center in Dublin during Bloomsday week 2013, the Center's director announced that "in this 99th year following the copyright of *Ulysses*, the Joyce family heirs released the book to the public for its free use." (Parts of the novel were first copyrighted in 1914 by Margaret Caroline Anderson for *The Little Review*.)

In sum, the purpose of **ULYSSES Abridged ~ *A Shorter Journey through James Joyce's Masterpiece*** is to enable aficionados of the classics and a general readership who have not undertaken reading all 768 pages of the lengthy, at times meandering *Ulysses,* to do so in measure; moreover, to respect its place in modern literature, Irish history, culture and politic; all the while entertaining Joycean ideas contemporary with their own lives; perhaps in turn motivating a fuller reading or scholarly inquiry. Like a travel guide, *Ulysses* is a *must read* before visiting Dublin. I ask forgiveness from Joyce scholars, acknowledging that I can in no way do justice to the entirety of this classic. But propriety be damned. With a sip of Irish whiskey and a pint of Guinness at hand, I commenced to re-read, judiciously select, surgically redact, and type, type, type the text originally typeset from the scrawling hand of the author! So raising pint, here's to the everyday reader who herein can journey with Joyce and proudly achieve familiarity with his classic *Ulysses.* Sláinte!

— But it's no use, says he. Force, hatred, history, all that. That's not life for men and women, insult and hatred. And everybody knows it's the opposite of that that is really life.

— What? says Alf.

— Love, says Bloom. I mean the opposite of hatred.

--- E12 The Cyclops

FOREWORD

The epic writing of James Joyce is the essence of this humble abridged rendition. (My written contributions are secondary.) A *day in the life* of one Leopold Bloom, his odyssey around Dublin town and his associations, should be entertaining, and lends itself to one's own imagination, experiences, and perhaps reminiscences of a visit to Ireland.

Homer's *The Odyssey* is the framework for Joyce's organization. My annotations provide overview and motifs. The text is original. The content prioritizes the central story, captures significant happenings, reflects critical themes, and retrains Joyce's writing, language and style. Granted, some passages simply appeal to this reader/ author, e.g., those related to religion… and horse racing!

Before the *redaction process notes* below, I encourage your enjoyment reading *Ulysses*! Don't overstrain to make sense of every part. Simply pass over foreign language phrases. Appreciate the changes in writing structure from Old English to narration to play script to Q/A to inner monologue. Don't be surprised when a character or notion from a previous episode pops up again later. Laugh with its humor; shake your head at its audacity; visualize the composite images. It's likely you'll be either dumbfounded or in awe of the expansive mind of Joyce and his creative and expansive vocabulary! (To be sure, the definition of *cuckold* is 'the husband of an unfaithful wife.') Take pleasure in the reading, aloud if you would, as one of the characters in the scene.

Editing the extraneous seemed possible because Joyce's stream of consciousness often extends beyond the story's skeleton. Thoughts may overlap or change abruptly such that it is not the editing that reads as a break in the novel's fluency but the original text itself. No words whatsoever were changed. Rarely, if ever, was a word omitted from a sentence. Overall, few sentences were redacted; only paragraphs deemed nonessential to the theme.

As stated, Joyce did not label chapters, nor follow chronologically those of *The Odyssey*. "Episodes" are identified by their Homeric titles and synchronized with the storyline, some parallels more or less obvious. A succinct outline of the episode and listing of motifs intends guidance for the reader. Motifs are multiple and nuanced over the course of episodes.

Many text passages are longer than preferred; but it was painful to truncate the wholeness of an action or dialogue. When in doubt, no edit was made. Progressing through episodes, it was necessary to revise earlier episodes where past-to-present connections were perceived.

Anyone attempting to compare this abridgement to the original text could do so. An ellipsis of **four** dots (. . . .) indicates an emission of a paragraph or page. A **tight** three dot ellipsis (...) signifies a phrase or sentence omitted within a paragraph. Note that Joyce himself employed the three spaced dot ellipsis (. . .) especially in Episodes 15-16-17. While unintentional, the four dot ellipsis created spacing in the otherwise dense text which further facilitates reading.

Transcribing original text and the possibility of misspellings was an issue. Because Joyce wrote in British English (e.g., 'honour') <u>and</u> created words, proofreading was a challenge. This text retains Joyce's writing style, e.g., Aeolus is written as news copy; Circe as play script; Ithaca as question-and-answer; Penelope as "wildly flowing monologue" as one scholar put it. May I demonstrate the difficulty of transcribing Episode 15 Circe in play script: Caps – Center Justify – Return – Left Justify – Italics – Parentheses – Stage Directions – Parentheses – Undo Italics – Standard Font – Return. Whew!

Let us commence our odyssey through *Ulysses* with an overview from the two scholars cited:

"Joyce's novel recalls and at the same time radically reconstructs the adventures of Ulysses, the protagonist of Homer's ancient epic called *The Odyssey*. Joyce's three principal characters are modeled on leading figures in Homer's poem. Ulysses – king of Ithaca, mastermind of the Greek war against Troy, heroic voyager, and merciless slayer of the suitors who besieged his wife during his long absence – is reincarnated as Leopold Bloom, a middle-aged Dubliner of Hungarian Jewish extraction who sells advertising space for a living. Ulysses' son Telemachus, who sets out to seek his long lost father at the beginning of *The Odyssey,* is reincarnated as

Stephen Dedalus, a fictionalized version of Joyce's younger self – a brilliant and restless young man who yearns to write but seems destined to drown in drink and dissipation. Penelope, the supremely faithful wife of Ulysses, is reincarnated as Molly, the adulterous wife of Leopold Bloom.

"This extraordinarily ambitious project raises challenging questions. How can the exploits of an ancient warrior king and heroic voyager be reenacted by a pacifist who has scarcely ever been to sea and who tolerates his wife's adultery, taking no revenge on her lover? How can Telemachus be reborn in Stephen, who has absolutely no wish to see his father at all? And how can the role of a supremely faithful wife be played by an adulteress?" – James A.W. Heffernan, Ph.D., Emeritus Professor of English, Dartmouth College

"Joyce's novel is about the humanity that exists behind the common events of daily existence. *Ulysses* is among the most moving, intimate, and profoundly human of epics. Beyond the complexity, the technique, and the difficulty, is a timeless story of a man and a woman, and a young man encountering the world and the issues we all face -- love, loss, doubt, passion, and uncertainty over our most fundamental relationships to one another, to our nation, to God. Bloom is every bit as heroic as Odysseus, an icon of the virtues extolled in the New Testament, a Jewish upholder of Mosaic Law, a reporter of city life. Bloom is the Everyman; and the characters of this story transcend their time and place and stand for all people, in all times and places. Every character is on a passage that will ultimately end in the grave, but Bloom speaks for the power of life." – Marc. C. Conner, Ph.D., Professor of English, Washington and Lee University.

This journey segues from Joyce's close to *A Portrait of the Artist as a Young Man*, Stephen Dedalus, with new protagonist Leopold Bloom:

"Mother is putting my new second hand clothes in order. She prays now, she says, that I may learn in my own life and away from home and friends what the heart is and what it feels. Amen. So be it. Welcome, O life! I go to encounter for the millionth time the reality of experience and to forge in the smithy of my soul the uncreated conscience of my race."

Episode 1 – Telemachus... son of Homer's Greek Hero Odysseus (Ulysses) who leaves Ithaca to seek his long lost father so that he and Odysseus can drive away the suitors who are despoiling the kingdom while they court his mother Penelope. ~ Stephen Dedalus is the prodigal son who lost his mother, feels estranged from his father, and seeks a paternal relationship with a metaphysical parent. His home is usurped by his suitor roommates.

Stephen Dedalus, an introverted young man bereaved of his mother, beset with remorse over their deathbed parting, just returned from Paris – awakens in the Martello Tower on Dublin Bay. Lodgers Buck Mulligan, Catholic, medical student; and Haines, Oxford student of Irish folklore, prone to nightmares – mock Stephen in his search for life's meaning, physical and spiritual. Mulligan similarly shows disdain for an old milkwoman. He aims to "usurp" both Stephen's house key and his wages for drink, leaving Stephen feeling impoverished and homeless.

THEMES
Life is a struggle. Losing one's mother. Being mired in the past. Broken glasses symbolically impair inner vision. True paternity. Reference to Hamlet. Breaking from Catholicism, a "server of a servant." Cynicism, patronization, antisemiticism. The Irish Renaissance is futile. Await the day the poor old lady of Irish lore turns into a beautiful young Gaelic queen. Key to Ireland's future?

I

STATELY, PLUMP Buck Mulligan came from the stairhead, bearing a bowl of lather on which a mirror and razor lay crossed. A yellow dressinggown, ungirdled, was sustained gently behind him by the mild morning air. He held the bowl aloft and intoned:

– *Introibo ad altare Dei.*

Halted, he peered down the dark winding stairs and called up coarsely:

– Come up, Kinch. Come up, you fearful jesuit.

Solemnly he came forward and mounted the round gunrest. He faced about and blessed gravely thrice the tower, the surrounding country and the awaking mountains. Then, catching sight of Stephen Dedalus, he bent towards him and made rapid crosses in the air, gurgling in his throat and shaking his head. Stephen Dedalus, displeased and sleepy, leaned his arms on the top of the staircase and looked coldly at the shaking gurgling face that blessed him, equine in its length, and at the light untonsured hair, grained and hued like pale oak.

Buck Mulligan peeped an instant under the mirror and then covered the bowl smartly.

--Back to the barracks, he said sternly.

He added in a preacher's tone

--For this, O dearly beloved, is the genuine Christine: body and soul and blood and ouns. Slow music, please. Shut your eyes, gents. One moment. A little trouble about those white corpuscles. Silence, all.

. . . .

He skipped off the gunrest and looked gravely at his watcher, gathering about his legs the loose fold of his gown. The plump shadowed face and sullen oval jowl recalled a prelate, patron of arts in the middle ages. A pleasant smile broke quietly over his lips.

--The mockery of it, he said gaily. Your absurd name, an ancient Greek.

He pointed his finger in friendly jest and went over to the parapet, laughing to himself. Stephen Dedalus stepped up, followed him wearily halfway and sat down on the edge of the gunrest, watching him still as he propped his mirror on the parapet, dipped the brush in the bowl and lathered cheeks and neck.

Buck Mulligan's gay voice went on.

--My name is absurd too: Malachi Mulligan, two dactyls. But it has a Hellenic ring, hasn't it? Tripping and sunny like the buck himself. We must go to Athens. Will you come if I can get the aunt to fork out twenty quid?

He laid the brush aside and, laughing with delight, cried:

--Will he come? The jejune jesuit.

Ceasing, he began to shave with care.

--Tell me, Mulligan, Stephen said quietly.

--Yes, my love?

--How long is Haines going to stay in this tower?

Buck Mulligan showed a shaven cheek over his right shoulder.

[2]

--God, isn't he dreadful? he said frankly. A ponderous
Saxon. He thinks you're not a gentleman. God, these bloody English.
Bursting with money and indigestion. Because he comes from
Oxford. You know, Dedalus; you have the real Oxford manner. He
can't make you out. O, my name for you is the best: Kinch, the
knife-blade.

He shaved warily over his chin.

– He was raving all night about a black panther, Stephen
said. Where is his guncase?

– A woeful lunatic, Mulligan said. Were you in a funk?

– I was, Stephen said with energy and growing fear. Out here
in the dark with a man I don't know raving and moaning to himself
about shooting a black panther. You saved men from drowning. I'm
not a hero, however. If he stays on here I am off.

. . . .

Stephen stood up and went over to the parapet. Leaning on it
he looked down on the water and on the mailboat clearing the
harbour mouth of Kingstown.

--Our mighty mother, Buck Mulligan said.

He turned abruptly his great searching eyes from the sea to
Stephen's face.

--The aunt thinks you killed your mother, he said. That's
why she won't let me have anything to do with you.

--Someone killed her, Stephen said gloomily.

--You could have knelt down, damn it, Kinch, when your
dying mother asked you, Buck Mulligan said. I'm hyperborean as
much as you. But to think of your mother begging you with her last
breath to kneel down and pray for her. And you refused. There is
something sinister in you . . .

He broke off and lathered again, lightly his farther cheek. A
tolerant smile curled his lips.

--But a lovely mummer, he murmured to himself. Kinch, the
loveliest mummer of them all.

He shaved evenly and with care, in silence, seriously.

Stephen, an elbow rested on the jagged granite, leaned his palm against his brow and gazed at the fraying edge of his shiny black coat-sleeve. Pain, that was not the pain of love, fretted his heart. Silently, in a dream she had come to him after her death, her wasted body within its loose brown graveclothes giving off an odour of wax and rosewood, her breath, that had been bent upon him, mute, reproachful, a faint odour of wetted ashes. Across the threadbare cuffedge he saw the sea hailed as a great sweet mother by the wellfed voice beside him. The ring of bay and skyline held a dull green mass of liquid. A bowl of white china had stood beside her deathbed holding the green sluggish bile which she had torn up from her rotting liver by fits of loud groaning vomiting.

. . . .

Stephen turned his gaze from the sea and to the plump face with its smokeblue mobile eyes.

– That fellow I was with in the Ship last night, said Buck Mulligan, says you have the g.p.i. He's up in the Dottyville with Conolly Norman. General paralysis of the insane.

He swept the mirror a half circle in the air to flash the tidings abroad in sunlight now radiant on the sea. His curling shaven lips laughed and the edges of his white glittering teeth. Laughter seized all his strong wellknit trunk.

– Look at yourself, he said, you dreadful bard.

Stephen bent forward and peered at the mirror held out to him, cleft by a crooked crack, hair on end. As he and others see me. Who chose this face for me? This dogsbody to rid of vermin.

. . . .

Buck Mulligan suddenly linked his arm in Stephen's and walked with him round the tower, his razor and mirror clacking in the pocket where he had thrust them.

– It's not fair to tease you like that, Kinch, is it? he said kindly. God knows you have more spirit than any of them.

Parried again. He fears the lancet of my art as I fear that of his. The cold steelpen.

. . . .

[4]

– Let him stay, Stephen said. There's nothing wrong with him except at night.

– Then what is it? Buck Mulligan asked impatiently. Cough it up. I'm quite frank with you. What have you against me now?

They halted, looking towards the blunt cape of Bray Head that lay on the water like the snout of a sleeping whale. Stephen freed his arm quietly.

– Do you wish me to tell you? he asked.

– Yes, what is it? Buck Mulligan answered.

He looked in Stephen's face as he spoke. A light wind passed his brow, fanning softly his fair uncombed hair and stirring silver points of anxiety in his eyes.

Stephen, depressed by his own voice, said:

– Do you remember the first day I went to your house after my mother's death?

Buck Mulligan frowned quickly and said:

– What? Where? I can't remember anything. I remember only ideas and sensations. Why? What happened in the name of God?

– You were making tea, Stephen said, and I went across the landing to get you more hot water. Your mother and some visitor came out of the drawingroom. She asked you who was in your room.

– Yes? Buck Mulligan said. What did I say? I forget.

– You said, Stephen answered, *O, it's only Dedalus whose mother is beastly dead.*

A flush which made him seem younger and more engaging rose to Buck Mulligan's cheek.

– Did I say that? he asked. Well? What harm is that?

He shook his constraint from him nervously.

– And what is death, he asked, your mother's or yours or my own? You saw only your mother die. I see them popoff every day in the Mater and Richmond and cut up into tripes in the dissecting room. It's a beastly thing and nothing else. It simply doesn't matter. You wouldn't kneel down to pray for your mother on her deathbed when she asked you. Why? Because you have the cursed jesuit strain

in you, only it's injected the wrong way. To me it's all a mockery
and beastly. Her cerebral lobes are not functioning. She calls the
doctor Sir Peter Teazle and picks buttercups off the quilt. Humour
her till it's over. You crossed her last wish in death and yet you sulk
with me because I don't whinge like some hired mute from
Laloutte's. Absurd! I suppose I did say it. I didn't mean to offend the
memory of your mother.

He had spoken himself into boldness. Stephen, shielding the
gaping wounds which the words had left in his heart, said very
coldly:

– I am not thinking of the offence to my mother.
– Of what, then? Buck Mulligan asked.
– Of the offence to me, Stephen answered.
Buck Mulligan swung round on his heel.
– O, an impossible person! he exclaimed.
He walked off quickly round the parapet. Stephen stood at
his post, gazing over the calm sea towards the headland.

. . . .

His head vanished but the drone of his descending voice
boomed out of the stairhead:

> *And no more turn aside and brood*
> *Upon love's bitter mystery*
> *For Fergus rules the brazen cars.*

. . . .

A cloud began to cover the sun slowly, shadowing the bay in
deeper green. It lay behind him, a bowl of bitter waters. Fergus'
song: I sang it alone in the house, holding down the long dark
chords. Her door was open: she wanted to hear my music. Silent with
awe and pity I went to her bedside. She was crying in her wretched
bed. For whose words, Stephen: love's bitter mystery.

Where now?

. . . .

In a dream, silently, she had come to him, her wasted body
within its loose graveclothes giving off an odour of wax and

[6]

rosewood, her breath bent over him with mute secret words, a faint odour of wetted ashes.

Her glazing eyes, staring out of death, to shake and bend my soul. On me alone. The ghostcandle to light her agony. Ghostly light on the tortured face. Her hoarse loud breath rattling in horror, while all prayed on their knees. Her eyes on me to strike me down. *Liliata rutilantium te confessorum turma circumdet: iubilantium te virginum chorus excipiat.*

Ghoul! Chewer of corpses!

No mother. Let me be and let me live.

--Kinch ahoy!

Buck Mulligan's voice sang from within the tower. It came nearer up the staircase, calling again. Stephen, still trembling at his soul's cry, heard warm running sunlight and in the air behind him friendly words.

--Dedalus, come down, like a good mosey. Breakfast is ready. Haines is apologizing for waking us last night. It's all right.

--I'm coming, Stephen said, turning.

--Do, for Jesus' sake, Buck Mulligan said. For my sake and all our sakes.

His head disappeared and reappeared.

--I told him your symbol of Irish art. He says it's very clever. Touch him for a quid, will you? A guinea, I mean.

--I get paid this morning, Stephen said.

--The school kip? Buck Mulligan said. How much? Four quid? Lend us one.

--If you want it, Stephen said.

--Four shining sovereigns, Buck Mulligan cried with delight. We'll have a glorious drunk to astonish the druidy druids. Four omnipotent sovereigns.

He flung up his hands and tramped down the stone stairs, singing out of tune with a Cockney accent:

> *O, won't we have a merry time*
> *Drinking whisky, beer and wine,*
> *On coronation,*

Coronation day?
O, won't we have a merry time
On coronation day?

Warm sunshine merrying over the sea. The nickel shaving bowl
forgotten, on the parapet. Why should I bring it down? Or leave it
there all day, forgotten friendship?

. . . .

     – Have you the key? a voice asked.

Dedalus has it, Buck Mulligan said. Janey Mack, I'm
choked. He howled without looking up from the fire:

     – Kinch!

     – It's in the lock, Stephen said, coming forward.

The key scraped round harshly twice and, when the heavy
door had been set ajar, welcome light and bright air entered.

Haines stood at the doorway, looking out. Stephen haled his
upended valise to the table and sat down to wait. Buck Mulligan
tossed the fry on to the dish beside him. Then he carried the dish and
a large teapot over to the table, set them down heavily and sighed
with relief.

     – I'm melting, he said, as the candle remarked when . . . But
hush. Not a word more on that subject. Kinch, wake up. Bread,
butter, honey. Haines, come in. The grub is ready. Bless us, O Lord,
and these thy gifts. Where's the sugar? O, jay, there's no milk.

Stephen fetched the loaf and pot of honey and the
buttercooler from the locker. Buck Mulligan sat down in a sudden
pet.

     – What sort of a kip is this? he said. I told her to come after
eight.

     – We can drink it black, Stephen said. There's a lemon in the
locker.

     – O, damn you and your Paris fads, Buck Mulligan said. I
want Sandycove milk.

Haines came in from the doorway and said quietly:

     – That woman is coming up with the milk.

[8]

– The blessings of God on you, Buck Mulligan cried, jumping up from his chair. Sit down. Pour out the tea there. The sugar is in the bag. Here, I can't go fumbling at the damned eggs. He hacked through the fry on the dish and slapped it out on three plates, saying:

– *In nomine Patris et Filii et Spiritus Sancti.*

Haines sat down to pour out the tea.

– I'm giving you two lumps each, he said. But, I say, Mulligan, you do make strong tea, don't you?

Buck Mulligan, hewing thick slices from the loaf, said in an old woman's wheedling voice:

– When I makes tea I makes tea, as old mother Grogan said. And when I makes water I makes water.

– By Jove, it is tea, Haines said.

. . . .

He crammed his mouth with fry and munched and droned.

The doorway was darkened by an entering form.

--The milk, sir.

--Come in, ma'am, Mulligan said. Kinch, get the jug.

An old woman came forward and stood by Stephen's elbow.

--That's a lovely morning, sir, she said. Glory be to God.

--To whom? Mulligan said, glancing at her. Ah, to be sure.

Stephen reached back and took the milkjug from the locker.

--The islanders, Mulligan said to Haines casually, speak frequently of the collector of prepuces.

--How much, sir? asked the woman.

--A quart, Stephen said.

He watched her pour into the measure and thence into the jug rich white milk, not hers. Old shrunken paps. She poured again a measureful and a tilly. Old secret she had entered from a morning world, maybe a messenger. She praised the goodness of the milk, pouring it out. Crouching by a patient cow at daybreak in the lush field, a witch on her toadstool, her wrinkled fingers quick at the squirting dugs. They lowed about her whom they knew, dewsilky cattle. Silk of the kine and poor old woman, names given her in old

times. A wandering crone, lowly form of an immortal serving her
conqueror and her gay betrayer, their common cuckquean a
messenger from the secret morning. To serve or to upbraid, whether
he could not tell: but scorned to beg her favour.

--It is indeed, ma'am, Buck Mulligan said, pouring milk into
their cups.

--Taste it, sir, she said.

He drank at her bidding.

--If we could only live on good food like that, he said to her
somewhat loudly, we wouldn't have the country full of rotten teeth
and rotten guts. Living in a bogswamp, eating cheap food and the
streets paved with dust, horsedung and consumptives' spits.

--Are you a medical student, sir? the old woman asked.

--I am, ma'am, Buck Mulligan answered.

Stephen listened in scornful silence. She bows her old head
to a voice that speaks to her loudly, her bonesetter, her medicineman;
me she slights. To the voice that will shrive and oil for the grave all
there is of her but her woman's unclean loins, of man's flesh made
not in God's likeness, the serpent's prey. And to the loud voice that
now bids her be silent with wondering unsteady eyes.

--Do you understand what he says? Stephen asked her.

--Is it French you are talking, sir? the old woman said to
Haines.

Haines spoke to her again a longer speech, confidently.

--Irish, Buck Mulligan said. Is there Gaelic on you?

--I thought it was Irish, she said, by the sound of it. Are you
from west, sir?

--I am an Englishman, Haines answered.

--He's English, Buck Mulligan said, and he thinks we ought
to speak Irish in Ireland.

--Sure we ought to, the old woman said, and I'm ashamed I
don't speak the language myself. I'm told it's a grand language by
them that knows.

[10]

--Grand is no name for it, said Buck Mulligan. Wonderful entirely. Fill us out some more tea, Kinch. Would you like a cup, ma'am?

--No, thank you, sir, the old woman said, slipping the ring of the milkcan on her forearm and about to go.

Haines said to her:

– Have you your bill? We had better pay her, Mulligan, hadn't we?

Stephen filled the three cups.

. . . .

She curtseyed and went out, followed by Buck Mulligan's tender chant:

> --*Heart of my heart, were it more,*
> *More would be laid at your feet.*

He turned to Stephen and said:

– Seriously, Dedalus. I'm stony. Hurry out to your school kip and bring us back some money. Today the bards must drink and junket. Ireland expects that every man this day will do his duty.

– That reminds me, Haines said, rising, that I have to visit your national library today.

– Our swim first, Buck Mulligan said.

He turned to Stephen and asked blandly:

– Is this the day for your monthly wash, Kinch?

Then he said to Haines:

– The unclean bard makes a point of washing once a month.

– All Ireland is washed by the gulfstream, Stephen said as he let honey trickle over a slice of the loaf.

Haines from the corner where he was knotting easily a scarf about the loose collar of his tennis shirt spoke:

– I intend to make a collection of your sayings if you will let me.

Speaking to me. They wash and tub and scrub. Agenbite of inwit. Conscience. Yet here's a spot.

– That one about the cracked lookingglass of a servant being the symbol of Irish art is deuced good.

Buck Mulligan kicked Stephen's foot under the table and said with warmth of tone:

– Wait till you hear him on Hamlet, Haines.

– Well, I mean it. Haines said, still speaking to Stephen. I was just thinking of it when that poor old creature came in.

– Would I make money by it? Stephen asked.

Haines laughed and, as he took his soft grey hat from the holdfast of the hammock, said:

– I don't know, I'm sure.

He strolled out to the doorway. Buck Mulligan bent across to Stephen and said with coarse vigour:

– You put your hoof in it now. What did you say that for?

– Well? Stephen said. The problem is to get money. From whom? From the milkwoman or from him. It's a toss up, I think.

. . . .

Haines called to them from the doorway:

– Are you coming, you fellows?

– I'm ready, Buck Mulligan answered, going towards the door. Come out, Kinch. You have eaten all we left, I suppose. Resigned he passed out with grave words and gait, saying, wellnigh with sorrow:

– And going forth he met Butterfly.

Stephen, taking his ashplant from its leaningplace, followed them out and, as they went down the ladder, pulled to the slow iron door and locked it. He put the huge key in his inner pocket.

At the foot of the ladder, Buck Mulligan asked:

– Did you bring the key?

– I have it, Stephen said, preceding them.

He walked on. Behind him he heard Buck Mulligan club with his heavy bathtowel the leader shoots of ferns or grasses.

– Down, sir. How dare you, sir?

Haines asked:

– Do you pay rent for this tower?

[12]

– Twelve quid, Buck Mulligan said.

– To the secretary of state for war, Stephen added over his shoulder.

They halted while Haines surveyed the tower and said at last:

– Rather bleak in wintertime, I should say. Martello you call it?

– Billy Pitt had them built, Buck Mulligan said, when the French were on the sea. But ours is the *omphalos*.

– What is your idea of Hamlet? Haines asked of Stephen.

– No, no, Buck Mulligan shouted in pain. I'm not equal to Thomas Aquinas and the fiftyfive reasons he has made to prop it up. Wait till I have a few pints in me first.

He turned to Stephen, saying as he pulled down neatly the peaks of his primrose waistcoat:

– You couldn't manage it under three pints, Kinch, could you?

– It has waited so long, Stephen said listlessly, it can wait longer.

– You pique my curiosity, Haines said amiably. Is it some paradox?

– Pooh! Buck Mulligan said. We have grown out of Wilde paradoxes. It's quite simple. He proves by algebra that Hamlet's grandson is Shakespeare's grandfather and that he himself is the ghost of his own father.

. . . .

– It's a wonderful tale, Haines said, bringing them to halt again.

Eyes, pale as the sea the wind had freshened, paler, firm and prudent. The seas' ruler, he gazed southward over the bay, empty save for the smokeplume of the mailboat, vague on the bright skyline, and a sail tacking by the Muglins.

– I read a theological interpretation of it somewhere, he said bemused. The Father and the Son idea. The Son striving to be atoned with the Father.

Buck Mulligan at once put on a blithe broadly smiling face. He looked at them, his wellshaped mouth open happily, his eyes, from which he had suddenly withdrawn all shrewd sense, blinking with mad gaiety. He moved a doll's head to and fro, the brims of his Panama hat quivering, and began to chant in a quiet happy foolish voice:

-- I'm the queerest young fellow that ever you heard.
My mother's a jew, my father's a bird.
With Joseph the joiner I cannot agree,
So here's to disciples and Calvary.

He held up a forefinger of warning.
-- If anyone thinks that I amn't divine
He'll get no free drinks when I'm making the wine
But have to drink water and wish it were plain
That I make when the wine becomes water again.

He tugged swiftly at Stephen's ashplant in farewell and, running forward to a brow of the cliff, fluttered his hands at his sides like fins or wings of one about to rise in the air, and chanted:

--Goodbye, now, goodbye. Write down all I said
And tell Tom, Dick and Harry I rose from the dead.
What's bred in the bone cannot fail me to fly
And Olivet's breezy . . . Goodbye, now, goodbye.

He capered before them down towards the fortyfoot hole, fluttering his winglike hands, leaping nimbly, Mercury's hat quivering in the fresh wind that bore back to them his brief birdlike cries.

Haines, who had been laughing guardedly, walked on beside Stephen and said:

-- We oughtn't to laugh, I suppose. He's rather blasphemous. I'm not a believer myself, that is to say. Still his gaiety takes the harm out of it somehow, doesn't it? What did he call it? Joseph the Joiner?

[14]

--The ballad of Joking Jesus, Stephen answered.

--O, Haines said, you have heard it before?

--Three times a day, after meals, Stephen said drily.

--You're not a believer, are you? Haines asked. I mean, a believer in the narrow sense of the word. Creation from nothing and miracles and a personal God.

--There's only one sense of the word, it seems to me, Stephen said.

Haines stopped to take out a smooth silver case in which twinkled a green stone. He sprang it open with his thumb and offered it.

--Thank you, Stephen said, taking a cigarette.

Haines helped himself and snapped the case to. He put it back in his sidepocket and took from this waistcoastpocket a nickel tinderbox, sprang it open too, and, having lit his cigarette, held the flaming spunk towards Stephen in the shell of his hands.

--Yes, of course, he said, as they went on again. Either you believe or you don't, isn't it? Personally I couldn't stomach that idea of a personal God. You don't stand for that, I suppose?

--You behold in me, Stephen said with grim displeasure, a horrible example of free thought.

He walked on, waiting to be spoken to, trailing his ashplant by his side. Its ferrule followed lightly on the path, squealing at his heels. My familiar, after me, calling Steeeeeeeeeephen. A wavering line along the path. They will walk on it tonight, coming here in the dark. He wants that key. It is mine, I paid the rent. Now I eat his salt bread. Give him the key too. All. He will ask for it. That was in his eyes.

--After all, Haines began . . .

Stephen turned and saw that the cold gaze which had measured him was not all unkind.

--After all, I should think you are able to free yourself. You are your own master, it seems to me.

--I am the servant of two masters, Stephen said, an English and an Italian.

--Italian? Haines said.

A crazy queen, old and jealous. Kneel down before me.

--And a third, Stephen said, there is who wants me for odd jobs.

--Italian? Haines said again. What do you mean?

-- The imperial British state, Stephen answered, his colour rising, and the holy Roman catholic and apostolic church.

Haines detached from his underlip some fibres of tobacco before he spoke.

--I can quite understand that, he said calmly. An Irishman must think like that, I daresay. We feel in England that we have treated you rather unfairly. It seems history is to blame.

. . . .

They followed the winding path down to the creek. Buck Mulligan stood on the stone, in shirtsleeves, his unclipped tie rippling over his shoulder. A young man clinging to a spur of rock near him moved slowly frogwise his green legs in the deep jelly of water.

. . . .

The young man shoved himself backward through the water and reached the middle of the creek in two long clean strokes. Haines sat down on a stone, smoking.

– Are you not coming in? Buck Mulligan asked.

– Later on, Haines said. Not on my breakfast.

Stephen turned away.

– I'm going, Mulligan, he said.

– Give us that key, Kinch, Buck Mulligan said, to keep my chemise flat.

Stephen handed him the key. Buck Mulligan laid it across his heaped clothes.

– And twopence, he said, for a pint. Throw it there.

Stephen threw two pennies on the soft heap. Dressing, undressing. Buck Mulligan erect, with joined hands before him, said solemnly:

[16]

– He who stealeth from the poor lendeth to the Lord. Thus spake Zarathustra.

His plump body plunged.

– We'll see you again, Haines said, turning as Stephen walked up the path and smiling at wild Irish.

Horn of a bull, hoof of a horse, smile of a Saxon.

– The Ship, Buck Mulligan cried. Half twelve.

– Good, Stephen said.

He walked along the upwardcurving path.

> *Liliata rutilantium.*
> *Turma circumdet.*
> *Iubilantium te virginum*

The priest's grey nimbus in niche where he dressed discreetly. I will not sleep here tonight. Home also I cannot go.

A voice, sweettoned and sustained, called to him from the sea. Turning the curve he waved his hand. It called again. A sleek brown head, a seal's, far out on the water, round.

Usurper.

Episode 2 – Nestor... aged Greek soldier and rhetorician of the Trojan War, first visited by Telemachus in search of his father Odysseus. Nestor helped keep order among the military principals, and also tamed horses. ~ Garret Deasy, school headmaster, affords Stephen no meaningful guidance. His words support military conquest in history. He has knowledge of animals.

Stephen taught Greek history and mythology at Headmaster Garrett Deasy's school. Counseling a a young boy, He realizes that the boy's mother must have loved this tired child in spite of his inadequacies. Stephen is reminded of the loss of his mother. He meets Deasy in his office to collect his pay. Deasy wants Stephen, with friends in newspaper, to deliver his article on the disease of Irish livestock. Conversation comes round to women and the evils of the world. Stephen is not destined for tenure at Deasy's school, feeling he was still a learner, rather than teacher; and Deasy was not one to learn from as he believed history, not Britain, was responsible for the plight of the Irish. Deasy was anti-Semitic, anti-women, and greedy.

THEMES

Students memorize great works rather than understand their doctrine. Personal history a microcosm of human history, a series of life-and-death battles. Ireland's imprisonment by England. Parnell betrayed by a sex scandal. Women blamed for the evils of history. Three faithless wives (precursor to Molly Bloom). Distorted view of Jews as wanderers over the earth (Leopold Bloom). Excessive stress on money, military conquest, greed destroying Ireland. Who will save the country?

YOU, COCHRANE, WHAT CITY SENT FOR HIM?

– Tarentum, sir.

– Very good. Well?

– There was a battle, sir.

– Very good. Where?

The boy's blank face asked the blank window.

Fabled by the daughters of memory. And yet it was in some way if not as memory fabled it. A phrase, then, of impatience, thud of Blake's wings of excess. I hear the ruin of all space, shattered glass and toppling masonry, and time one livid final flame. What's left us then?

– I forgot the place, sir. 279 B.C.

– Asculum, Stephen said, glancing at the name and date in the gorescarred book.

– Yes, sir. And he said: *Another victory like that and we are done for.*

[18]

That phrase the world had remembered. A dull ease of the
mind. From a hill above a corpsestrewn plain a general speaking to
his officers, leaned upon his spear. Any general to any officers. They
lend ear.

— You, Armstrong, Stephen said. What was the end of
Pyrrhus?

— End of Pyrrhus, sir?

— I know, sir. Ask me, sir, Comyn said.

— Wait. You, Armstrong. Do you know anything about
Pyrrhus?

A bag of figrolls lay snugly in Armstrong's satchel. He
curled them between his palms at whiles and swallowed them softly.
Crumbs adhered to the tissues of his lips. A sweetened boy's breath.
Welloff people, proud that their eldest son was in the navy. Vico
Road, Dalkey.

— Pyrrhus, sir? Pyrrhus, a pier.

All laughed. Mirthless high malicious laughter. Armstrong
looked round at his classmates, silly glee in profile. In a moment
they will laugh more loudly, aware of my lack of rule and of the fees
their papas pay.

Tell me now, Stephen said, poking the boy's shoulder with
the book, what is a pier.

-- A pier, sir, Armstrong said. A thing out in the waves. A
kind of bridge. Kingstown pier, sir.

Some laughed again: mirthless buy with meaning. Two in
the back bench whispered. Yes. They knew: had never learned nor
ever been innocent. All. With envy he watched their faces...

--Kingston pier, Stephen said. Yes, a disappointed bridge.
The words troubled their gaze.

-- How sir? Comyn asked. A bridge is across a river.

. . . .

Had Pyrrhus not fallen by a beldam's hand in Argos or Julius
Caesar not been knifed to death? They are not to be thought away.
Time has branded them and fettered they are lodged in the room of
infinite possibilities they have ousted. But can those have been

possible seeing that they never were? Or was that only possible which came to pass? Weave, weaver of the wind.

Tell us a story, sir.

– Oh, do, sir, a ghoststory.

– Where do you begin in this? Stephen asked, opening another book.

– *Weep no more,* Comyn said.

– Go on then, Talbot.

– And the history, sir?

– After, Stephen said. Go on, Talbot.

A swarthy boy opened a book and propped it nimbly under the breastwork of his satchel. He recited jerks of verse with odd glances at the text:

--Weep no more, woeful shepherd, weep no more
For Lycidas, your sorrow, is not dead,
Sunk though he be beneath the watery floor . . .

It must be a movement then, an actuality of the possible as possible. Aristotle's phrase formed itself within the gabbled verses and floated out into the studious silence of the library of Saint Genevieve where he had read, sheltered from the sin of Paris, night by night. By his elbow a delicate Siamese conned a handbook of strategy. Fed and feeding brains about me: under glowlamps, impaled, with faintly beating feelers: and in my mind's darkness a sloth of the underworld, reluctant, shy of brightness, shifting her dragon scaly folds. Thought is the thought of thought. Tranquil brightness. The soul is in a manner all that is: the soul is the form of forms. Tranquility sudden, vast, candescent: form of forms.

Talbot repeated:

--Through the dear might of Him that walked on waves,
Through the dear might . . .

-- Turn over, Stephen said quietly. I don't see anything.

-- What, sir? Talbot asked simply, bending forward..

His hand turned the page over. He leaned back and went on again having just remembered. Of him that walked on the waves. Here also over these craven hearts his shadow lies and on the scoffer's heart and lips and on mine. It lies upon their eager faces who offered him a coin of the tribute. To Caesar what is Caesar's, to God what is God's. A long look from dark eyes, a riddling sentence to be woven on the church's looms. Ay.

> *Riddle me, riddle me, randy ro.*
> *My father gave me seeds to sow.*

Talbot slid his closed book into his satchel.

-- Have I heard all? Stephen asked.

-- Yes, sir. Hockey at ten, sir.

. . . .

A stick struck the door and a voice in the corridor called:

– Hockey!

They broke asunder, sidling out of their benches, leaping them. Quickly they were gone and from the lumberroom came the rattle of sticks and clamour of their boots and tongues.

Sargent who alone had lingered came forward slowly, showing an open copybook. His tangled hair and scraggy neck gave witness of unreadiness and through his misty glasses weak eyes looked up pleading. On his cheek, dull and bloodless, a soft stain of ink lay, dateshaped, recent and damp as a snail's bed.

He held out his copybook. The word *Sums* was written on the headline. Beneath were sloping figures and at the foot a crooked signature with blind loops and a blot. Cyril Sargent: his name and seal.

– Mr Deasy told me to write them out all again, he said, and show them to you, sir.

Stephen touched the edges of the book. Futility.

– Do you understand how to do them now? he asked.

– Numbers eleven to fifteen, Sargent answered. Mr Deasy said I was to copy them off the board, sir.

– Can you do them yourself? Stephen asked.

– No, sir.

Ugly and futile: lean neck and tangled hair and a stain of ink, a snail's bed. Yet someone loved him, borne him in her arms and in her heart. But for her the race of the world would have trampled him under foot, a squashed boneless snail. She had loved his weak watery blood drained from her own. Was that then real? The only true thing in life? His mother's prostrate body the fiery Columbanus in holy zeal bestrode. She was no more: the trembling skeleton of a twig burnt in the fire, an odour of rosewood and wetted ashes. She had saved him from being trampled under foot and had gone, scarcely having been. A poor soul gone to heaven: an on a heath beneath winking stars a fox, red reek of rapine in his fur, with merciless bright eyes scraped in the earth, listened, scraped up the earth, listened, scraped and scraped."

Sitting at his side Stephen solved out the problem. He proves by algebra that Shakespeare's ghost is Hamlet's grandfather. Sargent peered askance through his slanted glasses. Hockeysticks rattled in the lumberoom: the hollow knock of a ball and calls from the field.

. . . .

In long shady strokes Sargent copied the data. Waiting always for a word of help his hand moved faithfully the unsteady symbols, a faint hue of shame flickering behind his dull skin. *Amor matris:* subjective and objective genitive. With her weak blood and wheysour milk she had fed him and hid from sight of others his swaddling bands.

Like him was I, these sloping shoulders, this gracelessness. My childhood bends beside me. Too far for me to lay a hand there once or lightly. Mine is far and his secret as our eyes. Secrets, silent, stony sit in the dark palaces of both our hearts: secrets weary of their tyranny: tyrants willing to be dethroned.

The sum was done.

. . . .

In the corridor his name was heard, called from the playfield.
– Sargent!
– Run on, Stephen said. Mr Deasy is calling you.

[22]

He stood in the porch and watched the laggard hurry toward the scrappy field where sharp voices were in strife. They were sorted in teams and Mr Deasy came stepping over wisps of grass with gaitered feet. When he had reached the schoolhouse voices again contending called to him. He turned his angry white moustache.

– What is it now? he cried continually without listening.

– Cochrane and Halliday are on the same side, sir, Stephen cried.

– Will you wait in my study for a moment, Mr Deasy said, till I restore order here.

. . . .

A hasty step over the stone porch and in the corridor. Blowing out his rare moustache Mr Deasy halted at the table.

-- First, our little financial settlement, he said.

He brought out of his coat a pocketbook bound by a leather thong. It slapped open and he took from it two notes, one of joined halves, and laid them carefully on the table.

-- Two, he said, strapping and stowing his pocketbook away.

And now his strongroom for the gold. Stephen's embarrassed hand moved over the shells heaped in the cold stone mortar: whelks and money, cowries and leopard shells: and this, whorled as an emir's turban, and this, the scallop of Saint James. An old pilgrim's hoard, dead treasure, hollow shells.

A sovereign fell, bright and new, on the soft pile of the tablecloth.

-- Three, Mr. Deasy said, turning his little savingsbox about in his hand. These are handy things to have. See. This is for sovereigns. This is for shillings, sixpences, halfcrowns. And here crowns. See.

He shot from it two crowns and two shillings.

-- Three twelve, he said. I think you'll find that's right.

-- Thank you, sir, Stephen said, gathering the money together with shy haste and putting it all in a pocket of his trousers.

-- No thanks at all, Mr Deasy said. You have earned it.

Stephen's hand, free again, went back to the hollow shells. Symbols too of beauty and of power. A lump in my pocket. Symbols soiled by greed and misery.

— Don't carry it like that, Mr Deasy said. You'll pull it out somewhere and lose it. You just buy one of these machines. You'll find them very handy.

Answer something.

— Mine would be often empty, Stephen said.

The same room and hour, the same wisdom: and I the same. Three times now. Three nooses round me here. Well. I can break them in this instant if I will.

— Because you don't save, Mr Deasy said, pointing his finger. You don't know what money is. Money is power, when you have lived as long as I have. I know, I know. If youth but knew. But what does Shakespeare say? *Put money in thy purse.*

— Iago, Stephen murmured.

He lifted his gaze from the idle shells to the old man's stare.

— He knew what money was, Mr Deasy said. He made money. A poet but an Englishman too. Do you know what is the pride of the English? Do you know what is the proudest word you will ever hear from an Englishman's mouth?

The seas' ruler. His seacold eyes looked on the empty bay: history is to blame: on me and on my words, unhating.

— That on his empire, Stephen said, the sun never sets.

— Ba! Mr Deasy cried. That's not English. A French Celt said that. He tapped his savingsbox against his thumbnail.

— I will tell you, he said solemnly, what is his proudest boast. *I paid my way.*

Good man, good man.

— *I paid my way. I never borrowed a shilling in my life.* Can you feel that? *I owe nothing.* Can you?

. . . .

Mr Deasy stared sternly for some moments over the mantelpiece at the shapely bulk of a man in tartan fillibegs: Albert Edward, Prince of Wales.

[24]

-- You think me an old fogey and an old tory, his thoughtful voice said. I saw three generations since O'Connell's time. I remember the famine. Do you know that the orange lodges agitated for repeal of the union twenty years before O'Connell did or before the prelates of your communion denounced him as a demagogue? You fenians forget some things.

Glorious, pious and immortal memory. The lodge of Diamond in Armagh the splendid be hung with corpses of papishes. Hoarse, masked and armed, the planters' covenant. The black north and true blue bible. Croppies lie down.

Stephen sketched a brief gesture.

-- I have rebel blood in me too, Mr Deasy said. On the spindle side. But I am descended from sir John Blackwood who voted for the union. We are all Irish, all kings' sons.

-- Alas, Stephen said.

. . . .

-- That reminds me, Mr Deasy said. You can do me a favour, Mr Dedalus, with some of your literary friends. I have a letter here for the press. Sit down a moment. I have just to copy the end.

. . . .

Shouts rang shrill from the boys playfield and a whirring whistle.

Again: a goal. I am among them, among their battling bodies in a medley, the joust of life. You mean that knockkneed mother's darling who seems to be slightly crawsick? Jousts. Time shocked rebounds, shock by shock. Jousts, slush and and uproar of battles, the frozen deathspew of the slain, a hout of the spear spikes baited with men's bloodied guts.

-- Now then, Mr Deasy said, rising.

He came to the table, pinning together his sheets. Stephen stood up.

-- I have put the matter into a nutshell, Mr Deasy said. It's about the foot and mouth disease. Just look through it. There can be no two opinions on the matter.

May I trespass on your valuable space. That doctrine of
laissez faire which so often in our history. Our cattle trade. The way
of all our old industries. Liverpool ring which jockeyed the Galway
harbour scheme. European conflagration. Grain supplies through the
narrow waters of the channel. The pluterperfect imperturbability of
the department of agriculture. Pardoned a classical allusion.
Cassandra. By a woman who was no better than she should be. To
come to the point at issue.

    -- I don't mince words, do I? Mr Deasy asked as Stephen
read on.

    Foot and mouth disease. Known as Koch's preparation.
Serum and virus. Percentage of salted horses… Veterinary
surgeons… Courteous offer a fair trial… In every sense of the word
take the bull by the horns. Thanking you for the hospitality of your
columns.

    – I want that to be printed and read, Mr Deasy said. You will
see at the next outbreak they will put an embargo on Irish cattle. And
it can be cured. It is cured… it is regularly treated and cured in
Austria by cattledoctors there. They offer to come over here. I am
trying to work up influence with the department. Now I'm going to
try publicity.

    – Mark my words, Mr Dedalus, he said. England is in the
hands of the jews. In all the highest places: her finance, her press.
And they are the signs of a nation's decay. Wherever they gather
they eat up the nation's vital strength. I have seen it coming these
years. As sure as we are standing here the jew merchants are already
at their work of destruction. Old England is dying….

    – Dying, he said, if not dead by now.

The harlot's cry from street to street
Shall weave old England's winding sheet.

    His eyes open wide in vision stared sternly across the
sunbeam in which he halted.

    – A merchant, Stephen said, is one who buys cheap and sells
dear, jew or gentile, is he not?

[26]

— They sinned against the light, Mr Deasy said gravely. And you can see the darkness in their eyes. And that is why they are wanderers on the earth to this day.

. . . .

— Who has not? Stephen said.

— What do you mean? Mr Deasy asked.

He came forward a pace and stood by the table. His underjaw fell sideways open uncertainly. Is this old wisdom? He waits to hear from me.

— History, Stephen said, is a nightmare from which I am trying to awake.

From the playfield the boys raised a shout. A whirring whistle: goal. What if that nightmare gave you a back kick?

— The ways of the Creator are not our ways, Mr Deasy said. All history moves towards one great goal, the manifestation of God.

— Stephen jerked his thumb towards the window, saying:

— That is God.

Hooray! Ay! Whrrwhee!

— What? Mr Deasy asked.

— A shout in the street, Stephen answered, shrugging his shoulders.

Mr Deasy looked down and held for a while the wings of his nose tweaked between his fingers. Looking up again, he set them free.

-- I am happier than you are, he said. We have committed many errors and many sins. A woman brought sin into the world. For a woman who was no better than she should be, Helen, the runaway wife of Menelaus, ten years the Greeks made war on Troy. A faithless wife first brought the strangers to our shore here, MacMurrough's wife and her leman O'Rourke, prince of Breffni. A woman too brought Parnell low. Many errors, many failures but not the one sin. I am a struggler now at the end of my days. But I will fight for the right till the end.

> *For Ulster will fight*
> *And Ulster will be right.*

Stephen raised the sheets in his hand.

-- Well, sir, he began.

-- I foresee, Mr Deasy said, that you will not remain here very long at this work. You were not born to be a teacher, I think. Perhaps I am wrong.

-- A learner rather, Stephen said.

And here what will you learn more?

Mr Deasy shook his head.

-- Who knows, he said. To learn one must be humble. But life is the great teacher.

. . . .

– Good morning, sir, Stephen said, putting the sheets in his pocket. Thank you.

– Not at all, Mr Deasy said as he searched the papers on his desk. I like to break a lance with you, as old as I am.

– Good morning, sir, Stephen said again, bowing to his bent back.

He went out by the open porch and down the gravel path under the trees, hearing the cries and voices and crack of sticks from the playfield. The lions couchant on the pillars as he passed out through the gate; toothless terrors. Still I will help him in his fight. Mulligan will dub me a new name: the bullockbefriending bard.

– Mr Dedalus!

Running after me. No more letters, I hope.

– Just one moment.

– Yes, sir, Stephen said, turning back at the gate.

Mr Deasy halted, breathing hard and swallowing his breath.

– I just wanted to say, he said. Ireland, they say, has the honour of being the only country which never persecuted the jews. Do you know that? No. And do you know why?

He frowned sternly on the bright air.

– Why, sir? Stephen asked, beginning to smile.

– Because she never let them in, Mr Deasy said solemnly.

[28]

– She never let them in, he cried again through his laughter as he stamped on the gaitered feet over the gravel of the path. That's why.

On his wise shoulders through the checkerwork of leaves the sun flung spangles, dancing coins.

Episode 3 -- Proteus... God of the sea who changes forms at will. Telemachus learns of Proteus from Menelaus, who describes how Proteus is ever shifting his being. ~ Looking out to sea, in his evolving consciousness, Stephen philosophizes on the inevitable (ineluctable) sea changes of life and death.

Wandering along the beach at Sandymount Strand, Stephen struggles to to disentangle the translucent *(diaphane)* realities of his past: objects he perceives in time *(nacheinander)* and space *(nebeneinander)*, and discover who he really is and not who he is perceived to be. Stephen sees Florence McCabe and friend, midwives, whose heavy bag sends Stephen's mind into birth, creation, life and death imagery. He debates whether to visit his aunt and uncle. A bloated dog carcass gives him pause. Stephen contemplates his parentage, and that of Christ. Stephen is aggrieved by his past transgressions, some in Paris. He ponders a recent drowning. Through the sight of three masts of a ship, he perceives that crucifixion is the means to a sea change and hope of resurrection. Thus ends part ONE, Stephen's saga.

THEMES
Is what we see real? Is what we hear real? Who are we really? As perceived by others? Life bound up in inescapable change. "Our mighty mother" the origin of our reality. The real father, physical man or God Himself? How to know one's self, better or worse. Change, transformation, patriotism, one's leadership in a national cause can be a crucifixion. Hope teeters with despair, sanity with madness, creativity with waste, death without redemption.

INELUCTABLE MODALITY OF THE VISIBLE: AT LEAST THAT IF NO more, thought through my eyes. Signatures of all things I am here to read, seaspawn and seawrack, the nearing tide, that rusty boot. Snotgreen, bluesilver, rust: coloured signs. Limits of the diaphane. But he adds: in bodies. Then he was aware of them bodies before of them coloured. How? By knocking his sconce against them, sure. Go easy. Bald he was and a millionaire, *maestro di color che sanno.* Limit of the diaphane in. Why in? Diaphane, adiaphane. If you can put your five fingers through it, it is a gate, if not, a door. Shut your eyes and see.

Stephen closed his eyes to hear his boots crush crackling wrack and shells. You are walking through it howsomever. I am, a stride at a time. A very short space of time through very short times of space. Five, six: the *nacheinander.* Exactly: and that is the ineluctable modality of the audible. Open your eyes. No. Jesus! If I fell over a cliff that beetles o'er his base, fell through the *nebeneinander* ineluctably. I am getting on nicely in the dark. My

[30]

ash sword hangs at my side. Tap with it: they do. My two feet in his boots are at the end of his legs, *nebeneinander.* Sounds solid: made by the mallet of Los Demiurgos. Am I walking into eternity along Sandymount strand? Crush, crack, crick, crick."

. . . .

Open your eyes now. I will. One moment. Has all vanished since? If I open and am for ever in the black adiaphane. *Basta!* I will see if I can see.

See now. There all the time without you: and ever shall be, world without end.

They came down the steps from Leahy's terrace prudently, *Frauenzimmer:* and down the shelving shore flabbily their splayed feet sinking in the silted sand. Like me, like Algy, coming down to our mighty mother. Number one swung lourdily her midwife's bag, the other's gamp poked in the beach. From the liberties, out for the day. Mrs. Florence MacCabe, relict of the late Patrick MacCabe, deeply lamented, of Bride Street. One of her sisterhood lugged me squealing into life. Creation from nothing. What has she in the bag? A misbirth with a trailing navelcord, hushed in rudy wool. The cords of all link back, strandentwining cable of all flesh. That is why mystic monks. Will you be as gods? Gaze in your omphalos. Hello. Kinch here. Put me on to Edenville. Aleph, alpha: nought, nought, one.

Spouse and helpmate of Adam Kadmon: Heva, naked Eve. She had no navel. Gaze. Belly without blemish, bulging big, a buckler of taut vellum, no whiteheaped corn, orient and immortal, standing from everlasting to everlasting. Womb of sin.

Wombed in sin darkness I was too, made not begotten. By them, the man with the voice and my eyes and a ghostwoman with ashes on her breath. They clasped and sundered, did the coupler's will. From before the ages He willed me and now may not will me away or ever. A *lex eterna* stays about him. Is that then the divine substance wherein Father and Son are consubstantial? Where is poor dear Arius to try conclusions? Warring his life long on the contransmagnificandjewbangtantiality. Illstarred heresiarch. In a

Greek watercloset he breathed his last: euthanasia. With beaded mitre and with crozier, stalled upon his throne, widower of a widowed see, with upstiffed omophorion, with clotted hinderparts.

Airs romped around him, nipping and eager airs. They are coming, waves. The whitemaned seahorses, champing, brightwindbridled, the steeds of Mananaan.

I mustn't forget his letter for the press. And after? The Ship, half twelve. By the way go easy with that money like a good young imbecile. Yes, I must.

. . . .

Cousin Stephen, you will never be a saint. Isle of saints. You were awfully holy, weren't you? You prayed to the Blessed Virgin that you might not have a red nose. You prayed to the devil in Serpentine avenue that the fubsy widow in the front might lift her clothes still more from the wet street. *O si, certo!* Sell your soul for that, do, dyed rags pinned round a squaw. More tell me, more still! On the top of Howth tram alone crying to the rain: *naked women!* What about that, eh?

What about what? What else were they invented for?

Reading two pages apiece of seven books every night, eh? I was young. You bowed to yourself in the mirror, stepping forward to applause earnestly, striking face. Hurray for the Goddamned idiot! Hray! No-one saw: tell no-one. Books you were going to write with letters for titles. Have you read his F? O yes, but I prefer Q. Yes, but W is wonderful. O yes, W. Remember your epiphanies on green oval leaves, deeply deep, copies to be sent if you died to all the great libraries of the world, including Alexandria? Someone was to read them there after a few thousand years, a mahamanvantara. Pico della Mirandola like. Ay, very like a whale. When one reads these strange pages of one long gone one feels that one is at one with one who once . . .

. . . .

He halted. I have passed the way to aunt Sara's. Am I not going there? Seems not. No-one about. He turned northeast and crossed the firmer sand towards the Pigeonhouse.

[32]

-- Qui vous a mis dans cette fichue position?

-- C'est le pigeon, Joseph.

Patrice, home on furlough, lapped warm milk with me in the bar MacMahon. Son of the wild goose, Kevin Egan of Paris. My father's a bird, he lapped the sweet *lait chaud* with pink young tongue, plump bunny's face. Lap, *lapin.* He hopes to win in the *gros lots.* About the nature of women he read in Michelet. But he must send me *La Vie de Jesus* by M. Leo Taxil. Lent it to his friend.

-- C'est tordant, vous savez. Moi je suis socialiste. Je ne crois pas en l'existence de Dieu. Faut pas le dire à mon père.

-- Il croit?

-- Mon père, oui.

Schluss. He laps.

. . . .

You were going to do wonders, what? Missionary to Europe after fiery Columbanus. Fiacre and Scotus on their creepystools in heaven spilt from their pintpots, loudlatinlaughing: *Euge! Euge!* Pretending to speak broken English as you dragged your valise, porter threepence, across the slimy pier at Newhaven. *Comment?* Rich booty you brought back; *Le Tutu,* five tattered numbers of *Pantalon Blanc et Culotte Rouge,* a blue French telegram, curiosity to show:

-- Mother dying come home father.

The aunt thinks you killed your mother. That's why she won't.

> *Then here's a health to Mulligan's aunt*
> *And I'll tell you the reason why.*
> *She always kept things decent in*
> *The Hannigan famileye.*

His feet marched in sudden proud rhythm over the sand furrows, along by the boulders of the south wall. He stared at them proudly, piled stone mammoth skulls. Gold light on sea, on sand, on boulders. The sun is there, the slender trees, the lemon houses.

Paris rawly waking, crude sunlight on her lemon streets. Moist pith of farls of bread, the froggreen wormwood, her matin incense, court the air. Belluomo rises from the bed of his wife's lover's wife, the kerchiefed housewife is astir, a saucer of acetic acid in hands. In Rodot's Yvone and Madeleine newmake their tumbled beauties, shattering with gold teeth *chaussons* of pastry, their mouths yellowed with the *pus* of *flan breton*. Faces of Paris men go by, their wellpleased pleasers, curled conquistadores.

. . . .

In gay Paree he hides, Egan of Paris, unsought by any save by me. Making his day's stations, the dingy printingcase, his three taverns, the Montmartre lair he sleeps short night in, rue de la Goutte-d'Or, damascened with flyblown faces of the gone. Loveless, landless, wifeless. She is quite nicey comfy without her outcastman, madame, in rue Gît-le-Coeur, canary and two buck lodgers. Peachy cheeks, a zebra skirt, frisky as a young thing's. Spurned and despairing. Tell Pat you saw me, won't you? I wanted to get poor Pat a job one time. *Mon fils,* soldier of France. I taught him to sing. *The boys of Kilkenny are stout roaring blades.* Know that old lay? I taught Patrice that. Old Kilkenny: saint Canice, Strongbow's castle on the Nore. Goes like this. *O, O.* He takes me, Napper Tandy, by the hand.

> *O, O the boys of*
> *Kilkenny . . .*

Weak wasting hand on mine. They have forgotten Kevin Egan, not he them. Remembering thee, O Sion.

He had come nearer the edge of the sea and wet sand slapped his boots. The new air greeted him, harping in wild nerves, wind of wild air of seeds of brightness. Here, I am not walking out to the Kish lightship, am I? He stood suddenly, his feet beginning to sink slowly in the quaking soil. Turn back.

Turning, he scanned the shore south, his feet sinking again slowly in new sockets. The cold domed room of the tower waits. Through the barbicans the shafts of light are moving ever, slowly

[34]

ever as my feet are sinking, creeping duskward over the dial floor. Blue dusk, nightfall, deep blue night. In the darkness of the dome they wait, their pushedback chairs, my obelisk valise, around a board of abandoned platters. Who to clear it? He has the key. I will not sleep there when this night comes. A shut door of a silent tower entombing their blind bodies, the panthersahib and his pointer. Call: no answer. He lifted his feet up from the suck and turned back by the mole of boulders. Take all, keep all. My soul walks with me, form of forms. So in the moon's midwatches I pace the path above the rocks, in sable silvered, hearing Elsinore's tempting flood.

The flood is following me. I can watch it flow past from here. Get back then by the Poolbeg road to the strand there. He climbed over the sedge and eely oarweeds and sat on a stool of rock, resting his ashplant in a grike.

A bloated carcass of a dog lay lolled on bladderwrack. Before him the gunwale of a boat, sunk in the sand. *Un coche ensablé,* Louis Veuillot called Gautier's prose. These heavy sands are language tide and wind have silted here. And there, the stoneheaps of dead builders, a warren of weasel rats. Hide gold there. Try it. You have some. Sands and stones. Heavy of the past. Sir Lout's toys. Mind you don't get one bang on the ear. I'm the bloody well gigant rolls all them bloody well boulders, bones for my steppingstones. Feefawfum. I zmellz de bloodz odz an Iridzman.

A point, live dog, grew into sight running across the sweep of sand. Lord, is he going to attack me? Respect his liberty. You will not be master of others or their slave. I have my stick. Sit tight. From farther away, walking shoreward across from the crested tide, figures, two. The two maries. They have tucked it safe among the bulrushes. Peekaboo. I see you. No, the dog. He is running back to them. Who?

Galleys of the Lochlanns ran here to the beach, in quest of prey, their bloodbeaked prows riding low on a molten pewter surf. Danevikings, torcs of tomahawks aglitter on their breasts when Malachi wore the collar of gold. A school of turlehide whales stranded in hot noon, spouting, hobbling in the shallows. Then from

the starving cagework city a horde of jerkind dwarfs, my people,
with flayers' knives, running, scaling, hacking in green blubbery
whalemeat. Famine, plague and slaughters. Their blood is in me,
their lusts my waves. I moved among them on the frozen Liffey, that
I, a changeling, among the spluttering resin fires. I spoke to no-one:
none to me.

. . . .

    We don't want any of your medieval abstrusiosities. Would
you do what he did? A boat would be near, a lifebuoy. *Natürlich*, put
there for you. Would you or would you not? The man that was
drowned nine days ago off Maiden's rock. They are waiting for him
now. The truth, spit it out. I would want to. I would try. I am not a
strong swimmer. Water cold soft. When I put my face into it in the
basin at Clongowes. Can't see! Who's behind me? Out quickly,
quickly! Do you see the tide flowing quickly in on all sides, sheeting
the lows of sands quickly, shelling cocoacoloured? If I had land
under my feet. I want his life still to be his, mine to be mine. A
drowning man. His human eyes scream to me out of horror of his
death, I . . . With him together down . . . I could not save her. Waters:
bitter death: lost.

    A woman and a man. I see her skirties. Pinned up, I bet.

    Their dog ambled about a bank of dwindling sand, trotting,
sniffing on all sides. Looking for something lost in a past life.
Suddenly he made off like a bounding hare, ears flung back, chasing
the shadow of a lowskimming gull. The man's shrieked whistle
struck its limp ears. He turned, bounded back, came nearer, trotted
on twinkling shanks. On a field tenney a buck, trippant, proper,
unattired. At the lacefringe of the tide he halted with stiff forehoofs,
seawardpointed ears. His snout lifted barked at the wavenoise, herds
of seamorse. They serpent towards his feet, curling, unfurling many
crests, every ninth, breaking, plashing, from far, from farther out,
waves and waves.

    Cocklepickers. They waded a little way in the water and,
stooping, soused their bags, and, lifting them again, waded out. The
dog yelped running to them, reared up and pawed them, dropping on

[36]

all fours, again reared up at them with mute bearish fawning.
Unheeded he kept by them as they came towards the drier sand, a rag
of wolf's tongue redpanting from his jaws. His speckled body
ambled ahead of them and then loped off at a calf's gallop. The
carcass lay on his path. He stopped, sniffed, stalked around it,
brother, nosing closer, went round it, sniffing rapidly like a dog all
over the dead dog's bedraggled fell. Dogskull, dogsniff, eyes on the
ground, moves to one great goal. Ah, poor dogsbody. Here lies poor
dogsbody's body.

    – Tatters! Out of that, you mongrel.

. . . .

    After he woke me up last night same dream or was it? Wait.
Open hallway. Street of harlots. Remember. Haroun al Raschid. I am
almosting it. That man led me, spoke. I was not afraid. The melon he
had he held against my face. Smiled: creamfruit smell. That was the
rule, said. In. Come. Red carpet spread. You will see who.

. . . .

    – His lips lipped and mouthed fleshless lips of air: mouth to
her womb. Oomb, allwombing tomb. His mouth moulded issuing
breath, unspeeched: ooeeehah: roar of cataractic planets, globed
blazing, roaring wayawayawayawayawayaway. Paper. The
banknotes, blast them. Old Deasy's letter. Here. Thanking you for
your hospitality tear the blank end off. Turning his back to the sun he
bent over far to a table of rock and scribbled words. That's twice I
forgot to take slips from the library counter.

    His shadow lay over the rocks as he bent, ending. Why not
endless till the farthest star? Darkly they are there behind this light,
darkness shining in the brightness, delta of Cassiopeia, worlds. Me
sits there with his augur's rod of ash, in borrowed sandals, by day
beside a livid sea, unbeheld, in violet night walking beneath a reign
of uncouth stars. I throw this ended shadow from me, manshape
ineluctable, call it back. Endless, would it be mine, form of my
form? Who watches me here? Who ever anywhere will read these
written words? Signs on a white field. Somewhere to someone in
your flutiest voice. The good bishop of Cloyne took the veil of the

[37]

temple out of his shovel hat: veil of space with coloured emblems hatched on its field. Hold hard. Coloured on a flat: yes, that's right. Flat I see, then think distance, near, far, flat I see, east, back. Ah, see now. Falls back suddenly, frozen in stereoscope. Click does the trick. You find my words dark. Darkness is in our souls, do you not think? Flutier. Our souls, shame-wounded by our sins, cling to us yet more, a woman to her lover clinging, the more the more.

She trusts me, her hand gentle, the longlashed eyes. Now where the blue hell am I bringing her beyond the veil? Into the ineluctable modality of the ineluctable visuality. She, she, she. What she? The virgin at Hodges Figgis' window on Monday looking in for one of the alphabet books you were going to write. Keen glance you gave her. Wrist through the braided jess of her sunshade. She lives in Leeson park, with a grief and kickshaws, a lady of letters. Talk that to someone else, Stevie: a pickmeup. Bet she wears those curse of God stay suspenders and yellow stockings, darned with lumpy wool. Talk about apple dumplings, *piuttosto*. Where are your wits?

Touch me. Soft eyes. Soft soft soft hand. I am lonely here. O, touch me soo, now. What is that word known to all men? I am quiet here alone. Sad too. Touch me, touch me.

He lay back at full stretch over the sharp rocks, cramming the scribbled note and pencil into a pocket, his hat tilted down on his eyes. That is Kevin Egan's movement I made nodding for his nap, sabbath sleep. *Et vidit Deus. Et erant valde bona.* Alo! *Bonjour,* welcome as the flowers in May. Under its leaf he watched through peacocktwittering lashes the southing sun. I am caught in this burning scene. Pan's hour, the faunal noon. Among gumheavy serpentplants, milkoozing fruits, where on the tawny waters leaves lie wide. Pain is far.

And no more turn aside and brood.

His gaze brooded on his broadtoed boots, a buck's castoffs *nebeneinander.* He counted the creases of rucked leather wherein another's foot had nested warm. The foot that beat the ground in tripudium, foot I dislove. But you were delighted when Esther Osvalt's shoe went on you: girl I knew in Paris. *Tiens, quel petit pied!* Staunch friend, a brother soul: Wilde's love that dare not speak its name. He now will leave me. And the blame? As I am. As I am. All or not at all.

. . . .

Five fathoms out there. Full fathom five thy father lies. At one he said. Found drowned. High water at Dublin bar. Driving before it a loose drift of rubble, fanshoals of fishes, silly shells. A corpse rising saltwhite from the undertow, bobbing landward, a pace a pace a porpoise. There he is. Hook it quick. Sunk though he be beneath the watery floor. We have him. Easy now.

Bag of corpsegas sopping in foul brine. A quiver of minnows, fat of a spongy titbit, flash through the slits of his buttoned trouserfly. God becomes man becomes fish becomes barnacle goose becomes featherbed mountain. Dead breaths I living breathe, tread dead dust, devour a urinous offal from all the dead. Hauled stark over the gunwale he breathes upward the stench of his green grave, his leprous nosehole snoring to the sun.

A seachange this, brown eyes saltblue. Seadeath, mildest of all deaths known to man. Old Father Ocean. *Prix de Paris:* beware of imitations. Just you give it a fair trial. We enjoyed ourselves immensely.

Come. I thirst. Clouding over. No black clouds anywhere, are there? Thunderstorm. Allbright he falls, proud lightning of the intellect. *Lucifer, dico, qui nescit occasum.* No. My cockle hat and staff and his my sandal shoon. Where? To evening lands. Evening will find itself.

He took the hilt of his ashplant, lunging with it softly, dallying still. Yes, evening will find itself in me, without me. All days make their end. By the way next when is it? Tuesday will be the longest day. Of all the glad new year, mother, the rum tum tiddledy tum. Lawn Tennyson, gentleman poet. *Gia.* For the old hag with the yellow teeth. And Monsieur Drumont, gentleman journalist. *Gia.* My teeth are very bad. Why, I wonder? Feel. That one is going too. Shells. Ought I go to a dentist, I wonder, with that money? That one.

Toothless Kinch, the superman. Why is that, I wonder, or does it mean something perhaps?

My handkerchief. He threw it. I remember. Did I not take it up?

His hand groped vainly in his pockets. No, I didn't. Better buy one.

He laid the dry snot picked from his nostril on a ledge of rock, carefully. For the rest let look who will.

Behind. Perhaps there is someone.

He turned his face over a shoulder, rere regardant. Moving through the air high spars of a threemaster, her sails brailed up on the crosstrees, homing, upstream, silently moving, a silent ship.

[40]

Episode 4 – Calypso... a beautiful nymph who held Odysseus as a love captive for seven years until Zeus compels her to let Odysseus resume his voyage home. ~ Leopold Bloom is captivated by his wife Molly who resembles the nymph pictured above their bed. Throughout the day Bloom is held back by his knowledge of her adultery that afternoon.

Leopold Bloom commences his day's odyssey as had Stephen Dedalus. With subtle similarities, Bloom prepares breakfast for his wife, Molly, and milk for his cat; hears Church bells reminding him of Dignam's funeral that day. He brings in the mail, a letter from Blazes Boylan to his wife, and a letter from daughter Milly.The cloud covering the sun depresses Bloom, causing him to think of death. His visit to Dlugacz's butchery and his encounter with the neighbors' serving girl arouse his sensuality. After breakfast and after his morning stool where he imagines his publishing a prize titbit, he leaves home and wife but without his latchkey.

THEMES
To be of Mind whilie accepting of Body functions. Death the "gray sunken cunt of the world." The death of Bloom's Jewish heritage. Death causes man to cherish the touch of warm flesh. We are keyless and dispossessed. Allusion to upcoming sexual affair of wife Molly and actor Blazes Boylan, and daughter Milly's sexual ripening -- "those seaside girls." Parallels similarities and differences between the odyssey of Leopold Bloom, man of earth and science, and that of Stephen Dedalus, philosopher-artist. Salvation through acceptance of the total self.

II

MR. Leopold Bloom ate with relish the inner organs of beasts and fowls. He liked thick giblet soup, nutty gizzards, a stuffed roast heart, liver slices fried with crustcrumbs, fried hencod's roes. Most of all he liked grilled mutton kidneys which gave to his palate a fine tang of faintly scented urine.

Kidneys were in his mind as he moved about the kitchen softly, righting her breakfast things on the humpy tray. Gelid light and air were in the kitchen but out of doors gentle summer morning everywhere. Made him feel a bit peckish.

The coals were reddening.

Another slice of bread and butter: three, four: right. She didn't like her plate full. Right. He turned from the tray, lifted the kettle off the hob and set it sideways on the fire. It sat there, dull and squat, its spout stuck out. Cup of tea soon. Good. Mouth dry. The cat walked stiffly round a leg of the table with tail on high.

-- Mkgnao!

-- O, there you are, Mr. Bloom said, turning from the fire.

The cat mewed in answer and stalked again stiffly round a leg of the table, mewing. Just how she stalks over my writingtable. Prr. Scratch my head. Prr.

Mr. Bloom watched curiously, kindly, the lithe black form. Clean to see: the gloss of her sleek hide, the white button under the butt of her tail, the green flashing eyes. He bent down to her, his hands on his knees.

-- Milk for the pussens, he said.

-- Mrkgnao! the cat cried.

. . . .

On quietly creaky boots he went up the staircase to the hall, paused by the bedroom door. She might like something tasty. Thin bread and butter she likes in the morning. Still perhaps: once in a way.

He said softly in the bare hall:

-- I am going round the corner. Be back in a minute.

And when he had heard his voice say it he added:

--You don't want anything for breakfast?

A sleepy soft grunt answered:

-- Mn.

No. She did not want anything. He heard then a warm heavy sigh, softer, as she turned over and the loose brass quoits of the bedstead jingled. Must get those settled really. Pity. All the way from Gibraltar. Forgotten any little Spanish she knew. Wonder what her father gave for it. Old style. Ah yes, of course. Bought it at the governor's auction. Got a short knock. Hard as nails at a bargain, old Tweedy. Yes, sir. At Plevna that was. I rose from the ranks, sir, and I'm proud of it. Still he had brains enough to make that corner in stamps. Now that was farseeing.

. . . .

On the doorstep he felt in his hip pocket for the latchkey. Not there. In the trousers I left off. Must get it. Potato I have. Creaky wardrobe. No use disturbing her. She turned over sleepily that time.

[42]

He pulled the halldoor to after him very quietly, more, till the footleaf dropped gently over the threshold, a limp lid. Looked shut. All right till I come back anyhow.

He crossed to the bright side, avoiding the loose cellarflap of number seventyfive. The sun was nearing the steeple of George's church. Be a warm day I fancy. Specially in these black clothes feel it more. Black conducts, reflects (refracts is it?), the heat. But I couldn't go in that light suit. Make a picnic of it. His eyelids sank quietly often as he walked in happy warmth. Boland's breadvan delivering with trays our daily but she prefers yesterday's loaves turnovers crisp crowns hot. Makes you feel young. Somewhere in the east: early morning: set off at dawn, travel round in front of the sun, steal a day's march on him. Keep it up for ever never grow a day older technically.

. . . .

He approached Larry O'Rourke's. From the cellar grating floated up the flabby gush of porter. Through the open doorway the bar squirted out whiffs of ginger, teadust, biscuitmush. Good house, however: just the end of the city traffic. For instance M'Auley's down there: n. g. as position. Of course if they ran a tramline along the North Circular from the cattle market to the quays value would go up like a shot.

Bald head over the blind. Cute old codger. No use canvassing him for an ad. Still he knows his own business best.

. . . .

— Where do they get the money? Coming up redheaded curates from the county Leitrim, rinsing empties and old man in the cellar. Then, lo and behold, they blossom out as Adam Findlaters or Dan Tallons. Then think of the competition. General thirst. Good puzzle would be cross Dublin without passing a pub.

. . . .

He halted before Dlugacz's window, staring at the hanks of sausages, polonies, black and white. Fifty multiplied by. The figures whitened in his mind unsolved: displeased, he let them fade. The shiny links packed with forcemeat fed his gaze and he breathed in tranquility the lukewarm breath of cooked spicy pig's blood.

A kidney oozed bloodgouts on the willowpatterned dish: the last. He stood by the nextdoor girl at the counter. Would she buy it too, calling the items from a slip in her hand. Chapped: washing soda. And a pound and a half of Denny's sausages. His eyes rested on her vigorous hips. Woods his name is. Wonder what he does. Wife is oldish. New blood. No followers allowed. Strong pair of arms. Whacking a carpet on the clothesline. She does whack it, by George. The way her crooked skirt swings at each whack.

The ferreteyed porkbutcher folded the sausages he had snipped off with blotchy fingers, sausagepink. Sound meat there like a stallfed heifer.

. . . .

The porkbutcher snapped two sheets from the pile, wrapped up her prime sausages and made a red grimace.

– Now, my miss, he said.

She tendered a coin, smiling boldly, holding her thick wrist out.

– Thank you, my miss. And one shilling threepence change. For you, please?

Mr. Bloom pointed quickly. To catch up and walk behind her if she went slowly, behind her moving hams. Pleasant to see first thing in the morning. Hurry up, damn it. Make hay while the sun shines. She stood outside the shop in sunlight and sauntered lazily to the right. He sighed down his nose: they never understand. Sodachapped hands. Crusted toenails too. Brown scapulars in tatters, defending her both ways. The sting of disregard glowed to weak pleasure within his breast. For another: a constable off duty cuddled her in Eccles Lane. They like them sizeable. Prime sausage. O please, Mr. Policeman, I'm lost in the wood.

-- Threepence, please.

His hand accepted the moist tender gland and slid it into a sidepocket. Then it fetched up three coins from his trousers' pocket

and laid them on the rubber prickles. They lay, were read quickly
and quickly slid, disc by disc, into the till.

-- Thank you, sir. Another time.

A speck of eager fire from foxeyes thanked him. He
withdrew his gaze after an instant. No: better not: another time.

-- Good morning, he said, moving away.

-- Good morning, sir.

No sign. Gone. What matter?

. . . .

A cloud began to cover the sun wholly slowly wholly. Grey.
Far.

No, not like that. A barren land, bare waste. Vulcanic lake,
the dead sea: no fish, weedless, sunk deep in the earth. No wind
would lift those waves, grey metal, poisonous foggy waters.
Brimstone they called it raining down: the cities of the plain: Sodom,
Gomorrah, Edom. All dead names. A dead sea in a dead land, grey
and old. Old now. It bore the oldest, the first race. A bent hag
crossed from Cassidy's clutching a noggin bottle by the neck. The
oldest people. Wandered far away over all the earth, captivity to
captivity, multiplying, dying, being born everywhere. It lay there
now. Now it could bear no more. Dead: an old woman's: the grey
sunken cunt of the world.

Desolation.

Grey horror seared his flesh. Folding the page into his pocket
he turned into Eccles Street, hurrying homeward.

. . . .

Two letters and a card lay on the hallfloor. He stopped and
gathered them. Mrs Marion Bloom. His quick heart slowed at once.
Bold hand. Mrs Marion.

– Poldy!

Entering the bedroom he halfclosed his eyes and walked
through warm yellow twilight towards her tousled head.

–Who are the letters for?

He looked at them. Mullingar. Milly.

-- A letter for me from Milly, he said carefully, and a card to you. And a letter to you.

He laid her card and letter on the twill bedspread near the curve of her knees.

-- Do you want the blind open?

Letting the blind up by gentle tugs halfway his backward eye saw her glance at the letter and tuck it under her pillow.

-- That do? he asked, turning.

She was reading the card, propped on her elbow.

-- She got the things, she said.

He waited till she had laid the card aside and curled herself back slowly with a snug sigh.

-- Hurry up with that tea, she said. I'm parched.

-- The kettle is boiling, he said.

But he delayed to clear the chair: her striped petticoat, tossed soiled linen: and lifted all in an armful on to the foot of the bed.

As he went down the kitchen stairs she called:

-- Poldly!

-- What?

-- Scald the teapot.

On the boil sure enough: a plume of steam from the spout. He scalded and rinsed out the teapot and put in four full spoons of tea, tilting the kettle then to let water flow in. Having set it to draw, he took off the kettle and crushed the pan flat on the live coals and watched the lump of butter slide and melt. While he unwrapped the kidney the cat mewed hungrily against him. Give her too much meat she won't mouse. Say they won't eat pork. Kosher. Here. He let the bloodsmeared paper fall to her and dropped the kidney amid the sizzling butter sauce. Pepper. He sprinkled it through his fingers, ringwise, from the chipped eggcup.

Then he slit open his letter, glancing down the page and over. Thanks: new tam: Mr. Coghlan: lough Owel picnic: young student: Blazes Boylan's seaside girls.

The tea was drawn. He filled his own moustachecup, sham crown Derby, smiling. Silly Milly's birthday gift. Only five she was

then. No wait: four. I gave her the amberoid necklace she broke.
Putting pieces of folded brown paper in the letterbox for her. He
smiled, pouring.

O, Milly Bloom, you are my darling.
You are my looking glass from night to morning.
I'd rather have you without a farthing
Than Katey Keogh with her ass and garden.

. . . .

He prodded a fork into the kidney and slapped it over: then
fitted the teapot on the tray. Its hump bumped as he took it up.
Everything on it? Bread and butter, four, sugar, a spoon, her cream.
Yes. He carried it upstairs, his thumb hooked in the teapot handle.

Nudging the door open with his knee he carried the tray and
set it on the chair by the bedhead.

-- What a time you were, she said.

She set the brasses jingling as she raised herself briskly, an
elbow on the pillow. He looked calmly down on her bulk and
between her large soft bubs, sloping within her nightdress like a
shegoat's udder. The warmth of her couched body rose on the air,
mingling with the fragrance of the tea she poured.

A strip of torn envelope peeped from under the dimpled
pillow. In the act of going he stayed to straighten the bedspread.

–Who was the letter from? he asked.

Bold hand. Marion.

–O, Boylan, she said. He's bringing the programme.

–What are you singing?

–*La ci darem* with J.C.Doyle, she said, and *Love's Old Sweet
Song.*

Her full lips, drinking, smiled. Rather stale smell that
incense leaves next day. Like foul flowerwater.

–Would you like the window open a little?

She doubled a slice of bread into her mouth, asking:

–What time is the funeral?

–Eleven, I think, he answered. I didn't see the paper.

Following the pointing of her finger he took up a leg of her
soiled drawers from the bed. No? Then, a twisted grey garter looped
round a stocking: rumpled, shiny sole.

– No: that book.

Other stocking. Her petticoat.

– It must have fell down, she said.

. . . .

The *Bath of the Nymph* over the bed. Given away with the
Easter number of *Photo Bits:* Splendid masterpiece in art colours.
Tea before you put milk in. Not unlike her with her hair down:
slimmer. Three and six I gave for the frame. She said it would look
nice over the bed. Naked nymphs: Greece: and for instance all the
people that lived then.

He turned the pages back.

– Metempsychosis, he said, is what the ancient Greeks called
it. They used to believe you could be changed into an animal or a
tree for instance. What they called nymphs, for example.

Her spoon ceased to stir up the sugar. She glazed straight
before her, inhaling through her arched nostrils.

– There's a smell of burn, she said. Did you leave something
on the fire?

– The kidney! he cried suddenly.

. . . .

Cup of tea now. He sat down, cut and buttered a slice of the
loaf. He shore away the burnt flesh and flung it to the cat. Then he
put a forkful into his mouth, chewing with discernment the
toothsome pliant meat. Done to a turn. A mouthful of tea. Then he
cut away dies of bread, sopped one in the gravy and put it in his
mouth. What was that about some young student and a picnic? He
creased out the letter at his side, reading it slowly as he chewed,
sopping another die of bread in the gravy and raising it to his mouth.

Dearest Papli,

Thanks ever so much for the lovely birthday present. It suits
me splendid. Everyone says I'm quite the belle in my new tam. I got

mummy's lovely box of creams and am writing. They are lovely. I am getting on swimming in the photo business now. Mr Coghlan took one of me and Mrs will send when developed. We did great biz yesterday. Fair day and all the beef to the heels were in. We are going to lough Owel on Monday with a few friends to make a scrap picnic. Give my love to mummy and to yourself a big kiss and thanks. I hear them at the piano downstairs. There is to be a concert in the Greville Arms on Saturday. There is a young student comes here some evenings named Bannon his cousin or something are big swells he sings Boylan's (I was on the pop of writing Blazes Boylan's) song about those seaside girls. Tell him silly Milly sends my best respects. Must now close with fondest love.

  Your fond daughter,

          MILLY

 P.S. Excuse bad writing, am in a hurry. Byby.

Fifteen yesterday. Curious, fifteenth of the month too. Her first birthday away from home. Separation. Remember the summer morning she was born, running to knock up Mrs Thornton in Denzille street. Jolly old woman. Lots of babies she must have helped into the world. She knew from the first poor little Rudy wouldn't live. Well, God is good, sir. She knew at once. He would be eleven now if he had lived.

. . . .

He felt full: then a gentle loosening of his bowels. He stood up, undoing the waistband of his trousers. The cat mewed to him.

-- Miaow! he said in answer. Wait till I'm ready.

Heaviness: hot day coming. Too much trouble to fag up the stairs to the landing.

A paper. He liked to read at stool. Hope no ape comes knocking just as I'm.

In the table drawer he found an old number of *Titbits*. He folded it under his armpit, went to the door and opened it. The cat went up in soft bounds. Ah, wanted to go upstairs, curl up in a ball on the bed.

Listening, he heard her voice:

-- Come, come pussy. Come.

He went out through the backdoor into the garden: stood to listen towards the next garden. No sound. Perhaps hanging clothes out to dry. The maid was in the garden. Fine morning.

. . . .

He kicked open the crazy door of the jakes. Better be careful not to get these trousers dirty for the funeral. He went in, bowing his head under the low lintel. Leaving the door ajar, amid the stench of mouldy limewash and stale cobwebs he undid his braces. Before sitting down he peered through a chink up at the nextdoor window. The king was in his counting house. Nobody.

Asquat on the cuckstool he folded out his paper turning its pages over his bared knees. Something new and easy. No great hurry. Keep it a bit. Our prie titbit. *Matcham's Masterstroke.* Written by Mr. Philip Beaufoy, Playgoers' club, London. Payment at the rate of one guinea a column has been made to the writer. Three and a half. Three pounds three. Three pounds thirteen and six.

Quietly he read, restraining himself, the first column and, yielding but resisting, began the second. Midway, his last resistance yielding, he allowed his bowels to ease themselves quietly as he read, reading patiently, that slight constipation of yesterday quite gone. Hope it's not too big bring on piles again. No, just right. So. Ah! Costive one tabloid of cascara sagrada. Life might be so. It did not move or touch him but it was something quick and neat. Print anything now. Silly season. He read on, seated calm above his own rising smell. Neat certainly. *Matcham often thinks of the masterstroke by which he won the laughing witch who now.* Begins and ends morally. *Hand in hand.* Smart. He glanced back through what he had read and, while feeling his water flow quietly, he envied kindly Mr. Beaufoy who had written it and received payment of three pounds thirteen and six.

Might manage a sketch. By Mr. and Mrs. L. M. Bloom. Invent a story for some proverb which? Time I used to try jotting down on my cuff what she said dressing. Dislike dressing together.

[50]

Nicked myself shaving. Biting her nether lip, hooking the placket of her skirt. Timing her. 9.15. Did Roberts pay you yet? 9.20. What had Gretta Conroy on? 9.23. What possessed me to buy this comb? 9.24. I'm swelled after that cabbage. A speck of dust on the patent leather of her boot.

. . . .

He tore away half the prize story sharply and wiped himself with it. Then he girded up his trousers, braced and buttoned himself. He pulled back the jerky shaky door of the jakes and came forth from the gloom of the air.

In the bright light, lightened and cooled in limb, he eyed carefully his black trousers, the ends, the knees, the houghs of the knees. What time is the funeral? Better find out in the paper.

A creak and a dark whirr in the air high up. The bells of George's church. They tolled the hour: loud dark iron.

Heigho! Heigho!
Heigho! Heigho!
Heigho! Heigho!

Quarter to. There again: the overtone following through the air, third.

Poor Dignam!

Episode 5 – The Lotus Eaters… a hospitable tribe who live off the narcotic fruit of the lotus, whose offerings of food and flowers make men forget their life quests. ~ With scenes of scents, flowers, and drugs; the people of Ireland may be seen as lotus eaters, drugged in their obedience to the Catholic Church, lost in unfulfilled sexual longings, and looking for means of escape and relief.

Leopold Bloom walks circuitous to the post office for a letter from Martha Clifford with whom he weighs a love duet. Before the Oriental Tea shop he dreams of the far east. He indulges a tiresome M'Coy before reading the letter. He visits All Hallow's church during a mass. At the chemist, having forgotten Molly's prescription, he buys a bar of lemon soap, its fragrance follows him into the night's escapade. Bumping into Bantam Lyons he leaves him a throwaway which Bantam perceives to be a tip to winning the Ascot Gold Cup Race. Bloom fantasizes on a Turkish Bath.

THEMES

Escapism, dreaminess, loneliness. Alienation as a Jew, a "Throwaway." Ireland's lethargic bondage to the Catholic Church. Holy Communion as a lollipop. Contrasting roles of scripture's Mary and Martha, e.g., Marion (Molly) Bloom and Martha Clifford. Christ's body as Eucharist contrasts Bloom's detachment from others. People's sexual yearning, sterility, jaded sex, emptiness. Avoidance or forgetfulness of the primary problems of their lives.

BY LORRIES ALONG SIR JOHN ROGERSON'S QUAY MR BLOOM walked soberly, past Windmill lane, Leask's the linseed crusher's, the postal telegraph office. Could have given that address too. And past the sailor's home. He turned from the morning noises of the quayside and walked through Lime street.

. . .

In Westland row he halted before the window of the Belfast and Oriental Tea Company and read the legends of leadpapered packets: choice blend, finest quality, family tea. Rather warm. Tea. Must get some from Tom Kernan. Couldn't ask him at a funeral though. While his eyes still read blandly he took off his hat quietly inhaling his hairoil and sent his right hand with slow grace over his brow and hair. Very warm morning. Under their dropped lids his eyes found the tiny bow of the leather headband inside his high grade hat. Just there. His right hand came down into the bowl of his hat. His fingers found quickly a card behind the headband and transferred it to his waistcoat pocket.

So warm. His right hand once more slowly went over again: choice blend, made of the finest Ceylon brands. The far east. Lovely

[52]

spot it must be: the garden of the world, big lazy leaves to float about
on, cactuses, flowery meads, snaky lianas they call them. Wonder is
it like that. Those Cinghalese lobbing around the sun, in *dolce far
niente*. Not doing a hand's turn all day. Sleep six months out of
twelve. Too hot to quarrel. Influence of the climate. Lethargy.
Flowers of idleness. The air feeds most. Azotes. Hothouse in Botanic
gardens. Sensitive plants. Waterlilies. Petals too tired to. Sleeping
sickness in the air. Walk on roseleaves.

. . . .

He turned away and sauntered across the road. How did she
walk with her sausages? Like that something. As he walked he took
the folded *Freeman* from his sidepocket, unfolded it, rolled it
lengthwise in a baton and tapped it at each sauntering step against his
trouserleg. Careless air: just drop in to see. Per second, per second.
Per second for every second it means. From the curbstone he darted a
keen glance through the door of the postoffice. Too late box. Post
here. No-one. In.

He handed the card through the brass grill.

-- Are there any letters for me? he asked.

While the postmistress searched a pigeonhole he gazed at the
recruiting poster with soldiers of all arms on parade: and held the tip
of his baton against his nostrils, smelling freshprinted rag paper. No
answer probably. Went too far last time.

The postmistress handed him back through the grill his card
with a letter. He thanked and glanced rapidly at the envelope.

> Henry Flower, Esq.
> % P. O. Westland Row, City

Answered anyhow. He slipped card and letter into his
sidepocket, reviewing again the soldiers on parade.

. . . .

He strolled out of the postoffice and turned to the right. Talk:
as if that would mend matters. His hand went into his pocket and a
forefinger felt its way under the flap of the envelope, ripping it open
in jerks. Women will pay a lot of heed, I don't think. His fingers

drew forth the letter and crumpled the envelope in his pocket.
Something pinned on: photo perhaps. Hair? No.

M'Coy. Get rid of him quickly. Take me out of my way.
Hate company when you.

-- Hello, Bloom. Where are you off to?

--Hello, M'Coy. Nowhere in particular.

-- How's the body?

-- Fine. How are you?

-- Just keeping alive, M'Coy said.

His eyes on the black tie and clothes he asked with low
respect:

-- Is there any . . . no trouble I hope? I see you're . . .

-- O no, Mr Bloom said. Poor Dignam, you know. The
funeral is today.

-- To be sure, poor fellow. So it is. What time?

A photo it isn't. A badge maybe.

-- E . . . eleven, Mr Bloom answered.

-- I must try to get out there, M'Coy said. Eleven, is it? I
only heard it last night. Who was telling me? Holohan. You know
Hoppy?

--I know.

Mr Bloom gazed across the road at the outsider drawn up
before the door of the Grosvenor. The porter hoisted the valise up on
the well. She stood still, waiting, while the man, husband, brother,
like her, searched his pockets for change.

. . . .

– I was with Bob Doran, he's on one of his periodical bends,
and what do you call him Bantam Lyons. Just down there in
Conway's we were. . . .

– And he said: *Sad thing about our poor friend Paddy! What
Paddy?* I said. *Poor little Paddy Dignam,* he said.

Off to the country: Broadstone probably. High brown boots
with laces dangling. Well turned foot. What is he fostering over that
for? Sees me looking. Eye out for other fellow always. Good
fallback. Two strings to her bow.

[54]

– *Why?* I said. *What's wrong with him?* I said.

Proud: rich: silk stockings.

– Yes, Mr Bloom said.

He moved a little to the side of M'Coy's talking head. Getting up in a minute.

– *What's wrong with him?* he said. *He's dead,* he said. And, faith, he filled up. *Is it Paddy Dignam?* I said. I couldn't believe it when I heard it. I was with him no later than Friday last or Thursday was it in the Arch. *Yes,* he said. *He's gone. He died on Monday, poor fellow.*

Watch! Watch! Silk flash rich stockings white. Watch!

. . . .

– Wife well, I suppose? M'Coy's changed voice said.

– O yes, Mr Bloom said. Tiptop. thanks.

He unrolled the newspaper baton idly and read idly:

> *What is home without*
> *Plumtree's Potted Meat?*
> *Incomplete.*
> *With it an abode of bliss.*

-- My missus has just got an engagement. At least it's not settled yet.

Valise tack again. By the way no harm. I'm off that, thanks.

Mr Bloom turned his largelidded eyes with unhasty friendliness.

-- My wife too, he said. She's going to sing at a swagger affair in Ulster hall, Belfast, on the twentyfifth.

That so? M'Coy said. Glad to hear that, old man. Who's getting it up?

Mrs Marion Bloom. Not up yet. Queen was in her bedroom eating bread and. No book. Blackened court cards laid along her thigh by sevens. Dark lady and fair man. Cat furry black ball. Torn strip of envelope.

> *Love's*
> *Old*

-- It's a kind of a tour, don't you see? Mr Bloom said thoughtfully. *Sweet song.* There's a committee formed. Part shares and part profits.

M'Coy nodded, picking at this moustache stubble.

-- O well, he said. That's good news.

He moved to go.

-- Well, glad to see you looking fit, he said. Meet you knocking around.

-- Yes, Mr Bloom said.

-- Tell you what, M'Coy said. You might put down my name at the funeral, will you? I'd like to go but I mightn't be able, you see. There's a drowning case at Sandycove may turn up and then the coroner and myself would have to go down if the body is found. You just shove in my name if I'm not there, will you?

-- I'll do that, Mr Bloom said, moving to get off. That'll be all right.

-- Right, M'Coy said brightly. Thanks, old man. I'd go if I possibly could. Well, tolloll. Just C.P. M'Coy will do.

-- That will be done, Mr Bloom answered firmly.

. . . .

Mr Bloom stood at the corner, his eyes wandering over the multicoloured hoardings. Cantrell and Cochrane's Ginger Ale (Aromatic). Clery's summer sale. No, he's going on straight. Hello. *Leah* tonight: Mrs Bandman Palmer. Like to see her in that again. *Hamlet* she played last night. Male impersonator. Perhaps he was a woman. Why Ophelia committed suicide? Poor papa! How he used to talk about Kate Bateman in that! Outside the Adelphi in London waited all the afternoon to get in. Year before I was born that was: sixtyfive. And Ristori in Vienna . What is this the right name is? By Mosenthal it is. Rachel, is it? No. The scene he was always talking

[56]

about where the old blind Abraham recognises the voice and puts his fingers on his face.

– Nathan's voice! His son's voice! I heard the voice of Nathan who left his father to die of grief and misery in my arms, who left the house of his father and left the God of his father.

Every word is so deep, Leopold.

Poor papa! Poor man! I'm glad I didn't go into the room to look at his face. That day! O dear! O dear! Ffoo! Well, perhaps it was the best for him.

Mr Bloom went round the corner and passed the drooping nags of the hazard. No use thinking of it anymore. Nosebag time. Wish I hadn't met that M'Coy fellow.

. . . .

He drew the letter from his pocket and folded it into the newspaper he carried. Might just walk into her here. The lane is safer.

He passed the cabman's shelter. Curious the life of drifting cabbies, all weathers, all places, time or setdown, no will of their own. . . .

He turned into Cumberland street and, going on some paces, halted in the lee of the station wall… He opened the letter within the newspaper.

A flower. I think it's a. A yellow flower with flattened petals. Not annoyed then? What does she say?

Dear Henry,

I got your last letter to me and thank you very much for it. I am sorry you did not like my last letter. Why did you enclose the stamps? I am awfully angry with you. I do wish I could punish you for that. I called you naughty boy because I do not like that other world. Please tell me what is the real meaning of that word. Are you not happy in your home you poor little naughty boy? I do wish I could do something for you. Please tell me what you think of poor me. I often think of the beautiful name you have. Dear Henry, when will we meet? I think of you so often you have no idea. I have never

felt myself so much drawn to a man as you. I feel so bad about.
Please write me a long letter and tell me more. Remember if you do
not I will punish you. So now you know what I will do to meet you.
Henry dear, do not deny my request before my patience are
exhausted. Then I will tell you all. Goodbye now, naughtly darling. I
have such a bad headache today and write *by return* to your longing

MARTHA

P.S. Do tell me what kind of perfume does your wife use. I
want to know.

He tore the flower gravely from its pinhold smelt its almost
no smell and placed it in his heart pocket. Language of flowers. They
like it because no-one can hear. Or a poison bouquet to strike him
down. Then, walking slowly forward, he read the letter again,
murmuring here and there a word. Angry tulips with you darling
manflower punish your cactus if you don't please poor forgetmenot
how I long violets to dear roses when we soon anemone meet all
naughty nightstalk wife Martha's perfume. Having read it all he took
it from the newspaper and put it back in his sidepocket.

Weak joy opened his lips. Changed since the first letter.
Wonder did she write it herself. Doing the indignant: a girl of good
family like me, respectable character. Could meet one Sunday after
the rosary. Thank you: not having any. Usual love scrimmage. Then
running round corners. Bad as a row with Molly. Cigar has a cooling
effect. Narcotic. Go further next time. Naughty boy: punish: afraid of
words of course. Brutal, why not? Try it anyhow. A bit at a time.

Fingering still the letter in his pocket he drew the pin out of
it. Common pin, eh? He threw it on the road. Out of her clothes
somewhere: pinned together. Queer the number of pins they always
have. No roses without thorns..

Flat Dublin voices bawled in his head. Those two sluts that
night in the Coombe, linked together in the rain.

> *O, Mary lost the pin of her drawers.*
> *She didn't know what to do*
> *To keep it up*

To keep it up.

It? Them. Such a bad headache. Has her roses probably. Or sitting all day typing. Eyefocus bad for stomach nerves. What perfume does your wife use? Now could you make out a thing like that?

To keep it up.

Martha, Mary. I saw that picture somewhere I forget now old master or faked for money. He is sitting in their house, talking. Mysterious. Also the two sluts in the Coombe would listen.

To keep it up.

Nice kind of evening feeling. No more wandering about. Just loll there: quiet dusk: let everything rip. Forget… Going under the railway arch he took out the envelope, tore it swiftly in shreds and scattered them towards the road. The shreds fluttered away, sank in the dank air: a white flutter then all sank.

. . . .

He had reached the open backdoor of All Hallows. Stepping into the porch he doffed his hat, took the card from his pocket and tucked it again behind the leather headband. Damn it. I might have tried to work M'Coy for a pass to Mullingar.

Same notice on the door. Sermon by the very reverend John Conmee S. J. on saint Peter Claver and the African mission. Save China's millions. Wonder how they explain it to the heathen Chinee. Prefer an ounce of opium. Celestials. Rank heresy for them. Prayers for the conversion of Gladstone they had too when he was almost unconscious. The protestants the same. Convert Dr. William J. Walsh D. D. to the true religion. Buddha their god lying on this side in the museum. Taking it easy with hand under his cheek. Josssticks burning. Not like Ecce Homo. Crown of thorns and cross. Clever idea Saint Patrick the shamrock. Chopsticks? Conmee: Martin Cunningham knows him: distinguished looking. Sorry I didn't work him about getting Molly into choir instead of that Father Farley who looked a fool but wasn't. They're taught that. He's not going out in bluey specs with the sweat rolling off him to baptise blacks, is he? The glasses would take their fancy, flashing. Like to see them sitting round in a ring with bulb lips, entranced, listening. Still life. Lap it up like milk, I suppose.

The cold smell of sacred stone called him. He trod the worn steps, pushed the swingdoor and entered softly by the rere.

Something going on: some sodality. Pity so empty. Nice discreet place to be next some girl. Who is my neighbour? Jammed by the hour to slow music. That woman at midnight mass. Seventh heaven. Women knelt in the benches with crimson halters round their necks, heads bowed. A batch knelt at the altar rails. The priest went along by them, murmuring, holding the thing in his hands. He stopped at each, took out a communion, shook a drop or two (are they in water?) off it and put it neatly into her mouth. Her hat and head sank. Then the next one: a small old woman. The priest bent down to put it into her mouth, murmuring all the time. Latin. The next one. Shut your eyes and open your mouth. What? *Corpus.* Body. Corpse. Good idea the Latin. Stupefies them first. Hospice for the dying. They don't seem to chew it; only swallow it down. Rum idea: eating bits of a corpse why the cannibals cotton to it.

He stood aside watching their blind masks pass down the aisle, one by one, and seek their places. He approached a bench and seated himself in its corner, nursing his hat and newspaper. These pots we have to wear. We ought to have hats modelled on our heads. They were about him here and there, with heads still bowed in their crimson halters, waiting for it to melt in their stomachs. Something like those mazzoth: it's that sort of bread: unleavened shewbread. Look at them. Now I bet it makes them feel happy. Lollipop. It does. Yes, bread of angels it's called. There's a big idea behind it, kind of kingdom of God is within you feel. First communicants. Hoky-poky penny a lump. Then feel all like one family party, same in the theatre, all in the same swim. They do. I'm sure of that. Not so lonely. In our confraternity. Then come out a big spreeish. Let off steam. Thing is if you really believe in it. Lourdes cure, waters of oblivion, and the Knock apparition, statues bleeding. Old fellow asleep near that confession box. Hence those snores. Blind faith. Safe

[60]

in the arms of kingdom come. Lulls all pain. Wake this time next year.

He saw the priest stow the communion cup away, well in, and kneel an instant before it, showing a large grey bootsole from under the lace affair he had on. Suppose he lost the pin of his. He wouldn't know what to do to. Bald spot behind. Letters on his back I. N. R. I.? No: I. H. S. Molly told me one time I asked her. I have sinned: or no: I have suffered, it is. And the other one? Iron nails ran in.

. . . .

The priest was rinsing out the chalice: then he tossed off the dregs smartly. Wine. Makes it more aristocratic than for example if he drank what they are used to Guinness's porter or some temperance beverage Wheatley's Dublin hop bitters or Cantrell and Cochrane's ginger ale (aromatic). Doesn't give them any of it: shew wine: only the other. Cold comfort. Pious fraud but quite right: otherwise they'd have one old booser worse than another coming along, cadging for a drink. Queer the whole atmosphere of the. Quite right. Perfectly right that is.

. . . .

The priest came down from the altar, holding the thing out from him, and he and the massboy answered each other in Latin. Then the priest knelt down and began to read off a card:

-- O God, our refuge and our strength…

Mr. Bloom put his face forward to catch the words. English. Throw them the bone. I remember slightly. How long since your last mass? Gloria and immaculate virgin. Joseph her spouse. Peter and Paul. More interesting if you understood what it is all about. Wonderful organisation certainly, goes like clockwork. Confession. Everyone wants to . Then I will tell you all. Penance. Punish me, please. Great weapon in their hands. More than a doctor or solicitor. Woman dying to. And I schschschschschsch. And did you chachachachacha? And why did you? Look down at her ring to find an excuse. Whispering gallery walls have ears. Husband learn to his surprise. God's little joke. Then out she comes. Repentance skindeep. Lovely shame. Pray at an altar. Hail Mary and Holy Mary. Flowers, incense, candles melting. Hide her blushes. Salvation army blatant imitation. Reformed prostitute will address the meeting. How I found the Lord. Squareheaded chaps those must be in Rome: they work the whole show. And don't they rake in the money too? Bequests also: to the P. P. for the time being in his absolute discretion. Masses for the repose of my soul to be said publicly with open doors. Monasteries and convents. The priest in the Fermanagh will case in the witness box. No browbeating him. He had his answer pat for everything. Liberty and exaltation of our holy mother the church. The doctors of the church: they mapped out the whole theology of it.

. . . .

The priest and the massboy stood up and walked off. All over. The women remained behind: thanksgiving.

Better be shoving along. Brother Buzz. Come around with the plate perhaps. Pay your Easter duty.

He stood up. Hello. Were those two buttons of my waistcoat open all the time. Women enjoy it. Annoyed if you don't. Why didn't you tell me before. Never tell you. But we. Excuse, miss, there's a (whh!) just a (whh!) fluff. Or their skirt behind, placket unhooked. Glimpses of the moon. Still like you better untidy. Good job it wasn't farther south. He passed, discreetly buttoning, down the aisle and out through the main door into the light. He stood a moment unseeing by the cold black marble bowl while before him and behind two worshippers dipped furtive hands in the low tide of holy water.

. . . .

He walked southward along Westland row. But the recipe is in the other trousers. O, and I forgot that latchkey too. Bore this funeral affair. O well, poor fellow, it's not his fault. When was it I got it made up last? Wait. I changed a sovereign I remember. First of the month it must have been or the second. O he can look it up in the prescriptions book.

[62]

The chemist turned back page after page. Sandy shrivelled smell he seems to have. Shrunken skull. And old. Quest for the philosopher's stone. The alchemists. Drugs age you after mental excitement. Lethargy then. Why? Reaction. A lifetime in a night. Gradually changes your character. Living all the day among herbs, ointments, disinfectants. All his alabaster lilypots. Mortar and pestle. As. Dist. Fol. Laur. Te Virid. Smell almost cure you like the dentist's doorbell. Doctor whack. He ought to physic himself a bit. Electuary or emulsion. The first fellow that picked an herb to cure himself had a bit of pluck. Simples. Want to be careful. Enough stuff here to chloroform you. Test: turns blue litmus paper red. Chloroform. Overdose of laudanum. Sleeping draughts. Lovephiltres. Paragoric poppysyrup bad for cough. Clogs the pores or the phlegm. Poisons the only cures, Remedy where you least expect it. Clever of nature.

    -- About a fortnight ago, sir?

    -- Yes, Mr Bloom said.

    He waited by the counter, inhaling the keen reek of drugs, the dusty dry smell of sponges and loofahs. Lot of time taken up telling your aches and pains.

. . . .

But you want a perfume too. What perfume does your? *Peau d'Espagne.* that orangeflower. Pure curd soap. Water is so fresh. Nice smell these soaps have. Time to get a bath round the corner. Hammam. Turkish. Massage. Dirt gets rolled up in your navel. Nicer if a nice girl did it. Also I think I. Yes I. Do it in the bath. Curious longing I. Water to water. Combine business with pleasure. Pity no time for massage. Feel fresh then all day. Funeral be rather glum.

    – Yes, sir, the chemist said. That was two and nine. Have you brought a bottle?

    – No, Mr Bloom said. Make it up, please. I'll call later in the day and I'll take one of those soaps. How much are they?

    – Fourpence, sir.

    Mr Bloom raised a cake to his nostrils. Sweet lemony wax.

    – I'll take this one, he said. That makes three and a penny.

– Yes, sir, the chemist said. You can pay all together, sir, when you come back.

– Good, Mr Bloom said.

He strolled out of the shop, the newspaper baton under his armpit, the coolwrapped soap in his left hand.

At his armpit Bantam Lyons' voice and hand said:

–Hello, Bloom, what's the best news? Is that today's? Show us a minute.

Shaved off his moustache again, by Jove! Long cold upper lip. To look younger. He does look balmy. Younger than I am.

Bantam Lyons' yellow blacknailed fingers unrolled the baton. Wants a wash too. Take off the rough dirt. Good morning, have you used Pear's soap? Dandruff on his shoulders. Scalp wants oiling.

–I want to see about that French horse that's running today, Bantam Lyons' said. Where the bugger is it?

He rustled the pleated pages, jerking his chin on his high collar. Barber's itch. Tight collar he'll lose his hair. Better leave him the paper and get shut of him.

–You can keep it, Mr Bloom said.

–Ascot. Gold cup. Wait, Bantam Lyons muttered. Half a mo. Maximum the second.

–I was just going to throw it away, Mr Bloom said.

Bantam Lyons raised his eyes suddenly and leered weakly.

–What's that? his sharp voice said.

–I say you can keep it, Mr Bloom answered. I was going to throw it away that moment.

Bantam Lyons doubted an instant, leering: then thrust the outspread sheets back on Mr Bloom's arms.

–I'll risk it, he said. Here, thanks.

. . . .

He walked cheerfully toward the mosque of the baths. Remind you of a mosque, redbaked bricks, the minarets…

Enjoy a bath now: clean trough of water, cool enamel, the gentle tepid stream. This is my body.

He foresaw his pale body reclined in it at full, naked, in a womb of warmth, oiled by scented melting soap, softly laved. He saw his trunk and limbs riprippled over and sustained, buoyed lightly upward, lemonyellow: his navel, bud of flesh: and saw the dark tangled curls of his bush floating, floating hair of the stream around the limp father of thousands, a languid floating flower.

Episode 6 – Hades... Lord of the realm of the dead. Odysseus visits the Underworld, across the four rivers of hell and past the guard dog entrance, where he meets the spirits of various Greek heroes. ~ Journeying across the four rivers of Dublin to a funeral at Glasnevin Cemetery, Bloom imagines the underworld, his head fills with thoughts of death, separation, and religion. He recalls his father's dying request to care for his dog, Athos.

Bloom joins acquaintances in a carriage ride to the funeral of Paddy Dignam, over the four Dublin rivers, passing by Stephen Dedalus and Blazes Boylan. In conversation Bloom feels much the outsider, dismissed as a social inferior. (In its news coverage, Bloom's name is mistaken, as was his act of the throwaway). His peers' pleasantries remind Bloom of his father's suicide, and of Molly's upcoming concert tour with Boylan. In opposition are his views on suicide, death and resurrection. Bloom is intermittently fixated on nails, finger and steel, feeling crucified by his life circumstances.

THEMES
Father-son relations. Suicide, afterlife, the underworld. Futility of debt caused by alcohol. The cold orthodoxy of Catholicism. Resurrection of the (nailed) body. Isolation, separateness, social inferiority. Choosing life over the aspects of death. Misnomers and (humorous) misunderstandings.

MARTIN CUNNINGHAM, FIRST, POKED HIS SILKHATTED HEAD INTO the creaking carriage and, entering deftly, seated himself. Mr. Power stepped in after him, curving his height with care.

-- Come on, Simon.

-- After you, Mr. Bloom said.

Mr. Dedalus covered himself quickly and got in, saying:

-- Yes, yes.

-- Are we all here now? Martin Cunningham asked. Come along, Bloom.

Mr Bloom entered and sat in the vacant place. He pulled the door to after him and slammed it tight till it shut tight. He passed an arm through the armstrap and looked seriously from the open carriage window at the lowered blinds of the avenue. One dragged aside: an old woman peeping. Nose whiteflattened against the pane. Thanking her stars she was passed over. Extraordinary the interest they take in a corpse. Glad to see us go we give them such trouble coming. Job seems to suit them. Huggermugger in corners. Slop about in slipperslappers for the fear he'd wake. Then getting it ready. Laying it out. Molly and Mrs Fleming making the bed. Pull it more

[66]

to your side. Our windingsheet. Never know who will touch you dead. Wash and shampoo. I believe they clip the nails and the hair. Keep a bit in an envelope. Grow all the same after. Unclean job.

. . . .

All watched awhile through their windows caps and hats lifted by passers. Respect. The carriage swerved from the tramtrack to the smoother road past Watery lane. Mr Bloom at gaze saw a lithe young man, clad in mourning, a wide hat.

-- There's a friend of yours gone by, Dedalus, he said.

-- Who is that?

-- Your son and heir.

-- Where is he? Mr Dedalus said, stretching over across.

The carriage, passing the open drains and mounds of rippedup roadway before the tenement houses, lurched round the corner and, swerving back to the tramtrack, rolled on noisily with chattering wheels. Mr Dedalus fell back, saying:

-- Was that Mulligan cad with him? His *fidus Achates?*

-- No, Mr Bloom said. He was alone.

-- Down with his aunt Sally, I suppose, Mr Dedalus said, the Goulding faction, the drunken little cost-drawer and Crissie, papa's little lump of dung, the wise child that knows her own father.

. . . .

Mr Bloom glanced from his angry moustache to Mr. Power's mild face and Martin Cunningham's eyes and beard gravely shaking. Noisy selfwilled man. Full of his son. He is right. Something to hand on. If little Rudy had lived. See him grow up. Hear his voice in the house. Walking beside Molly in an Eton suit. My son. Me in his eyes. Strange feeling it would be. From me. Just a chance. Must have been that morning in Raymond terrace she was at the window, watching the two dogs at it by the wall of the cease to do evil. And the sergeant grinning up. She had that cream gown on with the rip she never stitched. Give us a touch, Poldy. God, I'm dying for it. How life begins.

Got big then. Had to refuse the Greystones concert. My son inside her. I could have helped him on in life. I could. Make him independent. Learn German too.

. . . .

The carriage halted short.

-- What's wrong?

-- We're stopped.

-- Where are we?

Mr Bloom put his head out of the window.

-- The grand canal, he said.

Gasworks. Whooping cough they say it cures. Good job Milly never got it. Poor children! Doubles them up black and blue in convulsions. Shame really. Got off lightly with illness compared. Only measles. Flaxseed tea. Scarlatina, influenza epidemics. Canvassing for death. Don't miss this chance. Dog's home over there. Poor old Athos! Be good to Athos, Leopold, is my last wish. Thy will be done. We obey them in the grave. A dying scrawl. He took it to heart, pined away. Quiet brute. Old men's dogs usually are.

. . . .

The carriage turned again its stiff wheels and their trunks swayed gently. Martin Cunningham twirled more quickly the peak of his beard.

– Tom Kernan was immense last night, he said. And Paddy Leonard taking him off to his face.

– O draw him out, Martin, Mr Power said eagerly. Wait till you hear him sing, Simon, on Ben Dollard's singing of *The Croppy Boy.*

– Immense, Martin Cunningham said pompously. *His singing of that simple ballad, Martin, is the most trenchant rendering I ever heard in the whole course of my experience.*

– Trenchant, Mr Power said laughing. He's dead nuts on that. And the retrospective arrangement.

. . . .

They went past the bleak pulpit of Saint Mark's, under the railway bridge, past the Queen's theatre: in silence. . . .

[68]

Plasto's. Sir Philip Crampton's memorial fountain bust. Who was he?

-- How do you do? Martin Cunningham said, raising his palm to his brow in salute.

-- He doesn't see us, Mr Power said. Yes, he does. How do you do?

-- Who? Mr Dedalus asked.

-- Blazes Boylan, Mr Power said. There he is airing his quiff.

Just that moment I was thinking.

Mr Dedalus bent across to salute. From the door of the Red Bank the white disc of a straw hat flashed reply: passed.

Mr. Bloom reviewed the nails of his left hand, then those of his right hand. The nails, yes. Is there anything more in him that she sees? Fascination. Worst man in Dublin. That keeps him alive. They sometimes feel what a person is. Instinct. But a type like that. My nails. I am just looking at them: well pared. And after: thinking alone. Body getting a bit softly. I would notice that from remembering. What causes that I suppose the skin can't contract quickly enough when the flesh falls off. But the shape is there. The shape is there still. Shoulders. Hips. Plump. Night of the dance dressing. Shift stuck between the cheeks behind.

He clasped his hands between his knees and, satisfied, sent his vacant glance over their faces.

Mr Power asked:

-- How is the concert tour getting on, Bloom?

-- O very well, Mr Bloom said. I hear great accounts of it . It's a good idea, you see . . .

-- Are you going yourself?

-- Well no, Mr Bloom said. In point of fact I have to go down to the county Clare on some private business.

. . . .

They passed under the hugecloaked Liberator's form.

Martin Cunningham nudged Mr Power.

-- Of the tribe of Rueben, he said.

A tall blackbearded figure, bent on a stick, stumping round the corner of Elvery's elephant house showed them a curved hand open on his spine.

-- In all his pristine beauty, Mr Power said.

Mr Dedalus looked after the stumping figure and said mildly:

-- The devil break the hasp of your back!

Mr Power, collapsing in laughter, shaded his face from the wind as he carriage passed Gray's statue.

-- We have all been there, Mr Cunningham said broadly.

His eyes met Mr Bloom's eyes. He caressed his beard, adding:

-- Well, nearly all of us.

Mr Bloom began to speak with sudden eagerness to his companions' faces.

-- That's an awfully good one that's going the rounds about Reuben J. and the son.

-- About the boatman? Mr Power asked.

-- Yes. Isn't it awfully good?

-- What is that? Mr Dedalus asked. I didn't hear it.

-- There was a girl in the case, Mr Bloom began, and he determined to send him to the isle of Man out of harm's way but when they were both . . .

-- What? Mr Dedalus asked. That confirmed bloody hobbledehoy is it?

-- Yes, Mr Bloom said. They were both on the way to the boat and he tried to drown . . .

-- Drown Barabbas! Mr Dedalus cried. I wish to Christ he did!

Mr Power sent a long laugh down his shaded nostrils.

-- No, Mr Bloom said, the son himself. . . .

Martin Cunningham thwarted his speech rudely.

-- Reuben J. and the son were piking it down the quay next the river on their way to the isle of Man boat and the young chiseller suddenly got loose and over the wall with him into the Liffey.

[70]

-- For God's sake! Mr Dedalus exclaimed in fright. Is he dead?

-- Dead! Martin Cunningham cried. Not he! A boatman got a pole and fished him out by the slack of the breeches and he was landed up to the father on the quay. More dead than alive. Half the town was there.

-- Yes, Mr Bloom said. But the funny part is . . .

-- And Reuben J., Martin Cunningham said, gave the boatman a florin for saving his son's life.

A stifled sigh came from under Mr Power's hand.

-- O, he did, Martin Cunningham affirmed. Like a hero. A silver florin.

-- Isn't it awfully good? Mr Bloom said eagerly.

-- One and eightpence too much, Mr Dedalus said drily.

Mr Power's choked laugh burst quietly in the carriage.

Nelson's pillar.

-- Eight plums a penny! Eight for a penny!

-- We had better look a little serious, Martin Cunningham said.

Mr Dedalus sighed.

-- And then indeed, he said, poor little Paddy wouldn't grudge us a laugh. Many a good one he told himself.

-- The Lord forgive me! Mr Power said, wiping his wet eyes with his fingers. Poor Paddy! I little thought a week ago when I saw him last and he was in his usual health that I'd be driving after him like this. He's gone from us.

-- As decent a little man as ever wore a hat, Mr Dedalus said. He went very suddenly.

-- Breakdown, Martin Cunningham said. Heart.

He tapped his chest sadly.

Blazing face: redhot. Too much John Barleycorn. Cure for a red nose. Drink like the devil till it turns adelite. A lot of money he spent colouring it.

Mr Power gazed at the passing houses with rueful apprehension.

[71]

-- He had a sudden death, poor fellow, he said.

-- The best death, Mr Bloom said.

Their wide open eyes looked at him.

-- No suffering, he said. A moment and all is over. Like dying in sleep.

No-one spoke.

. . . .

White horses with white frontlet plumes came round the Rotunda corner, galloping. A tiny coffin flashed by. In a hurry to bury. A mourning coach. Unmarried. Black for the married. Piebald for bachelors. Dun for a nun.

– Sad, Martin Cunningham said. A child.

A dwarf's face mauve and wrinkled like little Rudy's was. Dwarf's body, weak as putty, in a whitelined deal box. Burial friendly society pays. Penny a week for sod of turf. Our. Little. Beggar. Baby. Meant nothing. Mistake of nature. If it's healthy it's from the mother. If not the man. Better luck next time.

– Poor little thing, Mr Dedalus said. It's well out of it.

The carriage climbed more slowly the hill of Rutland square. Rattle his bones. Over the stones. Only a pauper. Nobody owns.

-- In the midst of life, Martin Cunningham said.

-- But the worst of all, Mr Power said, is the man who takes his own life.

Martin Cunningham drew out his watch briskly, coughed and put it back.

-- The greatest disgrace to have in the family, Mr Power added.

-- Temporary insanity, of course, Martin Cunningham said decisively. We must take a charitable view of it.

-- They say a man who does it is a coward, Mr Dedalus said.

-- It is not for us to judge, Martin Cunningham said.

Mr Bloom, about to speak, closed his lips again. Martin Cunningham's large eyes. Looking away now. Sympathetic human man he is. Intelligent. Like Shakespeare's face. Always a good word to say. They have no mercy on that here or infanticide. Refuse

[72]

christian burial. They used to drive a stake of wood through his heart
in the grave. As if it wasn't broken already. Yet sometimes they
repent too late. Found in the riverbed clutching rushes. He looked at
me. And that awful drunkard of a wife of his. Setting up house for
her time after time and then pawning the furniture on him every
Saturday almost. Leading him the life of the damned. Wear the heart
out of a stone, that. Monday morning start afresh. Shoulder to the
wheel. Lord, she must have looked a sight that night, Dedalus told
me he was in there. Drunk about the place and capering with
Martin's umbrella:

> *And they call me the jewel of Asia,*
> *Of Asia,*
> *The geisha.*

He looked away from me. He knows. Rattle his bones

That afternoon of the inquest. The redlabelled bottle on the
table. The room in the hotel with hunting pictures. Stuffy it was.
Sunlight through the slats of the Venetian blinds. The coroner's ears,
big and hairy. Boots giving evidence. Thought he was asleep first.
Then saw like yellow streaks on his face. Had slipped down to the
foot of the bed. Verdict: overdose. Death by misadventure. The
letter. For my son Leopold.

No more pain. Wake no more. Nobody owns.

The carriage rattled swiftly along Blessington street. Over
the stones.

. . . .

Dunphy's corner. Mourning coaches drawn up drowning
their grief. A pause by the wayside. Tiptop position for a pub. Expect
we'll pull up here on the way back to drink his health. Pass round the
consolation. Elixir of life. . . .

In silence they drove along Phibsborough road. An empty
hearse trotted by, coming from the cemetery: looks relieved.

Crossguns bridge: the royal canal.

Water rushed roaring through the sluices. A man stood on his dropping barge between clamps of turf. On the towpath by the lock a slacktethered horse. Aboard of the *Bugabu.*

. . . .

Gloomy gardens then went by, one by one: gloomy houses.

Mr Power pointed.

– That is where Childs was murdered, he said. The last house.

– So it is, Mr Dedalus said. A gruesome case. Seymour Bushe got him off. Murdered his brother. Or so they said.

– The crown had no evidence, Mr Power said.

– Only circumstantial, Martin Cunningham said. That's the maxim of the law. Better for ninetynine to escape than for one innocent person to be wrongfully condemned.

. . . .

The felly harshed against the curbstone: stopped. Martin Cunningham put out his arm and, wrenching back the handle, he shoved the door open with his knee. He stepped out. Mr Power and Mr Dedalus followed.

Change that soap now. Mr Bloom's hand unbuttoned his hip pocket swiftly and transferred the paperstuck soap to his inner handkerchief pocket. He stepped out of the carriage, replacing the newspaper his other hand still held.

Paltry funeral: coach and three carriages. It's all the same. Pallbearers, gold reins, requiem mass, firing a volley. Pomp of death. Beyond the hind carriage a hawker stood by his barrow of cakes and fruit. Simnel cakes those are, stuck together: cakes of the dead. Dogbiscuits. Who ate them? Mourners coming out. . . .

Coffin now. Got here before us, dead as he is. Horse looking round at it with his plume skeowways. Dull eye: collar tight on his neck, pressing on a bloodvessel or something. Do they know what they cart out here every day? Must be twenty or thirty funerals every day. . . .

The mutes shouldered the coffin and bore it in through the gates. So much dead weight. Felt heavier myself stepping out of that bath. First the stiff: then the friends of the stiff. Corny Kelleher and the boy followed with their wreaths. Who is that beside them? Ah, the brother-in-law.

All walked after.

Martin Cunningham whispered:

-- I was in mortal agony with you talking of suicide before Bloom.

-- What? Mr Power whispered. How so?

-- His father poisoned himself, Martin Cunningham whispered. Had the Queen's hotel in Ennis. You heard him say he was going to Clare. Anniversary.

-- O God! Mr Power whispered. First I heard of it. Poisoned himself!

He glanced behind him to where a face with dark thinking eyes followed towards the cardinal's mausoleum. Speaking.

-- Was he insured? Mr Bloom asked.

-- I believe so, Mr Kernan answered, but the policy was heavily mortgaged. Martin is trying to get the youngster into Artane.

-- How many children did he leave?

-- Five. Ned Lambert says he'll try to get one of the girls into Todd's.

-- A sad case, Mr Bloom said gently. Five young children.

-- A great blow to the poor wife, Mr Kernan added.

-- Indeed yes, Mr Bloom agreed.

Has the laugh at him now.

. . . .

The mutes bore the coffin into the chapel. Which end is his head.

After a moment he followed the others in, blinking in the screened light. The coffin lay on its bier before the chancel, four tall yellow candles at its corners. Always in front of us. Corny Kelleher, laying a wreath at each fore corner, beckoned to the boy to kneel. The mourners knelt here and there in praying desks. Mr Bloom stood behind near the font and, when all had knelt dropped carefully his unfolded newspaper from his pocket and knelt his right knee upon it.

He fitted his black hat gently on his left knee and, holding its brim, bent over piously.

A server, bearing a brass bucket with something in it, came out through a door. The whitesmocked priest came after him tidying his stole with one hand, balancing with the other a little book against his toad's belly. Who'll read the book? I, said the rook.

They halted by the bier and the priest began to read out of his book with a fluent croak.

Father Coffey. I knew his name was like a coffin. *Domine-namine*. Bully about the muzzle he looks. Bosses the show. Muscular christian. Woe betide anyone that looks crooked at him: priest. Thou art Peter. Burst sideways like a sheep in clover Dedalus says he will. With a belly on him like a poisoned pup. Most amusing expressions that man finds. Hhhn: burst sideways.

-- *Non intres in judicium cum servo tuo, Domine.*

Makes them feel more important to be prayed over in Latin. Requiem mass.

. . . .

The priest closed his book and went off, followed by the server. Corny Kelleher opened the sidedoors and the gravediggers came in, hoisted the coffin again, carried it out and shoved it on their cart. Corny Kelleher gave one wreath to the boy and one to the brother-in-law. All followed them out of the sidedoors into the mild grey air. Mr Bloom came last, folding his paper again into his pocket. He gazed gravely at the ground till the coffincart wheeled off to the left. The metal wheels ground the gravel with a sharp grating cry and the pack of blunt boots followed the barrow along a lane of sepulchres.

The ree the ra the ree the ra the roo. Lord, I mustn't lilt here.

– The O'Connell circle, Mr Dedalus said about him.

Mr Power's soft eyes went up to the apex of the lofty cone.

– He's at rest, he said, in the middle of his people, old Dan O'. But his heart is buried in Rome. How many broken hearts are buried here, Simon!

[76]

– Her grave is over there, Jack, Mr Dedalus said. I'll soon be stretched beside her. Let Him take me whenever He likes.

Breaking down, he began to weep to himself quietly, stumbling a little in his walk. Mr Power took his arm.

– She's better where she is, he said kindly.

– I suppose so, Mr Dedalus said with a weak gasp. I suppose she is in heaven if there is a heaven.

. . . .

Mr Kernan said with solemnity:

-- *I am the resurrection and the life.* That touches a man's inmost heart.

-- It does, Mr Bloom said.

Your heart perhaps but what prices the fellow in the six feet by two with his toes to the daisies? No touching that. Seat of the affections. Broken heart. A pump after all, pumping thousands of gallons of blood every day. One fine day it gets bunged up and there you are. Lots of them lying around here: lungs, hearts, livers. Old rusty pumps: damn the thing else. The resurrection and the life. Once you are dead you are dead. That last day idea. Knocking them all up out of their graves. Come forth, Lazarus! And he came fifth and lost the job. Get up! Last day! Then every fellow mousing around for his liver and his lights and the rest of his traps. Find damn all of himself that morning. Pennyweight of powder in a skull. Twelve grammes one pennyweight. Troy measure.

Corny Kelleher fell into step at their side

-- Everything went off A 1, he said. What?

He looked on them from his drawling eye. Policeman's shoulders. With your tooraloom tooraloom.

-- As it should be, Mr Kernan said.

-- What? Eh? Corny Kelleher said.

Mr Kernan assured him.

-- Who is that chap behind with Tom Kernan? John Henry Menton asked. I know his face.

Ned Lambert glanced back.

-- Bloom, he said, Madam Marion Tweedy that was, is, I mean, the soprano. She's his wife.

-- O, to be sure, John Henry Menton said. I haven't seen her for some time. She was a finelooking woman. I danced with her, wait, fifteen seventeen golden years ago, at Mat Dillon's, in Roundtown. And an armful she was.

He looked behind the others.

-- What is he? he asked. What does he do? Wasn't he in the stationery line? I fell foul of him one evening, I remember, at bowls.

Ned Lambert smiled.

-- Yes, he was, he said, in Wisdom Hely's. A traveller for blottingpaper.

-- In God's name, John Henry Menton said, what did she marry a coon like that for? She had plenty of game in her then.

-- Has still, Ned Lambert said. He does some canvassing for ads.

John Henry Menton's large eyes stared ahead.

The barrow turned into a side lane. A portly man, ambushed among the grasses, raised his hat in homage. The gravediggers touched their caps.

– John O'Connell, Mr Power said, pleased. He never forgets a friend.

Mr O'Connell shook all their hands in silence. Mr Dedalus said:

– I am come to pay you another visit.

– My dear Simon, the caretaker answered in a low voice. I don't want your custom at all.

. . . .

He has seen a fair share go under in his time, lying around him field after field. Holy fields. More room if they buried them standing. Sitting or kneeling you couldn't. Standing? His head might come up some day above ground in a landslip with his hand pointing. All honeycombed the ground must be: oblong cells. . . .

I dare say the soil would be quite fat with corpse manure, bones, flesh, nails, charnelhouses. Dreadful. Turning green and pink,

[78]

decomposing. Rot quick in damp earth. The lean old one tougher. Then a kid of a tallowy kind of a cheesy. Then begin to get black, treacle oozing out of them. Then dried up. Deathmoths. Of course the cells or whatever they are go on living. Changing about. Live for ever practically. Nothing to feed on feed on themselves.

. . . .

The caretaker put the papers in his pocket. The barrow had ceased to trundle. The mourners split and moved to each side of the hole, stepping with care around the graves. The gravediggers bore the coffin and set its nose on the brink, looping the bands round it.

Burying him. We come to bury Caesar. His ides of March or June. He doesn't know who is here nor care.

Now who is that lankylooking galoot over there in the macintosh? Now, I'd give a trifle to know who he is. Always someone turns up you never dreamt of. A fellow could live on his lonesome all his life. Yes, he could. Still he'd have to get someone to sod him after he died though he could dig his own grave. We all do. Only man buries. No ants too. First thing strikes anybody. Bury the dead. Say Robinson Crusoe was true to life. Well then Friday buried him. Every Friday buries a Thursday if you come to look at it.

> *O, poor Robinson Crusoe,*
> *How could you possibly do so?*

Poor Dignam! His last lie on the earth in his box. When you think of them all it does seem a waste of good wood. All gnawed through. They could invent a handsome bier with a kind of panel sliding let it down that way. Ay but they might object to be buried out of another fellow's. They're so particular. Lay me in my native earth. Bit of clay from the holy land. Only a mother and deadborn child ever buried in the one coffin. I see what it means. I see. To protect him as long as possible even in the earth. The Irishman's house is his coffin. Enbalming in catacombs, mummies, the same idea.

Mr Bloom stood far back, his hat in his hand, counting the bared heads. Twelve. I'm thirteen. No. The chap in the macintosh is thirteen. Death's number. Where the deuce did he pop out of? He wasn't in the chapel, that I'll swear. Silly superstition that about thirteen.

. . . .

We are praying now for the repose of his soul. Hoping you're well and not in hell. Nice change of air. Out of the frying pan of life into the fire of purgatory.

Does he ever think of the hole waiting for himself? They say you do when you shiver in the sun. Someone walking over it. Callboy's warning. Near you. Mine over there towards Finglas, the plot I bought. Mamma poor mamma, and little Rudy.

The gravediggers took up their spades and flung heavy clods of clay in on the coffin. Mr Bloom turned his face. And if he was alive all the time? Whew! By Jingo, that would be awful! No, no: he is dead, of course. Of course he is dead. Monday he died. They ought to have some law to pierce the heart and make sure or an electric clock or telephone in the coffin and some kind of a canvas airhole. Flag of distress. Three days. Rather long to keep them in summer. Just as well to get shut of them as soon as you are sure there's no.

The clay fell softer. Begin to be forgotten. Out of sight, out of mind.

The caretaker moved away a few paces and put on his hat. Had enough of it. The mourners took heart of grace, one by one, covering themselves without show. Mr Bloom put on his hat and saw the portly figure make its way deftly through the maze of graves. Quietly, sure of his ground, he traversed the dismal fields.

Hynes jotting down something in his notebook. Ah, the names. But he knows them all. No: coming to me.

-- I am just taking the names, Hynes said below his breath. What is your christian name? I'm not sure.

-- L, Mr Bloom said. Leopold. And you might put down M'Coy's name too. He asked me too.

-- Charley, Hynes said writing. I know. He was on the *Freeman* once.

[80]

So he was before he got the job in the morgue under Louis Byrne. Good idea a postmortem for doctors. Find out what they imagine they know. He died of a Tuesday. Got the run. Levanted with the cash of a few ads. Charley, you're my darling. That was why he asked me to. O well, does no harm. I saw to that, M'Coy. Thanks, old chap: much obliged. Leave him under an obligation: costs nothing.

-- And tell us, Hynes said, do you know that fellow in the, fellow was over there in the . . .

He looked around.

-- Macintosh. Yes, I saw him, Mr Bloom said. Where is he now?

-- M'Intosh, Hynes said, scribbling, I don't know who he is. Is that his name?

He moved away, looking about him.

-- No, Mr Bloom began, turning and stopping. I say, Hynes!

Didn't hear. What? Where has he disappeared to? Not a sign. Well of all the. Has anybody here seen? Kay ee double ell. Become invisible. Good Lord, what became of him?

A seventh gravedigger came beside Mr Bloom to take up an idle spade.

-- O, excuse me!

He stepped aside nimbly.

. . . .

The mourners moved away slowly, without aim, by devious paths, staying awhile to read a name on a tomb.

– Let us go round by the chief's grave, Hynes said. We have time.

– Let us, Mr Power said.

They turned to the right, following their slow thoughts. With awe Mr Power's blank voice spoke:

– Some say he is not in that grave at all. That the coffin was filled with stones. That one day he will come again.

Hynes shook his head.

– Parnell will never come again, he said. He's there, all that was mortal of him. Peace to his ashes.

Mr Bloom walked unheeded along his grove by saddened angels, crosses, broken pillars, family vaults, stone hopes praying with upcast eyes, old Ireland's hearts and hands. More sensible to spend the money on some charity for the living. Pray for the repose of the soul of. Does anybody really? Plant him and have done with him. Like down a coalshoot. Then lump them together to save time. All souls' day. Twentyseventh I'll be at his grave. Ten shillings for the gardener. He keeps it free of weeds. Old man himself. Bent down double with his shears clipping. Near death's door. Who passed away. Who departed this life. As if they did it of their own accord. Got the shove, all of them. Who kicked the bucket. More interesting if they told you what they were. So and so, wheelwright. I travelled for cork lino. I paid five shillings in the pound. Or a woman's with her saucepan. I cooked good Irish stew. Eulogy in a country churchyard it ought to be that poem of whose is it Wordsworth or Thomas Campbell. Entered into rest the protestants put it. Old Dr Murren's. The great physician called him home. Well it's God's acre for them. Nice country residence. Newly plastered and painted. Ideal spot to have a quiet smoke and read the *Church Times.* Marriage ads they never try to beautify. Rusty wreaths hung on knobs, garlands of bronzefoil. Better value that for the money. Still, the flowers are more poetical. The other gets rather tiresome, never withering. Expresses nothing. Immortelles. . . .

How many! All these here once walked round Dublin. Faithful departed. As you are now so once were we.

. . . .

The gates glimmered in front: still open. Back to the world again. Enough of this place. Brings you a bit nearer every time. Last time I was here was Mrs Sinico's funeral. Poor papa too. The love that kills. And even scraping up the earth at night with a lantern like that case I read of to get at fresh buried females or even putrefied with running gravesores. Give you the creeps after a bit. I will appear to you after death. You will see my ghost after death. My ghost will

[82]

haunt you after death. There is another world after death named hell. I do not like that other world she wrote. No more do I. Plenty to see and hear and feel yet. Feel live warm beings near you. Let them sleep in their maggoty beds. They are not going to get me this innings. Warm beds: warm fullblooded life.

Martin Cunningham emerged from a sidepath, talking gravely.

Solicitor, I think. I know his face. Menton. John Henry, solicitor, commissioner for oaths and affidavits. Dignam used to be in his office. Mat Dillon's long ago. Jolly Mat convivial evenings. Cold fowl, cigars, the Tantalus glasses. Heart of gold really. Yes, Menton. Got his rag out that evening on the bowling green because I sailed inside him. Pure fluke of mine: the bias. Why he took such a rooted dislike to me. Hate at first sight. Molly and Floey Dillon linked under the lilactree, laughing. Fellow always like that, mortified if women are by. . . .

They walked on towards the gates. Mr Bloom, chapfallen, drew behind a few paces so as not to overhear. Martin laying down the law. Martin could wind a sappyhead like that round his little finger without his seeing it.

Oyster eyes. Never mind. Be sorry after perhaps when it dawns on him. Get the pull over him that way.

Thank you. How grand we are this morning.

Episode 7 – Aeolus... custodian of the winds who sealed all adverse winds tightly in a leather bag so as not to hamper Odysseus' sail homeward. Within sight of home, the crew opened the bag which blew the ship off course and back to Aeolus who angrily sends them away. ~ Aeolus' counterpart is Myles Crawford, newspaper editor, whose headlines parody windy, empty journalism. Bloom, headed to land an ad for Keyes, is blown off course by the editor's actions. Stephen Dedalus asserts his journalistic voice in two parables.

After the burial, Bloom departs the coach in Dublin center and enters the newspaper office to negotiate an advertisement for Alexander Keyes, but is unexpectedly foiled in his effort. Bloom is literally bumped around by office workers and mimicked by newsboys. Bloom's boss leaves him muddled with indecision. The office principals' behavior toward Bloom vis-a-vis their mutual congeniality causes Bloom to realize his inability to engage with fellow Dubliners. Stephen arrives and shares his vision of a stultified Dublin.

THEMES
Windy, ambiguous, empty journalism; creativity versus defecation. Windy conversations reflect disrespect for facts and realities of Irish history. Contrast of Bloom's Jewishness, his ridicule by and isolation from co-workers. The Gold Cup Race. Sexual affair of Molly and Boylan. Keyless plight of Bloom, and of Ireland in bondage to England with lifeless heroes of the past. Dublin as a sterile, paralyzed city in need of a vision.

IN THE HEART OF THE HIBERNIAN METROPOLIS

BEFORE NELSON'S PILLAR TRAMS SLOWED, SHUNTED, CHANGED trolley, started for Blackrod, Kingstown and Dalkey, Clonskea, Rathgar and Terenure, Palmerston park and upper Rathmines, Sandymount Green, Rathmines, Ringsend and Sandymount Tower, Harold's Cross. The hoarse Dublin United Tramway Company's timekeeper bawled them off:

-- Rathgar and Terenure!

-- Come on, Sandymount Green!

Right and left parallel clanging ringing a doubledecker and a singledeck moved from their railheads, swerved to the down line, glided parallel.

-- Start, Palmerston park!

. . . .

GENTLEMEN OF THE PRESS

Grossbooted draymen rolled barrels dullthudding out of Prince's stores and bumped them up on the brewery float. On the

[84]

brewery float bumped dullthudding barrels rolled by grossbooted draymen out of Prince's stores,

-- There it is Red Murray said. Alexander Keyes.

-- Just cut it out, will you? Mr Bloom said, and I'll take it round to the *Telegraph* office.

The door of Ruttledge's office creaked again. Davy Stephens, minute in a large capecoat, a small felt hat crowning his ringlets, passed out with a roll of papers under his cape, a king's courier.

Red Murray's long shears slice out the advertisement from the newspaper in four clean strokes. Scissors and paste.

-- I'll go through the printing works, Mr Bloom said, taking the cut square.

-- Of course, if he wants a par, Red Murray said earnestly, a pen behind his ear, we can do him one.

-- Right, Mr Bloom said with a nod. I'll rub that in.
We.

. . . .

WITH UNFEIGNED REGRET IT IS WE ANNOUNCE THE DISSOLUTION OF A MOST RESPECTED DUBLIN BURGESS

Hynes here too: account of the funeral probably. Thumping thump. This morning the remains of the late Mr Patrick Dignam. Machine. Smash a man to atoms if they got him caught. Rule the world today. His machineries are pegging away too. Like these, got out of hand: fermenting. Working away, tearing away. And that old grey rat tearing to get in.

. . . .

HOUSE OF KEYES

--Like that, see. Two crossed keys here. A circle. Then here the name Alexander Keyes, tea, wine and spirit merchant. So on.

Better not teach him his own business.

--You know yourself, councilor, just what he wants. The round the top in leaded: the house of keys. You see? Do you think that's a good idea?

The foreman moved his scratching hand to his lower ribs and scratched there quietly.

--The idea, Mr. Bloom said, is the house of keys. You know, councilor, the Manx parliament. Innuendo of home rule. Tourists, you know, from the isle of Man. Catches the eye, you see. Can you do that?

I could ask him perhaps about how to pronounce that *voglio.* But then if he didn't know only make it awkward for him. Better not.

-- We can do that, the foreman said. Have you the design?

-- I can get it, Mr Bloom said. It was in a Kilkenny paper. He has a house there too. I'll just run out and ask him. Well, you can do that and just a little par calling attention. You know the usual. High class licensed premises. Longfelt want. So on.

The foreman thought for an instant.

-- We can do that, he said. Let him give us a three months' renewal.

A typesetter brought him a limp galleypage. He began to check it silently. Mr Bloom stood by, hearing the loud throbs of cranks, watching the silent typesetters at their cases.

. . . .

AND IT WAS THE FEAST OF THE PASSOVER

He stayed in his walk to watch a typesetter neatly distributing type. Reads it backwards first. Quickly he does it. Must require some practice that. mangiD. kcirtaP. Poor papa with his hagadah book, reading backwards with his finger to me. Pessach. Next year in Jerusalem. Dear, O dear! All that long business about that brought us out of the land of Egypt and into the house of bondage *alleluia. Shema Israel Adonai Elohenu.* No, that's the other. Then the twelve brothers, Jacob's sons. And then the lamb and the cat and the dog and the stick and the water and the butcher and then the angel of death kills the butcher and he kills the ox and the dog kills the cat. Sounds a bit silly till you come to look into it well. Justice it means but it's everybody eating everyone else. That's what life is after all. How quickly he does that job. Practice makes perfect. Seems to see with his fingers.

[86]

Mr Bloom passed on out of the clanking noises through the gallery on to the landing. Now am I going to tram it out all the way and then catch him out perhaps? Better phone him up first. Number? Same as Citron's house. Twentyeight. Twentyeight double four.

. . . .

SAD

Cleverest fellow at the junior bar he used to be. Decline poor chap. That hectic flush spells finis for a man. Touch and go with him. What's in the wind, I wonder. Money worry.

-- *Or again if we but climb the serried mountain peaks.*

-- You're looking extra.

-- Is the editor to be seen? J. J. O'Molloy asked, looking towards the inner door.

-- Very much so, professor MacHugh said. To be seen and heard. He's in his sanctum with Lenehan.

J. J. O'Molloy strolled to the sloping desk and began to turn back the pink pages of the file.

Practice dwindling. A mighthavebeen. Losing heart. Gambling. Debts of honour. Reaping the whirlwind. Used to get good retainers from D. and T. Fitzgerald. Their wigs to show their grey matter. Brains on their sleeve like the statue in Glasnevin. Believe he does some literary work for the *Express* with Gabriel Conroy. Wellread fellow. Myles Crawford began on the *Independent.* Funny the way those newspaper men veer about when they get wind of a new opening. Weathercocks. Hot and cold in the same breath. Wouldn't you know which to believe. One story good till you hear the next. Go for one another baldheaded in the papers and then all blows over. Hailfellow well met the next moment.

-- Ah, listen to this for God's sake, Ned Lambert pleaded. *Or again if we but climb the serried mountain peaks . . .*

-- Bombast! the professor broke in testily. Enough of the inflated windbag!

-- *Peaks,* Ned Lambert went on, *towering high on high, to bathe our souls, as it were . . .*

-- Bathe his lips, Mr Dedalus said. Blessed and eternal God! Yes? Is he taking anything for it?

-- *As 'twere, in the peerless panorama of Ireland's portfolio, unmatched, despite their wellpraised prototypes in other vaunted prize regions, for very beauty, of bosky grove and undulating plain and luscious pastureland of vernal green, steeped in the transcendent translucent glow of our mild mysterious Irish twilight. . . . . .*

O, HARP EOLIAN

He took a reel of dental floss from his waistcoat pocket and, breaking off a piece, twanged it smartly between two and two of his resonant unwashed teeth.

-- Bingbang, bangbang.

Mr Bloom, seeing the coast clear, made for the inner door.

-- Just a moment, Mr Crawford, he said. I just want to phone about an ad.

He went in.

-- What about that leader this evening? professor MacHugh asked, coming to the editor and laying a firm hand on his shoulder.

-- That'll be all right, Myles Crawford said more calmly. Never you fret. Hello, Jack. That's all right.

-- Good day, Myles, J. J. O'Molloy said, letting the pages he held slip limply back on the file. Is that Canada swindle case on today?

The telephone whirred inside.

-- Twenty eight . . . No, twenty . . . Double four . . . Yes.

SPOT THE WINNER

Lenehan came out of the inner office with *Sports* tissues.

--Who wants a dead cert for the Gold cup? he asked. Sceptre with O. Madden up.

He tossed the tissues on to the table.

Screams of newsboys barefoot in the hall rushed near and the door was flung open.

-- Hush, Lenehan said. I hear footsteps.

Professor McHugh strode across the room and seized the cringing urchin by the collar as the others scampered out of the hall and down the steps. The tissues rustled up in the draught, floated softly in the air blue scrawls and under the table came to earth.

It wasn't me, sir. It was the big fellow shoved me, sir.

-- Throw him out and shut the door, the editor said. There's a hurricane blowing.

Lenehan began to paw the tissues up from the floor, grunting as he stooped twice.

-- Waiting for the racing special, sir, the newsboy said. It was Pat Farrel shoved me, sir.

He pointed to two faces peering in round the door-frame.

-- Him, sir.

-- Out of this with you, professor MacHugh said gruffly.

He hustled the boy out and banged the door to.

J. J. O'Molloy turned the files crackingly over, murmuring, seeking:

-- Continued on page six, column four.

-- Yes . . . *Evening Telegraph* here, Mr Bloom phoned from the inner office. Is the boss . . . ? Yes, *Telegraph* . . . To where? . . . Aha! Which auction rooms? . . . Aha! I see . . . Right. I'll catch him.

A COLLISION ENSUES

The bell whirred again as he rang off. He came in quickly and bumped against Lenehan who was struggling up with the second tissue.

-- *Pardon, monsieur,* Lenehan said, clutching him for an instant and making a grimace.

-- My fault, Mr Bloom said, suffering his grip. Are you hurt? I'm in a hurry.

-- Knee, Lenehan said.

He made a comic face and whined, rubbing his knee.

-- The accumulation of the *anno Domini.*

-- Sorry, Mr Bloom said.

He went to the door and, holding it ajar, paused. J. J. O'Molloy slapped the heavy pages over. The noise of two shrill voices, a mouthorgan, echoed in the bare hallway from the newsboys squatted on the doorsteps:

> *We are the boys of Wexford*
> *Who fought with heart and hand.*

EXIT BLOOM

--I'm just running round to Bachelor's walk, Mr Bloom said, about this ad of Keyes's. Want to fix it up. They tell me he's round there in Dillon's.

He looked indecisively for a moment at their faces. The editor who, leaning against the mantelshelf, had propped his head on his hand suddenly stretched forth an arm amply.

-- Begone! he said. The world is before you.

-- Back in no time, Mr Bloom said, hurrying out.

J. J. O'Molloy took the tissues from Lenehan's hand and read them, blowing them apart gently, without comment.

-- He'll get that advertisement, the professor said, staring through his blackrimmed spectacles over the crossblind. Look at the young scamps after him.

-- Show! Where? Lenehan cried, running to the window.

. . . .

THE GRANDEUR THAT WAS ROME

--Wait a moment, professor MacHugh said, raising two quiet claws. We mustn't be led away by words, by sounds of words. We think of Rome, imperial, imperious, imperative.

He extended elocutionary arms from frayed stained shirtcuffs pausing:

--What was their civilization? Vast, I allow: but vile. Cloacae: sewers. The Jews in the wilderness and on the mountaintop said: *It is meet to be here. Let us build an altar to Jehovah.* The Roman, like the Englishman who follows in his footsteps, brought to every new shore on which he set his foot (on our shore he never set

[90]

it) only his cloacal obsession. He gazed about him in his toga and he said: *It is meet to be here. Let us construct a watercloset.*

--Which they accordingly did do, Lenehan said. Our old ancient ancestors, as we read in the first chapter of Guinness's, were partial to the running stream.

--They were nature's gentlemen, J.J. O'Molloy murmured. But we have also Roman law.

--And Pontius Pilate is its prophet, professor McHugh responded.

-- Do you know that story about chief Baron Palles? J. J. O'Molloy asked. It was at the royal university dinner. Everything was going swimmingly . . .

-- First my riddle, Lenehan said. Are you ready?

Mr O'Madden Burke, tall in copious grey of Donegal tweed, came in from the hallway. Stephen Dedalus behind him, uncovered as he entered.

- *Entrez, mes enfants!* Lenehan cried.

-- I escort a suppliant, Mr O'Madden Burke said melodiously. Youth led by Experience visits Notoriety.

-- How do you do? the editor said, holding out a hand. Come in. Your governor is just gone.

?   ?   ?

Lenehan said to all:

-- Silence! What opera resembles a railway line? Reflect, ponder, excogitate, reply.

Stephen handed over the typed sheets, pointing to the title and signature.

-- Who? the editor asked.

Bit torn off.

-- Mr Garrett Deasy, Stephen said.

-- That old pelters, the editor said. Who tore it? Was he short taken.

> *On swift sail flaming*
> *From storm and south*
> *He comes, pale vampire,*

Mouth to my mouth.

-- Good day, Stephen, the professor said, coming to peer over their shoulders. Foot and mouth? Are you turned . . . ?

Bullockbefriending bard.

. . . .

LENEHAN'S LIMERICK

There's a ponderous pundit MacHugh
Who wears goggles of ebony hue.
As he mostly sees double
To wear them why trouble?
I can't see the Joe Miller. Can you?

In mourning for Sallust, Mulligan says. Whose mother is beastly dead.

Myles Crawford crammed the sheets into a sidepocket.

-- That'll be all right, he said. I'll read the rest after. That'll be all right.

Lenehan extended his hands in protest.

-- But my riddle! he said. What opera is like a railway line?

-- Opera? Mr O'Madden Burke's sphinx face reriddled.

Lenehan announced gladly:

-- *The Rose of Castille.* See the wheeze? Rows of cast steel. Gee!

He poked Mr O'Madden Burke mildly in the spleen. Mr O'Madden Burke fell back with grace on his umbrella, feigning a gasp.

-- Help! He sighed. I feel a strong weakness.

Lenehan, rising to tiptoe, fanned his face rapidly with the rustling tissues.

The professor, returning by way of the files, swept his hand across Stephen's and Mr O'Madden Burke's loose ties.

-- Paris, past and present, he said. You look like communards.

-- Like fellows who had blown up the bastille, J. J. O'Molloy said in quiet mockery. Or was it you shot the lord lieutenant of Finland between you? You look as though you had done the deed. General Bobrikoff.

OMNIUM GATHERUM

-- We were only thinking about it, Stephen said.

-- All the talents, Myles Crawford said. Law, the classics . . .

-- The turf, Lenehan put in.

-- Literature, the press.

--If Bloom were here, the professor said. The gentle art of advertisement.

-- And Madam Bloom, Mr O'Madden Burke added. The vocal muse. Dublin's prime favourite.

Lenehan gave a loud cough.

-- Ahem! he said very softly. O, for a fresh of breath air! I caught a cold in the park. The gate was open.

YOU CAN DO IT!

The editor laid a nervous hand on Stephen's shoulder.

– I want you to write something for me, he said. Something with a bite in it. You can do it. I see it in your face. *In the lexicon of youth . . .*

See it in your face. See it in your eye. Lazy idle little schemer.

– Foot and mouth disease! the editor cried in scornful invective. Great nationalist meeting in Borris-in-Ossory. All balls! Bulldosing the public! Give them something with a bite in it. Put us all into it, damn its soul. Father Son and Holy Ghost and Jakes M'Carthy.

– We can all supply mental pabulum, Mr O'Madden Burke said.

Stephen raised his eyes to the bold unheeding stare.

– He wants you for the pressgang, J. J. O'Molloy said.

. . . .

A MAN OF HIGH MORALE

— Professor Magennis was speaking to me about you, J. J. O'Molloy said to Stephen. What do you think really of that hermetic crowd, the opal hush poets: A. E. the master mystic? That Blavatsky woman started it. She was a nice old bag of tricks. A. E. has been telling some yankee interviewer that you came to him in the small hours of the morning to ask him about planes of consciousness. Magennis thinks you must have been pulling A. E.'s leg. He is a man of the very highest morale, Magennis.

Speaking about me. What did he say? What did he say? What did he say about me? Don't ask.

— No, thanks, professor MacHugh said, waving the cigarette case aside. Wait a moment. Let me say one thing. The finest display of oratory I ever heard was a speech made by John F. Taylor at the college historical society. . . .

. . . .

FROM THE FATHERS

It was revealed to me that those things are good which yet are corrupted which neither if they were supremely good nor unless they were good could be corrupted. Ah, curse you! That's saint Augustine.

— *Why will you jews not accept our culture, our religion and our language? You are a tribe of nomad herdsmen; we are a mighty people. You have no cities nor no wealth: our cities are hives of humanity and our galleys, trireme and quadrireme, laden with all manner merchandise furrow the waters of the known globe. You have but emerged from primitive conditions: we have a literature, a priesthood, an agelong history and a polity.*

Nile.

Child, man, effigy.

By the Nilebank the babemaries kneel, cradle of bulrushes: a man supple in combat: stonehorned, stonebearded, heart of stone.

— *You pray to a local and obscure idol: our temples, majestic and mysterious, are the abodes of Isis and Osiris, of Horus and Ammon Ra. Yours are serfdom, awe and humbleness: our thunder and the seas. Israel is weak and few are her children: Egypt is an host and terrible are her arms. Vagrants and daylabourers are you called: the world trembles at our name.*

A dumb belch of hunger cleft his speech. He lifted his voice above it boldly:

– But, ladies and gentlemen, had the youthful Moses listened to and accepted that view of life, had he bowed his head and bowed his will and bowed his spirit before that arrogant admonition he would never have brought the chosen people out of their house of bondage nor followed the pillar of the cloud by day. He would never have spoken with the Eternal amid lightnings on Sinai's mountaintop nor even have come down with the light of inspiration shining in his countenance and bearing in his arms the tablets of the law, graven in the language of the outlaw.

He ceased and looked at them, enjoying silence.

OMINOUS – FOR HIM!

J. J. O'Molloy said not without regret:

– And yet he died without having entered the land of promise.

– A sudden – at – the – moment – though – from – lingering – illness – often – previously – expectorated – demise, Lenehan said. And with a great future behind him.

The troop of bare feet was heard rushing along the hallway and pattering up the staircase.

– That is oratory, the professor said, uncontradicted.

Gone with the wind. Hosts at Mullaghmast and Tara of the kings. Miles of ears of porches. The tribune's words howled and scattered to the four winds. A people sheltered with his voice. Dead noise. Akasic records of all that ever anywhere wherever was. Love and laud him: me no more.

I have money.

– Gentlemen, Stephen said. As the next motion on the agenda paper may I suggest that the house now adjourn?

— You take my breath away. It is not perchance a French compliment? Mr O'Madden Burke asked. 'Tis the hour, methinks, when the winejug, metaphorically speaking, is most grateful in Ye ancient hostelry.

— That it be and hereby resolutely resolved. All who are in favour say ay, Lenehan announced. The contrary no. I declare it carried. To which particular boosing shed? . . My casting vote is: Mooney's!

He led the way, admonishing:

— We will sternly refuse to partake of strong waters, will we not? Yes, we will not. By no manner of means.

Mr O'Madden Burke, following close, said with an ally's lunge of his umbrella:

Lay on, Macduff!

— Chip of the old block! The editor cried, slapping Stephen on the shoulder. Let us go. Where are those blasted keys?

He fumbled in his pocket, pulling out the crushed typesheets.

— Foot and mouth. I know. That'll be all right. That'll go in. Where are they? That's all right.

He thrust the sheets back and went into the inner office.

. . . .

DEAR DIRTY DUBLIN

Dubliners.

-- Two Dublin vestals, Stephen said, elderly and pious, have lived fifty and fiftythree years in Fumbally's lane.

-- Where is that? the professor asked.

-- Off Blackpitts.

Damp night reeking of hungry dough. Against the wall. Face glistening tallow under her fustian shawl. Frantic hearts. Akasic records. Quicker, darlint!

On now. Dare it. Let there be life.

-- They want to see the views of Dublin from the top of Nelson's pillar. They save up three and tenpence in a red tin letterbox moneybox. They shake out the threepenny bits and a sixpence and coax out the pennies with the blade of a knife. Two and

[96]

three in silver and one and seven in coppers. They put on their bonnets and best clothes and take their umbrellas for fear it may come on to rain.

-- Wise virgins, professor MacHugh said.

. . . .

RETURN OF BLOOM

-- Yes, he said. I see them.

-- Mr Bloom, breathless, caught in a whirl of wild newsboys near the offices of the *Irish Catholic* and *Dublin Penny Journal,* called:

-- Mr Crawford! A moment!

-- *Telegraph!* Racing special!

-- What is it? Myles Crawford said, falling back a pace.

A newsboy cried in Mr Bloom's face:

-- Terrible tragedy in Rathmines! A child bit by a bellows!

INTERVIEW WITH THE EDITOR

-- Just this ad, Mr Bloom said, pushing through towards the steps, puffing, and taking the cutting from his pocket. I spoke with Mr Keyes just now. He'll give a renewal for two months, he says. After he'll see. But he wants a par to call attention in the *Telegraph* too, the Saturday pink. And he wants it if it's not too late I told councillor Nannetti from the *Kilkenny People.* I can have access to it in the national library. House of keys, don't you see? His name is Keyes. It's a play on the name. But he practically promised he'd give the renewal. But he wants just a little puff. What will I tell him, Mr Crawford?

K. M. A.

-- Will you tell him he can kiss my arse? Myles Crawford said, throwing out his arm for emphasis. Tell him that straight from the stable.

A bit nervy. Look out for squalls. All off for a drink. Arm in arm. Lenehan's yachting cap on the cadge beyond. Usual blarney. Wonder is that young Dedalus the moving spirit. Has a good pair of boots on him today. Last time I saw him he had his heels on view.

Been walking in muck somewhere. Careless chap. What was he doing in Irishtown?

-- Well, Mr Bloom said, his eyes returning, if I can get the design I suppose it's worth a short par. He'd give the ad I think. I'll tell him . . .

K. M. R. I. A.

-- He can kiss my royal Irish arse, Myles Crawford cried loudly over his shoulder. Any time he likes, tell him.

While Mr Bloom stood weighing the point and about to smile he strode on jerkily.

RAISING THE WIND

-- *Nulla bona,* Jack, he said, raising his hand to his chin. I'm up to here. I've been through the hoop myself. I was looking for a fellow to back a bill for me no later than last week. You must take the will for the deed. Sorry, Jack. With a heart and a half if I could raise the wind anyhow.

J. J. O'Molloy pulled a long face and walked on silently. They caught up on the others and walked abreast.

-- When they have eaten the brawn and the bread and wiped their twenty fingers in the paper the bread was wrapped in, they go nearer to the railing.

-- Something for you, the professor explained to Myles Craword. Two old Dublin women on the top of Nelson's pillar.

. . . .

THOSE SLIGHTLY RAMBUNCTIOUS FEMALES

-- Easy all, Myles Crawford said, no poetic licence. We're in the archdiocese here.

-- And settle down on their stripped petticoats, peering up at the statue of the onehandled adulterer.

-- Onehandled adulterer! the professor cried. I like that. I see the idea. I see what you mean.

DAMES DONATE DUBLIN'S CITS
SPEEDPILLS VELOCITOUS AEROLITHS, BELIEFS

[98]

-- It gives them a crick in their necks, Stephen said, and they are too tired to look up or down or to speak. They put the bag of plums between them and eat the plums out of it one after another, wiping off with their handkerchiefs the plumjuice that dribbles out of their mouths and spitting the plumstones slowly out between the railings.

He gave a sudden loud young laugh as a close. Lenehan and Mr O'Madden Burke, hearing, turned, beckoned and led on across toward Mooney's.

-- Finished? Myles Crawford said. So long as they do no worse.

. . . .

WHAT?--AND LIKEWISE--WHERE?

-- But what do you call it? Myles Crawford asked. Where did they get the plums?

VIRGILIAN, SAYS PEDAGOGUE.
SOPHOMORE PLUMPS FOR OLD MAN MOSES

-- Call it, wait, the professor said, opening his long lips wide to reflect. Call it, let me see. Call it: *deus nobis haec otia fecit.*

-- No, Stephen said, I call it *A Pisgah Sight of Palestine or the Parable of the Plums.*

-- I see, the professor said.

He laughed richly.

-- I see, he said again with new pleasure. Moses and the promised land. We gave him that idea, he added to J. J. O'Molloy.

HORATIO IS CYNOSURE THIS FAIR JUNE DAY

J. J. O'Molloy sent a weary sidelong glance towards the statue and held his peace.

-- I see, the professor said.

He halted on sir John Gray's pavement island and peered aloft at Nelson through the meshes of wry smile

Journeying through Dublin's streets, Bloom encounters various individuals engaged in the banalities of life. He is saddened to see Dilly Dedalus standing on the street, knowing her father is off drinking. Mrs. Breen's husband is driven mad by a postcard. Bloom feels concern for Mina Purefoy in labor. He reminisces on his romance with Molly. Bloom enters the Burton Hotel for lunch but is repulsed by the piggish eating of diners. He moves on, preoccupied with his wife's upcoming affair and their marital relationship. At Davy Byrne's pub over lunch he recalls lovemaking with Molly. Avoiding Boylan, he ducks into the National Library Museum where, pondering the digestive process, he looks at a naked goddess to see whether she has an anus.

THEMES
The passing of life, the madness of life, the humanity behind everyday events. Creativity and birth. The etiquette of eating and drinking. Molly's upcoming affair with Boylan vis-a-vis Bloom and Molly's lacking a physical-sexual relationship since their one-year-old Rudy's death. Romantic reminiscences of earlier years.

PINEAPPLE ROCK, LEMON PLATT, BUTTER SCOTCH. A SUGARSTICKY girl shoveling scoopfuls of creams for a christian brother. Some school treat. Bad for the tummies. Lozenge and comfit manufacturer to His Majesty the King. God. Save. Our. Sitting on his throne, sucking red jujubes white.

A sombre Y. M. C. A. young man, watchful among the warm sweet fumes of Graham Lemon's, placed a throwaway in a hand of Mr. Bloom.

Heart to heart talks.

Bloo . . . Me? No.

Blood of the Lamb.

His slow feet walked him riverward, reading. Are you saved? All are washed in the blood of the lamb. God wants blood victim. Birth, hymen, martyr, war, foundation of a building, sacrifice, kidney burntoffering, druid's altars. Elijah is coming. Dr John Alexander Dowie, restorer of the church in Zion, is coming.

Is coming! Is coming!! Is coming!!!
All heartily welcome.

[100]

Paying game. Torry and Alexander last year. Polygamy. His wife will put the stopper on that. Where was that ad some Birmingham firm the luminous crucifix? Our Saviour. Wake up the dead of night and see him on the wall, hanging. Pepper's ghost idea. Iron nails ran in.

. . . .

From Butler's monument house corner he glanced along Bachelor's walk. Dedalus' daughter there still outside Dillon's auctionrooms. Must be selling off some old furniture. Knew her eyes at once from the father. Lobbing about waiting for him. Home always breaks up when the mother goes. Fifteen children he had. Birth every year almost. That's in their theology or the priest won't give the poor woman the confession, the absolution. Increase and multiply. Did you ever hear such an idea? Eat you out of house and home. No families themselves to feed. Living on the fat of the land. Their butteries and larders. I'd like to see them do the black fast Yom Kippur. Crossbuns. One meal and a collation for fear he'd collapse on the altar. A housekeeper of one of those fellows if you could pick it out of her. Never pick it out of her. Like getting L.s.d. out of him. Does himself well. No guests. All for number one. Watching his water. Bring your own bread and butter. His reverence. Mum's the word.

Good Lord, that poor child's dress is in flitters. Underfed she looks too. Potatoes and marge, marge and potatoes. It's after they feel it. Proof of the pudding. Undermines the constitution.

. . . .

He halted again and bought from the old applewoman two Banbury cakes for a penny and broke the brittle paste and threw its fragments down into the Liffey. See that? The gulls swooped silently two, then all, from their heights, pouncing on the prey. Gone. Every morsel.

Aware of their greed and cunning he shook the powdery crumb from his hands. They never expected that. Manna. Live on fishy flesh they have to, all sea birds, gulls, seagoose. Swans from Anna Liffey swim down here sometimes to preen themselves. No account for tastes. Wonder what kid is swanmeat. Robinson Crusoe had to live on them.

. . . .

He crossed Westmoreland street when apostrophe S had plodded by. Rover cycleshop. Those races are on today. How long ago is that? Year Phil Gilligan died. We were in Lombard street west. Wait, was in Thom's. Got the job in Wisdom Hely's year we married. Six years. Ten years ago: ninetyfour he died, yes that's right, the big fire at Arnott's. Val Dillon was lord mayor. The Glencree dinner. Alderman Robert O'Reilly emptying the port into his soup before the flag fell, Bobbob lapping it for the inner alderman. Couldn't hear what the band played. For what we have already received may the Lord make us. Milly was a kid then. Molly had that elephantgrey dress with the braided frogs. Mantailored with selfcovered buttons. She didn't like it because I sprained my ankle first day she wore choir picnic at the Sugarloaf. As if that. Old Goodwin's tall hat done up with some sticky stuff. Flies' picnic too. Never put a dress on her back like it. Fitted her like a glove, shoulder and hips. Just beginning to plump it out well. Rabbit pie we had that day. People looking after her.

Happy. Happier then. Snug little room that was with the red wallpaper, Dockrell's, one and ninepence a dozen. Milly's tubbing night. American soap I bought: elderflower. Cosy smell of her bathwater. Funny she looked soaped all over. Shapely too. Now photography. Poor papa's daguerreotype atelier he told me of. Hereditary taste.

He walked along the curbstone.

Stream of life....

. . . .

Swish and soft flop her stays made on the bed. Always warm from her. Always liked to let herself out. Sitting three after till near two, taking out her hairpins. Milly tucked up in beddyhouse. Happy. Happy. That was the night . . .

-- O, Mr Bloom, how do you do?

-- Oh, how do you do, Mrs Breen?

[102]

-- No use complaining. How is Molly those times? Haven't seen her for ages.

-- In the pink, Mr Bloom said gaily, Milly had a position down in Mullingar, you know.

-- Go away! Isn't that grand for her?

-- Yes, in a photographer's there. Getting on like a house on fire. How are all your charges?

-- All on the baker's list, Mrs Breen said.

How many has she? No other in sight.

-- You're in black I see. You have no . . .

-- No, Mr Bloom said. I have just come from a funeral.

Going to crop up all day, I foresee. Who's dead, when and what did he die of? Turn up like a bad penny.

-- O dear me, Mrs Breen said, I hope it wasn't any near relation.

May as well get her sympathy.

-- Dignam, Mr Bloom said. An old friend of mine. He died quite suddenly, poor fellow. Heart trouble, I believe. Funeral was this morning.

> *Your funeral's tomorrow*
> *While you're coming through the rye.*
> *Diddlediddle dumdum*
> *Diddlediddle . . .*

--Sad to lose the old friends, Mrs Breen's womaneyes said melancholily.

Now that's quite enough about that. Just quietly: husband.

-- And your lord and master?

Mrs Breen turned up her two large eyes. Hasn't lost them anyhow.

-- O, don't be talking, she said. He's a caution to rattlesnakes. He's in there now with his lawbooks finding out the law of libel. He has me heartscalded. Wait till I show you.

. . . .

-- There must be a new moon out, she said. He's always bad then. Do you know what he did last night?

Her hand ceased to rummage. Her eyes fixed themselves on him wide in alarm, yet smiling.

--What? Mr. Bloom asked.

Let her speak. Look straight in her eyes. I believe you. Trust me.

-- Woke me up in the night, she said. Dream he had a nightmare.

Indiges.

-- Said the ace of spades was walking up the stairs.

-- The ace of spades! Mr Bloom said.

She took a folded postcard from her handbag.

-- Read that, she said. He got it in the morning.

-- What is it? Mr Bloom asked, taking the card. U.P.?

-- U.P.: up, she said. Someone taking a rise out of him. It's a great shame for them whoever he is.

-- Indeed it is, Mr Bloom said.

She took back the card, sighing.

-- And now he's going round to Mr Menton's office. He's going to take an action for ten thousand pounds, he says.

She folded the card into her untidy bag and snapped the catch.

Same blue serge dress she had two years ago, the nap bleaching. Seen its best days. Wispish hair over her ears. And that dowdy toque, three old grapes to take the harm out of it. Shabby genteel. She used to be a tasty dresser. Lines round her mouth. Only a year or so older than Molly.

See the eye that woman gave her, passing. Cruel. The unfair sex.

He looked still at her, holding back behind his look his discontent. Pungent mockturtle oxtail mulligatawny. I'm hungry too. Flakes of pastry on the gusset of her dress: daub of sugary flour stuck to her cheek. Rhubarb tart with liberal fillings, rich fruit interior.

[104]

Josie Powell that was. In Luke Doyle's long ago, Dolphin's Barn, the charades. U. P.: up.

Change the subject.

-- Do you ever see anything of Mrs Beaufoy, Mr Bloom asked.

-- Mina Purefoy? She said.

Philip Beaufoy I was thinking. Playgoer's club. Matcham often thinks of the masterstroke. Did I pull the chain? Yes. The last act.

-- Yes.

-- I just called to ask on the way in is she over it. She's in the lying-in hospital in Holles street. Dr Horne got her in. She's three days bad now.

-- O, Mr Bloom said. I'm sorry to hear that.

-- Yes, Mrs Breen said. And a household of kids at home. It's a very stiff birth, the nurse told me.

-- O, Mr Bloom said.

His heavy pitying gaze absorbed her news. His tongue clacked in compassion. Dth! Dth!

-- I'm sorry to hear that, he said. Poor thing! Three days! That's terrible for her.

Mrs Breen nodded.

-- She was taken bad on the Tuesday . . .

Mr Bloom touched her funnybone gently, warning her.

-- Mind! Let this man pass.

A bony form strode along the curbstone from the river, staring with a rapt gaze into the sunlight through a heavy stringed glass. Tight as a skullpiece a tiny hat gripped his head. From his arm a folded dustcoat, a stick and an umbrella dangled to this stride.

-- Watch him, Mr Bloom said. He always walks outside the lampposts. Watch!

-- Who is he if it's a fair question, Mrs Breen asked. Is he dotty?

-- His name is Cashel Boyle O'Connor Fitzmaurice Tisdall Farrell, Mr Bloom said, smiling. Watch!

-- He has enough of them, she said. Denis will be like that one of these days.

She broke off suddenly.

-- There he is, she said. I must go after him. Goodbye. Remember me to Molly, won't you?

-- I will, Mr Bloom said.

. . . .

Mr Bloom walked on again easily, seeing ahead of him in the sunlight the tight skullpiece, the dangling stick, umbrella, dustcoat. Going in two days. Watch him! Out he goes again. One way of getting on in the world. And that other old mosey lunatic in those duds. Hard time she must have with him.

U. P.: up. I'll take my oath that's Alf Bergan or Richie Goulding. Wrote it for a lark in the Scotch house, I bet anything. Round to Menton's office. His oyster eyes staring at the postcard. Be a feast for the gods.

He passed the *Irish Times*. There might be other answers lying there. Like to answer them all. Good system for criminals. Code. At their lunch now. Clerk with the glasses there doesn't know me. O, leave them there to simmer. Enough bother wading through forty-four of them. Wanted smart lady typist to aid gentleman in literary work. I called you naughty darling because I do not like that other world. Please tell me what is the meaning. Please tell me what perfume does your wife. Tell me who made the world. The way they spring those questions on you. And the other one Lizzie Twigg. My literary efforts have had the good fortune to me with the approval of the eminent poet A. E. (Mr Geo Russell). No time to do her hair drinking sloppy tea with a book of poetry.

. . . .

Poor Mrs Purefoy! Methodist husband. Method in his madness. Saffron bun and milk and soda lunch in the educational dairy. Eating with a stopwatch, thirtytwo chews to the minute. Still his muttonchop whiskers grew. Supposed to be well connected. Theodore's cousin in Dublin Castle. One tony relative in every family. Hardy annuals he presents her with. Saw him at the Three

[106]

Jolly Topers marching along bareheaded and his eldest boy carrying one in a marketnet. The squallers. Poor thing! Then having to give the breast year after year all hours of the night Selfish those t.t's are. Dog in the manger. Only one lump of sugar in my tea, if you please.

He stood at Fleet street crossing. Luncheon interval a sixpenny at Rowe's? Must look up that ad in the national library. An eightpenny in the Burton. Better. On my way.

He walked on past Bolton's Westmoreland house. Tea. Tea. Tea. I forgot to tap Tom Kernan.

Sss. Dth, dth, dth! Three days imagine groaning on a bed with a vinegared handkerchief round her forehead, her belly swelling out! Phew! Dreadful simply! Child's head too big: forceps. Doubled up inside her trying to butt its way out blindly, groping for the way out. Kill me that would. Lucky Molly got over hers lightly. They ought to invent something to stop that. Life with hard labour. Twilightsleep idea: queen Victoria was given that. Nine she had. A good layer. Old woman that lived in a shoe she had so many children. Suppose he was consumptive. Time someone thought about it instead of gassing about the what was it the pensive bosom of the silver effulgence. Flapdoodle to feed fools on. They could easily have big establishments. Whole thing quite painless out of all the taxes give every child born five quid at compound interest up to twentyone, five per cent is a hundred shillings and five tiresome pounds, multiply by twenty decimal system, encourage people to put by money save hundred and ten and a bit twentyone years want to work it out on paper come to a tidy sum, more than you think.

Not stillborn of course. They are not even registered. Trouble for nothing

. . . .

Before the huge high door of the Irish house of parliament a flock of pigeons flew. Their little frolic after meals. Who will we do it on? I pick the fellow in black. Here goes. Here's good luck. Must be thrilling from the air. Apjohn, myself and Owen Goldberg up in the trees near Goose green playing the monkeys. Mackerel they called me.

A squad of constables debouched from College street, marching in Indian file. Goose step. Foodheated faces, sweating helmets, patting their truncheons. After their feed with a good load of fat soup under their belts. Policeman's lot is oft a happy one. They split up into groups and scattered, saluting towards their beats. Let out to graze. Best moment to attack one in pudding time. A punch in his dinner. A squad of others, marching irregularly, rounded Trinity railings, making for the station. Bound for their troughs. Prepare to receive cavalry. Prepare to receive soup.

. . . .

His smile faded as he walked, a heavy cloud hiding the sun slowly, shadowing Trinity's surly front. Trams passed one another, ingoing, outgoing, clanging. Useless words. Things go on same: day after day: squads of police marching out, back: trams in, out. Those two loonies mooching about. Dignam carted off. Mina Purefoy swollen belly on a bed groaning to have a child tugged out of her. One born every second somewhere. Other dying every second. Since I fed the birds five minutes. Three hundred kicked the bucket. Other three hundred born, washing the blood off, all are washed in the blood of the lamb, bawling maaaaaa.

Cityful passing away, other cityful coming, passing away too: other coming on, passing on. Houses, lines of houses, streets, miles of pavements, piledup bricks, stones. Changing hands. This owner, that. Landlord never dies they say. Other steps into his shoes when he gets his notice to quit. They buy the place up with gold and still they have all the gold. Swindle in it somewhere. Piled up in cities, worn away age after age, Pyramids in sand. Built on bread and onions. Slaves. Chinese wall. Babylon. Big stones left. Round towers. Rest rubble, sprawling suburbs, jerrybuilt, Kerwan's mushroom houses, built of breeze. Shelter for the night.

No one is anything.

This is the very worst hour of the day. Vitality. Dull, gloomy: hate this hour. Feel as if I had been eaten and spewed.

. . . .

They passed from behind Mr Bloom along the curbstone. Beard and bicycle. Young woman.

And there he is too. Now that's really a coincidence: secondtime. Coming events cast their shadows before. With the approval of the eminent poet Mr Geo Russell. That might be Lizzie Twigg with him. A. E.: what does that mean? Initials perhaps. Albert Edward, Arthur Edmund, Alphonsus Eb Ed El Esquire. What was he saying? The ends of the world with a Scotch accent. Tentacles: octopus. Something occult: symbolism. Holding forth. She's taking it all in. Not saying a word. To aid gentleman in literary work.

His eyes followed the high figure in homespun, beard and bicycle, a listening woman at his side. Coming from the vegetarian. Only weggebobbles and fruit. Don't eat a beefsteak. If you do the eyes of that cow will pursue you through all eternity. They say it's healthier. Wind and watery though. Tried it. Keep you on the run all day. Bad as a bloater. Dreams all night. Why do they call that thing they gave me nutsteak? Nutarians. Fruitarians. To give you the idea you are eating rumpsteak. Absurd. Salty too. They cook in soda. Keep you sitting by the tap all night.

Her stockings are loose over her ankles. I detest that: so tasteless. Those literary ethereal people they are all. Dreamy, cloudy, symbolistic. Esthetes they are. I wouldn't be surprised if it was that kind of food you see produces the like waves of the brain the poetical. For example one of those policemen sweating Irish stew into their shirts; you couldn't squeeze a line of poetry out of him. Don't know what poetry is even. Must be in a certain mood.

> *The dreamy cloudy gull*
> *Waves o'er the waters dull.*

. . . .

His hand fell again to his side.

Never know anything about it. Waste of time. Gasballs spinning about, crossing each other, passing. Same old dingdong always. Gas, then solid, then world, then cold, then dead shell drifting around, frozen rock like that pineapple rock. The moon. Must be a new moon, she said. I believe there is.

[109]

He went on by la Maison Claire.

Wait. The full moon was the night we were Sunday fortnight exactly there is a new moon. Walking down by the Tolka. Not bad for a Fairview moon. She was humming: The young May moon she's beaming, love. He other side of her. Elbow, arm. He. Glowworm's la-amp is gleaming, love. Touch. Fingers. Asking. Answer. Yes.

Stop. Stop. If it was it was. Must.

Mr Bloom, quick breathing, slowlier walking, passed Adam court.

With a keep quiet relief, his eyes took note: this is street here middle of the day Bob Doran's bottle shoulders. On his usual bend, M'Coy said. They drink in order to say or do something or *cherchez la femme.* Up in the Coombe with chummies and streetwalkers and then the rest of the year as sober as a judge.

. . . .

I was happier then. Or was that I? Or am I now I? Twenty-eight I was. She twentythree when we left Lombard street west something changed. Could never like it again after Rudy. Can't bring back time. Like holding water in your hand. Would you go back to then? Just beginning then. Would you? Are you not happy in your home, you poor little naughty boy? Wants to sew on buttons for me. I must answer. Write it in the library.

Grafton street gay with housed awnings lured his senses. Muslin prints, silk, dames and dowagers, jingle of harnesses, hoofthuds lowringing in the baking causeway. Thick feet that woman has in the white stockings. Hope the rain mucks them up on her. Country bred chawbacon. All the beef to the heels were in. Always gives a woman clumsy feet. Molly looks out of plumb.

He passed, dallying, the windows of Brown Thomas, silk mercers. Cascades of ribbons. Flimsy China silks. A tilted urn poured from its mouth a flood of bloodhued poplin: lustrous blood. The huguenots brought that here. *La causa è santa!* Tara tara. Great chorus that. Tara. Must be washed in rainwater. Meyerbeer. Tara: bom bom bom.

[110]

Pincushions. I'm a long time threatening to buy one. Stick them all over the place. Needles in window curtains.

He bared slightly his left forearm. Scrape: nearly gone. Not today anyhow. Must go back for that lotion. For her birthday perhaps. Junejulyaugustseptember eighth. Nearly three months off. Then she mightn't like it. Women won't pick up pins. Say it cuts lo.

Gleaming silks, petticoats on slim brass rails, rays of flat silk stockings.

Useless to go back. Had to be. Tell me all.

High voices. Sunwarm silk. Jingling harnesses. All for a woman, home and houses, silk webs, silver, rich fruits, spicy from Jaffa. Agendath Netaim. Wealth of the world.

A warm human plumpness settled down his brain. His brain yielded. Perfume of embraces all him assailed. With hungered flesh obscurely, he mutely craved to adore.

Duke street. Here we are. Must eat. The Burton. Feel better then.

. . . .

His heart astir he pushed in the door of the Burton restaurant. Stink gripped his trembling breath: pungent meatjuice, slop of greens. See the animals feed.

Men, men, men.

Perched on high stools by the bar, hats shoved back, at the tables calling for more bread no charge, swilling, wolfing gobuls of sloppy food, their eyes bulging, wiping wetted moustaches. A pallid suetfaced young man polished his tubler knife fork and spoon with his napkin. New set of microbes. A man with an infant's saucestained napkin tucked round him on this plate: halfmasticated gristle: no teeth to chewchewchew it. Chump chop from the grill. Bolting to get it over. Sad booser's eyes. Bitten off more than he can chew. Am I like that? See ourselves as others see us. Hungry man is an angry man. Working tooth and jaw. Don't! O! A bone! That last pagan king of Ireland Cormac in the schoolpoem choked himself at Sletty southward of the Boyne. Wonder what he was eating. Something

galoptious. Saint Patrick converted him to Christianity. Couldn't
swallow it all however.

-- Roast beef and cabbage.

-- One stew.

Smells of men. His gorge rose. Spaton sawdust, sweetish
warmish cigarette smoke, reek of plug, spilt beer, men's beery piss,
the stale of ferment.

Couldn't eat a morsel here. Fellow sharpening his knife and
fork, to eat all before him, old chap picking his tootles. Slight spasm,
full, chewing the cud. Before and after. Grace after meals. Look on
this picture then on that. Scoffing up stewgravy with sopping sippets
of bread. Lick it off the plate, man! Get out of this.

He gazed round the stooled and tabled eaters, tightening the
wings of his nose.

--Two stouts here.

-- Once corned and cabbage.

That fellow ramming a knifeful of cabbage down as if his
life depended on it. Good stroke. Give me the fidgets to look. Safer
to eat from his three hands. Tear it limb from limb. Second nature to
him. Born with a silver knife in his mouth. That's witty, I think. Or
no. Silver means born rich. Born with a knife. But then the illusion is
lost.

An illgrit server gathered sticky clattering plates. Rock, the
bailiff, standing at the bar blew the foamy crown from his tankard.
Well up: it splashed yellow near his boot. A diner, knife and fork
upright, elbows on table, ready for a second helping stared towards
the foodlift across his stained square of newspaper. Other chap
telling him something with his mouth full. Sympathetic listener.
Table talk. I munched hum un thu Unchster Bunk un Munchday. Ha?
Did you, faith?

Mr Bloom raised two fingers doubtfully to his lips. His eyes
said.

-- Not here. Don't see him.

Out. I hate dirty eaters.

[112]

He backed towards the door. Get a light snack in Davy Byrne's. Stopgap. Keep me going. Had a good breakfast.

-- Roast and mashed here.

-- Pint of stout.

Every fellow for his own, tooth and nail. Gulp. Grub. Gulp. Gobstuff.

He came out into the clearer air and turned back towards Grafton street. Eat or be eaten. Kill! Kill!

. . . .

He entered Davy Byrne's. Moral pub. He doesn't chat. Stands a drink now and then. But in leapyear once in four. Cashed a cheque for me once.

What will I take now? He drew his watch. Let me see now. Shandygaff?

-- Hellow, Bloom! Nosey Flynn said from his nook.

-- Hello, Flynn.

-- How's things?

-- Tiptop . . . Let me see. I'll take a glass of burgundy and . . . let me see.

. . . .

-- Have you a cheese sandwich?

--Yes, sir.

Like a few olives too if they had them. Italian I prefer. Good glass of burgundy; take away that. Lubricate. A nice salad, cool as a cucumber. Tom Kernan can dress. Puts gusto into it. Pure olive oil. Milly served me that cutlet with a sprig of parsley. Take one Spanish onion. God made food, the devil the cooks. Devilled crab.

-- Wife well?

-- Quite well, thanks . . . A cheese sandwich, then. Gorgonzola, have you?

-- Yes, sir.

Nosey Flynn sipped his grog.

-- Doing any singing those times?

Look at his mouth. Could whistle in his own ear. Flap ears to match. Music. Knows as much about it as my coachman. Still better tell him. Does no harm. Free ad.

-- She's engaged for a big tour end of this month. You may have heard perhaps.

-- No. O, that's the style. Who's getting it up?

The curate served.

-- How much is that?

-- Seven d., sir . . . Thank you, sir.

Mr. Bloom cut his sandwich into slender strips. *Mr MacTrigger.* Easier than the dreamy creamy stuff. *His five hundred wives. Had the time of their lives.*

-- Mustard, sir?

-- Thank you.

He studded under each lifted strip yellow blobs. *Their lives.* I have it. *It grew bigger and bigger and bigger.*

-- Getting it up? he said. Well, it's like a company idea, you see. Part shares and part profits.

-- Ay, now I remember, Nosey Flynn said, putting his hand in his pocket to scratch his groin. Who is this was telling me? Isn't Blazes Boylan mixed up in it?

A warm shock of air heat of mustard hauched on Mr Bloom's heart. He raised his eyes and met the stare of a bilious clock. Two. Pub clock five minutes fast. Time going on. Hands moving. Two. Not yet.

His midriff yearned then upward, sank within him, yearned more longly, longingly.

Wine.

He smellsipped the cordial juice and, bidding his throat strongly to speed it, set his wineglass delicately down.

-- Yes, he said. He's the organiser in point of fact.

No fear. No brains.

Nosey Flynn snuffled and scratched. Flea having a good square meal.

. . . .

[114]

Davy Byrne came forward from the hindbar in tuckstictched shirtsleeves, cleaning his lips with two wipes of his napkin. Herring's blush. Whose smile upon each feature plays with such and such replete. Too much fat on the parsnips.

-- And here's himself and pepper on him, Nosey Flynn said. Can you give us a good one for the Gold cup?

-- I'm off that, Mr Flynn, Davy Byrne answered. I never put anything on a horse.

-- You're right there, Nosey Flynn said.

Mr Bloom ate his strips of sandwich, fresh clean bread, with relish of disgust, pungent mustard, the feety savour of green cheese. Sips of his wine soothed his palate. Not logwood that. Tastes fuller this weather with the chill off.

Nice quiet bar. Nice piece of wood in that counter. Nicely planed. Like the way it curves there.

-- I wouldn't do anything at all in that line, Davy Byrne said. It ruined many a man the same horses.

Vintners sweepstake. Licensed for the sale of beer, wine, spirits for consumption on the premises. Heads I win tails you lose.

-- True for you, Nosey Flynn said. Unless you're in the know. There's no straight sport now. Lenehan gets some good ones. He's giving Sceptre today. Zinfandel's the favourite, lord Howard de Walden's, won at Epsom. Morny Cannon is riding him. I could have got seven to one against Saint Amant a fortnight before.

-- That so? Davy Byrne said . . .

He went towards the window and, taking up the petty cash book, scanned its pages.

-- I could, faith, Nosey Flynn said snuffling. That was a rare bit of horseflesh. Saint Frusquin was her sire. She won in a thunderstorm, Rothschild's filly, with wadding in her ears. Blue jacket and yellow cap. Bad luck to big Ben Dollard and his John O'Gaunt. He put me off it. Ay.

He drank resignedly from his tumbler, running his fingers down the flutes.

-- Ay, he said, sighing.

Mr Bloom, champing standing, looked upon his sigh. Nosey numskull. Will I tell him that horse Lenehan? He knows already. Better let him forget. Go and lose more. Fool and his money. Dewdrop coming down again. Cold nose he'd have kissing a woman. Still they might like. Prickly beards they like. Dog's cold noses. Old Mrs Riordan with the rumbling stomach's Skye terrier in the City Arms hotel. Molly fondling him in her lap. O the big doggy-bowwowsywowsy!

Wine soaked and softened rolled pith of bread mustard a moment mawkish cheese. Nice wine it is. Taste it better because I'm not thirsty. Bath of course does that. Just a bite or two. Then about six o'clock I can. Six, six. Time will be gone then. She . . .

. . . .

Glowing wine on his palate lingered swallowed. Crushing in the winepress grapes of Burgundy. Sun's heat it is. Seems to a secret touch telling me memory. Touched his sense moistened remembered. Hidden under wild ferns on Howth. Below us bay sleeping sky. No sound. The sky. The bay purple by the Lion's head. Green by Drumleck. Yellowgreen towards Sutton. Fields of undersea, the lines faint brown in the grass, buried cities. Pillowed on my coat she had her hair, earwigs in the heather scrub my hand under her nape, you'll toss me all. O wonder! Coolsoft with ointments her hand touched me, caressed: her eyes upon me did not turn away. Ravished over her I lay, full lips open, kissed her mouth. Yum. Softly she gave me in my mouth the seedcake warm and chewed. Mawkish pulp her mouth had mumbled sweet and sour with spittle. Joy: I ate it: joy. Young life, her lips that gave me pouting. Soft, warm, sticky gumjelly lips. Flowers her eyes were, take me, willing eyes. Pebbles fell. She lay still. A goat. No-one. High on Ben Howth rhododendrons a nannygoat walking surefooted, dropping currants. Screened under ferns she laughed warmfolded. Wildly I lay on her, kissed her; eyes, her lips, her stretched nick, beating, woman's breasts full in her blouse of nun's veiling, fat nipples upright. Hot I tongued her. She kissed me. I was kissed. All yielding she tossed my hair. Kissed, she kissed me.

[116]

Me. And me now.

. . . .

Dribbling a quiet message from his bladder came to go to do not to do there to do. A man and ready he drained his glass to the lees and walked, to men too they gave themselves, manly conscious, lay with men lovers, a youth enjoyed her, to the yard.

When the sound of his boots had ceased Davy Byrnes said from his book:

-- What is this he is? Isn't he in the insurance line?

-- He's out of that long ago, Nosey Flynn said. He does canvassing for the *Freeman.*

-- I know him well to see, Davy Byrne said. Is he in trouble?

-- Trouble? Nosey Flynn said. Not that I heard of. Why?

-- I noticed he was in mourning.

-- Was he? Nosey Flynn said. So he was, faith. I asked him how was all at home. You're right, by God. So he was.

-- I never broach the subject, Davy Byrne said humanely, if I see a gentleman is in trouble that way. It only brings it up fresh in their minds.

-- It's not the wife anyhow, Nosey Flynn said. I met him the day before yesterday and he coming out of that Irish farm dairy John Wyse Nolan's wife has in Henry street with a jar of cream in his hand taking it home to his better half. She's well nourished, I tell you. Plovers on toast.

-- And he is doing for the *Freeman?* Davy Byrne said.

Nosey Flynn pursed his lips.

-- He doesn't buy cream on the ads he picks up. You can make bacon of that.

-- How so? Davy Byrne asked, coming from his book.

Nosey Flynn made swift passes in the air with juggling fingers. He winked.

-- He's in the craft, he said.

-- Do you tell me so? Davy Byrne said.

-- Very much so, Nosey Flynn said. Ancient free and accepted order. Light, life and love, by God. They give him a leg up. I was told that by a, well, I won't say who.

-- Is that a fact?

-- O, it is a fine order, Nosey Flynn said. They stick to you when you're down. I know a fellow was trying to get into it, but they're as close as damn it. By God they did right to keep the women out of it.

Davy Byrne smiledyawnednodded all in one:

-- Iiiiiichaaaaaaach!

-- There was one woman, Nosey Flynn said, hid herself in a clock to find out what they be doing. But be damned but they smelt her out and swore her in on the spot a master mason. That was one of the Saint Legers of Doneraile.

Davy Byrne, sated after his yawn, said with tearwashed eyes:

-- And is that a fact? Decent quiet man he is. I often saw him in here and I never once saw him, you know, over the line.

-- God Almighty couldn't make him drunk, Nosey Flynn said firmly. Slips off when the fun gets too hot. Didn't you see him look at his watch? Ah, you weren't there. If you ask him to have a drink first thing he does he outs with the watch to see what he ought to imbibe. Declare to God he does.

--There are some like that, Davy Byrne said. He's a safe man, I'd say.

-- He's not too bad, Nosey Flynn said, snuffling it up. He has been known to put his hand down too to help a fellow. Give the devil his due. O, Bloom has his good points. But there's one thing he'll never do.

His hand scrawled a dry pen signature beside his grog.

-- I know, Davy Byrne said.

-- Nothing in black and white, Nosey Flynn said.

Paddy Leonard and Bantam Lyons came in. Tom Rochford followed, a plaining had on his claret waistcoat.

-- Day, Mr Byrne.

-- Day, gentlemen.

They paused at the counter.

-- Who's standing? Paddy Leonard asked.

-- I'm sitting anyhow, Nosey Flynn answered.

-- Well, what'll it be? Paddy Leonard asked.

-- I'll take a stone ginger, Bantam Lyons said.

-- How much? Paddy Leonard cried. Since when, for God's sake? What's yours, Tom?

-- How is the drainage? Nosey Flynn asked, sipping.

For answer Tom Rochfold pressed his hand to his breastbone and hiccupped.

-- Would I trouble you for a glass of fresh water, Mr Byrne? he said.

-- Certainly, sir.

Paddy Leonard eyed his alemates.

-- Lord love a duck, he said, look at what I'm standing drinks to! Cold water and gingerpop! Two fellows that would suck whisky off a sore leg. He has some bloody horse up his sleeve for the Gold cup. A dead snip.

-- Zinfandel is it? Nosey Flynn asked.

Tom Rochfold spilt powder from a twisted paper into water set before him.

-- That cursed dyspepsia, he said before drinking.

-- Breadsoda is very good, Davy Byrne said.

Tom Rochfold nodded and drank.

-- Is it Zinfandel?

-- Say nothing, Bantam Lyons winked. I'm going to plunge five bob on my own.

-- Tell us if you're worth your salt and be damned to you, Paddy Leonard said. Who gave it to you?

Mr Bloom on his way out raised three fingers in greeting.

-- So long, Nosey Flynn said.

The others turned.

-- That's the man now that gave it to me, Bantam Lyons whispered.

-- Prrwht! Paddy Leonard said with scorn. Mr Byrne, sir, we'll take two of your small Jamesons after that and a . . .

-- Stone ginger, Davy Byrne added civilly.

-- Ay, Paddy Leonard said. A suckingbottle for the baby.

Mr Bloom walked toward Dawson street, his tongue brushing his teeth smooth. Something green it would have to be: spinach say. Then with those Rontgen rays searchlight you could.

. . . .

Keyes: two months if I get Nannetti to. That'll be two pounds ten, about two pounds eight. Three Hynes owes me. Two eleven. Prescott's ad. Two fifteen. Five guineas about. On the pig's back.

Could buy one of those silk petticoats for Molly, colour of her new garters.

Today. Today. Not think.

Tour the south then. What about English watering places? Brighton, Margate. Piers by moonlight. Her voice floating out. Those lovely seaside girls. Against John Long's a drowsing loafer lounged in heavy thought, gnawing a crusted knuckle. Handy man want job. Small wages. Will eat anything.

Mr Bloom turned at Gray's confectioner's window of unbought tarts and passed the reverend Thomas Connellan's bookstore. *Why I left the church of Rome? Bird's nest.* Women run him. They say they used to give pauper children soup to change to protestants in the time of the potato blight. Society over the way papa went to for the conversion of poor jews. Same bait. Why we left the church of Rome?

A blind stripling stood tapping the curbstone with his slender cane. No tram in sight. Wants to cross.

-- Do you want to cross? Mr Bloom asked.

The blind strapping did not answer. His wall face frowned weakly. He moved his head uncertainly.

-- You're in Dawson street, Mr Bloom said. Molesworth street is opposite. Do you want to cross? There's nothing in the way.

The cane moved out trembling to the left. Mr Bloom's eye followed its line and saw again the dyeworks' van drawn up before Drago's. Where I saw his brilliantined hair just when I was. Horse droppings. Driver in John Long's. Slaking his drouth.

-- There's a van there, Mr Bloom said, but it's not moving. I'll see you across. Do you want to go to Molesworth street?

-- Yes, the stripling answered. South Frederick street.

-- Come, Mr Bloom said.

He touched the thin elbow gently: then took the limp seeing hand to guide it forward.

Say something to him. Better not do the condescending. They mistrust what you tell them. Pass a common remark:

-- The rain kept off.

No answer.

Stains on his coat. Slobbers his food, I suppose. Tastes all different for him. Have to be spoonfed first. Like a child's hand his hand. Like Milly's was. Sensitive. Sizing me up I daresay from my hand. Wonder if he has a name. Van. Keep his cane clear of the horse's legs tired drudge get his doze. That's right. Clear. Behind a bull: in front of a horse.

-- Thanks, sir.

Knows I'm a man. Voice.

-- Right now? First turn to the left.

The blind stripling tapped the curbstone and went on his way, drawing his cane back, feeling again.

Mr Bloom walked behind the eyeless feet, a flatcut suit of herringbone tweed. Poor young fellow! How on earth did he know that van was there? Must have felt it. See things in their foreheads perhaps. Kind of sense of volume. Weight. Would he feel it if something was removed? Feel a gap. Queer idea of Dublin he must have, tapping his way round by the stones. Could he walk in a beeline if he hadn't that cane? Bloodless pious face like a fellow going to be a priest.

. . . .

Mr Bloom came to Kildare Street. First I must. Library.

Straw hat in sunlight. Tan shoes. Turnedup trousers. It is. It is.

His heart quopped softly. To the right. Museum. Goddesses. He swerved to the right.

Is it? Almost certain. Won't look. Wine in my face. Why did I? Too heady. Yes, it is. The walk. Not see. Not see. Get on.

Making for the museum gate with long windy strides he lifted his eyes. Handsome building. Sir Thomas Deane designed. Not following me?

Didn't see me perhaps. Light in his eyes.

The flutter of his breath came forth in short sighs. Quick. Cold statues: quiet there. Safe in a minute.

No, didn't see me. After two. Just at the gate.

My heart!

His eyes beating looked steadfastly at cream curves of stone. Sir Thomas Deane was the Greek architecture.

Look for something I.

His hasty hand went quick into a pocket, took out, read unfolded. Agendath Netaim. Where did I?

Busy looking for.

He thrust back quickly Agendath.

Afternoon she said.

I am looking for that. Yes, that. Try all pockets. Handker. *Freeman.* Where did I? Ah, yes. Trousers. Purse. Potato. Where did I?

Hurry. Walk quietly. Moment more. My heart.

His hand looking for the where did I put found in his hip pocket soap lotion have to call tepid paper stuck. Ah, soap there! Yes. Gate.

Safe!

[122]

Episode 9 – Scylla and Charybdis… a female, six-headed monster that snatched sailors from ships, and opposite the waters of a dangerous whirlpool that sucks down ships. Odysseus must carefully navigate between the two, but inclines toward Scylla. ~ Even as Stephen navigates between the monsters of mundane life and the whirlpool of neo-Irish literary movements, he personifies Scylla in his snappy arguments and displays Charybdis in a whirlpool of theories on Shakespeare.

In Dublin's National Library, Stephen theorizes on Shakespeare, his marriage, his *Hamlet*, impotence, adultery – to a group of literati. He disputes aesthetics and other matters, while thoughts intrude upon his consciousness: reactions to his talk, flashbacks to Mulligan and Haines, money spent on a prostitute, Father Conmee, and his mother's death. Apart from Stephen, the principals discuss the Irish Literary Renaissance and A.E.Russell's work. Later, Mulligan and Bloom appear. Mulligan revels that Bloom was staring at the anus of a goddess. Mulligan flatters Stephen's wit, is silent on Wilde's alleged homosexuality, poeticizes masturbation. In departing, Bloom passes between Stephen and Mulligan.

THEMES
A dissection and debate of Shakespeare's life, family, marriage, and plays, notably *Hamlet*. Reconciling flesh with spirit, mind with body, and with workaday concerns. Paternity, the (mystical) relationship of father and son. Self-doubt, past ghosts of life, skepticism of religious teachings. The whirlpool of arguments on the Irish nationalist and literary movement and its authors.

URBANE, TO COMFORT THEM, THE QUAKER LIBRARIAN PURRED:

-- And we have, have we not, those priceless pages of *Wilhelm Meister?* A great poet on a great brother poet. A hesitating soul taking arms against a sea of troubles, torn by conflicting doubts, as one sees in real life.

He came a step in a sinkapace forward on a neatsleather creaking and a step backward a sinkapace on the solemn floor.

A noiseless attendant setting open the door but slightly, made him a noiseless beck.

-- Directly, said he, creaking to go, albeit lingering. The beautiful ineffectual dreamer who comes to grief against hard facts. One always feels that Goethe's judgments are so true. True in the larger analysis.

Twicecreakingly analysis he corantoed off. Bald, most zealous by the door he gave his large ear all to the attendants's words: heard them: and was gone.

Two left.

-- Monsieur de la Palisse, Stephen sneered, was alive fifteen minutes before his death.

-- Have you found those six brave medicals, John Eglinton asked with elder's gall, to write *Paradise Lost* at your dictation? *The Sorrows of Satan* he calls it.

Smile. Smile. Cranly's smile.

> *First he tickled her*
> *Then he patted her*
> *Then he passed the female catheter.*
> *For he was a medical*
> *Jolly old medi . . .*

-- I feel you would need one more for *Hamlet.* Seven is dear to the mystic mind. The shining seven W. B. calls them.

. . . .

Mulligan has my telegram.

Folly. Persist.

-- Our young Irish bards, John Englinton censured, have yet to create a figure which the world will set beside Saxon Shakespeare's Hamlet though I admire him, as old Ben did, on this side idolatry.

-- All these questions are purely academic, Russell oracled out of his shadow. I mean, whether Hamlet is Shakespeare or James I or Essex. Clergymen's discussions of the historicity of Jesus. Art has to reveal to us ideas, formless spiritual essences. The supreme question about a work of art is out of how deep a life does it spring. The painting of Gustave Moreau is the painting of ideas. The deepest poetry of Shelley, the words of Hamlet bring our mind into contact with the eternal wisdom, Plato's world of ideas. All the rest is speculation of schoolboys for schoolboys.

A. E. has been telling some yankee interviewer. Wall, tarnation strike me!

-- The schoolmen were schoolboys first, Stephen said superpolitely. Aristotle was once Plato's schoolboy.

[124]

-- And has remained so, one should hope, John Eglinton
sedately said. One can see him, a model schoolboy with his diploma
under his arm.

He laughed again at the now smiling bearded face.

Formless spiritual. Father, Word and Holy Breath. Allfather,
the heavenly man. Hiesos Kristos, magician of the beautiful, the
Logos who suffers in us at every moment. This verily is that. I am
the fire upon the altar. I am the sacrificial butter.

Dunlop, Judge, the noblest Roman of them all, A. E., Arval,
the Name Ineffable, in heaven hight, K. H., their master, whose
identity is no secret to adepts. Brothers of the great white lodge
always watching to see if they can help. The Christ with the
bridesister, moisture of light, born of an ensouled virgin, repentant
sophia, departed to the plane of buddhi. The life esoteric is not for
ordinary person. O. P. must work off bad karma first. Mrs Cooper
Oakley once glimpsed our very illustrious sister H. P. B.'s elemental.

O, fie. Out on't! *Pfuiteufel!* You naughtn't to look missus, so
you naughtn't when a lady's showing of her elemental.

Mr Best entered, tall, young, mild, light. He bore in his hand
with grace a notebook, new, large, clean, bright.

-- That model schoolboy, Stephen said, would find Hamlet's
musings about the afterlife of his princely soul, the improbable,
insignificant and undramatic monologue, as shallow as Plato's.

John Eglinton, frowning, said, waxing wroth:

-- Upon my word it makes my blood boil to hear anyone
compare Aristotle to Plato.

-- Which of the two, Stephen asked, would have banished
me from his commonwealth?

Unsheathe your dagger definitions. Horseness is the
whatness of allhorse. Streams of tendency and eons they worship.
God: noise in the street: very peripatetic. Space: what you damn well
have to see. Through spaces smaller than red globules of man's
blood they creepycrawl after Blake's buttocks into eternity of which
this vegetable world is but a shadow. Hold to the now, the here,
through which all future plunges to the past.

Mr Best came forward, amiable, towards his colleague.

-- Haines is gone, he said.

-- Is he?

-- I was showing him Jubainville's book. He's quite enthusiastic, don't you know, about Hyde's *Lovesongs of Connacht.* I couldn't bring him in to hear the discussion. He's gone to Gill's to buy it.

> *Bound thee forth, my booklet, quick*
> *To greet the callous public.*
> *Writ, I ween, 'twas not my wish*
> *In lean unlovely English.*

-- The peatsmoke is going to his head, John Eglinton opined.

We feel in England. Penitent thief. Gone. I smoked his baccy. Green twinkling stone. An emerald set in the ring of the sea.

-- People do not know how dangerous lovesongs can be, the auric egg of Russell warned occultly. The movements which work revolutions in the world are born out of the dreams and visions in a peasant's heart on the hillside. For them the earth is not an exploitable ground but the living mother. The rarefied air of the academy and the arena produce the sixshilling novel, the musichall song, France produces the finest flower of corruption in Mallarme' but the desirable life is revealed only to the poor of heart, the life of Homer's Phaecians.

. . . .

Between the Saxon smile and the yankee yawp. The devil and the deep sea.

--He will have it that *Hamlet* is a ghoststory, John Eglinton said for Mr Best's behoof. Like the fat boy in Pickwick he wants to make our flesh creep.

> *List! List! O List!*

My flesh hears him: creeping, hears.

> *If thou didst ever . . .*

[126]

-- What is a ghost? Stephen said with tingling energy. One who has faded into impalpability through death, through absence, through change of manners. Elizabethan London lay as far from Stratford as corrupt Paris lies from virgin Dublin. Who is the ghost from *limbo patrum,* returning to the world that has forgotten him? Who is the king, Hamlet?

John Eglinton shifted his spare body, leaning back to judge.

. . . .

-- The play begins. A player comes on under the shadow, made up in the castoff mail of a court buck, a wellset man with a bass voice. It is the ghost, the king, a king and no king, and the player is Shakespeare who has studied *Hamlet* all the years of his life which were not vanity in order to play the part of the spectre. He speaks the words to Burbage, the young player who stands before him beyond the rack of cerecloth, calling him by a name:

Hamlet, I am thy father's spirit

bidding him list. To a son he speaks, the son of his soul, the prince, young Hamlet and to the son of his body, Hamnet Shakespeare, who has died in Stratford that his namesake may live for ever.

-- Is it possible that that player Shakespeare, a ghost by absence, and in the vesture of buried Denmark, a ghost by death, speaking his own words to his own son's name (had Hamnet Shakespeare lived he would have been prince Hamlet's twin) is it possible, I want to know, or probable that he did not draw or foresee the logical conclusion of those premises: you are the dispossessed son: I am the murdered father: you mother is the guilty queen. Ann Shakespeard, born Hathaway?

-- But this prying into the family life of a great man, Russell began impatiently.

Art thou there, truepenny?

-- Interesting only to the parish clerk. I mean, we have the plays. I mean when we read the poetry of *King Lear* what is it to us how the poet lived? As for living, our servants can do that for us, Villiers de l'Isle has said. Peeping and prying into greenroom gossip of the day, the poet's drinking, the poet's debts. We have *King Lear:* and it is immortal.

Mr Best's face appealed to, agreed.

. . . .

Buzz. Buzz.

But I, entelechy, form of forms, am I by memory because undee everchanging forms.

I that sinned and prayed and fasted.

A child. Conmee saved from pansies.

I, I and I. I.

A. E. I. O. U.

-- Do you mean to fly in the face of the tradition of three centuries? John Eglinton's carping voice asked. Her ghost at least has been laid for ever. She died, for literature at least, before she was born.

-- She died, Stephen retorted, sixtyseven years after she was born. She saw him into and out of the world. She took his first embraces. She bore his children and she laid pennies on his eyes to keep his eyelids closed when he lay on his deathbed.

Mother's deathbed. Candle. The sheeted mirror. Who brought me into this world lies there, bronzelidded, under few cheap flowers. *Liliata rutilantium.*

I wept alone.

John Eglinton looked in the tangled glowworm of his lamp.

-- The world believes that Shakespeare made a mistake, he said, and got out of it as quickly and as best he could.

-- Bosh! Stephen said rudely. A man of genius makes no mistakes. His errors are volitional and are the portals of discovery.

Portals of discovery opened to let in the quaker librarian, softcreakfooted, bald, eared and assiduous.

-- A shrew, John Eglinton said shrewdly, is not a useful portal of discovery, one should imagine. What useful discovery did Socrates learn from Xanthippe?

-- Dialectic, Stephen answered: and from his mother how to bring thoughts into the world. What he learnt from his other wife

[128]

Myrto (*absit nomen!*) Socratididion's Epipsychidion, no man, not a
woman, will ever know. But neither the midwife's lore nor the
caudlectures saved him from the archons of Sinn Fein and their
noggin of hemlock.

 -- But Ann Hathaway? Mr Best's quiet voice said
forgetfully. Yes, we seem to be forgetting her as Shakespeare
himself forgot her.

 His look went from brooder's beard to carper's skull, to
remind, to chide them not unkindly, then to the baldpink lollard
costard, guiltless though maligned.

. . . .

 -- Ryefield, Mr Best said brightly, gladly, raising his new
book, gladly, brightly.

 He murmured then with blonde delight for all:

> *Between the acres of the rye*
> *These pretty countryfolk would lie.*

Paris: the wellpleased pleaser.

 A tall figure in bearded homespun rose from shadow and
unveiled its cooperative watch.

 -- I am afraid I am due at the *Homestead.*

Whither away? Exploitable ground.

 -- Are you going, John Eglinton's active eyebrows asked.
Shall we see you at Moore's tonight? Piper is coming.

 -- Piper! Mr Best piped. Is Piper back?

 --I don't know if I can. Thursday. We have our meeting. If I
can get away in time.

. . . .

 -- They say we are to have a literary surprise, the quaker
librarian said, friendly and earnest. Mr Russell, rumour has it, is
gathering a sheaf of our younger poet's verses. We are all looking
forward anxiously.

 Anxiously he glanced in the cone of lamplight where three
faces, lighted, shone.

 See this. Remember.

Stephen looked down on a wide headless caubeen, hung on his ashplanthandle over his knee. My casque and sword. Touch lightly with two index fingers. Aristotle's experiment. One or two? Necessity is that in virtue of which it is impossible that one can be otherwise. Argal, one hat is one hat.

Listen.

Young Colum and Starkey. George Roberts is doing the commercial part. Longworth will give it a good puff in the *Express.* O, will he? I liked Colum's *Drover.* Yes, I think he has that queer thing, genius. Do you think he has genius really? Yeats admired his line: *As in wild earth a Grecian vase.* Did he? I hope you'll be able to come tonight. Malachi Mulligan is coming too. Moore asked him to bring Haines. Did you hear Miss Mitchell's joke about Moore the Martyn? That Moore is Martyn's wild oats? Awfully clever, isn't it? They remind one of don Quixote and Sancho Panza. Our national epic has yet to be written, Dr Sigerson says. Moore is the man for it. A knight of the rueful countenance here in Dublin. With a saffron kilt? O'Neill Russell? O, yes, he must speak the grand old tongue. And his Dulcinea? Jame Stephens is doing some clever sketches. We are becoming important, it seems.

. . . .

Stephen sat down.

The quaker librarian came from the leavetakers. Blushing his mask said:

-- Mr Dedalus, your views are most illuminating.

He creaked to and fro, tiptoing up nearer heaven by the altitude of a chopine, and, covered by the noise of outgoing, said low:

-- Is it your view, then, that she was not faithful to the poet?

Alarmed face asks me. Why did he come? Courtesy or an inward light?

-- Where there is a reconciliation, Stephen said, there must have been first a sundering.

-- Yes.

[130]

Christfox in leather trews, hiding, a runaway in blighted treeforks from hue and cry. Knowing no vixen, walking lonely in the chase. Women he won to him, tender people, a whore of Babylon, ladies of justices, bully tapsters' wives. Fox and geese. And in New Place a slack dishonoured body that once was comely, once as sweet, as fresh as cinnamon, now her leaves falling, all, bare, frighted of the narrow grave and unforgiven.

-- Yes. So you think.

The door closed behind the outgoer.

. . . .

They are still. Once quick in the brains of men. Still: but an itch of death is in them, to tell me in my ear a maudlin tale, urge me to wreak their will.

-- Certainly, John Eglinton mused, of all great men he is the most enigmatic. We know nothing but that he lived and suffered. Not even so much. Others abide our question. A shadow hangs over all the rest.

-- But *Hamlet* is so personal, isn't it? Mr Best pleaded. I mean, a kind of private paper, don't you know, of his private life. I mean I don't care a button, don't you know, who is killed or who is guilty . . .

He rested an innocent book on the edge of the desk, smiling his defiance. His private papers in the original. *Ta an bad ar an tir. Taim imo shagart.* Put beurla on it, littlejohn.

Quoth littlejohn Eglinton:

-- I was prepared for paradoxes from what Malachi Mulligan told us but I may as well warn you that if you want to shake my belief that Shakespeare is Hamlet you have a stern task before you.

Bear with me.

Stephen withstood the bane of miscreant eyes, glinting stern under wrinkled brows. A basilisk. *E quando vedel'uomo l'attosca.* Messer Brunetto, I thank thee for the word.

-- As we, or mother Dana, weave and unweave our bodies, Stephen said, from day to day, their molecules shuttled to and fro, so does the artist weave and unweave his image. And as the mole on my right breast is where it was when I was born, though all my body has been woven of new stuff time after time, so through the ghost of the unquiet father the image of the unliving son looks forth. In the intense instant of imagination, when the mind, Shelley says, is a fading coal, that which I was is that which I am and that which in possiblity I may come to be. So in the future, the sister of the past, I may see myself as I sit here now but by reflection from that which then I shall be.

Drummond of Hawthornden helped you at that stile.

-- Yes, Mr Best said youngly, I feel Hamlet quite young. The bitterness might be from the father but the passages with Ophelia are surely from the son.

Has the wrong sow by the lug. He is in my father. I am in his son.

-- That mole is the last to go, Stephen said, laughing.

John Eglinton made a nothing pleasing mow.

-- If that were the birthmark of genius, he said, genius would be a drug in the market. The plays of Shakespeare's later years which Renan admired so much breathe another spirit.

-- The spirit of reconciliation, the quaker librarian breathed.

-- There can be no reconciliation, Stephen said, if there has not been a sundering.

Said that.

-- If you want to know what are the events which cast their shadow over the hell of time of *King Lear, Othello, Hamlet, Troilus and Cressida,* look to see when and how the shadow lifts. What softens the heart of a man, Shipwrecked in storms dire, Tried, like another Ulysses, Pericles, prince of Tyre?

Head, redconecapped, buffeted, brineblinded.

. . . .

The benign forehead of the quaker librarian enkindled rosily with hope.

-- I hope Mr Dedalus will work out his theory for the enlightenment of the public. And we ought to mention another Irish commentator, Mr George Bernard Shaw. Nor should we forget Mr

[132]

Frank Harris. His articles on Shakespeare in the *Saturday Review* were surely brilliant. Oddly enough he too draws unhappy relation with the dark lady of the sonnets. The favoured rival is William Herbert, earl of Pembroke. I own that if the poet must be rejected, such a rejection would seem more in harmony with -- what shall I say? -- our notions of what ought not to have been.

Felicitously he ceased and held a meek head among them, auk's egg, prize of their fray.

He thous and thees her with grave husbandwords. Dost love, Miriam? Dost love thy man?

-- That may be too, Stephen said. There is a saying of Goethe's which Mr Magee likes to quote. Beware of what you wish for in youth because you will get it in middle life. Why does he send to one who is a *buonaroba,* a bay where all men ride, a maid of honour with a scandalous girlhood, a lordling to woo for him? He was himself a lord of language and had made himself a coistrel gentleman and had written *Romeo and Juliet.* Why? Belief in himself has been untimely killed. He was overborne in a cornfield first (ryefield, I should say) and he will never be a victor in his own eyes after nor play victoriously the game of laugh and lie down. Assumed dongiovannism will not save him. No later undoing will undo the first undoing. The tusk of the boar has wounded him there where love lies ableeding. If the shrew is worsted yet there remains to her woman's invisible weapon. There is, I feel in the words, some goad of the flesh driving him into a new passion, a darker shadow of the first, darkening even his own understanding of himself. A life fate awaits him and the two rages commingle in a whirlpool.

They list. And in the porches of their ears I pour.

-- The soul has been before stricken mortally, a poison poured in the porch of a sleeping ear. But those who are done to death in sleep cannot know the manner of their quell unless their Creator endow their souls with that knowledge in the life to come. The poisoning and the beast with two backs that urged it king Hamlet's ghost could not know of were he not endowed with knowledge by his creator. That is why the speech (his lean unlovely

English) is always turned elsewhere, backward. Ravisher and ravished, what he would but would not, go with him from Lucrece's bluecircled ivory globes to Imogen's breast, bare, with its mole cinquespotted. He goes back, weary of the creation he has piled up to hide him from himself, an old dog licking sore. But, because loss is his gain, he passes on towards eternity in undiminished personality, untaught by the wisdom he has written or by the laws he revealed. His beaver is up. He is a ghost, a shadow now, the wind by Elsinore's rocks or what you will, the sea's voice, a voice heard only in the heart of him who is the substance of his shadow, the son consubstantial with the father.

 -- Amen! responded from the doorway.

 Hast thou found me, O mine enemy?

 Entr'acte.

 A ribald face, sullen as a dean's, Buck Mulligan came forwards then blithe in motley, towards the greeting of their smiles. My telegram.

 -- You were speaking of the gaseous vertebrate, if I mistake not? he asked of Stephen.

 Primrosevested he greeted gaily with his doffed Panama as with a bauble.

 They make him welcome. *Was Du verlaschst wirst Du noch dienen.*

 Brood of mocker: Photios, pseudomalachi, Johann Most.

 He Who Himself begot, middler the Holy Ghost, and Himself sent himself, Agenbuyer, between Himself and others, Who, put upon by His fiends, stripped and whipped, was nailed like bat to barndoor, starved on crosstree, Who let Him bury, stood up, harrowed hell, fared into heaven and there these nineteen hundred years sitteth on the right hand of His Own Self but yet shall come in the latter day to doom the quick and dead when all the quick shall be dead already.

[Musical score for Gloria in excelsis Deo printed in original text]

 He lifts hands. Veils fall. O, flowers! Bells with bells with bells acquiring.

[134]

-- Yes, indeed, the quaker librarian said. A most instructive discussion, Mr Mulligan, I'll be bound, has his theory too of the play and of Shakespeare. All sides of life should be represented.

He smiled on all sides equally.

Buck Mulligan thought, puzzled:

-- Shakespeare? he said. I seem to know the name.

A flying sunny smile rayed in his loose features.

-- To be sure, he said, remembering brightly. The chap that writes like Synge.

Mr Best turned to him:

-- Haines missed you, he said. Did you meet him? He'll see you after at the D. B. C. He's gone to Gill's to buy Hyde's *Lovesongs of Connacht.*

-- I came through the museum, Buck Mulligan said. Was he here?

-- The bard's fellowcountrymen, John Eglinton answered, are rather tired perhaps of our brilliancies of theorising. I hear that an actress played Hamlet for the fourhundredandeighth time last night in Dublin. Vining held that the prince was a woman. Has no-one made him out to be an Irishman? Judge Barton, I believe, is searching for some clues. He swears (His Highness not His Lordship) by saint Patrick.

. . . .

Buck Mulligan's again heavy face eyed Stephen awhile. Then, his head wagging, he came near, drew a folded telegram from his pocket. His mobile lips read, smiling with new delight.

-- Telegram! he said. Wonderful inspiration! Telegram! A papal bull!

He sat on a corner of the unlit desk, reading aloud joyfully:

-- *The sentimentalist is he who would enjoy without incurring the immense debtorship for a thing done.* Signed: Dedalus. Where did you launch it from? The kips? No. College Green. Have you drunk the four quid? The aunt is going to call on your unsubstantial father. Telegram! Malachi Mulligan, the Ship, lower Abbey street. O, you peerless mummer! O, you priestified kinchite!

Joyfully he thrust the message and envelope into a pocket but keened in querulous brogue:

-- It's what I'm telling you, mister honey, it's queer and sick we were, Haines and myself, the time himself brought it in. 'Twas murmur we did for a gallus potion would rouse a friar, I'm thinking, and he limp with leching. And we one hour and two hours and three hours in Connery's sitting civil waiting for pints apiece.

He wailed!

-- And we to be there, mavrone, and you to be unbeknownst sending us your conglomerations the way we to have our tongues out a yard long like the drouthy clerics do be fainting for a pussful.

Stephen laughed.

Quickly, warningfully, Buck Mulligan bent down:

-- The tramper Synge is looking for you, he said, to murder you. He heard you pissed on his halldoor in Glasthule. He's out in pampooties to murder you.

-- Me! Stephen exclaimed. That was your contribution to literature.

Buck Mulligan gleefully bent back, laughing to the dark eavesdropping ceiling.

-- Murder you! he laughed.

Harsh gargoyle face that warred against me over our mess of hash of lights in rue Saint-Andres-des-Artes. In words of words for words, palabras. Oisin with Patrick. Faunman he met in Clamart woods, brandishing a winebottle, *C'est vendredi saint!* Muthering Irish. His image, wandering, he met. I mine. I met a fool i' the forest.

-- Mr Lyster, an attendant said from the door ajar.

--. . . in which everyone can find his own. So Mr Justice Madden in his *Diary of Master William Silence* has found the hunting terms . . . Yes? What is it?

-- There's a gentleman here, sir, the attendant said, coming forward and offering a card. From the *Freeman.* He wants to see the files of the *Kilkenny People* for last year.

-- Certainly, certainly, certainly. Is the gentleman? . . .

[136]

He took the eager card, glanced, not saw, laid down, unglanced, looked, asked, creaked, asked:

-- Is he? . . . O there!

Brisk in a galliard he was off and out. In the daylit corridor he talked with voluble pains of zeal, in duty bound, most fair, most kind, most honest broadbrim.

-- This gentleman? *Freeman's Journal? Kilkenny People?* To be sure. Good day, sir. *Kilkenny* . . . We have certainly . . .

A patient silhouette waited, listening.

-- All the leading provincial . . . *Northern Whig, Cork Examiner, Enniscorthy Guardian,* 1903 . . . Will you please? . . . Evans, conduct this gentleman . . . If you follow the atten . . . Or please allow me . . . This way . . . Please, sir . . .

Voluble, dutiful, he led the way to all the provincial papers, a bowing dark figure following his hasty heels.

The door closed.

-- The sheeny! Buck Mulligan cried.

He jumped up and snatched the card.

-- What's his name? Ikey Moses? Bloom.

He rattled on.

-- Jehovah, collector of prepuces, is no more. I found him over in the museum when I went to hail the foamborn Aphrodite. The Greek mouth that has never been twisted in prayer. Every day we must do homage to her. *Life of life, thy lips enkindle.*

Suddenly he turned to Stephen:

-- He knows you. He knows your old fellow. O, I fear me, he is Greeker than the Greeks. His pale Galilean eyes were upon her mesial groove. Venus Kallipyge. O, the thunder of those loins! *The god pursuing the maiden hid.*

--We want to hear more, John Eglinton decided with Mr Best's approval. We begin to be interested in Mrs S. Till now we had thought of her, if at all, as a patient Griselda, a Penelope stayathome.

. . . .

-- And Harry of six wives' daughter and other lady friends from neighbour seats, as Lawn Tennyson, gentleman poet, sings. But all those twenty years what do you suppose poor Penelope in Stratford was doing behind the diamond panes?

Do and do. Thing done. In a rosary of Fetter Lane of Gerard, herbalist, he walks, greyedauburn. An azure harebell like her veins. Lids of Juno's eyes, violets. He walks. One life is all. One body. Do. But do. Afar, in a reek of lust and squalor, hands are laid on whiteness.

Buck Mulligan rapped John Eglinton's desk sharply.

-- Whom do you suspect? he challenged.

-- Say that he is the spurned lover in the sonnets. Once spurned twice spurned. But the court wanton spurned him for a lord, his dearmylove.

Love that dare not speak its name.

-- As an Englishman, you mean, John sturdy Eglinton put in, he loved a lord.

Old wall where sudden lizards flash. At Charenton I watched them.

-- It seems so, Stephen said, when he wants to do for him, and for all other and singular uneared wombs, the holy office an ostler does for the stallion. Maybe, like Socrates, he had a midwife to mother as he had a shrew to wife. But she, the giglot wanton, did not break a bedvow. Two deeds are rank in that ghost's mind: a broken vow and the dullbrained yokel on whom her favour has declined, deceased husband's brother. Sweet Ann I take it, was hot in the blood. Once a wooer twice a wooer.

. . . .

Lovely! Buck Mulligan suspired amorously. I asked him what he thought of the charge of pederasty brought against the bard. He lifted his hands and said: *All we can say is that life ran very high in those days.* Lovely!

Catamite.

-- The sense of beauty leads us astray, said beautifulinsadness Best to ugling Eglinton.

Steadfast John replied severe:

[138]

-- The doctor can tell us what those words mean. You cannot eat your cake and have it.

Sayest thou so? Will they wrest from us, from me the palm of beauty?

-- And the sense of property, Stephen said.

. . . .

I think you're getting on very nicely. Just mix up a mixture of theolologicophilolological. *Mingo, minxi, mictum, mingere.*

-- Prove that he was a jew, John Eglinton dared, expectantly. Your dean of studies holds he was a holy Roman.

Suffaminandus sum.

-- He was made in Germany, Stephen replied, as the champion French polisher of Italian scandals.

-- A myriadminded man, Mr Best reminded. Coleridge called him myriadminded.

Amplius. In societate humana hoc est maxime necessarium ut sit amicitia inter multos.

-- Saint Thomas, Stephen began . . .

-- *Ora pro nobis,* Monk Mulligan groaned, sinking to a chair. There he keened a wailing rune.

-- *Pogue mahone! Acushla machree!* It's destroyed we are from this day! It's destroyed we are from this day! It's destroyed we are surely!

-- All smiled their smiles.

-- Saint Thomas, Stephen, smiling, said, whose gorbellied works I enjoy reading in the original, writing of incest from a standpoint different from that of the new Viennese school Mr Magee spoke of, likens it in his wise and curious way to an avarice of the emotions. He means that the love so given to one near in blood is covetously withheld from some stranger who, it may be, hungers for it. Jews, whom christians tax with avarice, are of all races the most given to inter-marriage. Accusations are made in anger. The christian laws which built up the hoards of the jews (for whom, as for the lollards, storm as shelter) bound their affections too with hoops of steel. Whether these be sins or virtues old Nobodaddy will tell us at doomsday leet. But a man who holds so tightly to what he calls his rights over what he calls his debts will hold tightly also to what he calls his rights over her whom he calls his wife. No sire smile neighbour shall cover his ox or his wife or his manservant or his maidservant or his jackass.

    -- Or his jennyass, Buck Mulligan antiphoned.

    -- Gentle Will is being roughly handled, gentle Mr Best said gently.

    -- Which Will? gagged sweetly Buck Mulligan. We are getting mixed.

    -- The will to live, John Eglinton philosophised, for poor Ann, Will's widow, is the will to die.

    -- *Requiescat!* Stephen prayed.

        What of all the will to do?
        It has vanished long ago . . .

. . . .

Your own? He knows your old fellow. The widower.

Hurrying to her squalid deathlair from gay Paris on the quayside I touched his hand. The voice, new warmth, speaking. Dr Bob Kenny is attending her. The eyes that wish me well. But do not know me.

    -- A father, Stephen said, battling against hopelessness, is a necessary evil. He wrote the play in the months that followed his father's death. If you hold that he, a greying man with two marriageable daughters, with thirtyfive years of life, *nel mezzo del cammin di nostra vita,* with fifty of experience, is the beardless undergraduate from Wittenberg then you must hold that his seventyyear old mother is the lustful queen. No. The corpse of John Shakespeare does not walk the night. From hour to hour it rots and rots. He rests, disarmed of fatherhood, having devised that mystical estate upon his son. Boccaccio's Calandrino was the first and last man who felt himself with child. Fatherhood, in the sense of conscious begetting, is unknown to man. It is a mystical estate, an apostolic succession, from only begetter to begotten. On that mystery and not on the madonna which the cunning Italian intellect flung to

[140]

the mob of Europe the church is founded and founded irremovably because founded, like the world, macro- and microcosm, upon the void. Upon incertitude, upon unlikelihood. *Amor matris,* subjective and objective genitive, may be the only true thing in life. Paternity may be a legal fiction . Who is the father of any son that any son should love him or he any son?

What the hell are you driving at?

I know. Shut up. Blast you! I have reasons.

Amplius. Adhuc. Iterum. Postea.

Are you condemned to do this?

-- They are sundered by a bodily shame so steadfast that the criminal annals of the world, stained with all other incests and bestialities, hardly record its breach. Sons with mother, sires with daughters, lesbic sisters, loves that dare not speak their name, nephews with grandmothers, jailbirds with keyholes, queens with prize bulls. The sun unborn mars beauty: born, he brings pain, divides affection, increases care. He is a male: his growth is his father's decline, this youth his father's envy, his friend his father's enemy.

In rue Monsieur-le-Prince I thought it.

-- What links them in nature? An instant of blind rut.

Am I father? If I were?

Shrunken uncertain hand.

-- Sabellius, the African, subtlest heresiarch of all the beasts of the field, held that the Father was Himself His Own Son. The bulldog of Aquin, with whom no word shall be impossible, refutes him. Well: if the father who has not a son be not a father can the son who has not a father be a son? When Rutlandbaconsouthamptonshakespeare or another poet of the same name in the comedy of errors wrote *Hamlet* he was not the father of his own son merely but, being no more a son, he was and felt himself the father of all his race, the father of his own grandfather, the father of his unborn grandson who, by the same token, never was born for nature, as Mr Magee understands her, abhors perfection.

[141]

Eglintoneyes, quick with pleasure, looked up shybrightly. Gladly glancing, a merry puritan, through the twisted eglantine.

Flatter. Rarely. But Flatter.

-- Himself his own father, Sonmulligan told himself. Wait. I am big with child. I have an unborn child in my brain. Pallas Athena! A play! The play's the thing! Let me parturiate!

He clasped his paunchbrow with both birthaiding hands.

. . . .

STEPHEN

He had three brothers, Gilbert, Edmund, Richard. Gilbert in his old age told some cavaliers he got a pass for nowt from Maister Gatherer one time mass he did and he seen his brud Maister Wull the playwriter up in Lunnon in a wrestling play wud a man on's back. The playhouse sausage filled Gilbert's soul. He is nowhere: but an Edmund and a Richard are recorded in the works of sweet William.

MAGEEGLINTON

Names! What's in a name?

BEST

That is my name, Richard, don't you know. I hope you are going to say a good word for Richard, don't you know, for my sake.

(Laughter)

. . . .

Read the skies. *Autontimerumenos. Bous Stehphanoumenos.* Where's your configuration? Stephen, Stephen, cut the bread even. S. D.: *sua donna. Già: di lui. Gelindo risolve di non amar. S. D.*

-- What is that, Mr. Dedalus? the quaker librarian asked.

Was it a celestial phenomenon?

-- A star by night, Stephen said, a pillar of the cloud by day.

What more's to speak?

Stephen looked on his hat, his stick, his boots.

Stephanous, my crown. My sword. His boots are spoiling the shape of my feet. Buy a pair. Holes in my socks. Handkerchief too.

[142]

-- You make good use of the name, John Eglinton allowed.
Your own name is strange enough. I suppose it explains your
fantastical humour.

Me, Magee, and Mulligan.

Fabulous artificer, the hawklike man. You flew. Whereto?
Newhaven-Dieppe, steerage passenger. Paris and back. Lapwing.
Icarus. *Pater, ait.* Seabedabbled, fallen, weltering. Lapwing you are.
Lapwing he.

Mr Best's eagerquietly lifted his book to say:

--That's very interesting because that brother motive, don't
you know, we find also in the old Irish myths. Just what you say. The
three brothers Shakespeare. In Grimm too, don't you know, the
fairytales. The third brother that marries the sleeping beauty and
wins the best prize.

Best of Best brothers. Good, better, best.

The quaker librarian springhalted near.

-- I should like to know, he said, which brother you . . . I
understand you to suggest there was misconduct with one of the
brothers . . . But perhaps I am anticipating?

He caught himself in the act: looked at all: refrained.

An attendant from the doorway called:

-- Mr Lyster! Father Dineen wants . . .

-- O! Father Dineen! Directly.

Swiftly rectly creaking rectly rectly he was rectly gone.

John Eglinton touched the foil.

-- Come, he said. Let us hear what you have to say of
Richard and Edmund. You kept them for the last, didn't you?

-- In asking you to remember those two noble kinsmen
nuncle Richie and nuncle Edmund, Stephen answered, I feel I am
asking too much perhaps. A brother is as easily forgotten as an
umbrella.

Lapwing.

Where is your brother? Apothecaries' hall. My whetstone.
Him, then Cranly, Mulligan: now these. Speech, speech. But act. Act
speech. They mock to try you. Act. Be acted on.

Lapwing.

I am tired of my voice, the voice of Esau. My kingdom for a drink.

. . . .

Why? Stephen answered himself. Because the theme of the false or the usurping or the adulterous brother or all three in one is to Shakespeare, what the poor is not, always with him. The note of banishment, banishment from the heart, banishment from home, sounds uninterruptedly from *The Two Gentlemen of Verona* onward till Prospero breaks his staff, buries certain fathoms in the earth and drowns his book. It doubles itself in the middle of his life, reflects itself in another, repeats itself, protasis, epitasis, catastasis, catastrophe. It repeats itself again when he is near the grave, when his married daughter Susan, chip of the old block, is accused of adultery. But it was the original sin that darkened his understanding, weakened his will and left in him a strong inclination to evil. The words are those of my lords bishops of Maynooth: an original sin and, like original sin, committed by another in whose sin he too has sinned. It is between the lines of his last written words, it is petrified on his tombstone under which her four bones are not to be laid. age has not withered it. Beauty and peace have not done it away. It is in infinite variety everywhere in the world he has created, in *Much Ado about Nothing,* twice in *As you like It,* in *The Tempest,* in *Hamlet,* in *Measure for Measure,* and in all the other plays which I have not read.

He laughed to free his mind from his mind's bondage.
Judge Eglinton summed up.

-- The truth is midway, he affirmed. He is the ghost and the prince. He is all in all.

. . . .

-- Man delights him not nor woman neither, Stephen said. He returns after a life of absence to that spot of earth where he was born, where he has always been, man and boy, a silent witness and there, his journey of life ended, he plants his mulberrytree in the earth. Then dies. The motion is ended. Gravediggers bury Hamlet *pere* and Hamlet *fils*. A king and a prince at last in death, with incidental music. And, what though murdered and betrayed, bewept by all frail tender hearts for, Dane or Dubliner, sorrow for the dead is the only husband from whom they refuse to be divorced. If you like the epilogue, look long on it: prosperous Prospero, the good man rewarded, Lizzie, grandpa's lump of love, and nuncle Richie, the bad man taken off by poetic justice to the place where the bad niggers go. Strong curtain. He found in the world without as actual what was in his world within as possible. Maeterlinck says: *If Socrates leave his house today will he find the sage seated on his doorstep. If Judas go forth tonight it is to Judas his steps will tend.* Every life is many days, day after day. We walk through ourselves, meeting robbers, ghosts, giants, old men, young men, wives, widows, brothers-in-love. But always meeting ourselves. The playwright who wrote the folio of this world and wrote it badly (He gave us light first and the sun two days later), the lord of things as they are whom the most Roman of catholics call *dio boia,* hangman god, is doubtless all in all in all of us, ostler and butcher, and would be bawd and cuckold too but that in the economy of heaven, foretold by Hamlet, there are no more marriages, glorified man, and androgynous angel, being a wife unto himself.

--*Eureka!* Buck Mulligan cried. *Eureka!*

Suddenly happied he jumped up and reached in stride John Eglinton's desk.

-- May I? he said. The Lord has spoken to Malachi.

He began to scribble on a slip of paper.

Take some slips from the counter going out.

-- Those who are married, Mr Best, douce herald, said, all save one shall live. The rest shall keep as they are.

He laughed, unmarried, at Eglinton Johannes, of arts a bachelor.

Unwed, unfancied, ware of wiles, they fingerponder nightly each his variorum edition of *The Taming of the Shrew.*

-- You are a delusion, said roundly John Eglinton to Stephen. You have brought us all this way to show us a French triangle. Do you believe your own theory?

-- No, Stephen said promptly.

-- Are you going to write it? Mr Best asked. You ought to make it a dialogue, don't you know, like the Platonic dialogues Wilde wrote.

John Eclecticon doubly smiled.

-- Well, in that case, he said, I don't see why you should expect payment for it since you don't believe it yourself. Dowden believes there is some mystery in *Hamlet* but will say no more. Herr Bleibtreu, the man Piper met in Berlin, who is working up that Rutland theory, believes that the secret is hidden in the Stratford monument. He is going to visit the present duke, Piper says, and prove to him that his ancestor wrote the plays. It will come as a surprise to his grace. But he believes his theory.

I believe, O Lord, help my unbelief. That is, help me to believe or help me to unbelieve? Who helps to believe? *Egomen.* Who to unbelieve? Other chap.

-- You are the only contributor to *Dana* who asks for pieces of silver. Then I don't know about the next number. Fred Ryan wants space for an article on economics.

Fraidrine. Two pieces of silver he lent me. Tide you over. Economics.

-- For a guinea, Stephen said, you can publish this interview.

Buck Mulligan stood up from his laughing scribbling, laughing: and then gravely said, honeying malice:

--I called upon the bard Kinch at his summer residence in upper Mecklenburgh street and found him deep in the study of the *Summa contra Gentiles* in the company of two gonorrheal ladies, Fresh Nelly and Rosalie, the coalquay whore.

He broke away.

-- Come, Kinch. Come, wandering AEngus of the birds.

Come, Kinch, you have eaten all we left. Ay, I will serve you your orts and offals.

[146]

Stephen rose.

Life is many days. This will end.

-- We shall see you tonight, John Eglinton said. *Notre ami* Moore says Malachi Mulligan must be there.

Buck Mulligan flaunted his slip and panama.

-- Monsieur Moore, he said, lecturer on French letters to the youth of Ireland. I'll be there. Come, Kinch, the bards must drink. Can you walk straight?

Laughing he . . .

Swill till eleven. Irish nights' entertainment.

Lubber . . .

Stephen followed a lubber . . .

One day in the national library we had a discussion. Shakes. After his lub back I followed. I gall his kibe.

. . . .

Puck Mulligan footed fealty, trilling:

> *I hardly hear the purlieu cry*
> *Or a Tommy talk as I pass by*
> *Before my thoughts begin to run*
> *On F. M'Curdy Atkinson,*
> *The same that had the wooden leg*
> *And that filibustering fillibeg*
> *That never dared to slake his drouth,*
> *Magee that had the chinless mouth.*
> *Being afraid to marry on earth*
> *They masturbated for all they were worth.*

Jest on. Know thyself.

Halted below me, a quizzer looks at me. I halt.

-- Mournful mummer, Buck Mulligan moaned. Synge has left off wearing black to be like nature. Only crows, priests and English coal are black.

A laugh tripped over his lips.

-- Longworth is awfully sick, he said, after what you wrote about that old hake Gregory. O you inquisitional drunken jew jesuit!

She gets you a job on the paper and then you go and slate her drivel to Jaysus. Couldn't you do the Yeats touch?

He went on and down, mopping, chanting with waving graceful arms:

-- The most beautiful book that has come out of our country in my time. One thinks of Homer.

He stopped at the stairfoot.

-- I have conceived a play for the mummers, he said solemnly.

The pillared Moorish hall, shadows entwined. Gone the nine men's morrice with caps of indices.

In sweetly varying voices Buck Mulligan read this tablet:

Everyman His own Wife

or

A Honeymoon in the Hand
(a national immortality in three orgasms)
by
Ballocky Mulligan

He laughed, lolling a to and fro head, walking on, followed by Stephen: and mirthfully he told the shadows, souls of men:

-- O, the night in the Camden hall when the daughters of Erin had to lift their skirts to step over you as you lay in your mulberrycoloured, multicoloured, multitudinous vomit!

-- The most innocent son of Erin, Stephen said, for whom they ever lifted them.

About to pass through the doorway, feeling one behind, he stood aside.

Part. The moment is now. Where then? If Socrates leave his house today, if Judas go forth tonight. Why? That lies in space which I in time must come to ineluctably.

My will: his will that fronts me. Seas between.

A man passed out between them, bowing, greeting.

-- Good day again, Buck Mulligan said.

The portico.

[148]

Here I watched the birds for augury. AEngus of the birds.
They go, they come. Last night I flew. Easily flew. Men wondered.
Street of harlots after. A creamfruit melon he held to me. In. You
will see.

-- The wandering jew, Buck Mulligan whispered with
clown's awe. Did you see his eye? He looked upon you to lust after
you. I fear thee, ancient mariner. O, Kinch, thou art in peril. Get thee
a breechpad.

Manner of Oxenford.

Day. Wheelbarrow sun over arch of bridge.

A dark back went before them. Step of a pard, down, out by
the gateway, under portcullis barbs.

They followed.

Offend me still. Speak on.

Kind air defined the coigns of houses in Kildare street. No
birds. Frail from the housetops two plumes of smoke ascended,
pluming, and in a flaw of softness softly were blown.

Cease to strive. Peace of the druid priests of Cymbeline,
hierophantic: from wide earth an altar.

Laud we the gods
And let our crooked smokes climb to their nostrils
From our bless'd altars.

Episode 10 – The Wandering Rocks… Circe told Odysseus that to return home he must sail either through the large, moving rocks that lie in his course, or pass between Scylla and Charybdis. Odysseus chose the latter. ~ Avoiding another S&C dis-course, Bloom and Stephen separately navigate their way around the various characters on the streets of Dublin, bumping, obstructing or passing with little communication.

Father Conmee meanders in mind and body to the O'Brien Institute to find a place for the late Dignam's son. As he encounters others, he reflects and prays. Molly Bloom home at 7 Eccles street arcs a coin toss to a crippled sailor. The Dedalus children struggle to get by. A crumbled throwaway on the coming of Elijah floats down the Liffey River. Boylan shops for Molly and flirts with the girl from Thornton's. Lenehan checks horse race odds, then delights in telling M'Coy of his liberties with Molly while Leopold stargazes. Bloom looks for a sexy novel for Molly. Mulligan and Haines speculate on Stephen. Patrick Dignam processes his father's death. Dubliners observe the viceregal cavalcade.

THEMES

Eighteen parts and a final *coda*. Key bookends: Father Conmee, symbol of the Catholic Church – and - Viceroy of England, symbol of British Rule both dominate Irish life. Simultaneous, oft repeated incidences of the various personages' city life; a panorama of Dublin's city dwellers with all their warts. Acceptance of and compassion for everyday people as they are.

THE SUPERIOR, THE VERY REVEREND JOHN CONMEE S. J., REST HIS smooth watch in his interior pocket as he came down the presbytery steps. Five to three. Just nice time to walk to Artane. What was that boy's name again? Dignam, yes. *Vere dignum et justum est.* Brother Swan was the person to see. Mr Cunningham's letter. Yes. Oblige him, if possible. Good practical catholic: useful at mission time.

A onelegged sailor, swinging himself onward by lazy jerks of his crutches, growled some notes. He jerked short before the convent of the sisters of charity and held out a peaked cap for alms towards the very reverend John Conmee S. J. Father Conmee blessed him in the sun for his purse held, he knew, one silver crown.

Father Conmee crossed to Mountjoy square. He thought but not for long, of soldiers and sailors, whose legs had been shot off by cannonballs, ending their days in some pauper ward, and of cardinal Wolsey's words: *If I had served my God as I have served my king He would not have abandoned me in my old days.* He walked by the treeshade of sunnywinking leaves and towards him came the wife of Mr David Sheehy M. P.

-- Very well, indeed, father. And you father?

Father Conmee was wonderfully well indeed. He would go to Buxton probably for the waters. And her boys, were they getting on well at Belvedere? Was that so? Father Conmee was very glad

[150]

indeed to hear that. And Mr Sheehy himself? Still in London. The house was still sitting, to be sure it was. Beautiful weather it was, delightful indeed. Yes, it was very probable that Father Bernard Vaughn would come again to preach. O, yes: a very great success. A wonderful man really.

Father Conmee was very glad to see the wife of Mr David Sheehy M. P. looking so well and he begged to be remembered to Mr David Sheehy M. P. Yes, he would certainly call.

. . . .

Father Conmee stopped three little schoolboys at the corner of Mountjoy square. Yes: they were from Belvedere. The little house: Aha. And were good boys at school? O. That was very good now. And what was his name? Jack Sohan. And his name? Ger. Gallaher. And the other little man? His name was Brunny Lynam. O, that was a very nice name to have.

Father Conmee gave a letter from his breast to master Brunny Lynam and pointed to the red pillarbox at the corner of Fitzgibbon street.

-- But mind you don't post yourself into the box, little man, he said.

The boys sixeyed Father Conmee and laughed.

-- O, sir.

-- Well, let me see if you can post a letter, Father Conmee said.

Master Brunny Lynam ran across the road and put Father Conmee's letter to father provincial into the mouth of the bright red letterbox, Father Conmee smiled and nodded and smiled and walked along Mountjoy square east.

. . . .

A band of satchelled schoolboys crossed from Richmond street. All raised untidy caps. Father Conmee greeted them more than once benignly. Christian brother boys.

Father Conmee smelled incense on his right hand as he walked. Saint Joseph's church, Portland row. For aged and virtuous females. Father Conmee raised his hat to the Blessed Sacrament. Virtuous: but occasionally they were also badtempered.

. . . .

Father Conmee passed H. J. O'Neill's funeral establishment where Corny Kelleher totted figures in the daybook while he chewed a blade of hay. A constable on his beat saluted Father Conmee and

Father Conmee saluted the constable. In Youkstetter's, the pork-butcher's, Father Conmee observed pig's puddings, white and black and red, lying neatly curled in tubes.

. . . .

At Newcomen bridge Father Conmee stepped into an outward bound tram for he disliked to traverse on foot the dingy way past Mud Island.

Father Conmee sat in a corner of the tramcar, a blue ticket tucked with care in the eye of one plump kid glove, while four shillings, a sixpence and five pennies chuted from his other plump glovepalm into his purse. Passing the ivy church he reflected that the ticket inspector usually made his visit when one had carelessly thrown away the ticket. The solemnity of the occupants of the car seemed to Father Conmee excessive for a journey so short and cheap. Father Conmee liked cheerful decorum.

It was a peaceful day. The gentleman with the glasses opposite Father Conmee had finished explaining and looked down. His wife, Father Conmee supposed. A tiny yawn opened the mouth of the wife of the gentleman with the glasses. She raised her small gloved fist, yawned ever so gently, tiptapping her small gloved fist on her opening mouth and smiled tinily, sweetly.

Father Conmee perceived her perfume in the car. He perceived also that the awkward man at the other side of her was sitting on the edge of the seat.

Father Conmee at the altarrails placed the host with difficulty in the mouth of the awkward old man who had the shaky head.

At Annesley bridge the tram halted, and when it was about to go, an old woman rose suddenly from her place to alight. The conductor pulled the bellstrap to stay the car for her. She passed out with her basket and a market net: and Father Conmee thought that, as she had nearly passed the end of the penny fare, she was one of those good souls who had always to be told twice *bless you, my child,* that they have been absolved, *pray for me.* But they had so many worries in life, so many cares, poor creatures.

From the hoardings Mr Eugene Stratton grinned with thick niggerlips at Father Conmee.

Father Conmee thought of the souls of black and brown and yellow men and of his sermon on saint Peter Claver S. J. and the African mission and of the propagation of the faith and of the

[152]

millions of black and brown and yellow souls that had not received
the baptism of water when their last hour came like a thief in the
night. That book by the Belgian jesuit, *Le Nombre des Élus,* seemed
to Father Conmee a reasonable plea. Those were millions of human
souls created by God in His Own likeness to whom the faith had not
(D. V.) been brought. But they were God's souls created by God. It
seemed to Father Conmee a pity that they should all be lost, a waste,
if one might say.

At the Howth road stop Father Conmee alighted, was saluted
by the conductor and saluted in his turn.

. . . .

Don John Conmee walked and moved in times of yore. He
was humane and honoured there. He bore in mind secrets confessed
and he smiled at smiling noble faces in a beeswaxed drawingroom,
ceiled with full fruit clusters. And the hands of a bride and of a
bridegroom, noble to noble, were impalmed by don John Conmee.

It was a charming day.

The lychgate of a field showed Father Conmee breadths of
cabbages, curtseying to him with ample underleaves. The sky
showed him a flock of small white clouds going slowly down the
wind. *Moutonner,* the French said. A homely and just word.

Father Conmee, reading his office, watched a flock of
muttoning clouds over Rathcoffey. His thinsocked ankles were
tickled by the stubble of Clongowes field. He walked there, reading
in the evening, and heard cries of the boys' lines at their play, young
cries in the quiet evening. He was their rector: his reign was mild.

Father Conmee drew off his gloves and took his rededged
breviary out. An ivory bookmark told him the page.

Nones. He should have read that before lunch. But lady
Maxwell had come.

Father Conmee read in secret *Pater* and *Ave* and crossed his
breast. *Deus in adiutorium.*

He walked calmly and read mutely the nones, walking and
reading till he came to *Res* in *Beati immaculati: Principium
verborum tuorum veritas: in eternum omnia iudicia iustitiae tuae.*

A flushed young man came from a gap of a hedge and after
him came a young woman with wild nodding daisies in her hand.
The young man raised his cap abruptly: the young woman abruptly
bent and with slow care detached from her light skirt a clinging twig.

Father Conmee blessed both gravely and turned a thin page of his breviary. *Sin: Principes persecuti sunt me gratis: et a verbis tuis formidavit cor meum.*

*

A onelegged sailor crutched himself round MacConnell's corner, skirting Rabaiotti's icecream car, and jerked himself up Eccles street. Towards Larry O'Rourke, in shirtsleeves in his doorway, he growled unamiably

-- *for England . . .*

He swung himself violently forward past Katey and Boody Dedalus, halted and growled:

-- *home and beauty.*

J. J. O'Molloy's white careworn face was told that Mr Lambert was in the warehouse with a visitor.

A stout lady stopped, took a copper coin from her purse and dropped it into the cap held out to her. The sailor grumbled thanks and glanced sourly at the unheeding windows, sank his head and swung himself forward four strides.

He halted and growled angrily:

-- *For England . . .*

Two barefoot urchins, sucking long liquorice laces, halted near him, gaping at his stump with their yellow-slobbered mouths.

He swung himself forward in vigorous jerks, halted, lifted his head towards a window and bayed deeply:

-- *home and beauty.*

The gay sweet chirping whistling within went on a bar or two, ceased. The blind of the window was drawn aside. A card *Unfurnished Apartments* slipped from the sash and fell. A plump bare generous arm shone, was seen, held forth from a white petticoatbodice and taut shiftstraps. A woman's hand flung forth a coin over the area railings. It fell on the path. One of the urchins ran to it, picked it up and dropped it into the minstrel's cap, saying:

-- There, sir.

*

Katey and Boody Dedalus shoved in the door of the closesteaming kitchen.

-- Did you put in the books? Boody asked.

Maggy at the range rammed down a greyish mass beneath bubbling suds twice with her potstick and wiped her brow.

-- They wouldn't give anything for them, she said.

[154]

Father Conmee walked through Clongowes fields, his thinsocked ankles tickled by stubble.

-- Where did you try? Boody asked.

-- M'Guinness's.

Boody stamped her foot and threw her satchel on the table.

-- Bad cess to her big face! she cried.

Katey went to the range and peered with squinting eyes.

-- What's in the pot? she asked.

-- Shirts, Maggy said.

Boody cried angrily:

-- Crickety, is there nothing for us to eat?

Katey, lifting the kettlelid in a pad of her stained skirt, asked:

-- And what is this?

A heavy fume gushed in answer.

-- Peasoup, Maggy said.

-- Where did you get it? Katey asked.

-- Sister Mary Patrick, Maggy said.

The lacquey rang his bell.

-- Barang!

Boody ast down at the table and said hungrily:

-- Give us it here!

Maggy poured yellow thick soup from the kettle into a bowl. Katey, sitting opposite Boody, said quietly, as her fingertip lifted to her mouth random crumbs.

-- A good job we have that much. Where's Dilly?

-- Gone to meet father, Maggy said.

Boody, breaking big chunks of bread into the yellow soup, added:

-- Our father who art not in heaven.

Maggy, pouring yellow soup in Katey's bowl, exclaimed:

-- Boody! For shame!

A skiff, a crumpled throwaway, Elijah is coming, rode lightly down the Liffey, under Loopline bridge, shooting the rapids where water chafed around the bridgepiers, sailing eastward past hulls and anchorchains, between the Customhouse old dock and George's quay.

*

The blond girl in Thornton's bedded the wicker basket with rustling fibre. Blazes Boylan handed her the bottle swathed in pink tissue paper and a small jar.

[155]

-- Put these in first, will you? he said.

-- Yes, sir, the blond girl said, and the fruit on top.

-- That'll do, game ball, Blazes Boylan said.

She bestowed fat pears neatly, head by tail, and among them ripe shamefaced peaches.

Blazes Boylan walked here and there in new tan shoes about the fruitsmelling shop, lifting fruits, young juicy crinkled and plump red tomatoes, sniffing smells.

H. E. L. Y.'S. filed before him, tallwhitehatted, past Tangier lane, plodding towards their goal.

He turned suddenly from a chip of strawberries, drew a gold watch from his fob and held it at its chain's length.

-- Can you send them by tram? Now?

A darkbacked figure under Merchants' arch scanned books on the hawker's car.

-- Certainly, sir. Is it in the city?

-- O, yes. Blazes Boylan said. Ten minutes.

The blond girl handed him a docket and pencil.

-- Will you write the address, sir?

Blazes Boylan at the counter wrote and pushed the docket to her.

-- Send it at once, will you? he said. It's for an invalid.

-- Yes, sir. I will, sir.

Blazes Boylan rattled merry money in his trousers' pocket.

-- What's the damage? he asked.

The blond girl's slim fingers reckoned the fruits.

Blazes Boylan looked into the cut of her blouse. A young pullet. He took a red carnation from the tall stemglass.

-- This for me? he asked gallantly.

The blond girl glanced sideways at him, got up regardless, with his tie a bit crooked, blushing.

-- Yes, sir, she said.

Bending archly she reckoned again fat pears and blushing peaches.

Blazes Boylan looked in her blouse with more favour, the stalk of the red flower between his smiling teeth.

-- May I say a word to your telephone, missy? he asked roguishly.

*

. . . .

[156]

Going down the path of Sycamore street beside the Empire musichall Lenehan showed M'Coy how the whole thing was. One of those manholes like a bloody gaspipe and there was the poor devil stuck down it half choked with sewer gas. Down went Tom Rochford anyhow, booky's vest and all, with the rope around him. And be damned but he got the rope round the poor devil and the two were hauled up.

-- The act of a hero, he said.

At the Dolphin they halted to allow the ambulance car to gallop past them for Jervis street.

-- This way, he said, walking to the right. I want to pop into Lynam's to see Sceptre's starting price. What's the time by your gold watch and chain?

M'Coy peered into Marcus Tertius Moses' sombre office, then at O'Neill's clock.

-- After three, he said. Who's riding her?

-- O. Madden, Lenehan said. And a game filly she is.

While he waited in Temple bar M'Coy dodged a banana peel with gentle pushes of his toe from the path to the gutter. Fellow might damn easyget a nasty fall there coming along tight in the dark.

The gates of the drive opened wide to give egress to the viceregal cavalcade.

-- Even money, Lenehan said returning. I knocked against Bantam Lyons in there going to back a bloody horse someone gave him that hasn't an earthly. Through here.

They went up the steps and under Merchants' arch. A darkbacked figure scanned books under a hawker's cart.

-- There he is, Lenehan said.

-- Wonder what he is buying, M'Coy said, glancing behind.

-- *Leopoldo or the Bloom is on the Rye,* Lenehan said.

-- He's dead nuts on sales, M'Coy said. I was with him one day and he bought a book from an old one in Liffey street for two bob. There were fine plates in it worth double the money, the stars and the moon and comets with long tails. Astronomy it was about.

Lenehan laughed.

-- I'll tell you a damn good one about comets' tails, he said. Come over in the sun.

They crossed to the metal bridge and went along Wellington quay by the river wall.

Master Patrick Aloysius Dignam came out of Mangan's, late Fehrenbach's, carrying a pound and a half of porksteaks.

-- There was a big spread out at Glencree reformatory, Lenehan said eagerly. The annual dinner you know. Boiled shirt affair. The lord mayor was there, Val Dillon it was, and sire Charles Cameron and Dan Dawson spoke and there was music. Bartell D'Arcy sang and Benjamin Dollard . . .

-- I know, M'Coy broke in. My missus sang there once.

-- Did she? Lenehan said.

A card *Unfurnished Apartments* reappeared on the window sash of number 7 Eccles street.

He checked his tale a moment but broke out in a wheezy laugh.

But wait till I tell you, he said. Delahunt of Camden street had the catering and yours truly was chief bottlewasher. Bloom and the wife were there. Lashings of stuff we put up: port wine and sherry and curacao to which we did ample justice. Fast and furious it was. After liquids came solids. Cold joints galore and mince pies . . .

-- I know, M'Coy said. The year the missus was there . . .

Lenehan linked his arm warmly.

-- But wait till I tell you, he said. We had a midnight lunch too after all the jollification and when we sallied forth it was blue o'clock the morning after the night before. Coming home it was a gorgeous winter's night on the Featherbed Mountain. Bloom and Chris Callinan were on one side of the car and I was with the wife on the other. We started singing glees and duets: *Lo, the early beam of morning.* She was well primed with a good load of Delahunt's port under her bellyband. Every jolt the bloody car gave I had her bumping up against me. Hell's delights! She has a fine pair, God bless her. Like that.

He held his caved hands a cubit from him frowning:

-- I was tucking the rug under her and settling her boa all the time. Know what I mean?

His hands moulded ample curves of air. He shut his eyes tight in delight, his body shrinking, and blew a sweet chirp from his lips.

-- The lad stood to attention anyhow, he said with a sigh. She's a gamey mare and no mistake. Bloom was pointing out all the stars and the comets in the heavens to Chris Callinan and the jarvey: the great bear and Hercules and the dragon and the whole jingbang

[158]

lot. But, by God, I was lost, so to speak, in the milky way. He knows them all by faith. At last she spotted a weeny weeshy one miles away. *And what star is that, Poldy?* says she. By God, she had Bloom cornered. *That one, is it?* says Chris Callinan, *sure that's only what you might call a pinprick.* By God, he wasn't far wide of the mark.

Lenehan stopped and leaned on the riverwall, panting with soft laughter.

-- I'm weak, he gasped.

M'Coy's white face smiled about it at instants and grew grave. Lenehan walked on again. He lifted his yachtingcap and scratched his hindhead rapidly. He glanced sideways in the sunlight at M'Coy.

--He's a cultured allroundman, Bloom is, he said seriously. He's not one of your common or garden . . . you know . . . There's a touch of the artist about old Bloom.

*

Mr Bloom turned over idly pages of *The Awful Disclosures of Maria Monk,* then of Aristotle's *Masterpiece.* Crooked botched print. Plates: infants cuddled in a ball in bloodred wombs like livers of slaughtered cows. Lots of them like that at this moment all over the world. All butting with their skulls to get out of it. Child born every minute somewhere. Mrs Purefoy.

He laid both books aside and glanced at the third: *Tales of the Ghetto* by Leopold von Sacher Masoch.

-- That I had, he said, pushing it by.

The shopman let two volumes fall on the counter.

-- Them are two good ones, he said.

Onions of his breath came across the counter out of his ruined mouth. He bent to make a bundle of the other books, hugged them against his unbuttoned waistcoat and bore them off behind the dingy curtain.

On O'Connell bridge many persons observed the grave deportment and gay apparel of Mr Denis J. Maginni, professor of dancing &c.

Mr Bloom, alone, looked at the titles. *Fair Tyrants* by James Lovebirch. Know the kind that is. Had it? Yes.

He opened it. Thought so.

A woman's voice behind the dingy curtains. Listen: The man.

[159]

No: she wouldn't like that much. Got her it once.

He read the other title: *Sweets of Sin.* More in her line. Let us see.

He read where his finger opened.

-- *All the dollarbills her husband gave her were spent in the stores on wondrous gowns and costliest frillies. For him! For Raoul!*

Yes, This. Here. Try.

-- *Her mouth glued on his in a luscious voluptuous kiss while his hands felt for the opulent curves inside her deshabille.*

Yes. Take this. The end.

-- *You are late, he spoke hoarsely, eyeing her with a suspicious glare. The beautiful woman threw off her sabletrimmed wrap, displaying her queenly shoulders and heaving embonpoint. An imperceptible smile played round her perfect lips as she turned to him calmly.*

Mr Bloom read again: *The beautiful woman.*

Warmth showered over him, cowing his flesh. Flesh yielded amid rumpled clothes. Whites of eyes swooning up. His nostrils arched themselves for prey. Melting breast ointments *(for him! For Raoul!)*. Armpits' oniony sweat. Fishgluey slime *(her heaving embonpoint!)* Feel! Press! Crushed! Sulphur dung of lions!

Young! Young!

An elderly female, no more young, left the building of the courts of chancery, king's bench, exchequer and common pleas, having heard in the lord's chancellor' court the case in lunacy of Potterton, in the admiralty division the summons, exparte motion, of the owners of the Lady Cairns versus the owners of the barque Mona, in the court of appeal reservation of judgment in the case of Harvey versus the Ocean Accident and Guarantee Corporation.

Phlegmy coughs shook the air of the bookshop, bulging out the dingy curtains. The shopman's uncombed grey head came out and his unshaven reddened face, coughing. He raked his throat rudely, spat phlegm on the floor. He put his boot on what he had spat, wiping his sole along it and bent, showing a rawskinned crown, scantily haired.

Mr Bloom beheld it.

Mastering his troubled breath, he said:

-- I'll take this one.

The shopman lifted eyes bleared with old rheum.

-- *Sweets of Sin,* he said, tapping on it. That's a good one.

[160]

*

The lacquey by the door of Dillon's auctionrooms shook his handbell twice again and viewed himself in the chalked mirror of the cabinet.

Dilly Dedalus, listening by the curbstone, heard the beats of the bell, the cries of the auctioneer within. Four and nine. Those lovely curtains. Five shillings. Cosy curtains. Selling new at two guineas. Any advance on five shillings? Going for five shillings.

The lacquey lifted his handbell and shook it:

-- Barang!

Bang of the last bell spurred the halfmile wheelmen to their sprint. J. A. Jackson, W. E. Wylie, A. Munro and H. T. Gahan, their stretched necks wagging, negotiated the curve by the College Library.

Mr Dedalus, tugging a long moustache, came round from William's row. He halted near his daughter.

-- It's time for you, she said.

-- Stand up straight for the love of the Lord Jesus, Mr Dedalus said. Are you trying to imitate your uncle John the cornetplayer, head upon shoulders? Mr Dedalus placed his hands on them and held them back.

-- Stand up straight, girl, he said. You'll get curvature of the spine. Do you know what you look like?

He let his head sink suddenly down and forward, hunching his shoulders and dropping his underjaw.

-- Give it up, father, Dilly said. All the people are looking at you.

Mr Dedalus drew himself upright and tugged again at his moustache.

-- Did you get any money? Dilly asked.

-- Where would I get money? Mr Dedalus said. There is no one in Dublin would lend me fourpence.

-- You got some, Dilly said, looking in his eyes.

-- How do you know that? Mr Dedalus asked, his tongue in his cheek.

Mr. Kernan, pleased with the order he had booked, walked boldly along James's street.

-- I know you did, Dilly answered. Were you in the Scotch house now?

-- I was not then, Mr Dedalus said, smiling. Was it the little nuns taught you to be so saucy? Here.

He handed her a shilling.

-- See if you can do anything with that, he said.

-- I suppose you got five, Dilly said. Give me more than that.

-- Wait awhile, Mr Dedalus said threateningly. You're like the rest of them, are you? An insolent pack of little bitches since your poor mother died. But wait awhile. You'll all get a short shrift and a long day from me. Low blackguardism! I'm going to get rid of you. Wouldn't care if I was stretched out stiff. He's dead. The man upstairs is dead.

He left her and walked on. Dilly followed quickly and pulled his coat.

-- Well, what is it? he said, stopping.

The lacquey rang his bell behind their backs.

-- Barang!

-- Curse your bloody blatant soul, Mr Dedalus cried, turning on him.

The lacquey, aware of comment, shook the lolling clapper of his bell but feebly:

-- Bang!

Mr Dedalus stared at him.

-- Watch him, he said. It's instructive. I wonder will he allow us to talk.

-- You got more than that, father, Dilly said.

-- I'm going to show you a little trick, Mr Dedalus said. I'll leave you all where Jesus left the jews. Look, that's all I have. I got two shillings from Jack Power and I spent twopence for a shave for the funeral.

He drew forth a handful of copper coins nervously.

-- Can't you look for some money somewhere? Dilly said.

Mr Dedalus thought and nodded.

-- I will, he said gravely. I looked all along the gutter in O'Connell street. I'll try this one now.

You're very funny, Dilly said, grinning.

-- Here, Mr Dedalus said, handing her two pennies. Get a glass of milk for yourself and a bun or something. I'll be home shortly.

He put the other coins in his pocket and started to walk on.

The viceregal cavalcade passed, greeted by obsequious policemen, out of Parkgate.

-- I'm sure you have another shilling, Dilly said.

The lacquey banged loudly.

Mr Dedalus amid the din walked off, murmuring to himself with a pursing mincing mouth:

-- The little nuns! Nice little things! O, sure they wouldn't do anything! O, sure they wouldn't really! Is it little sister Monica!

*

. . . .

North wall and sir John Rogerson's quay, with hulls and anchorchains, sailing westward, sailed by a skiff, a crumpled throwaway, rocked on the ferry-wash, Elijah is coming.

Mr Kernan glanced in farewell at his image. High colour, of course. Grizzled moustache. Returned Indian officer. Bravely he bore his stumpy body forward on spatted feet, squaring his shoulders. Is that Lambert's brother over the way, Sam? What? Yes. He's as like it as damn it. No. The windscreen of that motorcar in the sun there. Just a flash like that. Damn like him.

Aham! Hot spirit of juniper juice warmed his vitals and his breath. Good drop of gin, that was. His frocktails winked in bright sunshine to his fat strut.

Down there Emmet was hanged, drawn and quartered. Greasy black rope. Dogs licking the blood off the street when the lord lieutenant's wife drove by in her noddy.

Let me see. Is he buried in saint Michan's? Or no, there was a midnight burial in Glasnevin. Corpse brought in through a secret door in the wall. Dignam is there now. Went out in a puff. Well, well. Better turn down here. Make a detour.

Mr Kernan turned and walked down the slope of Watling street by the corner of Guinness' visitors' waitingroom. Outside the Dublin Distillers Company's stores an outside car without fare or or jarvey stood, the reins knotted to the wheel. Damn dangerous thing. Some Tipperary bosthoon endangering the lives of the citizens. Runaway horse.

Denis Breen with his tomes, weary of having waited an hour in John Henry Menton's office, led his wife over O'Connell bridge, bound for the office of Messrs Collis and Ward.

Mr Kernan approached Island street.

[163]

Times of the troubles. Must ask Ned Lambert to lend me
those reminiscences of sir Jonah Barrington. When you look back on
it all now in a kind of retrospective arrangement. Gaming at Daly's.
No cardsharping then. One of those fellows got his hand nailed to the
table by a dagger. Somewhere here Lord Edward Fitzgerald escaped
from major Sirr. Stables behind Moira house.

Damn good gin that was.

Fine dashing young nobleman. Good stock, of course. That
ruffian, that sham squire, with his violet gloves, gave him away.
Course they were on the wrong side. They rose in dare and evil days.
Fine poem that is: Ingram. They were gentlemen. Ben Dollard does
sing that ballad touchingly. Masterly rendition.

At the siege of Ross did my father fall.

A cavalcade in easy trot along Pembroke quay passed,
outriders leaping, leaping in their, in their saddles. Frockcoats.
Cream sunshades.

Mr Kernan hurried forward, blowing pursily.

His Excellency! Too bad! Just missed that by a hair. Damn
it! What a pity!

*

. . . .

Stephen went down Bedford row, the handle of the ash
clacking against his shoulderblade. In Clohissey's window a faded
1860 print of Heenan boxing Sayers held his eye. Staring backers
with square hats stood round the roped prizering. The heavyweights
in light loincloths proposed gently each to other his bulbous fists.
And they are throbbing: heroes' hearts.

He turned and halted by the slanted bookcart.

-- Twopence each, the huckster said. Four for sixpence.

Tattered pages. *The Irish Beekeeper. Life and Miracles of the
Curé of Arts. Pocket Guide to Killarney.*

I might find here one of my pawned schoolprizes. *Stephanos
Dedalo, alumno optimo, palmam ferenti.*

Father Conmee, having read his little hours, walked through
the hamlet of Donnycarney, murmuring vespers.

Binding too good probably, what is this? Eighth and ninth
book of Moses. Secret of all secrets. Seal of King David. Thumped
pages: read and read. Who has passed here before me? How to soften
chapped hands. Recipe for white wine vinegar. How to win a

[164]

woman's love. For me this. Say the following talisman three times
with hands folded:

    -- Se el yilo nebrakada femininum! Amor me solo. Sanktus!
Amen.

    Who wrote this? Charms and invocations of the most blessed
abbot Peter Salanka to all true believers divulged. As good as any
other abbot's charms, as mumbling Joachim's. Down, baldynoodle,
or we'll wool your wool.

    -- What are you doing here, Stephen.

    Dilly's high shoulders and shabby dress.

    Shut the book quick. Don't let see.

    -- What are you doing? Stephen said.

    A Stuart face of nonesuch Charles, lank locks falling at his
sides. It glowed as she crouched feeding the fire with broken boots. I
told her of Paris. Late lieabed under a quilt of old overcoats,
fingering a pinchbeck bracelet, Dan Kelly's token. *Nebrakada*
femininum.

    -- What have you there? Stephen asked.

    -- I bought it from the other cart for a penny, Dilly said,
laughing nervously. Is it any good?

    My eyes they say she has. Do others see me so? Quick, far
and daring. Shadow of my mind.

    He took the coverless book from her hand. Chardenal's
French primer.

    -- What did you buy that for? he asked. To learn French?

    She nodded, reddening and closing tight her lips.

    Show no surprise. Quite natural.

    -- Here, Stephen said. It's all right. Mind Maggy doesn't
pawn it on you. I suppose all my books are gone.

    -- Some, Dilly said. We had to.

    She is drowning. Agenbite. Save her. Agenbite. All against
us. She will drown me with her eyes and hair. Lank coils of seaweed
hair around me, my heart, my soul. Salt green death.

    We.

    Agenbite of inwit. Inwit's agenbite.

    Misery! Misery!

*

. . . .

    As they trod across the thick carpet Buck Mulligan
whispered behind his panama to Haines.

[165]

-- Parnell's brother. There in the corner.

They chose a small table near the window opposite a longfaced man whose beard and gaze hung intently down on a chessboard.

-- Is that he? Haines asked, twisting round in his seat.

-- Yes, Mulligan said. That's John Howard, his brother, our city marshal.

John Howard Parnell translated a white bishop quietly and his grey claw went up again to his forehead whereat it rested.

An instant after, under its screen, his eyes looked quickly, ghostbrigtht, at his foe and fell once more upon a working corner.

-- I'll take a *mélange,* Haines said to the waitress.

-- Two *mélanges,* Buck Mulligan said. And bring us some scones and butter and some cakes as well.

When she had gone he said laughing:

-- We call it D. B. C. because they have damn bad cakes. O, but you missed Dedalus on *Hamlet.*

Haines opened his newbought book.

-- I'm sorry, he said. Shakespeare is the happy huntingground of all minds that have lost their balance.

The onelegged sailor growled at the area of 14 Nelson street:

-- *England expects . . .*

Buck Mulligan's primrose waistcoat shook gaily to his laughter.

-- You should see him, he said, when his body loses its balance. Wandering AEngus, I call him.

-- I am sure he has an *idée fixe,* Haines said, pinching his chin thoughtfully with thumb and forefinger. Now I am speculating what it would be likely to be. Such persons always have.

Buck Mulligan bent across the table gravely.

-- They drove his wits astray, he said, by visions of hell. He will never capture the Attic note. The note of Swinburne, of all poets, the white death and the rudy birth. That is his tragedy. He can never be a poet. The joy of creation . . .

-- Eternal punishment, Haines said, nodding curtly. I see. I tackled him this morning on belief. There was something on his mind, I saw. It's rather interesting because Professor Pokorny of Vienna makes an interesting point out of that.

Buck Mulligan's watchful eyes saw the waitress come. He helped her to unload her tray.

[166]

-- He can find no trace of hell in ancient Irish myth, Haines
said, amid the cheerful cups. The moral idea seems lacking, the sense
of destiny, of retribution. Rather strange he should have just that
fixed idea. Does he write anything for your movement?

He sank two lumps of sugar deftly longwise through the
whipped cream. Buck Mulligan slit a steaming scone in two and
plastered butter over its smoking pith. He bit off a soft piece hungrily

-- Ten years, he said, chewing and laughing. He is going to
write something in ten years.

-- Seems a long way off, Haines said, thoughtfully lifting his
spoon. Still, I shouldn't wonder if he did after all.

He tasted a spoonful from the creamy cone of his cup.

-- This is real Irish cream I take it, he said with forbearance.
I don't want to be imposed on.

Elijah, skiff, light crumpled throwaway, sailed eastward by
flanks of ships and trawlers, amid archipelago of corks, beyond new
Wapping street past Benson's ferry, and by the threemasted schooner
Rosevean from Bridgwater with bricks.

*

. . . .

In Grafton street Master Dignam saw a red flower in a toff's
mouth and a swell pair of kicks on him and he listening to what the
drunk was telling him and grinning all the time.

No Sandymount tram.

Master Dignam walked along Nassau street, shifted the
porksteaks to his other hand. His collar sprang up again and he
tugged it down. The blooming stud was too small for the buttonhole
of the shirt, blooming end to it. He met schoolboys with satchels. I'm
not going tomorrow either, stay away till Monday. He met other
schoolboys. Do they notice I'm in mourning? Uncle Barney said
he'd get it into the paper tonight. Then they'll all see it in the paper
and read my name printed and pa's name.

His face got all grey instead of being red like it was and
there was a fly walking over it up to his eye. The scrunch that was
when they were screwing the screws into the coffin: and the bumps
when they were bringing it downstairs.

Pa was inside it and ma crying in the parlour and uncle
Barney telling the men how to get it round the bend. A big coffin it
was, and high and heavylooking . How was that? The last night pa
was boosed he was standing on the landing there bawling out for his

[167]

boots to go out to Tunney's for to boose more and he looked butty
and short in his shirt. Never see him again. Death, that is. Pa is dead.
My father is dead. He told me to be a good son to ma. I couldn't hear
the other things he said but I saw his tongue and his teeth trying to
say it better. Poor pa. That was Mr Dignam, my father. I hope he is
in purgatory now because he went to confession to father Conroy on
Saturday night.

*

William Humble, earl of Dudley, and Lady Dudley,
accompanied by lieutenantcolonel Hesseltine, drove out after
luncheon from the viceregal lodge. In the following carriage were the
honourable Mrs Paget, Miss de Courcy and the honourable Gerald
Wald, A. D. C. in attendance.

The cavalcade passed out by the lower gate of Phoenix Park
saluted by obsequious policemen and proceeded past Kingsbridge
along the northern quays. The viceroy was most cordially greeted on
his way through the metropolis. At Bloody bridge Mr Thomas
Kernan beyond the river greeted him vainly from afar. Between
Queen's and Whitworth bridges Lord Dudley's viceregal carriages
passed and were unsalted by Mr Dudley White, B. L. M. A. . . . On
Ormond quay Mr Simon Dedalus, steering his way from the
greenhouse for the subsheriff's office, stood still in midstreet and
brought his hat low. His Excellency graciously returned Mr Dedalus'
greeting. . . . On Grattan bridge Lenehan and M'Coy, taking leave of
each other, watched the carriages go by. . . . Beyond Lundy Foot's
from the shaded door of Kavanagh's winerooms John Wyse Nolan
smiled with unseen coldness towards the lord lieutenantgeneral and
general governor of Ireland. . . . From the window of the D. B. C.
Buck Mulligan gaily, and Haines gravely, gazed down on the
viceregal equipage over the shoulders of eager guests, whose mass of
forms darkened the chessboard whereon John Howard Parnell looked
intently. In Fownes street, Dilly Dedalus straining her sight upward
from Chardenal's first French primer, saw sunshades spanned and
wheelspokes spinning in the glare. . . . By the provost's wall came
jauntily Blazes Boylan, stepping in tan shoes and socks with skyblue
clocks to the refrain of *My girl's a Yorkshire girl.*

Blazes Boylan presented to the leaders' skyblue frontlets and
high action a skyblue tie, a widebrimmed straw hat at a rakish angle
and a suit of indigo serge. His hands in his jacket pockets forgot to
salute but he offered to the three ladies the bold admiration of his

[168]

eyes and the red flower between his lips. As they drove along Nassau street His Excellency drew the attention of his bowing consort to the programme of music which was being discoursed in College park. Unseen brazen highland laddies blared and drumthumped after the *cortège:*

> *But though she's a factory lass*
> *And wears no fancy clothes.*
> *Baraabum.*
> *Yet I've a sort of a*
> *Yorkshire relish for*
> *My little Yorkshire rose.*
> *Baraabum.*

Episode 11 – The Sirens… The seductive songs of mermaids induced sailors to crash their ships on the deadly island rocks. Odysseus stuffed wax in his crew's ears, but had himself tied to the mast so as to hear the Sirens' songs. ~ Two barmaids and a prostitute stir the emotions of Bloom, as do the musicians' songs of love and nationalism. Even as he witnesses the narcotic effect of the music, Bloom resists being seduced by empty emotions.

A fugue of lyrical strands intone this afternoon episode of Bloom's anticipation of his cuckoldry by Molly. He buys stationery to write his flirt, Martha; then follows Boylan into the Ormond Hotel from whom he sits unseen, joining Uncle Richie for dinner during which he writes to Martha in pseudonym. Two sexy barmaids taunt him, as Boylan flirts with them. Bar song lyrics conjure feelings of failure as husband and father. Bloom recognizes an air from the opera *Martha* and Lionel's love for her; and realizes that he is lonely for Molly's love. Upon hearing Simon Dedalus sing *The Croppy Boy*, an Irish patriot exposed by a fake British priest, Bloom reflects on the death of his son Rudy. A blind piano tuner returns for his tuner, Bloom departs and breaks wind as he reads the words of the martyred Emmet.

THEMES
57 techniques of musical composition echo sounds and actions of Dublin folk. The intoxicating power of music. The loss of love, of mother, of a son; a physical, political, moral sense of the false father theme. Betrayal by Molly. Bloom's loneliness, isolation; yet resilience and common sense. Parallels to the betrayal of Christ. The realism of life, of emotions, over empty rhetoric.

BRONZE BY GOLD HEARD THE HOOFIRONS, STEELYRINING

Impethnthn thnthnthn.

Chips, picking chips off rocky thumbnail, chips. Horrid! And gold flushed more.

A husky fifenote blew.

Blew. Blue bloom is on the

Gold pinnacled hair.

A jumping rose on satiny breasts of satin, rose of Castille.

Trilling, trilling: Idolores.

Peep! Who's in the . . . peepofgold?

Tink cried to bronze in pity.

And a call, pure, long and throbbing. Longindying call.

Decoy. Soft word. But look! The bright stars fade. O rose! Notes chirruping answer. Castille. The morn is breaking.

Jingle jingle jaunted jingling.

Coin rang. Clock clacked.

Avowal. *Sonnez.* I could. Rebound of garter. Not leave thee. Smack. *La cloche!* Thigh smack. Avowal. Warm. Sweetheart, goodbye!

Jingle. Bloo.

Boomed crashing chords. When love absorbs. War! War!

[170]

The tympanum.
A sail! A veil awave upon the waves.
Lost. Throstle fluted. All is lost now.
Horn. Hawhorn.
When first he saws. Alas!
Full tup. Full throb.
Warbling. Ah, lure! Alluring.
Martha! Come!
Clapclop. Clipclap. Clappyclap.
Goodgod henev erheard inall.
Deaf bald Pat brought pad knife took up.
A moonlight nightcall: far: far.
I feel so sad. P.S. So lonely blooming.
Listen!
The spiked and winding cold seahorn. Have you the? Each
and for other plash and silent roar.
Pearls: when she. Liszt's rhapsodies. Hissss.
You don't?
Did not: no, no: believe: Lidlyd. With a cock with a carra.
Black.
Deepsounding. Do, Ben, do.
Wait while you wait. Hee hee. Wait while you hee.
But wait!
Low in dark middle earth. Embedded ore.
Naminedamine. All gone. All fallen.
Tiny, her tremulous fernfoils of maidenhair.
Amen! He gnashed in fury.
Fro. To, fro. A baton cool protruding.
Bronzelydia by Minagold.
By bronze, by gold, in oceangreen of shadow. Bloom. Old
Bloom.
One rapped, one tapped with a carra, with a cock.
Pray for him! Pray, good people!
His gouty fingers nakkering.
Big Benaben. Big Benben.
Last rose Castille of summer left bloom I feel so sad alone.
Pwee! Little wind piped wee.
True men. Lid Ker Cow De and Dolly. Ay, ay. Like you
men.!
Will lift your tschink with tschunk.

Fff! Oo!

Where bronze from anear? Where gold from afar? Where hoofs?

Rrrpr. Kraa. Kraandl.

Then, not till then. My eppripfftaph. Be prfwritt.

Done.

Begin!

Bronze by gold, Miss Douce's head by Miss Kennedy's head, over the crossblind of the Ormond bar heard the viceregal hoofs go by, ringing steel.

-- Is that her? asked Miss Kennedy.

Miss Douce said yes, sitting with his ex, pearl grey and *eau de Nil.*

Exquisite contrast, Miss Kennedy said.

When all agog Miss Douce said eagerly:

-- Look at the fellow in the tall silk.

-- Who? Where? gold asked more eagerly.

-- In the second carriage. Miss Douce's wet lips said, laughing in the sun. He's looking. Mind till I see.

She darted, bronze, to the backmost corner, flattening her face against the pane in a halo of hurried breath.

Her wet lips tittered:

-- He's killed looking back.

She laughed:

-- O wept! Aren't men frightful idiots?

With sadness.

Miss Kennedy sauntered sadly from bright light, twinning a loose hair behind an ear. Sauntering sadly, gold no more, she twisted twined a hair. Sadly she twined in sauntering gold hair behind a curving ear.

-- It's them has the fine times, sadly then she said.

A man.

Bloomwho went by by Moulang's pipes, bearing in his breast the sweets of sin, by Wine's antiques in memory bearing sweet sinful words, by Carroll's dusky battered plate, for Raoul.

The boots to them, them in the bar, them barmaids came. For them unheeding him he banged on the counter his tray of chattering china. And

-- There's your teas, he said.

Miss Kennedy with manners transposed the teatray down to an upturned lithia crate, safe from eyes, low.

-- What is it? loud boots unmannerly asked.

-- Find out, Miss Douce retorted, leaving her spyingpoint.

-- Your *beau*, is it?

A haughty bronze replied:

-- I'll complain to Mrs de Massey on you if I hear any more of your impertinent insolence.

-- Imperthnthn thnthnthn, bootsnout sniffed rudely, as he retreated as she threatened as he had come.

Bloom.

On her flower frowning Miss Douce said:

-- Most aggravating that young brat is. If he doesn't conduct himself I'll wring his ear for him a yard long.

Ladylike in exquisite contrast.

-- Take no notice, Miss Kennedy rejoined.

She poured in a teacup tea, then back in the teapot tea. They covered under their reef of counter, waiting on footstools, crates upturned, waiting for their teas to draw. They pawed their blouses, both of black satin, two and nine a yard, waiting for their teas to draw, and two and seven.

Yes, bronze from anear, by gold from afar, heard steel from anear, hoofs ring from afar, and heard steelhoofs ringhoof ring steel.

. . . .

Bloowhose dark eye read Aaron Figatner's name. Why do I always think Figather? Gathering figs I think. And Prosper Lore's huguenot name. By Bassi's blessed virgins Bloom dark eyes went by. Bluerobed, white under, come to me. God they believe she is: or goddess. Those today. I could not see. That fellow spoke. A student. After with Dedalus' son. He might be Mulligan. All comely virgins. That brings those rakes of fellows in: her white.

By went his eyes. The sweets of sin. Sweet are the sweets. Of sin.

In a giggling peal young goldbronze voices blended, Douce with Kennedy your other eye. They threw young heads back, bronze gigglegold, to let freefly their laughter, screaming, your other, signals to each other, high piercing notes.

Ah, panting, sighing. Sighing, ah, fordone their mirth died down.

Miss Kennedy lipped her cup again, raised, drank a sip and giggle-giggled. Miss Douce, bending again over the teatray, ruffled again her nose and rolled droll fattened eyes. Again Kennygiggles, stooping her fair pinnacle of hair, stooping her tortoise napecomb showed, spluttered out of her mouth her tea, choking in tea and laughter, coughing with choking, crying:

-- O greasy eyes! Imagine being married to a man like that, she cried. With his bit of beard!

Douce gave full vent to a splendid yell, a full yell of full woman, delight, joy, indignation.

-- Married to the greasy nose! she yelled.

Shrill, with deep laughter, after bronze in gold, they urged each other to peal after peal, ringing in changes, bronzegold goldbronze, shrilldeep, to laughter after laughter. And then laughed more. Greasy I knows. Exhausted, breathless their shaken heads they laid, braided and pinnacled by glossycombed, against the counterledge. All flushed (O!), panting, sweating (O!), a breathless.

Married to Bloom, to greaseasabloom.

-- O saints above! Miss Douce said, sighed above her jumping rose. I wished I hadn't laughed so much. I feel all wet.

-- O, Miss Douce! Miss Kennedy protested. You horrid thing!

And flushed yet more (you horrid!), more goldenly.

By Cantwell's offices roved Greasebloom, by Ceppi's virgins, bright of their oils. Nannetti's father hawked those things about, wheedling at doors as I. Religion pays. Must see him about Keyes par. Eat first. I want. Not yet. At four, she said. Time ever passing. Clockhands turning. On. Where eat? The Clarence, Dolphin. On. For Raoul. Eat. If I net five guineas with those ads. The violet silk petticoats. Not yet. The sweets of sin.

Flushed less, still less, goldenly paled.

Into their bar strolled Mr Dedalus. Chips, picking chips off one of his rocky thumbnails. Chips. He strolled.

-- O welcome back, Miss Douce.

He held her hand. Enjoyed her holidays?

-- Tiptop.

He hoped she had nice weather in Rostrevor.

-- Gorgeous, she said. Look at the holy show I am. Lying out on the strand all day.

Bronze whiteness.

[174]

-- That was exceedingly naughty of you, Mr Dedalus told her and pressed her hand indulgently. Tempting poor simple males.

Miss Douce of satin doused her arm away.

-- O go away, she said. You're very simple, I don't think.

He was.

-- Well now, I am, he mused. I looked so simple in the cradle they christened me simple Simon.

-- You must have been a doaty, Miss Douce made answer. And what did the doctor order today?

-- Well now, he mused, whatever you say yourself. I think I'll trouble you for some fresh water and a half glass of whisky.

Jingle.

-- With the greatest alacrity, Miss Douce agreed.

With grace of alacrity towards the mirror gilt Cantrell and Cochrane's she turned herself. With grace she tapped a measure of gold whisky from her crystal keg. Forth from the skirt of his coat Mr Dedalus brought pouch and pipe. Alacrity she served. He blew through the flue two husky fifenotes.

-- By Jove, he mused. I often wanted to see the Mourne mountains. Must be a great tonic in the air down there. But a long threatening comes at last, they say. Yes, yes.

Yes. He fingered shreds of hair, her maidenhair, her mermaid's, into the bowl. Chips. Shreds. Musing. Mute.

None not said nothing. Yes.

Gaily Miss Douce polished a tumbler, trilling:

-- *O, Idolores, queen of the eastern seas!*

-- Was Mr Lidwell in today?

In came Lenehan. Round him peered Lenehan. Mr Bloom reached Essex bridge. Yes, Mr Bloom crossed bridge of Yessex. To Martha I must write. Buy paper. Daly's. Girl there civil. Bloom. Old Bloom. Blue Bloom is on the rye.

-- He was in at lunchtime, Miss Douce said.

Lenehan came forward.

-- Was Mr Boylan looking for me?

He asked. She answered:

-- Miss Kennedy, was Mr Boylan in while I was upstairs?

She asked. Miss voice of Kennedy answered, a second teacup poised, her gaze upon a page.

-- No. He was not.

Miss gaze of Kennedy, heard not seen, read on. Lenehan round the sandwichbell wound his round body round.

-- Peep! Who's in the corner?

No glance of Kennedy rewarding him he yet made overtures. To mind her stops. To read only the black ones: round o and crooked ess.

Jingle jaunty jingle.

Girlgold she read and did not glance. Take no notice. She took no notice while he read by rote a solfa fable for her, plappering flatly:

-- Ah fox met stork. Said thee fox too thee stork: will you put your bill down in my throat and pull upp ah bone?

He droned in vain. Miss Douce turned to her tea aside.

He sighed, aside:

-- Ah me! O my!

He greeted Mr Dedalus and got a nod.

-- Greetings from the famous son of a famous father.

-- Who may he be? Mr Dedalus asked.

Lenehan opened most genial arms. Who?

-- Who may he be? he asked. Can you ask? Stephen, the youthful bard.

Dry.

Mr Dedalus, famous fighter, laid by his dry filled pipe.

-- I see, he said. I didn't recognize him for the moment. I hear he is keeping select company. Have you seen him lately?

He had.

-- I quaffed the nectarbowl with him this very day, said Lenehan. In Mooney's *en ville* and in Mooney's *sur mer*. He had received the rhino for the labour of his muse.

He smiled at bronze's teabathed lips, at listening lips and eyes.

-- The *élite* of Erin hung upon his lips. The ponderous pundit, Hugh MacHugh, Dublin's most brilliant scribe and editor, and that minstrel boy of the wild wet west who is known by the euphonious appellation of the O'Madden Burke.

After an interval Mr Dedalus raised his grog and

-- That must have been highly diverting, said he. I see.

He see. He drank. With a faraway mourning mountain eye. Set down his glass.

He looked towards the saloon door.

-- I see you have moved the piano.

-- The tuner was in today, Miss Douce replied, tuning it for the smoking concert and I never heard such an exquisite player.

-- Is that a fact?

-- Didn't he, Miss Kennedy? The real classical, you know. And blind too, poor fellow. Not twenty I'm sure he was.

-- Is that a fact? Mr Dedalus said.

He drank and strayed away.

-- So sad to look at his face, Miss Douce condoled.

God's curse on bitch's bastard.

Tink to her pity cried a diner's bell. To the door of the diningroom came bald Pat , came bothered Pat, came Pat, waiter of Ormond. Lager for diner. Lager without alacrity she served.

With patience Lenehan waited for Boylan with impatience, for jingle jaunty blazes boy.

Upholding the lid he (who?) gazed in the coffin (coffin?) at the oblique triple (piano?) wires. He pressed (the same who pressed indulgently her hand), soft pedalling a triple of keys to see the thickness of felt advancing, to hear the muffled hammerfall in action.

Two sheets cream vellum paper on reserve two envelopes when I was in Wisdom Hely's wise Bloom in Daly's Henry Flower bought. Are you not happy in your home? Flower to console me and a pin cuts lo. Means something, language of flow. Was it a daisy? Innocence that is. Respectable girl meet after mass. Tanks awfully muchly. Wise Bloom eyed on the door a poster, a swaying mermaid smoking mid nice waves. Smoke mermaids, coolest whiff of all. Hair streaming: lovelorn. For some man. For Raoul. He eyed and saw afar on Essex bridge a gay hat riding on a jauntingcar. It is. Third time. Coincidence.

Jingling on supple rubbers it jaunted from the bridge to Ormond quay. Follow. Risk it. Go quick. At four. Near now. Out.

-- Two pence, sir, the shopgirl dared to say.

-- Aha . . . I was forgetting . . . Excuse . . .

And four.

At four she. Winsomely she on Bloomhimwhom smiled. Bloo smi qui go. Ternoon. Think you're the only pebble on the beach? Does that to all. For men.

In drowsy silence gold bent to her page.

From the saloon a call came, long in dying. That was a tuningfork the tuner had that he forgot that he now struck. A call again. That he now poised that it now throbbed. You hear? It throbbed, pure, pure, softly and softlier, its buzzing prongs. Longer in dying call.

Pat paid for diner's popcorked bottle: and over tumbler tray and popcorked bottle ere he went he whispered, bald and bothered, with Miss Douce.

-- *The bright stars fade . . .*

A voiceless song sang from within, singing:

--*. . . the morn is breaking.*

A duodene of birdnotes chirruped bright treble answer under sensitive hands. Brightly the keys, all twinkling, linked, all harpsichording, called to a voice to sing strain of dewy morn, of youth, of love's leavetaking, life's, love's morn.

-- *The dewdrops pearl . . .*

Lenehan's lips over the counter lisped a low whistle of decoy.

-- But look this way, he said, rose of Castille.

Jingle jaunted by the curb and stopped.

She rose and closed her reading, rose of Castille. Fretted forlorn, dreamily rose.

-- Did she fall or was she pushed? he asked her.

She answered, slighting:

-- Ask no questions and you'll hear no lies.

Like lady, ladylike.

Blazes Boylan's smart tan shoes creaked on the barfloor where he strode. Yes, gold from anear by bronze from afar. Lenehan heard and knew and hailed him:

-- See the conquering hero comes.

Between the car and window, warily walking, went Bloom, unconquered hero. See me he might. The seat he sat on: warm. Black wary hecat walked towards Richie Goulding's legal bag, lifted aloft saluting.

-- *And I from thee . . .*

-- I hear you were around, said Blazes Boylan.

He touched to fair Miss Kennedy a rim of his slanted straw. She smiled on him. But sister bronze outsmiled her, preening for him her richer hair, a bosom and a rose.

Boylan bespoke potions.

-- What's your cry? Glass of bitter? Glass of bitter, please, and a sloegin for me. Wire in yet?

[178]

Not yet. At four he. All said four.

Cowley's red lugs and Adam's apple in the door of the sheriff's office. Avoid. Goulding a chance. What is he doing in the Ormond? Car waiting. Wait.

Hello. Where off to? Something to eat? I too was just. In here. What, Ormond? Best value in Dublin. Is that so? Diningroom. Sit tight there. See, not be seen. I think I'll join you. Come on. Richie led on. Bloom followed bag. Dinner fit for a prince.

Miss Douce reached high to take a flagon, stretching her satin arm, her bust, that all but burst, so high.

-- O! O! jerked Lenehan, gasping at each stretch. O!

But easily she seized her prey and let it low in triumph.

-- Why don't you grow? asked Blazes Boylan.

Shebronze, dealing from her jar thick syrupy liquor for his lips, looked as it flowed (flower in his coat: who gave him?), and syrupped with her voice:

-- Fine goods in small parcels.

That is to say she. Neatly she poured slowsyruppy sloe.

-- Here's fortune, Blazes said.

He pitched a broad coin down. Coin rang.

-- Hold on, said Lenehan, till I . . .

-- Fortune, he wished, lifting his bubbled ale.

-- Sceptre will win in a canter, he said.

-- I plunged a bit, said Boylan winking and drinking. Not on my own, you know. Fancy a friend of mine.

Lenehan still drank and grinned at his tilted ale and at Miss Douce's lips that all but hummed, not shut, the oceansong her lips had trilled. Idolores. The eastern seas.

Clock whirred. Miss Kennedy passed their way (flower, wonder who gave), bearing away teatray. Clock clacked.

Miss Douce took Boylan's coin, struck boldly the cashregister. It clanged. Clock clanged. Fair one of Egypt teased and sorted in the till and hummed and handed coins in change. Look to the west. A clack. For me.

-- What time is that? asked Blazes Boylan. Four?

O'clock.

Lenehan, small eyes hunger on her humming, bust ahumming, tugged Blazes Boylan's elbowsleeve.

-- Let's hear the time, he said.

The bag of Goulding, Collis, Ward led Bloom by ryebloom flowered tables. Aimless he chose with agitated aim, bald Pat attending, a table near the door. Be near. At four. Has he forgotten? Perhaps a trick. Not come: whet appetite. I couldn't do. Wait, wait. Pat, waiter, waited.

Sparkling bronze azure eyed Blazure's skyblue bow and eyes.

-- Go on, pressed Lenehan. There's no-one. He never heard.

-- *. . . to Flora's lips did hie.*

High, a high note, pealed in the treble, clear.

Bronzedouce, communing with her rose that sank and rose, sought Blazes Boylan's flower and eyes.

-- Please, please.

He pleaded over returning phrases of avowal.

-- *I could not leave thee . . .*

Afterwits, Miss Douce promised coyly.

-- No, now, urged Lenehan. *Sonnezlacloche!* O do! There's no one.

She looked. Quick. Miss Kenn out of earshot. Sudden bent. Two kindling faces watched her bend.

Quavering the chords strayed from the air, found it again, lost chord, and lost and found it faltering.

-- Go on! *Sonnez!*

Bending, she nipped a peak of skirt above her knee. Delayed. Taunted them still, bending, suspending, with wilful eyes.

-- *Sonnez!*

Smack. She let free sudden in rebound her nipped elastic garter smackwarm against her smackable woman's warmhosed thigh.

-- *La cloche!* cried gleeful Lenehan. Trained by owner. No sawdust there.

She smilesmirked supercilious (wept! aren't men?), but, lightward gliding, mild she smiled on Boylan.

-- You're the essence of vulgarity, she in gliding said.

Boylan, eyed, eyed. Tossed to fat lips his chalice, drankoff his tiny chalice, sucking the last fat violet syrupy drops. He spellbound eyes went after her gliding head as it went down the bar by mirrors, gilded arch for ginger ale, hock and claret glasses shimmering, a spiky shell, where it concerted, mirrored, bronze with sunnier bronze.

Yes, bronze from anearby.

-- . . . *Sweetheart, goodbye!*

I'm off, said Boylan with impatience.

He slid his chalice brisk away, grasped his change.

-- Wait a shake, begged Lenehan, drinking quickly. I wanted to tell you. Tom Rochford . . .

-- Come on to blazes, said Blazes Boylan, going.

Lenehan gulped to go.

-- Got the horn or what? he said. Wait. I'm coming.

He followed the hasty creaking shoes but stood by nimbly by the threshold, saluting forms, a bulky with a slender.

-- How do you do Mr Dollard?

-- Eh? How do? How do? Ben Dollard's vague bass answered, turning an instant from Father Cowley's woe. He won't give you any trouble, Bob. Alf Bergan will speak to the long fellow. We'll put a barleystraw in that Judas Iscariot's ear this time.

Sighing, Mr Dedalus came through the saloon, a finger soothing an eyelid.

-- Hoho, we will, Ben Dollard yodled jollily. Come on, Simon, give us a ditty. We heard the piano.

Bald Pat, bothered waiter, waited for drink orders, Power for Richie. And Bloom? Let me see. Not make him walk twice. His corns. Four now. How warm this black is. Course nerves a bit. Refracts (is it?) heat. Let me see. Cider. Yes, bottle of cider.

-- What's that? Mr Dedalus said. I was only vamping, man.

-- Come on, come on, Ben Dollard called. Begone, dull care. Come, Bob.

He ambled Dollard, bulky slops, before them (hold that fellow with the: hold him now) into the saloon. He plumped him on the stool. His gouty plumped chords. Plumped stopped abrupt.

Bald Pat in the doorway met tealess gold returning. Bothered he wanted Power and cider. Bronze by the window watched, bronze from afar.

Jingle a tinkle jaunted.

Bloom heard a jing, a little sound. He's off. Light sob of breath Bloom sighed on the silent bluehued flowers. Jingling. He's gone. Jingle. Hear.

-- Love and war, Ben, Mr Dedalus said. God be with old times.

. . . .

Pat served uncovered dishes. Leopold cut liverslices. As said before he ate with relish the inner organs, nutty gizzards, fried cods' roes while Richie Goulding, Collis, Ward ate steak and kidney, steak then kidney, bite by bite of pie he ate Bloom ate they ate.

Bloom with Goulding, married in silence, ate. Dinner fit for princes.

By Bachelor's walk jogjaunty jingled Blazes Boylan, bachelor, in sun, in heat, mare's glossy rump tarot, with flick of whip, on bounding tyres: sprawled, warmseated, Boylan impatience, ardentbold. Horn. Have you the? Horn. Have you the? Haw haw horn.

Over their voices Dollard bassooned attack, blooming over bombarding chords:

-- *When love absorbs my ardent soul . . .*

Roll of Bensoulbenjamin rolled to the quivery loveshivery roof-panes.

-- War! War! cried Father Cowley. You're the warrior.

-- So I am, Ben Warrior laughed. I was thinking of your landlord. Love or money.

He stopped. He wagged huge beard, huge face over his blunder huge.

-- Sure, you'd burst the tympanum of her ear, man, Mr Dedalus said through smoke aroma, with an organ like yours.

In bearded abundant laughter Dollard shook upon the keyboard. He would.

-- Not to mention another membrane, Father Cowley added. Half time. Ben. *Amoroso ma non troppo.* Let me there.

. . . .

-- Which air is that? asked Leopold Bloom.

-- *All is lost now.*

Richie cocked his lips apout. A low incipient note sweet banshee murmured all. A thrush. A throstle. His breath, birdsweet, good teeth he's proud of, fluted with plaintive woe. Is lost. Rich sound. Two notes in one there. Blackbird I heard in the hawthorn valley. Taking my motives he twined and turned them. All most too new call is lost in all. Echo. How sweet the answer. How is that done? All lost now. Mournful he whistled. Fall, surrender, lost.

Bloom bent leopold ear, turning a fringe of doyley down under the vase. Order. Yes, I remember. Lovely air. In sleep she went to him. Innocence in the moon. Still hold her back. Brave, don't

know the danger. Call name. Touch water. Jingle jaunty. Too late.
She longed to go. That's why. Woman. As easy as stop the sea. Yes:
all is lost.

    -- A beautiful air, said Bloom lost Leopold. I know it well.

    Never in all his life had Richie Goulding.

    He knows it well too. Or he feels. Still harping on his
daughter. Wise child that knows her father, Dedalus said. Me?

    Bloom askance over liverless saw. Face of the all is lost.
Rollicking Richie once. Jokes stale now. Wagging his ear.
Napkinring in his eye. Now begging letters he sends his son with.
Crosseyed Walter sir I did sir. Wouldn't trouble only I was expecting
some money. Apologise.

    Piano again. Sounds better than last time I heard. Tuned
probably. Stopped again.

    . . . .

    Braintipped, cheek touched with flame, they listened feeling
that flow endearing flow over skin limbs human heart soul spine.
Bloom signed to Pat, bald Pat is a waiter hard of hearing, to set ajar
the door of the bar. The door of the bar. So. That will do. Pat, waiter,
waited, waiting to hear, for he was hard of hear by the door.

    -- *Sorrow from me seemed to depart.*

    Through the hush of air a voice sang to them, low, not rain,
not leaves in murmur, like no voice of strings of reeds or
whatdoyoucallthem dulcimers, touching their still ears with words,
still hearts of their each his remembered lives. Good, good to hear:
sorrow from them each seemed to from both depart when first they
heard. When first they saw, lost Richie, Poldy, mercy of beauty,
heard from a person wouldn't expect it in the least, her first merciful
lovesoft oftloved word.

    Love that is singing: love's old sweet song. Bloom unwound
slowly the elastic band of his packet. Love's old sweet *sonnez la*
gold. Bloom wound a skein round four forkfingers, stretched it,
relaxed, and wound it round his troubled double, fourfold, in octave,
gyved them fast.

    -- *Full of hope and all delighted . . .*

    Tenors get women by the score. Increase their flow. Throw
flower at his feet when will we meet? My head it simply. Jingle all
delighted. He can't sing for tall hats. Your head it simply swurls.
Perfumed for him. What perfume does your wife? I want to know.
Jing. Stop. Knock. Last look at mirror always before she answers the

door. The hall. There? How do you? I do well. There? What? Or? Phila of cachous, kissing comfits, in her satchel. Yes? Hands felt for the opulent.

Alas! The voice rose, sighing, changed: loud, full, shining, proud.

-- But alas, 'twas idle dreaming . . .

. . . .

Martha it is. Coincidence. Just going to write Lionel's song. Lovely name you have. Can't write. Accept my little pres. Play on her heartstrings pursestrings too. She's a. I called you naughty boy. Still the name: Martha. How strange! Today.

The voice of Lionel returned, weaker but unwearied. It sang again to Richie Poldy Lydia Lidwell also sang to Pat open mouth ear waiting to wait. How first he saw that form endearing, how sorrow seemed to part, how look, form, word charmed him Gould Lidwell, won Pat Bloom's heart.

Wish I could see his face, though. Explain better. Why the barber in Drago's always looked my face when I spoke his face in the glass. Still hear it better here than in the bar though farther.

-- Each graceful look . . .

First night when first I saw her at Mat Dillon's in Terenure. Yellow, black lace she wore. Musical chairs. We two the last. Fate. After her. Fate. Round and round slow. Quick round. We two. All looked. Halt. Down she sat. All ousted looked. Lips laughing. Yellow knees.

-- Charmed my eye . . .

Singing. *Waiting* she sang. I turned her music. Full voice of perfume of what perfume does your lilactrees. Bosom I saw, both full, throat warbling. First I saw. She thanked me. Why did she me? Fate. Spanish eyes. Under a peartree alone patio this hour in old Madrid one side in shadows Dolores shedolores. At me. Luring. Ah, alluring.

-- Martha! Ah, Martha!

Quitting all languor Lionel cried in grief, in cry of passion dominant to love to return with deepening yet with rising chords of harmony. In cry of lionel loneliness that she should know, must Martha feel. For only her he waited. Where? Here there try there here all try where. Somewhere.

-- Co-me, thou lost one!
Co-me thou dear one!

[184]

Alone. One love. One hope. One comfort me. Martha, chestnote, return.

-- *Come!*

It soared, a bird, it held its flight, a swift pure cry, soar silver or it leaped serene, speeding, sustained, to come, don't spin it out too long long breath he breath long life, soaring high, high resplendent, aflame, crowned, high in the effulgence symbolistic, high, or the ethereal bosom, high of the high vast irradiation everywhere all soaring all around about the all, the endlessnessnessness . . .

-- *To me!*

Siopold!

Consumed.

Come. Well sung. All clapped. She ought to. Come. to me, to him, to her, you too, me, us.

-- Bravo! Clapclap. Goodman, Simon. Clappyclapclap. Encore! Clapclipclap. Sound as a bell. Bravo, Simon! Clapclopcalp. Encore, enclap, said, cried, clapped all, Ben Dollard, Lydia Douce, George Lidwell, Pat, Mina, two gentlemen with two tankards, Cowley, first gent with tank and bronze Miss Douce and gold Miss Mina.

. . . .

Thou lost one. All songs on that theme. Yet more Bloom stretched his string. Cruel it seems. Let people get fond of each other: lure them on. Then tear asunder. Death. Explos. Knock on the head. Outtohelloutofthat. Human life. Dignam. Ugh, that rat's tail wriggling! Five bob I gave. *Corpus paradisum.* Corncrake croaker: belly like a poisoned pup. Gone. They sing. Forgotten. I too. And one day she with. Leave her: get tired. Suffer then. Snivel. Big Spanishy eyes goggling at nothing. Her wavyavyeavyheavyeavyevyevy hair un comb: 'd.

Yet too much happy bores. He stretched more, more. Are you not happy in your? Twang. It snapped.

Jingle into Dorset street.

Miss Douce withdrew her satiny arm, reproachful, pleased.

-- Don't make half so free, said she, till we are better acquainted.

George Lidwell told her really and truly: but she did not believe.

First gentleman told Mina that was so. She asked him was that so. And second tankard told her so. That that was so.

. . . .

Better write it here. Quills in the postoffice chewed and twisted.

Bald Pat at a sign drew nigh. A pen and ink. He went. A pad. He went. A pad to blot. He heard, deaf Pat.

-- Yes, Mr Bloom said, teasing the curling catgut fine. It certainly is. Few lines will do. My present. All that Italian florid music is. Who is this wrote? Know the name you know better. Take out sheet notepaper, envelope: unconcerned. It's so characteristic.

-- Grandest number in the whole opera, Goulding said.

-- It is, Bloom said.

. . . .

Down the edge of his *Freeman* baton ranged Bloom's your other eye, scanning for where did I see that. Callan, Coleman, Dignam Patrick. Heigho! Heigho! Fawcett. Aha! Just I was looking

. . .

Hope he's not looking, cute as a rat. He held unfurled his *Freeman.* Can't see now. Remember write Greek ees. Bloom dipped, Bloo mur: dear sir. Dear Henry wrote: dear Maddy. Got your lett and flow. Hell did I put? Some pock or oth. It is utterl imposs. Underline *imposs.* To write today.

Bore this. Bored Bloom tambourine gently with I am just reflecting fingers on flat pad Pat brought.

On. Know what I mean. No, change that ee. Accept my poor little pres enclos. Ask her no answ. Hold on. Five Dig. Two about here. Penny the gulls. Elijah is com. Seven Davy Byrne's. Is eight about. Say half a crown. My poor little pres: p. o. two and six. Write me a long. Do you despise? Jingle, have you the? So excited. Why do you call me naught? You naughty too? O, Mairy lost the pin of her. Bye for today. Yes, yes, will tell you. Want to. To keep it up. Call me that other. Other world she wrote. My patience are exhaust. To keep it up. You must believe. Believe. The tank. It. Is. True.

Folly am I writing? Husbands don't. That marriage does, their wives. Because I'm away from. Suppose. But how? She must. Keep young. If she found out. Card in my high grade ha. No, not tell all. Useless pain. If they don't see. Woman. Sauce for the gander.

. . . . .

-- Answering an ad? keen Richie's eyes asked Bloom.

-- Yes, Mr Bloom said. Town traveller. Nothing doing, I expect.

[186]

Bloom mur: best references. But Henry wrote: it will excite me. You know now. In haste. Henry. Greek ee. Better add postscript. What is he playing now? Improvising intermezzo. P. S. The rum tum tum. How will you pun? You punish me? Crooked skirt swinging, whack by. Tell me I want to. Know. O. Course if I didn't I wouldn't ask. La la la rere. Trails off there sad in minor. Why minor sad? Sign H. They like sad tail at end. P. P. S. La la la ree. I feel so sad today. La ree. So lonely. Dee.

He blotted quick on pad of Pat. Envel. Address. Just copy out of paper. Murmured: Messrs Callan, Coleman and Co, limited. Henry wrote:

Miss Martha Clifford
% P. O.
Dolphin's barn lane
Dublin.

Blot over the other so he can't read. Right. Idea prize titbit. Something detective read off blottingpad. Payment at the rate of guinea per col. Matcham often thinks the laughing witch. Poor Mrs Purefoy. U. p.: up.

Too poetical that about sad. Music did that. Music hath charms Shakespeare said. Quotations every day in the year. To be or not to be. Wisdom while you wait.

In Gerard's rosery of Fetter lane he walks, greyed-auburn. One life is all. One body. Do. But do.

Done anyhow. Postal order stamp. Postoffice lower down. Walk now. Enough. Barney Kiernan's I promised to meet them. Dislike that job. House of mourning. Walk. Pat! Doesn't hear. Deaf beetle he is.

Car near there now. Talk. Talk. Pat! Doesn't. Settling those napkins. Lot of ground he must cover in the day. Paint face behind on him then he'd be two. Wish they'd sing more. Keep my mind off.

Bald Pat who is bothered mitred the napkins. Pat is a waiter hard of hearing. Pat is a waiter who waits while you wait. Hee hee hee hee. He waits while you wait. Hee hee. A waiter is he. Hee hee hee hee. He waits while you wait. While you wait if you wait he will wait while you wait. Hee hee hee hee. Hoh. Wait while you wait.

Douce now. Douce Lydia. Bronze and rose.

She had a gorgeous, simply gorgeous, time. And look at the lovely shell she brought.

[187]

To the end of the bar to him she bore lightly the spiked and winding seahorn that he, George Lidwell, solicitor, might hear.

-- Listen! She bade him.

Under Tom Kiernan's ginhot words the accompanist wove music slow. Authentic fact. How Walter Bapty lost his voice. Well, sir, the husband took him by the throat. *Scoundrel,* said he. *You'll sing no more lovesongs.* He did, sir Tom. Bob Cowley wove. Tenors get wom. Cowley lay back.

Ah, now he heard, she holding it to his ear. Hear! He heard. Wonderful. She held it to her own and through the sifted light pale gold in contrast glided. To hear.

Tap.

Bloom through the bardoor saw a shell held at their ears. He heard more faintly that that they heard, each for herself alone, then each for other, hearing the plash of waves, loudly, a silent roar.

Bronze by a weary gold, anear, afar, they listened.

. . . .

That's joyful I can feel. Never have written it. Why? My joy is other joy. But both are joys. Yes, joy it must be. Mere fact of music shows you are. Often thought she was in the dumps till she began to lilt. Then know.

M'Coy valise. My wife and your wife. Squealing cat. Like tearing silk. When she talks like the clapper of a bellows. They can't manage men's intervals. Gap in their voices too. Fill me. I'm warm, dark, oen. Molly in *qui est homo:* Mercadante. My ear against the wall to hear. Want a woman who can deliver the goods.

Jog jig jogged stopped. Dandy tan shoe of dandy Boylan socks skyblue clocks came light to earth.

O, look we are so! Chamber music. could make a kind of pun on that. It is a kind of music I often thought when she. Acoustics that is. Tinkling. Empty vessels make most noise. Because the acoustics, the resonance changes according as the weight of gth water is equal to the law of falling wetter. Like those rhapsodies of Liszt's, Hungarian, gipsyeyed. Pearls. Drops. Rain. Diddle idle addle addle oodle oodle. Hiss. Now. Maybe now. Before.

One rapped on a door, one tapped with a knock, did he knock Paul de Kock, with a loud proud knocker, with a cock carracarraccarra cock. Cockcock.

Tap.

-- *Qui sdegno,* Ben, said Father Cowley.

[188]

-- No, Ben, Tom Kiernan interfered, *The Croppy Boy.* Our native Doric.

-- Ay do, Ben, Mr Dedalus said. Good men and true.

-- Do, do, they begged in one.

I'll go. Here, Pat, return. Come. He came, he came, he did not stay. To me. How much?

-- What key? Six sharps?

-- F sharp in major, Ben Dollard said.

Bob Cowley's outstretched talons gripped the black deepsounding chords.

Must go prince Bloom told Richie prince. No, Richie said. Yes, must. Got money somewhere. He's on for a razzle backache spree. Much? He seehears lipspeech. One and nine. Penny for yourself. Here. Give him twopence tip. Deaf, bothered. But perhaps he has wife and family waiting, waiting Patty come home. Hee hee hee hee. Deaf wait while they wait.

But wait. But hear. Chords dark. Lugugugubrious. Low. In a cave of the dark middle earth. Embedded ore. Lumpmusic.

The voice of dark age, of unlove, earth's fatigue made grave approach, and painful, come from afar, from hoary mountains, called on good men and true. The priest he sought, with him would he speak a word.

Tap. . . .

The priest's at home. A false priest's servant bade him welcome. Step in. The holy father. Curlycues of chords.

Ruin them. Wreck their lives. Then build them cubicles to end their days in. Hushaby. Lullaby. Die, dog. Little dog, die.

The voice of warning, solemn warning, told them the youth had entered a lonely hall, told them how solemn fell his footstep there, told them the gloomy chamber, the vested priest sitting to shrive. . . .

Listen. Bloom listened. Richie Goulding listened. And by the door deaf Pat, bald Pat, tipped Pat, listened.

The chords harped slower.

The voice of penance and of grief came slow, embellished, tremulous. Ben's contrite beard confessed: *in nomine Domini,* in God's name. He knelt. He beat his hand upon his breast, confessing: *mea culpa.*

Latin again. That holds them like birdlime. Priest with the communion corpus for those women. Chap in the mortuary, coffin or coffey, *corpusnomine.* Wonder where that rat is by now. Scrape.

Tap.

They listened: tankards and Miss Kennedy, George Lidwell eyelid well expressive, fullbusted satin, Kernan, Si.

The sighing voice of sorrow sang. His sins. Since easter he had cursed three times. You bitch's bast. And once at masstime he had gone to play. Once by the churchyard he had passed and for his mother's rest he had not prayed. A boy. A croppy boy.

Bronze, listening by the beerpull, gazed far away. Soulfully. Doesn't half know I'm. Molly great dab at seeing anyone looking.

Bronze gazed far sideways. Mirror there. Is that best side of her face? They always know. Knock at the door. Last tip to titivate.

Cockcarracarra.

. . . .

All gone. All fallen. At the siege of Ross, his father, at Gorey all his brothers fell. To Wexford, we are the boys of Wexford, he would. Last of his name and race.

I, too, last my race. Milly young student. Well, my fault perhaps. No son. Rudy. Too late now. Or if not? If not? If still?

He bore no hate.

Hate. Love. Those are names. Rudy. Soon I am old.

Big Ben his voice unfolded. Great voice, Richie Goulding said, a flush struggling in his pale, to Bloom, soon old but when he was young.

Ireland comes now. My country above the king. She listens. Who fears to speak of nineteen four? Time to be shoving. Looked enough.

-- *Bless me, father,* Dollard the croppy cried. *Bless me and let me go.*

Tap.

Bloom looked, unblessed to go. Got up to kill: on eighteen bob a week. Fellows shell out the dibs. Fellows shell out the dibs. Want to keep your weathereye open. Those girls, those lovely. By the sad sea waves. Chorusgirl's romance. Letters read out for the breach of promise. From Chickabiddy's own Mumpsypum. Laughter in court. Henry. I never signed it. The lovely name you.

Low sank the music, air and words. Then hastened. The false priest rustling soldier from his cassock. A yeoman captain. They know it all by heart. The thrill they itch for. Yeoman cap.

Tap. Tap.

Thrilled, she listened, bending in sympathy to hear.

Blank face. Virgin should say: or fingered only. Write something on it: page. If not what becomes them? Decline, despair. Keeps them young. Even admire themselves. See. Play on her. Lip blow. Body of a white woman, a flute alive. Blow gentle. Loud. Three holes all women. Goddess I didn't see. They want it: not too much polite. That's why he gets them. Gold in your pocket, brass in your face. With look to look: songs without words. Molly that hurdygurdy boy. She knew he meant the monkey was sick. Or because so like the Spanish. Understand animals too that way. Solomon did. Gift of nature.

Ventriloquise. My lips closed. Think in my stom. What?

Will? You? I. Want. You. To.

With hoarse rude fury the yeoman cursed. Swelling in apoplectic bitch's bastard. A good thought, boy, to come. One hour's your time to live, your last.

Tap. Tap.

Thrill now. Pity they feel. To wipe away a tear for martyrs. For all things dying, want to, dying to die. For that all things born. Poor Miss Purefoy. Hope she's over. Because their wombs.

. . . .

With a cock with a carra.

Tap. Tap. Tap.

I hold this house. Amen. He gnashed in fury. Traitors swing.

The chords consented. Very sad thing. But had to be.

Get out before the end. Thanks, that was heavenly. Where's my hat? Pass by her. Can leave that *Freeman.* Letter I have. Suppose she were the? No. Walk, walk, walk. Like Cashel Boylo Connoro Coylo Tisdall Maurice Tisntdall Farrell, Waaaaaalk.

Well, I must be. Are you off? Yrfmstbyes. Blmstup. O'er ryehigh blue. Bloom stood up. Ow. Soap feeling rather sticky behind. Must have sweated: music. That lotion, remember. Well, so long. High grade. Card inside, yes.

By deaf Pat in the doorway, straining ear, Bloom passed.

At Geneva barrack that young man died. At Passage was his body laid. Dolor! O, he dolores! The voice of the mournful chanter called to dolorous prayer.

By rose, by satiny bosom, by the fondling hand, by slops, by empties, by popped corks, greeting in going, past eyes and maidenhair, bronze and faint gold in deepseashadow, went Bloom, soft Bloom, I feel so lonely Bloom.

Tap. tap. Tap.

Pray for him, prayed the bass of Dollard. You who hear in peace. Breathe a prayer, drop a tear, good men, good people. He was the croppy boy.

Scaring eavesdropping boots croppy bootsboy Bloom in the Ormond hallway heard growls and roars of bravo, fat backslapping, their boots all treading, boots not the boots of the boy. General chorus off for a swill to wash it down. Glad I avoided.

-- Come on, Ben, Simon Dedalus said. By God, you're as good as ever you were.

-- Better, said Tomgin Kernan. Most trenchant rendition of that ballad, upon my soul and honour it is.

-- Lablache, said Father Cowley.

. . . .

'Tis the last rose of summer Dollard left Bloom felt wind wound round inside.

Gassy thing that cider: binding too. Wait. Postoffice near Reube J's one and eightpence too. Get shut of it. Dodge round by Greek street. Wish I hadn't promised to meet. Freer in air. Music. Gets your nerves. Beerpull. Her hand that rocks the cradle rule the. Ben Howth. That rules the world.

Far. Far. Far. Far.

Tap. Tap. Tap. Tap.

Up the quay went Lionelleopold, naughty Henry with letter for Mady, with sweets of sin with frillies for Raoul with met him pike hoses went Poldy on.

Tap blind walked tapping by the tap the curbstone tapping, tap by tap.

. . . .

Pwee! A wee little wind piped eeee. In Bloom's little wee.

Was he? Mr Dedalus said, returning, with fetched pipe. I was with him this morning at poor little Paddy Dignam's . . .

-- Ay, the Lord have mercy on him.

[192]

-- By the by there's a tuningfork in there on the . . .

Tap. Tap. Tap. Tap.

-- The wife has a fine voice. Or had. What? Lidwell asked.

-- O, that must be the tuner, Lydia said to Simonlionel first I saw, forgot it when he was here.

Blind he was she told George Lidwell second I saw. And played so exquisitely, treat to hear. Exquisite contrast: bronzelid minagold.

-- Shout! Ben Dollard shouted, pouring. Sing out!

Rrrrrr.

I feel I want . . .

Tap. Tap. Tap. Tap. Tap.

-- Very, Mr Dedalus said, staring hard at a headless sardine.

Under the sandwichbell lay on a bier of bread one last, one lonely, last sardine of summer. Bloom alone.

-- Very, he stared. The lower register, for choice.

Tap. Tap. Tap. Tap. Tap. Tap. Tap. Tap.

Bloom went by Barry's. Wish I could. Wait. That wonderworker if I had. Twentyfour solicitors in that one house. Litigation. Love one another. Piles of parchment. Messrs Pick and Pocket have power of attorney. Goulding, Collis, Ward. . . .

Tap. Tap. A stripling, blind, with a tapping cane, came taptaptapping by Daly's window where a mermaid, hair all streaming (but he couldn't see), blew whiffs of a mermaid (blind couldn't), mermaid coolest whiff of all.

Instruments. A blade of grass, shell of her hands, then blow. Even comb and tissuepaper you can knock a tune out of. Molly in her shift in Lombard street west, hair down. I suppose each kind of trade made its own, don't you see? Hunter with a horn. Haw. Have you the? *Cloche. Sonnez la!* Shepherd his pipe. Policeman a whistle. Locks and keys! Sweep! Four o'clock's all's well! Sleep! All is lost now. Drum? Pompey. Wait, I know. Towncrier, bumbailiff. Long John. Waken the dead. Pom. Dignam. Poor little *nominedomine.* Pom. It is music, I mean of course it's all pom pom pom very much what they call *da capo.* Still you can hear. As we march we march along, march along. Pom.

I must really. Fff. Now if I did that at a banquet. Just a question of custom shah of Persia. Breathe a prayer, drop a tear. All the same he must have been a bit of a natural not to see it was a yeoman cap. Muffled up. Wonder who was that chap at the grave in the brown mackin. O, the whore of the lane!

A frowsy whore with black straw sailor hat askew came glazily in the day along the quay towards Mr Boom. When first he saw that form endearing. Yes, it is. I feel so lonely. Wet night in the lane. Horn. Who had the? Heehaw. Shesaw. Off her beat here. What is hse? Hope she. Psst! Any chance of your wash. Knew Molly. Had me decked. Stout lady does be with you in the brown costume. Put you off your stroke. That appointment we made. Knowing we'd never, well hardly ever. Too dear too near to home sweet home. See me, does she? Looks a fright in the day. Face like dip. Damn her! O, well, she has to live like the rest. Look in here.

In Lionel Mark's antique saleshop window haughty Henry Lionel Leopold dear Henry Flower earnestly Mr Leopold Bloom envisaged candlestick melodeon oozing maggoty blowbags. Bargain: six bob. Might learn to play. Cheap. Let her pass. Course everything is dear if you don't want it. That's what good salesman is. Make you buy what he wants to sell. Chap sold me the Swedish razor he shaved me with. Wanted to charge me for the edge he gave it. She's passing now. Six bob.

Must be the cider or perhaps the burgund.

Near bronze from anear near gold from afar they chinked their clinking glasses all, brighteyed and gallant, before bronze Lydia's tempting last rose of summer, rose of Castille. First Lid, De, Cow, Ker, Doll, a fifth: Lidwell, Si Dedalus, Bob Cowley, Kernan and Big Ben Dollard.

Tap. A youth entered a lonely Ormond hall.

Bloom viewed a gallant pictured hero in Lionel Mark's window. Robert Emmet's last words. Seven last words. Of Meyerbeer that is.

-- True men like you men.
-- Ay, ay, Ben.
-- Will lift your glass with us.
They lifted.
Tschink. Tschunk.

Tip. An unseeing stripling stood in the door. He saw not bronze. He saw not gold. Nor Ben nor Bob nor Tom nor Si nor George nor tanks nor Richie nor Pat. Hee hee hee. He did not see.

Seabloom, greasebloom viewed last words. Softly. *When my country takes her place among.*

Prrprr.

Must be the bur.

Fff. Ol. Rrpr.

Nations of the earth. No-one behind. She's passed. *Then and not till then.* Tram. Kran, kran, kran. Good oppor. Coming. Krandlkrankran. I'm sure it's the burgund. Yes. One, two. *Let my epitaph be. Karaaaaaaa. Written. I have.*

Pprrpffrrppffff.

Done.

Episode 12 – Cyclops… a one-eyed Cyclop imprisoned Odysseus and his crewmen in his cave and began to devour them one by one. Odysseus plans their escape by getting the Cyclop drunk on wine and blinding him, driving a fiery stake into his eye. The surviving crewmen held onto the underbelly of the Cyclop's sheep as he let the flock out of the cave in the morning. As the voyagers sailed away, Odysseus taunts the blind Cyclop who then hurls a rock at the disembarking ship. ~ In the cave of a pub of patrons, Bloom's person and character is attacked by the drunken "citizen." With a pointed cigar in hand, Bloom deflects the scornful accusations, infuriates the citizen, and escapes as a tin biscuit box is flung at him.

An anonymous narrator and parodist accompanies patrons at Kiernan's' pub, the men making assertions and bantering back and forth over drinks. Bloom, awaiting associates to meet with the deceased Dignam's family, becomes a subject of criticism and the rantings of the citizen. Pub vitriol extends to literary styles, national aspirations, sports, classism, all eliciting the rage of the citizen. Bloom is perceived as self-righteous and a know-it-all, further antagonizing the citizen and his dog who affronts him. Equally frustrated by his business dealings and accused of stinginess, thought to have won money on *Throwaway*, Bloom asserts himself and escapes defending reality and love as opposed to blindness and hate, whereupon the citizen hurls a biscuit tin at his carriage.

THEMES
Satirizing persons who see things with one eye, having limited vision and being intellectually blind, and/or drunk, chauvinistic, faux-patriotic and hypocritical. 32 parodies related to nationalism and the Irish Literary Revival. Reference to cylindrical, phallic objects and eye metaphors. Representations of gladiators, drunkards. saints, martyrs, virgins, confessors. Pervading sense of darkness, hatred, violence set against temperance, mercy, love. Bloom as an imperfect Elijah.

I WAS JUST PASSING THE TIME OF DAY WITH OLD TROY OF THE D. M. P. at the corner of Arbour hill there and be damned but a bloody sweep came along and he near drove his gear into my eye. I turned around to let him have the weight of my tongue when who should I see dodging along Stony Batter only Joe Hynes.

    -- Lo, Joe, says I. How are you blowing? Did you see that bloody chimneysweep near shove my eye out with his brush?

    -- Soot's luck, says Joe. Who's the old ballocks you were talking to?

    -- Old Troy, says I, was in the force. I'm on two minds not to give that fellow in charge for obstructing the thoroughfare with his brooms and ladders.

    -- What are you round those parts? says Joe.

    -- Devil a much, says I. There is a bloody big foxy thief beyond the garrison church at the corner of Chicken Lane -- old Troy was just giving me a wrinkle about him -- lifted any God's quantity of tea and sugar to pay three bob a week said he had a farm in the

country Down off a hop of my thumb by the name of Moses Herzog
over there near Heytesbury street.

-- Circumcised! says Joe.

-- Ay, says I. A bit off the top. An old plumber named
Geraghty. I'm hanging on to his taw now for the past fortnight and I
can't get a penny out of him.

-- That the lay you're on now? says Joe.

-- Ay, says I. How are the mighty fallen! Collector of bad
and doubtful debts. But that's the most notorious bloody robber
you'd meet in a day's walk and the face on him all pockmarks would
hold a shower of rain. *Tell him,* says he, *I dare him,* says he, *and I
doubledare him to send you round here again or if he does,* says he,
*I'll have him summonsed up before the court, so will I, for trading
without licence.* And he after stuffing himself till he's fit to burst!
Jesus, I had to laugh at the little jewy getting his shirt out. *He drink
me my teas. He eat me my sugars. Because he no pay me my
moneys?*

. . . .

-- Are you a strict t. t.? says Joe.

-- Not taking anything between drinks, says I.

-- What about paying our respects to our friend? says Joe.

-- Who? says I. Sure, he's in John of God's off his head,
poor man.

-- Drinking his own stuff? says Joe.

-- Ay, says I. Whisky and water on the brain.

-- Come around to Barney Kiernan's, says Joe. I want to see
the citizen.

-- Barney mavourneen's be it, says I. Anything strange or
wonderful, Joe?

-- Not a word, says Joe. I was up at that meeting in the City
Arms.

-- What was that, Joe? says I.

-- Cattle traders, says Joe, about the foot and mouth disease.
I want to give the citizen the hard word about it.

So we went around by the Linenhall barracks and the back of
the courthouse talking of one thing or another. Decent fellow Joe
when he has it but sure like that he never has it. Jesus, I couldn't get
over that bloody foxy Geraghty, the daylight robber. For trading
without a licence, says he.

. . . .

So we turned into Barney Kiernan's and there sure enough was the citizen up in the corner having a great confab with himself and that bloody mangy mongrel, Garryowen, and he waiting for what the sky would drop in the way of a drink.

-- There he is, says I, in his gloryhole, with his cruiskeen lawn and his load of papers, working for the cause.

The bloody mongrel let a grouse out of him would give you the creeps. Be a corporal work of mercy if someone would take the life of that bloody dog. I'm told for a fact he ate a good part of the breeches off a constabulary man in Santry that came around one time with a blue paper about a licence.

-- Stand and deliver, says he.

-- That's all right, citizen, say Joe. Friends here.

-- Pass, friends, says he.

Then he rubs his hand in his eye and says he:

-- What's your opinion of the times?

Doing the rapparee and Rory of the hill. But begob, Joes was equal to the occasion.

-- I think the markets are on a rise, says he, sliding his hand down his fork.

So begob the citizen claps his paw on his knee and he says:

-- Foreign wars is the cause of it.

And says Joe, sticking his thumb in his pocket:

-- It's the Russians wish to tyrannise.

-- Arrah, give over your bloody codding, Joe says I, I've a thirst on me I wouldn't sell for half a crown.

-- Give it a name, citizen, says Joe.

-- Wine of the country, says he.

-- What's yours? says Joe.

-- Ditto MacAnaspey, says I.

-- Three pints, Terry, says Joe. And how's the old heart, citizen? says he.

-- Never better, *a chara,* says he. What Garry? Are we going to win? Eh?

And with that he took the bloody old towser by the scruff of the neck and, by Jesus, he near throttled him.

The figure seated on a large boulder at the foot of a round tower was that of a broadshouldered deepchested stronglimbed frankeyed redhaired freely freckled shaggybearded widemouthed largenosed longheaded deepvoiced barekneeed brawnyhanded

[198]

hairylegged ruddyfaced sinewyarmed hero. From shoulder to
shoulder he measured several ells and his rocklike mountainous
knees were covered, as was likewise the rest of his body wherever
visible, with a strong growth of tawny prickly hair in hue and
toughness similar to the mountain grose *(Ulex Europeus)*. The
widewinged nostrils, from which bristles of the same tawney hue
projected, were of such capaciousness that within their cavernous
obscurity the fieldlark might easily have lodged her nest. The eyes in
which a tear and a smile strove ever for the mastery were of the
dimensions of a goodsized cauliflower. A powerful current of warm
breath issued at regular intervals from the profound cavity of his
mouth while in rhythmic resonance the loud strong hale
reverberations of his formidable heart thundered rumbling causing
the ground, the summit of the lofty tower and the still loftier walls of
the cave to vibrated and tremble.

. . . .

From his girdle hung a row of seastones which dangled at every
movement of his portentous frame and on these were graven with
rude yet striking art the tribal images of many Irish heroes and
heroines of antiquity, Cuchulin, Conn of hundred battles, Niall of
nine hostages, Brian of Kincora, the Ardri Malachi, Art
MacMurragh, Shane O'Neill, Father John Murphy, Owen Roe,
Patrick Sarsfield, Red Hugh O'Donnell... A couched spear of
acuminated granite rested by him while at his feet reposed a savage
animal of the canine tribe whose stertorous gasps announced that he
was sunk in uneasy slumber, a supposition confirmed by hoarse
growls and spasmodic movements which his master repressed from
time to time by tranquillising blows of a might cudgel rudely
fashioned out of paleolithic stone.

So anyhow Terry brought the three pints Joe was standing
and begob the sight nearly left my eyes when I saw him land out a
quid. O, as true as I'm telling you. A goodlooking sovereign.

-- And there's more where that came from, says he.

-- Were you robbing the poorbox, Joe? says I.

-- Sweat of my brow, says Joe. 'Twas the prudent member
gave me the wheeze.

-- I saw him before I met you, says I, sloping around by Pill
lane and Greek street with his cod's eye counting up all the guts of
the fish.

Who comes through Michan's land, bedight in sable armour? O'Bloom, the son of Rory: it is he. Impervious to fear is Rory's son: he of the prudent soul.

-- For the old woman of Prince's street, says the citizen, the subsided organ. The pledgebound party on the floor of the house. And look at this blasted rag, says he. Look at this, says he. *The Irish Independent,* if you please, founded by Parnell to be the workingman's friend. Listen to the births and deaths in the *Irish all for Ireland Independent* and I'll thank you and the marriages.

And he starts reading them out:

. . . .

-- Ah, well, says Joe, handing round the boose. Thanks be to God they had the start of us. Drink
that, citizen.

-- I will, says he, honourable person.

-- Health, Joe, says I. And all down the form.

Ah! Ow! Don't be talking! I was blue mouldy for the want of that pint. Declare to God I could hear it hit the pit of my stomach with a click.

And lo, as they quaffed their cup of joy, a godlike messenger came swiftly in, radiant as the eye of heaven, a comely youth, and behind him there passed an elder of noble gait and countenance, bearing the sacred scrolls of law, and with him his lady wife, a dame of peerless lineage, fairest of her race.

Little Alf Bergan popped in around the door and hid behind Barney's snug, squeezed up with the laughing, and who was sitting up there in the corner that I hadn't seen snoring drunk, blind to the world, only Bob Doran. I didn't know what was up and Alf kept making signs out the door. And begob what was it only that bloody old pantaloon Denis Breen in his bath slippers with two bloody big books tucked under his oxter and the wife hotfoot after him, unfortunate wretched woman trotting like a poodle. I thought Alf would split.

-- Look at him, says he. Breen. He's traipsing all around Dublin with a postcard someone sent him with u. p.: up on it to take a li . . .

And he doubled up.

-- Take a what? says I.

-- Libel action, says he, for ten thousand pounds.

-- O hell! says I.

The bloody mongrel began to growl that'd put the fear of God in you seeing something was up but the citizen gave him a kick in the ribs.

-- *Bi i dho husht,* says he.

-- Who? says Joe.

-- Breen, says Alf. He was in John Henry Menton's and then he went round to Collis and Ward's and then Tom Rochford met him and sent him round to the subsheriff's for a lark. O God, I've a pain laughing. U. p.: up. The long fellow gave him an eye as good as a process and now the bloody old lunatic is gone round to Green Street to look for a G. man.

-- When is long John going to hang that fellow in Mountjoy? says Joe.

Bergan, says Bob Doran, waking up. Is that Alf Bergan?

-- Yes, says Alf. Hanging? Wait till I show you. Here, Terry, give us a pony. That bloody old fool! Ten thousand pounds. You should have seen long John's eye. U. p. . . . .

And he started laughing.

-- Who are you laughing at? says Bob Doran. Is that Bergan?

-- Hurray up, Terry boy, says Alf.

Terence O'Ryan heard him and straightway brought him a crystal cup full of the foaming ebon ale which the noble twin brothers Bungiveagh and Bungardilaun brew ever in their divine alevats, cunning as the sons of deathless Leda. For they garner the succulent berries of the hop and mass and sift and bruise and brew them and they mix therewith sour juices and bring the must to the sacred fire and cease not night or day from their toil, those cunning brothers, lords of the vat.

Then did you, chivalrous Terence, hand forth, as to the manner born, that nectarous beverage and you offered the crystal cup to him that thirsted, the soul of chivalry, in beauty akin to the immortals.

. . . .

-- What's that bloody freemason doing, say the citizen, prowling up and down outside?

-- What's that? says Joe.

-- Here you are, says Alf, chucking out the rhino. Talking about hanging. I'll show you something you never saw. Hangmen's letters. Look at here.

So he took a bundle of wisps of letters and envelopes out of his pocket.

-- Are you codding? says I.

-- Honest injun, says Alf. Read them.

So Joe took up the letters.

-- Who are you laughing at? says Bob Doran.

So I saw there was going to be a bit of dust. Bob's a queer chap when the porter's up in him so says I just to make talk:

-- How's Willy Murray those times, Alf?

-- I don't know, says Alf. I saw him just now in Capel Street with Paddy Dignam. Only I was running after that . . .

-- You what? says Joe, throwing down the letters. With who?

-- With Dignam, says Alf.

-- Is it Paddy? says Joe.

-- Yes, says Alf. Why?

-- Don't you know he's dead? says Joe.

-- Paddy Dignam dead? says Alf.

-- Ay, says Joe.

-- Sure I'm after seeing him not five minutes ago, says Alf, as plain as a pikestaff.

-- Who's dead? says Bob Doran.

-- You saw his ghost then, says Joe, God between us and harm.

-- What? says Alf. Good Christ, only five . . . What? . . . and Willie Murray with him, the two of them there near whatdoyoucallhim's . . . What? Dignam dead?

-- What about Dignam, says Bob Doran. Who's talking about . . . ?

-- Dead! says Alf. He is no more dead than you are.

-- Maybe so, says Joe. They took the liberty of burying him this morning anyhow.

-- Paddy? says Alf.

-- Ay, says Joe. He paid the debt of nature, God be merciful to him.

-- Good Christ! Says Alf.

Begob he was what you might call flabbergasted.

In the darkness spirit hands were felt to flutter and when by prayer by tantras had been directed to the proper quarter a faint but increasing luminosity of ruby light became gradually visible, the apparition of the etheric double being particularly lifelike owing to the discharge of jivic rays from the crown of the head and face. Communication was effected through the pituitary body and also by means of the orangefiery and scarlet rays emanating from the sacral region and solar plexus. Questioned by his earthname as to his whereabouts in the heaven world he stated that he was now on the path of pralaya or return but was still submitted to trial at the hands of certain bloodthirsty entities on the lower astral levels. In reply to a question as to his first sensations in the great divide beyond he stated that previously he had seen as in a glass darkly but that those who had passed over had summit possibilities of atomic development opened up to them. Interrogated as to whether life three resembled our experience in the flesh he stated that he had heard from more favoured beings now in the spirit that their abodes were equipped with every modern home comfort such as talafana, alavatar, hatakalda, wataklasat and that the highest adepts were steeped in waves of volupcy of the very purest nature. Having requested a quart of buttermilk this was brought and evidently afforded relief. Asked if he had any message for the living he exhorted all who were still at the wrong side of Maya to acknowledge the true path for it was reported in devanic circles that Mars and Jupiter were out for mischief on the eastern angle where the ram has power. It was queried whether there were any special desires on the part of the defunct and the reply was: *We greet you, friends of earth, who are still in the body. Mind C. K. doesn't pile it on.* It was ascertained that the reference was to Mr Cornelius Kelleher, manager of Messrs H. J. O'Neill's popular funeral establishment, a personal friend of the defunct, who had been responsible for the carrying out of the interment arrangements. Before departing he requested that it should be told to his dear son Patsy that the other boot which he had been looking for was at present under the commode in the return room and that the pair should be sent to Cullen's to be soled only as the heels were still good. He stated that this had greatly perturbed his peace of mind in the other region and earnestly requested that his desire should be made known.

Assurances were given that the matter would be attended to and it was intimated that this had given satisfaction.

He is gone from mortal haunts: O'Dignam, sun of our morning. Fleet was his foot on the bracken: Patrick of the beamy brow. Wail, Banba, with your wind: and wail, O ocean, with your whirlwind.

-- There he is again, says the citizen, starting out.

-- Who? says I.

-- Bloom, says he. He's on point duty up and down there for the last ten minutes.

And begog, I saw his physog do a peep in and then slidder off again.

Little Alf was knocked bawways. Faith, he was.

-- Good Christ! says he. I could have sworn it was him.

And says Bob Doran, with the hat on the back of his poll, lowest blackguard in Dublin when he's under the influence:

-- Who said Christ is good?

-- I beg your parsnips, says Alf.

-- Is that a good Christ, say Bob Doran, to take away poor little Willy Dignam?

-- Ah well, says Alf, trying to pass it off. He's over all his troubles.

But Bob Doran shouts out of him.

-- He's a bloody ruffian I say, to take away poor little Willy Dignam.

Terry came down and tipped him the wink to keep quiet, that they didn't want that kind of talk in a respectable licensed premises. And Bob Doran starts doing the weeps about Paddy Dignam, true as you are there.

-- The finest man, says he, sniveling, the finest purest character.

The tear is bloody near your eye. Talking through his bloody hat. Fitter for him to go home to the little sleepwalking bitch he married, Mooney, the bumbailiff's daughter. Mother kept a kip in Hardwicke street that used to be stravaging about the landings Bantam Lyons told me that was stopping there at two in the morning without a stitch on her, exposing her person, open to all comers, fair field and no favour.

-- The noblest, the truest, says he. And he's gone, poor little Willy, poor little Paddy Dignam.

And mournful and with heavy heart he bewept the extinction of that beam of heaven.

Old Garryowen started growling again at Bloom that was skeezing round the door.

-- Come in, come in, he won't eat you, says the citizen.

So Bloom slopes in with his cod's eye on the dog and he asks Terry was Martin Cunningham there.

-- O, Christ M'Keown, says Joe, reading one of the letters. Listen to this, will you?

And he starts reading out one.

. . . .

Hello, Bloom, say he, what will you have?

So they started arguing about the point, Bloom saying he wouldn't and couldn't and excuse him no offence and all to that and then he said well he'd just take a cigar. Gob, he's a prudent member and no mistake.

-- Give us one of your prime stinkers, Terry, says Joe.

And Alf was telling us there was one chap sent in a mourning card with a black border round it.

-- They're all barbers, says he, from the black country that would hang their own fathers for five quid down and travelling expenses.

And he was telling us there's two fellows waiting below to pull his heels down when he gets the drop and choke him properly and then they chop up the rope after and sell the bits for a few bob a skull.

In the dark land they bide, the vengeful knights of the razor. Their deadly coil they grasp: yea, and therein they lead to Erebus whatsoever wight hath done a deed of blood for I will on nowise suffer it even so saith the Lord.

So they started talking about capital punishment and of course Bloom comes out with the why and the wherefore and all the codology of the business and the old dog smelling him all the time I'm told those jewies does have a sort of a queer odour coming off them for doges about I don't know what all deterrent effect and so forth and so on.

-- There's one thing it hasn't a deterrent effect on, Say Alf.

-- What's that? says Joe.

-- The poor bugger's tool that's being hanged, says Alf.

--That so? says Joe.

-- The poor bugger's tool that's being hanged, says Alf.

-- That so? says Joe.

-- God's truth, says Alf. I heard that from the head warder that was in Kilmainham when they hanged Joe Brady, the invincible.

He told me when they cut him down after the drop it was standing up in their faces like a poker.

    -- Ruling passion strong in death, says Joe, as someone said.

    -- That can be explained by science, says Bloom. It's only a natural phenomenon, don't you see, because on account of the . . .

    And then he starts with his jawbreakers about phenomenon and science and this phenomenon and the other phenomenon.

. . . .

    So of course the citizen was only waiting for the wink of the word and he starts gassing out of him about the invincibles and the old guard and the men of sixtyseven and who fears to speak of ninetyeight and Joe with him about all the fellows that were hanged, drawn and transported for the cause by drumhead courtmartial and a new Ireland and new this, that and the other. Talking about new Ireland he ought to go and get a new dog so he ought. Mangy ravenous brute sniffling and sneezing all round the place and scratching his scabs and round he goes to Bob Doran that was standing Alf a half one sucking up for what he could get. So of course Bob Doran starts doing the bloody fool with him:

    -- Give us the paw! Give the paw, doggy! Good old doggy. Give us the paw here! Give us the paw!

    Arrah! bloody end to the paw he'd paw and Alf trying to keep him from tumbling off the bloody stool atop of the bloody old dog and he talking all kinds of drivel about training by kindness and thoroughbred dog and intelligent dog: give you the bloody pip. Then he starts scraping a few bits of old biscuit out of the bottom of a Jacob's tin he told Terry to bring. Gob, he golloped it down like old boots and his tongue hanging out of him a yard long for more. Near ate the tin and all, hungry bloody mongrel.

    And the citizen and Bloom having an argument about the point, the brothers Sheares and Wolfe Tone beyond on Arbour Hill and Robert Emmet and die for your country, the Tommy Moore touch about Sara Curran and she's far from the land. And Bloom, of course, with his knockmedown cigar putting on swank with his lardy face. Phenomenal! The fat heap he married is a nice old phenomenon with a back on her like a ballalley. Time they were stopping up in the *City Arms* Pisser Burke told me there was an old one there with a cracked loodheramaun of a nephew and Bloom trying to get the soft side of her doing the mollycoddle playing bezique to come in for a bit of the wampum in her will and not eating meat of a Friday

[206]

because the old one was always thumping her craw and taking the lout out for a walk. And one time he led him the rounds of Dublin and, by the holy farmer, he never cried crack till he brought him home as drunk as a boiled owl and he said he did it to teach him the evils of alcohol and by herrings if the three women didn't roast him it's a queer story, the old one, Bloom's wife and Mrs O'Dowd that kept the hotel. Jesus, I had to laugh at Pisser Burke taking them off chewing the fat and Bloom with his *but don't you see?* and *but on the other hand*. And sure, more be token, the lout I'm told was in Power's after the blender's, round in Cope street going home footless in a cab five times in a week after drinking his way through all the samples in the bloody establishment. Phenomenon!

    -- The memory of the dead, says the citizen taking up his pintglass and glaring at Bloom.

    -- Ay, ay, says Joe.

    --You don't grasp my point, says Bloom. What I mean is . . .

    -- *Sinn Fein!* says the citizen. *Sinn fein amhain*! The friends we love are by our side and the foes we hate before us.

    The last farewell was affecting in the extreme. From the belfries far and near the funereal deathbell tolled unceasingly while all around the gloomy precincts rolled the ominous warning of a hundred muffled drums punctuated by the hollow booming of pieces of ordnance. The deafening claps of thunder and the dazzling flashes of lightning which lit up the ghastly scene testified that the artillery of heaven had leny its supernatural pomp to the already gruesome spectacle. A torrential rain poured down from the floodgates of the angry heavens upon the bared heads of the assembled multitude which numbered at the lowest computation five hundred thousand persons.

   . . . .

It was exactly seventeen o'clock. The signal for prayer was then promptly given by megaphone and in an instant all heads were bared, the commendatore's patriarchal sombrero, which has been in the possession of his family since the revolution of Rienzi, being removed by his medical adviser in attendance, Dr Pippi. The learned prelate who administered the last comforts of holy religion to the hero martyr when about to pay the death penalty knelt in a most christian spirit in a pool of rainwater, his cassock above his hoary head, and offered up to the throne of grace fervent prayers of supplication. Hard by the block stood the grim figure of the

[207]

executioner, his visage being concealed in a tengallon pot with two circular perforated apertures through which his eyes glowered furiously. As he awaited the fatal signal he tested the edge of his horrible weapon by honing it upon his brawny forearm or decapitated in rapid succession a flock of sheep which had been provided by the admirers of his fell but necessary office. . . . The *nec* and *non plus ultra* of emotion were reached when the blushing bride elect burst her way through the serried ranks of the bystanders and flung herself upon the muscular bosom of him who was about to be launched into eternity for her sake. The hero folded her willowy form in a living embrace murmuring fondly *Sheila, my own.* Encouraged by this use of her christian name she kissed passionately all the various suitable areas of his person which the decencies of prison garf permitted her ardour to reach. She swore to him as they mingled the salt streams of their tears that she would cherish his memory, that she would never forget her hero boy who went to his death with a song on his lips as if he were but going to a hurling match in Clonturk park. She brought back to his recollection the happy days of blissful childhood together on the banks of Anna Liffey when they had indulged in the innocent pastimes of the young and, oblivious of the dreadful present, they both laughed heartily, all the spectators, including the venerable pastor, joining in the general merriment. That monster audience simply rocked with delight. But anon they were overcome with grief and clasped their hands for the last time. A fresh torrent of tears burst from their lachrymal ducts and the vast concourse of people, touched to the inmost core, broke into heartrending sobs, not the least affected being the aged prebendary himself. . . .

-- God blimey if she aint a clinker, that there bleeding tart. Blimey it makes me kind of bleeding cry, straight, it does, when I sees her cause I thinks of my old mashtub what's waiting for me down Limehouse way.

So then the citizen begins talking about the Irish language and the corporation meeting and all to that and the shoneens that can't speak their own language and Joe chipping in because he stuck someone for a quid and Bloom in his old goo with his twopenny stump that he cadged off Joe and talking about the Gaelic league and the antitreating league and drink, the curse of Ireland. Antitreating is about the size of it. Gob, he'd let you pour all manner of drink down his throat till the Lord would call him before you'd ever see the froth of his pint. And one night I went in with a fellow into one of their musical evenings, song and dance about she get up on a truss of hay she could my Maureen Lay, and there was a fellow with a Ballyhooly blue ribbon badge spiffing out of him in Irish and a lot of colleen bawns going about with temperance beverages and selling medals and oranges and lemonade and a few old dry buns, gob, flahoolagh entertainment, don't be talking. Ireland sober is Ireland free. And then an old fellow starts blowing into his bagpipes and all the gouges shuffling their feet to the tune the old cow died of. And one or two sky pilots having an eye around that there was no goings on with females hitting below the belt.

    -- So howandever, as I was saying, the old dog seeing the tin was empty starts mousing around by Joe and me. I'd train him by kindness, so I would, if he was my dog. Give him a rousing fine kick now and again where it wouldn't blind him.

    -- Afraid he'll bite you? says the citizen, sneering.

    --No, says I. But he might take my leg for a lampost.

    So he calls the old dog over.

    -- What's on you, Garry? says he.

    Then he starts hauling and mauling and talking to him in Irish and the old towser growling, letting on to answer, like a duet in the opera. Such growling you never heard as they let off between them. Someone that has nothing better to do ought to write a letter *pro bono publico* to the papers about the muzzling order for a dog the like of that. Growling and grousing and his eye all bloodshot from the drouth is in it and the hydrophobia dropping out of his jaws.

  . . . .

    The metrical system of the canine original, which recalls the intricate alliterative and isosyllabic rules of the Welsh englyn, is infinitely more complicated but we believe our readers will agree that the spirit has been well caught. Perhaps it should be added that the effect is greatly increased if Owen's verse be spoken womewhat slowly and indistinctly in a tone suggestive of suppressed rancour.

> *The curse of my curses*
> *Seven days every day*
> *And seven dry Thursdays*
> *On you, Barney Kiernan,*
> *Has no sup of water*
> *To cool my courage,*

And my guts red roaring
After Lowry's lights.

So he told Terry to bring some water for the dog and, gob,
you could hear him lappin it up a mile off. And Joe asked him would
he have another.

-- I will, says he, *a chara,* to show there's no ill feeling.

Gob, he's not as green as he's cabbagelooking. Arsing
around from one pub to another, leaving it to your own honour, with
old Giltrap's dog and getting fed up by the ratepayers and
corporators. Entertainment for man and beat. And says Joe:

-- Could you make a hole in another pint?

-- Could a swim duck? says I.

-- Same again, Terry, says Joe. Are you sure you won't have
anything in the way of liquid refreshments? says he.

-- Thank you, no, says Bloom. As a matter of fact I just
wanted to meet Martin Cunningham, don't you see, about this
insurance of poor Dignam's. Martin asked me to go to the house.
You see, he, Dignam, I mean, didn't serve any notice of the
assignment on the company at the time and nominally under the act
the mortgagee can't recover on the policy.

-- Holy Wars, says Joe laughing, that's a good one if the old
Shylock is landed. So the wife comes out top dog, what?

-- Well, that's a point, says Bloom, for the wife's admirers.

-- Whose admirers? says Joe.

-- The wife's advisers, I mean, says Bloom.

. . . .

So Bob Doran comes lurching around asking Bloom to tell
Mrs. Dignam he was sorry for her trouble and he was very sorry
about the funeral and to tell her that he said and everyone who knew
him said that there was never a truer, finer that poor little Willy
that's dead to tell her. Choking with bloody foolery. And shaking
Bloom's hand doing the tragic to tell her that. Shake hands, brother.
You're a rogue and I'm another.

-- Let me, said he, so far presume upon our acquaintance
which, however slight it may appear if judged by the standard of
mere time, is founded, as I hope and believe, on a sentiment of
mutual esteem, as to request of you this favour. But, should I have
overstepped the limits of reserve let the sincerity of my feelings be
the excuse for my boldness.

[210]

-- No, rejoined the other, I appreciate to the full the motives which actuate your conduct and I shall discharge the office you entrust to me consoled by the reflection that, though the errand be one of sorrow, this proof of your confidence sweetens in some measure the bitterness of the cup.

-- Then suffer me to take your hand, said he. The goodness of your heart, I feel sure, will dictate to you better than my inadequate words the expressions which are most suitable to convey and emotion whose poignancy, were I to give vent to my feelings, would deprive me even of speech.

And off with him and out trying to walk straight. Boosed at five o'clock.

. . . .

So Joe starts telling the citizen about the foot and mouth disease and the cattle traders and taking action in the matter and the citizen sending them all to the rightabout and Bloom coming out with his sheepdip for the scab and a hoose drench for coughing calves and the guaranteed remedy for timber tongue. Because he was up one time in a knacker's yard. Walking about with his book and pencil here's my head and my heels are coming till Joe Cuffe gave him the order of the boot for giving lip to a grazier. Mister Knowall. Teach your grandmother how to milk ducks. Pisser Burke was telling me in the hotel the wife used to be in rivers of tears sometimes with Mrs O'Dowd crying her eyes out with her eight inches of fat all over her. Couldn't loosen her farting strings but old cod's eye was waltzing around her showing her how to do it. What's your programme today? Ay. Humane methods. Because the poor animals suffer and experts say the best known remedy that doesn't cause pain to the animal and on the sore spot administer gently. Gob, he'd have a soft hand under a hen.

Ga Ga Gara. Klook Klook Klook. Black Liz is our hen. She lays eggs for us. When she lays her egg she is so glad. Gara. Klook Klook Klook. Then comes good uncle Leo. He puts his hand under black Liz and takes her fresh egg. Ga ga ga ga Gara. Klook Klook Klook.

-- Anyhow, says Joe. Field and Nannetti are going over tonight to London to ask about it on the floor of the House of Commons.

-- Are you sure, says Bloom, the councillor is going? I wanted to see him, as it happens.

-- Well, he's going off by the mailboat, says Joe, tonight.

-- That's too bad, says Bloom. I wanted particularly. Perhaps only Mr Field is going. I couldn't phone. No. You're sure.

-- Nannan's going too, says Joe. The league told him to ask a question tomorrow about the commissioner of police forbidding Irish games in the park. What do you think of that, citizen. *The Sluagh na h-Eireann.*

. . . .

-- There's the man, says Joe, that made the Gaelic sports revival. There he is sitting there. The man that got away James Stephens. The champion of all Ireland at putting the sixteen pound shot. What was your best throw, citizen?

-- *Na bacleis,* says the citizen, letting on to be modest. There was a time I was good as the next fellow anyhow.

-- Put it there, citizen, says Joe. You were and a bloody sight better.

-- Is that really a fact? says Alf.

-- Yes, says Bloom. That's well known. Do you know that?

So off they started about Irish sport and shoneen games the like of the lawn tennis and about hurley and putting the stone and racy of the soil and building up a nation once again and all of that. And of course Bloom had to have his say too about if a fellow had a rower's heart violent exercise was bad. I declare to my antimacassar if you took up a straw from the bloody floor and if you said to Bloom: *Look at, Bloom. Do you see that straw? That's a straw.* Declare to my aunt he'd talk about it for an hour so he would and talk steady.

A most interesting discussion took place in the ancient hall of *Brian O'Ciarnain's* in *Sraid no Bretaine Bheag,* under the auspices of *Sluag na n-Eireann,* on the revival of ancient Gaelic sports and the importance of physical culture, as understood in ancient Greece and ancient Rome and ancient Ireland, for the development of the race. The venerable president of this noble order was in the chair and the attendance was of large dimensions. After an instructive discourse by the chairman, a magnificent oration eloquently and forcibly expressed, a most interesting and instructive discussion of the usual high standard of excellence ensued as to the desirability of the revivability of the ancient games and sports of our ancient pancetic forefathers. The wellknown and highly respected worker in the cause of our old tongue, Mr Joseph M'Carthy Hynes,

[212]

made an eloquent appeal for the resuscitation of the ancient Gaelic sports and pastimes, practised morning and evening by Finn MacCool, as calculated to revive the best traditions of manly strength and power handed down to us from ancient ages. L.Bloom, who met with a mixed reception of applause and hisses, having espoused the negative the vocalist chairman brought the discussion to a close, in response to repeated requests and hearty plaudits from all parts of a bumper house, by a remarkably noteworthy rendering of the immortal Thomas Osborne Davis' evergreen verses (happily too familiar to need recalling here) *A nation once again* in the execution of which the veteran patriot champion may be said without fear of contradiction to have fairly excelled himself.

. . . .

-- Talking about violent exercise, says Alf, were you at that Keogh-Bennett match?

-- No, says Joe.

-- I heard So and So made a cool hundred quid over it, says Alf.

-- Who? Blazes? says Joe.

And says Bloom:

-- What I meant about tennis for example,is the agility and training of the eye.

-- Ay, Blazers, says Alf. He let out that Myler was on the beer to run the odds and he swatting all the time.

-- We know him, says the citizen. The traitor's son. We know what put English gold in his pocket.

-- True for you, says Joe.

And Bloom cuts in again about lawn tennis and the circulation of the blood, asking Alf:

-- Now don't you think, Bergan?

-- Myler dusted the floor with him, says Alf. Heenan and Sayers was only a bloody fool to it. Handed him the father and mother of a beating. See the little kipper not up to his navel and the big fellow swiping. God, he gave him one last puck in the wind. Queensberry rules and all, made him puke what he never ate.

It was a historic and a hefty battle when Myler and Percy were scheduled to don the gloves for the purse of fifty sovereigns. Handicapped as he was by lack of poundage, Dublin's pet lamb made up for it by superlative skill in righcraft. The final bout of fireworks was a gruelling for both champions. The welterweight sergeantmajor had tapped some lively claret in the previous mixup during which Keogh had been receiver-general of rights and lefts, the artilleryman putting in some neat work on the pet's nose, and Myler came on looking groggy. The soldier got to business leading off with a powerful left jab to which the Irish gladiator retaliated by shooting out a stiff one flush to the point of Bennett's jaw. The redcoat ducked but the Dubliner lifted him with a left hook, the body punch being a fine one. The men came to handgrips. Myler quickly became busy and got his man under, the bout ending with the bulkier man on the ropes, Myler punishing him. The Englishman, whose right eye was nearly closed, took his corner where he was liberally drenched with water and, when the bell went, came on gamey and brimful of pluck, confident of knocking out the fistic Eblanite in jigtime. It was a fight to a finish and the best man for it. The two fought like tigers and excitement ran fever high. The referee twice cautioned Pucking Percy for holding but the pet was tricky and his footwork a treat to watch. After a brisk exchange of courtesies during which a smart upper cut of the military man brought blood freely from his opponent's mouth the lamb suddenly waded in all over his man and landed a terrific left to Battling Bennett's stomach, flooring him flat. It was a knockout clean and clever. Amid tense expectation the Portobello bruiser was being counted out when Bennett's second Ole Pfotts Wettstein threw in the towel and the Santry boy was declared victor to the frenzied cheers of the public who broke through the ringropes and fairly mobbed him with delight.

-- He knows which side his bread is buttered, say Alf. I hear he's running a concert tour now up in the north.

-- He is, says Joe. Isn't he?

--Who? says Bloom. Ah, yes. That's quite true. Yes, a kind of summer tour, you see. Just a holiday.

-- Mrs B. is the bright particular star, isn't she? says Joe.

-- My wife? says Bloom. She's singing, yes. I think it will be a success too. He's an excellent man to organise. Excellent.

Hoho, begob, says I to myself, says I. That explains the milk in the cocoanut and absence of hair on the animal's chest. Blazes doing the tootle on the flute. Concert tour. Dirty Dan the dodger's son off Island bridge that sold the same horses twice over to the government to fight the Boers. Old Whatwhat. I called about the poor and water rate, Mr Boylan. You what? That's the bucko that'll organise her, take my tip. 'Twixt me and you Caddereesh.

[214]

Pride of Calpe's rocky mount, the ravenhaired daughter of Tweedy. There grew she to peerless beauty where loquat and almond scent the air. The gardens of Alameda knew her step: the garths of olives knew and bowed. The chaste spouse of Leopold is she: Marion of the bountiful bosoms.

And lo, there entered one of the clan of the O'Molloys, a comely hero of white face yet withal somewhat ruddy, his majesty's counsel learned in the law, and with him the prince and heir of the noble line of Lambert.

-- Hello, Ned.

-- Hello, Alf.

-- Hello, Jack.

-- Hello, Joe.

-- God save you, says the citizen.

-- Save you kindly, says J. J. What'll it be, Ned?

-- Half one, says Ned.

So J. J. ordered the drinks.

-- Were you round at the court? says Joe.

-- Yes, says J. J. He'll square that, Ned, says he.

-- Hope so, says Ned. . . .

-- Did you see that bloody lunatic Breen round there, says Alf. U. p. up.

-- Yes, says J. J. Looking for a private detective.

-- Ay, says Ned, and he wanted right go wrong to address the court only Corny Kelleher got round him telling him to get the handwriting examined first.

-- Ten thousand pounds, says Alf laughing. God I'd give anything to hear him before a judge and jury.

--Was it you did it, Alf? says Joe. The truth, the whole truth and nothing but the truth, so help you Jimmy Johnson.

-- Me? says Alf. Don't cast your nasturtiums on my character.

-- Whatever statement you make, says Joe, will be taken down in evidence against you.

-- Of course an action would lie, say J. J. It implies that he is not *compos mentis*. U. p. up.

-- *Compos* your eye! says Alf laughing. Do you know that he's balmy? Look at his head. Do you know that some mornings he has to get his hat on with a shoehorn?

-- Yes, says J. J., but the truth of a libel is no deference to an indictment for publishing it in the eyes of the law.

-- Ha, ha, Alf, says Joe.

-- Still, says Bloom, on account of the poor woman, I mean his wife.

-- Pity about her, says the citizen. Or any other woman marries a half and half.

-- How half and half? says Bloom. Do you mean he . . .

-- Half and half I mean, says the citizen. A fellow that's neither fish nor flesh.

-- Nor good red herring, says Joe.

-- That what's I mean, says the citizen. A pishogue, if you know what that is.

Begob I saw there was trouble coming. And Bloom explained he meant on account of it being cruel for the wife having to go round after the stuttering fool. Cruelty to animals so it is to let that bloody povertystricken Breen out on grass with his beard out tripping him, bringing down the rain. And she with her nose cockahoop after she married him because a cousin of his old fellow's was pew opener to the pope. Picture of him on the wall with his smashall sweeney's moustaches. The signor Birini from Summerhill, the eyetallyano, papal zouave to the Holy Father, has left the quay and gone to Moss street. And who was he, tell us? A nobody, two pair back and passages, at seven shillings a week, and he covered with all kinds of breastplates bidding defiance to the world.

-- And moreover, says J. J., a postcard is publication. It was held to be sufficient evidence of malice in the testcase Sadgrove v. Hole. In my opinion an action might lie.

Six and eightpence, please. Who wants your opinion? Let us drink our pints in peace. Gob, we won't be let even do that much itself.

-- Well, good health, Jack says Ned.

-- Good health, Ned, says J. J.

-- There he is again, says Joe.

-- Where? says Alf.

And begob there he was passing the door with his books under his oxter and the wife beside him and Corny Kelleher with his wall eye looking in as they went past, talking to him like a father, trying to sell him a secondhand coffin.

. . . .

[216]

So Bloom lets on he heard nothing and he starts talking with Joe telling him he needn't trouble about that little matter till the first but if he would just say a word to Mr Crawford. And so Joe swore high and holy by this and by that he'd do the devil and all.

-- Because you see, says Bloom, for an advertisement you must have repetition. That's the whole secret.

-- Rely on me, says Joe.

-- Swindling the peasants, says the citizen, and the poor of Ireland. We want no more strangers in our house.

-- O I'm sure that will be all right, Hynes, says Bloom. It's just that Keyes you see.

-- Consider that done, says Joe.

-- Very kind of you, says Bloom.

-- The strangers, says the citizen. Our own fault. We let them come in. We brought them. The adulteress and her paramour brought the Saxon robbers here.

-- Decree *nisi*, says J. J.

And Bloom letting on to be awfully deeply interested in nothing, a spider's web in the corner behind the barrel, and the citizen scowling after him and the old dog at his feet looking up to know who to bite and when.

-- A dishonoured wife, says the citizen, that's what's the cause of all our misfortunes.

-- And here she is, says Alf, that was giggling over the *Police Gazette* with Terry on the counter, in all her warpaint.

-- Give us a squint at her, says I.

And what was it only one of the smutty yankee pictures Terry borrows off of Corny Kelleher. Secrets for enlarging your private parts. Misconduct of society belle. Norman W. Tupper, wealthy Chicago contractor, finds pretty but faithless wife in lap of officer Taylor. Belle in her bloomers misconducting herself and her fancy man feeling for her tickles and Norman W. Tupper bouncing in with his peashooter just in time to be late after she doing the trick of the loop with officer Taylor.

-- O Jakers, Jenny, says Joe, how short your shirt is!

-- There's hair, Joe, says I. Get a queer old tailend of corned beef off of that one, what?

So anyhow in came John Wyse Nolan and Lenehan with him with a face as long as a late breakfast.

-- Well, says the citizen, what's the latest from the scene of action? What did those tinkers in the cityhall at their caucus meeting decide about the Irish language?

O'Nolan, clad in shining armour, low bending made obeisance to the puissant and high and mighty chief of all Erin and did him to wit of that which had befallen, how that the grave elders of the most obedient city, second of the realm, had met them in the tholsel, and there, after due prayers to the gods who dwell in ether supernal, had taken solemn counsel whereby they might, if so be it might be, bring once more into honour among mortal men the winged speech of the sea-divided Gael.

-- It's on the march, says the citizen. To hell with the bloody brutal Sassenachs and their *patois.*

So J. J. puts in a word doing the toff about one story was good till you heard another and blinking facts and the Nelson policy putting your blind eye to the telescope and drawing up a bill of attainder to impeach a nation and Bloom trying to back him up moderation and botheration and their colonies and their civilisation.

-- Their syphilisation, you mean, says the citizen. To hell with them! The curse of a goodfornothing God light sideways on the bloody thicklugged sons of whores' gets! No music and no art and no literature worthy of the name. Any civilisation they have stole from us. Tonguetied sons of bastards' ghosts.

-- The European family, says J. J. . . .

-- They're not European, says the citizen. I was in Europe with Kevin Egan of Paris. You wouldn't see a trace of them or their language anywhere in Europe except in a *cabinet d'aisance.*

And says John Wyse:

-- Full many a flower is born to blush unseen.

And says Lenehan that knows a bit of the lingo:

-- *Conspuez les Anglais! Perfide Albion!*

He said and then lifted he in his rude great brawny strengthy hands the medher of dark strong foamy ale and, uttering his tribal slogan *Lamh Dearg Abu,* he drank to the undoing of his foes, a race of mighty valorous heroes, rulers of the waves, who sit on thrones of alabaster silent as the deathless gods.

-- What's up with you, says I to Lenehan. You look like a fellow that had lost a bob and found a tanner.

-- Gold cup, says he.

-- Who won, Mr Lenehan? says Terry.

[218]

-- *Throwaway,* says he, at twenty to one. A rank outsider.
And the rest nowhere.

-- And Bass's mare? says Terry.

-- Still running, says he. We're all in a cart. Boylan plunged
two quid on my tip *Sceptre* for himself and a lady friend.

-- I had half a crown myself, says Terry, on *Zinfandel* that
Mr Flynn gave me. Lord Howard de Walden's.

-- Twenty to one, says Lenehan. Such is life in an outhouse.
Throwaway, says he. Takes the biscuit and talking about bunions.
Fraility, thy name is *Sceptre.*

-- So he went over to the biscuit tin Bob Doran left to see if
there was anything he could lift on the nod, the old cur after him
backing his luck with his mangy snout up. Old mother Hubbard went
to the cupboard.

-- Not there, my child, says he.

-- Keep your pecker up, says Joe. She'd have won the money
only for the other dog.

And J. J. and the citizen arguing about law and history with
Bloom sticking in an odd word.

-- Some people, says Bloom, can see the mote in other's eyes
but they can't see the beam in their own.

-- *Raimeis,* says the citizen. There's no-one as blind as the
fellow who won't see, if you know what that means. Where are our
missing twenty millions of Irish should be here today instead of four,
our lost tribes?... What do the yellowjohns of Anglia owe us for our
ruined trade and ruined hearths? And the beds of the Barrow and
Shannon they won't deepen with millions of acres of march and bog
to make ua all die of consumption.

-- As treeless as Portugal we'll be soon, says John Wyse, or
Heligoland with its one tree if something is not done to re-afforest
the land. Larches, firs, all the trees of the conifer family are going
fast. I was reading a report of lord Casstletown's . . .

-- Save them, says the citizen, the giant ashof Galway and
the chieftain elm of Kildare with a fortyfoot bole and an acre of
foliage. Save the trees of Ireland for the future men of Ireland on the
fair hills of Eire, O.

-- Europe has its eyes on you, says Lenehan.

. . . .

-- And our eyes are on Europe, says the citizen. We had our
trade with Spain and the French and with the Flemings before those

mongrels were pupped, Spanish ale in Galway, the winebark on the winedark waterway.

-- And will again, says Joe.

-- And with the help of the holy mother of God we will again, says the citizen, clapping his thigh. Our harbours that are empty will be full again, Queenstown, Kinsale, Galway, Blacksod Bay, Ventry in the kingdom of Kerry, Killybegs the third largest harbour in the wide world with a fleet of masts of the Galway Lynches and the Cavan O'Reillys and the O'Kennedys of Dublin when the earl of Desmond could make a treaty with the emperor Charles the Fifth himself. And will again, says he, when the first Irish battleship is seen breasting the waves with our own flag to the fore, none of your Henry Tudor's harps, no, the oldest flag afloat, the flag of the province of Desmond and Thomond, three crowns on a blue field,the three sons of Milesius.

And he took the last swig out of the pint, Moya. All wind and piss like a tanyard cat. Cows in Connacht have long horns. As much as his bloody life is worth to go down and address his tall talk to the assembled multitude in Shanagolden where he daren't show his nose with the Molly Maguires looking for him to let daylight through him for grabbing the holding of an evicted tenant.

-- Hear, hear to that, says John Wyse. What will you have?

-- An imperial yeomanry, says Lenehan, to celebrate the occasion.

-- Half one, Terry, says John Wyse, and a hands up. Terry! Are you asleep?

-- Yes, sir, says Terry. Small whisky and bottle of Allsop. Right sir....

-- But what about the fighting navy, says Ned, that keeps our foes at bay?

-- I'll tell you what about it, says the citizen. Hell upon earth it is. Read the revelations that's going on in the papers about flogging on the training ships at Portsmouth. a fellow writes that calls himself *Disgusted One.*

So he starts telling us about corporal punishment and about the crew of tars and officers and rearadmirals drawn up in cocked hats and the parson with his protestant bible to witness punishment and a young lad brought out, howling for his ma, and they tie him down on the buttend of a gun.

-- A rump and dozen, says the citizen, was what that old
ruffian sir John Beresford called it but the modern God's Englishman
calls it caning on the breech.

And says John Wyse:

-- 'Tis a custom more honoured in the breach than in the
observance.

Then he was telling us the master at arms comes along with
a long cane and he draws out and he flogs the bloody backside off of
the poor lad till he yells meila murder.

-- That's your glorious British navy, says the citizen, that
bosses the earth. The fellows that never will be slaves, with only the
hereditary chamber on the face of God's earth and their land in the
hands of a dozen gamehogs and cottonball barons. That's the great
empire they boast about of drudges and whipped serfs.

-- On which the sun never rises, says Joe.

-- And the tragedy of it is, says the citizen, they believe it.
The unfortunate yahoos believe it.

They believe in the rod, the scourger almighty, creator of
hell upon earth and in Jack Tar, the son of a gun, who was conceived
of unholy boast, born of the fighting navy, suffered under rump and
dozen, was scarified, flayed and curried, yelled like bloody hell, the
third day he rose again from the bed, steered into haven, sitteth on
his beamend till further orders whence he shall come to drudge for a
living and be paid.

-- But, says Bloom, isn't discipline the same everywhere? I
mean wouldn't it be the same here if you put force against force?

-- Didn't I tell you? As true as I'm drinking this porter if he
was at his last gasp he'd try to downface you that dying was living.

-- We'll put force against force, says the citizen. We have
our greater Ireland beyond the sea. They were driven out of house
and home in the black 47. Their mudcabins and their shielings by the
roadside were laid low by the batteringram and the *Times* rubbed its
hands and told the whitelivered Saxons there would soon be as few
Irish in Ireland as redskins in America. Even the grand Turk sent us
his piastres.

But the Sassenach tried to starve the nation at home while
the land was full of crops that the British hyenas bought and sold in
Rio de Janeiro. Ay, they drove out the peasants in hordes. Twenty
thousand of them died in the coffinships. But those that came to the
land of the free remember the land of bondage. And they will come

again and with a venegeance, no cravens, the sons of Granuaile, the champions of Kathleen ni Houlihan.

-- Perfectly true, says Bloom. But my point was . . .

-- We are a long time waiting for that day, citizen, says Ned. Since the poor old woman told us that the French were on the sea and landed at Killala.

-- Ay, says John Wyse. We fought for the royal Stuarts that reneged us against the Williamites and they betrayed us. Remember Limerick and the broken treatystone. We gave our best blood to France and Spain, the wild geese. Fontenoy, eh? And Sarsfield and O'Donnell, duke of Tetuan in Spain, and Ulysses Browne of Camus that was fieldmarshal to Maria Teresa. But what did we ever get for it?

-- The French! says the citizen. Set of dancing masters. Do you know what it is? They were never worth a roasted fart to Ireland. Aren't they trying to make an *Entente cordiale* now at Tay Pay's dinnerparty with perfidious Albion? Firebrands of Europe and they always were.

-- *Conspuez les Français,* says Lenehan. . . .

-- And what do you think, says Joe, of the holy boys, the priests and bishops of Ireland doing up his room in Maynooth in his Satanic Majesty's racing colours and sticking up pictures of all the horses his jockeys rode. The earl of Dublin, no less.

-- They ought to have stuck up all the women he rode himself, says little Alf.

And says J. J.:

-- Considerations of space influenced their lordship's decisions.

-- Will you try another, citizen? says Joe.

-- Yes, sir, says he, I will.

-- You? says Joe.

-- Beholden to you, Joe, says I. May your shadow never grow less.

-- Repeat that dose, says Joe.

Bloom was talking and talking with John Wyse and he quite excited with his dunducketymudcoloured mug on him and his old plumeyes rolling about.

-- Persecution, says he, all the history of the world is full of it. Perpetuating national hatred among nations.

-- But do you know what a nation means? says John Wyse.

-- Yes, says Bloom.

-- What is it? says John Wyse.

-- A nation? says Bloom. A nation is the same people living in the same place.

-- By God, then, says Ned, laughing, if that's so I'm a nation for I'm living in the same place for the past five years.

So of course everyone had a laugh at Bloom and says he, trying to muck out of it:

-- Or also living in different places.

-- That covers my case, says Joe.

-- What is your nation if I may ask, says the citizen.

-- Ireland, says Bloom. I was born here. Ireland.

The citizen said nothing only cleared the spit out of his gullet and, gob, he spat a Red bank oyster out of him right in the corner.

. . . .

-- Shove us over the drink, says I. Which is which?

-- That's mine, says Joe, as the devil said to the dead policeman.

-- And I belong to a race too, says Bloom, that is hated and persecuted. Also now. This very moment. This very instant.

Gob, he near burnt his fingers with the butt of his old cigar.

-- Robbed, say he. Plundered. Insulted. Persecuted. Taking what belongs to us by right. At this very moment, says he, putting up his fist, sold by auction off in Morocco like slaves or cattles.

-- Are you talking about the new Jerusalem? says the citizen.

-- I'm talking about injustice, says Bloom.

-- Right, says John Wyse. Stand up to it then with force like men.

That's an almanac picture for you. Mark for a softnosed bullet. Old lardyface standing up to the business end of a gun. Gob, he'd adorn a sweepingbrush so he would, if he only had a nurse's apron on him. And then he collapses all of a sudden, twisting around all the opposite, as limp as a wet rag.

-- But it's no use, says he. Force, hatred, history, all that. That's not life for men and women, insult and hatred. And everybody knows it's the very opposite of that that is really life.

-- What? says Alf.

-- Love, says Bloom. I mean the opposite of hatred. I must go now, says he to John Wyse. Just round to the court a moment to

see if Martin is there. If he comes just say I'll be back in a second.
Just a moment.

-- Who's hindering you? And off he pops like greased
lightning.

-- A new apostle to the gentiles, says the citizen. Universal
love.

-- Well, says John Wyse, isn't that what we're told? Love
your neighbours.

-- That chap? says the citizen. Beggar my neighbour is his
motto. Love, Moya! He's a nice pattern of a Romeo and Juliet.

Love loves to love love. Nurse loves the new chemist.
Constable 14A loves Mary Kelly. Gerty MacDowell loves the boy
that has the bicycle. M. B. loves a fair gentleman. Li Chi Han lovey
up kissy Cha Pu Chow. Jumbo the elephant, loves Alice, the
elephant. Old Mr Verschoyle with the ear trumpet loves old Mrs
Verescholyle with the turnedin eye. The man in the brown macintosh
loves a lady who is dead. His Majesty the King loves Her Majesty
the Queen. Mrs Norman W. Tupper loves officer Taylor. You love a
person. And this person loves that other person because everybody
loves somebody but God loves everybody.

-- Well, Joe, says I, your very good health and song. More
power, citizen.

-- Hurrah, there, says Joe.

-- The blessing of God and Mary and Patrick on you, says
the citizen.

And he ups with his pint to wet his whistle.

-- We know those canters, says he, preaching and picking
your pocket. What about sanctimonious Cromwell and his ironsides
that put the women and children of Drogheda to the sword with the
bible text *God is love* pasted around the mouth of his cannon? The
bible! Did you read that skit in the *United Irishman* today about that
Zulu chief that's visiting England?

-- What's that? says Joe.

So the citizen takes up on of his paraphernalia papers and he
starts reading out:

...the reverend Ananias Praisegod Barebones, tendered his
best thanks to Massa Walkup and emphasised the cordial relations
existing between Abeakuta and the British Empire, stating that he
treasured as one of his dearest possessions an illuminated bible, the
volume of the word of God and the secret of England's greatness,

[224]

graciously presented to him by the white chief woman, the great squaw Victoria, with personal dedication from the august hand of the Royal Donor. The Alaki then drank a lovingcup of firstshot usquebaugh to the toast *Black and White* from the skull of his immediate predecessor...

-- Widow woman, says Ned, I wouldn't doubt her. Wonder did he put that bible to the same use as I would.

-- Same only more so, says Lenehan. And thereafter in that fruitful land the broadleaved mango flourished exceedingly.

. . . .

-- I know where he's gone, says Lenehan, cracking his fingers.

-- Who? says I.

-- Bloom, says he, the courthouse is a blind. He had a few bob on *Throwaway* and he's gone to gather in the shekels.

-- Is it that whiteyed kaffir? says the citizen, that never backed a horse in anger in his life.

-- That's where he's gone, says Lenehan. I met Bantam Lyons going to back that horse only I put him off it and he told me Bloom gave him the tip. Bet you what you like he has a hundred shillings to five on. He's the only man in Dublin has it. A dark horse.

-- He's a bloody dark horse himself, says Joe.

-- Mind, Joe, say I. Show us the entrance out.

-- There you are, says Terry.

Goodbye Ireland I'm going to Gort. So I just went round to the back of they yard to pumpship and begob (hundred shillings to five) while I was letting off my (*Throwaway* twenty to) letting off my load bob says I to myself I knew he was uneasy in his (two pints off of joe and one in Slattery's off) in his mind to get off the mark to (hundred shillings is five quid) and when they were in the (dark horse) Pisser Burke was telling me card party and letting on the child was sick (gob, must have done about a gallon) flabbyarse of a wife speaking down the tube *she's better* or *she's* (ow!) all a plan so he could vamoose with the pool if he won or (Jesus, full up I was) trading without licence (ow!) Ireland my nation says he (hoik! phthook!) neve be up to those bloody (there's the last of it) Jerusalem (ah!) cuckoos.

So anyhow when I got back they were at it dingdong, John Wyse saying it was Bloom gave the idea for Sinn Fein to Griffith to put in his paper all kinds of jerrymandering, packed juries and swindling the taxes off of the Government and appointing consuls all over the world to walk about selling Irish industries. Robbing Peter to pay Paul. Gob, that puts the bloody kybosh on it if old sloppy eyes is mucking up the show. Give us a bloody chance. God save Ireland from the likes of that bloody mouseabout. Mr Bloom with his argol bargol. And his old fellow before him perpetrating frauds, old Thethusalem Bloom, the robbing gagman, that poisoned himself with the prussic acid after he swamping the country with his baubles and his penny diamonds. Loans by post on easy terms. Any amount of money advanced on note of hand. Distance no object. No security. Gob he's like Lanty MacHale's goat that'd go a piece of the road with everyone.

-- Well, it's a fact, says John Wyse. And there's the man now that'll tell you about it, Martin Cunningham.

Sure enough the castle car drove up with Martin on it and Jack Power with him and a fellow named Crofter or Crofton, pensioner out of the collector general's, an orangeman Blackburn does have on the registration and he drawing his pay or Crawford gallivanting around the country at the king's expense.

. . . .

So in comes Martin asking where was Bloom.

--Where is he? says Lenehan. Defrauding widows and orphans.

-- Isn't that a fact, says John Wyse, what I was telling the citizen about Bloom and Sinn Fein?

-- That's so, says Martin. Or so they allege.

-- Who made those allegations? says Alf.

-- I, says Joe. I'm the alligator.

-- And after all, says John Wyse, why can't a jew love his country like the next fellow?

-- Why not? says J.J., when he's quite sure which country it is.

-- Is he a jew or a gentile or a holy Roman or a swaddler or what the hell is he? says Ned. Or who is he? No offence, Crofton.

-- We don't want him, says Crofter the Orangeman or presbyterian.

-- Who is Junius? says J. J.

-- He's a perverted jew, says Martin, from a place in Hungary and it was he drew up all the plans according to the Hungarian system. We know that in the castle.

[226]

-- Isn't he a cousin of Bloom the dentist? says Jack Power.

-- Not at all, says Martin. Only namesakes. His name was Virag. The father's name that poisoned himself. He changed it by deed poll, the father did.

-- That's the new Messiah for Ireland! says the citizen. Island of saints and sages!

-- Well, they're still waiting for their redeemer, says Martin. For that matter so are we.

-- Yes, says J. J., and every male that's born they think it may be their Messiah. And every jew is in a tall state of excitement, I believe, till he knows if a father or a mother.

-- Expecting every moment will be his next, says Lenehan.

-- O, by God, say Ned, you should have seen Bloom before that son of his that died was born. I met him on eday in the south city markets buying a tin of Neave's food six weeks before the wife was delivered.

-- *En ventre sa mère,* says J. J.

-- Do you call that a man? says the citizen.

-- I wonder did he ever put it out of sight, says Joe.

-- Well, there were two children born anyhow, says Jack Power.

-- And who does he suspect? says the citizen.

Gob, there's many a true word spoken in jest. One of those mixed middlings he is. Lying up in the hotel Pisser was telling me once a month with headache like a totty with her courses. Do you know what I'm telling you? It'd be an act of God to take a hold of a fellow the like of that and throw him in the bloody sea. Justifiable homicide, so it would. Then sloping off with his five quid without putting up a pint of stuff like a man. Give us your blessing. Not as much as would blind your eye.

-- Charity to the neighbour, says Martin. But where is he? We can't wait.

-- A wolf in sheep's clothing, says the citizen. That's what he is. Virag from Hungary! Ahasuerus I call him. Cursed by God.

-- Have you time for a brief libation, Martin? says Ned.

-- Only one, says Martin. We must be quick. J. J. and S.

-- You Jack? Crofton? Three half ones, Terry.

-- Saint Patrick would want to land again at Ballykinlar and convert us, says the citizen, after allowing things like that to contaminate our shores.

-- Well, says Martin, rapping for his glass. God bless all here is my prayer.

-- Amen, says the citizen.

-- And I'm sure he will, says Joe.

And at the sound of the sacring bell, headed by a crucifer with acolytes, thurifers, boatbearers, readers, ostiarii, deacons and subdeacons, the blessed company drew nigh of mitred abbots and priors and guardians and monks and friars...

. . . .

And when the good fathers had reached the appointed place, the house of Bernard Kiernan and Co, limited, 8, 9 and 10 little Britain street, wholesale grocers, wine and brandy shippers, licensed for the sale of beer, wine and spirits for consumption on the premises, the celebrant blessed the house and censed the mullioned windows and the groynes and the vaults and the arrises and the capitals and the pediments and the cornices and the engrailed arches and the spires and the cupolas and sprinkled the lintels thereof with blessed water and prayed that God might bless that house as he blessed the house of Abraham and Isaac and Jacob and make the angels of His light to inhabit therein. And entering he blessed the viands and the beverages and the company of all the blessed answered his prayers.

-- *Adiutorium nostrum in nomine Domini.*

-- *Que fecit coelum and terram.*

-- *Dominus vobiscum.*

-- *Et cum spiritu tuo.*

And he laid his hands upon the blessed and gave thanks and he prayed and they all with him prayed: . . .

-- And so say all of us, says Jack.

-- Thousand a year, Lambert says Crofton or Crawford.

-- Right, says Ned, taking up his John Jameson. And butter for the fish.

I was just looking round to see who the happy thought would strike when be damned but in he comes again letting on to be in a hell of a hurry.

-- I was just round at the courthouse, says he, looking for you. I hope I'm not . . .

-- No, says Martin, we're ready.

Courthouse my eye and your pockets hanging down with gold and silver. Mean bloody scut. Stand us a drink itself. Devil for a

[228]

sweet fear! There's a jew for you! All for number one. Cute as a shithouse rat. Hundred to five.

-- Don't tell anyone, says the citizen.

-- Beg your pardon, says he.

-- Come on boys, says Martin, seeing it was looking blue. Come along now.

-- Don't tell anyone, says the citizen, letting a bawl out of him. It's a secret.

And the bloody dog woke up and let a growl.

-- Bye bye all, says Martin.

And he got them out as quick as he could, Jack Power and Crofton or whatever you call him and him in the middle of them letting on to be all at sea up with them on the bloody jaunting car.

Off with you, says Martin to the jarvey.

The milkwhite dolphin tossed his mane and, rising in the golden poop, the helmsman spread the bellying sail upon the wind and stood off forward with all sail set, the spinnaker to larboard and, clinging to the sides of the noble bark, they linked their shining forms as doth the cunning wheelwright when he fashions about the heart of his wheel the equidistant rays whereof each one is sister to another and he binds them all with an outer ring and giveth speed to the feet of men whenas they ride to a hosting or contend for the smile of ladies fair. Even so did they come and set them, those willing nymphs, the undying sisters. And they laughed, sporting in a circle of their foam: and the bark clave the waves.

But begob I was just lowering the heel of the pint when I saw the citizen getting up to waddle to the door, puffing and blowing with the dropsy and he cursing the curse of Cromwell on him, bell, book and candle in Irish, spitting and spatting out of him and Joe and little Alf round him like a leprechaun trying to peacify him.

-- Let me alone, says he.

And begob he got as far as the door and they holding him and he bawls out of him:

-- Three cheers for Israel!

Arrah, sit down on the parliamentary side of your arse for Christ's sake and don't be making a public exhibition of yourself. Jesus, there's always some bloody clown or other kicking up a bloody murder about bloody nothing. Gob, it'd turn the porter sour in your guts, so it would.

[229]

And all the ragamuffins and sluts of the nation round the
door and Martin telling the jarvey to drive ahead and the citizen
bawling and Alf and Joe at him to whisht and he on his high horse
about the jews and the loafers calling for a speech and Jack Power
trying to get him to sit down on the car and hold his bloody jaw and
a loafer with a patch over his eye starts singing *If the man in the
moon was a jew, jew, jew* and a slut shouts out of her:

-- Eh, mister! Your fly is open, mister!

-- And says he:

-- Mendelssohn was a jew and Karl Marx and Mercadante
and Spinoza. And the Saviour was a jew and his father was a jew.
Your God.

-- He had no father, says Martin. That'll do now. Drive
ahead.

-- Whose God? says the citizen.

-- Well, his uncle was a jew, says he. Your God was a jew.
Christ was a jew like me.

Gob, the citizen made a plunge back into the shop.

-- By Jesus, says he, I'll brain that bloody jewman for using
the holy name. By Jesus, I'll crucify him so I will. Give us that
biscuitbox here.

-- Stop! Stop! says Joe.

. . . .

Gob, the devil wouldn't stop him till he got hold of the
bloody tin anyhow and out with him and little Alf hanging on to his
elbow and he shouting like a stuck pig, as good as any bloody play in
the Queen's royal theatre.

-- Where is he till I murder him?

And Ned and J. G. paralysed with the laughing.

-- Bloody wars, says I, I'll be in for the last gospel.

But as luck would have it the jarvey got the nag's head
round the other way and off with him.

-- Hold on, citizen, says Joe. Stop.

Begob he drew his hand and made a swipe and let it fly.
Mercy of God the sun was in his eyes or he'd have left him for dead.
Gob, he near sent it into the county Longford. The bloody nag took
fright and the old mongrel after the car like bloody hell and all the
populace shouting and laughing and the old tinbox clattering along
the street.

. . . .

[230]

You never saw the like of it in all your born puff. Gob, if he got that lottery ticket on the side of his poll he'd remember the gold cup, he would so, but begob the citizen would have been lagged for assault and battery and Joe or aiding and abetting. The jarvey saved his life by furious driving as sure as God made Moses. What? O, Jesus, he did. And he let a volley of oaths after him.

-- Did I kill him, says he, or what?

And he shouting to the bloody dog:

-- After him, Garry! After him, boy!

And the last we saw was the bloody car rounding the corner and old sheepface on it gesticulating and the bloody mongrel after it with his lugs back for all he was bloody well worth to tear him limb from limb. Hundred to five! Jesus, he took the value of it out of him, I promise you.

When lo, there came about them all a great brightness and they beheld the chariot wherein He stood ascend to heaven. And they beheld Him in the chariot, clothed upon in the glory of the brightness, having raiment as of the sun, fair as the moon and terrible that for awe they durst not look upon Him. And there came a voice out of heaven, calling: *Elijah! Elijah!* And he answered with a main cry: *Abba! Adonai!* And they beheld Him even Him, ben Bloom Elijah, amid clouds of angels ascend to the glory of brightness at an angle of fortyfive degrees over Donohoe's in Little Green Street like a shot off a shovel.

Episode 13 – Nausicaa... a princess of Phaecia comes upon a naked Odysseus washed ashore after a shipwreck and swimming for two days. Odysseus, magically glamorized by the gods, is seen by Nausicaa, a young and resourceful woman, as someone to marry. She ushered Odysseus to her father's palace to receive the king's aid, where he is royally entertained. Learning he wants to return home, they furnish his continuing voyage. ~ On the beach at Sandymount Strand, Bloom and Gerty MacDowell find deep mutual attraction and in each other's nearby presence, enjoy entertainment, fantasy, and sexual pleasure beneath royal fireworks.

Around 8pm Bloom, seeking relief after the Kiernan's pub encounter with the citizen et al and after visiting the bereaved Dignam home, walks to Sandymount Strand. He fixates on Gerty MacDowell, young, attractive, and fantasizing a new romance, whose two friends with little brothers play on the beach. Sensing Bloom's attention, Gerty arouses him with the tantalizing display of her undergarments, exciting him to masturbate in his pants as fireworks explode above the bay. Observing her limp away, Bloom feels sympathetic to her and similarly to women. Bloom ruminates on persons, scenes and the status of his life; drawing letters in the sand expressive of some deeper thought.

THEMES

The arc, the rising and falling of emotions and objects. Comparisons to the Blessed Mary, Refuge of Sinners. The hidden side of Irish womanhood and their repressed passions. The commingling of sex and religion. A clutch of contradictions in the good and the bad persuasions and actions of individuals.

THE SUMMER EVENING HAD BEGUN TO FOLD THE WORLD IN ITS mysterious embrace. Far away in the west the sun was setting and the last glow of all too fleeting day lingered lovingly on sea and strand, on the proud promontory of dear old Howth guarding as ever the waters of the bay, on the weedgrown rocks along Sandymount shore and, last but not the least, on the quiet church whence there streamed forth at times upon the stillness the voice of prayers to her who is in her pure radiance a beacon ever to the storm-tossed heart of man, Mary, star of the sea.

The three girl friends were seated on the rocks, enjoying the evening scene and the air which was fresh but not too chilly. Many a time and oft were they wont to come there to that favourite nook to have a cosy chat beside the sparkling waves and discuss matters feminine, Cissy Caffrey and Edy Boardman with the baby in the pushcar and Tommy and Jacky Caffrey, two little curlyheaded boys, dressed in sailor suits with caps to match and the name H.M.S. Belleisle printed on both. For Tommy and Jacky Chaffrey were twins, scarce four years old and very noisy and spoiled twins sometimes but endearing ways about them. They were dabbling in the sand with their spades and buckets, building castles as children do, or playing with their big coloured ball happy as the day was long,

[232]

And Edy Boardman was rocking the chubby baby to and fro in the pushcar while that young gentleman fairly chuckled with delight. He was but eleven months and nine days old and, though still a tiny toddler, was just beginning to lips his first babyish words. Cissy Caffrey bent over him to tease his fat little plucks and the dainty dimple in his chin.

-- Now, baby, Cissy Caffrey said. Say out big, big. I want a drink of water.

And baby prattled after her:

-- A jink a jink of jawbo.

. . . .

Gerty MacDowell who was seated near her companions, lost in thought, gazing far away into the distance, was in very truth as fair a specimen of winsome Irish girlhood as one would wish to see. She was pronounced beautiful by all who knew her though, as folks often said, she was more a Giltrap than a MacDowell. Her figure was slight and graceful, inclining even to fragility but those iron jelloids she had been taking of late had done her a world of good much better than the Widow Welch's female pills and she was much better of those discharges she used to get and that tired feeling. The waxen pallor of her face was almost spiritual in its ivorylike purity though her rosebud mouth was a genuine Cupid's bow, Greekly perfect.... There was an innate refinement, a languid queenly *hauteur* about Gerty which was unmistakably evidenced in her delicate hands and higharched instep. Had kind fate but willed her to be born a gentlewoman of high degree in her own right and had she only received the benefit of a good education Gerty MacDowell might easily have held her own beside any lady in the land and have seen herself exquisitely gowned with jewels on her brow and patrician suitors at her feet vying with one another to pay their devoirs to her. Mayhap it was this, the love that might have been, that lent tro her softlyfeatured face at whiles a look, tense with suppressed meaning that imparted a strange yearning tendency to the beautiful eyes a charm few could resist. Why have women such eyes of witchery? Gerty's were of the bluest Irish blue, set off by lustrous lashes and dark expressive brows... But Gerty's crowning glory was her wealth of wonderful hair. It was dark brown with a natural wave in it. She had cut it that very morning on account of the new moon and it nestled about her pretty head in a profusion of luxuriant clusters and pared her nails too, Thursday for wealth. And just now at Edy's words as a telltale flush, delicate as the faintest rosebloom, crept into her cheeks she looked so lovely in her sweet girlish shyness that of a surety God's fair land of Ireland did not hold equal.

For an instant she was silent with rather sad downcast eyes. She was about to retort but something checked the words on her tongue. Inclination prompted her to speak out: dignity told her to be silent. The pretty lips pouted a while but then she glanced up and broke out into a joyous little laugh which had in it all the freshness of a young May morning. She knew right well, no-one better, what made squinty Edy say that because of him cooling on his attentions when it was simply a lovers' quarrel. As per usual somebody's nose was out of joint about the boy that had the bicycle always riding up and down in front of her window. Only now his father kept him in the evenings studying hard to get an exhibition in the intermediate that was on and he was going to Trinity college to study for a doctor when he left the high school like his brother W. E. Wylie who was racing in the bicycle races in Trinity college university. Little recked he perhaps for what she felt, that dull aching void in her heart sometimes, piercing to the core. Yet he was young and perchance he might learn to love her in time. They were protestants in his family and of course Gerty knew Who came first and after Him the blessed Virgin and then Saint Joseph. But he was undeniably handsome with an exquisite nose and he was what he looked every inch a gentleman, the shape of his head too at the back without his cap on that she would know anywhere something off the common and the way he turned the bicycle at the lamp with his hands off the bars and also the nice perfume of those good cigarettes and besides they were both of a size and that was why Edy Boardman thought she was so frightfully clever because he didn't go and ride up and down in front of her bit of a garden.

Gerty was dressed simply but with the instinctive taste of a votary of Dame Fashion for she felt that there was just a might that he might be out. A neat blouse of electric blue, selftinted by dolly dyes (because it was expected in the *Lady's Pictorial* that electric blue would be worn), with a smart vee opening down to the division and kerchief pocket (in which she always kept a piece of cottonwood scented with her favourite perfume because the handkerchief spoiled the sit) and a navy threequarter skirt cut to the stride showed off her slim graceful figure to perfection. She wore a coquettish little love of a hat of wideleaved nigger straw contrast trimmed with an underbrim

[234]

of eggblue chenille and at the side a butterfly bow to tone…. Her wellturned ankle displayed its perfect proportions beneath her skirt and just the proper amount and no more of her shapely limbs encased in finespun hose with high spliced heels and wide garter tops. As for undies they were Gerty's chief care and who that knows the fluttering hopes and fears of sweet seventeen (thought Gerty would never see seventeen again) can find it in his heart to blame her? She had four dinky sets, with awfully pretty stitchery, three garments and nighties extra, and each set slotted with different coloured ribbons, rosepink, pale blue, mauve, and peagreen and she aired them herself and blued them when they came home from the wash and ironed them and she had a brickbat to keep the iron on because she wouldn't trust those washerwomen as far as she'd see them scorching the things. She was wearing the blue for luck, hoping against hope, her own colour and the lucky colour too for a bride to have a bit of blue somewhere on her …

And yet and yet! That strained look on her face! A gnawing sorrow is there all the time. Her very soul is in her eyes and she would give worlds to be in the privacy of her own familiar chamber where, giving way to tears, she could have a good cry and relieve her pentup feelings. Though not too much because she knew how to cry nicely before the mirror. You are lovely, Gerty, it said. The paly light of evening falls upon a face infinitely sad and wistful. Gerty MacDowell yearns in vain. Yes, she had known from the first that her daydream of a marriage has been arranged and the weddingbells ringing for Mrs Reggy Wilie T. C. D. (because the one who married the elder brother would be Mrs Wylie) and in the fashionable intelligence Mrs Gertrude Wylie was wearing a sumptuous confection of grey trimmed with expensive blue fox was not to be. He was too young to understand. He would not believe in love, a woman's birthright… he who would woo and win Gerty MacDowell must be a man among men. But waiting, always waiting to be asked and it was leap year too and would soon be over. No prince charming is her beau ideal to lay a rare and wondrous love at her feet but rather a manly man with a strong quiet face who had not found his ideal, perhaps his hair slightly flecked with grey, and who would understand, take her in his sheltering arms, strain her to him in all the strength of his deep passionate nature and comfort her with a long long kiss. It would be like heaven. For such a one she yearns this balmy summer eve. With all the heart of her she longs to be his only, his affianced bride for riches for poor, in sickness in health, till death us two part, from this day to this day forward.

. . . .

And then there came out upon the air the sound of voices and the pealing anthem of the organ. It was the men's temperance retreat conducted by the missioner, the reverend John Hughes S. J., rosary, sermon and benediction of the Most Blessed Sacrament. They were gathered together without distinction of social class (and a most edifying spectacle it was to see) in that simple fane beside the waves, after the storms of this weary world, kneeling before the feet of the immaculate, reciting the litany of Our Lady of Loreto, beseeching her to intercede for them, the old familiar words, holy Mary, holy virgin of virgins. How sad to poor Gerty's ears! Had her father only avoided the clutches of the demon drink, by taking the pledge or those powders the drink habit cured in Pearson's Weekly, she might now be rolling in her carriage, second to none. Over and over had she told herself that as she mused by the dying embers in a brown study without the lamp because she hated two lights or oftentimes gazing out of the window dreamily by the hour at the rain falling on the rusty bucket, thinking. But that vile decoction which has ruined so many hearths and homes had cast its shadow over her childhood days. Nay, she had even witnessed in the home circle deeds of violence caused by intemperance and had seen her own father, a prey to the fumes of intoxication, forget himself completely for if there was one thing of all things that Gerty knew it was the man who lifts his hand to a woman save in the way of kindness deserves to be branded as the lowest of the low.

And still the voices sang in supplication to the Virgin most powerful, Virgin most merciful. And Gerty, wrapt in thought, scarce saw or heard her companions or the twins at their boyish gambols or the gentleman off Sandymount green that Cissy Caffrey called the man that was so like himself passing along the strand taking a short walk....

A sterling good daughter was Gerty just like a second mother in the house, a ministering angel too with a little heart worth its weight in gold. And when her mother had those raging splitting headaches who was it rubbed on the menthol cone on her forehead but Gerty though she didn't like her mother taking pinches of snuff and that was the only single thing they ever had words about, taking snuff. Everyone thought the world of her for her gentle ways. It was

[236]

Gerty who tacked up on the wall of that place where she never forgot every fortnight the chlorate of lime Mr Tunney the grocer's christmas almanac the picture of halcyon days where a young gentleman in the costume they used to wear then with a three-cornered hat was offering a bunch of flowers to his ladylove with oldtime chivalry through her lattice window. You could see there was a story behind it....

The twins were now playing in the most approved brotherly fashion, till at last Master Jacky who was really as bold as brass there was no getting behind that deliberately kicked the ball as hard as ever he could down towards the seaweedy rocks. Needless to say poor Tommy was not slow to voice his dismay but luckily the gentleman in black who was sitting there by himself came gallantly to the rescue and intercepted the ball. Our two champions claimed their plaything with lusty cries and to avoid trouble Cissy Caffrey called to the gentleman to throw it to her please. The gentleman aimed the ball once or twice and then threw it up the strand towards Cissy Caffrey but it rolled down the slope and stopped right under Gerty's skirt near the little pool by the rock. The twins clamoured again for it and Cissy told her to kick it away and let them fight for it so Gerty drew back her foot but she wished their stupid ball hadn't come rolling down to her and she gave a kick but she missed and Edy and Cissy laughed.

-- If you fail try again, Edy Boardman said.

Gerty smiled assent and bit her lip. A delicate pink crept into her pretty cheek but she was determined to let them see so she just lifted her skirt a little but just enough and took good aim and gave the ball a jolly good kick and it went ever so far and the two twins after it down towards the shingle. Pure jealousy of course it was nothing to draw attention on account of the gentleman opposite looking. She felt the warm flush, a danger signal always with Gerty MacDowell, surging and flaming into her cheeks. Till then they had only exchanged glances of the most casual but now under the brim of her new hat she ventured a look at him and the face that met her gaze there in the twilight, wan and strangely drawn, seemed to her the saddest she had ever seen.

Through the open window of the church the fragrant incense was wafted and with it the fragrant names of her who was conceived without stain of original sin, spiritual vessel, pray for us, honourable vessel, pray for us, vessel of singular devotion, pray for us, mystical rose. And careworn hearts were there and toilers for their daily bread and many who had erred and wandered, their eyes wet with contrition but for all that bright with hope for the reverend father Hughes had told them what the great saint Bernard said in his famous prayer of Mary, the most pious Virgin's intercessory power that it was not recorded in any age that those who implored her powerful protection were ever abandoned by her.

Gerty wished to goodness they would take their squalling baby home out of that and not get on her nerves no hour to be out and the little brats of twins. She gazed out towards the distant sea. It was like the paintings that man used to do on the pavement with all the coloured chalks and such a pity too leaving them there to be all blotted out, the evening and the clouds coming out and the Bailey light on Howth and to hear the music like that and the perfume of those incense they burned in the church like a kind of waft. And while she gazed her heart went pitapat. Yes, it was her he was looking at and here was meaning in his look. His eyes burned into her as though they would search her through and through read her very soul. Wonderful eyes they were, superbly expressive, but could you trust them? People were so queer. She could see at once by his dark eyes and his pale intellectual face that he was a foreigner, the image of the photo she had of Martin Harvey, the matinee idol, only for the moustache which she preferred because she wasn't stagestruck like Winny Rippingham that wanted they two to always dress the same on account of a play but she could not see whether he had an aquiline nose or a slightly *retrousse'* from where he was sitting. He was in deep mourning, she could see that, and the story of a haunting sorrow was written on his face. She would have given worlds to know what it was. He was looking up so intently, so still and he saw her kick the ball and perhaps he could see the bright steel buckles of her shoes if she swung them like that thoughtfully with the toes down. She was glad that something told her to put on the transparent stockings thinking Reggy Wylie might be out but that was far away. Here was that of which she had so often dreamed. It was he who mattered and there was joy on her face because she wanted him because she felt instinctively that he was like no-one else. The very heart of the girlwoman went out to him, her dreamhusband, because she knew on the instant it was him. If he had suffered, more sinned against than sinning, or even, even, if he had been himself a sinner, a wicked man, she cared not. Even if he was a

[238]

protestant or methodist she could convert him easily if he truly loved
her. There were wounds that wanted healing with heartbalm. She
was a womanly woman not like other flighty girls, unfeminine, he
had known, those cyclists showing off what they hadn't got and she
just yearned to know all, to forgive all if she could make him fall in
love with her, make him forget the memory of the past. Then
mayhap he would embrace her gently, like a real man, crushing her
soft body to him, and love her, his ownest girlie, for her alone.

Refuge of sinners. Comfortress of the afflicted. *Ora pro
nobis.* Well has it been said that whosoever prays to her with faith
and constancy can never be lost or cast away: and fitly is she too a
haven of refuge for the afflicted because of the seven dolours which
transpierced her own heart. Gerty could picture the whole scene in
the church, the stained glass windows lighted up, the candles, the
flowers and the blue banners of the blessed Virgin's sodality and
Father Conroy was helping Canon O'Hanlon at the altar, carrying
things in and out with his eyes cast down. He looked almost a saint
and his confessional box was so quiet and clean and dark and his
hands were just like white wax and if ever she became a Dominican
nun in their white habit perhaps he might come to the convent for the
novena of Saint Dominic. He told her that time when she told him
about that in confession crimsoning up to the roots of her hair for fer
he could see, not to be troubled because that was only the voice of
nature and we were all subject to nature's laws, he said, in this life
and that that was no sin because that came from the nature of woman
instituted by God, he said, and that Our Blessed Lady herself said to
the archangel Gabriel be it done unto me according to Thy Word.
. . . .

Queen of angels, queen of patriarchs, queen of prophets, of
all saints, they prayed, queen of the most holy rosary and then Father
Conroy handed the thurible to Canon O'Hanlon and he put in the
incense and censed the Blessed Sacrament and Cissy Caffrey caught
the two twins and she was itching to give them a good clip on the ear
but she didn't because she thought he might be watching but she
never made a bigger mistake in all her life because Gerty could see
without looking that he never took his eyes off of her and then Canon
O'Hanlon handed the thurible back to Father Conroy and knelt down
looking up at the Blessed Sacrament and the choir began to sing
Tantum ergo and she just swung her foot in and out in time as the
music rose and fell to the *Tantumer gosa cramen tum.* Three and

eleven she paid for those stockings in Sparrow's of George's street on the Tuesday, no the Monday before Easter and there wasn't a brack on them and that was what he was looking at, transparent, and not at her insignificant ones that had neither shape nor form (the cheek of her!) because he had eyes in his head to see the difference for himself....

Gerty just took off her hat for a moment to settle her hair and a prettier, daintier head of nutbrown tresses was never seen on a girl's shoulders, a radiant little vision, in sooth, almost maddening in its sweetness. You would have to travel many a long mile before you found a head of hair the like of that. She could almost see the swift answering flush of admiration in his eyes that set her tingling in every nerve. She put on her hat so that she could see from underneath the brim and swung her buckled shoe faster for her breath caught as she caught the expression in his eyes. He was eyeing her as a snake eyes its prey. Her woman's instinct told her that she had raised the devil in him and at the thought a burning scarlet swept from throat to brow till the lovely colour of her face became a glorious rose.

Edy Boardman was noticing it too because she was squinting at Gerty, half smiling, with her specs, like an old maid, pretending to nurse the baby. Irritable little gnat she was and always would be and that was why no-one could get on with her, poking her nose into what was no concern of hers. And she said to Gerty:

-- A penny for your thoughts.

-- What? replied Gerty with a smile reinforced by the whitest of teeth. I was only wondering was it late.

Because she wished to goodness they'd take the snottynosed twins and their baby home to the mischief out of that so that was why she just gave a gentle hint about its being late. And when Cissy came up Edy asked her the time and Miss Cissy, as glib as you like, said it was half past kissing time, time to kiss again. But Edy wanted to know because they were told to be in early.

-- Wait, said Cissy, I'll ask my uncle Peter over there what's the time by his conundrum.

So over she went and when he saw her coming she could see him take his hand out of his pocket, getting nervous, and beginning to play with his watchchain, looking at the church. Passionate nature though he was Gerty could see that he had enormous control over himself. One moment he had been there, fascinated by a loveliness

that made him gaze, and the next moment it was the quiet gravefaced
gentleman, selfcontrol expressed in every line of his
distinguishedlooking figure.

Cissy said to excuse her would he mind telling her what was
the right time and Gerty could see him taking out his watch, listening
to it and looking up and clearing his throat and he said he was very
sorry his watch stopped but he thought it must be after eight because
the sun was set. His voice had a cultured ring in it and though he
spoke in measured accents there was a suspicion of a quiver in the
mellow tones. Cissy said thanks and came back with her tongue out
and said uncle said his waterworks were out of order.

Then they sang the second verse of the *Tantum ergo* and
Canon O'Hanlon got up again and censed the Blessed Sacrament and
knelt down and he told Father Conroy that one of the candles was
just going to set fire to the flowers and Father Conroy got up and
settled it all right and she could see the gentleman winding his watch
and listening to the works and she swung her leg more in and out of
time. It was getting darker but he could see and he was looking all
the time that he was winding the watch or whatever he was doing to
it and then he put it back and put his hands back into his pockets. She
felt a kind of sensation rushing all over her and she knew by the feel
of her scalp and that irritation against her stays that that thing must
be coming on because the last time too was when she clipped her
hair on account of the moon. His dark eyes fixed themselves on her
again drinking in her every contour, literally worshipping at her
shrine. If ever there was undisguised admiration in a man's
passionate gaze it was there plain to be seen on that man's face. It is
for you, Gertrude MacDowell, and you know it.

. . . .

How moving the scene there in the gathering twilight, the
last glimpse of Erin, the touching chime of those evening bells and at
the same time a bat flew forth from the ivied belfry through the dusk,
hither, thither, with a tiny lost cry. And she could see far away the
lights of the lighthouses so picturesque she would have loved to do
with a box of paints because it was easier than to make a man and
soon the lamplighter would be along by shady Tritonville avenue
where the couples walked and lighting the lamp near her window
where Reggie Wylie used to turn his freewheel like she read in that
book *The Lamplighter* by Miss Cummins, author of *Mabel Vaughan*
and other tales. For Gerty had her dreams that no-one knew of. She

[241]

loved to read poetry and when she got a keepsake from Bertha Supple of that lovely confession album with the coralpink cover to write her thoughts in she laid it in the drawer of her toilettable which, though it did not err on the side of luxury, was scrupulously neat and clean. It was there she kept her girlish treasures trove, the tortoiseshell combs, her child of Mary badge, the whiterose scent, the eyebrowleine, her alabaster pouncetbox and the ribbons to change when her things came home from the wash and there were some beautiful thoughts written in it in violet ink that she bought in Hely's of Dame Street for she felt that she too could write poetry if she could only express herself like that poem that appealed to her so deeply that she had copied out of the newspaper she found one evening round the potherbs. *Art thou real, my ideal?* it was called by Louis J. Walsh, Magherafelt, and after there was something about *twilight, wilt thou ever?* and ofttimes the beauty of poetry, so sad in its transient loveliness, had misted her eyes with silent tears that the years were slipping by for her, one by one, and but for that one shortcoming she knew she need fear no competition and that was an accident coming down Dalkey hill and she always tried to conceal it. But it must end she felt. If she saw that magic lure in his eyes there would be no holding back for her. Love laughs at locksmiths. She would make the great sacrifice. Her every effort would be to share his thoughts. Dearer than the whole world would she be to him and gild his days with happiness. There was the allimportant question and she was dying to know was he a married man or a widower who had lost his wife or some tragedy like the nobleman with the foreign name from the land of song had to have her put into a madhouse, cruel only to be kind. But even if -- what then? Would it make a very great difference? From everything in the least indelicate her finebred nature instinctively recoiled. She loathed that sort of person, the fallen women off the accommodation walk beside the Dodder that went with the soldiers and coarse men, with no respect for a girl's honour, degrading the sex and being taken up to the police station. No, no: not that. They would be just good friends like a big brother and sister without all that other in spite of the conventions of Society with a big ess. Perhaps it was an old flame he was in mourning for from the days beyond recall. She thought she understood. She would try to understand him because men were so different. The old love was waiting, waiting with little white hands stretched out, with blue appealing eyes. Heart of mine! She would follow her dream of love,

[242]

the dictates of her heart that told her he was her all in all, the only man in all the world for her for love was the master guide. Nothing else mattered. Come what might she would be wild, untrammelled, free.

Canon O'Hanlon put the Blessed Sacrament back into the tabernacle and the choir sang *Laudate Dominum omnes gentes* and then he locked the tabernacle door because the benediction was over and Father Conroy handed him his hat to put on and crosscat Edy asked wasn't she coming but Jacky Caffrey called out:

-- O, look, Cissy!

And they all looked was it sheet lightning but Tommy saw it too over the trees beside the church, blue and then green and purple.

-- It's fireworks, Cissy Caffrey said.

And they all ran down the strand to see over the houses and the church, helterskelter, Edy with the pushcar with baby Boardman in it and Cissy holding Tommy and Jacky by the hand so they wouldn't fall running.

-- Come on, Gerty, Cissy called. It's the bazaar fireworks.

But Gerty was adamant. She had no intention of being at their beck and call. If they could run like rossies she could sit so she could see from where she was. The eyes that were fastened upon her set her pulses tingling. She looked at him a moment, meeting his glance, and a light broke in upon her. Whitehot passion was in that face, passion silent as the grave, and it had made her his. At last they were left alone without the others to pry and pass remarks and she knew he could be trusted to the death, steadfast, a sterling man, a man of inflexible honour to his fingertips. His hands and face were working and a tremor went over her. She leaned back far to look up where the fireworks were and she caught her knee in her hands so as not to fall back looking up and there was no one to see only him and her when she revealed all her graceful beautifully shaped legs like that, supply soft and delicately rounded, and she seemed to hear the panting of his heart, his hoarse breathing, because she knew about the passion of men like that, hot-blooded, because Bertha Supple told her once in a dead secret and made her swear she'd never about the gentleman lodger that was staying with them out of the Congested Districts Board that had pictures cut out of papers of those skirtdancers and highkickers and she said he used to do something not very nice that you could imagine sometimes in the bed. But this was altogether different from a thing like that because there was all the difference because she could almost feel him draw her face to his and the first quick hot touch of his handsome lips. Besides there was absolution so long as you didn't do the other thing before being married and there ought to be women priests that would understand without your telling out and Cissy Caffrey too sometimes had that dreamy kind of dreamy look in her eyes so that she too, my dear, and Winny Rippingham so mad about actors' photographs and besides it was on account of that other thing coming on the way it did.

And Jacky Caffrey shouted to look, there was another and she leaned back and the garters were blue to match on account of the transparent and they all saw it and shouted to look, look there it was and she leaned back ever so far to see the fireworks and something queer was flying about through the air, a soft thing to and fro, dark. And she saw a long Roman candle going up over the trees up, up, and, in the tense hush, they were all breathless with excitement as it went higher and higher and she had to lean back more and more to look up after it, high, high, almost out of sight, and her face was suffused with a divine, an entrancing blush from straining back and he could see her other things too, nainsook knickers, the fabric that caresses the skin, better than those other pettiwidth, the green, four, and eleven, on account of being white and she let him and she saw that he saw and then it went so high it went out of sight a moment and she was trembling in every limb from being bent so far back he had a full view high up above her knee on-one ever not even on the swing or wading and she wasn't ashamed and he wasn't either to look in that immodest way like that because he couldn't resist the sight of the wondrous revealment half offered like those skirtdancers behaving so immodest before gentlemen looking and he kept on looking, looking. She would fain have cried to him chokingly, held out her snowy slender arms to him to come, to feel his lips laid on her white brow the cry of a young girl's love, a little strangled cry, wrung from her, that cry that has rung through the ages. And then a rocket sprang and bang shot blind and O! then the Roman candle burst and it was like a sigh of O! and everyone cried O! O! in raptures and it gushed out of it a stream of rain gold hair threads and they shed and ah! they were all greeny dewy stars falling with golden, O so lively! O so soft, sweet, soft!

Then all melted away dewily in the grey air: all was silent. Ah! She glanced at him as she bent forward quickly, a pathetic little glance of piteous protest, of shy reproach under which he coloured

[244]

like a girl. He was leaning back against the rock behind. Leopold
Bloom (for it is he) stands silent, with bowed head before those
young guileless eyes. What a brute he had been! At it again? A fair
unsullied soul had called to him and, wretch that he was, how had he
answered? An utter cad he had been. He of all men! But there was an
infinite store of mercy in those eyes, for him too a word of pardon
even though he had erred and sinned and wandered. She a girl tell?
No, a thousand times no. That was their secret, only theirs, alone in
the hiding twilight and there was none to know or tell save the little
bat that flew so softly through the evening to and fro and little bats
don't tell.

Cissy Caffrey whistled, imitating the boys in the football
field to show what a great person she was: and then she cried:

-- Gerty! Gerty! We're going. Come on. We can see further
up.

Gerty had an idea, one of love's little ruses. She slipped a
hand into her kerchief pocket and took out the wadding and waved in
reply of course without letting him and then slipped it back. Wonder
if he's too far to. She rose. Was it goodbye? No. She had to go but
they would meet again, there, and she would dream of that till then,
tomorrow, of her dream of yester eve. She drew herself up to her full
height. Their souls met in a last lingering glance and the eyes that
reached her heart, full of a strange shining, hung enraptured on her
sweet flowerlike face. She half smiled at him wanly, a sweet
forgiving smile, a smile that verged on tears, and then they parted.

Slowly without looking back she went down the uneven
strand to Cissy, to Edy, to Jacky and Tommy Caffrey, to baby
Boardman. It was darker now and there were stones and bits of wood
on the strand and slippy seaweed. She walked with a certain quiet
dignity characteristic of her but with care and very slowly because
Gerty MacDowell was . . .

Tight boots? No. She's lame! O!

Mr Bloom watched her as she limped away. Poor girl! That's
why she's left on the shelf and the others did a sprint. Thought
something was wrong by the cut of her jib. Jilted beauty. A defect is
ten times worse in a woman. But makes them polite. Glad I didn't
know it when she was on show. Hot little devil all the same.
Wouldn't mind. Curiosity like a nun or a negress or a girl with
glasses. That squinty one is delicate. Near her monthlies, I expect,
makes them feel ticklish. I have such a bad headache today. Where

did I put the letter? Yes, all right. all kinds of crazy longings. Licking
pennies. Girl in Tranquilla convent that nun told me liked to smell
rock oil. Virgins go mad in the end I suppose. Sister? How many
women in Dublin have it today? Martha, she. Something in the air.
That's the moon. But then why don't all women menstruate at the
same time with the same moon, I mean? Depends on the time they
were born, I suppose. Or all start scratch then get out of step.
Sometimes Molly and Milly together. Anyhow I got the best of that.
Damned glad I didn't do it in the bath this morning over her silly I
will punish you letter.

. . . .

Didn't let her see me in profile. Still, you never know. Still, you
never know. Pretty girls and ugly men marrying. Beauty and the
beast. Besides I can't be so if Molly. Took off her hat to show her
hair. Wide brim bought to hide her face, meeting someone might
know her, bend down or carry a bunch of flowers to smell. Hair
strong in rut. Ten bob I got for Molly's combings when we were on
the rocks in Holles street. Why not? Suppose he gave her money.
Why not? All a prejudice. She's worth ten fifteen, more a pound. All
that for nothing. Bold hand. Mrs Marion. Did I forget to write
address on that letter like the postcard I sent to Flynn? And the day I
went to Drimmie's without a necktie. Wrangle with Molly it was put
me off. No, I remember. Richie Goulding. He's another. Weighs on
my mind. Funny my watch stopped at half past four. Dust. Shark
liver oil they use to clean could do it myself. Save. Was that just
when he, she?

O, he did. Into her. She did. Done.

Ah!

Mr Bloom with careful hand recomposed his wet shirt. O
Lord, that little limping devil. Begins to feel cold and clammy.
Aftereffect not pleasant. Still you have to get rid of it someway.
They don't care. Complimented perhaps. Go home to nicey bread
and milky and say night prayers with the kiddies. Well, aren't they.
See her as she is spoil all. Must have the stage setting, the rouge,
costume, position, music. The name too. *Amours* of actresses. Nell
Gwynn, Mrs Bracegirdle, Maud Branscombe. Curtain up. Moonlight
silver effulgence. Maiden discovered with pensive bosom. Little
sweetheart come and kiss me. Still I feel. The strength it gives a man.
That's the secret of it. Good job I let off there behind coming out of
Dignam's. Cider that was. Otherwise I couldn't have. Makes you

[246]

want to sing after. *Lacaus esant taratara.* Suppose I spoke to her. What about? Bad plan however if you don't know how to end the conversation. Ask them a question they ask you another.

. . . .

Ask you do you like mushrooms because she once knew a gentleman who. Or ask you what someone was going to say when he changed his mind and stopped. Yet if I went the whole hog, say: I want to, something like that. Because I did. She too. Offend her. Then make it up. Pretend to want something awfully, then cry off for her sake. Flatters them. She must have been thinking of someone else all the time. What harm? Must since she came to the use of reason, he, he and he. First kiss does the trick. The propitious moment. Something inside them goes pop. Mushy like, tell by their eye, on the sly. First thoughts are best. Remember that till their dying day. Molly, lieutenant Mulvey that kissed her under the Moorish wall beside the gardens. Fifteen she told me. But her breasts were developed. Fell asleep then. After Glencree dinner that was when we drove home the featherbed mountain. Gnashing her teeth in sleep. Lord mayor had his eye on her too. Val Dillon. Apoplectic.

There she is with them down there for the fireworks. My fireworks. Up like a rocket, down like a stick. And the children, twins they must be, waiting for something to happen. Want to be grownups. Dressing in mother's clothes. Time enough, understand all the ways of the world. And the dark one with the mop head and nigger mouth. I knew she could whistle. Mouth made for that. Like Molly. Why that high class whore in Jammet's wore her veil only to her nose. Would you mind, please, telling me the right time? I'll tell you the right time up a dark lane. Say prunes and prisms forty times every morning, cure for fat lips. Caressing the little boy too. Onlookers see most of the game. Of course they understand birds, animals, babies. In their line.

Didn't look back when she was going down the strand. Wouldn't give that satisfaction. Those girls, those girls, those lovely seaside girls. Fine eyes she had, clear. It's the white of the eye brings that out not so much the pupil. Did she know what I? Course. Like a cat sitting beyond a dog's jump.

. . . .

Lord!

Did me good all the same. Off colour after Kiernan's, Dignam's. For this relief much thanks. In *Hamlet,* that is. Lord! It was all things combined. Excitement. When she leaned back felt an ache at the butt of my tongue. Your head it simply swirls. He's right. Might have made a worse fool of myself however. Instead of talking about nothing. Then I will tell you all. Still it was a kind of language between us. It couldn't be? No, Gerty they called her. Might be a false name however like the address Dolphin's barn a blind.

> *Her maiden name was Jemina Brown*
> *And she lived with her mother in Irishtown.*

. . . .

This wet is very unpleasant. Stuck. Well the foreskin is not back. Better detach.

Ow!

Other hand a sixfooter with a wifey up to his waistpocket. Long and short of it. Big he and little she. Very strange about my watch. Wristwatches are always going wrong. Wonder is there any magnetic influences between the person because that was about the time he. Yes, I suppose at once. Cat's away the mice will play.

. . . .

Wait. Hm. Hm. Yes. That's her perfume. That's her perfume. Why she waved her hand. I leave you this to think of me when I'm far away on the pillow. What is it? Heliotrope? No Hyacinth? Hm. Roses, I think. She'd like scent of that kind. Sweet and cheap: soon sour. Why Molly likes opoponax. Suits her with a little jessamine mixed. Her high notes and her low notes. At the dance night she met him dance of the hours. Heat brought it out. She was wearing her black and it had the perfume of the time before. Good conductor, is it? Or bad? Light too. Suppose there's some connection. For instance if you go into a cellar where it's dark. Mysterious thing too. Why did I smell it only now? took its time in coming like herself, slow but sure. Suppose it;s ever so many millions of tiny grains blown across. Yet, it is.

. . . .

Perhaps they get a man smell off us. What though? Cigary gloves Long John had on his desk the other. Breath? What you eat and drink gives that. No Mansmell, I mean. Must be connected with that because priests that are supposed to be are different. Women buzz round it like flies round treacle. Railed off the altar get on to it at any cost. The tree of forbidden priest. O father, will you? Let me be the first to. That diffuses itself all through the body, permeates.

[248]

Source of life and it's extremely curious the smell. Celery sauce. Let me.

Mr Bloom inserted his nose. Hm. Into the. Hm. Opening of his waistcoat. Almonds or. No Lemons it is. Ah, no, that's the soap.

O by the by that lotion. I knew there was something on my mind. Never went back and the soap not paid. Dislike carrying bottles like that hag this morning. Hynes might have paid me that three shillings. I could mention Meagher's just to remind him . Still if he works that paragraph. Two and nine. Bad opinion of me he'll have. Call tomorrow. How much do I owe you Three and nine? Two and nine, sir. Ah. Might stop him giving credit another time. Lose your customers that way. Pubs do. Fellow run up a bill on the slate and then slinking around the back streets into somewhere else.

Here's this nobleman passed before. Blown in from the bay. Just went as far as turn back. Always at home at dinnertime. Looks mangled out: had a good tuck in. Enjoying nature now. Grace after meals. After supper walk a mile. Sure he has a small bank balance somewhere, government sit. Walk after him now make him awkward like those newsboys me today. Still you learn something. See ourselves as others see us. So long as women don't mock what matter? That's the way to find out. Ask yourself who is he now. *The Mystery Man on the Beach,* prize titbit story by Mr Leopold Bloom. Payment at the rate of one guinea per column. And that fellow today at the graveside in the brown macintosh. Corns on his kismet however. Healthy perhaps absorb all the. Whistle brings rain they say. Must be some somewhere. Old Betty's joints are on the rack. Mother Shipton's prophecy that is about ships around they fly in the twinkling. No. Signs of rain it is. The royal reader. And distant hills seem coming nigh.

. . . .

All quiet on Howth now. The distant hills seem. Where we. The rhododendrons. I am a fool perhaps. He gets the plums and I the plumstones. Where I come in. All that old hill has seen. Names change: that's all. Lovers: yum yum.

Tired I feel now. Will I get up? O wait. Drained all the manhood out of me, little wretch. She kissed me. My youth. Never again. Only once it comes. Or hers. Take the train there tomorrow. No. Returning not the same. Like kids your second visit to a house. The new I want. Nothing new under the sun. Care of P. O. Dolphin's barn. Are you not happy in your? Naughty darling. At Dolphin's barn charades in Luke Doyle's house. Mat Dillon and his bevy of daughters: Tiny, Atty, Foley, Miami, Louy, Hetty. Molly too. Eightyseven that was. Year before we. And the old major partial to his drop of spirits. Curious she an only child, I an only child. So it returns. Think you're escaping and run into yourself. Longest way round is the shortest way home. And just when he and she. Circus horse walking in a ring. Rip van Winkle we played. Rip: tear in Henny Doyle's overcoat. Van: breadvan delivering. Winkle: cockles and periwinkles. Then I did Rip van Winkle coming back. She leaned on the sideboard watching. Moorish eyes. Twenty years asleep in Sleepy Hollow. All changed. Forgotten. The young are old. His gun rusty from the dew.

. . . .

A long lost candle wandered up the sky from Mirus bazaar in search of funds for Mercer's hospital and broke, drooping, and shed a cluster of violet but one white stars. They floated, fell: they faded. The shepherd's hour: the hour of holding: hour of tryst. From house to house, giving his everwelcome double knock, went the nine o'clock postman, the glowworm's lamp at his belt gleaming here and there through the laurel hedges. And among the five young trees a hoisted lintstock lit the lamp at Leahy's terrace. By screens of lighted windows, by equal gardens a shrill voice wnt crying, wailing: *Evening Telegraph, stop the press edition! Result of the Gold Cup race!* and from the door of Dignam's house a boy ran out and called. Twittering the bat flew here, flew there. Far out over the sands the coming surf crept, grey. Howth settled for slumber tired of long days, of yumyum rhododendrons (he was old) and felt gladly the night breeze lift, ruffle his fell of ferns. He lay but opened a red eye unsleeping, deep and slowly breathing, slumberous but awake. And far on Kish bank the anchored lightship dwindled, winked at Mr Bloom.

. . . .

Better not stick here all night like a limpet. This weather makes you dull. Must be getting on for nine by the light. Go home. Too late for *Leah, Lily of Killarney.* No. Might be still up. Call to hospital to see. Hope she's over. Long day I've had. Martha, the bath, funeral, house of keys, museum with those goddesses, Dedalus' song. Then that bawler in Barney Kiernan's . Got my own back there. Drunken ranters. What I said about his God made him wince. Mistake to hit back. Or? No. Ought to go home and laugh at

[250]

themselves. Always want to be swilling in company. Afraid to be alone like a child of two. Suppose he hit me. Look at it other way round. Not so bad then. Perhaps not to hurt he meant. Three cheers for Israel, Three cheers for the sister-in-law he hawked about, three fangs in her mouth. Same style of beauty. Particularly nice old party for a cup of tea. The sister of the wife of the wild man of Borneo has just come to town. Imagine that in the early morning at close range. Everyone to his taste as Morris said when he kissed the cow. But Dignam's put the boots on it. Houses of mourning so depressing because you never know. Anyhow she wants the money. Must call to those Scottish widows as I promised. Strange name. Takes it for granted we're going to pop off first. That widow on Monday was it outside Cramer's that looked at me. Buried the poor husband but progressing favourably on the premium, Her widow's mite. Well? What do you expect her to do? Must wheedle her way along. Widower I hate to see. looks so forlorn. Poor man O'Connor wife and five children poisoned by mussels. here. The sewage. Hopeless. Some good matronly woman in a porkpie hat to mother him. Take him in tow, platterface and a large apron. Ladies' grey flannelette bloomers, three shillings a pair, astonishing bargain. Plain and loved, loved for ever, they say. Ugly: no woman thinks she is. Love, lie and be handsome for tomorrow we die. See him sometimes walking about trying to find out who played the trick. U. p.: up. Fate that is. He, not me. Also a shop often noticed. Curse seems to dog it. Dreamt last night? Wait. Something confused. She had red slippers on. Turkish. Wore the breeches. Suppose she does. Would I like her in pyjamas? Damned hard to answer. Nanetti's gone. Mailboat. Near Holyhead by now. Must nail that ad of Keyes's. Work Hynes and Crawford. Petticoats for Molly. She has something to put in them. What's that? Might be money.

Mr Bloom stooped and turned over a piece of paper on the strand. He brought it near his eyes and peered. Letter? No. Can't read. Better go. Better. I'm tired to move. Page of an old copybook. All those holes and pebbles. Who could count them? Never know what you find. Bottle with story of a treasure in it thrown from a wreck. Parcels post. Children always want to throw things in the sea. Trust? Bread cast in the waters. What's this? Bit of stick.

O! Exhausted that female has me. Not so young now. Will she come here tomorrow? Wait for her somewhere for ever. Must come back. Murderers do. Will I?

Mr Bloom with his stick gently vexed the thick sand at his foot. Write a message for her. Might remain. What?

I.

Some flatfoot tramp on it in the morning. Useless. Washed away. Tide comes here a pool near her foot. Bend, see my face there, dark mirror, breathe on it, stirs. All these rocks with lines and scars and letters. O, those transparent! Besides they don't know. What is the meaning of that other world. I called you naiughty boy because I do not like.

AM. A.

No room. Let it go.

Mr Bloom effaced the letters with his slow boot. Hopeless thing sand. Nothing grows in it. All fades. No fear of big vessels coming in here. Except Guinness's barges. Round the Kish in eighty days. Done half by design.

He flung his wooden pen away. The stick fell in silted sand, stuck. Now if you were trying to do that for a week on end you couldn't. Chance. We'll never meet again. But it was lovely. Goodbye, dear. Thanks. Made me feel so young.

Short snooze now if I had. Must be near nine. Liverpool boat long gone. Not even the smoke. And she can do the other. Did too. And Belfast. I won't go. Race there, race back to Ennis. Let him. Just close my eyes a moment. Won't sleep though. Half dream. It never comes the same. Bat again. No harm in him. Just a few.

O sweety all your little girlwhite up I saw dirty bracegirdle made me do love sticky we two naughty Grace darling she him half past the bed met him pike hoses frillies for Raoul to perfume your wife black hair heave under embon *senorita* young eyes Mulvey plump years dreams return tail end Agendath swoony lovey showed me her next year in drawers return next in her next her next.

A bat flew. Here. There. Far in the grey a bell chimed. Mr Bloom with open mouth, his left boot sanded sideways, leaned, breathed. Just for a few.

Cuckoo

Cuckoo

Cuckoo

The clock on the mantelpiece in the priest's house cooed where Canon O'Hanlon and Father Conroy and the reverend John

Hughes S. J. were taking tea and sodabread and butter and fried mutton chops with catsup and talking about

> *Cuckoo*
> *Cuckoo*
> *Cuckoo*

Because it was a little canarybird bird that came out of its little house to tell the time that Gerty MacDowell noticed the time she was there because she was as quick as anything about a thing like that, was Gerty MacDowell, and she noticed at once that foreign gentleman that was sitting on the rocks looking was

> *Cuckoo*
> *Cuckoo*
> *Cuckoo*

[253]

Episode 14 – The Oxen of the Sun… disembarking on the island of the Sun God, Helios, Odysseus' men, despite his dire warnings, slaughter the oxen of the Sun God whose curse upon the men leads to their death in a storm at sea, leaving Odysseus as the lone survivor on his voyage home. ~ Sitting in a hospital amidst insensitive young men drinking and joking of childbirth, Bloom hears mention of the slaughter of cows. Now at a nearby pub, the disrespectful remarks on fecundity and sterility repeat, leaving Bloom alone in his beliefs.

Nearing 11pm Bloom visits the National Maternity Hospital concerned for Mina Purefoy three days in labor, who at last, births a son. In the hospital Stephen Dedalus is drinking with medical students and acquaintances, all unconcerned and jocular over Mina. Stephen and friends with Bloom following, move on to Burke's pub where Stephen becomes thoroughly drunk on absinthe. Mulligan and Bannon enter, the latter reminiscing on his liaison with Milly Bloom in Mullingar. Departing, Stephen and Mulligan scuffle and Stephen hurts his hand. Stephen and Lynch head for the brothel district. Bloom decides to watch over Stephen as a surrogate father, and follows him to Nighttown, but via the wrong train stop.

THEMES
Slaughter of diseased Kerry cows. Fecundity, the birth process, productiveness. Life, its prevention by birth control and sterility, opposite narcissistic sex as the decay of Ireland. Medical care within the poverty of Ireland. Metaphorically, a running analogy of the gestation of the English language and its nine stages and forms. A cosmic and comic perspective of Western culture and its language.

DESHIL HOLLES EAMUS. DESHIL HOLLES EAMUS. DESHIL HOLLES EAMUS.

Send us, bright one, light one, Horhorn, quickening and wombfruit. Send us, bright one, light one, Horhorn, quickening and wombfruit. Send us, bright one, light one, Horhorn, quickening and wombfruit.

Hoopsa, boyaboy, hoopsa! Hoopsa, boyaboy, hoopsa! Hoopsa, boyaboy, hoopsa.

Universally that person's acumen is esteemed very little perceptive concerning whatsoever matters are being held as most profitable by mortals with sapience endowed to be studied who is ignorant of that which the most in doctrine erudite and certainly by reason of that in them high minds ornament deserving of veneration constantly maintain when by general consent they affirm that other circumstances being equal by no exterior splendour is the prosperity of a nation more efficaciously asserted than by the measure of how far forward may have progressed the tribute of its solicitude for that proliferent continuance which of evils the original if it be absent when fortunately present constitutes the certain sign of omnipotent nature's incorrupted benefaction.

. . . .

[254]

It is not why therefore we shall wonder if, as the best historians relate, among the Celts, who nothing that was not in its nature admirable admired, the art of medicine shall have been highly honoured. Not to speak of hostels, leperyards, sweating chambers, plague graves, their greatest doctors, the O'Shiels, the O'Hickeys, the O'Lees, have sedulously set down the divers methods by which the sick and the relapsed found again health whether the malady had been trembling withering or loose boyconnell flux. Certainly in every public work which in it anything of gravity contains preparation should be with importance commensurate and therefore a plan was by them adopted (whether by having preconsidered or as the maturation of experience it is difficult in being said which the discrepant opinions of subsequent inquirers are not up to the present concurred to render manifest) whereby maternity was so far from all accident possibility removed that whatever care the patient in that allhardest of woman hour chiefly required and not solely for the copiously opulent but also for her who not being sufficiently moneyed scarcely and often not even scarcely could subsist valiantly and for an inconsiderable emolument was provided.

. . . .

Before born babe bliss had. Within womb won he worship. Whatever in that one case done commodiously done was. A couch by midwives attended with wholesome food reposeful cleanest swaddles as though forthbringing were now done and by wise foresight set: but to this no less of what drugs there is need and surgical implements which are pertaining to her case not omitting aspect of all very distraction spectacles in various latitudes by our terrestrial orb offered together with images, divine and human, the cogitation of which by sejunct females is to tumescence conducive or eases issue in the high sunbright wellbuilt fair home of mothers when, ostensibly far gone and reproductive, it is come by her thereto to lie in, her term up.

Some man that wayfaring was stood by housedoor at night's oncoming. Of Israel's folk was that man that on earth wandering far had fared. Stark ruth of man his errand that him lone let till that house.

Of that house A. Horne is lord. Seventy beds keeps he there teeming mothers are wont that they lie for to thole and bring forth bairns hale so God'angel to Mary quoth. Watchers they there walk, white sisters in ward sleepless. Smarts they still sickness soothing:

in twelve moons thrice an hundred. Truest bedthanes they twain are, for Horne holding wariest ward.

In ward wary the watcher hearing come that man mildhearted eft rising with swire ywimpled to him her gate wide undid. Lo, levin leaping lightens in eyeblink Ireland's westward welkin! Full she dread that God the Wreaker all mankind would fordo with water for his evil sins. Christ's rood made she on breastbone and him drew that he would rathe infare under her thatch. That man her will wotting worthful went in Horne's House.

. . . .

As her eyes then ongot his weeds swart therefor sorrow she feared. Glad after she was that ere adread was. Her he asked if O'Hare Doctor tidings sent from far coast and she with grateful sigh him answered that O'Hare Doctor in heaven was. Sad was the man that word to hear that him so heavied in bowels ruthful. All she there told him, ruing death for friend so young, algate sore unwilling God's rightwiseness to withsay. She said that he had a fair sweet death through God His goodness with masspriest to be shriven, holy housel and sick men's oil to his limbs. The man then right earnest asked the nun of which death the dead man was died and the nun answered him and said that he was died in Mona island through bellycrab three year agone come Childermas and she prayed to God the Alltruthful to have his dear soul in his undeathliness. He heard her sad words, in held hat sad staring. So stood there both awhile in wanhope, sorrowing one with other.

Therefore, everyman, look to the last end that is thy death and dust that gripeth on every man that is born of woman for as he came naked forth from his mother's womb so naked shall he wend him at the last for to go as he came.

The man that was come into the house then spoke to the nursingwoman and he asked her how it fared with the woman that lay there in childbed. The nursingwoman answered him and said that that woman was in throes now full three days and that it would be a hard birth unneth to bear but that now in a little it would be. She said thereto that she had seen many births of women but never was none so hard as was that woman's birth. Then she set it forth all to him that time was had lived in that house. The man hearkened to her words for he felt with wonder women's woe in the travail that they have of motherhood and he wondered to look on her face that was a

[256]

young face for any man to see but yet was she left after long years a handmaid. Nine twelve bloodflows chiding her childless.

And whiles they spake the door of the castle was opened and there nighed them a mickle noise as of many that sat there at meat. And there came against the place as they stood a young learning knight yclept Dixon. And the traveller Leopold was couth to him sithen it had happened that they had had ado each with other in the house of misericord where this learning knight lay by cause the traveller Leopold came there with to be healed for he was sore wounded in his breast by a spear wherewith a horrible and dreadful dragon was smitten him for which he did do make a salve of volatile salt and chrism as much as he might suffice. And he said now that he should go into that castle for to make merry with them that were there. And the traveller Leopold said that he should go otherwhither for he was a man of cautels and a subtle. Also the lady was of his avis and reproved the learning knight would not hear say nay nor do her mandement ne have him in aught contrarious to his list and he said how it was a marvellous castle. And the traveller Leopold went into the castle for to rest him for a space being sore of limb after many marches environing in divers lands and sometimes venery.

. . . .

And the learning knight let pour for childe Leopold a draught and halp thereto the while all they that were there drank every each. And childe Leopold did up his beaver for to pleasure him and took apertly somewhat in amity for he never drank no manner of mead which he then put by and anon full privily he voided the more part in his neighbour glass and his neighbour wist not of his wile. And he sat down in that castle with them for to rest him there awhile. Thanked be Almighty God.

This meanwhile this good sister stood by the door and begged them at the reverence of Jesu our alther liege lord to leave their wassailing for there was one above one quick with child a gentle dame, whose time hied fast. Sir Leopold heard on the upfloor cry on high and he wondered what cry that it was whether of child or woman and I marvel, said he, that it be not come or now. Meseems it dureth overlong. And he was ware and saw a franklin that hight Lenehan on that side the table that was older than any of the tother and for that they both were knights virtuous in the one emprise and eke by cause that he was elder he spoke to him full gently. But, said he, or it be long too she will bring forth by God His bounty and have

[257]

joy of her childing for she hath waited marvellous long. And the franklin that had drunken said, Expecting each moment to be her next. Also he took the cup that stood tofore him for him needed never none asking nor desiring of him to drink and, Now drink, said he, fully delectably, and he quaffed as far as he might to their both's health for he was a passing good man of his lustiness. And sir Leoppld that was the goodliest guest that ever sat in scholars' hall and that was the meekest man and the kindness that ever laid husbandly hand under hen and that was the very truest knight of the world one that ever did minion service to lady gentle pledged him courtly in the cup. Woman's woe with wonder pondering.

Now let us speak of that fellowship that was there to the intent to be drunken an they might. There was a sort of scholars along either side the board, that is to wit, Dixon yclept junior of saint Mary Merciable's with other his fellow Lynch and Madden, scholars of medicine, and the franklin that hight Lenehan and on from Alba Longa, one Crotther, and young Stephen that had mien of a frere that was at head of the board and Costello that men clepen Punch Costello all long of a mastery of him erewhile gested (and of all them, reserved young Stephen, he was the most drunken that demanded still of more mead) and beside the meek sir Leopold. But on young Malachi they waited for that he promised to have come and such as intended to no goodness said how he had broke his avow. And sir Leopold sat with them for he bore fast friendship to sir Simon and to this his son young Stephen and for that his languor becalmed him there after longest wanderings insomuch as they feasted him for that time in the honourablest manner. Ruth red him, love led on with will to wander, loth to leave.

For they were right witty scholars. And he heard their aresouns each gen other as touching birth and righteousness, young Madden maintaining that put such case it were hard the wife to die (for so it had fallen out a matter of some year agone with a woman of Eblana in Horne's house that now was trespassed out of this world and the self night next before her death all leeches and pothecaries had taken counsel of her case). And they said farther she should live because in the beginning they said the woman should bring forth in pain and wherefore they that were of this imagination affirmed how young Madden had said truth for he had conscience to let her die. And not few and of these was young Lynch were in doubt that the world was now right evil governed as it was never other howbeit the

[258]

mean people believed it otherwise but the law nor his judges did provide no remedy. A redress God grant. This was scant said but all cried with one acclaim nay, by our Virgin Mother, the wife should live and the babe to die. In colour whereof they waxed hot upon that head what with argument and what for their drinking but the franklin Lenehan was prompt each when to pour them ale so that at the least way mirth might not lack. Then young Madden showed all the whole affair and when he said how that she was dead and how for holy religion sake by rede of palmer and bedesman and for a vow he had made to Saint Ultan of Arbraccan her goodman husband would not let her death whereby they were all wondrous grieved. To whom young Stephen had these words following, Murmur, sirs, is eke oft among lay folk. Both babe and parent now glorify their Maker, the one in limbo gloom, the other in purge fire. But, gramercy, what of those Godpossibled souls that we nightly impossibilise, which is the sin against the Holy Ghost, Very God, Lord and Giver of Life? For, sirs, he said, our lust is brief. We are means to those small creatures within us and nature has other ends than we.

. . . .

Then spoke young Stephen orgulous of mother Church that would cast him out of her bosom, of law of canons, of Lilith, patron of abortions, of bigness wrought by wind of seeds of brightness or by potency of vampires mouth to mouth or, as of moonflower or an she lie with a woman which her man has but lain with, *effectu secuto,* or peradventure in her bath according to the opinions of Averroes and Moses Maimonides. He said also how at the end of the second month a human soul was infused and how in all our holy mother foldeth ever souls for God's greater glory whereas that earthly mother which was but a dam to bring forth beastly should die by canon for so saith he that holdeth the fisherman's seal, even that blessed Peter on which rock was holy church for all ages founded. All they bachelors then asked of sir Leopold would he in like case so jeopard her person as risk life to save life. A wariness of mind he would answer as fitted all and laying hand to jaw, he said dissembling, as his wont was, that as it was informed him, who had ever love the art of physic as might a layman, and agreeing also with his experience of so seldom seen an accident it was good for that Mother Church belike at one blow had birth and death pence and in such sort deliverly he scaped their questions. That is truth, pardy, said Dixon, and, or I err, a pregnant word. Which hearing young Stephen was a marvellous glad man and he averred that he who stealeth from the poor lendeth to the Lord for he was of a wild manner when he was drunken and that he was now in that taking it appeared eftsoons.

But sir Leopold was passing grave maugre his word by cause he still had pity of the terrorcausing shrieking of shrill women in their labour and as he was minded of his good lady Marion that had borne him an only manchild which on this eleventh day on live had died and no man of art could save so dark is destiny. And she was wondrous stricken of heart for that evil hap and for his burial did him on a fair corselet of lamb's wool, the flower of the flock, lest he might perish utterly and lie akeled (for it was then about the midst of the winter) and now sir Leopold that had of his body no manchild for an heir looked upon him his friend's son and was shut up in sorrow for this forepassed happiness and as sad as he was that him failed a son of such gently courage (for all accounted him of real parts) so grieved he also in no less measure for young Stephen for that he lived riotously with those wastrels and murdered his goods with whores.

About that present time young Stephen filled all cups that stood empty so as there remained but little mo if the prudenter had not shadowed their approach from him that still plied it very busily who, praying for the intentions of the sovereign pontiff, he gave them for a pledge the vicar of Christ, which also as he said is vicar of Bray. Now drink we, quod he, of this mazer and quaff ye this mead which is not indeed parcel of my body but my soul's embodiment. Leave ye fraction of bread to them that live by bread alone. Be not afeard neither for any want for this will comfort more than the other will dismay. See ye here. And he showed them glistering coins of the tribute and goldsmith's notes the worth of two pounds nineteen shilling that he had, he said, for a song which he writ. They all admired to see the aforesaid riches in such dearth of money as was herebefore. His words were then these as followeth: Know all men, he said, time's ruins build eternity's mansions. What means this? Desire's wind blasts the thorntree but after it becomes from a bramblebush to be a rose upon the rood of time. Mark me now. In woman's womb word is made flesh but in the spirit of the maker all flesh that passes becomes the word that shall not pass away. This is the postcreation. *Omnis caro ad te veniet.*

. . . .

[260]

To be short this passage was scarce by when Master Dixon of Mary in Eccles, goodly grinning, asked young Stephen what was the reason why he had not cided to take friar's vows and he answered him obedience in the womb, chastity in the tomb but involuntary poverty all his days. Master Lenehan at this made return that he had heard of those nefarious deeds and how, as he heard hereof counted, he had besmirched the lily virtue of a confiding female which was corruption of minors and they all intershowed it too, waxing merry and toasting to his fathership. But he said very entirely it was clean contrary to their suppose for he was the eternal son and ever virgin. Thereat mirth grew in them the more and they rehearsed to him his curious rite of wedlock for the disrobing and deflowering of spouses, as the priests us in Madagascar island, she to be in guise of white and saffron, her groom in white and grain, with burning of nard and tapers, on a bridebed while clerks sung kyries and the anthem *Ut novetur sexu omnis corporis mysterium* till she was there unmaided.

. . . .

Young Stephen said indeed to his best remembrance they had but the one doxy be them and she of the stews to make shift with in delights amorous for life ran very high in those days and the custom of the country approved with it. Greater love than this, he said, no man hath that a man lay down his wife for his friend. Go thou and do likewise. Thus, or words to that effect, said Zarathustra, sometimes regius professor of French letters to the university of Oxtail nor breathed there ever that man to whom mankind was more beholden. bring the secondbest bed. *Orate, fratres, pro memetipso.* And all the people shall say, Amen. Remember, Erin, thy generations and thy days of old, how thou settedst little by me and by my word broughtest in a stranger to my gates to commit fornication in my sight and to wax fat and kick like Jeshurum. Therefore has thou sinned against the light and hast made me, thy lord, to be the slave of servants. Return, return, Clan Milly: forget me not, O Milesian. Why hast thou done this abomination before me that thou didst spurn me for a merchant of jalaps and didst deny me to the Roman and Indian of dark speech with whom thy daughters did lie luxuriously.

. . . .

A black crack of noise in the street here, alack, bawled, back. Loud on left Thor thundered: in anger awful the hammerhurler. Came now the storm that hist his heart. And Master Lynch bade him have a care to flout and witwanton as the god self was angered for his hellprate and paganry. And he that had erst challenged to be so doughty waxed pale as they might all mark and shrank together and his pitch that was before so haught uplift was now of a sudden quite plucked down and his heart shook within the cage of his breast as he tasted the rumour of that storm. Then did some mock and some jeer and Punch Costello fell hard again to his yale which Master Lenehan vowed he would do after and he was indeed but a word and a blow on any the least colour. But the braggart boaster cried that an old Nobodaddy was in his cups it was muchwhat indifferent and he would not lag behind his lead. But this was only to dye his desperation as cowed he crouched in Horne's hall. He drank indeed at one draught to pluck up a heart of any grace for it thundered long rumbling over all the heavens so that Master Madden, being godly certain whiles, knocked him on his ribs upon that crack of doom and Master Bloom at the braggart's side spoke to him calming words to slumber his great fear, advertising how it was no other thing but a hubbub noise that he heard, the discharge of fluid from the thunderhead, look you, having taken place, and all of the order of a natural phenomenon.

But was young Boasthard's fear vanquished by Calmer's words? No, for he had in his bosom a spike named Bitterness which could not by words be done away. And was he then neither calm like the one nor godly like the other? He was neither as much as he would have liked to be either. But could he not have endeavoured to have found again as in his youth the bottle Holiness that then he lived withal? Indeed not for Grace was not there to find that bottle. Heard he then in that clap the voice of the god Bringforth or, what Calmer said, a hubbub of Phenomenon? Heard? Why, he could not but hear unless he had plugged up the tube Understanding (which he had not done). For through that tube he saw that he was in the land of Phenomenon where he must for a certain one day die as he was like the rest too a passing show. And would he not accept to die like the rest and pass away? By no means would he and make more shows according as men do with wives which Phenomenon has commanded them to do by the book Law. Then wotted he nought of that other land which is called Believe-on-Me, that is the land of promise which behoves to the king Delightful and shall be for ever where there is no death and no birth neither wiving nor mothering at which all shall come as many as believe on it? Yes, Pious had told him of that land and Chaste had pointed him to the way but the reason was

[262]

that in the way he fell in with a certain whore of an eyepleasing
exterior whose name, she said, is Bird-in-the-Hand and she beguiled
him wrongways from the true path by her flatteries that she said to
him as, Ho, you pretty man, turn aside hither and I will show you a
brave place, and she lay at him so flatteringly that she had him in her
grot which is named Two-in-the-Bush or, by some learned, Carnal
Concupiscence.

  This was it what all that company that sat there at commons
in Manse of Mothers the most lusted after and if they met with this
whore Bird-in-the-Hand (which was within all foul plagues,
monsters and a wicked devil) they would strain the last but they
would make at her and know her. For regarding Believe-on-Me they
said it was nought else but notion and they could conceive no
thought of it for, first, Two-in-the-Bush whither she ticed them was
the very goodliest grot.

. . . .

Wherein, O wretched company, were ye all deceived for that was the
voice of the god that was in a very grievous rage that he would
presently lift his arm and spill their souls for their abuses and their
spillings done by them contrariwise to his word which forth to bring
brenningly biddeth.

. . . .

Over against the Rt. Hon. Mr Justice Fitzgibbon's door (that is to sit
with Mr Healy the lawyer upon the college lands) Mal. Mulligan a
gentleman's gentleman that had but come from Mr Moore's the
writer's (that was a papish but is now, folk say, a good Williamite)
chanced against Alec. Bannon in a cut bob (which are now in with
dance cloaks of Kendal green) that he was new got to town from
Mullingar with the stage where his coz and Mal M's brother will stay
a month yet till Saint Swithin and asks what in the earth he does
there, he bound home and he to Andrew Horne's being stayed for to
crush a cup of wine, so he said, but would tell him of a skittish
heifer, big of her age and beef to the heel and all this while poured
with rain and so both together on to Horne's. There Leop. Bloom of
Crawford's journal sitting snug with a covey of wags, likely
brangling fellows, Dixon jun., scholar of my lady Mercy, Vin.
Lynch, a Scots fellow, Will. Madden, T. Lenehan, very sad for a
racinghorse he fancied and Stephen D. Leop. Bloom there for a
languor he had but was now better, he having dreamed tonight a
strange fancy of his dame Mrs Moll with red slippers on in a pair of

Turkey trunks which is thought by those in ken to be for a change and Mistress Purefoy there, that got in through pleading her belly, and now on the stools, poor body, two days past her term, the midwives sore put to it and can't deliver, she queasy for a bowl of riceslop that is a shrewd drier up of the insides and her breath very heavy more than good and should be a bullyboy from the knocks they say, but God give her soon issue. 'This her ninth chick to live, I hear, and Lady day bit off her last chick's nails that was then a twelvemonth and with other three all breastfed that died written out in a fair hand in the king's bible. Her hub fifty odd and a methodist but takes the Sacrament and is to be seen any fair sabbath with a pair of boys off Bullock harbour dapping on the sound with a heavybraked reel or in a punt he has trailing for flounder and pollock and catches a fine bag, I hear. In sum an infinite great fall of rain and all refreshed and will much increase the harvest yet those in kensay after wind and water fire shall come for a prognostication of Malachi's almanac (and I hear that Mr Russell has done a prophetical charm of the same gist out of the Hindustanish for his farmer's gazette) to have three things in all but this a mere fetch without bottom of reason for old crones and bairns yet sometimes they are round in the right guess with their queerities no telling how.

  With this came up Lenehan to the feet of the table to say how the letter was in that night's gazette and he made a show to find it about him (for he swore with an oath that he had been at pains about it) but on Stephen's persuasion he gave over to search and was bidden to sit near by which he did mighty brisk.

. . . .

The other, Costello, that is, hearing this talk asked was it poetry or a tale. Faith, no, he says, Frank (that was his name), 'tis all about Kerry cows that are to be butchered along of the plague. But they can go hang, says he with a wink, for me with their bully beef, a pox on it. There's a good fish in this tin as ever came out of it and very friendly he offered to take of some salty sprats that stood by which he had eyed wishly in the meantime and found the place which was indeed the chief design of his embassy as he was sharpset. *Mort aux vaches,* says Frank then in the French language that had been indentured to a brandy shipper that has a winelodge in Bordeaux and he spoke French like a gentleman too.

. . . .

[264]

What, says Mr Leopold with his hands across, that was earnest to know the drift of it, will they slaughter all? I protest I saw them but this day morning going to the Liverpool boats, says he. I can scarce believe 'tis so bad, says he. And he had experience of the like brood beasts and of springers, greasy hoggets and wether wools, having been some years before actuary for Mr Joseph Cuffe, a worthy salemaster that drove his trade for live stock and meadow auctions hard by Mr Gavin Low's yard in Prussia street. I question with you there, says he. More like 'tis the hoose of the timber tongue. Mr Stephen, a little moved but very handsomely, told him no such matter and that he had dispatches from the emperor's chief tailtickler thanking him for the hospitality, that was sending over Doctor Rinderpest, the bestquoted cowcatcher in all Muscovy, with a bolus or two of physic to take the bull by the horns. Come, come, says Mr Vincent, plain dealing. He'll find himself on the horns of a dilemma if he meddles with a bull that's Irish, says he. Irish by name and irish by nature, says Mr Stephen, and he sent the ale purling about. An Irish bull in an English chinashop. I conceive you, says Mr Dixon. It is that same bull that was sent to our island by farmer Nicholas, the bravest cattle breeder of them all, with an emerald ring in his nose. True for you, says Mr Vincent cross the table, and a bullseye into the bargain, says he, and a plumper and a portlier bull, says he, never shit on shamrock. He had horns galore, a coat of gold and sweet smoky breath coming out of his nostrils so that women of our island, leaving doughballs and rollingpins, followed after him hanging his bulliness in daisychains. What for that, says Mr Dixon, but before he came over farmer Nicholas that was a eunuch had him properly gelded by a college of doctors, who were no better off than himself. So be off now, says he, and do all my cousin german the Lord Harry tells you and take a farmer's blessing, and with that he slapped his posteriors very soundly. But the slap and the blessing stood him friend, says Mr Vincent, for to make up he taught him a trick worth two of the other so that maid, wife, abbess and widow to this day affirm that they would rather any time of the month whisper in his ear in the dark of a cowhouse or get a lick on the nape from his long holy tongue then lie with the finest strapping young ravisher in the four fields of all Ireland.

. . . .

Our worthy acquaintance, Mr Malachi Mulligan, now appeared in the doorway as the students were finishing their apologue accompanied with a friend whom he had just rencountered, a young gentleman, his name Alec Bannon, who had late come to town, it being his intention to buy a colour or a cornetcy in the fencibles and list for the wars. Mr Mulligan was civil enough to express some relish of it all the more as it jumped with a project of his own for the cure of the very evil that had been touched on. Whereat he handed round to the company a set of pasteboard cards which he had had printed that day at Mr Quinnell's bearing a legend printed in fair italics: *Mr Malachi Mulligan, Fertiliser and Incubator, Lambay Island.* His project, as he went on to expound, was to withdraw from the round of idle pleasures such as form the chief business of sir Fopling Popinjay and sir Milksop Quidnunc in town and to devote himself to the boblest task for which our bodily organism has been framed. Well, let us hear of it, good my friend, said Mr Dixon. I make no doubt it smacks of wenching. Come, be seated, both. 'Tis as cheap sitting as standing. Mr Mulligan accepted of the invitation and, expatiating on his design, told his hearers that he had been led into this thought by a consideration of the causes of sterility, both the inhibitory and the prohibitory, whether the inhibition in its turn were due to conjugal vexations or to a parsimony of the balance as well as whether the prohibition proceeded from defects congenital or from proclivities acquired. It grieved him plaguily, he said, to see the nuptial couch defrauded of its dearest pledges: and to reflect upon so many agreeable females with rich jointures, a prey for the vilest bonzes, who hide their flambeau under a bushel in an uncongenial cloister or lose their womanly bloom in the embraces of some unaccountable muskin when they might multiply the inlets of happiness, sacrificing the inestimable jewel of their sex when a hundred pretty fellows were at hand to caress, this, he assured them, made his heart weep. To curb this inconvenience (which he concluded due to a suppression of latent heat), having advised with certain counsellors of worth and inspected into this matter, he had resolved to purchase in fee simple for ever the freehold of Lambay island from it holder, lord Talbot de Malahide, a Tory gentleman of not much in favour with our ascendancy party. He proposed to set up there a national fertilising farm to be named *Omphalos* with an obelisk hewn and erected after the fashion of Egypt and to offer his dutiful yeoman services for the fecundation of any female of what grade of life soever who should there direct to him with the desire of fulfilling the functions of her

[266]

natural. Money was no object, he said, nor would he take a penny for his pains. The poorest kitchenwench no less than the opulent lady of fashion, if so be their constructions, and their tempers were warm persuaders for their petitions, would find in him their man. For his nutriment he shewed how he would feed himself exclusively upon a diet of savoury tubercles and fish and coneys there, the flesh of these latter prolific rodents being highly recommended for this purpose, both broiled and stewed with a blade of mace and a pod or two of capsicum chillies.

. . . .

Mr Mulligan, now perceiving the table, asked for whom were those loaves and fishes and, seeing the stranger, he made a civil bow and said, Pray, sir, was you in need of any professional assistance we could give? Who, upon his offer, thanked him very heartily, though preserving his proper distance, and replied that he was come there about a lady, now an inmate of Horne's house, that was in an interesting condition, poor lady, from woman's woe (and here he fetched a deep sigh) to know if her happiness had yet taken place. Mr Dixon to turn the table, took on to ask Mr Mulligan himself whether his incipient ventripotence, upon which he rallied him, betokened an ovoblastic gestation in the prostatic utricle or male womb or was due was with the noted physician, Mr Austin Meldon, to a wolf in the stomach. For answer Mr Mulligan, in a gale of laughter at his smalls, smote himself bravely below the diaphragm, exclaiming with an admirable droll mimic of Mother Grogan (the most excellent creature of her sex though 'tis pity she'a a trollop): There's a belly that never bore a bastard. This was so happy a conceit that it renewed the storms of mirth and threw the whole room into the most violent agitations of delight. The spry rattle had run on in the same vein of mimicry but for some larum in the antechamber.

. . . .

Amid the general vacant hilarity of the assembly a bell rang and while all were conjecturing what might be the cause Miss Callan entered and, having spoken a few words in a low tone to young Mr Dixon, retired with a profound bow to the company. The presence even for a moment among a party of debauchees of a woman endued with every quality of modesty and not less severe than beautiful refrained humorous sallies even of the most licentious but her departure was the signal for an outbreak of ribaldry. Strike me silly, said Costello, a low fellow who was fuddled. A monstrous fine bit of cowflesh! I'll be sworn she has rendezvoused you. What, you dog? Have you a way with them? Gad's bud. Immensely so, said Mr Lynch. The bedside manner it is that they use in the Mater hospice. Demme, does not Doctor O'Gargle chuck the nuns there under the chin? As I look to be saved I had it from my Kitty who has been wardmaid there any time these seven months. Lawksamercy, doctor, cried the young blood in the primrose vest, feigning a womanish simper and immodest squirmings of his body, how you do trade a body! Drat the man! Bless me, I'm all of a wibblywobbly. Why, you're as bad as dear little Father Cantekissem that you are! May this pot of four half choke me, cried Costello, if she ain't in the family way I knows a lady what's got a white swelling quick as I claps eyes on her. The young surgeon, however, rose and begged the company to excuse his retreat as the nurse had just then informed him that he was needed in the ward. Merciful providence had been pleased to put a period to the sufferings of the lady who was *enceinte* which she had borne with a laudable fortitude and she had given birth to a bouncing boy. I want patience, said he, with those who without wit to enliven or learning to instruct, revile an ennobling profession which, saving the reverence due to the Deity, is the greatest power for happiness upon the earth. I am positive when I say that if need were I could produce a cloud of witnesses to the excellence of her noble exercitations which, so far from being a byword, should be a glorious incentive in the human breast. I cannot away with them. What? Malign such an one, the amiable Miss Callan, who is the lustre of her own sex and the astonishment of ours and at an instant the most momentous that can befall a puny child of clay? Perish the thought I shudder to think of the future of a race where the seeds of such malice have been sown and where no right reverence is rendered to mother and maid in house of Horne. Having delivered himself of this rebuke he saluted those present on the by and repaired to the door.

. . . .

To revert to Mr Bloom who, after his first entry, had been conscious of some impudent mocks which he, however, had borne with being the fruits of that age upon which it is commonly charged that it knows not pity. The young sparks, it is true, were full of extravagances as overgrown children: the words of their tumultuary discussions were difficultly understood and not often nice: their testiness and outrageous *mots* were such that his intellects resiled

[268]

from: nor were they scrupulously sensible of the proprieties though their fund of strong animal spirits spoke in their behalf. But the word of Mr Costello was an unwelcome language for him for he nauseated the wretch that seemed to him a cropeared creature of a misshapen gibbosity born out of wedlock and thrust like a crookback teethed and feet first into the world, which the dint of the surgeon's pliers in his skull lent indeed a colour to, so as it put him in thought of that missing link of creation's chain desiderated by the late ingenious Mr Darwin. It was now for more than the middle span of our allotted years that he had passed through the thousand vicissitudes of existence and, being of a wary ascendancy and self a man of a rare forecast, he had enjoined his heart to repress all motions of a rising cholera and, be intercepting them with the readiest precaution, foster within his breast that plenitude of sufferance which base minds jeer at, rash judgers scorn and all find tolerable and but tolerable. To those who create themselves wits as the cost of feminine delicacy (a habit of mind which he never did hold with) to them he would concede neither to bear the name nor to herit the tradition of a proper breeding: while for such that, having lost all forbearance, can lose no more, there remained the sharp antidote of experience to cause their insolvency to beat a precipitate and inglorious retreat. Not but what he could feel with mettlesome youth which, caring nought for the mows of dotards or the gruntlings of the severe, is ever (as the chaste fancy of the Holy Writer express it) for eating of the tree forbid it yet not so far forth as to pretermit humanity upon any condition soever towards a gentlewoman when she was about her lawful occasions. To conclude, while from the sister's words he had reckoned upon a speedy delivery he was, however, it must be owned, not a little alleviated by the intelligence that the issue so auspicated after an ordeal of such duress now testified once more to the mercy as well as to the bounty of the Supreme Being.

Accordingly he broke his mind to his neighbour, saying that to express his notion of the thing, his opinion (who ought not perchance to express one) was that one must have a cold constitution and a frigid genius not to be rejoiced by this freshest news of the fruition of her confinement since she had been in such pain through no fault of hers.

. . . .

The news was imparted with a circumspection recalling the ceremonial usages of the Sublime Porte by the second female

infirmarian to the junior medical officer in residence, who in his turn announced to the delegation that an heir had been born. When he had betaken himself to the women's apartment to assist at the prescribed ceremony of the afterbirth in the presence of the secretary of state for domestic affairs and the members of the privy council, silent in unanimous exhaustion and probation, the delegates, chafing under the length and solemnity of their vigil and hoping that the joyful occurrence would palliate a licence which the simultaneous absence of abigail and offer rendered the easier, broke out at once into a strife of tongues. In vain the voice of Mr Canvasser Bloom was heard endeavoring to urge, to mollify, to restrain. The moment was too propitious for the display of that discursiveness which seemed the only bond of union among tempers so divergent. Every phase of the situation was successively eviscerated: the prenatal repugnance of uterine brothers, the Caesarean section, posthumity with respect to the father and, that rarer form, with respect to the mother, the fratricidal case known as the Childs murder and rendered memorable by the impassioned plea of Mr Advocate Buseh which secured the acquittal of the wrongfully accused, the rights of primogeniture and king's bounty touching twins and triplets, miscarriages and infanticides, simulated and dissimulated, acardiac *foetus in foetu.*
. . . .

The impression made by his words was immediate but shortlived. It was effaced as easily as it had been evoked by an allocution from Mr Candidate Mulligan in that vein of pleasantry which none better than he knew know to affect, postulating as the supremest object of desire a nice clean old man. Contemporaneously, a heated argument having arisen between Mr Delegate Madden and Mr Candidate Lynch regarding the juridical and theological dilemma in the event of one Siamese twin predeceasing the other, the difficulty by mutual consent was referred to Mr Canvasser Bloom for instant submittal to Mr Coadjutor Deacon Dedalus. Hitherto silent, whether the better to show by preternatural gravity that curious dignity of the garb with which he was invested or in obedience to an inward voice, he delivered briefly, and as some thought perfunctorily, the ecclesiastical ordinance forbidding man to put asunder what God has joined.

But Malachias' tale began to freeze them with horror. He conjured up the scene before them. The secret panel beside the chimney slid back and in the recess appeared . . . Haines! Which of

[270]

us did not feel his flesh creep? He had a portfolio full of Celtic literature in one hand, in the other a phial marked *Poison.* Surprise, horror, loathing were depicted on all faces while he eyed them with a ghastly grin. I anticipated some such reception, he began with an eldritch laugh, for which, it seems, history is to blame. Yes, it is true. I am the murderer of Samuel Childs. And how I am punished! The inferno has no terrors for me. This is the appearance is on me. Tare and ages, what way would I be resting at all, he muttered thickly, and I tramping Dublin this while back with my share of songs and himself after me the like of a soulth or a bullawurrus? My hell, and Ireland's, is in this life. It is what I tried to obliterate my crime. Distractions, rookshooting, the Erse language (he recited some), laudanum (he raised the phial to his lips), camping out. In vain! His spectre stalks me. Dope is my only hope . . . Ah! Destruction! The black panther! With a cry he suddenly vanished and the panel slid back. An instant later his head appeared in the door opposite and said: Meet me at Westland row station at ten past eleven. He was gone! Tears gushed from the eyes of the dissipated host. The seer raised his hand to heaven, murmuring: The vendetta of Mananaan! The sage repeated *Lex talionis.* The sentimentalist is he who would enjoy without incurring the immense debtorship for a thing done. Malachias, overcome by emotion, ceased. The mystery was unveiled. Haines was the third brother. His real name was Childs. The black panther was himself the ghost of his own father. He drank drugs to obliterate. For this relief much thanks. The lonely house by the graveyard is uninhabited. No soul will live there. The spider pitches her web in the solitude. The nocturnal rat peers from his hole. A curse is on it. It is haunted. Murderer's ground.

What is the age of the soul of man? As she hath the virtue of the chameleon to change her hue to every new approach, to be gay with the merry and mournful with the downcast, so too is her age changeable as her mood. No longer is Leopold, as he sits there, ruminating, chewing the cud of reminiscence, that staid agent of publicity and holder of a modest substance in the funds. He is young Leopold, as in a retrospective arrangement, a mirror within a mirror (hey, presto!), he beholdeth himself. That young figure of then is seen, precociously manly, walking on a nipping morning from the old house in Clambrassil street to the high school, his book satchel on him bandolierwise, and in it a goodly hunk of wheaten loaf, a mother's thought. Or it is the same figure, a year or so gone over, in his first hard hat (ah, that was a day!), already on the road, a fullfledged traveller for the family firm, equipped with an orderbook, a scented handkerchief (not for show only), his case of bright trinketware (alas, a thing now of the past!), and a quiverful of compliant smiles for this or that halfwon housewife reckoning it out upon her fingertips or for a budding virgin shyly acknowledging (but the heart? tell me!) his studied baisemoins. The scent, the smile but more than these, the dark eyes and oleaginous address brought home at duskfall many a commission to the head of the firm seated with Jacob's pipe after like labours in the paternal ingle (a meal of noodles, you may be sure, is aheating), reading through round horned spectacles some paper from the Europe of a month before. But hey, presto, the mirror is breathed on and the young knighterrant recedes, shrivels, to a tiny speck within the mist. Now he is himself paternal and these about him might be his sons. Who can say? The wise father knows his own child. He thinks of a drizzling night in Hatch street hard by the bonded stores there, the first. Together (she is a poor waif, a child of shame, yours and mine and of all for a bare shilling and her luckpenny), together they hear the heavy tread of the watch as two raincapped shadows pass the new royal university. Bridie! Bridie Kelly! He will never forget the name, ever remember the night, first night, bridenight. They are entwined in nethermost darkness, the willer with the willed, and in an instant (*fiat!*) light shall flood the world. Did heart leap to heart? Nay, fair reader. In a breath 'twas done but – hold! Back! It must not be! In terror the poor girl flees away through the murk. She is the bride of darkness, a daughter of the night. She dare not bear the sunny golden babe of day. No Leopold! Name and memory solace thee not. That youthful illusion of thy strength was taken from thee and in vain. No son of thy loins is by thee. There is none now to be for Leopold, what Leopold was for Rudolph.

. . . .

Francis was reminding Stephen of years before when they had been at school together in Conmee's time. He asked about Glaucon, Alcibiades, Pisistratus. Where were they now? Neither knew. You have spoken of the past and its phantoms, Stephen said. Why think of them? If I call them into life across the waters of Lethe will not the poor ghosts troop to my call? Who supposed it? I, Bous Stephanoumenos, bullockbefriending bard, am lord and giver of their life. He encircled his gadding hair with a coronal of vineleaves,

[272]

smiling at Vincent. That answer and those leaves, Vincent said to him, will adorn you more fitly when something more, and greatly more, than a capful of light odes can call your genius father. All who wish you well hope this for you. All desire to see you bring forth the work you meditate. I heartily wish you may not fail them. O no, Vincent, Lenehan said, laying a hand on the shoulder near him, have no fear. He could not leave his mother an orphan. The young man's face grew dark. All could see how hard it was for him to be reminded of his promise and of his recent loss. He would have withdrawn from the feast had not the noise of voices allayed the smart. Madden had lost five drachmas on Sceptre for a whim of the rider's name: Lenehan as much more. He told them of the race. The flag fell and, huuh, off, scamper, the mare ran out freshly with O. Madden up. She was leading the field: all hearts were beating. Even Phyllis could not contain herself. She waved her scarf and cried: Huzzah! Sceptre wins! But in the straight on the run home when all were in close order the dark horse Throwaway drew level, reached, outstripped her. All was lost now. Phyllis was silent: her eyes were sad anemones. Juno, she cried, I am undone. But her lover consoled her and brought her a bright casket of gold in which lay some oval sugarplums which she partook. A tear fell: one only. A whacking fine whip, said Lenehan, is W. Lane. Four winners yesterday and three today. What rider is like him? Mount him on the camel or the boisterous buffalo the victory in a hack canter is still his. But let us bear it as was the ancient wont. Mercy on the luckless! Poor Sceptre! he said with a light sigh. She is not the filly that she was. Never, by this hand, shall we behold such another.

. . . .

The debate which ensued was in its scope and progress an epitome of the course of life. Neither place nor council was lacking in dignity. The debaters were the keenest in the land, the theme they were engaged on the loftiest and most vital. The high hall of Horne's house had never beheld an assembly so representative and so varied nor had the old rafters of that establishment ever listened to a language so encyclopaedic.

. . . .

It had better be stated here and now at the outset that the perverted transcendentalism to which Mr S. Dedalus' (Div. Scep) contentions would appear to prove him pretty badly addicted runs directly counter to accepted scientific methods. Science, it cannot be too repeated, deals with tangible phenomena. The man of science like the man in the street has to face hardheaded facts that cannot be blinked and explain them as best he can. There may be, it is true, some questions which science cannot answer – at present – such as the first problem submitted by Mr L. Bloom (Pubb. Canv.) regarding the future determination of sex. . . . The other problem raised by the same inquirer is scarcely less vital: infant mortality. It is interesting because, as he pertinently remarks, we are all born in the same way but we all die in different ways. . . . Mr J. Crotthers (Disc. Bacc.) attributes some of these demises to abnormal trauma in the case of women workers subjected to heavy labours in the workshop and to marital discipline in the home but by far the vast majority to neglect, private or official, culminating in the exposure of newborn infants, the practice of criminal abortion or in the atrocious crime of infanticide.

. . . .

In a recent public controversy with Mr L. Bloom (Pubb. Canv.) which took place in the commons' hall of the National Maternity Hospital, 29, 30 and 31 Holles street, of which, as is well known, Dr A. Horne (Lic. in Mdw., F. K. Q. C. P. I.) is the able and popular master, he is reported by eyewitnesses as having stated that once a woman has let the cat into the bag (an esthetic allusion, presumably, to one of the most complicated and marvellous of all nature's processes, the act of sexual congress) she must let it out again or give it life, as he phrased it, to save her own. At the risk of her own was the telling rejoinder of his interlocutor none the less effective for the moderate and measured tone in which it was delivered.

Meanwhile the skill and patience of the physician had brought about a happy *accouchement*. It had been a weary weary while for both patient and doctor. All that surgical skill could do was done and the brave woman had manfully helped. She had. She had fought the good fight and now she was very very happy. Those who have passed on, who have gone before, are happy too as they gaze down and smile upon the touching scene. Reverently look at her as she reclines there with the motherlight in her eyes, that longing hunger for baby fingers (a pretty sight it is to see), in the first bloom of her new motherhood, breathing a silent prayer of thanksgiving to One above, the Universal Husband. And as her loving eyes behold her babe she wishes only one blessing more, to have her dear Doady there with her to share her joy, to lay in his arms that mite of God's

[274]

clay, the fruit of their lawful embraces. He is older now (you and I may whisper it) and in a trifle stooped in the shoulders yet in the whirligig of years a grave dignity has come to the conscientious second accountant of the Ulster bank, College Green branch. O Doady, loved one of old, faithful lifemate now, it may never be again, that faroff time of the roses! With the old shake of her pretty head she recalls those days. God, how beautiful now across the mist of years! But their children are grouped in her imagination about the bedside, hers and his, Charley, Mary Alics, Frederick Albert (if he had lived), Mamy, Budgie (Victoria Frances), Tom, Violet Constance Louisa, darling little Bobsy (called our famous hero of the South African war, lord Bobs of Waterford and Candahar) and now this last little pledge of their union, a Purefoy if ever there was one, with the true Purefoy nose. Young hopeful will be christened Mortimer Edward after the influential third cousin of Mr Purefoy in the Treasury Remembrancer's office, Dublin Castle. And so time wags on: but father Cronion has dealt lightly here. No, let no sigh break from that bosom, dear gentle Mina. And Doady, knock the ashes from your pipe, the seasoned briar you still fancy when the curfew rings for you (may it be the distant day!) and dout the light whereby you read in the Sacred Book for the oil too has run low and so with a tranquil heart to bed, to rest. He knows and will call in His own good time. You too have fought the good fight and played loyally your man's part. Sir, to you my hand. Well done, thou good and faithful servant.

There are sins or (let us call them as the world calls them) evil memories which are hidden away by man in the darkest places of the heart but they abide there and wait. He may suffer their memory to grow dim, let them be as though they had not been and all but persuade himself that they were not or at least otherwise. Yet a chance word will call them forth suddenly and they will rise up to confront him in the most various circumstances, a vision or a dream, or while timbrel and harp soothe his senses or amid the cool silver tranquillity of the evening or at the feast at midnight when he is now filled with wine. Not to insult over him will the vision come as over one that lies under her wrath, not for vengeance to cut off from the living but shrouded in the piteous vesture of the past, silent, remote, reproachful.

. . . .

[275]

Mark this farther and remember. The end comes suddenly. Enter that antechamber of birth where the studious are assembled and note their faces. Nothing, as it seems, there of rash or violent. Quietude of custody rather, befitting their station in that house, the vigilant watch of shepherds and of angels about a crib in Bethlehem of Juda long ago. But as before the lightning the serried stormclouds, heavy with preponderant excess of moisture, in swelling masses turgidly distended, compass earth and sky in one vast slumber, impending above parched field and drowsy oxen and blighted growth of shrub and verdure till in an instant a flash rives their centres and with the reverberation of the thunder the cloudburst pours its torrent so and not otherwise was the transformation, violent and instantaneous, upon the utterance of the Word.

Burke's! Outflings my lord Stephen, giving a cry, and a tag and bobtail of all them after, cockerel, jackanapes, welsher, pilldoctor, punctual Bloom at heels with a universal grabbing at headgear, ashplants, bilbos, Panama hats and scabbards, Zermatt alpenstocks and what not. A dedale of lusty youth, noble every student there. Nurse Callan taken aback in the hallway cannot stay them or smiling surgeon coming downstairs with news of placentation ended, a full pound if a milligramme. They hark him on. The door! It is open? Ha! They are out tumultuously, off for a minute's race, all bravely legging it, Burke's of Denzille and Holles their ulterior goal. Dixon follows, giving them sharp language but raps out an oath, he too, and on. Bloom stays with nurse a thought to send a kind word to happy mother and nurseling up there. Doctor Diet and Doctor Quiet. Looks she too not other now? Ward of watching in Horne's house has told its tale in that washedout pallor. Them all being gone, a glance of motherwit helping he whispers close in going: Madam, when comes the storkbird for thee?

. . . .

Query. Who's astanding this here do? Proud possessor of damnall. Declare misery. Bet to the ropes. Me nantee saltee. Not a red at me this week gone. Yours? Mead of our fathers for the *Ubermensch.* Ditto. Five number ones. You, sir? Ginger cordial. Chase me, the cabby's caudle. Stimulate the caloric. Winding of his ticker. Stopped short never to go again when the old. Absinthe for me, savvy. *Caramba!* Have an eggnog or a prairie oyster. Enemy? Avuncular's got my timepiece. Ten to. Obligated awful. Don't mention it. Got a pectoral trauma, eh, Dix? Pos fact. Got bet be a boomblebee whenever he was settin sleepin in hes bit garten. Digs up near the Mater. Buckled he is. Know his dona? Yup, sartin, I do. Full of a dure. See her in her dishybilly. Peels off a credit. Lovey lovekin. None of your lean kine, not much. Pull down the blind, love. Two Ardilauns. Same here. Look slippery. If you fall don't wait to get up. Five, seven, nine. Fine! Got a prime pair of mincepies, no kid. And her take me to rests and her anker allbeplastered neck you stole my heart, O gluepot. Sir? Spud again the rheumatiz? All poppycock, you'll scuse me saying. For the hoi polloi. I vear thee beest a gert vool. Well doc? Back fro Lapland? Your corporosity sagaciating O K? How's the squaws and papooses? Womanbody after going on the straw? Stand and deliver. Password. There's hair. Ours the white death and the ruddy birth. Hi! Spit in your own eye, boss. Mummer's wire. Cribbed out of Meredith. Jesified orchidised polycimical jesuit! Aunty mine's writing Pa Kinch. Baddybad Stephen lead astray goodygood Malachi.

. . . .

You move a motion? Steve boy, you're going it some. More bluggy drunkables? Will immensely splendiferous stander permit one stooder of most extreme poverty and one largesize gracious thirst to terminate one expensive inaugurated libation? Give's a breather. Landlord, landlord, have you good wine, sttaboo? Hoots, mon, wee drap to pree. Cut and come again. Right Boniface! Absinthe the lot. *Nos omnes biberimus viridum toxicum diabolus capiat posteriora nostra.* Closing time, gents. Eh? Rome boose for the Bloom toff. I hear you say onions? Bloo? Cadges ads? Photo's papli, by all that's gorgeous! Play low, pardner. Slide. *Bonsoir la compagnie.* And snares of the poxfiend. Where's the buck and Namby Amby? Skunked? Leg bail. Aweel, ye maun e'en gang yer gates. Checkmate. King to tower. Kind Kristyann will yu help, yung man hoose frend tuk bungalo kee to find plais whear to lay crown off his hed 2 night. Crickey, I'm about sprung. Tarnally dog gone my shins if this beent the bestest puttiest longbreakyet. Item, courage, couple of cookies for this child. Cot's plood and prandypalls, none! Not a pite of sheeses? Thrust syphilis down to hell and with him those other licensed spirits. Time. Who wander through the world. Health all. *A la vôtre!*

. . . .

Your attention! We're nae tha fou. The Leith police dismisseth us. The least tholice. Ware hawks for the chap puking.

Unwell in his abominable regions. Yooka. Night. Mona, my thrue love. Yook. Mona, my own love. Ook.

Hark! Shut your obstropolos. Pflaap! Pflaap! Blaze on. There she goes. Brigade! Bout ship. Mount street way. Cut up. Pflaap! Tally ho. You not come? Run, skelter, race. Pflaaaap!

Lynch! Hey? Sign on long o me. Denzille lane this way. Change here for Bawdyhouse. We two, she said, will seek the kips where shady Mary is. Righto, any old time. *Laetabuntur in cubilibus suis.* You coming long? Whisper, who the sooty hell's the johnny in the black duds? Hush! Sinned against the light and even now that day is at hand when he shall come to judge the world by fire. Pflaap! *Ut implerentur scripturae.* Strike up a ballad. Then outspake medical Dick to his comrade medical Davy. Christicle, who's this excrement yellow gospeller on the Merrion hall? Elijah is coming washed in the Blood of the Lamb. Come on, you winefizzling ginsizzling booseguzzling existences! Come on, you dog-gone, bullnecked, beetlebrowed, hogjowled, peanutbrained, weaseleyed fourflushers, false alarms and excess baggage! Come on, you triple extract of infamy! Alexander J. Christ Dowie, that's yanked to glory most half this planet from 'Frisco Beach to Vladivostok. The Deity ain't no nickel dime bumshow. I put it to you that he's on the square and a corking fine business proposition. He's the grandest thing yet and don't you forget it. Shout salvation in king Jesus. You'll need to rise precious early, you sinner there, if you want ro diddle the Almighty God. Pflaaaap! Not half. He's got a coughmixture with a punch in it for you, my friend, in his backpocket. Just you try it on.

Episode 15 – Circe... an enchantress who turns Odysseus' men into swines. Odysseus, with the aid of a magical plant, resists Circe's transformative powers, makes her restore his men to their human form, and enjoys her sensual pleasures for a year before resuming his voyage home. ~ Bloom, Stephen and friend, visit a brothel where Bloom gives up his talisman and suffers hallucinations while Stephen is too inebriated to control himself. Bloom retakes his talisman, recovers his sanity, resolves all situations, and leads Stephen towards his home.

Written as a play of bizarre hallucinations and transformations, Bloom follows Stephen to Nighttown and Bella Cohen's brothel, passing Army Privates en route. There in a trance, Bloom is chastised, glorified, vilified. Bloom experiences hallucinations from his past, admonishment by his father and mother, is menaced by his wife, and faces accusations by women for whom he lusted. The whore Zoe takes his talisman potato and they taunt each other. He imagines himself a king, then is denounced. Bloom is transformed into a pig, into a woman; Bello/Bella further humiliates him. Bloom hallucinates on his cuckolding by Molly. Stephen struggles to vanquish the specter of his dead mother and her forced guilt upon him, breaking the chandelier with his ashplant. A trouser button bip brings Bloom to reality. He stands up to Bella, asserts himself for Stephen. Stephen, accosted by the English Privates for threatening their King, is rescued by Bloom in a paternal way. Bloom sees an apparition of his deceased son Rudy.

THEMES
Poverty and shady nightlife in parts of Dublin. Fear that sexual expression might turn participants into animals. The Irish potato famine and its tragic effects. Masochism as a universal trait in men and women. The dreamlike experience as cathartic purging of the individual. Defenseless Ireland captive of the tyrantical Catholic Church and England. Man's capacity for wonder and beauty.

The Mabbot street entrance of nighttown, before which stretches an uncobbled transiding set with skeleton tracks, red and green will-o'-the-wisps and danger signals. Rows of flimsy houses with gaping doors. Rare lamps with faint rainbow fans... Whistles call and answer.

THE CALLS

Wait, my love, and I'll be with you.

THE ANSWERS

Round behind the stable.

(A deafmute idiot with goggle eyes, his shapeless mouth dribbling, jerks past, shaken in Saint Vitus' dance. A chain of children's hands imprisons him.)

THE CHILDREN

Kithogue! Salute.

THE IDIOT

(Lifts a palsied left arm and gurgles.) Grhahute!

THE CHILDREN

Where's the green light?

THE IDIOT

(Gobbing.) Ghaghahest.

(They release him. He jerks on. A pigmy woman swings on a rope slung between the railings, counting. A form sprawled against a dustbin and muffled by its arm and hat moves, groans, grinding growling teeth, and snores again. On a step a gnome totting among rubbishtip crouches to shoulder a sack of rags and bones. A crone standing by with a smoky oil lamp rams the last bottle in the maw of his sack. He heaves his booty, tugs askew his peaked cap and hobbles off mutely. The crone makes back for her lair swaying her lamp. A bandy child, asquat on the doorstep with a papershuttlecock, crawls sidling after her in spurts, clutches her skirt, scrambles up. A drunken navvy grips with both hands the railings of an area, lurching heavily. At a corner two night watch in shoulder capes, their hands upon their staffholsters, loom tall. A plate crashes; a woman screams; a child wails. Oaths of a man roar, mutter, cease. Figures wander, lurk, peer from warrens. In a room lit by a candle stuck in a bottleneck a slut combs out the tatts from the hair of a scrofulous child. Cissy Caffrey's voice, still young, sings shrill from a lane.)

CISSY CAFFREY

I gave it to Molly
Because she was jolly,
The leg of the duck
The leg of the duck

(Private Carr and Private Compton, swaggersticks tight in their oxters, as they march unsteadily rightaboutface and burst together from their mouths a volleyed fart. Laughter of men from the lane. A hoarse virago retorts.)

THE VIRAGO

Signs on you, hairy arse. More power the Cavan girl.

CISSY CAFFREY

More luck to me. Cavan, Cootehill and Belturbet. *(She sings.)*

[280]

I gave it to Nelly
To stick in her belly
The leg of the duck
The leg of the duck.

(Private Carr and Private Compton turn and counterretort, their tunics bloodbright in a lampglow, black sockets of caps on their blond copper polls. Stephen Dedalus and Lynch pass through the crowd close to the redcoats.)

PRIVATE COMPTON

(Jerks his finger.) Way for the parson.

PRIVATE CARR

(Turns and calls.) What ho, parson!

CISSY CAFFREY

(Her voice soaring higher.)
She has it, she got it,
Wherever she put it
The leg of the duck.

(Stephen, flourishing the ashplant in his left hand, chants with joy the introit for paschal time. Lynch, his jockey cap low on his brow, attends him, a sneer of discontent wrinkling his face.)

STEPHEN

Vidi aquam egredientem de tempo a latere dextro. Alleluia.

(The famished snaggletusks of an elderly bawd protrude from a doorway.)

THE BAWD

(Her voice whispering huskily.) Sst! Come here till I tell you. Maidenhead inside. Sst.

STEPHEN

(Altius aliquantulum.) Et omnes ad quos pervenit aqua ista.

THE BAWD

(Spits in their trail her jet of venom.) Trinity medicals. Fallopian tube. All prick and no pence.

(Edy Boardman, sniffling, crouched with Bertha Supple, draws her shawl across nostrils.)

EDY BOARDMAN

(Bickering.) And say the one: I see you up Faithful place with your squarepusher, the greaser off the railway, in his cometobed hat. Did you, says I. That's not for you to say, says I. You never seen me in the mantrap with a married highlander, says I. The likes of her! Stag that one is. Stubborn as a mule! And her walking with two fellows the one time, Kildbride the enginedriver and lancecorporal Oliphant.

STEPHEN

(Triumphaliter.) Salvi facti i sunt.

(He flourishes his ashplant shivering the lamp image, shattering light over the world. A liver and white spaniel on the prowl slinks after him, growling. Lynch scares it with a kick.)

LYNCH

So that?

STEPHEN

(Looks behind.) So that gesture, not music, not odours, would be a universal language, the gift of tongues rendering visible not the lay sense but the first entelechy, the structural rhythm.

LYNCH

Pornosophical philotheology. Metaphysics in Mecklenburg street!

STEPHEN

We have shrewridden Shakespeare and henpecked Socrates. Even the allwisest stagyrite was bitted, bridled and mounted by a light of love.

LYNCH

Ba!

STEPHEN

Anyway, who wants two gestures to illustrate a loaf and a jug? This movement illustrates the loaf and jug of bread and wine in Omar. Hold my stick.

[282]

LYNCH

Damn your yellow stick. Where are we going?

STEPHEN

Lecherous lynx, to *la belle dame sans merci,* Georgina Johnson, *ad deam qui laetificat juventutem meam.*

(Stephen thrusts the ashplant on him and slowly holds out his hands, his head going back till both hands are a span from his breast, down turned in planes intersecting, the fingers about to part, the left being higher.)

. . . .

Snakes of river fog creep slowly. From drains, clefts, cesspools, middens arise on all sides stagnant fumes. A glow leaps in the south beyond the seaward reaches of the river. The navvy staggering forward cleaves the crowd and lurches towards the tramsiding. On the farther side under the railway bridge Bloom appears flushed, panting, cramming bread and chocolate into a side pocket. From Gillen's hairdresser's window a composite portrait shows him gallant Nelson's image. A concave mirror at the side presents to him lovelorn longlost lugubru Booloohoom. Grave Gladstone sees him level, Bloom for Bloom. He passes, struck by the stare of truculent Wellington but in the convex mirror grin unstruck the bonham eyes and fatchuck cheekchops of Jollypoldy the rixdix doldy. At Antonio Rabaiotto's door Bloom halts, sweated under the bright arclamps. He disappears. In a moment reappears and hurries on.)

BLOOM

Fish and taters. N. g. Ah!

(He disappears into Olhousen's, the pork butcher's, under the downcoming rollshutter. A few moments later he emerges from under the shutter, puffing Poldy, blowing Bloohoom. In each hand he holds a parcel, one containing a lukewarm pig's crubeen, the other a cold sheep's trotter, sprinkled with wholepepper. He gasps, standing upright. Then bending to one side he presses a parcel against his rib and groans.

BLOOM

Stitch in my side. Why did I run?

(He takes breath with care and goes forward slowly towards the lampset siding. The glow leaps again.)

. . . .

BLOOM

Beware of pickpockets. Old thieves' dodge. Collide. Then snatch your purse.

(The retriever approaches sniffling, nose to the ground. A sprawled form sneezes. A stooped bearded figure appears garbed in the long caftan of an elder in Zion and a smoking cap with magenta tassels. Horned spectacles hang down at the wings of the nose. Yellow poison streaks are on the drawn face.)

RUDOLPH

Second halfcrown waste money today. I told you not to go with drunken goy ever. So. You catch no money.

BLOOM

(Hides the crubeen and trotter behind his back and, crestfallen, feels warm and cold feetmeat) Ja, ich weiss, papachi.

RUDOLPH

What you making down this place? Have you no soul? *(With feeble vulture talons he feels the silent face of Bloom)* Are you not my son Leopold, the grandson of Leopold? Are you not my dear son Leopold who left the house of his father and left the god of his fathers Abraham and Jacob?

BLOOM

(With precaution.) I suppose so, father. Mosenthal. All that's left of him.

RUDOLPH

(Severely.) One night they bring you home drunk as dog after spend your good money. What you call them running chaps?

BLOOM

(In youth's smart blue Oxford suit with white vestlips, narrowshouldered, in brown Alpine hat, wearing gent's sterling silver waterbury keyless watch and double curb Albert with seal attached, one side of him coated with stiffening mud.) Harriers, father. Only that once.

[284]

RUDOLPH

Once! Mud head to foot. Cut your hand open. Lockjaw. They make you kaput, Leopoldleben. You watch them chaps.

BLOOM

(Weakly.) They challenged me to a sprint. It was muddy. I slipped.

RUDOLPH

(With contempt.) Goim natchez. Nice spectacles for your poor mother!

BLOOM

Mamma!

ELLEN BLOOM

(In pantomime dame's stringed mobcap, crinoline and bustle, widow Twankey's blouse with muttonleg sleeves buttoned behind, grey mittens and cameo brooch, her hair plaited in a crispine net, appears over the staircase banisters, a slanted candlestick in her hand and cries out in shrill alarm.) O blessed Redeemer, what have they done to him! My smelling salts! *(She hauls up a reef of skirt and ransacks the pouch of her striped blay petticoat. A phial, an Agnus Dei, a shrievelled potato and a celluloid doll fall out.)* Sacred Heart of Mary, where were you at all, at all?

(Bloom, mumbling, his eyes downcast, begins to bestow his parcels in his filled pockets but desists, muttering.)

A VOICE

(Sharply.) Poldy!

BLOOM

Who? *(He ducks and wards off a blow clumsily.)* At your service.

(He looks up. Beside her mirage of datepalms a handsome woman in Turkish costume stands before him. Opulent curves fill out her scarlet trousers and jacket slashed with gold. A wide yellow cummerbund girdles her. A white yashmak violet in the night, covers her face, leaving free only her large dark eyes and raven hair.)

BLOOM

Molly!

[285]

MARION

Welly? Mrs Marion from this out, my dear man, when you speak to me. *(Satirically.)* Has poor little hubby cold feet waiting so long?

BLOOM

(Shifts from foot to foot.) No, no. Not the least little bit.

(He breathes in deep agitation, swallowing gulps of air, questions, hopes, crubeens for her supper, things to tell her, excuses, desire, spellbound. A coin gleams on her forehead. On her feet are jewelled toerings. Her ankles are linked by a slender fetterchain. Beside her a camel, hooded with a turreting turban, waits. A silk ladder of innumerable rungs climbs to his bobbing howdah. He ambles near with disgruntled hindquarters. Fiercely she slaps his haunch, her goldcurb wristbangles angriling, scolding him in Moorish.)

MARION

Nebrakada! Feminimum.

(The camel, lifting a foreleg, plucks from a tree a large mango fruit, offers it to his mistress, blinking, in his cloven hoof, then droops his head and, grunting, with uplifted neck, fumbles to kneel. Bloom stoops his back for leapfrog.)

BLOOM

I can give you . . . I mean as your business menagerie . . . Mrs Marion . . . if you . . .

MARION

So you notice some change? *(Her hands passing slowly over her trinketed stomacher. A slow friendly mockery in her eyes.)* O Poldy, Poldy, you are a poor old stick in the mud! Go and see life. See the wide world.

BLOOM

I was just going back for that lotion whitewax, orangeflower water. Shop closes early on Thursday. But the first thing in the morning. *(He pats divers pockets.)* This moving kidney. Ah!
(He points to the south, then to the east. A cake of new clean lemon soap arises, diffusing light and perfume.)

THE SOAP
We're a capital couple are Bloom and I;

[286]

He brightens the earth, I polish the sky.

*(The freckled face of Sweny, the druggist, appears in the disc of the
soapsun.)*

SWENY

Three and a penny, please.

BLOOM

Yes. For my wife, Mrs Marion. Special recipe.

MARION

(Softly.) Poldy!

BLOOM

Yes, ma'am?

MARION

Ti trema un poco il cuore?
*(In disdain she saunters away, plump as a pampered pouter pigeon,
humming the duet from* Don Giovanni.*)*

BLOOM

Are you sure about that *Voglio?* I mean the pronunciati . . .
*(He follows, followed by the sniffing terrier. The elderly bawd seizes
his sleeve, the bristles of her chinmole glittering.)*

THE BAWD

Ten shillings a maidenhead. Fresh thing was never touched. Fifteen.
There's no one in it only her old father that's dead drunk.
*(She points. In the gap of her dark den furtive, rainbedraggled Bridie
Kelly stands.)*

BRIDIE

Hatch street. Any good in your mind?
*(With a squeak she flaps her bat shawl and runs. A burly rough
pursues with booted strides. He stumbles on the steps, recovers,
plunges into gloom. Weak squeaks of laughter are heard, weaker.)*

THE BAWD

(Her wolfeyes shining.) He's getting his pleasure. You won't get a
virgin in the flash houses. Ten shillings. Don't be all night before the
polis in plain clothes sees us. Sixtyseven is a bitch.)

(Leering, Gerty MacDowell limps forward. She draws from behind ogling, and shows coyly her bloodied clout.)

GERTY

With all my worldly goods I thee and thor. *(She murmurs.)* You did that. I hate you.

BLOOM

I? When? You're dreaming. I never saw you.

THE BAWD

Leave the gentleman alone, you cheat. Writing the gentleman false letters. Streetwalking and soliciting. Better for your mother take the strap to you at the bedpost, hussy like you.

GERTY

(To Bloom.) When you saw all the secrets of my bottom drawer. *(She paws his sleeve, slobbering.)* Dirty married man! I love you for doing that to me.
(She slides away crookedly. Mrs Breen in man's frieze overcoat with loose bellows pockets, stands in the causeway, her roguish eyes wideopen, smiling in all her herbivorous buckteeth.)

MRS BREEN

Mr . . .

BLOOM

(Coughs gravely.) Madam, when we last had this pleasure by letter dated the sixteenth instant . . .

MRS BREEN

Mr Bloom! You down here in the haunts of sin! I caught you nicely! Scamp!

BLOOM

(Hurriedly.) Not so loud my name. Whatever do you think me? Don't give me away. Walls have ears. How do you do? It's ages since I. You're looking splendid. Absolutely it. Seasonable weather we are having this time of year. Black refracts heat. Short cut home here. Interesting quarter. Rescue of fallen women Magdalen asylum. I am the secretary . . .

MRS BREEN

(Holds up a finger.) Now don't tell a big fib! I know somebody
won't like that. O just wait till I see Molly! *(Slily.)* Account for
yourself this very minute or woe betide you!

BLOOM

(Looks behind.) She often said she'd like to visit. Slumming. The
exotic, you see. Negro servants too in livery if she had money.
Othello black brute. Eugene Stratton. Even the bones and cornerman
at the Livermore christies. Bohee brothers. Sweep for that matter.

. . . .

BLOOM

(Seizes her wrist with his free hand.) Josie Powell that was, prettiest
deb in Dublin. How time flies by! Do you remember, harking back in
a retrospective arrangement, Old Christmas night Georgina
Simpson's housewarming while they were playing the Irving Bishop
game, finding the pin blindfolded and thoughtreading? Subject, what
is in the snuffbox?

MRS BREEN

You were the lion of the night with your seriocomic recitation and
you looked the part. You were always a favourite with the ladies.

BLOOM

*(Squire of dames, in dinner jacket, with watered-silk facings, blue
masonic badge in his buttonhole, black bow and mother-of-pearl
studs, a prismatic champagne glass tilted in his hand.)* Ladies and
gentlemen, I give you Ireland, home and beauty.

MRS BREEN

The dear dead days beyond recall. Love's old sweet song.

. . . .

BLOOM

When you made your present choice they said it was beauty and the
beast. I can never forgive you for that. *(His clenched fist at his
brow.)* Think what it means. All you meant to me then. *(Hoarsely.)*
Woman, it's breaking me!

*(Dennis Breen, whitetailhatted, with Wisdom Hely's sandwichboard,
shuffles past them in carpet slippers, his dull beard thrust out,
muttering to the right and left. Little Alf Bergan, cloaked in the pall*

of the ace of spades, dogs him to the left and right, doubled in laughter.)

ALF BERGAN

(Points jeering at the sandwich boards.) U.p: Up.

MRS BREEN

(To Bloom.) High jinks below stairs. *(She gives him the glad eye.)* Why didn't you kiss the spot to make it well? You wanted to.

BLOOM

(Shocked.) Molly's best friend! Could you?

MRS BREEN

(Her pulpy tongue between her lips, offers a pigeon kiss.) Hnhn. The answer is a lemon. Have you a little present for me there?

BLOOM

(Offhandedly.) Kosher. A snack for supper. The home without potted meat is incomplete. I was at *Leah.* Mrs Bandman Palmer. Trenchant exponent of Shakespeare. Unfortunately threw away the programme. Rattling good place round there for pig's feet. Feel.

. . . .

MRS BREEN

Humbugging and deluthering as per usual with your cock and bull story.

BLOOM

I want to tell you a little secret about how I came to be here. But you must never tell. Not even Molly. I have a most particular reason.

MRS BREEN

(All agog.) O, not for worlds.

BLOOM

Let's walk on. Shall us?

MRS BREEN

(Eagerly.) Yes, yes, yes, yes, yes, yes, yes, yes.
(She fades from his side. Followed by the whining dog he walks on towards hellsgates. In an archway a standing woman, bent forward, her feet apart, pisses cowily. Outside a shuttered pub a bunch of loiterers listen to a tale which their broken snouted gaffer rasps out

[290]

*with a raucous humour. An armless pair of them flop wrestling,
growling, in maimed sodden playfight.)*

*(Bloom passes. Cheap whores, singly, coupled, shawled, dishevelled,
call from lanes, doors, corners.)*

THE WHORES

Are you going far, queer fellow?
How's your middle leg?
Got a match on you?
Eh, come here till I stiffen it for you.

*(He plodges through their sump towards the lighted street beyond.
From a bulge of window curtains a gramophone rears a battered
brazen trunk. In the shadow a shebeenkeeper haggles with the navvy
and the two redcoats.)*

. . . .

BLOOM

Wildgoose chase this. Disorderly houses. Lord knows where they are
gone. Drunks cover distance double quick. Nice mixup. Scene at
Westland row. Then jump in first class with third ticket. Then too
far. Train with engine behind. Might have taken me to Malahide or a
siding for the night or collision. Second drink does it. Once is a dose.
What am I following him for? Still, he's the best of that lot. If I
hadn't heard about Mrs Beaufoy Purefoy I wouldn't have gone and
wouldn't have met. Kismet. He'll lose that cash. Relieving office
here. Good biz for cheaptricks, organs. What do you lack? Soon got,
soon gone. Might have lost my life too with that mangongwheel-
tracktrolleyglarejuggernaut only for presence of mind. Can't always
save you though. If I had passed Truelock's window that day two
minutes later would have been shot. Absence of body. Still if bullet
went through my coat get damages for shock, five hundred pounds.
What was he? Kildare street club toff. God help his gamekeeper.

(He gazes ahead reading on the wall a scrawled chalk legend Wet
Dream *and a phallic design.)*

Odd! Molly drawing on the frosted carriagepane at Kingstown.
What's that like? *(Gaudy dollwomen loll in the lighted doorways, in
window embrasures, smoking birdseye cigarettes. The odour of the
sicksweet week floats towards him in slow round ovalling wreaths.)*

THE WREATHS

Sweet are the sweets. Sweets of sin.

BLOOM

My spine's a bit limp. Go or turn? And this food? Eat it and get all pigsticky. Absurd I am. Waste of money. One and eight pence too much. *(The retriever drives a cold snivelling muzzle against his hand, wagging his tail.)* Strange how they take to me. Even the brute today. Better speak to him first. Like women they like *rencontres*. Stinks like a polecat. *Chacun son gout.* He might be mad. Fido. Uncertain his movements. Good fellow! Garryowen! *(The wolfdog sprawls on his back, wriggling obscenely with begging paws, his long black tongue lolling out.)* Influence of his surroundings. Give and have done with it. Provided nobody. *(Calling encouraging words he shambles back with a furtive poacher's tread, dogged by the setter into a dark stalestunk corner. He unrolls one parcel and goes to dump the crubeen softly but holds back and feels the trotter.)* Sizeable for threepence. But then I have it in my left hand. Calls for more effort. Why? Smaller from want of use. O, let it slide. Two and six.
(With regret he lets unrolled crubeen and trotter slide. The mastiff mauls the bundle clumsily and gluts himself with growling greed, crunching the bones. Two raincapped watch approach, silent, vigilant. They murmur together.)

THE WATCH

Bloom. Of Bloom. For Bloom. Bloom.
(Each lays a hand on Bloom's shoulder.)

FIRST WATCH

Caught in the act. Commit no nuisance.

BLOOM

(Stammers.) I am doing good to others.
(A covey of gulls, storm petrels, rises hungrily from Liffey slime with Banbury cakes in their beaks.)
. . . .

THE FIRST WATCH

Come. Name and address.

[292]

BLOOM

I have forgotten for the moment. Ah, yes! *(He takes off his high grade hat, saluting.)* Dr Bloom, Leopold, dental surgeon. You have heard of von Bloom Pasha. Umpteen millions. *Donnerwetter!* Owns half Austria. Egypt. Cousin.

FIRST WATCH

Proof.
(A card falls from inside the leather headband of Bloom's hat.)

BLOOM

(In red fez, cadi's dress coat with broad green sash, wearing a false badge of the Legion of Honour, picks up the card hastily and offers it.) Allow me. My club is the Junior Army and Navy. Solicitors: Messrs John Henry Menton, 27 Bachelor's Walk.

FIRST WATCH

(Reads.) Henry Flower. No fixed abode. Unlawfully watching and besetting.

SECOND WATCH

An alibi. You are cautioned.

BLOOM

(Produces from his heartpocket a crumpled yellow flower.) This is the flower in question. It was given me by a man I don't know his name. *(Plausibly.)* You know that old joke, rose of Castille. Bloom. The change of name Virag. *(He murmurs privately and confidentially.)* We are engaged you see, sergeant. Lady in the case. Love entanglement. *(He shoulders the second watch gently.)* Dash it all. It's a way we gallants have in the navy. Uniform that does it. *(He turns gravely to the first watch.)* Still, of course, you do get your Waterloo sometimes. Drop in some evening and have a glass of old Burgundy. *(To the second watch gaily.)* I'll introduce you, inspector. She's game. Do it in shake of a lamb's tail.

(A dark mercurialised face appears, leading a veiled figure.)

THE DARK MERCURY

The Castle is looking for him. He was drummed out of the army.

MARTHA

(Thickveiled, a crimson halter round her neck, a copy of the Irish Times *in her hand, in tone of reproach, pointing.)* Henry! Leopold! Leopold! Lionel, thou lost one! Clear my name.

FIRST WATCH

(Sternly.) Come to the station.

BLOOM

(Scared, hats himself, steps back, then, plucking at his heart and lifting his right forearm on the square, he gives the sign and dueguard of fellowcraft.) No, no, worshipful master, light of love. Mistaken identity. The Lyons mail. Lesurques and Dubosc. You remember the Childs fratricide case. We medical men. By striking him dead with a hatchet. I am wrongfully accused. Better one guilty escape than ninetynine wrongfully condemned.

MARTHA

(Sobbing behind her veil.) Breach of promise. My real name is Peggy Griffin. He wrote to me that he was miserable. I'll tell my brother, the Bective rugger fullback, on you, heartless flirt.

BLOOM

(Behind his hand). She's drunk. The woman is inebriated. *(He murmurs vaguely the past of Ephraim.)* Shitbroleeth.

SECOND WATCH

(Tears in his eyes, to Bloom.) You ought to be thoroughly well ashamed of yourself.

BLOOM

Gentleman of the jury, let me explain. A pure mare's nest. I am a man misunderstood. I am being made a scapegoat of. I am a respectable married man, without a stain on my character. I live in Eccles street. My wife, I am the daughter of a most distinguished commander, a gallant upstanding gentleman, who do you call him, Majorgeneral Brian Tweedy, one of Britain's fighting men who helped to win our battles. Got his majority for the heroic defence of Rorke's Drift.

FIRST WATCH

Regiment.

[294]

BLOOM

(Turns to the gallery.) The royal Dublins, boys, the salt of the earth, known the world over. I think I see some old comrades in arms up there among you. The R. D. F. With our own Metropolitan police, guardians of our homes, the pluckiest lads and finest body of men, as physique, in the service of our sovereign.

FIRST WATCH

Profession or trade.

BLOOM

Well, I follow a literary occupation. Author-journalist. In fact we are just bringing out a collection of prize stories of which I am the inventor, something that is an entirely new departure. I am connected with the British and Irish press. If you ring up . . .

(Myles Crawford strides out jerkily, a quill between his teeth. His scarlet beak blazes with the aureole of his straw hat. He dangles a hank of Spanish onions in one hand and holds with the other hand a telephone receiver nozzle to his ear.)

MYLES CRAWFORD

(His cock's wattles wagging.) Hello, seventyseven eightfour. Hello. *Freeman's Urinal* and *Weekly Arsewiper* here. Paralyse Europe. You which? Bluebags? Who writes. Is it Bloom?

BEAUFOY

(Drawls.) No, you aren't, not by a long shot if I know it. I don't see it, that's all. No born gentleman, no one with the most rudimentary promptings of a gentleman would stoop to such particularly loathsome conduct. One of those, my lord. A plagiarist. A soapy sneak masquerading as a literateur. It's perfectly obvious that with the most inherent baseness he has cribbed some of my bestselling books, really gorgeous stuff, a perfect gem, the love passages in which are beneath suspicion. The Beaufoy books of love and great possessions with which your lordship is doubtless familiar, are a household word throughout the kingdom.

BLOOM

(Murmurs with hangdog meekness.) That bit about the laughing witch hand in hand I take exception to, if I may . . .

BEAUFOY

(Shouts.) It's a damnably foul lie showing the moral rottenness of the man! *(He extends his portfolio.)* We have here damning evidence, the *corpus delicti,* my lord, a specimen of my maturer work disfigured by the hallmark of the beast.

A VOICE FROM THE GALLERY
Moses, Moses, king of the jews,
Wiped his arse in the Daily News.

BLOOM

(Bravely.) Overdrawn.

BEAUFOY

You low cad! You ought to be ducked in the horsepond, you rotter! *(To the court.)* Why, look at the man's private life! Leading a quadruple existence! Street angel and house devil. Not fit to be mentioned in mix society. The arch conspirator of the age.

BLOOM

(To the court.) And he, a bachelor, how . . .

FIRST WATCH
The King versus Bloom. Call the woman Driscoll.

THE CRIER
Mary Driscoll, scullerymaid!
(Mary Driscoll, a slipshod servant girl, approaches. She has a bucket on the crook of her arm and a scouringbrush in her hand.)

SECOND WATCH
Another! Are you of the unfortunate class?

MARY DRISCOLL

(Indignantly.) I'm not a bad one. I bear respectable character and was four months in my last place. I was in a situation, six pounds a year and my chances with Fridays out, and I had to leave owing to his carryings on.
FIRST WATCH
What do you charge him with?

MARY DRISCOLL

He surprised me in the rere of the premises, your honour, when the
missus was out shopping one morning with a request for a safety pin.
He held me and I was discoloured in four places as a result. And he
interfered twitch with my clothing.

BLOOM

She counterassaulted.

MARY DRISCOLL

(Scornfully.) I had more respect for the scouringbrush, so I had. I
remonstrated with him, your lord, and he remarked: Keep it quiet!
(General laughter.)

GEORGES FOTRELL

(Clerk of the crown and peace, resonantly.) Order in court! The
accused will now make a bogus statement.

*(Bloom, pleading not guilty and holding a fullblown water lily,
begins a long unintelligible speech.)*

. . . .

J. J. O'MOLLOY

*(In barrister's grey wig and stuffgown, speaking with a voice of
pained protest.)* This is no place for indecent levity at the expense of
an erring mortal disguised in liquor. We are not in a beargarden nor
at an Oxford rag nor is this a travesty of justice. My client is an
infant, a poor foreign immigrant who started scratch as a stowaway
and is now trying to turn an honest penny. The trumped up
misdemeanor was due to a momentary aberration of heredity,
brought on by hallucination, such familiarities as the alleged guilty
occurrence being quite permitted in my client's native place, the land
of the Pharaoh. *Prima facie,* I put it to you that there was no attempt
at carnally knowing. Intimacy did not occur and the offence
complained by Driscoll, that her virtue was solicited, was not
repeated. I would deal in especial with atavism. There have been
cases of shipwreck and somnambulism in my client's family. If the
accused could speak he could a tale unfold one of the strangest that
have ever been narrated between the covers of a book. He himself,
my lord, is a physical wreck from cobbler's weak chest. His
submission is that he is of Mongolian extraction and irresponsible for
his actions. Not all there, in fact.

[297]

BLOOM

(Barefoot, pigeonbreasted, in lascar's vest and trousers, apologetic toes turned in, opens his tiny mole's eyes and looks about him dazedly, passing a slow hand across his forehead. Then he hitches his belt sailor fashion and with a shrug of oriental obeisance salutes the court, pointing one thumb heavenward.) Him makee velly muchee fine night. *(He begins to lilt simply.)*

> Li li poo lil chile,
> Blingee pigfoot evly night.
> Payee two shilly . . .

(He is howled down.)

J. J. O'MOLLOY

(Hotly to the populace.) This is a lonehand fight. By Hades, I will not have any client of mine gagged and badgered in this fashion by a pack of curs and laughing hyenas. The Mosaic code has superseded the law of the jungle. I say it and I say it emphatically without wishing for one moment to defeat the ends of justice, accused was not accessory before the act and prosecutrix has not been tampered with. The young person was treated by defendant as if she were his very own daughter. *(Bloom takes J. J. O'Molloy's hand and raises it to his lips.)* I shall call rebutting evidence to prove up to the hilt that the hidden hand is again at its old game. When in doubt persecute Bloom. My client, an innately bashful man, would be the last man in the world to do anything ungentlemanly which injured modesty could object to or cast a stone at a girl who took the wrong turning when some dastard, responsible for her condition, had worked his own sweet will on her. He wants to go straight. I regard him as the whitest man I know. He is down on his luck at present owing to the mortgaging of his extensive property at Agendath Netaim in faraway Asis Minor, slides of which will now be shown. *(To Bloom.)* I suggest that you will do the handsome thing.

BLOOM

A penny in the pound.

J. J. O'MOLLOY

(Almost voicelessly.) Excuse me, I am suffering from a severe chill, have recently come from a sickbed. A few wellchosen words. *(He assumes the avine head, foxy moustache and proboscidal eloquence*

[298]

of Seymour Bushe.) When the angel's book comes to be opened if aught that the pensive bosom has inaugurated of soultransfigured and of soultransfiguring deserves to live I say accord the prisoner at the bar the sacred benefit of the doubt. *(A paper with something written on it is handed into the court.)*

MRS YELVERTON BARRY

(In lowcorsaged opal balldress and elbowlength ivory gloves, wearing a sabletrimmed brick quilted dolman, a comb of brilliants and panache of osprey in her hair.) Arrest him constable. He wrote me an anonymous letter in prentice backhand when my husband was in North Riding of Tipperary on the Munster circuit, signed James Lovebirch. He said that he had seen from the gods my peerless globes as I sat in a box of the *Theatre Royal* at a command performance of *La Cigale.* I deeply inflamed him, he said. He made improper overtures to me to misconduct myself at half past four p.m. on the following Thursday, Dunsink time. He offered to send me through the post a work of fiction by Monsieur Paul de Kock, entitled *The Girl with the Three Pairs of Stays.*

THE HONORABLE MRS MERVYN TALBOYS

(In amazon costume, hard hat, jackboots, cockspurred, vermilion waistcoat, fawn musketeer gauntlets with braided drums, long train held up and hunting crop with which she strikes her welt constantly.) Also me. Because he saw me on the polo ground of the Phoenix park at the match All Ireland versus the Rest of Ireland. My eyes, I know, shone divinely as I watched Captain Slogger Dennehy of the Inniskillings win the final chukkar on his darling cob *Centaur.* This plebeian Don Juan observed me from behind a hackney car and sent me in double envelopes an obscene photograph, such as are sold after dark on Paris boulevards, insulting to any lady. I have it still. It represents a partially nude senorita, frail and lovely (his wife as he solemnly assured me, taken by him from nature), practising illicit intercourse with a muscular torero, evidently a blackguard. He urged me to do likewise, to misbehave, to sin with officers of the garrison. He implored me to soil his letter in an unspeakable manner, to chastise him as he richly deserves, to bestride and ride him, to give him a most vicious horsewhipping.
(Several highly respectable Dublin ladies hold up improper letters received from Bloom.)

THE HONOURABLE MRS MERVYN TALBOYS

(Stamps her jingling spurs in a sudden paroxysm of sudden fury.) I will, by the God above me. I'll scourge the pigeonlivered cur as long as I can stand over him. I'll flay him alive.

. . . .

BLOOM

(Shuddering, shrinking, joins his hands with hangdog mien.) O cold! O shivery! It was your ambrosial beauty. Forget, forgive. Kismet. Let me off this once. *(He offers the other cheek.)*

(Davy Stephens, ringleted, passes with a bevy of barefoot newsboys.)

DAVY STEPHENS

Messenger of the Sacred Heart and *Evening Telegraph* with Saint Patrick's Day Supplement. Containing the new addresses of all the cuckolds in Dublin.

(The very reverend Canon O'Hanlon in cloth of gold cope elevates and exposes a marble timepiece. Before him Father Conroy and the reverend John Hughes S.J. bend low.)

THE TIMEPIECE

(Unportalling.)

Cuckoo
Cuckoo
Cuckoo

(The brass quoits of a bed are heard to jingle.)

THE QUOITS

Jigjag, Jigajiga. Jigjag.

(A panel of fog rolls back rapidly, revealing rapidly in the jurybox the faces of Martin Cunningham, foreman silkhatted, Jack Power, Simon Dedalus, Tom Kernan, Ned Lambert, John Henry Menton, Myles Crawford, Lenehan, Paddy Leonard, Nosey Flynn, M'Coy and the featureless face of a Nameless One.)

THE NAMELESS ONE

Bareback riding. Weight for age. Gob, he organised her.

THE JURORS

(All their heads turned to his voice.) Really?

THE NAMELESS ONE

(Snarls.) Arse over tip. Hundred shillings to five.

THE JURORS

(All their heads lowered in assent.) Most of us thought as much.

FIRST WATCH

He is a marked man. Another girl's plait cut. Wanted: Jack the Ripper. A thousand pounds reward.

SECOND WATCH

(Awed, whispers.) And in black. A mormon. Anarchist.

THE CRIER

(Loudly.) Whereas Leopold Bloom of no fixed abode is a well known dynamitard, forger, bigamist, bawd and cuckold and a public nuisance to the citizens of Dublin and whereas at this commission of assizes the most honourable . . .

(His Honour, sir Frederick Falkiner, recorder of Dublin, in judicial garb of grey stone rises from the bench, stonebearded. He bears in his arms an umbrella sceptre. From his forehead arise starkly the Mosaic ramshorns.)

THE RECORDER

I will put an end to this white slave traffic and rid Dublin of this odious pest. Scandalous! *(He dons the black cap.)* Let him be taken, Mr Subsheriff, from the dock where he now stands and detained in custody in Mountjoy prison during His Majesty's pleasure and there be hanged by the neck until he is dead and therein fail not at your peril on may the Lord have mercy on your soul. Remove him. *(A black skullcap descends upon his head.)*

. . . .

SECOND WATCH

(Points to the corner.) The bomb is here.

FIRST WATCH

Infernal machine with a time fuse.

BLOOM

No, no. Pig's feet. I was at a funeral.

FIRST WATCH

(Draws his truncheon.) Liar!

(The beagle lifts his snout, showing the grey scorbutic face of Paddy Dignam. He has gnawed all. He exhales a putrid carcasefed breath. He grows to human size and shape. His dachshund coat becomes a brown mortuary habit. His green eye flashes bloodshot. Half of one ear, all the nose and both thumbs are ghouleaten.)

PADDY DIGNAM

(In a hollow voice.) It is true. It was my funeral. Doctor Finucane pronounced life extinct when I succumbed to the disease from natural causes.
(He lifts his mutilated ashen face moonwards and bays lugubriously.)

BLOOM

(In triumph.) You hear?

. . . .

PADDY DIGNAM

Pray for the repose of his soul.

(He worms down through a coalhole, his brown habit trailing its tether over rattling pebbles. After him toddles an obese grandfather rat on fungus turtle paws under a grey carapace. Dignam's voice, muffled, is heard baying under ground: Dignam's dead and gone below.
(All recedes. Bloom plodges forward again. He stands before a lighted house listening. The kisses, winging from their bowers, fly about him, twittering, warbling, cooing.)

THE KISSES

(Warbling.) Leo! *(Twittering.)* Icky licky micky sticky for Leo! *(Cooing.)* Coo coocoo! Yummyumm Womwom! *(Warbling.)* Big comebig! Pirouette! Leopold! *(Twittering.)* Leeolee! *(Warbling.)* O Leo!
(They rustle, flutter upon his garments, alight, bright giddy flecks, silvery sequins.)

BLOOM

A man's touch. Sad music. Church music. Perhaps here.

(Zoe Higgins, a young whore in a sapphire slip, closed with three bronze buckles, a slim black velvet fillet round her throat, nods, trips down the steps and accosts him.)

ZOE

Are you looking for someone? He's inside with his friend.

BLOOM

Is this Mrs Mack's?

ZOE

No, eightyone. Mrs Cohen's. You might go farther and fare worse. Mother Slipperslapper. *(Familiarly.)* She's on the job herself tonight with the vet, her tipster, that gives her all the winners and pays for her son in Oxford. Working overtime but her luck's turned today. *(Suspiciously.)* You're not his father, are you?

BLOOM

Not I!

ZOE

You both in black. Has little mousey any tickles tonight?
(His skin, alert, feels her fingertips approach. A hand slides over his left thigh.)

ZOE

How's the nuts?

BLOOM

Off side. Curiously they are on the right. Heavier I suppose. One in a million my tailor, Mesias, says.

ZOE

(In sudden alarm.) You're a hard chancre.

BLOOM

Not likely.

[303]

ZOE

I feel it.
(Her hand slides into his left trouser pocket and brings out a hard black shrivelled potato. She regards it and Bloom with dumb moist lips.)

BLOOM

A talisman. Heirloom.

ZOE

For Zoe? For keeps? For being so nice, eh?
(She puts the potato greedily into a pocket, then links his arm, cuddling him with supple warmth. He smiles uneasily. Slowly, note by note, oriental music is played. He gazes in the tawny crystal of her eyes, ringed with kohol. His smile softens.)

ZOE

You'll know me the next time.

BLOOM

(Fascinated.) I thought you were of good stock by your accent.

ZOE

And you know what thought did?
(She bites his ear gently with little goldstopped teeth sending him a cloying breath of stale garlic. The roses draw apart, disclose a sepulchre of the gold kings and their mouldering bones.

BLOOM

(Draws back, mechanically caressing her right bub with a flat awkward hand.) Are you a Dublin girl?

ZOE

(Catches a stray hair deftly and twists it to her coil.) No bloody fear. I'm English. Have you a swaggerroot?

BLOOM

(As before.) Rarely smoke, dear. Cigar now and then. Childish device. *(Lewdly.)* The mouth can be better engaged than with a cylinder of rank week.

ZOE

Go on. Make a stump speech out of it.

[304]

BLOOM

(In workman's corduroy overalls, black gansy with red floating tie and apache cap.) Mankind is incorrigible. Sir Walter Raleigh brought from the new world that potato and that weed, the one a killer of pestilence by absorption, the other a poisoner of the ear, eye, heart, memory, will, understanding, all. That is to say, he brought the poison a hundred years before another person whose name I forgot brought the food. Suicide. Lies. All our habits. Why, look at our public life!

(Midnight chimes from distant steeples.)

THE CHIMES

Turn again, Leopold! Lord mayor of Dublin!

BLOOM

(In alderman's gown and chain.) Electors of Arran Quay, Inns Quay, Rotunda, Mountjoy and North Dock, better run a tramline, I say, from the cattlemarket to the river. That's the music of the future. That's my programme. *Cui bono?* But our buccaneering Vanderdeckens in their phantom ship of finance . . .

AN ELECTOR

Three times four for our future chief magistrate!

(The aurora borealis of the torchlight procession leaps.)

(Several wellknown burgesses, city magnates and freemen of the city shake hands with Bloom and congratulate him....)

LATE LORD MAYOR HARRINGTON

(In scarlet robe with mace, gold mayoral chain and large white silk scarf.) That alderman sir Leo Bloom's speech be printed at the expense of the ratepayers. That the house in which he was born be ornamented with commemorative tablet and that the thoroughfare hitherto known as Cow Parlour off Cork street be henceforth designated Boulevard Bloom.

. . . .

(Prolonged applause. Venetian masts, maypoles and festal arches spring up. A streamer bearing the legends Cead Mille Failte *and* Mah Ttob Melek Israel *spans the street.*

. . . .

(Under an arch of triumph Bloom appears bareheaded, in a crimson velvet mantle trimmed with ermine, bearing Saint Edward's staff, the orb and sceptre with the dove, the curtana. He is seated on a milkwhite horse with long flowing crimson tail, richly caparisoned, with golden headstall. Wild excitement. The ladies from their balconies throw down rosepetals. The air is perfumed with essences. The men cheer. Bloom's boys run amid the bystanders with branches of hawthorn and wrenbushes.)

BLOOM'S BOYS
The wren, the wren,
The king of all birds
Saint Stephen's his day.
Was caught in the furze.

A BLACKSMITH
(Murmurs.) For the Honour of God! And is that Bloom? He scarcely looks thirtyone.
A PAVIOR AND FLAGGER
That's the famous Bloom now, the world's greatest reformer. Hats off!
(All uncover their heads. Women whisper eagerly.)

A NOBLEWOMAN
(Nobly.) All that man has seen!
A FEMINIST
(Masculinely.) And done!
A BELLHANGER
A classic face! He has the forehead of a thinker.
(Bloom's weather. A sunburst appears in the northwest.)

THE BISHOP OF DOWN AND CONNOR
I here present your undoubted emperor president and king chairman, the most serene and potent and very puissant ruler of this realm. God save Leopold the First!

[306]

ALL

God save Leopold the First!

BLOOM

(In dalmatic and purple mantle, to the bishop of Down and Connor, with dignity.) Thanks, somewhat eminent sir.

WILLIAM, ARCHBISHOP OF ARMAGH

(In purple stock and shovel hat.) Will you to your power cause law and mercy to be executed in all your judgments in Ireland and territories thereunto belonging?

BLOOM

(Placing his right hand on his testicles, swears.) So may the Creator deal with me. All this I promise to do.

MICHAEL, ARCHBISHOP OF ARMAGH

(Pours a cruse of hairoil over Bloom's head.) Gaudium magnum annuntio vobis. Habemus carneficem. Leopold, Patrick, Andrew, David, George, be thou anointed!

(Bloom holds up his right hand on which sparkles the Koh-i-Noor diamond. His palfrey neighs. Immediate silence. Wireless intercontinental and interplanetary transmitters are set for reception of message.)

BLOOM

My subjects! We hereby nominate our faithful charger Copula Felix hereditary Grand Vizier and announce that we have this day repudiated four former spouse and have bestowed our royal hand upon the princess Selene, the splendour of night.

(The former morganatic spouse of Bloom is hastily removed in the Black Maria. The princess Selene, in moonblue robes, a silver crescent on her head, descends from a Sedan chair, borne by two giants. An outburst of cheering.)

JOHN HOWARD PARNELL

(Raises the royal standard.) Illustrious Bloom! Successor to my famous brother!

[307]

BLOOM

(Embraces John Howard Parnell.) We thank you from our heart,
John, for this right royal welcome to green Erin, the promised land of
our common ancestors.
*(The freedom of the city is presented to him embodied in a charter.
The keys of Dublin, crossed on a crimson cushion, are given to him.
He shows all that he is wearing green socks.)*

BLOOM

My beloved subjects, a new era is about to dawn. I, Bloom, tell you
verily it is even now at hand. Yea, on the word of a Bloom, ye shall
ere long enter into the golden city which is to be the new
Bloomusalem in the Nova Hibernia of the future.

*(Thirtytwo workmen wearing rosettes, from all the counties of
Ireland, under the guidance of Derwan the builder, construct the
new Bloomusalem. It is a colossal edifice, with crystal roof, built in
the shape of a huge pork kidney, containing forty thousand rooms. In
the course of its extension several buildings and monuments are
demolished. Government offices are temporarily transferred to
railway sheds. Numerous houses are razed to the ground. The
inhabitants are lodged in barrels and boxes, all marked in red with
the letters: L. B. Several paupers fall from a ladder. A part of the
walls of Dublin, crowded with loyal sightseers, collapses.)*

THE SIGHTSEERS

(Dying.) Morituri te salutant. (They die.)

*(A man in a brown macintosh springs up through a trapdoor. He
points an elongated finger at Bloom.)*

THE MAN IN THE MACINTOSH

Don't you believe a word he says. That man is Leopold M'Intosh,
the notorious fireraiser. His real name is Higgins.

BLOOM

Shoot him! Dog of a christian! So much for M'Intosh!
*(A cannonshot. The man in the macintosh disappears. Bloom with his
sceptre strikes down poppies. The instantaneous deaths of many
powerful enemies, graziers, members of parliament, members of the*

[308]

*standing committees, are reported. . . Women press forward to touch
the hem of Bloom's robe. The lady Gwendolen Dubedat bursts
through the throng, leaps on his horse and kisses him on both cheeks
amid a great acclamation. A magnesium flashlight photograph is
taken. Babes and sucklings are held up.)*

THE WOMEN

Little father! Little father!

THE BABES AND SUCKLIINGS
Clap clap hands till Poldy comes home,
Cakes in his pocket for Leo alone.

*(Bloom, bending down, pokes Baby Boardman gently in the
stomach.)*

BABY BOARDMAN

(Hiccups, curdled milk flowing from his mouth.) Hajajaja.

BLOOM

(Shaking hands with a blind stripling.) My more than Brother!
(Placing his arms around the shoulders of an old couple.) Dear old
friends! *(He plays pussy fourcorners with ragged boys and girls.)*
Peep! Bopeep! *(He wheels twins in a perambulator.)* Ticktacktwo
wouldyousetashoe? …

THE CITIZEN

(Choked with emotion, brushes aside a tear in his emerald muffler.)
May the good God bless him!
(The rams' horns sound for silence. The standard of Zion is hoisted.)

BLOOM

*(Unclocks impressively, revealing obesity, unrolls a paper and reads
solemnly.)* Aleph Beth Ghimel Daleth Hagadah Tephilim Kosher
Yom Kippur Hanukah Roschaschana Beni Brith Bar Mitzvah
Mazzoth Askenazim Meshuggah Talith.
*(An official translation is read by Jimmy Henry, assistant town
clerk.)*

JIMMY HENRY

The Court of Conscience is now open. His Most Catholic Majesty
will now administer open air justice. Free medical and legal advice,

solution of doubles and other problems. All cordially invited. Given at this our loyal city of Dublin in the year 1 of the Paradisiacal Era.

PADDY LEONARD

What am I to do about my rates and taxes?

BLOOM

Pay them, my friend.

PADDY LEONARD

Thank you.

NOSEY FLYNN

Can I raise a mortgage on my fire insurance?

BLOOM

(Obdurately.) Sirs, take notice that by the law of torts you are bound over in your own recognisances for six months in the sum of five pounds.

. . . .

LARRY O'ROURKE

An eight day licence for my new premises. You remember me, sir Leo, when you were in number seven. I'm sending around a dozen of stout for the missus.

BLOOM

(Coldly.) You have the advantage of me. Lady Bloom accepts no presents.

CROFTON

This is indeed a festivity.

BLOOM

(Solemnly.) You call it a festivity. I call it a sacrament.

ALEXANDER KEYES

When will we have our own house of keys?

BLOOM

I stand for the reform of municipal morals and the plain ten commandments. New worlds for old. Union of all, jews, moslem and gentile. Three acres and a cow for all children of nature. Saloon motor hearses. Compulsory manual labor for all. All parks open to the public day and night. Electric dishscrubbers. Tuberculosis,

[310]

lunacy, war and mendicancy must now cease. General amnesty, weekly carnival, with masked licence, bonuses for all, esperanto the universal brotherhood. No more patriotism of barspongers and dropsical impostors. Free money, free love and a free lay church in a free lay state.

O'MADDEN BURKE

Free fox in a free henroost.

BLOOM

Mixed races and marriage.

LENEHAN

What about mixed bathing?

(Bloom explains to those near him his schemes for social regeneration. All agree with him. The keeper of the Kildare Street Museum appears, dragging a lorry on which are the shaking statues of several naked goddesses...)

FATHER FARLEY

He is an episcopalian, an agnostic, an anythingarian seeking to overthrow our holy faith.

MRS RIORDAN

(Tears up her will.) I'm disappointed in you! You bad man!

MOTHER GROGAN

(Removes her boot to throw it at Bloom.) You beast! You abominable person!

NOSEY FLYNN

Give us a tune, Bloom. One of the old sweet songs.

BLOOM

(With rollicking humour.)

    I vowed that I never would leave her,
    She turned out a cruel deceiver.
    With my tooraloom tooraloom tooraloom tooraloom.

HOPPY HOLOHAN

Good old Bloom! There's nobody like him after all.

PADDY LEONARD

Stage Irishman!

[311]

BLOOM

What railway opera is like a tramline in Gibraltar? The Rows of Casteele. *(Laughter.)*

LENEHAN

Plagiarist! Down with Bloom!

THE VEILED SIBYL

(Enthusiastically.) I'm a Bloomite and I glory in it. I believe in him spite of all. I'd give my life for him, the funniest man on earth.

BLOOM

(Winks at the bystanders.) I bet she's a bonnie lassie.

THEODORE PUREFOY

(In fishing cap and oilskin jacket.) He employs a mechanical device to frustrate the sacred ends of nature.

THE VEILED SIBYL

(Stabs herself.) My hero god! *(She dies.)*
(Many most attractive and enthusiastic women also commit suicide....)

ALEXANDER J. DOWIE

(Violently.) Fellowchristians and anti-Bloomites, the man called Bloom is from the roots of hell, a disgrace to christian men. A fiendish libertine from his earliest years this stinking goat of Mendes gave precocious signs of infantile debauchery recalling the cities of the plain, with a dissolute granddam. This vile hypocrite, bronzed with infamy, is the white bull mentioned in the Apocalypse. A worshipper of the Scarlet Woman, intrigue is the very breath of his nostrils. The stake faggots and the caldron of boiling oil are for him. Caliban!

THE MOB

Lynch him! Roast him! He's as bad as Parnell was. Mr Fox!

(Mother Grogran throws her boot at Bloom. Several shopkeepers from the upper and lower Dorset street throw objects of little or no commercial value, hambones, condensed milk tins, unsaleable cabbage, stale bread, sheeps' tails, odd pieces of fat.)

[312]

BLOOM

(Excitedly.) This is midsummer madness, some ghastly joke again.
By heaven, I am guileless as the unsunned snow! It was my brother
Henry. He is my double. He lives in number 2 Dolphin's Barn.
Slander, the viper, has wrongfully accused me. Fellowcountrymen,
sgenl inn bata coisde gan capall. I call on my old friend, Dr Malachi
Mulligan, sex specialist, to give medical testimony on my behalf.

DR MULLIGAN

(In motor jerkin, green motorgoggles on his brow.) Dr Bloom is
bisexually abnormal. He has recently escaped from Dr Eustace's
private asylum for demented gentlemen. Born out of bedlock
hereditary epilepsy is present, the consequence of unbridled lust.
Traces of elephantiasis have been discovered among his ascendants.
There are marked symptoms of chronic exhibitionism.
Ambidexterity is also latent. He is prematurely bald from selfabuse,
perversely idealistic in consequence, a reformed rake, and has metal
teeth. In consequence of a family complex he has temporarily lost his
memory and I believe him to be more sinned against than sinning. I
have made a pervaginal examination and, after application of the
acid test to 5427 anal, axillary, pectoral and pubic hairs, I declare
him to be *virgo intacta.*
(Bloom holds his high grade hat over his gential organs.)

. . . .

DR DIXON

(Reads a bill of health.) Professor Bloom is a finished example of the
new womanly man. His moral nature is simple and lovable. Many
have found him a dear man, a dear person. He is a rather quaint
fellow on the whole, coy though not feebleminded in the medical
sense. He has written a really beautiful letter, a poem in itself, to the
court missionary of the Reformed Priests' Protection Society which
clears up everything. He is practically a total abstainer and I can
affirm that he sleeps on a straw litter and eats the most Spartan food,
cold dried grocer's peas. He wears a hairshirt in winter and summer
and scourges himself every Saturday. He was, I understand, at one
time a firstclass misdemeanant in Glencree reformatory. Another
report states that he was a very posthumous child. I appeal for
clemency in the name of the most sacred word our vocal organs have
ever been called upon to speak. He is about to have a baby.
(General commotion and compassion. Women faint.)

BLOOM

O, I so want to be a mother.

MRS THORNTON

(In nursetender's gown.) Embrace me tight, dear. You'll be soon over it. Tight dear.
(Bloom embraces her tightly and bears eight male yellow and white children. They appear on a redcarpeted staircase adorned with expensive plants. All are handsome, with valuable metallic faces, wellmade, respectably dressed and wellconducted, speaking five modern languages fluently and interested in various arts and sciences....)

A VOICE

Bloom, are you the Messiah ben Joseph or ben David?

BLOOM

(Darkly.) You have said it.

BROTHER BUZZ

Then perform a miracle.

BANTAM LYONS

Prophesy who will win the Saint Leger.
(Bloom walks on a net, covers his left eye with his left ear, passes through several walls, climbs Nelson's Pillar, hangs from the top ledge by his eyelids, eats twelve dozen oysters (shells included), heals several sufferers from king's evil, contracts his face so as to resemble many historical personages....)

A DEADHAND

(Writes on the wall.) Bloom is a cod.

A CRAB

(In bushranger's kit.) What did you do in the cattlecreep behind Kilbarrack?

A FEMALE INFANT

(Shakes a rattle.) And under Ballybough bridge?

A HOLLYBUSH

And in the devil's glen?

[314]

BLOOM

(Blushes furiously all over from front to nates, three tears falling from his left eye. Spare my past.

THE IRISH EVICTED TENANTS

(In bodycoats, kneebreeches, with Donnybrook fair shillelaghs.) Sjambok him!

(Bloom with asses' ears seats himself in the pillory with crossed arms, his feet protruding. He whistles Don Giovanni, a cenar teco. *Artane orphans, joining hands, caper round him. Girls of the Prison Gate Mission, joining hands, caper round in the opposite direction.)*

THE ARTANE ORPHANS

You hig, you hog, you dirty dog!
You think the ladies love you!

THE PRISON GATE GIRLS

If you see kay
Tell him he may
See you in tea
Tell him from me.

. . . .

(All the people cast soft pantomime stones at Bloom. Many bonafide travelers and ownerless dogs come near him and defile him...)

(Invests Bloom in a yellow habit with embroidery of painted flames and high pointed hat. He places a bag of gunpowder round his neck and hands him over to the civil power, saying.) Forgive him his trespasses.

(Lieutenant Myers of the Dublin Fire Brigade by general request sets fire to Bloom. Lamentations.)

THE CITIZEN

Thank heaven!

BLOOM

(In a seamless garment marked I. H. S. stands upright amid phoenix flames.) Weep not for me, O daughters of Erin.

(He exhibits to Dublin reporters traces of burning. The daughters of Erin, in black garments with large prayerbooks and long lighted candles in their hands, kneel down and pray.)

THE DAUGHTERS OF ERIN

Kidney of Bloom, pray for us.
Flower of the Bath, pray for us.
Mentor of Menton, pray for us.
Canvasser for the Freeman, pray for us.
Charitable Mason, pray for us.
Wandering Soap, pray for us.
Sweets of Sin, pray for us.
Music without Words, pray for us.
Reprover of the Citizen, pray for us.
Friend of all Frillies, pray for us.
Midwife Most Merciful, pray for us.
Potato Preservative against the Plague and Pestilence, pray for us.
(A choir of six hundred voices, conducted by Mr Vincent O'Brien, sings the Alleluia chorus, accompanied on the organ by Joseph Glynn. Bloom becomes mute, shrunken, carbonised.)

ZOE

Talk away till you're black in the face.

BLOOM

(In caubeen with clay pipe stuck in the band, dusty brogues, an emigrant's red handkerchief bundle in his hand, leading a black bogoak pig by a sugaun, with a smile in his eye.) Let me be going now, woman of the house, for by all goats in Connemara I'm after having the father and mother of a bating. *(With a tear in his eye.)* All insanity. Patriotism, sorrow for the dead, music, future of the race. To be or not to be. Life's dream is o'er. End it peacefully. They can live on. *(He gazes far away mournfully.)* I am ruined. A few pastilles of aconite. The blinds drawn. A letter. Then lie back to rest. *(He breathes softly.)* No more. I have lived. Fare. Farewell.

ZOE

(Stiffly, her finger in her neckfillet.) Honest? Till the next time. *(She sneers.)* Suppose you got up the wrong side of the bed or came too quick with your best girl. O, I can read your thoughts.

[316]

BLOOM

(Bitterly.) Man and woman, love, what is it? A cork and bottle.

ZOE

(In sudden sulks.) I hate a rotter that's insincere. Give a bleeding whore a chance.

BLOOM

(Repentantly.) I am very disagreeable. You are a necessary evil. Where are you from? London?

ZOE

(Glibly.) Hog's Norton where the pigs play the organ. I'm Yorkshire born. *(She holds his hand which is feeling for her nipple.)* I say, Tommy Tittlemouse. Stop that and begin worse. Have you cash for a short time? Ten shillings?

BLOOM

(Smiles, nods slowly.) More, houri, more.

ZOE

And more's mother? *(She pats him offhandedly with velvet paws.)* Are you coming into the musicroom to see our new pianola? Come and I'll peel off.

BLOOM

(Feeling his occiput dubiously with the unparalleled embarrassment of a harassed pedlar gauging the symmetry of her peeled pears.) Somebody would be dreadfully jealous if she knew. The greeneyed monster. *(Earnestly.)* You know how difficult it is. I needn't tell you.

ZOE

(Flattered.) What the eye can't see the heart can't grieve for. *(She pats him.)* Come.

BLOOM

Laughing witch! The hand that rocks the cradle.

ZOE

Babby!

BLOOM

(In babylinen and pelisse, bigheaded, with a caul of dark hair, fixes big eyes on her fluid slip and counts its bronze buckles with a chubby finger, his moist tongue tolling and lisping.)

[317]

THE BUCKLES

Love me. Love me not. Love me.

ZOE

Silent means consent. *(With little parted talons she captures his hand, her forefinger giving to his palm the passtouch of secret monitor, luring him to doom.)* Hot hands cold gizzard.

(He hesitates amid scents, music, temptations. She leads him towards the steps, drawing him by the odour of her armpits, the vice of her painted eyes, the rustle of her slip in whose sinuous folds lurks the lion reek of all the male brutes that have possessed her.)

THE MALE BRUTES

(Exhaling sulphur of rut and dung and ramping in their loosebox, faintly roaring, their drugged heads swaying to and fro.) Good!

(Zoe and Bloom reach the doorway where two sister whores are seated. They examine him curiously from under their pencilled brows and smile to his hasty bow. He trips awkwardly.)

ZOE

(Her lucky hand instantly saving him. Hoopsa! Don't fall upstairs.

BLOOM

The just man falls seven times. *(He stands aside at the threshold.)* After you is good manners.

ZOE

Ladies first, gentlemen after.

(She crosses the threshold. He hesitates. She turns and, holding out her hands, draws him over. He hops. On the antlered rack of the hall hang a man's hat and waterproof. Bloom uncovers himself but, seeing them, frowns, then smiles, preoccupied. A door on the return landing is thrown open.... Lynch squats crosslegged on the hearthrug of matted hair, his cap back to the front. With a wand he beats time slowly. Kitty Ricketts, a bony pallid whore in navy costume, doeskin gloves rolled back from a coral wristlet, a chain purse in her hand, sits perched on the edge of the table swinging her leg and glancing at herself in the gilt mirror over the mantelpiece. A

[318]

tag of her corset lace hangs slightly below her jacket. Lynch indicates mockingly the couple at the piano.)

KITTY

(Coughs behind her hand.) She's a bit imbecillic. *(She signs with a waggling forefinger.)* Blemblem. *(Lynch lifts up her skirt and white petticoat with the wand. She settles them down quickly.)* Respect yourself. *(She hiccups, then bends quickly her sailor hat under which her hair glows, red with henna.)*
O, excuse!

ZOE

More limelight, Charley. *(She goes to the chandelier and turns the gas full cock.)*

KITTY

(Peers at the gasjet.) What ails it tonight?

LYNCH

(Deeply.) Enter a ghost and hobgoblins.

ZOE

Clap on the back for Zoe.

(The wand in Lynch's hand flashes: a brass poker. Stephen stands at the pianola on which sprawl his hat and ashplant. With two fingers he repeats once more the series of empty fifths. Florry Talbot, a blond feeble goosefat whore in a tatterdemalion gown of mildewed strawberry, lolls spreadeagle in the sofa corner, her limp forearm pendent over the bolster, listening. A heavy stye droops over her sleepy eyelid.)
. . . .
(Outside the gramophone begins to blare The Holy City.*)*

STEPHEN

(Abruptly.) What went forth to the ends of the world to traverse not itself. God, the sun, Shakespeare, a commercial traveller, having itself traversed in reality itself, becomes that self. Wait a moment. Wait a second. Damn that fellow's noise in the street. Self which it itself was ineluctably preconditioned to becomes. *Ecco!*

LYNCH

(With a mocking whinny of laughter grins at Bloom and Zoe Higgins.) What a learned speech, eh?

ZOE

(Briskly.) God help your head, he knows more than you have forgotten.
(With obese stupidity Florry Talbot regards Stephen.)

FLORRY

They say the last day is coming this summer.

ZOE

(Explodes in laughter.) Great unjust God!

FLORRY

(Offended.) Well, it was in the papers about Antichrist. O, my foot's tickling.
(Ragged barefoot newsboys, jogging a wagtail kite, patter past, yelling.)

THE NEWSBOYS

Stop press edition. Result of the rockinghorse races. Sea serpent in the royal canal. Safe arrival of Antichrist.

(Stephen turns and sees Bloom.)

STEPHEN

A time, times and half a time.

(Reuben J. Antichrist, wandering jew, a clutching hand open on his spine, stumps forward. Across his loins is slung a pilgrim's wallet from which protrude promissory notes and dishonoured bills. Aloft over his shoulder he bears a long boatpole from the hook of which a sodden huddled mass of his only son, saved from Liffey waters, hangs from the slack of its breeches. A hobgoblin in the image of Punch Costello, hipshot, crookbacked, hydrocephalic, prognathic with receding forehead and Ally Sloper nose, tumbles in somersaults through the gathering darkness.)...

FLORRY

(Sinking into torpor, crosses herself secretly.) The end of the world!

[320]

(A female tepid effluvium leaks out from her. Nebulous obscurity occupies space. Through the drifting fog without the gramophone blares over coughs and feetshuffling.)

THE GRAMOPHONE
Jerusalem!
Open your gates and sing
Hosanna . . .

(A rocket rushes up the sky and bursts. A white star falls from it, proclaiming the consummation of all things and second coming of Elijah. Along an infinite invisible tightrope taut from zenith to nadir the End of the World, a twoheaded octopus in gillie's kilts, busby and tartan filibegs, whirls through the murk, head over heels, in the form of the Three Legs of Man.)

THE END OF THE WORLD
(With a Scotch accent.) Wha'll dance the keel row, the keel row, the keel row?
(Over the passing drift and choking breathcoughs, Elijah's voice, harsh as a corncrake's, jars on high. Perspiring in a loose lawn surplice with funnel sleeves he is seen, vergerfaced, above a rostrum about which the banner of old glory is draped. He thumps the parapet.)

ELIJAH
No yapping, if you please, in this booth. Jake Crane, Creole Sue, Dave Campbell, Abe Kirschner, do you coughing with your mouths shut. Say, I am operating all this trunk line. Boys, do it now. God's time is 12.25. Tell mother you'll be there. Rush your order and you play a slick ace. Join on right here! Book through to eternity junction, the nonstop run. Just one word more. Are you a god or a doggone clod? If the second advent came to Coney Island are we ready ? Florry Christ, Stephen Christ, Zoe Christ, Bloom Christ, Kitty Christ, Lynch Christ, it's up to you to sense the cosmic force. Have we cold feet about the cosmos? No. Be on the side of the angels. Be a prism. You have that something within, the higher self. You can rub shoulders with a Jesus, a Gautama, and Ingersoll. Are you all in the vibration? I say you are. You once nobble that, congregation, and a buck joyride to heaven becomes a back number.

You got me? It's a lifebrightener, sure. The hottest stuff ever was. It's the whole pie with jam in it. It's just the cutest snappiest line out. It is immense, supersumptuous. It restores. It vibrates. I know and I am some vibrator. Joking apart and getting down to bedrock, A. J. Christ Dowie and the harmonial philosophy, have you got that? O.K. Seventyseven west sixtyninth street. Got me? That's it. You call me up by sunphone any old time. Bumboosers, save your stamps. *(He shouts.)* Now then our glory song. All join heartily in the singing. Encore! *(He sings.)* Jeru . . .

. . . .

STEPHEN

In the beginning was the word, in the end the world without end. Blessed be the eight beatitudes.
(The beatitudes, Dixon, Madden, Crotthers, Costello, Lenehan, Bannon, Mulligan and Lynch in white surgical students' gowns, four abreast, goosestepping, tramp fast past the noising marching.)

THE BEATITUDES

(Incoherently.) Beer beef battledog buybull businum barnum buggerum bishop.

LYSTER

(In quakergrey kneebreeches and broadbrimmed hat, says discreetly.) He is our friend. I need not mention names. Seek thou the light.
(He corantos by. Best enters in hairdresser attire, shinily lingered, his locks in curlpapers. He leads John Eglinton who wears a mandarin's kimono of Nankeen yellow, lizard lettered, and a high pagoda hat.)

BEST

(Smiling, lifts the hat and displays a shaven poll from the crown of which bristles a pigtail toupee tied with an orange topknot.) I was just beautifying him, don't you know. A thing of beauty, don't you know. Yeats says, or I mean, Keats says.

JOHN EGLINTON

(Produces a greencapped dark lantern and flashes it towards a corner; with carping accent.) Esthetics and cosmetics are for the boudoir. I am out for truth. Plain truth for a plain man. Tanderagee wants the facts and means to get them.

. . . .

[322]

ZOE

Who has a fag as I'm here?

LYNCH

(Tossing a cigarette on to the table.) Here.

ZOE

(Her head perched aside in mock pride.) Is that the way to hand the pot to a lady? *(She stretches up to light the cigarette over the flame, twirling it slowly, showing the brown tufts of her armpits. Lynch with his poker lifts boldly a side of her slip. Bare from her garters up her flesh appears under the sapphire a nixie's green. She puffs calmly at her cigarette.)* Can you see the beauty spot of my behind?

LYNCH

I'm not looking.

ZOE

(Makes sheep's eyes.) No? You wouldn't do a less thing. Would you suck a lemon?

(Squinting in mock shame she glances with sidelong meaning at Bloom, then twists round towards him, pulling her slip free of the poker. Blue fluid again flows over her flesh. Bloom stands, smiling desirously, twirling his thumbs. Kitty Ricketts licks her middle finger with her spittle and gazing into the mirror, smooths both eyebrows. Lipoti Virag, basilicogrammate, chutes rapidly down through the chimneyflute and struts two steps to the left on gawky pink stilts....

VIRAG

(Heels together, bows.) My name is Virag Lipoti, of Szombathely. *(He coughs thoughtfully, drily.)* Promiscuous nakedness is much in evidence hereabouts, eh? Inadvertently her backview revealed the fact that she is not wearing those rather intimate garments of which you are a particular devotee. The injection mark on the thigh I hope you perceived? Good.

BLOOM

Granpappachi. But . . .

VIRAG

Number two on the other hand, she of the cherry rouge and coiffeuse white, whose hair owes not a little to our tribal elixir of gopherwood, is in walking costume and tightly staysed by her sit, I should opine.

[323]

Backbone in front, so to say. Correct me but I always understood that the act so performed by skittish humans with glimpses of lingerie appealed to you in virtue of its exhibitionisticicity. In a word. Hippogriff. Am I right?

BLOOM

She is rather lean.

. . . .

(Bloom surveys uncertainly the three whores, then gazes at the veiled mauve light, hearing the everflying moth.)

BLOOM

I wanted then to have now concluded. Nightdress was never. Hence this. But tomorrow is a new day will be. Past was is today. What now is will then tomorrow as now was be past yester.

VIRAG

(Prompts into his ear in a pig's whisper.) Insects of the day spend their brief existence in reiterated coition, lured by the smell of the inferiorly pulchritudinous female possessing extendified pudendal verve in dorsal region. Pretty Poll! *(His yellow parrotbeak gabbles nasally.)* They had a proverb in the Carpathians in or about the year five thousand five hundred and fifty of our era. One tablespoon of honey will attract friend Bruin more than half a dozen barrels of first choice malt vinegar. Bear's buzz bothers bees. But of this apart. At another time we may resume. We were very pleased, we others. *(He coughs and, bending his brow, rubs his nose thoughtfully with a scooping hand.)* You shall find that these night insects follow the light. An illusion for remember their complex unadjustable eye. For all these knotty points see the seventeenth book of my Fundamentals of Sexology or the Love Passion which Doctor L. B. says is the book sensation of the year. Some, to example, there are again whose movements are automatic. Perceive. That is his appropriate sun. Nightbird nightsun nighttown. Chase me, Charley! Buzz!

. . . .

BLOOM

(Absently.) Ocularly woman's bivalve case is worse. Always open sesame. The cloven sex. Why they fear vermin, creeping things. Yet Eve and the serpent contradict. Not a historical fact. Obvious analogy to my idea. Serpents too are gluttons for woman's milk. Wind their way through miles of omnivorous forest to sucksucculent

[324]

her breast dry. Like those bubblyjocular Roman matrons one reads of in Elephantuliasis.

VIRAG

(His mouth projected in hard wrinkles, eyes stonily forlornly closed, psalms in outlandish monotone.) That the cows with their those distended udders that they have been the known . . .

BLOOM

I am going to scream. I beg your pardon. Ah? So. *(He repeats.)* Spontaneously to seek out the saurian's lair in order to entrust their teats to his avid suction. Ant milks aphis. *(Profoundly.)* Instinct rules the world. In life. In death.

VIRAG

(Head askew, arches his back and hunched wingshoulders, peers at the moth out of blear bulged eyes, points a horning claw and cries.) Who's Ger Ger? Who's dear Gerald? O, I much fear he shall be most badly burned. Will some pleashe pershon not now impediment so catastrophic mit agitation of firstclass tablenumpkin? *(He mews.)* Luss puss puss puss! *(He sighs, draws back and stares sideways down with dropping underjaw.)* Well, well. He doth rest anon.

> I'm a tiny tiny thing
> Ever flying in the spring
> Round and round a ringaring.
> Long ago I was a king,
> Now I do this kind of thing
> On the wing, on the wing!
> Bing!

(He rushes against the mauve shade flapping noisily.) Pretty pretty pretty pretty pretty pretty petticoats.

(From left upper entrance with two sliding steps Henry Flower comes forward to left front centre. He wears a dark mantle and drooping plumed sombrero. He carries a sliverstringed inlaid dulcimer and a longstemmed bamboo Jacob's pipe, its clay bowl fashioned as a female head. He wears dark velvet hose and silverbuckled pumps. He has the romantic Saviour's face with flowing locks, thin beard and moustache. His spindlelegs and sparrow feet are those of the tenor Mario, prince of Candia. He

[325]

settles down his goffered ruffs and moistens his lips with a passage
of his amorous tongue.)*
                        HENRY
(In a low dulcet voice, touching the strings of his guitar.) There is a
flower that bloometh.

*(Virag truculent, his jowl set, stares at the lamp. Grave Bloom
regards Zoe's neck. Henry gallant turns with pendent dewlap to the
piano.)*
                        STEPHEN
(To himself.) Play with your eyes shut. Imitate pa. Filling my belly
with husks of swine. Too much of this. I will arise and go to my.
Expect this is the. Steve, thou art in a parlous way. Must visit old
Deasy or telegraph. Our interview of this morning has left on me a
deep impression. Though our ages. Will write fully tomorrow. I'm
partially drunk, by the way. *(He touches the keys again.)* Minor
chord comes now. Yes. Not much however.

*(Almidano Artifoni holds out a batonfoll of music with vigorous
moustachework.)*
                        ARTIFONI
Ci rifletta. Lei rovina tutto.
                        FLORRY
Sing us something. Love's old sweet song.

                        STEPHEN
No voice. I am a most finished artist. Lynch, did I show you the
letter about the lute?
                        FLORRY
(Smirking.) The bird that can sing and won't sing.
. . . .

                        STEPHEN
Spirit is willing but the flesh is weak.

                        FLORRY
Are you out of Maynooth? You're like someone I knew once.

                        STEPHEN
Out of it now. *(To himself.)* Clever.
. . . .

[326]

ZOE

There was a priest down here two nights ago to do his bit of business
with his coat buttoned up. You needn't try to hide, I says to him. I
know you've a Roman collar.

VIRAG

Perfectly logical from his standpoint. Fall of man. *(Harshly, his
pupils waxing.)* To hell with the pope! Nothing new under the sun. I
am the Virag who disclosed the sex secrets of monks and maidens.
Why I left the Church of Rome. Read the Priest, the Woman and the
Confessional. Penrose. Flipperty Jippert. *(He wriggles.)* Woman,
undoing with sweet pudor her belt of rushrope, offers her all moist
yoni to man's lingam. Short time after man presents woman with
pieces of jungle meat. Woman shows joy and covers herself with
featherskins. Man loves her yoni fiercely with big lingam, the stiff
one. *(He cries.) Coactus volui.* Then giddy woman will run about.
Strong man grasps woman's wrist. Woman squeals, bites, spucks.
Man, now fierce angry, strikes woman's fat yadgana. *(He chases his
tail.)* Piffpaff! Popo! *(He stops, sneezes.)* Pchp! *(He worries his
butt.)* Prrrrrht!

LYNCH

I hope you gave the good father a penance. Nine glorias for shooting
a bishop.

ZOE

(Spouts walrus smoke through her nostrils.) He couldn't get a
connection. Only, you know, sensation. A dry rush.

BLOOM

Poor man!

. . . .

HENRY

(Caressing on his breast a severed female head, murmurs.) Thin
heart, mine love. *(He plucks his lutestrings.)* When first I saw . . .

VIRAG

(Sloughing his skins, his multitudinous plumage moulting.) Rats! *(He
yawns, showing a coalblack throat and closes his jaws by an upward
push of his parchment roll.)* After having said which I took my
departure. Farewell. Fare thee well. *Dreck!*

. . . .

STEPHEN

(Over his shoulder to Zoe.) You would have preferred the fighting parson who founded the protestant error. But beware Antisthenes, the dog sage, and the last end of Arius Heresiarchus. The agony in the closet.

LYNCH

All one and the same god to her.

STEPHEN

(Devoutly.) And Sovereign Lord of all things.

FLORRY

(To Stephen.) I'm sure you are a spoiled priest. Or a monk.

LYNCH

He is. A Cardinal's son.

STEPHEN

Cardinal sin. Monks of the screw.

(Hi Eminence, Simon Stephen Cardinal Dedalus, Primate of all Ireland, appears in the doorway, dressed in red soutane, sandals and socks. Seven dwarf simian acolytes, also in red, cardinal sins, uphold his train, peeping under it. He wears a battered silk hat sideways on his head. His thumbs are stuck in his armpits and his palms outspread. Round his neck hangs a rosary of corks ending on his breast in a corkscrew cross. Releasing his thumbs, he invokes grace from on high with large wave gestures and proclaims with bloated pomp.)

THE CARDINAL
Conservio lies captured.
He lies in the lowest dungeon.
With manacles and chains around his limbs
Weighing upwards of three tons.

(He looks at all for a moment, his right eye closed tight, his left cheek puffed out. Then, unable to repress his merriment, he rocks to and fro, arms akimbo, and sings with broad rollicking humour.)

O, the poor little fellow
Hi-hi-hi-hi-his legs they were yellow

[328]

He was plump, fat and heavy and brisk as a snake
But some bloody savage
To graze his white cabbage
He murdered Nell Flaherty's duckloving drake.

*(A multitude of midges swarms over his robe. He scratches himself
with crossed arms at his ribs, grimacing, and exclaims.)*

I'm suffering the agony of the damned. By the hoky fiddle, thanks be
to Jesus those funny little chaps are not unanimous. If they were
they'd walk me off the face of the bloody globe.

*(His head aslant, he blesses curtly with fore and middle fingers,
imparts his Easter kiss and doubleshuffles off comically, swaying his
hat from side to side, shrinking quickly to the size of his trainbearers.
The dwarf acolytes, giggling, peeping, nudging, ogling,
Easterkissing, zigzag behind him. His voice is heard mellow from
afar, merciful, male, melodious.)*

Shall carry my heart to thee,
Shall carry my heart to thee,
And the breath of the balmy night
Shall carry my heart to thee.

(The trick doorhandle turns.)

THE DOORHANDLE

Theeee.

ZOE

The devil is in that door.

*(A male form passes down the creaking staircase and is heard taking
the waterproof and hat from the rack. Bloom starts forward
involuntarily and, half closing the door as he passes, takes the
chocolate from his pocket and offers it nervously to Zoe.)*

ZOE

(Sniffs his hair briskly.) Hum. Thank your mother for the rabbits. I'm
very fond of what I like.

BLOOM

(Hearing a male voice talk with the whores on the doorstep, pricks his ears.) If it were he? After? Or because not? Or the double event? . . . .

(In Svengali's fur overcoat, with folded arms and Napoleonic forelock, frowns in ventriloquial exorcism with piercing eagle glance toward the door. Then, rigid, with left foot advanced, he makes a swift pass with impelling fingers and gives the sign of past master, drawing his right arm downwards from his left shoulder.) Go, go, go, I conjure you, whoever you are.

(A male cough and tread are heard passing through the mist outside. Bloom's features relax. He places a hand in his waistcoat, posing calmly. Zoe offers him chocolate.)

(The door opens. Bella Cohen, a massive whoremistress enters. She is dressed in a threequarter ivory gown, fringed round the hem with tasselled selvedge, and cools herself, flirting a black horn fan like Minnie Hauck in Carmen. *On her left hand are wedding and keeper rings. Her eyes are deeply carboned. She has a sprouting moustache. Her olive face is heavy, slightly sweated and fullnosed, with orangetainted nostrils. She has large pendant beryl eardrops.)*

BELLA

My word! I'm all of a mucksweat.
(She glances around her at the couples. Then her eyes rest on Bloom with hard insistence. Her large fan winnows wind towards her heated face, neck and embonpoint. Her falcon eyes glitter.)

THE FAN

(Flirting quickly, then slowly.) Married, I see.

BLOOM

Yes . . . Partly, I have mislaid . . .
THE FAN
(Half opening, then closing.) And the missus is master. Petticoat government.
BLOOM
(Looks down with sheepish grin.) That is so.

[330]

THE FAN

(Folding together, rests against her eardrop.) Have you forgotten me?

BLOOM

Yes. No.

THE FAN

(Folded akimbo against her waist.) Is me her was you dreamed before? Was then she him you us since knew? Am all them and the same now we?

(Bella approaches, gently tapping with the fan.)

BLOOM

(Wincing.) Powerful being. In my eyes read that slumber which women love.

THE FAN

(Tapping.) We have met. You are mine. It is fate.

BLOOM

(Cowed.) Exuberant female. Enormously I desiderate your domination. I am exhausted, abandoned, no more young. I stand, so to speak, with an unposted letter bearing the extra regulation fee before the too late box of the general postoffice of human life. The door and window open at a right angle cause a draught of thirtytwo feet per second according to the law of falling bodies. I have felt this instant a twinge of sciatica in my left glutear muscle. It runs in our family. Poor dear papa, a widower, was a regular barometer from it. He believed in animal heat. A skin of tabby lined his winter waistcoat. Near the end, remembering king David and the Sunamite, he shared his bed with Athos, faithful after death. A dog's spittle, as you probably . . . *(He winces.)* Ah!

THE FAN

(Tapping.) All things end. Be mine. Now.

BLOOM

(Undecided.) All now? I should not have parted with my talisman. Rain, exposure at dewfall on the sea rocks, a peccadillo at my time of life. Every phenomenon has a natural cause.

THE FAN

(Points downward slowly.) You may.

BLOOM

(Looks downwards and perceives her unfastened bootlace.) We are
observed.

THE FAN

(Points downward quickly.) You must.

BLOOM

(With desire, with reluctance.) I can make a true black knot. Learned
when I served my time and worked the mail order line for Kellet's.
Experienced hand. Every knot says a lot. Let me. In courtesy. I knelt
once before today. Ah!
*(Bella raises her gown slightly and, steadying her pose, lifts to the
edge of a chair a plump buskined hoof and a full pastern, silksocked.
Bloom, stifflegged, ageing, bends over her hoof and with gentle
fingers draws out and in her laces.)*

THE HOOF

Smell my hot goathide. Feel my royal weight.

BLOOM

(Crosslacing.) Too tight??

THE HOOF

If you bungle, Handy Andy, I'll kick your football for you.

BLOOM

Not to lace the wrong eyelet as I did the night of the bazaar dance.
Bad luck. Nook in wrong tache of her . . . person you mentioned.
That night she met . . . Now!
*(He knots the lace. Bella places her foot on the floor. Bloom raises
his head. Her heavy face, her eyes strike him in midbrow. His eyes
grow dull, darker and pouched, his nose thickens.)*

BLOOM

(Mumbles.) Awaiting your further orders, we remain, gentlemen . . .

[332]

BELLO

(With a hard basilisk stare, in a baritone voice.) Hound of
dishonour!

BLOOM

(Infatuated.) Empress!

BELLO

(His heavy cheekchops sagging.) Adorer of the adulterous rump!

BLOOM

(With sinews semiflexed.) Magnificence.

BELLO

Down! *(He taps her on the shoulder with his fan.)* Incline feet
forward! Slide left foot one pace back. You will fall. You are falling.
On the hands down!

BLOOM

(Her eyes upturned in the sign of admiration, closing.) Truffles!

*(With a piercing epileptic cry she sinks on all fours, grunting,
snuffing, rooting at his feet, then lies, shamming dead with eyes shut
tight, trembling eyelids, bowed upon the ground in the attitude of
most excellent master.)*

BELLO

*(With bobbed hair, purple gills, fat moustache rings round his
shaven mouth, in mountaineer's puttees, green silverbuttoned coast,
sport skirt and alpine hat with moorcock's feather, his hands stuck
deep in his breeches pockets, places his heel on her neck and grinds
it in.)* Feel my entire weight. Bow, bondslave, before the throne of
your despot's glorious heels, so glistening in their proud erectness.

BLOOM

(Enthralled, bleats.) I promise never to disobey.

BELLO

(Laughs loudly.) Holy smoke! You little know what's in store for
you. I'm the tartar to settle your little lot and break you in! I'll bet
Kentucky cocktails all round I shame it out of you, old son. Cheek
me, I dare you. If you do tremble in anticipation of heel discipline to
be inflicted in gym costume.
(Bloom creeps under the sofa and peers out through the fringe.)

ZOE

(Widening her slip to screen her.) She's not here.

BLOOM

(Closing her eyes.) She's not here.

BELLO

(Coaxingly.) Come, ducky dear. I want a word with you, darling, just to administer correction. Just a little heart to heart talk, sweety. *(Bloom puts out her timid head.)* There's a good girly now. *(Bello grabs her violently and drags her forward.)* I only want to correct you for your own good on a soft safe spot. How's that tender behind? O, ever so gently, pet. Begin to get ready.

BLOOM

(Fainting.) Don't tear my . . .

BELLO

(Savagely.) The nosering, the pliers, the bastinado, the hanging hook, the knout I'll make you kiss while the flutes play like the Nubian slave of old. You're in for it this time. I'll make you remember me for the balance of your natural life. *(His forehead veins swollen, his face congested.)*
(He twists her arm. Bloom squeaks, turning turtle.)

BLOOM

(Screams.) O, it's hell itself! Every nerve in my body aches like mad!

BELLO

(Shouts.) Good, by the rumping jumping general! That's the best bit of news I heard these six weeks. Here, don't keep me waiting, damn you. *(He slaps her face.)*

BLOOM

(Whimpers.) You're after hitting me. I'll tell . . .

BELLO

Hold him down, girls, till I squat on him.

ZOE

Yes. Walk on him! I will.

[334]

(The brothel cook, Mrs Keogh, wrinkled, greybearded, in a greasy bib, men's grey and green socks and brogues, floursmeared, a rollingpin stuck with raw pastry in her bare red hand, appears at the door.)

MRS KEOGH

(Ferociously.) Can I help? *(They hold and pinion Bloom.)*

BELLO

(Squats, with a grunt, on Bloom's upturned face, puffing cigarsmoke, nursing a fat leg.) I see Keating Clay is elected chairman of the Richmond Asylum and bytheby Guinness's preference shares are at sixteen three quarters. Curse me for a fool that I didn't buy that lot Craig and Gardner told me about. Just my infernal luck, curse it. And that Goddamned outsider *Throwaway* at twenty to one. *(He quenches his cigar angrily on Bloom's ear.)* Where's that Goddamned cursed ashtray?

BLOOM

(Goaded, buttocksmothered.) O! O! Monsters! Cruel one!

BELLO

Ask for that every ten minutes. Beg, pray for it as you never prayed before. *(He thrusts out a figged fist and foul cigar.)* Here, kiss that. Both. Kiss. *(He throws a leg astride and, pressing with horseman's knees, calls in a hard voice.)* Gee up! A cockhorse to Banbury cross. I'll ride him for the Eclipse stakes. *(He bends sideways and squeezes his mount's testicles roughly, shouting.)* Ho! off we pop! I'll nurse you in proper fashion. *(He horserides cockhorse, leaping in the saddle.)* The lady goes a pace a pace and the coachman goes a trot a trot and the gentleman goes a gallop a gallop a gallop a gallop.

BLOOM

(A sweat breaking out over him.) Not man. *(He sniffs.)* Woman.

BELLO

(Stands up.) No more blow hot and cold. What you longed for has come to pass. Henceforth you are unmanned and mine in earnest, a thing under the yoke. Now for your punishment frock. You will shed your male garments, you understand, Ruby Cohen? and don the shot

silk luxuriously rustling over your head and shoulders and quickly too.

BLOOM

(Shrinks.) Silk, mistress said! O crinkly! Scrapy! Must I tiptouch it with my nails?

BELLO

(Points to his whores.) As they are now, so will you be, wigged, singed, perfumesprayed, ricepowdered, with smoothshaven armpits. Tape measurements will be taken next your skin. You will be laced with cruel force into vicelike corsets of soft dove coutille, with whalebone busk, to the diamond trimmed pelvis, the absolute outside edge, while your figure, plumper than when at large, will be restrained in nettight frocks, pretty two ounce petticoats and fringes and things stamped, of course, with my houseflag, creations of lovely lingerie for Alice and nice scent for Alice. Alice will feel the pullpull. Martha and Mary will be a little chilly at first in such delicate thighcasting but the filly flimsiness of lace around your bare knees will remind you . . .

BLOOM

(A charming soubrette with dauby cheeks, mustard hair and large male hands and nose, leering mouth.) I tried her things on only once, a small prank, in Holles street. When we were hardup I washed them to save the laundry bill. My own shirts I turned. It was the purest thrift.

BELLO

(Jeers.) Little jobs that make mother pleased, eh! and showed off coquettishly in your domino at the mirror behind closedrawn blinds your unskirted thighs and hegoat's udders, in various poses of surrender, eh? Ho! Ho! I have to laugh! That secondhand black operatop shift and short trunk leg naughties all split up the stitches at her last rape that Mrs Miriam Dandrade sold you from the Shelbourne Hotel, eh?

BLOOM

(Her hands and features working.) It was Gerald converted me to be a true corsetlover when I was female impersonator in the High School play *Vice Versa.* It was dear Gerald. He got that kink, fascinated by sister's stays. Now dearest Gerald uses pinky greasepaint and gilds his eyelids. Cult of the beautiful.

[336]

BELLO

(With wicked glee.) Beautiful! Give us a breather! When you took your seat with womanish care, lifting your billowy flounces, on the smoothworn throat.

BLOOM

Science. To compare the various joys we each enjoy. *(Earnestly.)* And really it's better the position . . . because I used to wet . . .

BELLO

(Sternly.) No insubordination. The saw dust is there in the corner for you. I gave you strict instructions, didn't I? Do it standing, sir! I'll teach you to behave like a jinkleman! If I catch a trace on your swaddles. Aha! By the ass of the Dorans you'll find I'm a martinet. The sins of your past are rising against you. Many. Hundreds.

BELLO

(Whistles loudly.) Say! What was the most revolting piece of obscenity in all your career of crime? Go the whole hog. Puke it out. Be candid for once.

BLOOM

Don't ask me. Our mutual faith. Pleasants street. I only thought the half of the . . . I swear my sacred oath . . .

BELLO

(Peremptorily.) Answer. Repugnant wretch! I insist on knowing. Tell me something to amuse me, smut or a bloody goodghoststory or a line of poetry, quick, quick, quick! Where? How? What time? With how many? I give you just three seconds. One! Two! The . . . !

BLOOM

(Docile, gurgles.) I rererepugnosed in rerererepugnant . . .

BELLO

(Imperiously.) O get out, you skunk! Hold your tongue! Speak when you're spoken to.

BLOOM

(Bows.) Master! Mistress! Mantamer!
(He lifts his arms. His bangle bracelets fall.)

BELLO

(Satirically.) By day you will souse and bat our smelling
underclothes, also when we ladies are unwell, and swab out our
latrines with dress pinned up and a dishclout tied to your tail. Won't
that be nice? *(He places a ruby ring on her finger.)* And there now!
With this ring I thee own. Say, thank you, mistress.

BLOOM

Thank you, mistress.

BELLO

You will make the beds, get my tub ready, empty the pisspots in the
different rooms, including old Mrs Keogh's the cook's, a sandy one.
Ay, and rinse the seven of them well, mind, or lap it up like
champagne. Drink me piping hot. Hop! you will dance attendance or
I'll lecture you on your misdeeds, Miss Ruby, and spank your bare
bot right well, miss, with the hairbrush. You'll be taught the errors of
your ways. At night your wellcreamed braceleted hands will wear
fortythreebutton gloves newpowdered with talc and having delicately
scented fingertips. For such favours knights of old laid down their
lives. *(He chuckles.)* My boys will be no end charmed to see you so
ladylike, the colonel above all. When they come here the night
before the wedding to fondle my new attraction in gilded heels. First,
I'll have a go at you myself. A man I know on the turf named
Charles Alberta Marsh (I was in bed with him just now and another
gentleman out of the Hanaper and Petty Bag office) is on the lookout
for a maid of all work at short knock. Swell the bust. Smile. Droop
shoulders. What offers? *(He points.)* For that lot trained by owner to
fetch and carry, basket in mouth. *(He bares his arm and plunges it
elbowdeep in Bloom's vulva.)* There's fine depth for you! What,
boys? That give you a hardon? *(He shoves his arm in a bidder's
face.)* Here, wet the deck and wipe it round!

A BIDDER

A florin!
(Dillon's lacquey rings his handbell.)

A VOICE

One and eightpence too much.

THE LACQUEY

Barang!

[338]

CHARLES ALBERTA MARSH

Must be virgin. Good breath. Clean.

. . . .

BELLO

What else are you good for, an impotent thing like you ? *(He stoops
and, peering, pokes with his fan rudely under the fat suet folds of
Bloom's haunches.)* Up! Up! Manx cat! What have we here?
Where's your curly teapot gone to or who docked it on you,
cockyolly? Sing, birdy, sing. It's as limp as a boy of six's doing his
pooly behind a cart. But a bucket or sell your pump. *(Loudly.)* Can
you do a man's job?

BLOOM

Eccles Street . . .

BELLO

(Sarcastically.) I wouldn't hurt your feelings for the world but
there's a man of brawn in possession there. The tables are turned, my
gay young fellow! He is something like a fullgrown outdoor man.
Well for you, you muff, if you had that weapon with knobs and
lumps and warts all over it. He shot his bolt, I can tell you! Foot to
foot, knee to knee, belly to belly, bubs to breast! He's no eunuch. A
shock of red hair he has sticking out of him behind like a furzebush!
Wait for nine months, my lad! Holy ginger, it's kicking and
coughing up and down in her guts already! That makes you wild,
don't it? Touches the spot? *(He spits in contempt.)* Spittoon!

BLOOM

I was indecently treated, I . . . inform the police. Hundred pounds.
Unmentionable. I . . .

BELLO

Would if you could, lame duck. A downpour we want, not your
drizzle.

BLOOM

To drive me mad! Moll! I forgot! Forgive! Moll! . . . We . . . Still . . .

BELLO

(Ruthlessly.) No, Leopold Bloom, all is changed by woman's will
since you slept horizontal in Sleepy Hollow your night of twenty
years. Return and see.

(Old Sleepy Hollow calls over the wold.)

SLEEPY HOLLOW

Rip Van Winkle! Rip Van Winkle!

BLOOM

(In tattered moccasins with a rusty fowlingpiece, tiptoeing, fingertipping, his haggard bony bearded face peering through the diamond panes, cries out.) I see her! It's she! The first night at Mat Dillon's! But that dress, the green! And her hair is dyed gold and he . . .

BELLO

(Laughs mockingly.) That's your daughter, you owl, with a Mullingar student.
(Milly Bloom, fairhaired, greenvested, slimsandalled, her blue scarf in the seawind simply swirling, breaks from the arms of her lover and calls, her young eyes wonderwide.)

MILLY

My! It's Papli! But. O Papli, how old you've grown.

BELLO

(Cuttingly.) Their heelmarks will stamp the Brusselette carpet you bought at Wren's auction. In their horseplay with Moll the romp to find the buck flea in her breeches they will deface the little statue you carried home in the rain for art for art's sake. They will violate the secrets of your bottom drawer. Pages will be torn from your handbook of astronomy to make them pipespills. And they will spit in you ten shilling brass fender from Hampton Leedom's.

BLOOM

Ten and six. The act of low scoundrels. Let me go. I will return. I will prove . . .

BELLO

As a paying guest or a kept man? Too late. You have made your secondbest bed and others must lie in it. Your epitaph is written. You are down and out and don't you forget it, old bean.

BLOOM

Justice! All Ireland versus one! Has nobody . . . ?

BELLO

Die and be damned to you if you have any sense of decency or grace
about you. I can give you a rare old wine that'll send you skipping to
hell and back. Sign a will and leave us any coin you have. If you
have none see you damn well get it, steal it, rob it! We'll bury you in
our shrubbery jakes where you'll be dead and dirty with old Cuck
Cohen, my stepnephew I married, the bloody old gouty procurator
and sodomite with a crick in his neck, and my other ten or eleven
husbands, whatever the buggers' names were, suffocated in the one
cesspool. *(He explodes in a loud phlegm laugh.)* We'll manure you,
Mr Flower! *(He pipes scoffingly.)* Byby, Poldy! Byby, Papli!

BLOOM

(Clasps his head.) My will power! Memory! I have sinned! I have
stuff . . .
(He weeps tearlessly.)

BELLO

(Sneers.) Crybabby! Crocodile tears!

*(Bloom, broken, closely veiled for the sacrifice, sobs, his face to the
earth. The passing bell is heard. Darkshawled figures of the
circumcised in sackcloth and ashes, stand by the wailing wall. With
swaying arms they wail in pneuma over the recreant Bloom.)*

THE CIRCUMCISED

*(In a dark guttural chant as they cast dead sea fruit upon him, no
flowers). Shema Israel Adonai Elohenu Adonai Echad.*

VOICES

(Sighing.) So he's gone. Ah, yes. Yes, indeed. Bloom? Never heard
of him. No? Queer kind of chap. There's the widow. That so? Ah,
yes.
*(From the suttee pyre the flame of gum camphire ascends. The pall
of incense smoke screens and disperses. Out of her oak frame a
nymph with hair unbound, lightly clad in tea brown art colours,
descends from her grotto and passing under interlacing yews, stands
over Bloom.)*

THE YEWS

(Their leaves whispering.) Sister. Our sister. Ssh.

THE NYMPH

(Softly.) Mortal! *(Kindly.)* Nay, dost not weepest!

BLOOM

(Crawls jellily forward under the boughs, streaked by sunlight, with dignity.) This position. I felt it was expected of me. Force of habit.)

THE NYMPH

Mortal! You found me in evil company, highkickers, coster picnic makers, pugilists, popular generals, immoral panto boys in flesh tights and the nifty shimmy dancers, La Aurora and Karini, musical act, the hit of the century. I was hidden in cheap pink paper that smelt of rock oil. I was surrounded by the stale smut of clubmen, stories to disturb callow youth, ads for transparencies, truedup dice and bustpads, proprietary articles and why wear a truss with testimonial from ruptured gentleman. Useful hints to the married.

BLOOM

(Lifts a turtle head towards her lap.) We have met before. On another star.

THE NYMPH

(Sadly.) Rubber goods. Neverrip. Brand as supplied to the aristocracy. Corsets for men. I cure fits or money refunded. Unsolicited testimonials for Professor Waldman's wonderful chest exuber. My bust developed four inches in three weeks, reports Mrs Gus Rublin with photo.

BLOOM

You mean *Photo Bits?*

THE NYMPH

I do. You bore me away, framed me in oak and tinsel, set me above your marriage couch. Unseen, one summer eve, you kissed me in four places. And with loving pencil you shaded my eyes, my bosom and my shame.

BLOOM

(Humbly kisses her long hair.) Your classic curves, beautiful immortal. I was glad to look on you, to praise you, a thing of beauty, almost to pray.

THE NYMPH

During dark nights I heard your praise.

[342]

BLOOM

(Quickly.) Yes, yes. You mean that I . . . Sleep reveals the worst side of everyone, children perhaps excepted. I know I fell out of my bed or rather was pushed. Steel wine is said to cure snoring. For the rest there is that English invention, pamphlet of which I received some days ago, incorrectly addressed. It claims to afford a noiseless inoffensive vent. *(He sighs.)* 'Twas ever thus. Frailty, thy name is marriage.

THE NYMPH

(Her fingers in her ears.) And words. They are not in my dictionary.

BLOOM

You understood them?

THE NYMPH

(Covers her face with her hand.) What have I not seen in that chamber? What must my eyes look down on?

BLOOM

(Apologetically.) I know. Soiled personal linen, wrong side up with care. The quoits are loose. From Gibraltar by long sea, long ago.

THE NYMPH

(Bends her head.) Worse! Worse!

BLOOM

(Reflects precautiously.) That antiquated commode. It wasn't her weight. She scaled just eleven stone nine. She put on nine pounds after weaning. It was a crack and want of glue. Eh? And that absurd orangekeyed utensil which has only one handle.
(The sound of a waterfall is heard in bright cascade.)

BLOOM

(Pigeonbreasted, bottleshouldered, padded, in nondescript juvenile grey and black striped suit, too small for him, white tennis shoes, bordered stockings with turnover tops, and a red school cap with badge.) I was in my teens, a growing boy. A little then sufficed, a jolting car, the mingling odours of the ladies' cloakroom and lavatory, the throng penned tight on the old Royal stairs, for they love crushes, instincts of the herd, and the dark sexsmelling theatre unbridles vice. Even a pricelist of their hosiery. And then the heat.

There were sunspots that summer. End of school. And tipsycake. Halcyon days.

THE NYMPH

(With wide fingers.) O! Infamy!

BLOOM

I was precocious. Youth. The fauns. I sacrificed to the god of the forest. The flowers that bloom in the spring. It was pairing time. Capillary attraction is a natural phenomenon. Lotty Clarke, flaxenhaired, I saw at her night toilette through illclosed curtains, with poor papa's operaglasses. The wanton ate grass wildly. She rolled downhill at Rialto Bridge to tempt me with her flow of animal spirits. She climbed their crooked tree and I . . . A saint couldn't resist it. The demon possessed me. Besides, who saw?
(Staggering Bob, a whitepolled calf, thrusts a ruminating head with humid nostrils through the foliage.)

STAGGERING BOB

Me. Me see.

BLOOM

Simply satisfying a need. *(With pathos.)* No girl would when I went girling. Too ugly. They wouldn't play . . .

(High on Ben Howth through rhododendrons a nannygoat passes, plumpuddered, buttytailed, dropping currants.)

BLOOM

(Hatless, flushed, covered with burrs of thistledown and gorsepine. Regularly engaged. Circumstances alter cases. (He gazes intently downwards on the water.) Thirtytwo head over heels per second. Press nightmare. Giddy Elijah. Fall from the cliff. Sad end of government printer's clerk. *(Through silversilent summer air the dummy of Bloom, rolled in a mummy, rolls rotatingly from the Lion's Head cliff into the purple waiting waters.)*

(Far out in the bay between Bailey and Kish lights the Erin's King *sails, sending a broadening plume of coalsmoke from her funnel towards the land.)*

[344]

COUNCILLOR NANNETTI

(Alone on deck, in dark alpaca, yellow kitefaced, his hand in his waistcoat opening, declaims.) When my country takes her place among the nations of the earth, then, and not till then, let my epitaph be written. I have . . .

BLOOM

Done. Prff.

THE NYMPH

(Loftily.) We immortals, as you saw today, have not such a place and no hair there either. We are stonecold and pure. We eat electric light. *(She arches her body in lascivious crispation, placing her forefinger in her mouth.)* Spoke to me. Heard from behind. How then could you . . . ?

BLOOM

(Pacing the heather abjectly.) O, I have been a perfect pig. Enemas too I have administered. One third of a pint of quassia, to which add a tablespoon of rocksalt. Up the fundament. With Hamilton Long's syringe, the ladies friend.

THE NYMPH

In my presence. The powderpuff. *(She blushes and makes a knee.)* And the rest.

BLOOM

It overpowers me. The warm impress of her warm form. Even to sit where a woman has sat, especially with divaricated thighs, as though to grant last favours, most especially with previously well uplifted white sateen coatpants. So womanly full. It fills me full.

THE YEWS

Ssh! Sister, speak!

THE NYMPH

(Eyeless, in nun's white habit, coif and huge winged wimple, softly, with remote eyes.) Tranquilla convent. Sister Agatha. Mount Carmel, the apparitions of Knock and Lourdes. No more desire. *(She reclines her head, sighing.)* Only the ethereal. Where dreamy creamy gull waves o'er the waters dull.)

(Bloom half rises. His back trousers' button snaps.)

THE BUTTON

Bip!

(Two sluts of the Coombe dance rainily by, shawled, yelling flatly.)

THE SLUTS
O Leopold lost the pin of his drawers
He didn't know what to do,
To keep it up,
To keep it up.

BLOOM
(Coldly.) You have broken the spell. The last straw. If there were only ethereal where would you all be, postulants and novices? Shy but willing, like an ass pissing.

THE YEWS
(Their silverfoil of leaves precipitating, their skinny arms ageing and swaying.) Deciduously!

THE NYMPH
Sacrilege! To attempt my virtue! *(A large moist stain appears on her robe.)* Sully my innocence! You are not fit to touch the garment of a pure woman. *(She clutches in her robe.)* Wait, Satan. You'll sing no more lovesongs. Amen. Amen. Amen. Amen. *(She draws a poniard and, clad in the sheathmail of an elected knight of nine, strikes at his loins.)* Nekum!

BLOOM
(Starts up, seizes her hand.) Hoy! Nebrakada! Cat of nine lives! Fair play, madam. No pruning knife. The fox and the grapes, is it? What do we lack with your barbed wire? Crucifix not thick enough? *(He clutches her veil.)* A holy abbot you want or Brophy, the lame gardener, or the spoutless statue of the watercarrier or good Mother Alphonsus, eh, Reynard?

THE NYMPH
(With a cry, flees from him unveiled, her plaster cast cracking, a cloud of stench escaping from the cracks.) Poli . . . !

BLOOM
(Calls after her.) As if you didn't get it on the double yourselves. No jerks and multiple mucosities all over you. I tried it. Your strength our weakness. What's our studfee? What will you pay on the nail? You fee men dancers on the Riviera, I read. *(The fleeing nymph*

raises a keen.) Eh! I have sixteen years of black slave labour behind me. And would a jury give me five shillings alimony tomorrow, eh? Fool someone else, not me. *(He sniffs.)* But. Onions. Stale. Sulphur. Grease.

(The figure of Bella Cohen stands before him.)

BELLA

You'll know me next time.

BLOOM

(Composed, regards her.) Passee. Mutton dressed as lamb. Long in the tooth and superfluous hairs. A raw onion the last thing at night would benefit your complexion. And take some double chin drill. Your eyes are as vapid as the glass eyes of your stuffed fox. They have the dimensions of your other features, that's all. I'm not a triple screw propeller.

BELLA

(Contemptuously.) You're not game, in fact. *(Her sowcunt barks.)* Fohracht!

BLOOM

(Contemptuously.) Clean our nailless middle finger first, the cold spunk of your bully is dripping from your cockscomb. Take a handful of hay and wipe yourself.

BELLA

I know you, canvasser! Dead cod!

BLOOM

I saw him, kipkeeper! Pox and gleet vendor.

BELLA

(Turns to the piano.) Which of you was playing the dead march from *Saul?*

ZOE

Me. Mind your cornflowers. *(She darts to the piano and bangs chords on it with crossed arms.)* The cat's ramble through the slag. *(She glances back.)* Eh? Who's making love to my sweeties? *(She darts back to the table.)* What's yours is mine and what's mine is my own.)

(Kitty disconcerted coats her teeth with silver paper. Bloom approaches Zoe.)

[347]

BLOOM

(Gently.) Give me back that potato, will you?

ZOE

Forfeits, a fine thing and a superfine thing.

BLOOM

(With feeling.) It is nothing, but still a relic of poor mamma.

ZOE

Give a thing and take it back
God'll ask you where is that
You'll say you don't know
God'll send you down below.

BLOOM

There is a memory attached to it. I should like to have it.

STEPHEN

To have or not to have, that is the question.

ZOE

Here. *(She hauls up a reef of her slip, revealing her bare thigh and unrolls the potato from the top of her stocking.)* Those that hides knows where to find.

BELLA

(Frowns.) Here. This isn't a musical peepshow. And don't you smash that piano. Who's paying here?
(She goes to the pianola. Stephen fumbles in his pocket and, taking out a banknote by its corner, hands it to her.)

STEPHEN

(With exaggerated politeness.) This silken purse I made out of the sow's ear of the public. Madam, excuse me. If you allow me. *(He indicates vaguely Lynch and Bloom.)* We are all in the same sweepstake, Kinch and Lynch. *Dans ce bordel ou tenons nostre etat.*

LYNCH

(Calls from the hearth.) Dedalus! Give her your blessing for me.

[348]

STEPHEN

(Hands Bella a coin.) Gold. She has it.

BELLA

(Looks at the money, then at Zoe, Florry and Kitty.) Do you want
three girls? It's ten shillings here.

STEPHEN

(Delightedly.) A hundred thousand apologies. *(He fumbles again and
takes out and hands her two crowns.)* Permit, *brevi manu,* my sight is
somewhat troubled.
*(Bella goes to the table to count the money while Stephen talks to
himself in monosyllables. Zoe bounds over to the table. Kitty leans
over Zoe's neck. Lynch gets up, rights his cap and clasping Kitty's
waist, add his head to the group.)*
FLORRY

(Strives heavily to rise.) Ow! My foot's asleep. *(She limps over to the
table. Bloom approaches.)*

BELLA, ZOE, KITTY, LYNCH, BLOOM

(Chattering and squabbling.) The gentleman . . . ten shillings . . .
paying for the three . . . allow me a moment . . . this gentleman pays
separate . . . who's touching it? . . . ow . . . mind who you're
pinching . . . are you staying the night or a short time? . . . who did? .
. . you're a liar, excuse me . . . the gentleman paid down like a
gentleman . . . drink . . . it's long after eleven.

STEPHEN

(At the pianola, making a gesture of abhorrence.) No bottles! What,
eleven? A riddle.

ZOE

*(Lifting up her pettigown and folding half a sovereign into the top of
her stocking.)* Hard earned on the flat of my back.

STEPHEN

The fox crew, the cocks flew,
The bells in heaven
Were striking eleven.
'Tis time for her poor soul
To get out of heaven.

BLOOM

(Quietly lays half a sovereign on the table between Bella and Florry.) So. Allow me. *(He takes up the poundnote.)* Three times ten. We're square.

BELLA

(Admiringly.) You're such a slyboots, old cocky. I could kiss you.

ZOE

(Points.) Hum? Deep as a drawwell. *(Lynch bends Kitty back over the sofa and kisses her. Bloom goes with the poundnote to Stephen.)*

BLOOM

This is yours.

STEPHEN

How is that? *Le distrait* or absentminded beggar. *(He fumbles again in his pocket and draws out a handful of coins. An object falls.)* That fell.

BLOOM

(Stooping, picks up and hands a box of matches.) This.

STEPHEN

Lucifer. Thanks.

BLOOM

(Quietly.) You had better hand over that cash to me to take care of. Why pay more?

STEPHEN

(Hands him all his coins.) Be just before you are generous.

BLOOM

I will but is it wise? *(He counts.)* One, seven, eleven and five. Six. Eleven. I don't answer for what you may have lost.

STEPHEN

(Comes to the table.) Cigarette, please. *(Lynch tosses a cigarette from the sofa to the table.)* And so Georgina Johnson is dead and married. *(A cigarette appears on the table. Stephen looks at it.)* Wonder. Parlour magic. Married. Hm. *(He strikes a match and proceeds to light the cigarette with enigmatic melancholy.)*

[350]

LYNCH

(Watching him.) You would have a better chance of lighting it if you held the match nearer.

STEPHEN

(Brings the match nearer his eye.) Lynx eye. Must get glasses. Broke them yesterday. Sixteen years ago. Distance. The eye sees all flat. *(He draws the match away. It goes out.)* Brain thinks. Near: far. Ineluctable modality of the visible. *(He frowns mysteriously.)* Hm, Sphinx. The beast that has two backs at midnight. Married.

ZOE

It was a commercial traveller married her and took her away with him.

FLORRY

(Nods.) Mr Lambe from London.

STEPHEN

Lamb of London, who takest away the sins of our world.
(The cigarette slips from Stephen's fingers. Bloom picks it up and throws it into the grate.)

BLOOM

Don't smoke. You ought to eat. Cursed dog I met. *(To Zoe.)* You have nothing?

ZOE

Is he hungry?

STEPHEN
Hagende Hunger,
Fragende Frau,
Macht uns alle kaput.

ZOE

(Tragically. Hamlet, I am thy father's gimlet! *(She takes his hand.)* Blue eyed beauty, I'll read your hand. *(She points to his forehead.)* No wit, no wrinkles. *(She counts.)* Two, three, Mars, that's courage. *(Stephen shakes his head.)* No kid.

BLOOM

(Detaches her fingers and offers his palm.) More harm than good. Here. Read mine.

[351]

BELLA

Show. *(She turns up Bloom's hand.)* I thought so. Knobby knuckles, for the women.

ZOE

(Peering at Bloom's palm.) Gridiron. Travels beyond the sea and marry money.

BLOOM

Wrong.

ZOE

(Quickly.) O, I see. Short little finger. Henpecked husband. That wrong?

BLOOM

(Points to his hand.) That weal there is an accident. Fell and cut it twenty-two years ago. I was sixteen.

ZOE

I see, says the blind man. Tell us news.

STEPHEN

See? Moves to one great goal. I am twentytwo too. Sixteen years ago I twentytwo tumbled, twentytwo years ago he sixteen fell off his hobbyhorse. *(He winces.)* Hurt my hand somewhere. Must see a dentist. Money?
(Zoe whispers to Florry. They giggle. Bloom releases his hand and writes idly on the table in backhand, pencilling slow curves.)

FLORRY

What?
(A hackneycar, number three hundred and twentyfour, with a gallantbuttocked mare, driven by James Barton, Harmony Avenue, Donnybrook, trots past. Blazes Boylan and Lenehan sprawl swaying on the sideseats. The Ormond boots crouches behind on the axle. Sadly over the crossblind Lydia Douce and Mina Kennedy gaze.)

(Over the well of the car Blazes Boylan leans, his boater straw set sideways, a red flower in his mouth. Lenehan, in a yachtsman's cap and white shoes, officiously detaches a long hair from Blazes Boylan's shoulder.)

[352]

LENEHAN

Ho! What do I here behold? Were you brushing the cobwebs off a few quims?

BOYLAN

(Seated, smiles.) Plucking a turkey.

LENEHAN

A good night's work.

BOYLAN

(Holding up four thick bluntungulated fingers, winks.) Blazes Kate! Up to sample or your money back. *(He holds out a forefinger.)* Smell that.

LENEHAN

(Smells gleefully.) Ah! Lobster and mayonnaise. Ah!

ZOE AND FLORRY

(Laugh together.) Ha ha ha ha.

BOYLAN

(Jumps surely from the car and calls loudly for all to hear.) Hello, Bloom! Mrs Bloom up yet?

BLOOM

(In a flunkey's plum plush coat and kneebreeches, buff stockings and powdered wig.) I'm afraid not, sir, the last articles . . .

BOYLAN

(Tosses him sixpence.) here, to buy yourself a gin and splash. *(He hangs his hat smartly on a peg of Bloom's antlered head.)* Show me in. I have a little private business with your wife. You understand?

BLOOM

Thank you, sir. Yes, sir, Madam Tweedy is in her bath, sir.

MARION

He ought to feel himself highly honoured. *(She plops splashing out of the water.)* Raoul, darling, come and dry me. I'm in my pelt. Only my new hat and carriage sponge.

BOYLAN

(A merry twinkling in his eye.) Topping!

BELLA

What? What is it?
(Zoe whispers to her.)

MARION

Let him look, the pishogue! Pimp! And scourge himself! I'll write to a powerful prostitute or Bartholomona, the bearded woman, to raise weals out on him an inch thick and make him bring me back a signed and stamped receipt.

BELLA

(Laughing.) Ho ho ho ho.

BOYLAN

(To Bloom, over his shoulder.) You can apply your eye to the keyhole and play with yourself while I just go through her a few times.

BLOOM

Thank you, sir, I will, sir. May I bring two men chums to witness the deed and take a snapshot? *(He holds an ointment jar.)* Vaseline, sir? Orangeflower? . . . Lukewarm water? . . .

MINA KENNEDY

(Her eyes upturned.) O, it must be like the scent of geraniums and lovely peaches! O, he simply idolises every bit of her! Stuck together! Covered with kisses!

LYDIA DOUCE

(Her mouth opening.) Yumyum. O, he's carrying her round the room doing it! Ride a cock horse. You could hear them in Paris and New York. Like mouthfuls of strawberries and cream.

BOYLAN'S VOICE

(Sweetly, hoarsely, in the pit of his stomach.) Ah! Gooblazqruk brukarchkrasht!

MARION'S VOICE

(Hoarsely, sweetly rising to her throat.) O! Weeshwashtkissimapooisthnapoohuck!

BLOOM

(His eyes wildly dilated, clasps himself.) Show! Hide! Show! Plough her! More! Shoot!

[354]

LYNCH

(Points.) The mirror up to nature. *(He laughs.)* Hu hu hu hu hu hu. *(Stephen and Bloom gaze in the mirror. The face of William Shakespeare, beardless, appears there, rigid in facial paralysis, crowned by the reflection of the reindeer antlered hatrack in the hall.)*

SHAKESPEARE

(In dignified ventriloquy.) 'Tis the loud laugh bespeaks the vacant mind. *(To Bloom.)* Thou toughest as how thou wastest invisible. Gaze. *(He crows with a black capon's laugh.)* Iagogo! How my Oldfellow chokit his Thursdaymomun. Iagogo!

BLOOM

(Smiles yellowly at the whores.) When will I hear the joke?

ZOE

Before you're twice married and once a widower.

BLOOM

Lapses are condoned. Even the great Napoleon, when measurements were taken near the skin after his death . . .

STEPHEN

Et exaltabuntur cornua iusti. Queens lay with prize bulls. Remember Pasiphae for whose lust my grandoldgrossfather made the first confessionbox. Forget not Madam Grissel Steevens nor the suine scions of the house of Lambert. And Noah was drunk with wine. And his ark was open.

BELLA

None of that here. Come to the wrong shop.

LYNCH

Let him alone. He's back from Paris.

ZOE

(Runs to Stephen and links him.) O go on! Give us some parleyvoo.

(Stephen claps hot on head and leaps over to the fireplace, where he stands with shrugged shoulders, finny hands outspread, a painted smile on his face.)

STEPHEN

(Gabbles, with marionette jerks.) Thousand places of entertainment
to expenses your evenings with lovely ladies saling gloves and other
things perhaps her heart beerchops perfect fashionable house very
eccentric where lots cocottes beautiful dressed much about
princesses like are dancing cancan and walking there parisian
clowneries extra foolish for bachelors foreigners the same if talking a
poor english how much smart they are on things love and sensations
voluptuous. Misters very selects for is pleasure must to visit heaven
and hell show with mortuary candles and they tears silver which
occur every night. Perfectly shocking terrific of religion's things
mockery seen in universal world. All chic womans which arrive full
of modesty then disrobe and squeal loud to see vampire man debauch
nun very fresh young with *dessous troublants. (He clacks his tongue
loudly.) Ho, la la! Ce pif qu'il a!*

LYNCH

Vive le vampire!

THE WHORES

Bravo! Parleyvoo!

STEPHEN

(Grimacing with head back, laughs loudly, clapping himself.) Great
success of laughing. Angels much prostitutes like and holy apostles
big damn ruffians. *Demimondaines* nicely handsome sparkling of
diamonds very amiable costumed. Or do you are fond better what
belongs they moderns pleasure turpitude of old mans? *(He points
about him with grotesque gestures with Lynch and the whores reply
to.)* Caoutchouc statue woman reversible or lifesize tompeeptoms
virgins nudities very lesbic the kiss five ten times. Enter gentlemen
to see in mirrors every positions trapezes all that machine there
besides also if desire act awfully bestial butcher's boy pollutes in
warm veal liver or omelette on the belly *piece de Shakespeare.*

BELLA

(Clapping her belly, sinks back on the sofa with a shout of laughter.)
An omelette on the . . . Ho! ho! ho! Ho! . . . Omelette on the . . .

STEPHEN

(Mincingly.) I love you, Sir darling. Speak you englishman tongue
for *double entente cordiale.* O yes, *mon loup.* How much cost?

[356]

Waterloo. Watercloset. *(He ceases suddenly and holds up a forefinger.)*

ZOE

Go abroad and love a foreign lady.

STEPHEN

(Extending his arms.) It was here. Street of harlots. In Serpentine Avenue Beelzebub showed me her, a fubsy widow. Where's the red carpet spread?

BLOOM

(Approaching Stephen.) Look . . .

STEPHEN

No, I flew. My foes beneath me. And ever shall be. World without end. *(He cries.) Pater!* Free!

BLOOM

I say, look . . .

STEPHEN

Break my spirit, will he? *O merde alors! (He cries, his vulture talons sharpened.)* Hola! Hillyho!

(The fronds and spaces of the wallpaper file rapidly across country... The crowd bawls of dicers, crown and anchor players, thimbleriggers, broadsmen. Crows and touts, hoarse bookies in high wizard hats clamour deafeningly.)

THE CROWD
Card of the races. Racing card!
Ten to one on the field!
Tommy on the clay here! Tommy on the clay!
Ten to one bar one. Ten to one bar one.
Try your luck on spinning Jenny!
Ten to one bar one!
Sell the monkey, boys! Sell the monkey!
I'll give ten to one!
Ten to one bar one!

(A dark horse, riderless, bolts like a phantom past the winningposts, his mane moonfoaming, his eyeballs stars. The field follows, a bunch of bucking mounts. Skeleton horses: Sceptre, Maximum the Second,

Zinfandel, the Duke of Westminster's Shotover, Repulse, the Duke of Beaufort's Ceylon, prix de Paris. Dwarfs ride them, rusty armoured, leaping, leaping in their saddles. Last in a drizzle of rain, on a broken-winded isabelle nag, Cock of the North, the favourite, honey cap, green jacket, orange sleeves, Garrett Deasy up, gripping the reins, a hockey stick at the ready. His nag, stumbling on whitegaitered feet, jogs along the rocky road.)

(Private Carr, Private Compton and Cissy Caffrey pass beneath the windows, singing in discord.)

STEPHEN

Hark! Our friend, noise in the street.

ZOE

(Holds up her hand.) Stop!

PRIVATE CARR, PRIVATE COMPTON and CISSY CAFREY
Yet I've a sort a
Yorkshire relish for . . .

ZOE

That's me. *(She claps her hands.)* Dance! Dance! *(She runs to the pianola.)* Who has twopence?

BLOOM

Who'll . . .

LYNCH

(Handing her coins.) Here.

STEPHEN

(Cracking his fingers impatiently.) Quick! Quick! Where's my augur's rod? *(He runs to the piano and takes his ashplant, beating his foot in tripudium.)*

ZOE

(Turns the drumhandle.) There.

(She drops two pennies in the slot. Gold pink and violet lights start forth. The drum turns purring in low hesitation waltz.)

[358]

ZOE

(Twirls around herself, heeltapping.) Dance. Anybody here for there? Who'll dance?

(The pianola with changing lights, plays in waltz time the prelude to My Girl's a Yorkshire Girl. Stephen throws his ashplant on the table and seizes Zoe around the waist. Florry and Bella push the table towards the fireplace. Stephen, arming Zoe with exaggerated grace, begins to waltz her around the room. Her sleeve, falling from gracing arms, reveals a white fleshflower of vaccination. Bloom stands aside.)

THE PIANOLA
My little shy little lass has a waist.

(Zoe and Stephen turn boldly with looser swing. The twilight hours advance, from long shadows, dispersed, lagging, languideyed, their cheeks delicate with cipria and false faint bloom. They are in a grey gauze with dark bat sleeves that flutter in the land breeze.)

ZOE

I'm giddy.
(She frees herself, droops on a chair, Stephen seizes Florry and turns with her.)

KITTY

(Jumps up.) O, they played that on the hobbyhorses at the Mirus bazaar!
(She runs to Stephen. He leaves Florry brusquely and seizes Kitty. A screaming bittern's harsh high whistle shrieks.)

THE PIANOLA
My girl's a Yorkshire girl.

ZOE

Yorkshire through and through.

Come on all!
(She seizes Florry and waltzes her.)

STEPHEN

Pas seul!

(He wheels Kitty into Lynch's arms, snatches up his ashplant from the table and takes the floor. All wheel, whirl, waltz, twirl. Bloombella, Kittylynch, Florryzoe, jujuby women. Stephen with hat ashplant frogsplits in middle highkicks with skykicking mouth shut hand clasp part under thigh, with clang tinkle boomhammer tallyho hornblower blue green yellow flashes.)

THE PIANOLA
Though she's a factory lass
And wears no fancy clothes.

STEPHEN
Dance of death.
(The couples fall aside. Stephen whirls giddily. Room whirls back. Eyes closed, he totters. Red rails fly spacewards. Stars all around suns turn roundabout. Bright midges dance on wall. He stops dead.)

STEPHEN
Ho!
(Stephen's mother, emaciated, rises stark through the floor in leper grey with a wreath of faded orange blossoms and a torn bridal veil, her face worn and noseless, green with grave mould. Her hair is scant and lank. She fixes her bluecircled hollow eyesockets on Stephen and opens her toothless mouth uttering a silent word. A choir of virgins and confessors sing voicelessly.)

THE CHOIR
Liliata rutilantium te confessorum . . .
Iubilantium te virginum . . .

(From the top of a tower Buck Mulligan, in particoloured jester's dress of puce and yellow and clown's cap with curling bells, stands gaping at her, a smoking buttered split scone in his hand.)

BUCK MULLIGAN
She's beastly dead. The pity of it! Mulligan meets the afflicted mother. *(He upturns his eyes.)* Mercurial Malachi.

[360]

THE MOTHER

(With the subtle smile of death's madness.) I was once the beautiful Mary Goulding. I am dead.

STEPHEN

(Horrorstruck.) Lemur, who are you? What bogeyman's trick is this?

BUCK MULLIGAN

(Shakes his curling capbell.) The memory of it! Kinch killed her dogsbody bitchbody. She kicked the bucket. *(Tears of molten butter fall from his eyes into the scone.)* Our great sweet mother! *Epi oinopa ponton.*

THE MOTHER

(Comes nearer, breathing upon him softly her breath of wetted ashes.) All must go through it, Stephen. More women than men in the world. You too. Time will come.

STEPHEN

(Choking with fright, remorse and horror.) They said I killed you, mother. He offended your memory. Cancer did it, not I. Destiny.

THE MOTHER

(A green rill of bile trickling from a side of her mouth.) You sang that song to me. *Love's bitter mystery.*

STEPHEN

(Eagerly.) Tell me the word, mother, if you know now. The word known to all men.

THE MOTHER

Who saved you the night you jumped into the train at Dalkey with Paddy Lee? Who had pity for you when you were sad among the strangers? Prayer is all powerful. Prayer for the suffering souls in the Ursuline manual, and forty days' indulgence. Repent, Stephen.

STEPHEN

The ghoul. Hyena!

THE MOTHER

I pray for you in my other world. Get Dilly to make you that boiled rice every night after your brain work. Years and years I loved you, O my son, my firstborn, when you lay in my womb.

ZOE

(Fanning herself with the grate fan.) I'm melting.

FLORRY

(Points to Stephen.) Look! He's white.

BLOOM

(Goes to the window to open it more.) Giddy.

THE MOTHER

(With smouldering eyes.) Repent! O, the fire of hell!

STEPHEN

(Panting.) The corpsechewer! Raw head and bloody bones!

THE MOTHER

(Her face drawing near and nearer, sending out an ashen breath.) Beware! *(She raises her blackened withered right arm slowly toward Stephen's breast with outstretched fingers.)* Beware! God's hand! *(A green crab with malignant red eyes sticks deep its grinning claws into Stephen's heart.)*

STEPHEN

(Strangled with rage.) Shite! *(His features grow drawn and grey and old.)*

BLOOM

(At the window.) What?

STEPHEN

Ah non, par exemple! The intellectual imagination! With me all or not at all. *Non serviam!*

THE MOTHER

(Wrings her hands slowly, moaning desperately.) O Sacred Heart of Jesus, have mercy on him! Save him from hell, O divine Sacred Heart!

STEPHEN

No! No! No! Break my spirit all of you if you can! I'll bring you all to heel!

THE MOTHER

(In the agony of her deathrattle.) Have mercy on Stephen, Lord, for my sake! Inexpressible was my anguish when expiring with love, grief and agony on Mount Calvary.

[362]

STEPHEN

Nothung!
(He lifts his ashplant high with both hands and smashes the chandelier. Time's livid final flame leaps and, in the following darkness, ruin of all space, shattered glass and toppling masonry.)

BLOOM

Stop!

LYNCH

(Rushes forward and seizes Stephen's hand.) Here! Hold on! Don't run amok!

BELLA

Police!
(Stephen, abandoning his ashplant, his head and arms thrown back stark, beats the ground and flees from the room past the whores at the door.)

BELLA

(Screams.) After him!
(The two whores rush to the halldoors. Lynch and Kitty and Zoe stampede from the room. They talk excitedly. Bloom follows, returns.)

BELLA

Who pays for the lamp? *(She seizes Bloom's coattail.)* There. You were with him. The lamp's broken.

BLOOM

(Rushes to the hall, rushes back.) What lamp, woman?

BELLA

(Her eyes hard with anger and cupidity, points.) Who's to pay for that? Ten shillings. You're a witness.

BLOOM

(Snatches up Stephen's ashplant.) Me? Ten shillings? Haven't you lifted enough off him? Didn't he . . . !

BELLA

(Loudly.) Here, none of your tall talk. This isn't a brothel. A ten shilling house.

[363]

BLOOM

(His hand under the lamp, pulls the chain. Pulling, the gasket lights up a crushed mauve purple shade. He raises the ashplant.) Only the chimney's broken. Here is all he . . .

BELLA

(Shrinks back and screams.) Jesus! Don't!

BLOOM

(Warding off a blow.) To show you how he hit the paper. There's not a sixpenceworth of damage done. Ten shillings!

BELLA

Do you want me to call the police?

BLOOM

O, I know. Bulldog on the premises. But he's a Trinity student. Patrons of your establishment. Gentlemen that pay the rent. *(He makes a masonic sign.)* Know what I mean? Nephew of the vice-chancellor. You don't want a scandal.

BELLA

(Angrily.) Trinity! Coming down here ragging after the boat races and paying nothing. Are you my commander here? Where is he? I'll charge him. Disgrace him, I will. *(She shouts.)* Zoe! Zoe!

BLOOM

(Urgently.) And if it were your own son in Oxford! *(Warningly.)* I know.

BELLA

(Almost speechless.) Who are you incog?

ZOE

(In the doorway.) There's a row on.

BLOOM

What? Where? *(He throws a shilling on the table and shouts.)* That's for the chimney. Where? I need mountain air.

[364]

(He hurries out through the hall. The whores point. From the left arrives a jingling hackney car. It slows to in front of the house. Bloom at the halldoor perceives Corny Kelleher who is about to dismount from the car with two silent lechers. He averts his face. Bella from within the hall urges on her whores. They blow ickylickysticky yumyum kisses. Corny Kelleher replies with a ghostly lewd smile. The silent lechers turn to pay the jarvey. Zoe and Kitty still point right. Bloom, parting them swiftly, draws his caliph's hood and poncho and hurries down the steps with sideways face. The ashplant marks his stride. He walks, runs, zigzags, gallops, lugs laid back. He is pelted with gravel, cabbagestumps, biscuitboxes, eggs, potatoes, dead codfish, woman's slipperslappers. After him, freshfound, the hue and cry zigzag gallops in hot pursuit of follow my leader....)

THE HUE AND CRY

(Helterskelterpelterwelter.) He's Bloom! Stop Bloom! Stopabloom! Stopperrobber! Hi! Hi! Stop him at the corner!
(At the corner of Beaver Street beneath the scaffolding Bloom panting stops on the fringe of the noisy quarrelling knot, a lot not knowing a jot what hi! hi! row and wrangle round the whowhat brawlaltogether.)

STEPHEN

(With elaborate gestures, breathing deeply and slowly.) You are my guests. The uninvited. By virtue of the fifth of George and seventh of Edward. History to blame. Fabled by mothers of memory.

PRIVATE CARR

(To Cissy Caffrey.) Was he insulting you?

STEPHEN

Addressed her in vocative feminine. Probably neuter. Ungenitive.

VOICES

No, he didn't. The girl's telling lies. He was in Mrs Cohen's. What's up? Soldiers and civilians.

CISSY CAFFREY

I was in company with the soldiers and they left me to do – you know and the young man ran up behind me. But I'm faithful to the man that's treating me though I'm only a shilling whore.

STEPHEN

(Catches sight of Kitty's and Lynch's heads.) Hail, Sisyphus. *(He points to himself and the others.* Poetic. Neopoetic.

VOICES

She's faithfultheman.

CISSY CAFFREY

Yes, to go with him. And me with a soldier friend.

PRIVATE COMPTON

He doesn't half want a thick ear, the blighter. Biff him one, Harry.

PRIVATE CARR

(To Cissy.) Was he insulting you while me and him was having a piss?

STEPHEN

(To Private Compton.) I don't know your name but you are quite right. Doctor Swift says one man in armour will beat ten men in their shirts. Shirt is synechdoche. Part for the whole.

CISSY CAFFREY

(To the crowd.) No, I was with the private.

STEPHEN

(Amiably.) Why not? The bold soldier boy. In my opinion every lady for example . . .

PRIVATE CARR

(His cap awry, advancing to Stephen.) Say, how would it be, governor, if I was to bash in your jaw?

STEPHEN

(Looks up in the sky.) how? Very unpleasant. Noble art of self-pretence. Personally, I detest action. *(He waves his hand.)* Hand hurts me slightly. *Enfin, ce sont vos oignons. (To Cissy Caffrey.)* Some trouble is on here. What is it, precisely?

BLOOM

(Elbowing through the crowd, plucks Stephen's sleeve vigorously. Come now, professor, that carman is waiting.

[366]

STEPHEN

(Turns.) Eh? *(He disengages himself.)* Why should I not speak to him
or to any human being who walks upright upon this oblate orange?
(He points his finger.) I'm not afraid of what I can talk to if I see his
eye. Retaining the perpendicular.
(He staggers a pace back.)

BLOOM

(Propping him up.) Retain your own.

STEPHEN

(Laughs emptily.) My centre of gravity is displaced. I have forgotten
the trick. Let us sit down somewhere and discuss. Struggle for life is
the law or existence but modern philirenists, notably the tsar and the
king of England, have invented arbitration. *(He taps his brow.)* But
in here it is I must kill the priest and the king.

PRIVATE CARR

(Pulls himself free and comes forward.) What's that you're saying
about my king?

STEPHEN

(Nervous, friendly, pulls himself up.) I understand your point of
view, though I have no king myself for the moment. This is the age
of patent medicine. A discussion is difficult down here. But this is
the point. You die for your country, suppose. *(He places his arm on
Private Carr's sleeve.)* Not that I wish it for you. But I say: Let my
country die for me. Up to the present it has done so. I don't want it to
die. Damn death. Long live life!

PRIVATE COMPTON

Eh, Harry, give him a kick in the knackers. Stick one into Jerry.

BLOOM

(To the privates, softly.) He doesn't know what he's saying. Taking a
little more than is good for him. Absinthe, the greeneyed monster. I
know him. He's a gentleman, a poet. It's all right.

STEPHEN

(Nods, smiling and laughing.) Gentleman, patriot, scholar and judge
of impostors.

PRIVATE CARR

I don't give a bugger who he is.

STEPHEN

I seem to annoy them. Green rag to a bull.

BLOOM

(To Stephen.) Come home. You'll get into trouble.

STEPHEN

(Swaying.) I don't avoid it. He provokes my intelligence.

THE CITIZEN

(With a huge emerald muffler and shillelagh, calls.)
May the God above
Send down a cove
With teeth as sharp as razors
To slit the throat
Of the English dogs
That hanged our Irish leaders.

THE CROPPY BOY

(The rope noose round his neck, gripes in his issuing bowels with both hand.)
I bear no hate to a living thing,
But love my country beyond the king.

RUMBOLD, DEMON BARBER

(Accompanied by two blackmasked assistants, advances with a gladstone bag which he opens…. He jerks the rope, the assistants leap at the victim's legs and drag him downward, grunting: the croppy boy's tongue protrudes violently.)

THE CROPPY BOY

Horhot ho hray ho rhother's hest.

(He gives up the ghost.) A violent erection of the hanged sends gouts of sperm spouting through his death clothes on to the cobblestones.)

RUMBOLD

I'm near it myself. *(He undoes the noose.)* Rope which hanged the awful rebel. Ten shillings a time as applied to His Royal Highness.... My painful duty has now been done. God save the king!

EDWARD THE SEVENTH

(Dances slowly, solemnly , rattling his bucket and sings with soft contentment.)

On coronation day, on coronation day,
O, won't we have a merry time,
Drinking whisky, beer and wine!

PRIVATE CARR

Here. What are you saying about my king?

STEPHEN

(Throws up his hands.) O, this is too monotonous! Nothing. He wants my money and my life, though want must be his master, for some brutish empire of his. Money I haven't. *(He searches his pockets vaguely.)* Gave it to someone.

PRIVATE CARR

Who wants your bleeding money?

STEPHEN

(Tries to move off.) Will some one tell me where I am least likely to meet these necessary evils? *Ça se voit aussi à Paris.* Not that I . . . But by St. Patrick! . . .

(The women's heads coalesce. Old Gummy Granny in sugarloaf hat appears seated on a toadstool, the deathflower of the potato blight on her breast.)

STEPHEN

Aha! I know you, grammer! Hamlet revenge! The old sow that eats her farrow!

OLD GUMMY GRANNY

(Rocking to and fro.) Ireland's sweetheart, the king of Spain's daughter, alanna. Strangers in my house, bad manners to them! *(She keens with banshee woe.)* Ochone! Ochone! Silk of the kine. *(She waits.)* You met with poor old Ireland and how does she stand?

STEPHEN

How do I stand you? The hat trick? Where's the third person of the Blessed Trinity? Soggarth Aroon? The reverend Carrion Crow.

CISSY CAFFREY

(Shrill.) Stop them from fighting!

PRIVATE CARR

(Tugging at his belt.) I'll wring the neck of any bugger says a word against my fucking king.

BLOOM

(Terrified.) He said nothing. Not a word. A pure misunderstanding.

THE CITIZEN

Erin go bragh!

PRIVATE COMPTON

Go it, Harry. Do him one in the eye. He's a proboer.

BLOOM

(To the redcoats.) We fought for you in South Africa, Irish missile troops. Isn't that history? Royal Dublin Fusiliers. Honoured by our monarch.

PRIVATE CARR

I'll do him in.

PRIVATE COMPTON

(Waves the crowd back.) Fair play, here. Make a bleeding butcher's shop of the bugger.
(Massed bands blare Garryowen *and* God save the king.*)*

CISSY CAFFREY

They're going to fight. For me!

STEPHEN

The harlot's cry from street to street
Shall weave old Ireland's windingsheet.

PRIVATE CARR

(Loosening his belt, shouts.) I'll wring the neck of any fucking bastard says a word against my bleeding fucking king.

[370]

BLOOM

(Shakes Cissy Caffrey's shoulders.) Speak, you! Are you struck dumb? You are the link between nations and generations. Speak, women, sacred lifegiver.

CISSY CAFFREY

(Alarmed, seizes Private Carr's sleeve.) Amn't I with you? Amn't I your girl? Cissy's your girl. *(She cries.)* Police!

STEPHEN

(Ecstatically, to Cissy Caffrey.)
       White thy fambles, red thy gan
       And thy quarrons dainty is.

VOICES

Police!

DISTANT VOICES

Dublin's burning! Dublin's burning. On fire, on fire!

(Brimstone fires spring up. Dense clouds roll past. Heavy Gatling guns boom. Pandemonium. Troops deploy. Gallop of hoofs. Artillery. Hoarse commands. Bells clang. Backers shout. Drunkards bawl. Whores screech. Foghorns loot. Cries of valour. Shrieks of dying. . . .

PRIVATE CARR

(With ferocious articulation.) I'll do him in, so help me fucking Christ! I'll wring the bastard fucker's bleeding blasted fucking windpipe.

OLD GUMMY GRANNY

(Thrusts a dagger toward Stephen's hand.) Remove him, acushla. At 8:35 a.m. you will be in heaven and Ireland will be free. *(She prays.)* O good God, take him!

BLOOM

(Runs to Lynch.) Can't you get him away?

LYNCH

He likes dialectic, the universal language. Kitty! *(To Bloom.)* Get him away, you. He won't listen to me. *(He drags Kitty away.)*

STEPHEN

(Points.) Exit Judas. Et laqueo se suspendit.

BLOOM

(Runs to Stephen.) Come along with me now before worse happens.
Here's your stick.

STEPHEN

Stick, no. Reason. This feast of pure reason.

CISSY CAFFREY

(Pulling Private Carr.) Come on, you're boosted. He insulted me but
I forgive him. *(Shouting in his ear.)* I forgive him for insulting me.

BLOOM

(Over Stephen's shoulder.) Yes, go. You see he's incapable.

PRIVATE CARR

(Breaks loose.) I'll insult him.
*(He rushes towards Stephen, fists outstretched, and strikes him in the
face. Stephen totters, collapses, falls stunned. He lies prone, his face
to the sky, his hat rolling to the wall. Bloom follows and picks it up.)*

THE CROWD

Let him up! Don't strike him when he's down! Air! Who? The
soldier hit him. He's a professor. Is he hurted? Don't manhandle
him! He's fainted!

A HAG

What call had the redcoat to strike the gentleman and he under the
influence? Let them go and fight the Boers!

THE BAWD

Listen to who's talking! Hasn't the soldier a right to go with his girl?
He gave him the coward's blow.

BLOOM

(Shoves them back, loudly.) Get back, stand back!

PRIVATE COMPTON

(Tugging his comrade.) Here bugger off, Harry. There's the cops!
(Two raincaped watch, tall, stand in the group.)

[372]

FIRST WATCH

What's wrong here?

PRIVATE COMPTON

We were with this lady and he insulted us and assaulted my chum.

BLOOM

(Glances sharply at the man.) Leave him to me. I can easily . . .

SECOND WATCH

Who are you? Do you know him?

PRIVATE CARR

(Lurches towards the watch.) He insulted my lady friend.

BLOOM

(Angrily.) You hit him without provocation. I'm a witness. Constable, take his regimental number.

SECOND WATCH

I don't want your instructions in the discharge of my duty.

PRIVATE COMPTON

(Pulling his comrade.) Here, bugger off, Harry. Or Bennett'll have you in the lockup.

PRIVATE CARR

(Staggering as he is pulled away.) God fuck old Bennett! He's a whitearsed bugger, I don't give a shit for him.

FIRST WATCH

(Taking out his notebook.) What's his name?

BLOOM

(Peering over the crowd.) I just see a car there. If you give me a hand a second, sergeant . . .

FIRST WATCH

Name and address..

(Corny Kelleher, weepers round his hat, a death wreath in his hand, appears among the bystanders.)

(Quickly.) O, the very man! *(He whispers.)* Simon Dedalus' son. A bit sprung. Get those policemen to move those loafers back.

SECOND WATCH

Night, Mr Kelleher.

CORNY KELLEHER

(To the watch, with drawling eye.) That's all right. I know him. Won a bit on the races. Gold cup. Throwaway. *(He laughs.)* Twenty to one. Do you follow me?

FIRST WATCH

(Turns to the crowd.) Here, what are you all gaping at? Move on out of that.

(The crowd disperses slowly, muttering, down the lane.)

CORNY KELLEHER

Leave it to me, sergeant. That'll be all right. *(He laughs, shaking his head.)* We were often as bad ourselves, ay or worse. What? Eh, what?

FIRST WATCH

(Laughs.) I suppose so.

CORNY KELLEHER

(Nudges the second watch.) Come and wipe your name off the slate. *(He lilts, wagging his head.)* With my tooraloom tooraloom tooraloom tooraloom. What, eh, do you follow me?

SECOND WATCH

(Genially.) Ah, sure we were too.

CORNY KELLEHER

(Winking.) Boys will be boys. I've a car round there.

SECOND WATCH

All right, Mr Kelleher. Good night.

BLOOM

(Shakes hands with both of the watch in turn.) Thank you very much gentlemen, thank you. *(He mumbles confidentially.)* We don't want

[374]

any scandal, you understand. Father is well known, highly respected citizen. Just a little wild oats, you understand.

CORNY KELLEHER

Good night, men.

THE WATCH

(Saluting together.) Night, gentlemen. *(They move off with slow heavy tread.)*

BLOOM

(Blows.) Providential you came on the scene. You have a car? . . .

CORNY KELLEHER

(Laughs, pointing his thumb over his right shoulder to the car brought up against the scaffolding.) Two commercials that were standing fizz in Jammet's. Like princes, faith. One of them lost two quid on the race. Drowning his grief and were on for a go with the jolly girls. So I landed them up on Behan's car and down to nighttown.

BLOOM

I was just going home by Gardiner street when I happened to . . .

CORNY KELLEHER

(Laughs.) Sure they wanted me to join in with the mots. No, by God, says I. Not for old stagers like myself and yourself. *(He laughs again and leers with lackluster eye.)* Thanks be to God we have it in the house what, eh, do you follow me? Hah! hah! hah!

BLOOM

(Tries to laugh.) He, he, he! Yes. Matter of fact I was just visiting an old friend of mine there, Virag, you don't know him (poor fellow he's laid up for the past week) and we had a liquor together and I was just making my way home . . .
(The horse neighs.)

CORNY KELLEHER

Sure it was Behan, our jarvey there, that told me after we left the two commercials in Mrs Cohen's and I told him to pull up and got off to see. *(He laughs.)* Sober hearsedrivers a specialty. Will I give him a lift home? Where does he hang out? Somewhere in Cabra, what?

BLOOM

No, in Sandycove, I believe, from what he let drop.
(Stephen, prone, breathes to the stars. Corny Kelleher, asquint, drawls at the horse. Bloom in gloom, looms down.)

CORNY KELLEHER

(Scratches his nape.) Sandycove! *(He bends down and calls to Stephen.)* Eh! *(He calls again.)* Eh! He's covered with shavings anyhow. Take care they didn't lift anything off him.

BLOOM

No, no, no. I have his money and his hat here and stick.

CORNY KELLEHER

Ah well, he'll get over it. No bones broken. Well, I'll shove along. *(He laughs.)* I've a rendezvous in the morning. Burying the dead. Safe home!

BLOOM

Good night. I'll just wait and take him along in a few . . .
(Corny Kelleher returns to the outside car and mounts it. The horse harness jingles.)
CORNY KELLEHER

(From the car, standing.) Night.

BLOOM

Night.
(The jarvey chucks the reins and raises his whip encouragingly. The car and horse back slowly, awkwardly and turn. Corny Kelleher on the sideseat sways his head to and from in sign of mirth at Bloom's plight.... Bloom, holding in his hand Stephen's hat festooned with shavings and ashplant, stands irresolute. Then he bends to him and shakes him by the shoulder.)

BLOOM

Eh! Ho! *(There is no answer; he bends again.)* Mr Dedalus! *(There is no answer.)* The name if you call. Somnambulist. *(He bends again and hesitating, brings his mouth near the face of the prostrate form.)* Stephen! *(There is no answer. He calls again.)* Stephen!

[376]

STEPHEN

(Groans.) Who? Black panther vampire. *(He sighs and stretches himself, then murmurs thickly with prolonged vowels.)*

Who . . . drive . . . Fergus now.
And pierce . . . wood's woven shade? . . .

(He turns on his left side, sighing, doubling himself together.)

BLOOM

Poetry. Well educated. Pity. *(He bends again and undoes the buttons of Stephen's waistcoat.)* To breathe. *(He brushes the wood shavings from Stephen's clothes with light hands and fingers.)* One pound seven. Not hurt anyhow. *(He listens.)* What!

STEPHEN

(Murmurs.)

. . . shadows . . . the woods.
. . . white breast . . . dim . . .

(He stretches out his arms, sighs again and curls his body. Bloom holding his hat and ashplant stands erect. A dog barks in the distance. Bloom tightens and loosens his grip on the ashplant. He looks down on Stephen's face and form.)

BLOOM

(Communes with the night.) Face reminds me of his poor mother. In the shady wood. The deep white breast. Ferguson, I think I caught. A girl. Some girl. Best thing could happen him . . . *(He murmurs.)* . . . swear that I will always hail, ever conceal, never reveal, any part or parts, art or arts . . . *(He murmurs.)* in the rough sands of the sea . . . a cabletow's length from the shore . . . where the tide ebbs . . . and flows . . .
(Silent, thoughtful, alert, he stands guard, his fingers at his lips in the attitude of secret master. Against the dark wall a figure appears slowly, a fairy boy of eleven, a changeling, kidnapped, dressed in an Elon suit with glass shoes and a little bronze helmet, holding a book in his hand. He reads from right to left inaudibly, smiling, kissing the page.)

[377]

BLOOM
(*Wonderstruck, calls inaudibly.*) Rudy!

RUDY
(*Gazes unseeing into Bloom's eyes and goes on reading, kissing, smiling. He has a delicate mauve face. On his suit he has diamond and ruby buttons. In his free left hand he holds a slim ivory cane with a violet bowknot. A white lambkin peeps out of his waistcoat pocket.*)

[378]

Episode 16 – Eumaeus … faithful swineherd whom Odysseus meets upon returning home to Ithaca. Though disguised as a stranger, Eumaeus treats him hospitably and expresses desire for his return. Odysseus reunites with his son Telemachus, and together they kill the suitors of his wife Penelope. ~ The cabmen's shelter serves as a hospitable place for these two near-strangers as a fatherly Bloom attempts to establish a relationship with Stephen. Both dismiss of the interesting personages there. Each imagines the future.

Bloom and Stephen move on to Fitzharris' cabmen's shelter where they discuss many subjects: wandering, sensuality, nationalism, religion, the "simple" soul. En route Stephen is engaged by Corley. Shelter clientele are entertained by sailor W.B. Murphy's on his return home from sea. Bloom equivocates on his Jewishness. Biding time as Stephen sobers, Bloom reads the *Telegraph*. Bloom speculates on Parnell's return, a story the cabmen laugh off, though they've ideas about the Phoenix Park Murders. He recollects his exchange with Parnell. Bloom shares words on his Martha (Molly). He cajoles Stephen to work. Contemplating bringing Stephen home, the paternal Bloom assesses Stephen's character, and despite contradictory notions, thinks how they might benefit each other. They set out to Bloom's home at 7 Eccles Street.

THEMES
Wandering and misunderstanding. Disguises of our real selves. Recognizing and accepting differences. Robust but superficial persons. Dissolution of friendship. Need for acceptance. Exhaustion, emptiness, futile wandering (reflected in unfinished sentences and language as clichés). One's perspective of Dublin.

III

PREPARATORY TO ANYTHING else Mr Bloom brushed off the greater bulk of the shavings and handed Stephen the hat and ashplant and bucked him up generally in orthodox Samaritan fashion, which he very badly needed. His (Stephen's) mind was not exactly what you would call wandering but a bit unsteady and on his expressed desire for some beverage to drink Mr Bloom, in view of the hour it was and there being no pumps to Vartry water available for their ablutions, let alone drinking purposes, hit upon an expedient by suggesting, off the reel, the propriety of the cabman's shelter, as it was called, hardly a stonesthrow away near Butt Bridge, where they might hit upon some drinkables in the shape of milk and soda or a mineral. But how to get there was the rub. For the nonce he was rather nonplussed but inasmuch as the duty plainly devolved upon him to take some measures on the subject he pondered suitable ways and means during which Stephen repeatedly yawned. So far as he could see he was rather pale in the face so that it occurred to him as highly advisable to get a conveyance of some description which would answer in their then condition, both of them being e. d. ed,

[379]

particularly Stephen, always assuming that there was such a thing to be found. Accordingly, after a few such preliminaries, as, in spite of his having forgotten to take up his rather soapsuddy handkerchief after it had done yeoman service in the shaving line, brushing, they both walked together along Beaver street, or more properly, lane, as far as the farrier's and the distinctly fetid atmosphere of the livery stables at the corner of Montgomery street where they made tracks to the left from thence debouching into Amiens Street round by the corner of Dan Bergin's. But, as he confidently anticipated, there was not a sign of a Jehu plying for hire anywhere to be seen except a fourwheeler, probably engaged by some fellows inside on the spree, outside the North Star Hotel and there was no symptom of its budging a quarter of an inch when Mr Bloom, who was anything but a professional whistler, endeavoured to hail it by emitting a kind of a whistle, holding his arms arched over this head twice.

This was a quandary but, bringing commonsense to bear on it, evidently there was nothing for it but put a good face on the matter and foot it which they accordingly did. So, bevelling around by Mullet's and the Signal House, which they shortly reached, they proceeded perforce in the direction of Amiens street railway terminus, Mr Bloom being handicapped by the circumstance that one of the back buttons of his trousers had, to vary the timehonoured adage, gone the way of all buttons, though, entering thoroughly into the spirit of the thing, he heroically made light of the mischance. So, as neither of them were particularly pressed for time, as it happened, and the temperature refreshing since it cleared up after the recent visitation of Jupiter Pluvius, they dandered along … Between this point and the high, at present unlit, warehouses of Beresford Place Stephen thought to think of Ibsen, associated with Baird's, the stonecutter's, in his mind somehow Talbot Place, first turning to the right, while the other, who was acting as his *fidus Achates,* inhaled with internal satisfaction the smell of James Rourke's city bakery, situated quite close to where they were, the very palatable odour indeed of our daily bread, of all commodities of the public the primary and most indispensable. Bread, the staff of life, earn your bread, O tell me where is fancy bread? At Rourke's the baker's, it said.

En route, to his taciturn, and, not to put too fine a point on it, not yet perfectly sober companion, Mr Bloom, who at all events, was in complete possession of his faculties, never more so, in fact

[380]

disgustingly sober, spoke a word of caution *re* the dangers of nighttown, women of ill fame and swell mobsmen, which, barely permissible once in a while, though not as a habitual practice, was of the nature of a regular deathtrap for young fellows of his age particularly if they had acquired drinking habits under the influence of liquor unless you knew a little juijitsu for every contingency as even a fellow on the broad of his back could administer a nasty kick if you didn't look out…. Another thing he commented on was equipping soldiers with firearms or sidearms of any description, liable to go off at any time, which was tantamount to inciting them against civilians should by any chance they fall out over anything. You frittered away your time, he very sensibly maintained, and health and also character besides which the squandermania of the thing, fast women of the *demimonde* ran away with a lot of L. s.d. Into the bargain and the greatest danger of all was who you got drunk with though, touching the much vexed question of stimulants, he relished a glass of choice old wine in season as both nourishing and blood-making and possessing aperient virtues (notably a good burgundy which he was a staunch believer in) still never beyond a certain point where he invariably drew the line as it simply led to trouble all round to say nothing of your being at the tender mercy of others practically. Most of all he commented adversely on the desertion of Stephen by all his pubhunting *confrères* but one, a most glaring piece of ratting on the part of his brother medicos under all the circs.

    – And that one was Judas, said Stephen, who up to then had said nothing whatsoever of any kind.

  . . . .

    – Someone saluted you, Mr Bloom said.

    A figure of middle height on the prowl, evidently, under the arches saluted again, calling: *Night!* Stephen, of course, started rather dizzily and stopped to return the compliment. Mr Bloom, actuated by motives of inherent delicacy, inasmuch as he always believed in minding his own business, moved off but nevertheless remained on the *qui vive* with just a shade of anxiety though funkyish in the least….

    Stephen, that is when the accosting figure came to close quarters, though he was not in any over sober state himself, recognised Corley's breath redolent of rotten cornjuice. Lord John Corley, some called him, and his genealogy came about in the wise.

He was the eldest son of Inspector Corley of the G Division, lately deceased, who had married a certain Katherine Brophy, the daughter of a Lough farmer.…

Taking Stephen on one side he had the customary doleful ditty to tell. Not as much as a farthing to purchase a night's lodgings. His friends had all deserted him. Furthermore, he had a row with Lenehan and called him to Stephen a mean bloody swab with a sprinkling of other uncalled-for expressions. He was out of a job and implored of Stephen to tell him where on God's earth he could get something, anything at all to do. No, it was the daughter of the mother in the washkitchen that was fostersister to the heir of the house or else they were connected through the mother in some way, both occurrences happening at the same time if the whole thing wasn't a complete fabrication from start to finish. Anyhow, he was all in.

— I wouldn't ask you, only, pursued he, on my solemn oath and God knows I'm on the rocks.

— There'll be a job tomorrow or the next day, Stephen told him, in a boys' school at Dalkey for a gentleman usher. Mr Garret Deasy. Try it. You may mention my name.

— Ah, God, Corley replied, sure I couldn't teach in a school, man. I was never one of your bright ones, he added with a half laugh. Got stuck twice in the junior at Christian Brothers.

— I have no place to sleep myself, Stephen informed him.

Corley, at the first go-off, was inclined to suspect it was something to do with Stephen being fired out of his digs for bringing in a bloody tart off the street… He was starving too though he hadn't said a word about it.

Though this sort of thing went on every other night or very near it still Stephen's feelings got the better of him… But the cream of the joke was nothing would get it out of Corley's head that he was living in affluence and hadn't a thing to do but hand out the needful— whereas. He put his hand in a pocket anyhow, not with the idea of finding any food there, but thinking he might lend him anything up to a bob or so in lieu so that he might endeavour at all events and get sufficient to eat. But the result was in the negative for, to his chagrin, he found his cash missing. A few broken biscuits were all the result of his investigation. He tried his hardest to recollect for the moment whether he had lost, as well he might have, or left, because in that contingency it was not a pleasant lookout, very much the reverse, in

[382]

fact. He was altogether too fagged out to institute a thorough search though he tried to recollect about biscuits he dimly remembered. Who now exactly gave them, or where was, or did he buy? However, in another pocket he came across what he surmised in the dark were pennies, erroneously, however, as it turned out.

— Those are halfcrowns, man, Corley corrected him.

And so in point of fact they turned out to be. Stephen lent him one of them.

— Thanks, Corley answered. You're a gentleman. I'll pay you back some time. Who's that with you? I saw him a few times in the Bleeding Horse in Camden street with Boylan the billsticker. You might put in a good word for us to get me taken on there. I'd carry a sandwichboard only the girl in the office told me they're full up for the next three weeks, man. God, you've got to book ahead, man, you'd think it was for Carl Rosa. I don't give a shite anyway so long as I get a job even as a crossing sweeper.

. . . .

The pair parted company and Stephen rejoined Mr Bloom who, with his practised eye, was not without perceiving that he had succumbed to the blandiloquence of the other parasite. Alluding to the encounter he said, laughingly, Stephen, that is:

— He's down on his luck. He asked me to ask you to ask somebody named Boylan, a billsticker, to give him a job as a sandwichman.

At this intelligence, in which he seemingly evinced little interest, Mr Bloom gazed abstractedly for the space of a half a second or so in the direction of a bucket dredger, rejoicing in the farfamed name of Eblana, moored alongside Customhouse Quay and quite possibly out of repair, whereupon he observed evasively:

— Everybody gets their own ration of luck, they say. Now you mention it his face was familiar to me. But leaving that for the moment, how much did you part with, he queried, if I am not too inquisitive?

— Half-a-crown, Stephen responded. I daresay he needs it to sleep somewhere.

— Needs, Mr Bloom ejaculated, professing not the least surprise at the intelligence, I can quite credit the assertion and I guarantee he invariably does. Everyone according to his needs and everyone according to his deeds. But talking about things in general, where, added he with a smile, will you sleep yourself? Walking to

Sandycove is out of the question, and, even supposing you did, won't you get in after what occurred at Westland Row station. Simply fag out there for nothing. I don't mean to presume to dictate to you in the slightest degree but why did you leave your father's house?

— To seek misfortune, was Stephen's answer.

— I met your respected father on a recent occasion, Mr Bloom diplomatically returned. Today, in fact, or, to be strictly accurate, on yesterday. Where does he live at present? I gathered in the course of the conversation that he had moved .

— I believe he is in Dublin somewhere, Stephen answered unconcernedly. Why?

— A gifted man, Mr Bloom said of Mr Dedalus senior, in more respects than one and a born *raconteur* if ever there was one. He takes great pride, quite legitimately, out of you. You could go back, perhaps, he hazarded, still thinking of the very unpleasant scene at Westland Row terminus when it was perfectly evident that the other two, Mulligan, that is, and that English tourist friend of his, who eventually euchred their third companion, were patently trying as if the whole bally station belonged to them, to give Stephen the slip in the confusion.

There was no response forthcoming to the suggestion, however, such as it was, Stephen's mind's eye being too busily engaged in repicturing his family hearth the last time he saw it.

. . . .

— No, Mr Bloom repeated again, I wouldn't personally repose much trust in that boon companion of yours who contributes the humorous element, Dr Mulligan, as a guide, philosopher, and friend, if I were in your shoes. He knows which side of his bread is buttered on though in all probability he never realised what it is to be without regular meals. Of course you didn't notice as much as I did but it wouldn't occasion me the least surprise to learn that a pinch of tobacco or some narcotic was put in your drink for some ulterior object.

. . . .

— Except it simply amounts to one thing and he is what they call picking your brains, he ventured to throw out.

The guarded glance of half solicitude, half curiosity, augmented by friendliness, which he gave at Stephen's at present morose expression of features did not throw a flood of light, none at all in fact, on the problem as to whether he had let himself be

[384]

bamboozled, to judge by two or three lowspirited remarks he let drop, or, the other way about, saw through the affair, and, for some reason or other best known to himself, allowed matters to more or less . . . Grinding poverty did have that effect and he more than conjectured that, high educational abilities though he possessed, he experienced no little difficulty in making both ends meet.

. . . .

Mr Bloom and Stephen entered the cabman's shelter, an unpretentious wooden structure, where, prior to then, he had rarely, if ever, been before; the former having previously whispered to the latter a few hints anent the keeper of it, said to be the once famous Skin-the-Goat, Fitzharris, the invincible, though he wouldn't vouch for the actual facts, which quite possibly there was not one vestige of truth in. A few moments later saw our two noctambules safely seated in a discreet corner, only to be greeted by stares from the decidedly miscellaneous collection of waifs and strays and other nondescript specimens of the genus *homo,* already there engaged in eating and drinking, diversified by conversation, for whom they seemingly formed an object of marked curiosity.

– Now touching a cup of coffee, Mr Bloom ventured to plausibly suggest to break the ice, it occurs to me you ought to sample something in the shape of solid food, say a roll of some description.

Accordingly his first act was with characteristic *sangfroid* to order these commodities quietly. The *hoi polloi* of jarvies or stevedores, or whatever they were, after a cursory examination, turned their eyes, apparently dissatisfied, away, though one redbearded bibulous individual, a portion of whose hair was greyish, a sailor, probably, still stared for some appreciable time before transferring his rapt attention to the floor.

. . . .

The keeper of the shelter in the middle of this *tête-à-tête* put a boiling swimming cup of a choice concoction labelled coffee on the table and a rather antediluvian specimen of a bun, or so it seemed, after which he beat a retreat to his counter. Mr Bloom determining to have a good square look at him later on so as not to appear to . . . for which reason he encouraged Stephen to proceed with his eyes while he did the honours by surreptitiously pushing the cup of what was temporarily supposed to be called coffee gradually near him.

[385]

– Sounds are impostures, Stephen said after a pause of some little time. Like names, Cicero, Podmore, Napoleon, Mr Goodbody, Jesus, Mr Doyle. Shakespeares were as common as Murphies. What's in a name?

– Yes, to be sure, Mr Bloom unaffectedly concurred. Of course. Our name was changed too, he added, pushing the socalled roll across.

The redbearded sailor, who had his weather eye on the newcomers, boarded Stephen, whom he had singled out for attention in particular, squarely by asking:

– And what might your name be?

Just in the nick of time Mr Bloom touched his companion's boot but Stephen, apparently disregarding the warm pressure, from an unexpected quarter, answered:

– Dedalus.

The sailor stared at him heavily from a pair of drowsy baggy eyes, rather bunged up from excessive use of boose, preferably good old Hollands and water.

– You know Simon Dedalus? he asked at length.

– I've heard of him, Stephen said.

Mr Bloom was all at sea for a moment, seeing the others evidently eavesdropping too.

– He's Irish, the seaman bold affirmed, staring still in much the same way and nodding. All Irish.

– All too Irish, Stephen rejoined.

As for Mr Bloom he could neither make head or tail of the whole business and he was just asking himself what possible connection when the sailor, of his own accord, turned to the other occupants of the shelter and remarked:

– I seen him shoot two eggs off two bottles at fifty yards over his shoulder. The left hand dead shot.

Though he was slightly hampered by an occasional stammer and his gestures being also clumsy as it was still he did his best to explain.

– Bottle out there, say. Fifty yards measured. Eggs on the bottles. Cocks his gun over his shoulder. Aims.

He turned his body half around, shut up right eye completely, then he screwed his features up some way sideways and glared out into the night with an unprepossessing cast of countenance.

[386]

– Pom, he then shouted once.

The entire audience waited, anticipating an additional detonation, there being still a further egg.

– Pom, he shouted twice.

Egg two evidently demolished, he nodded and winked, adding bloodthirstily:

> *– Buffalo Bill shoots to kill,*
> *Never missed nor he never will.*

. . . .

– Murphy's my name, the sailor continued, W. B. Murphy, of Carrigaloe. Know where that is?

– Queenstown Harbour, Stephen replied.

– That's right, the sailor said. Fort Camden and Fort Carlisle. That's where I hails from. My little woman's down there. She's waiting for me, I know. *For England, home and beauty.* She's my own true wife I haven't seen for seven years now, sailing about.

Mr Bloom could easily picture his advent on this scene – the homecoming to the mariner's roadside shieling after having diddled Davy Jones – a rainy night with a blind moon. Across the world for a wife. Quite a number of stories there were on that particular Alice Ben Bolt topic, Enoch Arden and Rip Van Winkle and does anybody hereabouts remember Caoc O' Leary, a favourite and most trying declamation piece, by the way, of poor John Casey and a bit of perfect poetry in its own small way? Never about the runaway wife coming back, however much devoted to the absentee. The face at the window! Judge of his astonishment when he finally did breast the tape and the awful truth dawned upon him anent his better half, wrecked in his affections. You little expected me but I've come to stay and make a fresh start. There she sits, a grass widow, at the selfsame fireside. Believes me dead. Rocked in the cradle of the deep. And there sits uncle Chubb or Tomkin, as the case might be, the publican of the Crown and Anchor, in shirtsleeves, eating rumpsteak and onions. No chair for father. Boo! The wind! Her brandnew arrival is on her knee, *post mortem* child. With a high ro! and a randy ro! And my galloping tearing tandy O! Bow to the inevitable. Grin and bear it. I remain with much love your brokenhearted husband, W. B. Murphy. . . .

– We come up this morning eleven o'clock. The threemaster *Rosevean* from Bridgewater with bricks. I shipped to get over. Paid off this afternoon. There's my discharge. See? W. B. Murphy, A.B.S.

In confirmation of which statement he extricated from an inside pocket and handed to his neighbours a not very cleanlooking folded document.

– You must have seen a fair share of the world, the keeper remarked, leaning on the counter.

– Why, the sailor answered, upon reflection upon it, I've circumnavigated a bit since I first joined on. I was in the Red Sea. I was in China and North America and South America. I seen icebergs plenty, growlers. I was in Stockholm and the Black Sea, the Dardanelles, under Captain Dalton the best bloody man that ever scuttled a ship. I seen Russia. *Gospodi pomilooy.* That's how the Russian prays.

– You seen queer sights, don't be talking, put in a jarvey.

– Why, the sailor said, shifting his partially chewed plug, I seen queer things too, ups and downs. I seen a crocodile bite the fluke of an anchor same as I chew that quid.

He took out of his mouth the pulpy quid and, lodging it between his teeth, bit ferociously.

– Khaan! Like that. And I seen maneaters in Peru that eats corpses and the livers of horses. Look here. Here they are. A friend of mine sent me.

He fumbled out a picture postcard from his inside pocket, which seemed to be in its say a species of repository, and pushed it along the table. The printed matter on it stated:
Choza de Indios. Beni, Bolivia.

All focused their attention on the scene exhibited, at a group of savage women in striped loincloths, squatted, blinking, sucking, frowning, sleeping, amid a swarm of infants (there must have been quite a score of them) outside some primitive shanties of osier.

– Chews coca all day long, the communicative tarpaulin added. Stomachs like breadgraters. Cuts off their diddies when they can't bear no more children. See them there stark ballocknaked eating a dead horse's liver raw.

His postcard proved a centre of attraction for Messrs the greenhorns for several minutes, if not more.

– Know how to keep them off? he inquired genially.

Nobody volunteering a statement, he winked, saying:

– Glass. That boggles 'em. Glass.

Mr Bloom without evincing surprise, ostentatiously turned over the card to peruse the partially obliterated address and

[388]

postmark… There was no message evidently, as he took particular notice. Though not an implicit believer in the lurid story narrated (or the eggsniping transaction for that matter despite William Tell…), having detected a discrepancy between his name (assuming he was the person he represented himself to be and not sailing under false colours after having boxed the compass on the strict q.t. somewhere) and the fictitious addressee of the missive which made him nourish some suspicions of our friend's *bona fides,* nevertheless it reminded him in a way of a longcherished plan he meant to one day realise some Wednesday or Saturday of travelling to London *via* long sea not to say that he had ever travelled extensively to any great extent but he was at heart a born adventurer though by a trick of fate he had consistently remained a landlubber except you call going to Holyhead which was his longest… A great opportunity there certainly was for push and enterprise to meet the travelling needs of the public at large, the average man, i.e. Brown, Robinson and Co.

It was a subject of regret and absurd as well on the face of it and no small blame to our vaunted society that the man in the street, when the system really needed toning up, for a matter of a couple of paltry pounds, was debarred from seeing more of the world they lived in instead of being always cooped up since my old stick-in-the-mud took me for a wife. After all, hang it, they had their eleven and more humdrum months of it and merited a radical change of *venue* after the grind of city life in the summertime, for choice, when Dame Nature is at her spectacular best, constituting nothing short of a new lease of life. There were equally excellent opportunities for vacationists in the home island, delightful sylvan spots for rejuvenation offering a plethora of attractions as well as a bracing tonic for the system in and around Dublin and its picturesque environs, even, Poulaphouca, to which there was a steam tram, but also farther away from the madding crowd, in Wicklow, rightly termed the garden of Ireland, an ideal neighbourhood for elderly wheelmen, so long as it didn't come down, and in the wilds of Donegal, where if report spoke true, the *coup d'oeil* was exceedingly grand, though the lastnamed locality was not easily getatable so that the influx of visitors was not as yet all that it might be considering the signal benefits to be derived from it, while Howth with its historic associations and otherwise, Silken Thomas, Grace O'Malley, George IV, rhododendrons several hundred feet above sealevel was a favourite haunt with all sorts and conditions of men, especially in the spring when young men's fancy, though it had its own toll of deaths by falling off the cliffs by design or accidentally, usually, by the way, on their left leg, it being only about three quarters of an hour's run from the pillar. Because of course uptodate tourist travelling was as yet merely in its infancy, so to speak, and the accommodation left much to be desired. Interesting to fathom, it seemed to him, from a motive of curiosity pure and simple, was whether it was the traffic that created the route or vice-versa or the two sides in fact. He turned back the other side of the card picture and passed it to Stephen.

— I seen a Chinese one time, related the doughty narrator, that had little pills like putty and he would put them in the water and they opened, and every pill was something different. One was a ship, another was a house, another was a flower. Cooks rats in your soup, he appetisingly added, the Chinese does.

Possibly perceiving an expression of dubiosity on their faces, the globetrotter went on adhering to his adventures.

— And I seen a man killed in Trieste by an Italian chap. Knife in his back. Knife like that.

Whilst speaking he produced a dangerous looking claspknife, quite in keeping with his character, and held it in the striking position.

— In a knockingshop it was count of a tryon between two smugglers. Fellow hid behind a door, come up behind him. Like that. *Prepare to meet your God,* says he. Chuck! It went into his back up to the butt.

His heavy glance, drowsily roaming about, kind of defied their further questions even should they by any chance want to. That's a good bit of steel, repeated he, examining his formidable *stiletto.*

After which harrowing *dénouement* sufficient to appal the stoutest he snapped the blade to and stowed the weapon in question away as before in his chamber of horrors, otherwise pocket.

— They're great for the cold steel, somebody who was evidently quite in the dark said for the benefit of them all. That was why they thought the park murders of the invincibles was done by foreigners on account of them using knives.

At this remark, passed obviously in the spirit of *where ignorance is bliss,* Mr Bloom and Stephen, each in his own particular way, both instinctively exchanged meaningful glances, in a religious silence of the strictly *entre nous* variety however, towards the Skin-

[390]

the-Goat, *alias* the keeper, was drawing spurts of liquid from his boiler affair. His inscrutable face, which was really a work of art, a perfect study in itself, beggaring description, conveyed the impression that he didn't understand one jot of what was going on. Funny very.

There ensued a somewhat lengthy pause. One man was reading by fits and starts a stained by coffee evening journal; another, the card with the natives *choza de;* another, the seaman's discharge. Mr Bloom, so far as he was personally concerned, was just pondering in pensive mood. He vividly recollected when the occurrence alluded to took place as well as yesterday, some score of years previously, in the days of the land troubles when it took the civilised world by storm, figuratively speaking, early in the eighties, eightyone to be correct, when he was just turned fifteen.

. . . .

– There was a fellow sailed with me in the *Rover*, the old seadog, himself a rover, proceeded. Went ashore and took up a soft job as gentleman's valet at six quid a month. Them are his trousers I've on me and he gave me an oilskin and that jackknife. I'm game for that job, shaving and brushup. I hate roaming about. There's my son now, Danny, run off to sea and his mother got him took in a draper's in Cork where he could be drawing easy money.

– What age is he? queried one hearer who, by the way, seen from the side, bore a distant resemblance to Henry Campbell, from the townclerk, away from the carking cares of office, unwashed, of course, and in a seedy getup and a strong suspicion of nosepaint about the nasal appendage.

– Why, the sailor answered with a slow puzzled utterance. My son Danny? He'd be about eighteen now, way I figure it.

The Skibbereen father hereupon tore open his grey or unclean anyhow shirt with his two hands and scratched away at his chest on which was to be seen an image tattooed in blue Chinese ink, intended to represent an anchor.

– There was lice in that bunk in Bridgewater, he remarked. Sure as nuts. I must get a wash tomorrow or next day. It's them black lads I objects to. I hate those buggers. Sucks your blood dry, they does.

Seeing they were all looking at his chest, he accommodatingly dragged his shirt more open so that, on top of the time honoured symbol of the mariner's hope and rest, they had a full view of the figure 16 and a young man's sideface looking frowningly rather.

— Tattoo, the exhibitor explained. That was done when we were lying becalmed off Odessa in the Black Sea under Captain Dalton. Fellow the name of Antonio done that. There he is himself, a Greek.

— Did it hurt much doing it? one asked the sailor.

That worthy, however, was busily engaged in collecting round the someway in his. Squeezing or . . .

— See here, he said, showing Antonio. There he is, cursing the mate. And there he is now, he added. The same fellow, pulling the skin with his fingers, some special knack evidently, and he laughing at a yarn.

And in point of fact the young man named Antonio's livid face did actually look like forced smiling and the curious effect excited the unreserved admiration of everybody, including Skin-the-Goat who this time stretched over.

— Ay, ay, sighed the sailor, looking down on his manly chest. He's gone too. Ate by sharks after. Ay, ay.

He let go of the skin so that the profile resumed the normal expression of before.

— Neat bit of work, longshoreman one said.

— And what's the number for? Loafer number two queried.

— Eaten alive? a third asked the sailor.

— Ay, ay, sighed again the latter personage, more cheerily this time, with some sort of a half smile, for a brief duration only, in the direction of the questioner about the number. A Greek he was.

And then he added, with rather gallowsbird humour, considering his alleged end:

> — *As bad as old Antonio*
> *For he left me on my ownio.*

The face of a streetwalker, glazed and haggard under a black straw hat, peered askew round the door of the shelter, palpably reconnoitering on her own with the object of bring more grist to the mill. Mr Bloom scarcely knowing which way to look, turned away on the moment, flusterfied but outwardly calm... His reason for doing so was he recognised on the moment round the door the same face he had caught a fleeting glimpse of that afternoon on Ormond Quay, the partially idiotic female, namely, of the lane. . . Round the

[392]

side of the *Evening Telegraph* he just caught a fleeting glimpse of
her face round the side of the door with a kind of demented glassy
grin showing that she was not exactly all there...

    – It beats me, Mr Bloom confided to Stephen, medically I
am speaking, how a wretched creature like that from the Lock
Hospital, reeking with disease, can be barefaced enough to solicit or
how any man in his sober senses, if he values his health in the least.
Unfortunate creature! Of course, I suppose some man is ultimately
responsible for her condition. Still no matter what the cause is from
. . .   Stephen had not noticed her and shrugged his shoulders,
merely remarking:

    – In this country people sell much more than she ever had
and do a roaring trade. Fear them not that sell the body but have not
power to buy the soul. She is a bad merchant. She buys dear and sells
cheap. . . .

    – You, as a good catholic, he observed, talking of body and
soul, believe in the soul. Or do you mean the intelligence, the
brainpower as such, as distinct from any outside object, the table, let
us say, that cup? I believe in that myself because it has been
explained by competent men as the convolutions of the grey matter.
Otherwise we would never have such inventions as X rays, for
instance. Do you?

    Thus cornered, Stephen had to make a superhuman effort of
memory to try and concentrate and remember before he could say:

    – They tell me on the best authority it is a simple substance
and therefore incorruptible. It would be immortal, I understand, but
for the possibility of annihilation by its First Cause, Who, from all I
can hear, is quite capable of adding that to the number of His other
practical jokes, *corruptio per se* and *corruptio per accidens* both
being excluded by court etiquette.

    Mr Bloom thoroughly acquiesced in the general gist of this
though the mystical finesse involved was a bit out of his sublunary
depth still he felt bound to enter a demurrer on the head of simple,
promptly rejoining:

    – Simple? I shouldn't think that is the proper word. Of
course, I grant you, to concede a point, you do knock across a simple
soul once in a blue moon. But what I am anxious to arrive at is it is
one thing for instance to invent those rays Rontgen did, or the
telescope like Edison, though I believe it was before his time, Galileo
was the man I mean. The same applies to the laws, for example, of a

farreaching natural phenomenon such as electricity but it's a horse of quite another colour to say you believe in the existence of a supernatural God.

— O, that, Stephen expostulated, has been proved conclusively by several of the best known passages in Holy Writ, apart from circumstantial evidence.

On this knotty point, however the views of the pair, poles apart as they were, both in schooling and everything else, with the marked difference in their respective ages, clashed.

— Has been? the more experience of the two objected, sticking to his original point. I'm not so sure about that. That's a matter of every man's opinion and, without dragging in the sectarian side of the business, I beg to differ with you *in toto* there. My belief is, to tell you the candid truth, that those bits were genuine forgeries all of them put in by monks most probably or it's the big question of our national poet over again, who precisely wrote them, like *Hamlet* and Bacon, as you who know your Shakespeare infinitely better than I, of course, I needn't tell you. Can't you drink that coffee, by the way? Let me stir it and take a piece of that bun. It's like one of our skipper's bricks disguised. Still, no one can give what he hasn't got. Try a bit.

— Couldn't, Stephen contrived to get out, his mental organs for the moment refusing to dictate further.

Faultfinding being a proverbially bad hat, Mr Bloom thought well to stir, or try to, the clotted sugar from the bottom and reflected with something approaching acrimony on the Coffee Palace and its temperance (and lucrative) work. To be sure it was a legitimate object and beyond yea or nay did a world of good. Shelters such as the present one they were in run on teetotal lines for vagrants at night, concerts, dramatic evenings, and useful lectures (admittance free) by qualified men for the lower orders. On the other hand, he had a distinct and painful recollection they paid his wife, Madam Marion Tweedy who had been prominently associated with it at one time, a very modest remuneration indeed for her pianoplaying. The idea, he was strongly inclined to believe, was to do good and net a profit, there being no competition to speak of. Sulphate of copper poison, SO$_4$ or something in some dried peas he remembered reading of in a cheap eatinghouse somewhere but he couldn't remember when it was or where. Anyhow, inspection, medical inspection, of all eatables, seemed to him more than ever necessary which possibly accounted for the vogue of Dr Tibble's Vi-Cocoa on account of the medical analysis involved.

– Have a shot at it now, he ventured to say of the coffee after having been stirred.

Thus prevailed on to at any rate taste it, Stephen lifted the heavy mug from the brown puddle – it clopped out of it when taken up – by the handle and took a sip of the offending beverage.

– Still, it's solid food, his good genius urged, I'm a stickler for solid food, his one and only reason being not gormandising in the least but regular meals as the *sine qua non* for any kind of proper work, mental or manual. You ought to eat more solid food. You would feel a different man.

– Liquids I can eat, Stephen said. But oblige me by taking away that knife. I can't look at the point of it. It reminds me of Roman history.

Mr Bloom promptly did as suggested and removed the incriminated article, a blunt hornhandled ordinary knife with nothing particularly Roman or antique about it to the eye, observing that the point was the least conspicuous point about it.

– Our mutual friend's stories are like himself, Mr Bloom, *apropos* of knives, remarked to his *confidente sotto voce.* Do you think they are genuine? He could spin those yarns for hours on end all night long and lie like old boots. Look at him.

Yet still, though his eyes were thick with sleep and sea air, life was full of a host of things and coincidences of a terrible nature and it was quite within the bounds of possibility that it was not an entire fabrication though at first blush there was not much inherent probability in all the spoof he got off his chest being strictly accurate gospel.

He had been meantime taking stock of the individual in front of him and Sherlockhomesing him up, ever since he clapped eyes on him.

. . . .

– Mind you, I'm not saying that it's all a pure invention, he resumed. Analogous scenes are occasionally, if not often, met with. Giants, though, that is rather a far cry you see once in a way. Marcella, the midget queen. In those waxworks in Henry street I myself saw some Aztecs, as they are called, sitting bowlegged. They couldn't straighten their legs if you paid them because the muscles here, you see, he proceeded, indicating on his companion the brief outline, the sinews, or whatever you like to call them, behind the right knee, were utterly powerless from sitting that way so long cramped up, being adored as gods. There's an example again of simple souls.

. . . .

— Spaniards, for instance, he continued, passionate temperaments like that, impetuous as Old Nick, are given to taking the law into their own hands and give you your quietus double quick with those poignards they carry in the abdomen. It comes from the great heat, climate generally. My wife is, so to speak, Spanish, half, that is. Point of fact she could actually claim Spanish nationality if she wanted, having been born in (technically) Spain, i.e., Gibraltar. She has the Spanish type. Quite dark, regular brunette, black. I, for one, certainly believe climate accounts for character. That's why I asked you if you wrote your poetry in Italian.

— The temperaments at the door, Stephen interposed with, were very passionate about tenshllings. *Roberto ruba roba sua.*

— Quite so, Mr Bloom dittoed.

— Then, Stephen said, staring and rambling on to himself or some unknown listener somewhere, we have the impetuosity of Dante and the isosceles triangle, Miss Portinari, he fell in love with and Leonardo and san Tommaso Mastino.

— It's in the blood, Mr Bloom acceded at once. All are washed in the blood of the sun. Coincidence, I just happened to be in the Kildare street Museum today, shortly prior to our meeting, if I can so call it, and I was just looking at those antique statues there. The splendid proportions of hips, bosom. You simply don't knock against those kind of women here. An exception here and there. Handsome, yes, pretty in a way you find, but what I'm talking about is the female form. Besides, they have so little taste in dress, most of them, which greatly enhances a woman's natural beauty, no matter what you say. Rumpled stockings — it may be, possibly is, a foible of mine, but still it's a thing I simply hate to see.

Interest, however, was starting to flag somewhat all around and the others got on to talking about accidents at sea, ships lost in a fog, collisions with icebergs, all that sort of thing. Shipahoy, of course, had his own say to say. He had doubled the Cape a few odd times and weathered a monsoon, a kind of wind, in the China seas and through all those perils of the deep there was one thing, he

[396]

declared, stood to him, or words to that effect, a pious medal he had that saved him....

At this stage an incident happened. It having become necessary for him to unfurl a reef, the sailor vacated his seat.

– Let me cross your bows, mate, he said to his neighbour, who was just gently dropping off into a peaceful doze.

He made tracks heavily, slowly, with a dumpy sort of a gait to the door, stepped heavily down the one step there was out of the shelter and bore due left. While he was in the act of getting his bearings, Mr Bloom, who noticed when he stood up that he had two flasks of presumably ship's rum sticking one out of each pocket for the private consumption of his burning interior, saw him produce a bottle and uncork it, or unscrew, and applying its nozzle to his lips, take a good old delectable swig out of it with a gurgling noise. The irrepressible Bloom, who also had a shrewd suspicion that the old stager went out on a maneuvere after the counterattraction in the shape of a female, who, however, had disappeared to all intents and purposes, could, by straining, just perceive him, when duly refreshed by his rum puncheon exploit, gazing up at the piers and girders of the Loop Line, rather out of his depth, as of course it was all radically altered since his last visit and greatly improved. Some person or persons invisible directed him to the male urinal erected by the cleansing committee all over the place for the purpose but, after a brief space of time during which silence reigned supreme, the sailor, evidently giving it a wide berth, eased himself close at hand, the noise of his bilgewater some little time subsequently splashing on the ground where it apparently woke a horse of the cabrank....

All, the meantime, were loudly lamenting the falling off in Irish shipping, coastwise and foreign as well, which was all part and parcel of the same thing. A Palgrave Murphy boat was put off the ways at Alexandra Basin, the only launch that year. Right enough the harbours were there only no ships ever called.

There were wrecks and wrecks, the keeper said, who was evidently *au fait*.

What he wanted to ascertain was why that ship ran bang against the only rock in Galway Bay when the Galway Harbour scheme was mooted by a Mr Worthington or some name like that, eh? Ask her captain, he advised them, how much palmoil the British Government gave him for that day's work. Captain John Lever of the Lever line.

[397]

– Am I right, skipper? he queried of the sailor now returning
after his private potation and the rest of his exertions.

That worthy, picking up the scent of the fagend of the song
or words, growled in wouldbe music, but with great vim, some kind
of chanty or other in seconds or thirds. Mr Bloom's sharp ears heard
him then expectorate the plug probably (which it was), so that he
must have lodged it for the time being in his fist while he did the
drinking and making water jobs and found it a bit sour but after the
liquid fire in question. Anyhow in he rolled after his successful
libation – *cum* – potation, introducing an atmosphere of drink into
the *soiree,* boisterously trolling, like a veritable son of a seacook:

> *– The biscuits was as hard as brass,*
> *And the beef as salt as Lot's wife's arse.*
> *O Johnny Lever!*
> *Johnny Lever, O!*

After which effusion the redoubtable specimen duly arrived
on the scene and, regaining his seat, he sank rather than sat heavily
on the form provided.

Skin-the-Goat, assuming he was he, evidently with an axe to
grind, was airing his grievances in a forcible-feeble philippic anent
the natural resources of Ireland, or something of that sort, which he
described in his lengthy dissertation as the richest country bar one on
the face of God's earth, far and away superior to England, with coal
in large quantities, six million pounds' worth of pork exported every
year, ten millions between butter and eggs, and all the riches drained
out of it by England levying taxes on the poor people that paid
through the nose always, and gobbling up the best meat in the
market, and a lot more surplus steam in the same vein. Their
conversation accordingly became general and all agreed that that was
a fact. You could grow any mortal thing in Irish soil, he stated, and
there was Colonel Everard down there in Cavan growing tobacco.
Where would you find anywhere the like of Irish bacon? But a day of
reckoning, he stated *crescendo* with no uncertain voice – thoroughly
monopolising all the conversation – was in store for mighty England,
despite her power of pelf on account of her crimes. There would be a
fall and the greatest in history...
His advice to every Irishman was: stay in the land of your birth and
work for Ireland and live for Ireland. Ireland, Parnell said, could not
spare a single one of her sons.

[398]

Silence all around marked the termination of his *finale.* The impervious navigator heard these lurid tidings undismayed. . . .

While allowing him his individual opinions, as every man, the keeper added he cared nothing for any empire, ours or his, and considered no Irishman worthy of his salt that served it. Then they began to have a few irascible words, when it waxed hotter, both needless to say, appealing to the listeners who followed the passage of arms with interest so long as they didn't indulge in recriminations and come to blows.

From inside information extending over a series of years Mr Bloom was rather inclined to poohpooh the suggestion as egregious balderdash for, pending that consummation devoutly to be or not to be wished for, he was fully cognizant of the fact that their neighbours across the channel, unless they were much bigger fools than he took them for, rather concealed their strength than the opposite. It was quite on a par with the quixotic idea in certain quarters that in a hundred million years the coal seam of the sister island would be played out and if, as time went on , that turned out to be how the cat jumped all he could personally say on the matter was that as a host of contingencies, equally relevant to the issue, might occur ere then it was highly advisable in the interim to try to make the most of both countries, even though poles apart. Another little interesting point, the amours of whores and chummies, to put it in common parlance, reminded him Irish soldiers had as often fought for England as against her, more so in fact. And now, why? So the scene between the pair of them, the licensee of the place, rumoured to be or have been Fitzharris, the famous invincible, and the other, obviously bogus, reminded him forcibly as being on all fours with the confidence trick, supposing, that is, it was prearranged, as the lookeron, a student of the human soul, if anything, the others seeing least of the game. And as for the lessee or keeper, who probably wasn't the other person at all, he (Bloom) couldn't help feeling, and most properly, it was better to give people like that the goby unless you were a blithering idiot altogether and refuse to have anything to do with them as a golden rule in private life and their felonsetting, there always being the offchance of a Dannyman coming forward and turning queen's evidence – or king's now – like Denis or Peter Carey, an idea he utterly repudiated. Quite apart from that, he disliked those careers of wrongdoing and crime on principle. Yet, though such criminal propensities had never been an inmate of his

bosom in any shape or form, he certainly did feel, and no denying it
(while inwardly remaining what he was), a certain kind of admiration
for a man who had actually brandished a knife, cold steel, with the
courage of his political convictions though, personally, he would
never be party to any such thing, off the same bat as those love
vendettas of the south – have her or swing for her – when the
husband frequently, after some words passed between the two
concerning her relations with the other lucky mortal (the man having
had the pair watched), inflicted fatal injuries on his adored one as a
result of an alternative postnuptial *liaison* by plunging his knife into
her until it just struck him that Fitz, nicknamed Skin-the-Goat,
merely drove the car for the actual perpetrators of the outrage and so
was not, if he was reliably informed, actually party to the ambush
which inpoint of fact, was the plea some legal luminary saved his
skin on. In any case that was very ancient history by now and as for
our friend, the pseudo Skin-the-etcetera, he had transparently
outlived this welcome. He ought to have either died naturally or on
the scaffold high. Like actresses, always farewell – positively last
performance then come up smiling again. Generous to a fault, of
course, temperamental, no economising or any idea of the sort,
always snapping at the bone for the shadow. So similarly he had a
very shrewd suspicion that Mr Johnny Lever got rid of some L. s. d.
In the course of his perambulations round the docks in the congenial
atmosphere of the *Old Ireland* tavern, come back to Erin and so on.
Then as for the others, he had heard not so long before the same
identical lingo, as he told Stephen how he simply but effectually
silenced the offender.

– He took umbrage at something or other, that muchinjured
but on the whole eventempered person declared, I let slip. He called
me a jew, and in a heated fashion, offensively. So I, without
deviating from plain facts in the least, told him his God, I mean
Christ, was a jew too, and all his family, like me, though in reality
I'm not. That was one for him. A soft answer turns away wrath. He
hadn't a word to say for himself as everyone saw. Am I not right?

He turned a long you are wrong gaze on Stephen of timorous
dark pride at the soft impeachment, with a glance also of entreaty for
he seemed to glean in a kind of way that it wasn't all exactly . . .

– *Ex quibus,* Stephen mumbled in a noncommittal accent,
their two or four eyes conversing, *Christus* or Bloom his name is, or,
after all, any other, *secundum carnem.*

[400]

– Of course, Mr Bloom proceeded to stipulate, you must look at both sides of the question. It is hard to lay down any hard and fast rules as to right and wrong but room for improvement all round there certainly is though every country, they say, our own distressful included, has the government it deserves. But with a little goodwill all around. It's all very fine to boast of mutual superiority but what about mutual equality? I resent violence or intolerance in any shape or form. It never reaches anything or stops anything. A revolution must come on the due instalments plan. It's a patent absurdity on the face of it to hate people because they live round the corner and speak another vernacular, so to speak.

– Memorable bloody bridge battle and seven minutes' war, Stephen assented between Skinner's alley and Ormond market.

– Yes, Mr Bloom thoroughly agreed, entirely endorsing the remark, that was overwhelmingly right and the whole world was overwhelmingly full of that sort of thing.

– You just took the words out of my mouth, he said. A hocuspocus of conflicting evidence that candidly you couldn't remotely . . .

All those wretched quarrels, in his humble opinion, stirring up bad blood – bump of combativeness or gland of some kind, erroneously supposed to be about a punctilio of honour and a flag – were very largely a question of the money question which was at the back of everything, greed and jealousy, people never knowing when to stop.

– They accuse – remarked he audibly. He turned away from the others, who probably . . . and spoke nearer to, so as the others . . . in case they . . .

– Jews, he softly imparted in an aside in Stephen's ear, are accused of ruining. Not a vestige of truth in it, I can safely say. History – would you be surprised to learn? – proves up to the hilt Spain decayed when the Inquisition hounded jews out and England prospered when Cromwell, an uncommonly able ruffian, who, in other respects, has much to answer for, imported them. Why? Because they are practical and are proved to be so. I don't want to indulge in any . . . because you know the standard works on the subject, and then, orthodox as you are . . . But in the economic, not touching religion, domain, the priest spells poverty. Spain again, you saw in the war, compared with goahead America. Turks, it's in the dogma. Because if they didn't believe they'd go straight to heaven when they die they'd try to live better – at least, so I think. That's the juggle on which the p.p.'s raise the wind on false pretences. I'm, he resumed, with dramatic force, as good an Irishman as that rude person I told you about at the outset and I want to see everyone, concluded he, all creeds and classes *pro rata* having a comfortable tidysized income, in no niggard fashion either, something in the neighbourhood of L300 per annum. That's the vital issue at stake and it's feasible and would be provocative of friendlier intercourse between man and man. At least that's my idea for what it's worth. I call that patriotism. *Ubi patria,* as we learned a small smattering of in our classical day in *Alma Mater, vita bene.* Where you can live well, the sense is, if you work.

Over his untasteable apology for a cup of coffee, listening to this synopsis of things in general, Stephen stared at nothing in particular. He could hear, of course, all kinds of words changing colour like those crabs about Ringsend in the morning, burrowing quickly into all colours of different sorts of the same sand where they had a home somewhere beneath or seemed to. Then he looked up and saw the eyes that said or didn't say the words the voice he heard said – if you work.

– Count me out, he managed to remark, meaning to work.

The eyes were surprised at this observation, because as he, the person who owned them pro. tem. Observed, or rather, his voice speaking did: All must work, have to, together.

– I mean, of course, the other hastened to affirm, work in the widest possible sense. Also literary labour, not merely for the kudos of the thing. Writing for the newspapers which is the readiest channel nowadays. That's work too. Important work. After all, from the little I know of you, after all the money expended on your education, you are entitled to recoup yourself and command your price. You have every bit as much right to live by your pen in pursuit of your philosophy as the peasant has. What? You both belong to Ireland, the brain and the brawn. Each is equally important.

– You suspect, Stephen retorted with a sort of a half laugh, that I may be important because I belong to the *faubourg Saint Patrice* called Ireland for short.

– I would go a step farther, Mr Bloom insinuated.

– But I suspect, Stephen interrupted, that Ireland must be important because it belongs to me.

[402]

– What belongs? queried Mr Bloom, bending, fancying he was perhaps under some misapprehension. Excuse me. Unfortunately I didn't catch the latter portion. What was it you? . . .

Stephen, patently crosstempered, repeated and shoved aside his mug of coffee, or whatever you like to call it, none too politely, adding:

– We can't change the country. Let us change the subject.

At this pertinent suggestion, Mr Bloom, to change the subject, looked down, but in a quandary, as he couldn't tell exactly what construction to put on belongs to which sounded rather a far cry. The rebuke of some kind was clearer than the other part. Needless to say, the fumes of his recent orgy spoke then with some asperity in a curious bitter way, foreign to his sober state. Probably the home life, to which Mr Bloom attached the utmost importance, had not been all that was needful or he hadn't been familiarised with the right sort of people. With a touch of fear for the young man beside him, whom he furtively scrutinised with an air of some consternation remembering he had just come back from Paris, the eyes more especially reminding him forcibly of father and sister, failing to throw much light on the subject, however, he brought to mind instances of cultured fellows that promised so brilliantly, nipped in the bud of premature decay, and nobody to blame but themselves.

. . . .

For which and further reasons he felt it was interest and duty even to wait on and profit by the unlookedfor occasion, though why, he could not exactly tell, being as it was, already several shillings to the bad, having in fact, let himself in for it. Still, to cultivate the acquaintance of someone of no uncommon calibre who could provide food for reflection would amply repay any small . . . Intellectual stimulation as such was, he felt, from time to time a firstrate tonic for the mind. Added to which was the coincidence of meeting, discussion, dance, row, old salt, of the here today and gone tomorrow type, night loafers, the whole galaxy of events, all went to make up a miniature cameo of the world we live in, especially as the lives of the submerged then, viz., coalminers, divers, scavengers, etc., were very much under the microscope lately. To improve the shining hour he wondered whether he might meet with anything approaching the same luck as Mr Philip Beaufoy if taken down in writing. Suppose he were to pen something out of the common groove (as he fully intended doing) at the rate of one guinea per column, *My Experiences,* let's say, *in a Cabman's Shelter.*

The pink edition, extra sporting, of the *Telegraph,* tell a graphic lie, lay, as luck would have it, beside his elbow and as he was just puzzling again, far from satisfied, over a country belonging to him and the preceding rebus the vessel came from Bridgewater and the postcard was addressed to A. Boudin, find the captain's age, his eyes went aimlessly over the respective captions which came under his special province, the allembracing give us this day our daily press. First he got a bit of a start but it turned out to be only something about somebody named H. du Boyes, agent for typewriters or something like that. Great battle Tokio. Lovemaking in Irish L 200 damages. Gordon Bennett. Emigration swindle. Letter from His Grace William +. Ascot *Throwaway* recalls Derby of '92 when Captain Marshall's dark horse, *Sir Hugo,* captured the blue riband at long odds. New York disaster, thousand lives lost. Foot and Mouth. Funeral of the late Mr Patrick Dignam.

So to change the subject he read about Dignam, R.I.P., which, he reflected, was anything be a gay sendoff.

– *This morning* (Hynes put it in, of course), *the remains of the late Mr Patrick Dignam were removed from his residence, no 9 Newbridge Avenue, Sandymount, for interment in Glasnevin. The deceased gentleman was a most popular and genial personality in city life and his demise, after a brief illness, came as great shock to citizens of all classes by whom he is deeply regretted. The obsequies, at which many friends of the deceased were present, were carried out* (certainly Hynes wrote it with a nudge from Corny) *by Messrs. H. J. O'Neill & Son, 164 North Strand road. The mourners included: Patk. Dignam (son), Bernard Corrigan (brother-in-law), John Henry Menton, solr., Martin Cunningham, John Power eatonph ⅛ ador dorador douradora* (must be where he called Monks the dayfather about Keyes's ad), *Thomas Kernan, Simon Dedalus, Stephen Dedalus, B. A., Edward J. Lambert, Cornelius Kelleher, Joseph M'C. Hynes, L. Boom, C. P. M'Coy, – M'Intosh, and several others.*

Nettled not a little by *L. Boom* (as it incorrectly stated) and the line of bitched type, but tickled to death simultaneously by C. P. M'Coy and Stephen Dedalus, B. A., who were conspicuous, needless to say, by their total absence (to say nothing of M'Intosh), L. Boom pointed it out to his companion B. A., engaged in stifling another yawn, half nervousness, not forgetting the usual crop of nonsensical howlers of misprints.

– Is that first epistle to the Hebrews, he asked, as soon as his bottom jaw would let him, in? Text: open thy mouth and put thy foot in it.

– It is, really, Mr Bloom said (though first he fancied he alluded to the archbishop till he added about foot and mouth with which there could be no possible connection) overjoyed to set his mind at rest and a bit flabbergasted at Myles Crawford's after all managing the thing, there.

While the other was reading it on page two Boom (to give him for the nonce his new misnomer) whiled away a few odd leisure moments in fits and starts with the account of the third event at Ascot on page three, his sidevalue 1,000 sovs., with 3,000 sovs. in specie added for the colts and fillies, Mr. F. Alexander's *Throwaway,* b.h. by *Rightaway,* 5 yrs, 9 st 4 lbs. Thrale (W. Lane) 1. Lord Howard de Walden's *Zinfandel* (M. Cannon) 2. Mr W. Bass's *Sceptre,* 3. Betting 5 to 4 on *Zinfandel,* 20 to 1 *Throwaway* (off). *Throwaway* and *Zinfandel* stood close order. It was anybody's race then the rank outsider drew to the fore got long lead, beating lord Howard de Walden's chestnut colt and Mr W. Bass's bay filly *Sceptre* on a 2 ½ mile course....

– Who? the other, whose hand by the way was hurt, said.

One morning you would open the paper, the cabman affirmed, and read, *Return of Parnell.* He bet them what they liked. A Dublin fusilier was in that shelter one night and said he saw him in South Africa. Pride it was killed him, He ought to have done away with himself or lain low for a time after Committee Room No. 15 until he was his old self again with no-one to point a finger at him. Then they would all to a man have gone down to their marrowbones to him to come back when he had recovered his senses. Dead he wasn't. Simply absconded somewhere. The coffin they brought over was full of stones. He changed his name to De Wet, the Boer general. He made a mistake to fight the priests. And so forth and so on.

All the same Bloom (properly so dubbed) was rather surprised at their memories for in nine cases out of ten it was a case of tarbarrels, and not singly but in their thousands, and then complete oblivion because it was twenty odd years. Highly unlikely, of course, there was even a shadow of truth in the stories and, even supposing,

he thought a return highly inadvisable, all things considered.
Something evidently riled them in his death. . . . He saw him once on
the auspicious occasion when they broke up the type in the
Insuppressible or was it *United Ireland,* a privilege he keenly
appreciated, and, in point of fact, handed him his silk hat when it was
knocked off and he said *Thank you,* excited as he undoubtedly was
under his frigid expression notwithstanding the little misadventure
mentioned between the cup and the lip – what's bred in the bone.
Still, as regards return, you were a lucky dog if they didn't set the
terrier at you directly you got back. Then a lot of shillyshally usually
followed. . . .

    –That bitch, that English whore, did for him, the shebeen
proprietor commented. She put the first nail in his coffin.

    – Fine lump of a woman, all the same, the *soi-disant*
townclerk, Henry Campbell remarked and plenty of her. I seen her
picture in a barber's. Her husband was a captain or an officer.

    – Ay, Skin-the-Goat amusingly added. He was, and a
cottonball one.

    This gratuitous contribution of a humorous character
occasioned a fair amount of laughter among his *entourage.* As
regards Bloom, he, without the faintest suspicion of a smile, merely
gazed in the direction of the door and reflected upon the historic
story which had aroused extraordinary interest at the time when the
facts, to make matters worse, were made public with the usual
affectionate letters that passed between them, full of sweet nothings.
. . . Since their names were coupled, though, since he was her
declared favourite, where was the particular necessity to proclaim it
to the rank and file from the housetops, the fact namely, that he had
shared her bedroom, which came out in the witnessbox on oath when
a thrill went through the packed court literally electrifying everybody
in the shape of witnesses swearing to having witnessed him on such
and such a particular date in the act of scrambling out of an upstairs
apartment with the assistance of a ladder in night apparel, having
gained admittance in the same fashion, a fact that the weeklies,
addicted to the lubric a litte, simply coined shoals of money out of.
Whereas the simple fact of the case was it was simply a case of the
husband not being up to the scratch with nothing in common
between them beyond the name and then a real man arriving on the
scene, strong to the verge of weakness, falling a victim to her siren
charms and forgetting home ties. The usual sequel, to bask in the

[406]

loved one's smiles. The eternal question of the life connubial, needless to say, cropped up. Can real love, supposing there happens to be another chap in the case, exist between married folk? Though it was no concern of theirs absolutely if he regarded her with affection carried away by a wave of folly. A magnificent specimen of manhood he was truly, augmented obviously by gifts of a high order as compared with the other military supernumerary. . . . Looking back now in a retrospective kind of arrangement, all seemed like a dream. And the coming back was the worst thing you ever did because it went without saying you would feel out of place as things always moved with the times. Why, as he reflected, Irishtown Strand, a locality he had not been in for quite a number of years, looked different somehow since, as it happened, he went to reside on the north side. North or south however, it was just the wellknown case of hot passion, pure and simple, upsetting the applecart with a vengeance and just bore out the very thing he was saying, as she was also Spanish or half so, types that wouldn't do things by halves, passionate abandon of the south, casting every shred of decency to the winds.

– Just bears out what I am saying, he with glowing bosom said to Stephen. And, if I don't greatly mistake, she was Spanish too.

The king of Spain's daughter, Stephen answered, adding something or other rather muddled about farewell and adieu to you Spanish onions and the first land called the Deadman and from Ramhead to Scilly was so and so many . . .

– Was she? Bloom ejaculated surprised, though not astonished by any means. I never heard that rumor before. Possible, especially there it was, as she lived there. So, Spain.

Carefully avoiding a book in his pocket *Sweets of,* which reminded him by the by of that Capel street library book out of date, he took out his pocketbook and, turning over the various contents rapidly, finally he . . .

Do you consider, by the by, he said, thoughtfully selecting a faded photo which he laid on the table, that a Spanish type?

Stephen, obviously addressed, looked down on the photo showing a large sized lady, with her fleshy charms on evidence in an open fashion, as she was in the full bloom of womanhood, in evening dress cut ostentatiously low for the occasion to give a liberal display of bosom, with more than vision of breasts, her full lips parted, and some perfect teeth, standing near, ostensibly with gravity, a piano, on

the rest of which was *In old Madrid,* a ballad, pretty in its way,
which was then all the vogue. Her (the lady's) eyes, dark, large,
looked at Stephen, about to smile about something to be admired.
Lafayette of Westmoreland street, Dublin's premier photographic
artist, being responsible for the esthetic execution.

– Mrs Bloom, my wife the *prima donna,* Madam Marion
Tweedy, Bloom indicated. Taken a few years since. In or about '96.
Very like her then.

Beside the young man he looked also at the photo of the lady
now his legal wife who, he intimated, was the accomplished
daughter of Major Brian Tweedy and displayed at an early age
remarkable proficiency as a singer having even made her bow to the
public when her years numbered barely sweet sixteen. As for the
face, it was a speaking likeness in expression but it did not do justice
to her figure, which came in for a lot of notice usually and which did
not come out to the best advantage in that getup. She could without
difficulty, he said, have posed for the ensemble, not to dwell on
certain opulent curves of the . . . He dwelt, being a bit of an artist in
his spare time, on the female form in general developmentally
because, as it so happened, no later than that afternoon, he had seen
those Grecian statues, perfectly developed as works of art, in the
National Museum. Marble could give the original, shoulders, back
all the symmetry. All the rest, yes, Puritanism. It does though, St.
Joseph's sovereign . . . whereas no photo could, because it simply
wasn't art, in a word.

. . . .

And he did feel a kind of need there and then to follow suit
like a kind of inward voice and satisfy a possible need by moving a
motion. Nevertheless, he sat tight, just viewing the slightly soiled
photo creased by opulent curves, none the worse for wear, however,
and looked away thoughtfully with the intention of not further
increasing the other's possible embarrassment while gauging her
symmetry of heaving *embonpoint.* In fact, the slight soiling was only
an added charm, like the case of linen slightly soiled, good as new,
much better in fact, with the starch out. Suppose she was gone when
he? . . .

The vicinity of the young man he certainly relished,
educated, *distingué,* and impulsive into the bargain, far and away the
pick of the bunch, though you wouldn't think he had it in him . . . yet
you would. Besides he said the picture was handsome which, say

[408]

what you like, it was, though at the moment she was distinctly
stouter. And why not? An awful lot of makebelieve went on about
that sort of thing involving a lifelong slur with the usual splash page
of letterpress about the same old matrimonial tangle alleging
misconduct with professional golfer or the newest stage favourite
instead of being honest and aboveboard about the whole business.
How they were fated to meet and an attachment sprang up between
the two so that their names were coupled in the public eye was told
in court with letters containing the habitual mushy and
compromising expressions, leaving no loophole to show that they
openly cohabited two or three times a week at so wellknown seaside
hotel and relations, when the thing ran it normal course, became in
due course intimate. Then the decree *nisi* and the King's Proctor to
show cause why and, he failing to quash it, *nisi* was made absolute...
He, Bloom, enjoyed the distinction of being close to Erin's
uncrowned king in the flesh when the thing occurred in the historic
fracas... even when clothed in the mantle of adultery... Though
palpably a radically altered man, he was still a commanding figure,
though carelessly garbed as usual, with that look of settled purpose
which went a long way with the shillyshallyers till they discovered to
their vast discomfiture that their idol had feet of clay, after placing
him upon a pedestal, which she, however, was the first to perceive.
As those were particularly hot times in the general hullabaloo Bloom
sustained a minor injury from a nasty prod of some chap's elbow in
the crowd that of course congregated lodging some place about the
pit of the stomach, fortunately not of a grave character. His hat
(Parnell's) was inadvertently knocked off and, as a matter of strict
history, Bloom was the man who picked it up in the crush after
witnessing the occurrence meaning to return it to him (and return it
to him he did with the utmost celerity) who, panting and hatless and
whose thoughts were miles away from his hat at the time, being a
gentleman born with a stake in the country, he, as a matter of fact,
having gone into it more for the kudos of the thing than anyone else,
what's bred in the bone, instilled into him in infancy at his mother's
knee in the shape of knowing what good form was came out at once
because he turned round to the donor and thanked him with perfect
aplomb, saying: *Thank you, sir* though in a very different tone of
voice from the ornament of the legal profession whose headgear
Bloom also set to rights earlier in the course of the day, history
repeating itself with a difference; after the burial of a mutual friend

when they had left him alone in his glory after the grim task of having committed his remains to the grave.

On the other hand what incensed him more inwardly was the blatant jokes of the cabmen and so on, who passed it all off as a jest, laughing immoderately, pretending to understand everything, the why and the wherefore, and in reality not knowing their own minds, it being a case for the two parties themselves unless it ensued that the legitimate husband happened to be a party to it owing to some anonymous letter from the usual boy Jones, who happened to come across them at the crucial moment in a loving position locked in one another's arms drawing attention to their illicit proceedings and leading up to a domestic rumpus.... He personally, being of a skeptical bias, believed, and didn't make the smallest bones about saying so either, that man or men in the plural, were always hanging around on the waiting list about a lady, even supposing she was the best wife in the world and they got on fairly well together for the sake of argument, when, neglecting her duties, she chose to be tired of wedded life, and was on for a little flutter in polite debauchery to press their attentions on with her with improper intent, the upshot being that her affections centred on another, the cause of many *liaisons* between still attractive married women getting on for fair and forty and younger men, no doubt as several famous cases of feminine infatuation proved up to the hilt.

It was a thousand pities a young fellow blessed with an allowance of brains, as his neighbour obviously was, should waste his valuable time with profligate women, who might present him with a nice dose to last him his lifetime. In the nature of single blessedness he would one day take unto himself a wife when Miss Right came on the scene but in the interim ladies' society was a *conditio sine qua non* though he had the gravest possible doubts, not that he wanted in the smallest to pump Stephen about Miss Ferguson (who was very possibly the particular lodestar who brought him down to Irishtown so early in the morning), as to whether he would find much satisfaction basking in the boy and girl courtship idea and the company of smirking misses without a penny to their names bi- or tri-weekly with the orthodox preliminary canter of complimentpaying and walking out leading up to fond lovers' ways and flowers and chocs. To think of him house and homeless, rooked by some landlady worse than any stepmother, was really too bad at this age. The queer suddenly things he popped out with attracted the

[410]

elder man who was several years the other's senior or like his father.
But something substantial he certainly ought to eat, were it only an
eggflip made on unadulterated maternal nutriment or, failing that, the
homely Humpty Dumpty boiled.

– At what o'clock did you dine? he questioned of the slim
form and tired though unwrinkled face.

– Some time yesterday, Stephen said.

–Yesterday, exclaimed Bloom till he remembered it was
already tomorrow, Friday. Ah, you mean it's after twelve!

– The day before yesterday, Stephen said, improving on
himself.

Literally astounded at this piece of intelligence, Bloom
reflected. Though they didn't see eye to eye in everything, a certain
analogy there somehow was, as if both their minds were travelling,
so to speak, in the one train of thought. At his age when dabbling in
politics roughly some score of years previously when he had been a
quasi aspirant to parliamentary honours in the Buckshot Foster days
he too recollected in retrospect (which was a source of keen
satisfaction in itself) he had a sneaking regard for those same ultra
ideas. . . . so far as politics themselves were concerned, he was only
too conscious of the casualties invariably resulting from propaganda
and displays of mutual animosity and the misery and suffering it
entailed as a foregone conclusion on fine young fellows, chiefly,
destruction of the fittest, in a word.

Anyhow, upon weighing the pros and cons, getting on for
one as it was, it was high time to be retiring for the night. The crux
was it was a bit risky to bring him home as eventualities might
possibly ensue (somebody having a temper of her own sometimes)
and spoil the hash altogether as on the night he misguidedly brought
home a dog (breed unknown) with a lame paw, not that the cases
were either identical or the reverse, though he had hurt his hand too,
to Ontario Terrace, as he very distinctly remembered, having been
there, so to speak. On the other hand it was altogether far and away
too late for the Sandymount or Sandycove suggestion so that he was
in some perplexity as to which of the two alternatives . . . Everything
pointed to the fact that it behooved him to avail himself to the full of
the opportunity, all things considered. His initial impression was that
he was a bit standoffish or not over effusive but it grew on him
someway. For one thing he mightn't what you call jump at the idea,
if approached, and what mostly worried him was he didn't know

how to lead up to it or word it exactly, supposing he did entertain the proposal, as it would afford him very great personal pleasure if he would allow him to help to put a coin in his way or some wardrobe, if found suitable. At all events he wound up by concluding, eschewing for the nonce hidebound precedent, a cup of Epp's cocoa and a shakedown for the night plus the use of a rug or two and overcoat doubled into a pillow. At least he would be in safe hands and as warm as a toast on a trivet. He failed to perceive any very vast amount of harm in that always with the proviso no rumpus of any sort was kicked up. A move had to be made because that merry old soul, the grasswidower in question, who appeared to be glued to the spot, didn't appear in any particular hurry to wend his way home to his dearly beloved Queenstown. . . .

— I propose, our hero eventually suggested, after mature reflection while prudently pocketing her photo, as it's rather stuffy here, you just come with me and talk things over. My diggings are quite close in the vicinity. You can't drink that stuff. Wait, I'll just pay this lot.

The best plan clearly being to clear out, the remainder being plain sailing, he beckoned, while prudently pocketing the photo, to the keeper of the shanty, who didn't seem to . . .

— Yes, that's the best, he assured Stephen, to whom for the matter of that Brazen Head or him or anywhere else was all more or less . . .

All kinds of Utopian plans were flashing through his (Bloom's) busy brain. Education (the genuine article), literature, journalism, prize titbits, up to date billing, hydros and concert tours in English watering resorts packed with theatres, turning money away, duets in Italian with the accent perfectly true to nature and a quantity of other things, no necessity of course to tell the world and his wife from the housetops about it and a slice of luck. An opening was all was wanted. Because he more than suspected he had his father's voice to bank his hopes on which it was quite on the cards he had so it would be just as well, by the way no harm, to trail the conversation in the direction of that particular red herring just to . . .
. . . .

To cut a long story short, Bloom, grasping the situation, was the first to rise to his feet so as not to outstay their welcome having first and foremost, being as good as his word that he would foot the bill for the occasion, taken the wise precaution to unobtrusively motion to mine host as a parting shot a scarcely perceptible sign when the others were not looking to the effect that the amount due was forthcoming, making a grand total of fourpence (the amount he deposited unobtrusively in four coppers, literally the last of the Mohicans) he having previously spotted on the printed pricelist for all who ran to read opposite to him in unmistakable figures, coffee 2d., confectionery do., and honestly well worth twice the money once in a way, as Wetherup used to remark.

– Come, he counselled, to close the *séance.*

Seeing that the ruse worked and the coast was clear, they left the shelter or shanty together and the *elite* society of oilskin and company whom nothing short of an earthquake would move out of their *dolce far niente.* Stephen, who confessed to still feeling poorly and fagged out, paused at the, for a moment . . . the door to . . .

– One thing I never understood, he said, to be original on the spur of the moment, why they put tables upside down at night, I mean chairs upside down on the tables in cafes.

To which impromptu the never failing Bloom replied without a moment's hesitation, saying straight off:

– To sweep the floor in the morning.

So saying he skipped around nimbly, considering frankly, at the same time apologetic, to get on his companion's right, a habit of his, by the by, the right side being, in classical idiom, his tender Achilles. The night air was certainly now a treat to breathe though Stephen was a bit weak on his pins.

– It will (the air) do you good, Bloom said, meaning also the walk, in a moment. The only thing is to walk then you'll feel a different man. It's not far. Lean on me.

Accordingly he passed his left arm in Stephen's right and led him on accordingly.

– Yes, Stephen said uncertainly, because he thought he felt a strange kind of flesh of a different man approach him, sinewless and wobbly and all that.

Anyhow, they passed the sentrybox with stones, brazier, etc. where the municipal supernumerary, ex-Gumley, was still to all intents and purposes wrapped in the arms of Murphy, as the adage has it, dreaming of fresh fields and pastures new. And *apropos* of coffin stones, the analogy was not at all bad, as it was in fact a stoning to death on the part of the seventytwo out of eighty odd constituencies that ratted at the time of the split and chiefly the belauded peasant class, probably the selfsame evicted tenants he had put in their holdings.

So they passed on to chatting about music, a form of art for which Bloom, as a pure amateur, possessed the greatest love, as they made tracks arm-in-arm across Beresford place. Wagnerian music, though confessedly grand in its way, was a bit too heavy for Bloom and hard to follow at the first go-off but the music of Mercadante's *Huguenots,* Meyerbeer's *Seven Last Words on the Cross,* and Mozart's *Twelfth Mass,* he simply revelled in, the *Gloria* in that being to his mind the acme of first class music as such, literally knocking everything else into a cocked hat. He infinitely preferred the sacred music of the catholic church to anything the opposite shop could offer in that line such as those Moody and Sankey hymns or *Bid me to live and I will live thy protestant to be.* He also yielded to none in his admiration of Rossini's *Stabat Mater,* a work simply abounding in immortal numbers, in which his wife, Madam Marion Tweedy, made a hit, a veritable sensation, he might safely say greatly adding to her other laurels and putting the others totally in the shade in the jesuit fathers' church in Upper Gardiner street, the sacred edifice being thronged to the doors to hear her with virtuosos, or *virtuosi* rather. There was the unanimous opinion that there was none to come up to her and, suffice it to say in a place of worship for music or a sacred character, there was a generally voiced desire for an encore. On the whole, though favouring preferably light opera of the *Don Giovanni* description, and *Martha,* a gem in its line, he had a *penchant,* though with only a surface knowledge, for the severe classical school such as Mendelssohn.

. . . .

On the roadway which they were approaching whilst still speaking beyond the swing chain, a horse, dragging a sweeper, paced on the paven ground, brushing a long swathe of mire up so that with the noise Bloom was not perfectly certain whether he had caught aright the allusion to sixtyfive guineas and John Bull. He inquired if it was John Bull the political celebrity of that ilk, as it struck him, the two identical names, as a striking coincidence.

By the chains, the horse slowly swerved to turn, which perceiving Bloom, who was keeping a sharp lookout as usual plucked the other's sleeve gently, jocosely remarking:

– Our lives are in peril tonight. Beware the steamroller.

. . . .

[414]

– What's this I was saying? Ah, yes! My wife, he intimated, plunging *in medias res,* would have the greatest of pleasure in making your acquaintance as she is passionately attached to music of any kind.

He looked sideways in a friendly fashion at the sideface of Stephen, image of his mother, which was not quite the same as the usual blackguard type they unquestionably had and indubitable hankering after as he was perhaps not that way built.

Still, supposing he had his father's gift, as he more than suspected, it opened up new vistas in his mind, such as Lady Fingall's Irish industries concert on the preceding Monday, and aristocracy in general.

Exquisite variations he was now describing on an air *Youth here has End* by Jans Pieter Sweelinck, a Dutchman of Amsterdam where the frows come from. Even more he liked an old German song of *Johannes Jeep* about the clear sea and the voices of sirens, sweet murderers of men, which boggled Bloom a bit:

> *Von der Sirenen Listigkeit*
> *Tun die Poeten dichten.*

These opening bars he sang and translated *extempore.* Bloom, nodding, said he perfectly understood and begged him to go on by all means, which he did.

A phenomenally beautiful tenor voice like that, the rarest of boons, which Bloom appreciated at the very first note he got out, could easily, if properly handled by some recognised authority on voice production such as Barraclough and being able to read music into the bargain, command its own price. . . .
It was in fact only a matter of months and he could easily foresee him participating in their musical and artistic *conversaziones* during the festivities of the Christmas season, for choice, causing a slight flutter in the dovecotes of the fair sex and being made a lot of by ladies out for sensation, cases of which, as he happened to know, were on record, in fact, without giving the show away, he himself once upon a time, if he cared to, could easily have . . . . Besides, though taste latterly had deteriorated to a degree, original music like that, different from the conventional rut, would rapidly have a great vogue, as it would be a decided novelty for Dublin's musical world after the usual hackneyed run of catchy tenor solos foisted on a confiding public by Ivan St Austell and Hilton St Just and their

genus omne. Yes, beyond a shadow of a doubt, he could, with all the cards in his hand and he had a capital opening to make a name for himself and win a high place in the city's esteem where he could command a stiff figure . . . . being his own master, he would have heaps of time to practise literature in his spare moments when desirous of so doing with its clashing with his vocal career of containing anything derogatory whatsoever as it was a matter for himself alone. In fact, he had the ball at his feet and that was the very reason why the other, possessed of a remarkably sharp nose for smelling a rat of any sort, hung on to him at all.

The horse was just then . . . and later on, at a propitious opportunity he purposed (Bloom did), without anyway prying into his private affairs on the *fools step in where angels* principle advising him to sever his connection with a certain budding practitioner, who, he noticed, was prone to disparage, and even to a slight extent, with some hilarious pretext, when not present, deprecate him, or whatever you like to call it, which, in Bloom's humble opinion, threw a nasty sidelight on that side of a person's character – no pun intended.

The horse, having reached the end of his tether, so to speak, halted, and, rearing high a proud feathering tail, added his quota by letting fall on the floor, which the brush would soon brush up and polish, three smoking globes of turds. Slowly, three times, one after another, from a full crupper, he mired. And humanely his driver waited till he (or she) had ended, patient in his scythed car.

Side by side Bloom, profiting by the *contretemps,* with Stephen passed through the gap of chains, divided by the upright, and, stepping over a strand of mire, went across towards Gardiner street lower, Stephen singing more boldly, but not loudly, the end of the ballad:

Und alle Schiffe brucken

The driver never said a word, good, bad or indifferent. He merely watched the two figures, as he sat on his lowbacked car, both black – one full, one lean – walk towards the railway bridge, *to be married by Father Maher.* As they walked, they at times stopped and walked again, continuing their *tête-à-tête* (which of course he was utterly out of), about sirens, enemies of man's reason, mingled with a number of other topics of the same category, usupers, historical cases of the kind while the man in the sweeper car or you might as well call it in the sleeper car who in any case couldn't possibly hear

[416]

because they were too far simply sat in his seat near the end of lower Gardiner street *and looked after their lowbacked car.*

[417]

Episode 17 – Ithaca … island kingdom of Odysseus. Disguised as an old beggar who suffers the insults of his wife's suitors, and struck with a stool; Odysseus strings the great bow and with his son Telemachus kills the suitors and is united with his wife Penelope. ~ Bloom hosts Stephen in his home, as if a surrogate son. Under heavenly bodies, they urinate in a great arc (bow). Bloom strikes his head. He reflects on the suitor of his wife, and joins his wife in bed.

Having forgotten his key, Bloom enters his house through the basement door, then lets in Stephen. They sit, drink cocoa and talk, exchanging thoughts on cultures, experiences, the universe. Stephen declines an invitation to spend the night. They step out into the garden to pee and admire the heavens. Then Stephen leaves. Bloom assesses his day's activities, and the adultery. He fancies his future. On his way upstairs to bed, Bloom strikes his head on a sideboard moved for Boylan's visit, among other signs of lechery. Molly questions what he's done all day. Tired from it all, Bloom finds equanimity and falls asleep.

THEMES
A catechetical series of questions and answers, a scientific textbook. Homecoming. Significance of keys. Recollecting characters of the day's journey. Marital infidelity as natural pattern of the universe. Objectivity as logic for coping with the pain of separation from others. Fancy and imagination to disguise the painful blatancy of adultery. Religious imagery in numbers 3 and 9. Religious symbolism in actions perceived as rituals. Mortals and their actions in the perspective of a cosmic consciousness, perhaps a comedy at that.

WHAT PARALLEL COURSES DID BLOOM AND STEPHEN FOLLOW RE-turning?

Starting united both at normal walking pace from Beresford place they followed in the order named Lower and Middle Gardiner streets and Mountjoy square, west: then, at reduced pace, each bearing left, Gardiner's place by an inadvertance as far as the farther corner of Temple street, north: then at reduced pace with interruptions of halt, bearing right, Temple street, north, as far as Hardwicke place. Approaching, disparate, at relaxed walking pace they crossed both the circus before George's church diametrically, the chord in any circle being less than the arc which it subtends.

Of what did the duumvirate deliberate during their itinerary?

Music, literature, Ireland, Dublin, Paris, friendship, woman, prostitution, diet, the influence of gaslight or the light of arc and glow-lamps on the growth of adjoining paraheliotropic trees, exposed corporation emergency dustbuckets, the Roman catholic church, ecclesiastical celibacy, the Irish nation, jesuit education, careers, the study of medicine, the past day, the maleficent influence of the presabbath, Stephen's collapse.

[418]

Did Bloom discover common factors of similarity between their respective like and unlike reactions to experience?

Both were sensitive to artistic impressions musical in preference to plastic or pictorial. Both preferred a continental to an insular manner of life, a cisatlantic to a transatlantic place of residence. Both indurated by early domestic training and an inherited tenacity of heterodox resistance professed their disbelief in many orthodox religious, national, social and ethical doctrines. Both admitted the alternately stimulating and obtunding influence of heterosexual magnetism.

Were their views on some points divergent?

Stephen dissented openly from Bloom's view on the importance of dietary and civic selfhelp while Bloom dissented tacitly from Stephen's views on the eternal affirmation of the spirit of man in literature. Bloom assented covertly to Stephen's rectification of the anachronism involved in assigning the date of the conversion of the Irish nation to christianity from druidism by Patrick son of Calpornus, son of Potitus, son of Odyssus, sent by pope Celestine I in the year 432 in the reign of Leary to the year 260 or thereabouts in the reign of Cormac MacArt (+ 266 A.D.) suffocated by imperfect deglutition of aliment of Sletty and interred at Rossnaree.

. . . .

What action did Bloom make on their arrival at their destination?

At the housesteps of the 4th of the equidifferent uneven numbers, number 7 Eccles street, he inserted his hand mechanically into the back pocket of his trousers to obtain his latchkey.

Was it there?

It was in the corresponding pocket of the trousers which he had worn on the day but one proceeding.

Why was he doubly irritated?

Because he had forgotten and because he remembered that he had reminded himself twice not to forget.

What were then the alternatives before the, premeditatively (respectively) and inadvertently, keyless couple?

To enter or not to enter. To knock or not to knock.

Bloom's decision?

A stratagem. Resting his feet on the dwarf wall, he climbed over the area railings, compressed his hat on his head, grasped two points at the lower union of rails and stiles, lowered his body gradually by its length of five feet nine inches and a half to within two feet ten inches of the area pavement, and allowed his body to move freely in space by separating himself from the railings and crouching in preparation for the impact of the fall.

. . . .

Did he rise uninjured by concussion?

Regaining new stable equilibrium he rose uninjure though concussed by the impact, raised the latch of the area door by the exertion of force at its freely moving flange and by leverage of the first kind applied at its fulcrum gained retarded access to the kitchen through the subadjacent scullery, ignited a lucifer match by friction, set free inflammable coal gas by turning on the ventcock, lit a high flame which, by regulating, he reduced to quiescent candescence and lit finally a portable candle.

What discrete succession of images did Stephen meanwhile perceive?

Reclined against the area railings he perceived through the transparent kitchen panes a man regulating a gasflame of 14 C P, a man lighting a candle, a man removing in turn each of his two boots, a man leaving the kitchen holding a candle of 1 C P.

Did the man reappear elsewhere?

After a lapse of four minutes the glimmer of his candle was discernible through the semitransparent semicircular glass fanlight over the halldoor. The halldoor turned gradually on its hinges. In the open space of the doorway the man reappeared with his hat, with his candle.

Did Stephen obey his sign?

Yes, entering softly, he helped to close and chain the door and followed softly along the hallway the man's back and listed feet and lighted candle past a lighted crevice of doorway on the left and carefully down a turning staircase of more than five steps into the kitchen of Bloom's house.

[420]

What did Bloom do?

He extinguished the candle by a sharp expiration of breath upon its flame, drew two spoonseat deal chairs to the hearthstone, one for Stephen with its back to the area window, the other for himself when necessary, knelt on one knee, composed in the grate a pyre of crosslaid resintipped sticks and various coloured papers and irregular polygons of bet Abram coal at twentyone shillings a ton from the yard of Messrs Flower and M'Donald of 14 D'Olier street, kindled it at three projecting points of paper with one ignited lucifer match, thereby releasing the potential energy contained in the fuel by allowing its carbon and hydrogen elements to enter into free union with oxygen of the air.

Of what similar apparitions did Stephen think?

Of others elsewhere in other times who, kneeling on one knee or two, had kindled fires for him, of Brother Michael in the infirmary of the college of the Society of Jesus at Clongowes Wood, Sallins, in the county of Kildare: of his father, Simon Dedalus, in an unfurnished room of his first residence in Dublin, number thirteen Fitzgibbon street: of his godmother Miss Kate Morkan in the house of her dying sister Miss Julia Morkan at 15 Usher's Island: of his mother Mary, wife of Simon Dedalus, in the kitchen of number twelve North Richmond street on the morning of the feast of Saint FrancisXavier 1898, of the dean of studies, Father Butt, in the physics' theatre of university College, 16 Stephen's green, north: of his sister Dilly (Delia) in his father's house in Cabra.

. . . .

What did Bloom do at the range?

He removed the saucepan to the left hob, rose and carried the iron kettle to the sink in order to tap the current by turning the faucet to let it flow.

Did it flow?

Yes. From Roundwood reservoir in county Wicklow of a cubic capacity of 2,400 million gallons, percolating through a subterranean aqueduct of filter mains of single and double pipeage...to the 26 acre reservoir at Stillorgan, a distance of 22 statute miles, and thence, through a system of relieving tanks, by a gradient of 250 feet to the city boundary at Eustace bridge. . . .

[421]

What in water did Bloom, waterlover, drawer of water, watercarrier returning to range, admire?

Its universality: its democratic equality and constancy to its nature in seeking its own level: its vastness in the ocean of Mercator's projection: its unplumbed profundity in the Sundam trench of the Pacific exceeding 8,000 fathoms: the restlessness of its waves and surface particles visiting in turn all points of its seaboard: the independence of its units: the variability of states of sea: its hydrostatic quiescence in calm: its hydrokinetic turgidity in neap and spring tides: its subsidence after devastation: its sterility in the circumpolar icecaps, arctic and antarctic: its climatic and commercial significance: its preponderance of 3 to 1 over the dry land of the globe: . . . its capacity to dissolve and hold in solution all soluble substances including millions of tons of the most precious metals: . . . its vehicular ramifications in continental lakecontained streams and confluent oceanflowing rivers with their tributaries and transoceanic currents: . . . the simplicity of its composition, two constituent parts of hydrogen with one constituent part of oxygen: its healing virtues: its buoyancy in the waters of the Dead Sea: . . . its properties for cleansing, quenching thirst and fire, nourishing vegetation: its infallibility as paradigm and paragon: its metamorphoses as vapour, mist, cloud, rain, sleet, snow, hail: . . . its docility in working hydraulic millwheels, turbines, dynamos, electric power stations, bleachworks, tanneries, scutchmills: its utility in canals, rivers, if navigable, floating and graving docks: . . . its ubiquity as constituting 90% of the human body: . . .

Having set the halffilled kettle on the now burning coals, why did he return to the stillflowing tap?

To wash his soiled hands with a partially consumed tablet of Barrington's lemonflavoured soap, to which paper still adhered (bought thirteen hours previously for fourpence and still unpaid for), in fresh cold neverchanging everchanging water and dry them, face and hands, in a long redbordered holland cloth passed over a wooden revolving roller.

. . . .

Which seemed to the host to be the predominant qualities of his guest?

[422]

Confidence in himself, an equal and opposite power of abandonment and recuperation.

. . . .

Why did absence of light disturb him less than presence of noise?

Because of the surety of the sense of touch in his firm full masculine feminine passive active hand.

What quality did it (his hand) possess but with what counteracting influence?

The operative surgical quality but that he was reluctant to shed human blood even when the end justified the means, preferring in their natural order heliotherapy, pyschophysicotherapeutics, osteopathic surgery.

What lay under exposure on the lower middle and upper shelves of the kitchen dresser opened by Bloom?

On the lower shelf five vertical breakfast plates, six horizontal breakfast saucers on which rested inverted breakfast cups, a moustachecup, univerted, and saucer of Crown Derby, four white goldrimmed eggcups, and open shammy purse displaying coins, mostly copper, and a phial of aromatic violet comfits. On the middle shelf a chipped eggcup containing pepper, a drum of table salt, four conglomerated black olives in oleaginous paper, an empty pot of Plumtree's potted meat, an oval wicker basket bedded with fibre and containing one Jersey pear, a halfempty bottle of William Gilbey and Co's white invalid port, half disrobed of its swathe of coral pink tissue paper, a packet of Epp's soluble cocoa, five ounces of Anne Lynch's choice tea at 2/- per lb. in a crinkled leadpaper bag, a cylindrical canister containing the best crystallised lump sugar, two onions, one the larger, Spanish, entire, the other, smaller, Irish, bisected with augmented surface and more redolent, a jar of Irish Model Dairy's cream, a jug of brown crockery containing a noggin and a quarter of soured adulterated milk, converted by heat into water, acidulous serum and semisolidified curds, which added to the quantity subtracted for Mr Bloom's and Mrs Fleming's breakfasts made one imperial pint, the total quantity originally delivered, two cloves, a halfpenny and a small dish containing a slice of fresh ribsteak. On the upper shelf a battery of jamjars of various sizes and proveniences.

. . . .

What reminiscences temporarily corrugated his brow?

Reminiscences of coincidences, truth stranger than fiction, preindicative of the result of the Gold Cup flat handicap, the official and definitive result of which he had read in the *Evening Telegraph,* late pink edition, in the cabman's shelter, at Butt bridge.

Where had previous intimations of the result, effected or projected, been received by him?

In Bernard Kiernan's licensed premises 8, 9 and 10 Little Britain street: in David Byrne's licensed premises, 14 Duke street: in O'Connell street lower, outside Graham Lemon's when a dark man placed in his hand in a throwaway (subsequently thrown away), advertising Elijah, restorer of the church in Zion: in Lincoln place outside the premises of F. W. Sweny and Co (Limited) dispensing chemists, when, when Frederick M. (Bantam) Lyons had rapidly and successively requested, perused and restituted the copy of the current issue of the *Freeman's Journal* and *National Press* which he had been about to throw away (subsequently thrown away), he had proceeded towards the oriental edifice of the Turkish and Warm Baths, 11 Leinster street, with the light of inspiration shining in his countenance and bearing in his arms the secret of race, graven in the language of prediction.

What qualifying considerations allayed his perturbations?

The difficulties of interpretation since the significance of any event followed its occurrence as variably as the acoustic report followed the electrical discharge and of counterestimating against an actual loss by failure to interpret the total sum of possible losses proceeding originally from a successful interpretation.

His mood?

He had not risked, he did not expect, he had not been disappointed, he was satisfied.

What satisfied him?

To have sustained no positive loss. To have brought a positive gain to others. Light to the gentiles.

How did Bloom prepare a collation for a gentile?

[424]

He poured into two teacups two level spoonfuls, four in all, of Epp's soluble cocoa and proceeded according to the directions for use printed on the label, to each adding after sufficient time for infusion the prescribed ingredients for diffusion in the manner and in the quantity prescribed.

What supererogatory marks of special hospitality did the host show his guest?

Relinquishing his symposiarchal right to the moustache cup of imitation Crown Derby presented to him by his only daughter, Millicent (Milly), he substituted a cup identical with that of his guest and served extraordinarily to his guest and, in reduced measure, to himself the viscous cream ordinarily reserved for the breakfast of his wife Marion (Molly).

Was the guest conscious of and did he acknowledge these marks of hospitality?

His attention was directed to them by his host jocosely and he accepted them seriously as they drank in jocoserious silence Epp's massproduct, the creature cocoa.

Were there marks of hospitality which he contemplated but suppressed, reserving them for another and for himself on future occasions to complete the act begun?

The reparation of a fissure of the length of 1 ½ inches in the right side of his guest's jacket. A gift to his guest of one of the four lady's handkerchiefs, if and when ascertained to be in a presentable condition.

. . . .

What cerebration accompanied his frequentative act?

Concluding by inspection but erroneously that his silent companion was engaged in mental composition he reflected on the pleasures derived from literature of instruction rather than of amusement as he himself had applied to the works of William Shakespeare more than once for the solution of difficult problems in imaginary or real life.

. . . .

What lines concluded his first piece of original verse written by him, potential poet, at the age of 11 in 1877 on the occasion of the offering of three prizes at 10/- 5/- and 2/6 respectively by the *Shamrock,* a weekly newspaper?

> *An ambition to squint*
> *At my verses in print*
> *Makes me hope that for these you'll find room.*
> *If you so condescend*
> *Then please place at the end*
> *The name of yours truly, L. Bloom.*

Did he find four separating forces between his temporary guest and him?

Name, age, race, creed.

. . . .

What acrostic upon the abbreviation of his first name had he (kinetic poet) sent to Miss Marion Tweedy on the 14th February 1888?

> ***P**oets oft have sung in rhyme*
> ***O**f music sweet their praise divine.*
> ***L**et them hymn it nine times nine.*
> ***D**earer far than song or wine,*
> ***Y**ou are mine. The world is mine.*

. . . .

What relation existed between their ages?

16 years before in 1888 when Bloom was of Stephen's present age Stephen was 6. 16 years after in 1920 when Stephen would be of Bloom's present age Bloom would be 54. In 1936 when Bloom would be 70 and Stephen 54 their ages initially in the ratio of 16 to 0 would be as 17 ½ to 13 ½, the proposition increasing and the disparity diminishing according as arbitrary future years were added, for if the proportion existing in 1883 and continued immutable, conceiving that to be possible, till 1904 when Stephen was 22 Bloom would be 374…

What events might nullify these calculations?

The cessation of existence of both or either, the inauguration of a new era or calendar, the annihilation of the world and consequent extermination of the human species, inevitable but impredictable.

[426]

How many previous encounters proved their preexisting acquaintance?

Two. The first in the lilacgarden of Matthew Dillon's house, Medina Villa, Kimmage road, Roundtown, in 1887, in the company of Stephen's mother, Stephen being then of the age of 5 and reluctant to give his hand in salutation. The second in the coffeeroom of Breslin's hotel on a rainy Sunday in the January of 1892, in the company of Stephen's father and Stephen's granduncle, Stephen being then 5 years older.

Did Bloom accept the invitation to dinner given then by the son and afterwards seconded by the father?

Very gratefully, with grateful appreciation, with sincere appreciative gratitude, in appreciatively grateful sincerity of regret, he declined.

Did their conversation on the subject of these reminiscences reveal a third connecting link between them?

Mrs Riordan, a widow of independent means, had resided in the house of Stephen's parents from 1 September 1888 to 29 December 1891 and had also resided during the years 1892, 1893 and 1894 in the City Arms Hotel … she had been a constant informant of Bloom who resided also in the same hotel …

Had he performed any special corporal work of mercy for her?

He had sometimes propelled her on warm summer evenings, an infirm widow of independent, if limited means, in her convalescent bathchair with slow revolutions of its wheels as far as the corner of the North Circular road opposite Mr Gavin Low's place of business where she had remained for a certain time scanning through his onelensed binocular fieldglasses unrecognisable citizens on tramcars, roadster bicycles, equipped with inflated pneumatic tyres, hackney carriages, tandems, private and hired landaus, dogcarts, ponytraps and brakes passing from the city to the Phoenix Park and *vice versa.*

Why could he then support that his vigil with the greater equanimity?

Because in middle youth he had often sat observing through a rondel of bossed glass of a multicoloured pane the spectacle offered with continual changes of the thoroughfare without, pedestrians, quadrupeds, velocipedes, vehicles, passing slowly, a quickly, evenly, round and round and round the rim of a round precipitous globe.

What distinct different memories had each of her now eight years deceased?

The older, her bezique cards and counters, her Skye terrier, her suppositious wealth, her lapses of responsiveness and incipient catarrhal deafness: the younger, her lamp of colza oil before the statue of the Immaculate Conception, her green and maroon brushes for Charles Stewardt Parnell and for Michael Davitt, her tissue papers.

Were there no means still remaining to him to achieve the rejuvenation which these reminiscences divulged to a younger companion rendered the more desirable?

The indoor exercises, formerly intermittently practised, subsequently abandoned, prescribed in Eugen Sandow's *Physical Strength and How To Obtain It* which, designed particularly for commercial men engaged in sedentary occupations, were to be made with mental concentration in front of a mirror so as to bring into play the various families of muscles and produce successively a pleasant relaxation and the most pleasant repristination of juvenile agility.

Had any special agility been his in earlier youth?

Though ringweight lifting had been beyond his strength and the full circle gyration beyond his courage yet as a High School scholar he had excelled in his table and protracted execution of the half lever movement on the parallel bars in consequence of his abnormally developed abdominal muscles.

Did either openly allude to their racial difference?
Neither.

What, reduced to their simplest reciprocal form, were Bloom's thoughts about Stephen's thoughts about Bloom and Bloom's thoughts about Stephen's thoughts about Bloom's thoughts about Stephen?

[428]

He thought that he thought that he was a jew whereas he knew that he knew that he knew that he was not.

What , the enclosures of reticence removed, were their respective parentages?
Bloom, only born male transubstantial heir of Rudolf Virag (subsequently Rudolf Bloom) of Szombathely, Vienna, Budapest, Milan, London and Dublin and of Ellen Higgins, second daughter of Julius Higgins (born Karoly) and Fanny Higgins (born Hegarty); Stephen, eldest surviving male consubstantial heir of Simon Dedalus of Cork and Dublin and of Mary, daughter of Richard and Christina Goulding (born Grier).

Had Bloom and Stephen been baptised, and where and by whom, cleric or layman?
Bloom (three times) by the reverend Mr Gilmer Johnston M. A. alone in the protestant church of Saint Nicolas Without, Coombe; by James O'Connor, Philip Gilligan and James Fitzpatrick, together, under a pump in the village of Swords; and by the reverend Charles Malone C. C., in the church of the Three Patrons, Rathgar. Stephen (once) by the reverend Charles Malone, C. C., alone, in the church of the Three Patrons, Rathgar.

Did they find their educational careers similar?
Substituting Stephen for Bloom Stoom would have passed successively through a dame's school and the high school. Substituting Bloom for Stephen Blephen would have passed successively through the preparatory, junior, middle and senior grades of the intermediate and through the matriculation, first arts, second arts and arts degree course of the royal university.

Why did Bloom refrain from stating that he had frequented the university of life?
Because of his fluctuating incertitude as to whether this observation had or had not been already made by him to Stephen or by Stephen to him.

What two temperaments did they individually represent?
The scientific. The artistic.

What proofs did Bloom adduce to prove that his tendency was towards applied, rather than towards pure science?

Certain possible inventions of which he had cogitated when reclining in a state of supine repletion to aid digestion, stimulated by his appreciation of the importance of inventions now common but once revolutionary for example, the aeronautic parachute, the reflecting telescope, the spiral corkscrew, the safety pin, the mineral water siphon, the canal lock with winch and sluice, the suction pump.

. . . .

What also stimulated him in his cogitations?

The financial success achieved by Ephraim Marks and Charles A. James, the former by his 1d. bazaar, the latter at his 6 ½d. shop and world's fancy fair and waxwork exhibition; and the infinite possibilities hitherto unexploited of the modern art of advertisement if condensed in trilateral monideal symbols, vertically of maximum visibility (divined), horizontally of maximum legibility (deciphered) and of magnetising efficacy to arrest involuntary attention, to interest, to convince, to decide.

Such as?
K. 11. Kino's 11/- Trousers.
House of Keys. Alexander J. Keyes.

. . . .

Such as never?
What is home without Plumtree's Potted Meat?
Incomplete.
With it an abode of bliss.
Manufactured by George Plumtree, 23 Merchants' quay, Dublin, put up in 4 oz. pots, and inserted by Councillor Joseph P. Nannetti, M. P., Rotunda Ward, 19 Hardwicke street, under the obituary notices and anniversaries of deceases. The name on the label is Plumtree. A plumtree is a meatpot, registered trade mark. Beware of imitations. Peatmot. Trumplee. Montpat. Plamtroo.

Which example did he adduce to induce Stephen to deduce that originality, though producing its own reward, does not invariably conduce to success?

His own ideated and rejected project of an illuminated showcart, drawn by a beast of burden, in which two smartly dressed girls were to be seated engaged in writing.

What suggested scene was then constructed by Stephen?
Solitary hotel in mountain pass. Autumn. Twilight. Fire lit. In dark corner young man seated. Young woman enters. Restless. Solitary. She sits. She goes to the window. She stands. She sits. Twilight. She thinks. On solitary hotel paper she writes. She thinks. She writes. She sighs. Wheels and hoofs. She hurries out. He comes from his dark corner. He seizes solitary paper. He holds it towards fire. Twilight. He reads. Solitary.

What?
In sloping, upright and backhands: Queen's hotel, Queen's hotel, Queen's Ho . . .

What suggested scene was then constructed by Bloom?
The Queen's Hotel, Ennis County Clare, where Rudolph Bloom (Rudolf Virag) died on the evening of the 27 June 1886, at some hour unstated, in consequence of an overdose of monkshood (aconite) selfadministered in the form of a neuralgic liniment, composed of 2 parts of aconite liniment to 1 of chloroform liniment (purchased by him at 10:20 a.m. on the morning of 27 June 1886 at the medical hall of Francis Dennehy, 17 Church street, Ennis) after having, though not in consequence of having, purchased at 3:15 p.m. on the afternoon of 27 June 1886 a new boater straw hat, extra smart (after having, though not in consequence of having, purchased at the hour and in the place aforesaid, the toxin aforesaid), at the general drapery store of James Cullen, 4 Main street, Ennis.

Did he attribute his homonymity to information or coincidence or intuition?
Coincidence.

Did he depict the scene verbally for his guest to see?
He preferred himself to see another's face and listen to another's words by which potential narration was realised and kinetic temperament relieved.

. . . .

Which domestic problem as much as, if not more than, any other frequently engaged his mind?

What to do with our wives.

What had been his hypothetical singular solutions?

Parlour games (dominos, halma, tiddledy winks, spillkins, cup and ball, nap, spoil five, bezique, twentyfive, beggar my neighbour, draughts, chess or backgammon): embroidery, darning or knitting for the policeaided clothing society: musical duets, mandoline and guitar, piano and flute, guitar and piano: legal scrivenery or envelope addressing: biweekly visits to variety entertainments: commercial activity as pleasantly commanding and pleasingly obeyed mistress proprietress in a cool dairy shop or warm cigar divan: the clandestine satisfaction of erotic irritation in masculine brothels, state inspected and medically controlled: social visits, at regular infrequent prevented intervals and with regular frequent preventive superintendence, to and from female acquaintances of recognised respectability in the vicinity: courses of evening instruction specially designed to render liberal instruction agreeable.

What instances of deficient mental development in his wife inclined him in favour of the lastmentioned (ninth) solution?

In disoccupied moments she had more than once covered a sheet of paper with signs and hieroglyphics which she stated were Greek and Irish and Hebrew characters. She had interrogated constantly at varying intervals as to the correct method of writing the capital initial of the name of a city in Canada, Quebec. She understood little of political complications, internal, or balance of power, external. . . .

What compensated in the false balance of her intelligence for these and such deficiencies of judgment regardings persons, places and things?

The false apparent parallelism of all perpendicular arms of all balances, proved true by construction. The counterbalance of her proficiency of judgment regarding one person, proved true by experiment.

[432]

How had he attempted to remedy this state of comparative ignorance?

Variously. By leaving in a conspicuous place a certain book open at a certain page: by assuming in her, when alluding explanatorily, latent knowledge: by open ridicule in her presence of some absent other's ignorant lapse.

With what success had he attempted direct instruction?

She followed not all, a part of the whole, gave attention with interest, comprehended with surprise, with care repeated, with greater difficulty remembered, forgot with ease, with misgiving remembered, rerepeated with error.

What system had proved more effective?

Indirect suggestion implicating self-interest.

Example?

She disliked umbrella with rain, he liked woman with umbrella, she disliked new hat with rain, he liked woman with new hat, he bought new hat with rain, she carried umbrella with new hat.

Accepting the analogy implied in his guest's parable which examples of postexilic eminence did he adduce?

Three seekers of the pure truth, Moses of Egypt, Moses Maimonides, author of *More Neubkim* (Guide of the Perplexed) and Moses Mendelssohn of such eminence that from Moses (of Egypt) to Moses (Mendelssohn) there arose none like Moses (Maimonides).

What statement was made, under correction, by Bloom concerning a fourth seeker of pure truth, by name Aristotle, mentioned, with permission, by Stephen?

That the seeker mentioned had been a pupil of a rabbinical philosopher, name uncertain.

. . . .

What fragments of verse from the ancient Hebrew and ancient Irish languages were cited with modulations of voice and translation of texts by guest to host and by host to guest?

By Stephen: *suil, suil, suil arun, suil go siocair agus, suil go cuin* (walk, walk, walk your way, walk in safety, walk with care).

[433]

By Bloom: *Kifeloch, harimon rakatejch m'baad l'zamatejch* (thy temple amid thy hair is as a slice of pomegranate).

How was a glyphic comparison of the phonic symbols of both languages made in substantiation of the oral comparison?

On the penultimate blank page of a book of inferior literary style, entitled *Sweets of Sin* (produced by Bloom and so manipulated that its front cover came in contact with the surface of the table) with a pencil (supplied by Stephen) Stephen wrote the Irish characters for gee, eh, dee, em, simple and modified, and Bloom in turn wrote the Hebrew characters ghimel, aleph, daleth and (in the absence of mem) a substituted goph, explaining their arithmetical values as ordinal and cardinal numbers, videlicet 3, 1, 4 and 100.

. . . .

In what common study did their mutual reflections merge?

The increasing simplification traceable from the Egyptian epigraphic hieroglyphs to the Greek and Roman alphabets and the anticipation of modern stenography and telegraphic code in the cuneiform inscriptions (Semitic) and the virgular quinquecostate ogham writing (Celtic).

Did the guest comply with his host's request?

Doubly, by appending his signature in Irish and Roman characters.

What was Stephen's auditive sensation?

He heard in a profound ancient male unfamiliar melody the accumulation of the past.

What was Bloom's visual sensation?

He saw in a quick young male familiar form the predestination of a future.

. . . .

Did the host encourage his guest to chant in a modulated voice a strange legend on an allied theme?

Reassuringly, their place where none could hear them talk being secluded, reassured, the decocted beverages, allowing for subsolid residual sediment of a mechanical mixture, water plus sugar plus cream plus cocoa, having been consumed.

[434]

Recite the first (major) part of the chanted legend?

Little Harry Hughes and his schoolfellows all
Went out for to play ball.
And the very first ball little Harry Hughes played
He drove it o'er the jew's garden wall.
And the very second ball little Harry Hughes played
He broke the jew's windows all.

How did the son of Rudolph receive this first part?
With unmixed feeling. Smiling, a jew, he heard with
pleasure and saw the unbroken kitchen window.

Recite the second part (minor) of the legend.
Then out there came the jew's daughter
And she all dressed in green.
'Come back, come back, you pretty little boy,
And play your ball again.'
'I can't come back and I won't come back
Without my schoolfellows all,
For if my master he did hear
He'd make it a sorry ball.'

She took him by the lilywhite hand
And led him along the hall
Until she led him to a room
Where none could hear him call.

She took a penknife out of her pocket
And cut off his little head,
And now he'll play his ball no more
For he lies among the dead.

[Musical score for verses one and two of this chanted legend printed
in original text.]

How did the father of Millicent receive the second part?
With mixed feelings. Unsmiling, he heard and saw with
wonder a jew's daughter, all dressed in green.

[435]

Condense Stephen's commentary.

One of all, the least of all, is the victim predestined. Once by inadvertence, twice by design he challenges his destiny. It comes when he is abandoned and challenges him reluctant and, as an apparition of hope and youth holds him unresisting. It leads him to a strange habitation, to a secret infidel apartment, and there, implacable, immolates him, consenting.

Why was the host (victim predestined) sad?
He wished that a tale of deed should be told of a deed not by him should by him not be told.

Why was the host (reluctant, unresisting) still?
In accordance with the law of the conservation of energy.

Why was the host (secret infidel) silent?
He weighed the possible evidences for and against ritual murder: the incitation of the hierarchy, the superstition of the populace, the propagation of rumour in continued fraction of veridicity, the envy of opulence, the influence of retaliation, the sporadic reappearance of atavistic delinquency, the mitigating circumstances of fanaticism, hypnotic suggestion and somnambulism.

. . . .

Had this latter or any cognate phenomenon declared itself in any member of his family?
Twice, in Holles street and in Ontario terrace, his daughter Millicent (Milly) at the ages of 6 and 8 years had uttered in sleep and exclamation of terror and had replied to the interrogations of two figures in night attire with a vacant mute expression.

. . . .

What memories had he of her adolescence?
She relegated her hoop and skippingrope to a recess. On the duke's lawn entreated by an English visitor, she declined to permit him to make and take away her photographic image (objection not stated). On the South Circular road in the company of Elsa Potter, followed by an individual of sinister aspect, she went half way down Stamer street and turned abruptly back (reason of change not stated). On the vigil of the 15th anniversary of her birth she wrote a letter

from Mullingar, county Westmeath, making a brief allusion to a local student (faculty and year not stated).

. . . .

What proposal did Bloom, diambulist, father of Milly, somnambulist, make to Stephen, noctambulist?

To pass in repose the hours intervening between Thursday (proper) and Friday (normal) on an extemporised cubicle in the apartment immediately above the kitchen and immediately adjacent to the sleeping apartment of his host and hostess.

What various advantages would or might have resulted from a prolongation of such extemporisation?

For the guest: security of domicile and seclusion of study. For the host: rejuvenation of intelligence, vicarious satisfaction. For the hostess: disintegration of obsession, acquisition of correct Italian pronunciation.

Why might these several provisional contingencies between a guest and a hostess not necessarily preclude or be precluded by a permanent eventuality of reconciliatory union between a schoolfellow and a jew's daughter?

Because the way to daughter led through mother, the way to mother through daughter.

To what inconsequent polysyllabic question of his host did the guest return a monosyllabic negative answer?

If he had known the late Mrs Emily Sinico, accidentally killed at Sydney Parade railway, 14 October 1903.

What inchoate corollary statement was consequently suppressed by the host?

A statement explanatory of his absence on the occasion of the internment of Mrs Mary Dedalus, born Goulding, 26 June 1903, vigil of the anniversary of the decease of Rudolph Bloom (born Virag).

Was the proposal of asylum accepted?

Promptly, inexplicably, with amicability, gratefully it was declined.

[437]

What exchange of money took place between host and guest?

The former returned to the latter, without interest, a sum of money (L1. 7s. 0.), one pound seven shillings, advanced by the latter to the former.

. . . .

Why would a recurrent frustration the more depress him?

Because at the critical turningpoint of human existence he desired to amend many social conditions, the product of inequality and avarice and international animosity.

He believed then that human life was infinitely perfectible, eliminating these conditions?

There remained the generic conditions imposed by natural, as distinct from human law, as integral parts of the human whole: the necessity of destruction to procure alimentary sustenance: the painful character of the ultimate functions of separate existence, the agonies of birth and death: the monotonous menstruation of simian and (particularly) human females extending from the age of puberty to the menopause: inevitable accidents at sea, in mines and factories: certain very painful maladies and their resultant surgical operations, innate lunacy and congenital criminality, decimating epidemics: catastrophic cataclyms which make terror the basis of human mentality: seismic upheavals the epicentres of which are located in densely populated regions: the fact of vital growth, through convulsions of metamorphosis from infancy through maturity to decay.

Why did he desist from speculation?

Because it was a task for a superior intelligence to substitute other more acceptable phenomena in place of the less acceptable phenomena to be removed.

Did Stephen participate in his dejection?

He affirmed his significance as a conscious rational animal proceeding syllogistically from the known to the unknown and a conscious rational reagent between a micro- and a macrocosm ineluctably constructed upon the incertitude of the void.

Was this affirmation apprehended by Bloom?

Not verbally. Substantially.

[438]

What comforted his misapprehension?

That as a competent keyless citizen he had proceeded energetically from the unknown to the known through the incertitude of the void.

In what order of precedence, with what attendant ceremony was the exodus from the house of bondage to the wilderness of inhabitation effected.

Lighted Candle in Stick borne by

BLOOM.

Diaconal Hat on Ashplant borne by

STEPHEN.

With what intonation *secreto* of what commemorative psalm?

The 113th, *modus peregrinus: In exitu Israel de Egypto: domus Jacob de populo barbaro.*

What did each do at the door of egress?

Bloom set the candlestick on the floor. Stephen put the hat on his head.

For what creature was the door of egress a door of ingress?

For a cat.

What spectacle confronted them when they, first the host, then the guest, emerged silently, doubly dark, from obscurity by a passage from the rere of the house into the penumbra of the garden?

The heaventree of stars hung with humid nightblue fruit.

With what meditations did Bloom accompany his demonstration to his companion of various constellations?

Meditations of evolution increasingly vaster: of the moon invisible in incipent lunation, approaching perigee: of the infinite lattiginous scintillating uncondensed milky way... of Sirius (alpha in Canis Major) ... of Arcturus: of the precession of equinoxes ... of Orion with belt and sextuple sun theta and nebula ... of moribund and of nascent new stars such as Nova in 1901: of our system plunging towards the constellation of Hercules ... of the parallax or

[439]

parallactic drift of socalled fixed stars, in reality evermoving from immeasurably remote eons to infinitely remote futures in comparison with which the years, threescore and ten, of allotted human life formed a parenthesis of infinitesimal brevity.

. . . .

Did he find the problem of the inhabitability of the planets and their satellites by a race, given in species, and of the possible social and moral redemption of said race by a redeemer, easier of solution?

Of a different order of difficulty. Conscious that the human organism, normally capable of sustaining an atmospheric pressure of 19 tons, when elevated to a considerable altitude in the terrestrial atmosphere suffered with arithmetical progression of intensity, according as the line of demarcation between troposphere and stratosphere was approximated, from nasal hemorrhage, impeded respiration and vertigo, when proposing this problem for solution he had conjectured as a working hypothesis which could not be proved impossible that a more adaptable and differently anatomically constructed race of beings might subsist otherwise...

And the problem of possible redemption?
The minor was proved by the major.

. . . .

His (Bloom's) logical conclusion, having weighed the matter and allowed for possible error?

That it was not a heaventree, not a heavengrot, not a heavenbeast, not a heavenman. That it was a Utopia, there being no known method from the known to the unknown: an infinity, renderable equally finite by the suppositious probable appostion of one or more bodies equally of the same and of different magnitudes: a mobility of illusory forms immobilised in space, remobilised in air: a past which possibly has ceased to exist as a present before its future spectators had entered actual present existence.

. . . .

What special affinities appeared to him to exist between the moon and woman?

Her antiquity in preceding and surviving successive tellurian generations: her nocturnal predominance: her satellitic dependence: her luminary reflection: her constancy under all her phases, rising and setting by her appointed times, waxing and waning: the forced

[440]

invariably of her aspect: her indeterminate response to affirmative interrogation: her potency over effluent and refluent waters: her power to enamour, to mortify, to invest with beauty, to render insane, to incite to and aid delinquency: the tranquil inscrutability of her visage: the terribility of her isolated dominant implacable resplendent propinquity: her omens of tempest and of calm: the stimulation of her light, her motion and her presence: the admonition of her craters, her arid seas, her silence: her splendour, when visible: her attraction, when invisible.

What visible luminous sign attracted Bloom's, who attracted Stephen's gaze?

In the second storey (rere) of his (Bloom's) house the light of a paraffin oil lamp with oblique shade projected on a screen of roller blind supplied by Frank O'Hara, window blind, curtain pole and revolving shutter manufacturer, 16 Aungier street.

How did he elucidate the mystery of an invisible person, his wife Marion (Molly) Bloom, denoted by a visible splendid sign, a lamp?

With indirect and direct verbal allusions or affirmations: with subdued affection and admiration: with description: with impediment: with suggestion.

Both then were silent?

Silent, each contemplating the other in both mirrors of the reciprocal flesh of theirhisnothis fellowfaces.

Were they indefinitely inactive?

At Stephen's suggestion, at Bloom's instigation both, first Stephen, then Bloom, in penumbra urinated, their sides contiguous, their organs of micturition reciprocally rendered invisible by manual circumposition, their gazes, first Bloom's, then Stephen's, elevated to the projected luminous and semiluminous shadow.

Similarly?

The trajectories of their, first sequent, then simultaneous, urinations were dissimilar: Bloom's longer, less irruent, in the incomplete form of the bifurcated penultimate alphabetical letter who in his ultimate year at High School (1880) had been capable of attaining the point of greatest altitude against the whole concurrent strength of the institution, 210 scholars: Stephen's higher, more sibilant, who in the ultimate hours of the previous day had augmented by diuretic consumption an insistent vesical pressure.

What different problems presented themselves to each concerning the invisible audible collateral organ of the other?

To Bloom: the problems of irritability, tumescence, rigidity, reactivity, dimension, sanitariness, pelosity. To Stephen: the problem of the sacerdotal integrity of Jesus circumcised (1st January, holiday of obligation to hear mass and abstain from unnecessary servile work) and the problem as to whether the divine prepuce, the carnal bridal ring of the holy Roman catholic apostolic church, conserved in Calcata, were deserving of simple hyperduly or of the fourth degree of latria accorded to the abscission of such divine excrescences as hair and toenails.

What celestial sign was by both simultaneously observed?

A star precipitated with great apparent velocity across the firmament from Vega in the Lyre above the zenith beyond the stargroup of the Tress of Berenice towards the zodiacal sign of Leo.

How did the centripetal remainer afford egress to the centrifugal departer?

By inserting the barrel of an arruginated male key in the hole of an unstable female lock, obtaining a purchase on the bow of the key and turning its wards from right to left, withdrawing a bolt from its staple, pulling inward spasmodically an obsolescent unhinged door and revealing an aperture for free egress and free ingress.

How did they take leave, one of the other, in separation?

Standing perpendicular at the same door and on different sides of its base, the lines of their valedictory arms, meeting at any point and forming any angle less than the sum of two right angles.

What sound accompanied the union of their tangent, the disunion of their (respectively) centrifugal and centripetal hands?

The sound of the peal of the hour of the night by the chime of the bells in the church of Saint George.

. . . .

[442]

Where were the several members of the company which with Bloom that day at the bidding of that peal had travelled from Sandymount in the south to Glasnevin in the north?

Martin Cunningham (in bed), Jack Power (in bed), Simon Dedalus (in bed), Tom Kernan (in bed), Ned Lambert (in bed), Joe Hynes (in bed), John-Henry Menton (in bed), Bernard Corrigan (in bed), Patsy Dignam (in bed), Paddy Dignam (in the grave).

Alone, what did Bloom hear?

The double reverberation of retreating feet on the heavenborn earth, the double vibration of a jew's harp in the resonant lane.

Alone, what did Bloom feel?

The cold of interstellar space, thousands of degrees below freezing point or the absolute zero of Fahrenheit, Centigrade or Reaumur: the incipient intimations of proximate dawn.

. . . .

Did he remain?

With deep inspiration he returned, retraversing the garden, reentering the passage, reclosing the door. With brief suspiration he reassumed the candle, reascended the stairs, reapproached the door of the front room, hallfloor, and reentered.

What suddenly arrested his ingress?

The right temporal lobe of the hollow sphere of his cranium came into contact with a solid timber angle where, an infinitesimal but sensible fraction of a second later, a painful sensation was located in consequence of antecedent sensations transmitted and registered.

Describe the alterations effected in the disposition of the articles of furniture?

A sofa upholstered in prune plush had been translocated from opposite the door to the ingleside near the compactly furled Union Jack (an alteration which he had frequently intended to execute): the blue and white checkered inlaid majolicatopped table had been placed opposite the door in the place vacated by the prune plush sofa: the walnut sideboard (a projecting angle of which had momentarily arrested his ingress) had been moved from its position beside the door to a more advantageous but more perilous position in front of the door: two chairs had been moved from right and left of the ingleside to the position originally occupied by the blue and white checker inlaid majolicatopped table.

. . . .

What significances attend to these two chairs?
Significances of similitude, of posture, of symbolism, of circumstantial evidence, of testimonial supermanence.

What occupied the position originally occupied by the sideboard?
A vertical piano (Cadby) with exposed keyboard, its closed coffin supporting a pair of long yellow ladies' gloves and an emerald ashtray containing four consumed matched, a partly consumed cigarette and two discoloured ends of cigarettes, its musicrest supporting the music in the key of G natural for voice and piano of *Love's Old Sweet Song* (words by G. Clifton Bingham, composed by J. L. Molloy, sung by Madam Antoinette Sterling) open at the page with the final indications *ad libitum, forte,* pedal, *animato,* sustained, pedal, *ritirando,* close.

. . . .

His next proceeding?
From an open box on the majolicatopped table he extracted a black diminutive cone, one inch in height, placed it on its circular base on a small tin plate, placed his candlestick on the right corner of the mantelpiece, produced from his waistcoat a folded page of prospectus (illustrated) entitled Agendath Netaim, unfolded the same, examined it superficially, rolled it into a thin cylinder, ignited it in the candleflame, applied it when ignited to the apex of the cone till the latter reached the stage of rutilance, placed the cylinder in the basin of the candlestick disposing its unconsumed part in such a manner as to facilitate total combustion.

What followed this operation?
That truncated conical crater summit of the diminutive volcano emitted a vertical and serpentine fune redolent of aromatic oriental incense.

What homothetic objects, other than the candlestick, stood on the mantelpiece?

[444]

A timepiece of striated Connemara marble, stopped at the hour of 4.46 a.m. on the 21 March 1896, matrimonial gift of Matthew Dillon: a dwarf tree of glacial arborescence under a transparent bellshade, matrimonial gift of Luke and Caroline Doyle: an embalmed owl, matrimonial gift of Alderman John Hooper.

What interchanges of looks took place between these three objects and Bloom?

In the mirror of the giltbordered pierglass the undecorated back of the dwarf tree regarded the upright back of the embalmed owl. Before the mirror the matrimonial gift of Alderman John Hooper with a clear melancholy wise bright motionless compassionate gaze regarded Bloom while Bloom with obscure tranquil profound motionless compassionated gaze regarded the matrimonial gift of Luke and Caroline Doyle.

What composite asymmetrical image in the mirror then attracted his attention?

The image of a solitary (ipsorelative) mutable (aliorelative) man.

Why solitary (ipsorelative)?

Brothers and sisters had he non,
Yet that man's father was his grandfather's son.

Why mutable (aliorelative)?

From infancy to maturity he had resembled his maternal procreatrix. From maturity to senility he would increasingly resemble his paternal creator.

What final visual impression was communicated to him by the mirror?

The optical reflection of several inverted volumes improperly arranged and not in the order of their common letters with scintillating titles on the two bookshelves opposite.

Catalogue these books.
Thom's Dublin Post Office Directory, 1886
Denis Florence M'Carthy's *Poetical Works* (copper beechleaf bookmark at p. 5)
Shakespeare's *Works* (dark crimson morocco, goldtooled)....

The Child's Guide (blue cloth).
When We Were Boys by William O'Brien M.P. (green cloth, slightly faded, envelope bookmark at p. 217).
Thoughts from Spinoza (maroon leather).
The Story of the Heavens by Sir Robert Ball (blue cloth)....
Philosophy of the Talmud (sewn pamphlet).
Lockhart's *Life of Napoleon* (cover wanting, marginal annotations, minimising victories, aggrandising defeats of the protagonist)....
Laurence Bloomfield in Ireland by William Allingham (second edition, green cloth, gilt trefoil design, previous owner's name on recto of flyleaf erased).
A Handbook of Astronomy (cover, brown leather, detached, 5 plates, antique letterpress long primer, author's footnotes nonpareil, marginal clues, brevier, captions small pica).
The Hidden Life of Christ (black boards)....
Physical Strength and How to Obtain It by Eugene Sandow (red cloth)....

What reflections occupied his mind during the process of reversion of the inverted volumes?

The necessity of order, a place for everything and everything in its place: the deficient appreciation of literature possessed by females: the incongruity of an apple incubated in a tumbler and of an umbrella inclined in a closetool: the insecurity of hiding any secret document behind, beneath or between the pages of a book.

. . . .

What caused him consolation in his sitting posture?

The candour, nudity, pose, tranquility, youth, grace, sex, counsel of a statue erect in the centre of the table, an image of Narcissus purchased by auction from P. A. Wren, 9 Bachelor's Walk.

What caused him irritation in his sitting posture?

Inhibitory pressure of collar (size 17) and waistcoat (5 buttons), two articles of clothing superfluous in the costume of mature males and inelastic to alterations of mass by expansion.

How was the irritation allayed?

He removed his collar, with contained black necktie and collapsible stud, from his neck to a position on the left of the table.

[446]

He unbuttoned successively in reversed direction waistcoat, trousers,
shirt and vest.

. . . .

   [Compile the budget for 16 June 1904 . . . . printed in text.]

   Did the process of divestiture continue?
   Sensible of a benignant persistent ache in his footsoles he
extended his foot to one side and observed the creases, protuberances
and salient points caused by foot pressure in the course of walking
repeatedly in several different directions, then, inclined, he disnoded
the laceknots, unhooked and loosened the laces, took off each of his
two boots for the second time, detached the partially moistened right
sock through the fore part of which the nail of his great toes had
again effracted, raised his right foot and, having unhooked a purple
elastic sock suspender, took off his right sock, placed his unclothed
right foot on the margin of the seat of his chair, picked at and gently
lacerated the protruding part of the great toenail, raised the part
lacerated to his nostrils and inhaled the odour of the quick, then with
satisfaction threw away the lacerated unguical fragment.

   Why with satisfaction?
   Because the odour inhaled corresponded to other odours
inhaled of other unguical fragments, picked and lacerated by Master
Bloom, pupil of Mrs Ellis's juvenile school, patiently each night in
the act of brief genuflection and nocturnal prayer and ambitious
meditation.

   In what ultimate ambition had all concurrent and consecutive
ambitions now coalesced?
   Not to inherit by right of primogeniture.... but to purchase
by private treaty in fee simple a thatched bungalowshaped 2 storey
dwelling house of southerly aspect, surmounted by vane and
lightning conductor, connected with the earth, with porch covered by
parasitic plants (ivy or Virginia creeper), halldoor, olive green, with
smart carriage finish and neat doorbrasses, stucco front with gilt
tracery at eaves and gable, rising, if possible, upon a gentle eminence
with agreeable prospect from balcony with stone pillar parapet over
unoccupied and unoccupyable interjacent pastures and standing in 5
or 6 acres of its own ground, at such a distance from the nearest
public thoroughfare as to render its houselights visible at night above

[447]

and through a quickset hornbeam hedge of topiary cutting, situate at a given point not less than 1 statute mile from the periphery of the metropolis, within a time limit of not more than 5 minutes from tram or train line....

What additional attractions might the grounds contain?
An addenda, a tennis and fives court, a shrubbery, a glass summerhouse with tropical palms, equipped in the best botanical manner, a rockery with waterspray, a beehive arranged on humane principles, oval flowerbeds in rectangular grassplots set with eccentric ellipses of scarlet and chrome tulips, bleu scillas, crocuses, polyanthus, sweet William, sweat pea, lily of the valley... an orchard, kitchen garden and vinery, protected against illegal trespassers by glasstopped mural enclosures, a lumbershed with padlock for various inventoried implements.

. . . .

What might be the name of this erigible or erected residence?
Bloom Cottage. Saint Leopold's. Flowerville.

Could Bloom of 7 Eccles street foresee Bloom of Flowerville?
In loose allwool garments with Harris tweed cap, price 8/6, and useful garden boots with elastic gussets and wateringcan, planting aligned young firtrees, syringing, pruning, staking, sowing hayseed, trundling a weedladen wheelbarrow without excessive fatigue at sunset amid the scent of newmown hay, ameliorating the soil, multiplying wisdom, achieving longevity.

What syllabus of intellectual pursuits was simultaneously possible?
Snapshot photography, comparative study of religions, folklore relative to various amatory and superstitious practices, contemplation of the celestial constellations.

. . . .

Might he become a gentleman farmer of field produce and live stock?
Not impossibly, with 1 or 2 stripper cows, 1 pike of upland hay and requisite farming implements, e.g., an end-to-end churn, a turnip pulper etc.

[448]

What would be his civic functions and social status among the county families and landed gentry?

Arranged successively in ascending powers of hierarchical order, that of gardener, groundsman, cultivator, breeder, and at the zenith of his career, resident magistrate or justice of the peace with a family crest and coat of arms and appropriate classical motto (*Semper paratus*), duly recorded in the court directory (Bloom, Leopold P., M. P., P. C., K. P., L. L. D. *honoris causa,* Bloomville, Dundrum) and mentioned in court and fashionable intelligence (Mr and Mrs Leopold Bloom have left Kingston for England.)

What course of action did he outline for himself in such capacity?

A course that lay between undue clemency and excessive rigour: the dispensation in a heterogeneous society of arbitrary classes, incessantly rearranged in terms of greater and lesser social inequality of unbiassed homogenous indisputable justice,… Loyal to the highest constituted power in the land, actuated by an innate love of rectitude his aim would be the strict maintenance of public order, the repression of many abuses… the upholding of the letter of the law (common, statute and law merchant) against all traversers….

Prove that he had loved rectitude from his earliest youth.

To master Percy Apjohn at High School in 1880 he had divulged his disbelief in the tenets of the Irish (protestant) church (to which his father Rudolf Virag, later Rudolph Bloom, had been converted from the Israelitic faith and communion in 1865 by the Society for promoting Christianity among the Jews) subsequently abjured by him in favour of Roman catholicism at the epoch of and with a view to his matrimony in 1888…. he had advocated during nocturnal perambulations of the political theory of colonial (e.g. Canadian) expansion and the evolutionary theories of Charles Darwin, expounded in *The Descent of Man* and *The Origin of the Species.* In 1885 he had publicly expressed his adherence to the collective and national economic programme advocated by James Fintan Lalor, … the constitutional agitation of Charles Stewart Parnell (M. P. for Cork City), the programme of peace retrenchment and reform of William Ewart Gladstone (M. P. for Midlothian, N. B.)….

How much and how did he propose to pay for this country residence?

As per prospectus of the Industrious Foreign Acclimatised Nationalised Friendly Stateaided Building Society (incorporated 1874), a maximum of L60 per annum, ...

What rapid but insecure means to opulence might facilitate immediate purchase?

A private wireless telegraph which would transmit by dot and dash system the result of a national equine handicap (flat or steeplechase) of 1 or more miles and furlongs won by an outsider at odds of 50 to 1 at 3 hr. 8 m. p.m. at Ascot (Greenwich time) the message being received and available for betting purposes in Dublin at 2.59 p.m. (Dunsink time). The unexpected discovery of an object of great monetary value: precious stone, valuable adhesive of impressed postage stamps... A Spanish prisoner's donation of a distant treasure of valuables or specie or bullion.... A contract with an inconsiderate contractee for the delivery of 32 consignments of some given commodity.... A prepared scheme based on a study of the laws of probability to break the bank at Monte Carlo....
. . . .

Were there schemes of a wider scope?

A scheme to be formulated and submitted for approval to the harbour commissioners for the exploitation of white coal (hydraulic power), obtained by hydroelectric plant at peak of tide at Dublin bar or at head of water at Poulaphouca or Powerscourt.... A scheme for the use of dogvans and goatvans for the delivery of early morning milk. A scheme for the development of Irish tourist traffic in and around Dublin.... A scheme for the repristination of passenger and goods traffics over Irish waterways....
. . . .

For what reason did he meditate on schemes so difficult of realisation?

It was one of his axioms that similar meditations or the automatic relation to himself of a narrative concerning himself or tranquil recollection of the past when practised habitually before retiring for the night alleviated fatigue and produced as a result sound repose and renovated vitality.
. . . .

[450]

What did he fear?

The committal of homicide or suicide during sleep by an aberration of the light or reason, the incommensurable categorical intelligence situated in the cerebral convolutions.

What were habitually his final meditations?

Of some one sole unique advertisement to cause passers to stop in wonder, a poster novelty, with all extraneous accretions excluded, reduced to its simplest and most efficient terms not exceeding the span of casual vision and congruous with the velocity of modern life.

What did the first drawer unlocked contain?

A Vere Foster's handwriting copybook, property of Milly (Millicent) Bloom, certain pages of which bore diagram drawings marked *Papli,* which showed a large globular head with 5 hairs erect, 2 eyes in profile, the trunk full front with 3 large buttons, 1 triangular foot: 2 fading photographs of queen Alexandra of England and of Maud Branscombe, actress and professional beauty: a Yuletide card, bearing on it a pictorial representation of a parasitic plant, the legend *Mizpah,* the date Xmas 1892, the name of the senders, from Mr and Mrs M. Comerford, the versicle: *May this Yuletide bring to thee, Joy and peace and welcome glee:* a butt of red partly liquefied sealing wax,... a sealed prophecy (never unsealed) written by Leopold Bloom in 1886 concerning the consequences of the passing into law of William Ewart Gladstone's Home Rule bill of 1886 (never passed into law):... A cameo brooch, property of Ellen Bloom (born Higgins), deceased: 3 typewritten letters, addressee, Henry Flower, % P. O. Westland Row, addresser, Martha Clifford, % P. O. Dolphin's Barn:... a lowpower magnifying glass: 2 erotic photocards showing: a) buccal coition between nude senorita (rere presentation, superior position) and nude torero (fore presentation, inferior position): b) anal violation by male religious (fully clothed, eyes abject) of female religious (partly clothed, eyes direct),... 1 prospectus of the Wonderworker, the world's greatest remedy for rectal complaints direct from Wonderworker, Coventry House, South Place, London E. C., addressed to Mrs L. Bloom with brief accompanying note commencing: Dear Madam.

. . . .

What object did Bloom add to this collection of objects?

A 4th typewritten letter received by Henry Flower (let H. F. be L. B.) from Martha Clifford (find M. C.).

What pleasant reflection accompanied this action?
The reflection that, apart from the letter in question, his magnetic face, form and address had been favourably received during the course of the preceding day by a wife (Mrs Josephine Breen, born Josie Powell); a nurse, Miss Callan (Christian name unknown), a maid, Gertrude (Gerty, family name unknown).

What possibility suggested itself?
The possibility of exercising virile power of fascination in the most immediate future after an expensive repast in a private apartment in the company of an elegant courtesan, of corporal beauty, moderately mercenary, variously instructed, a lady by origin.

What did the 2nd drawer contain?
Documents: the birth certificate of Leopold Paula Bloom: and endowment assurance policy of L500 in the Scottish Widows' Assurance Society intestate Millicent (Milly) Bloom, coming into force at 25 years as with profit policy of L430.... Dockets of the Catholic Cemeteries' (Glasnevin) Committee, relative to a graveplot purchased: a local press cutting concerning change of name by deedpoll.
Quote the textual terms of this notice.
I, Rudolph Virag, now resident at no. 52 Clanbrassil street, Dublin, formerly of Szombathely in the kingdom of Hungary, hereby give notice that I have assumed and intend henceforth upon all occasions and at all times to be known by the name Rudolph Bloom.

What other objects relative to Rudolph Bloom (born Virag) were in the 2nd drawer?
An indistinct daguerreotype of Rudolph Virag and his father Leopold Virag executed in the year 1852.... an envelope addressed *To my Dear Son Leopold.*

What fractions of phrases did the lecture of those five whole words evoke?
Tomorrow will be a week that I received . . . it is no use Leopold to be . . . with your dear mother . . . that is not more to stand

[452]

. . . to her . . . all for me is out . . . be kind to Athos, Leopold . . . my
dear son . . . always . . . of me . . . *das Herz . . . Gott . . . dein . . .*

What reminiscences of a human subject suffering from
progressive melancholia did these objects evoke in Bloom?

An old man widower, unkempt hair, in bed, with head
covered, sighing: an infirm dog, Athos: aconite, resorted to by
increasing doses of grains and scruples as a palliative of recrudescent
neuralgia: the face of death of a septuagenarian suicide by poison.

Why did Bloom experience a sentiment of remorse?

Because in immature impatience he had treated with
disrespect certain beliefs and practices.

As?

The prohibition of the use of fleshmeat and milk at one meal,
the hebdomadary symposium of inordinately abstract, perfervidly
concrete mercantile coexreligionist excompatriots: the circumcision
of male infants: the supernatural character of Judaic scripture: the
ineffability of the tetragrammaron: the sanctity of the sabbath.

How did these beliefs and practices now appear to him?

Not more rational than they had then appeared, not less
rational than other beliefs and practices now appeared.

. . . .

Had time equally but differently obliterated the memory of
these migrations of narrator and listener?

In narrator by the access of years and in consequence of the
use of narcotic toxin: in listener by the access of years and in
consequence of the action of distraction upon vicarious experiences.

. . . .

By what could such a situation be precluded?

By decease (change of state), by departure (change of place).

Which preferably?

The latter, by the line of least resistance.

What considerations rendered it not entirely undesirable?

Constant cohabitation impeding mutual toleration of
personal defects. The habit of independent purchase increasingly

[453]

cultivated. The necessity to counteract by impermanent sojourn the permanence of arrest.

What considerations rendered it not irrational?

The parties concerned, uniting, had increased and multiplied, which being done, offspring produced and educed to maturity, the parties, if now disunited were obliged to reunite for increase and multiplication, which was absurd, to form by reunion the original couple of uniting parties, which was impossible.

What considerations rendered it desirable?

The attractive character of certain localities in Ireland and abroad, as represented in general geographical maps of polychrome design or in special ordnance survey charts by employment of scale numerals and hachures.

In Ireland?

The cliffs of Moher, the windy wilds of Connemara, lough Neagh with submerged petrified city, the Giant's Causeway, Fort Camden and Fort Carlisle, the Golden Vale of Tipperary, the islands of Aran, the pastures of royal Meath, Brigid's elm in Kildare, the Queen's Island shipyard in Belfast, the Salmon Leap, the lakes of Killarney.

Abroad?

Ceylon (with spicegardens…), Jerusalem, the holy city (with mosque of Omar and gate of Damascus, goal of aspiration), the straits of Gibraltar (the unique birthplace of Marion Tweedy), the Parthenon (containing statues, nude Greek divinities), the Wall street money market (which controlled international finance), the Plaza de Toros at La Linea, Spain (where O'Hara of the Camerons had slain the bull), Niagara (over which no human being had passed with impunity), the land of the Eskimos (eaters of soap), the forbidden country of Thibet (from which no traveller returns), the bay of Naples (to see which was to die), the Dead Sea.

. . . .

What public advertisement would divulge the occultation of the departed?

L5, reward lost, stolen or strayed from his residence 7 Eccles street, missing gent about 40, answering to the name of Bloom, Leopold (Poldy), height 5 ft 9½ inches, full build, olive complexion,

[454]

may have since grown a beard, when last seen was wearing a black
suit. Above sum will be paid for information leading to his
discovery.

What universal binomial denominations would be his as
entity and nonentity?

Assumed by any or known to none. Everyman or Noman.

What tributes his?

Honour and gifts of strangers, the friends of Everyman. A
nymph immortal, beauty, the bride of Noman.

Would the departed never nowhere nohow reappear?

Ever he would wander, selfcompelled, to the extreme limit
of his cometary orbit, beyond the fixed stars and variable suns and
telescopic planets, astronomical waifs and strays, to the extreme
boundary of space, passing from land to land, among peoples, amid
events. Somewhere imperceptibly he would hear and somehow
reluctantly, suncompelled, obey the summons of recall. Whence,
disappearing from the constellation of the Northern Crown he would
somehow reappear reborn above delta in the constellation of
Cassiopeia and after incalculable eons of peregrination return an
estranged avenger, a wreaker of justice on malefactors, a dark
crusader, a sleeper awakened, with financial resources (by
supposition) surpassing those of Rothschild or of the silver king.

What would render such return irrational?

An unsatisfactory equation between an exodus and return in
time through reversible space and an exodus and return in space
through irreversible time.

What play of forces, inducing inertia, rendered departure
undesirable?

The lateness of the hour, rendering procrastinatory: the
obscurity of the night, rendering invisible: the uncertainty of
thoroughfares, rendering perilous: the necessity for repose, obviating
movement: the proximity of an occupied bed, obviating research: the
anticipation of warmth (human) tempered with coolness (linen),
obviating desire and rendering desirable: the statue of Narcissus,
sound without echo, desired desire.

What advantages were possessed by an occupied, as distinct from an unoccupied bed?

The removal of nocturnal solitude, the superior quality of human (mature female) to inhuman (hotwaterjar) calefaction, the stimulation of matutinal contact, the economy of mangling done on the premises in the case of trousers accurately folded and placed lengthwise between the spring mattress (striped) and the woollen mattress (biscuit section).

What past consecutive causes, before rising preapprehended, of accumulated fatigue did Bloom, before rising, silently recapitulate?

The preparation of breakfast (burnt offering): intestinal congestion and premeditative defecation (holy of holies): the bath (rite of John): the funeral (rite of Samuel): the advertisement of Alexander Keyes (Urim and Thummin): the unsubstantial lunch (rite of Melchizedek): the visit to museum and national library (holy place): the bookhunt along Bedford row, Merchant's Arch, Wellington Quay (Simchath Torah): the music in the Ormond Hotel (Shira Shirim): the altercation with a truculent troglodyte in Bernard Kiernan's premises (holocaust): a blank period of time including a cardrive, a visit to a house of mourning, a leavetaking (wilderness): the eroticism produced by feminine exhibitionism (rite of Onan): the prolonged delivery of Mrs Mina Purefoy (heave offering): the visit to the disorderly house of Mrs Bella Cohen, 82 Tyrone street, lower, and subsequent brawl and chance medley in Beaver street (Armageddon): nocturnal perambulations to and from the cabman's shelter, Butt Bridge (atonement).

. . . .

Bloom's acts?

He deposited the articles of clothing on a chair, removed his remaining article of clothing, took from beneath the bolster at the head of the bed a folded long white nightshirt, inserted his head and arms into the proper apertures of the nightshirt, removed a pillow from the head to the foot of the bed, prepared the bedlinen accordingly and entered the bed.

How?

With circumspection, as invariably when entering an abode (his own or not his own): with solicitude, the snakespiral springs of the mattress being old, the brass quoits and pendent viper radii loose and tremulous under stress and strain: prudently, as entering a lair or ambush of lust or adder: lightly, the less to disturb: reverently, the bed of conception and of birth, of consummation of marriage and of breach of marriage, of sleep and of death.

What did his limbs, when gradually extended, encounter?
New clean bedlinen, additional odours, the presence of a human form, female, hers, the imprint of a human form, male, not his, some crumbs, some flakes of potted meat, recooked, which he removed.

If he had smiled why would he have smiled?
To reflect that each one who enters imagines himself to be the first to enter whereas he is always the last term of a preceding series even if the first term of a succeeding one, each imagining himself to be first, last, only and alone, whereas he is neither first nor last nor only nor alone in a series of originating in and repeated to infinity.

. . . .

What were his reflections concerning the last member of this series and late occupant of the bed?
Reflections on his vigour (a bounder), corporal proportion (a billsticker), commercial ability (a bester), impressionability (a boaster).

. . . .

With what antagonistic sentiments were his subsequent reflections affected?
Envy, jealousy, abnegation, equanimity.

. . . .

Why more abnegation than jealousy, less envy than equanimity?
From outrage (matrimony) to outrage (adultery) there arose nought but outrage (copulation) yet the matrimonial violator of the matrimonially violated had not been outraged by the adulterous violator of the adulterously violated.

What retribution, if any?
Assassination, never, as two wrongs did not make one right. Duel by combat, no. Divorce, not now. Exposure by mechanical

artifice (automatic bed) or individual testimony (concealed by ocular witness), not yet. Suit for damages by legal influence or simulation of assault with evidence of injuries sustained (selfinflected), not impossibly. If any, positively, connivance, introduction of emulation (material, a prosperous rival agency of publicity: moral, a successful rival agent of intimacy), depreciation, alienation, humiliation, separation protecting the one separated from the other, protecting separator from both.

By what reflection did he, a conscious reactor against the void incertitude, justify to himself his sentiments?

The preordained frangibility of the hymen, the presupposed intangibility of the thing in itself: the incongruity and disproportion between the selfprolonging tension of the thing proposed to be done and the self abbreviating relaxation of the thing done: the fallaciously inferred debility of the female, the muscularity of the male: the variations of ethical codes:... the continued product of seminators by generation: the continual production of semen by distillation: the futility of triumph or protest or vindication: the inanity of extolled virtue: the lethargy of nescient matter: the apathy of the stars.

. . . .

The visible signs of antesatisfaction?

An approximate erection: a solicitous adversion: a gradual elevation: a tentative revelation: a silent contemplation.

Then?

He kissed the plump mellow yellow smellow melons of her rump, on each plump melonous hemisphere, in their mellow yellow furrow, with obscure prolonged provocative melonsmellonous osculation.

The visible signs of postsatisfaction?

A silent contemplation: a tentative velation: a gradual abasement: a solicitous aversion: a proximate erection.

What followed the silent action?

Somnolent invocation, less somnolent recognition, incipient excitation, catechetical interrogation.

[458]

With what modifications did the narrator reply to this interrogation?

Negative: he omitted to mention the clandestine correspondence between Martha Clifford and Henry Flower, the public altercation at, in and in vicinity of the licensed premises of Bernard Kiernan and Co, the erotic provocation and response thereto caused by the exhibitionism of Gertrude (Gerty), surname unknown. Positive: he included mention of a performance by Mrs Bandman Palmer of *Leah* at the Gaiety Theatre, an invitation to supper at Wynn's (Murphy's) Hotel, a volume of peccaminous pornographical tendency entitled *Sweets of Sin,* anonymous, author a gentleman of fashion, a temporary concussion caused by a falsely calculated movement in the course of postcenal gymnastic display, the victim (since completely recovered) being Stephen Dedalus, professor and author, eldest surviving son of Simon Dedalus, of no fixed occupation, an aeronautical feat executed by him (narrator) in the presence of a witness, the professor and author aforesaid, with promptitude of decision and gymnastic flexibility.

Was the narration otherwise unaltered by modifications?
Absolutely.

Which event or person emerged as the salient point of his narration?
Stephen Dedalus, professor and author.

What limitations of activity and inhibitions of conjugal rights were perceived by listener and narrator concerning themselves during the course of this intermittent and increasingly more laconic narration?

By the listener a limitation of fertility inasmuch as marriage had been celebrated 1 calendar month after the 18th anniversary of her birth (8 September 1870), viz. 8 October, and consummated on the same date with female issue born 15 June 1889, having been anticipatorily consummated on the 10 September of the same year and complete carnal intercourse, with ejaculation of the semen within the natural female organ, having last taken place 5 weeks previous, viz. 27 November 1893, to the birth on 29 December 1893 of second (and only male) issue, deceased 9 January 1894, aged 11 days, there remained a period of 10 years, 5 months and 18 days

during which carnal intercourse had been incomplete, without
ejaculation of semen within the natural female organ. By the narrator
a limitation of activity, mental and corporal, inasmuch as complete
mental intercourse between himself and the listener had not taken
place since the consummation of puberty, indicated by catamenic
hemorrhage, of the female issue of narrator and listener, 15
September 1903, there remained a period of 9 months and 1 day
during which in consequence of a preestablished natural
comprehension in incomprehension between the consummated
females (listener and issue), complete corporal liberty of action had
been circumscribed.

How?
By various reiterated feminine interrogation concerning
masculine destination whither, the place where, the time at which,
the duration for which, the object with which in the case of
temporary absences, projected or effected.

What moved visibly above the listener's and the narrator's
invisible thoughts?
The upcast reflection of a lamp and shade, an inconstant
series of concentric circles of varying gradations of light and
shadow.

In what directions did listener and narrator lie?
Listener, S. E. by E.; Narrator, N. W. by W.: on the 53rd
parallel of latitude, N. and 6th meridian of longitude, W.: at an angle
of 45° to the terrestrial equator.

In what state of rest or motion?
At rest relatively to themselves and to each other. In motion
being each and both carried westward, forward and rereward
respectively, by the proper perpetual motion of the earth through
everchanging tracks of neverchanging space.

In what posture?
Listener: reclined semilaterally, left, left hand under head,
right leg extended in a straight line and resting on left leg, flexed, in
the attitude of Gea-Tellus, fulfilled, recumbent, big with seed.
Narrator: reclined laterally, left, with right and left legs flexed, the

[460]

indexfinger and thumb of the right hand resting on the bridge of the nose, in the attitude depicted on a snapshot photograph made by Percy Apjohn, the childman weary, the manchild in the womb.

    Womb? Weary?
    He rests. He has travelled.

. . . .

    Where?

    ●

Episode 18 – Penelope… wife of Odysseus, faithfully resisted all suitors awaiting his return. She delayed proposal stating she must complete weaving a burial shroud for Odysseus' father, while she unravels her weaving at night. Penelope does not recognize her husband after his long absence. Upon his describing the unique construction of their bed, known only to each other, she becomes convinced Odysseus is her husband. ~ From their bed with Bloom aside her, Molly speaks her mind on myriad aspects of her life, including would-be suitors. She references the sweater knit for deceased Rudy.

Bloom's wife Molly tells her story in this disjointed, self-contradictory stream of consciousness in only eight infinitely long sentences with no punctuation, bookended by the key word *yes*. Molly examines herself, her life. Reminisces on her suitors, on her children. She exhibits her feminine traits and her jealousy in disparaging other women. She expresses appreciation for Leopold, even as she directs criticism of him and Boylan for their deception, disrespect, and sexual habits. She yearns for sexual adventures and a "bit of fun." She affirms her love for her husband Leopold Bloom.

THEMES
Eight, the horizontal 8, symbol of infinity, the infinite variety of womanhood. Physical aspects of female personality. "Four cardinal points … the female breast, arse, womb and cunt." What Irish women were thinking. The loveless Irish marriage. Acceptance of oneself. Reconciliation. Symbols of rebirth. The power of love.

YES BECAUSE HE NEVER DID A THING LIKE THAT BEFORE AS ASK to get his breakfast in bed with a couple of eggs since the *City Arms* hotel when he used to be pretending to be laid up with a sick voice doing his highness to make himself interesting to that old faggot Mrs Riordan that he thought he had a great leg of and she never left us a farthing all for masses for herself and her soul greatest miser ever was actually afraid to lay out 4d for her methylated spirit telling me all her ailments she had too much old chat in her about politics and earthquakes and the end of the world let us have a bit of fun first God help the world if all the women were her sort down on bathingsuits and lownecks of course nobody wanted her to wear I suppose she was pious because no man would look at her twice I hope Ill never be like her a wonder she didn't want us to cover our faces but she was a welleducated woman certainly and her gabby talk about Mr Riordan here and Mr Riordan there I suppose he was glad to get shut of her and her dog smelling my fur and always edging to get up under my petticoats especially then still I like that in him polite to old women like that and waiters and beggars too hes not proud out of nothing . . . . I'm sure by his appetite anyway love its not or hed be off his feed thinking of her so either it was one of those night women if it was down there he was really and the hotel story he made up a pack of lies to hide it planning it Hynes kept me who did I meet ah yes I met do you remember Menton and who else who

[462]

let me see that big babbyface I saw him and he not long married
flirting with a young girl at Pooles Myriorama and turned my back
on him when he slinked out looking quite conscious what harm but
he had the impudence to make up to me one time well done to him
mouth almighty and his boiled eyes of all the big stupoes I ever met
and that called a solicitor only I hate having a long wrangle in bed or
else if its not that its some little bitch or other he got in with
somewhere or picked up on the sly if they only knew him as I do yes
because the day before yesterday he was scribbling something a
letter when I came into the front room for the matches to show him
Dignams death in the paper as if something told me and he covered it
up with the blottingpaper pretending to be thinking about business so
very probably that was it to somebody who thinks she has a softy in
him because all men get a bit like that at his age especially getting on
to forty he is now so as to wheedle any money she can out of him no
fool like an old fool and then the usual kissing my bottom was to
hide it not that I care two straws who he does it with or knew before
that way though Id like to find out so long as I dont have the two of
them under my nose all the time like that slut Mary we had in
Ontario terrace… 1 woman is not enough for them it was all his fault
of course ruining servants then proposing that she could eat at our
table on Christmas if you please O no thank you not in my house
stealing my potatoes and the oysters and the oysters 2/6 per doz
going out to see her aunt if you please common robbery so it was but
I was sure he had something on with that one it takes me to find out a
thing like that he said you have no proof it was her proof O yes… I
gave it to him anyhow either she or me leaves the house I couldn't
even touch him if I thought he was with a dirty barefaced liar and
sloven like that one denying it up to my face and singing about the
place in the W C too because she knew she was too well off yes
because he couldn't possibly do without it that long so he must do it
somewhere and the last time he came on my bottom when was it the
night Boylan gave my hand a great squeeze going along by the Tolka
in my hand there steals another I just pressed the back of his like that
with my thumb to squeeze back singing the young May Moon she
beaming love because he has an idea about him and me hes not such
a fool he said Im dining out and going to the Gaiety though Im not
going to give him the satisfaction in any case God knows hes change
in a way not to be always and ever wearing the same old hat unless I
paid some nicelooking boy to do it since I cant do it myself a young

[463]

boy would like me Id confuse him a little alone with him if we were
Id let him see my garters the new ones and make him turn red
looking at him seduce him I know what boys feel with that down on
their cheek doing that frigging drawing out the thing by the hour
question and answer would you do this that and the other with the
coalman yes with a bishop yes I would because I told him about
some Dean or Bishop was sitting beside me in the jews Temples
gardens when I was knitting that woollen thing a stranger to Dublin
what place was it and so on about the monuments and he tired me
out with statues encouraging him making him worse than he is who
is in your mind now tell me who are you thinking of who is it tell me
his name who tell me who the German Emperor is it yes imagine I'm
him think of him can you feel him trying to make a whore of me
what he never will he ought to give it up now at this age of his life
simply ruination for any woman and no satisfaction in it pretending
to like it till he comes and then finish it off myself anyway and it
makes your lips pale anyhow its done now once and for all with all
the talk of the world about it people make its only the first time after
that its just the ordinary do it and think no more about it why cant
you kiss a man without going and marrying him first you sometimes
love to wildly when you feel that way so nice all over you cant help
yourself I wish some man or other would take me sometime when
hes there and kiss me in his arms theres nothing like a kiss long and
hot down to your soul almost paralyses you then I hate that
confession when I used to go to Father Corrigan he touched me
father and what harm if he did where and I said on the canal bank
like a fool but whereabouts on your person my child on the leg
behind high up was it yes rather high up was it where you sit down
yes O Lord couldnt he say bottom right out and have done with it …
still his eyes were red when his father died theyre lost for a woman
of course must be terrible when a man cries let alone them Id like to
be embraced by one in his vestments and the smell of incense off
him like the pope besides theres no danger with a priest if youre
married hes too careful about himself then give something to H H the
pope for a penance I wonder was he satisfied with me one thing I
didn't like his slapping me behind going away so familiarly in the
hall though I laughed Im not a horse or an ass am I I suppose he was
thinking of his father I wonder is he awake thinking of me or
dreaming am I in it who gave him that flower he said he bought he
smelt of some kind of drink not whisky or stout… he had all he

[464]

could do to keep himself from falling asleep after the last time we took the port and potted meat it had a fine salty taste yes because I felt lovely and tired myself and fell asleep as sound as a top the moment I popped straight into bed till that thunder woke me up as if the world was coming to an end God be merciful to us I thought the heavens were coming down about us to punish when I blessed myself and said a Hail Mary like those awful thunderbolts in Gibraltar and they come and tell you theres no God… hed scoff if he heard because he never goes to church mass or meeting he says your soul you have no soul inside only grey matter because he doesnt know what it is to have one yes when I lit the lamp yes because he must have come 3 or 4 times with that tremendous big red brute of a thing he has I thought the vein or whatever the dickens they call it was going to burst through his nose is not so big after I took off all my things with the blinds down after my hours dressing and perfuming and combing it like iron or some kind of a thick crowbar standing all the time he must have eaten oysters I think a few dozen he was in great singing voice no I never in all my life felt anyone had one the size of that to make you feel full up… supposing I risked having another not off him though still if he was married Im sure hed have a fine strong child but I dont know Poldy has more spunk in him yes thatd be awfully jolly I suppose it was meeting Josie Powell and the funeral and thinking about me and Boylan set him off well he can think what he likes now if thatll do him any good… that was why we had the standup row over politics he began it not me when he said Our Lord being a carpenter at last he made me cry of course a woman is so sensitive about everything I was fuming with myself after for giving in only for I knew he was gone on me and the first socialist he said He was he annoyed me so much I couldnt put him into a temper still he knows a lot of mixed up things especially about the body and the insides… he used to be a bit on the jealous side whenever he asked who are you going to and I said over to Floey and he made me the present of lord Byrons poems and the three pairs of gloves so that finished that I could quite easily get him to make it up any time I know how Id even supposing he got in with her again and was going out to see her somewhere… possible the women are always egging on to that putting it on thick when hes there they know by his sly eye blinking a bit putting on the indifferent when they come out with something the kind he is what spoils him I dont wonder in the least because he was very handsome at that time trying

[465]

to look like lord Byron I said I liked though he was too beautiful for a man and he was a little before we got engaged afterwards though she didnt like it so much the day I was in fits of laughing with the giggles I couldnt stop about all my hairpins falling one after another with the mass of hair I had youre always in great humour she said yes because it grigged her because she knew what it meant because I used to tell her a good bit of what went on between us not all but just enough to make her mouth water but that wasnt my fault she didnt darken the door much after we were married… I saw on the moment she was edging to draw down a conversation about husbands and talk about him to run him down what was it she told me O yes that sometimes he used to go to bed with his muddy boots on when the maggot takes him just imagine having to get into bed with a thing like that that might murder you any moment what a man well its not the one way everyone goes mad Poldy anyway whatever he does always wipes his feet on the mat when he comes in wet or shine and always blacks his own boots too and he always takes off his hat when he come up in the street like that and now hes going about in his slippers…

theyre all so different Boylan talking about the shape of my foot he noticed at once even before he was introduced when I was in the D B C with Poldy laughing and trying to listen I was waggling my foot we both ordered 2 teas and plain bread and butter I saw him looking with his two old maids of sisters when I stood up and asked the girl where it was what do I care with it dropping out of me and that black closed breeches he made me buy take you half an hour to let them down wetting all myself always with some brandnew fad every other week such a long one I did I forgot my suede gloves on the seat behind that I never got after some robber of a woman and he wanted me to put it in the Irish Times lost in the ladies lavatory D B C Dame street finder return to Mrs Marion Bloom and I saw his eyes on my feet going out through the turning door he was looking when I looked back and I went there for tea 2 days after in the hope but he wasnt now how did that excite him because I was crossing them when we were in the other room first he meant the shoes that are too tight to walk in my hand is nice like that if I only had a ring with the stone for my month a nice aquamarine Ill stick him for one and a gold bracelet I dont like my foot so much still I made him spend once with my foot the night after Goodwins botch up of a concert so cold and windy it was well we had that rum in the house to mull and

[466]

the fire wasnt black out when he asked to take off my stockings lying on the hearthrug in Lombard street well and another time it was my muddy boots hed like me to walk in all the horses dung I could find but of course hes not natural like the rest of the world… he thinks nothing can happen without him knowing he hadnt an idea about my mother till we were engaged otherwise hed never have got me so cheap as he did he was 10 times worse himself anyhow begging me to give him a tiny bit cut off my drawers that was the evening coming along Kenilworth square he kissed me in the eye of my glove and I had to take it off asking me questions is it permitted to inquire the shape of my bedroom so I let him keep it as if I forgot it to think of me when I saw him slip it into his pocket of course hes mad on the subject of drawers thats plain to be seen always skeezing at those brazenfaced things on the bicycles with their skirts blowing up to their navels even when Milly and I were out with him at the open air fete that one in the cream muslin standing right against the sun so he could see every atom she had on when he saw me however standing at the corner of the Harolds cross road with a new raincoat on him with the muffler in the Zingari colours to show off his complexion and the brown hat looking slyboots as usual what was he doing there where hed no business they can go and get whatever they like from anything at all with a skirt on it and were not to ask any questions but they want to know where you were are you going I could feel him coming along skulking after me his eyes on my neck he had been keeping away from the house he felt it was getting too warm for him so I half turned and stopped then he pestered me to say yes till I took off my glove… he did look a big fool dripping in the rain splendid set of teeth he had made me hungry to look at them and beseeched of me to lift the petticoat I had on… I lifted them a bit and touched his trousers outside the way I used to Gardiner after with my ring hand to keep him from doing worse where it was too public I was dying to find out was he circumcised he was shaking like a jelly all over they want to do everything too quick take all the pleasure out of it and father waiting all the time for his dinner he told me to say I left my purse in the butchers and had to go back for it what a Deceiver then he wrote me that letter with all those words in it… then writing a letter every morning sometimes twice a day I liked the way he made love then he knew the way to take a woman when he sent me the 8 big poppies because mine was the 8th then I wrote the night he kissed my heart at Dolphins barn I couldnt describe it simply it

makes you feel like nothing on earth but he never knew how to
embrace well…I never know the time even that watch he gave me
never seems to go properly Id want to get it looked after when I
threw the penny to that lame sailor for England home and beauty
when I was whistling theres a charming girl I love and I hadnt even
put on my clean shift or powdered myself or a thing then this day
week were to go to Belfast just as well he had to go to Ennis his
fathers anniversary the 27th it wouldnt be pleasant if he did suppose
our rooms at the hotel were beside each other and any fooling went
on in the new bed I couldnt tell him to stop and not bother me with
him in the next room or perhaps some protestant clergyman with a
cough knocking on the wall then he wouldnt believe next day we
didnt do something its all very well a husband but you cant fool a
lover after me telling him we never did anything of course he didn't
believe me no its better hes going where he is… O I love jaunting in
a train or a car with lovely cushions I wonder will he take a 1st class
for me he might want to do it in the train by tipping the guard well O
I suppose therell be the usual idiots of men gaping at us with their
eyes as stupid as ever they can possibly be that was an exceptional
man that common workman that left us alone in the carriage that day
going to Howth…suppose I never came back what would they say
eloped with him that gets you on on the stage the last concert I sang
at where its over a year ago when was it St Teresas hall Clarendon St
little chits of missies they have now signing Kathleen Kearney and
her like on account of father being in the army and my singing the
absentminded beggar and wearing a brooch for lord Roberts when I
had the map of it all and Poldy not Irish enough was it him managed
it this time I wouldnt put it past him up to that till the jesuits found
out he was a freemason thumping the piano lead Thou me on copied
from some old opera yes and he was going about with some of them
Sinn Fein lately or whatever they call themselves talking his usual
trash and nonsense… O let them all go and smother themselves for
the fat lot I care he has plenty of money and hes not a marrying man
so somebody better get it out of him if I could find out whether he
likes me I looked a bit washy of course when I looked close in the
handglass powdering a mirror never gives you the expression besides
scrooching down on me like that all the time with his big hipbones
hes heavy to with his hairy chest for this heat always having to lie
down for them better for him put it into me from behind the way Mrs
Mastiansky told me her husband made her like the dogs do it and

[468]

stick out her tongue as far as ever she could and he so quiet and mild
with his tingating either can you ever be up to men the way it takes
them lovely stuff in that blue suit he had on and stylish tie and socks
with the skyblue silk things on them hes certainly welloff I know by
the cut his clothes have and his heavy watch but he was like a perfect
devil for a few minutes after he came back with the stop press tearing
up the tickets and swearing blazes because he lost 20 quid he said he
lost over that outsider that won and half he put on for me on account
of Lenehans tip cursing him to the lowest pits that sponger he was
making free with me after the Glencree dinner coming back that long
joult over the featherbed mountain after the lord Mayor looking at
me with his dirty eyes Val Dillon that big heathen I first noticed him
at dessert when I was cracking the nuts with my teeth I wished I
could have picked every morsel of that chicken out of my fingers it
was so tasty and browned and as tendered as anything… my belly is
a bit too big Ill have to knock off the stout at dinner or am I getting
too fond of it the last they sent from ORourkes was as flat as a
pancake he makes his money easy Larry they call him the old mangy
parcel he sent at Xmas a cottage cake and a bottle of hogwash he
tried to palm off as claret that he couldn't get anyone to drink God
spare his spit for fear hed die of the drouth or I must do a few
breathing exercises I wonder is that antifat any good might overdo it
thin ones are not so much the fashion now… Ive no clothes at all the
brown costume and the skirt and jacket and the one at the cleaners 3
whats that for any woman cutting up this old hat and patching up the
other the men wont look at you and women try to walk on you
because they know youve no man then with all the things getting
dearer every day for the 4 years more I have of life up to 35 no Im
what am I at all Ill be 33 in September will I what O well look at that
Mrs. Galbraith shes much older than me I saw her when I was out
last week her beautys on the wane she was a lovely woman
magnificent head of hair on her down to her waist tossing it back like
that like Kitty OShea in Grantham street 1st thing I did every
morning to look across see her combing it as if she loved it and was
full of it pity I only got to know her the day before we left… theres
nothing for a woman in that all invention made up about he drinking
the champagne out of her slipper after the ball was over like the
infant Jesus in the crib at Inchicore in the Blessed Virgins arms sure
no woman could have a child that big taken out of her and I thought
first it came out of her side because how could she go to the chamber

when she wanted to and she is a rich lady of course she felt honoured
H. R. H. he was in Gibraltar the year I was born I bet he found lilies
there too where he planted the tree he planted more than that in his
time he might have planted me too if hed come a bit sooner then I
wouldnt be here as I am… I hate those rich shops get on your nerves
nothing kills me altogether only he thinks he knows a great lot about
a womans dress and cooking mathering everything he can scour off
the shelves into it if I went by his advices every blessed hat I put on
does that suit me yes take that thats alright the one like the wedding
cake standing up miles off my head he said suited me… yes he was
awfully stiff and no wonder he changed the second time he looked
Poldy pigheaded as usual like the soup but I could see him looking
very hard at my chest when he stood up to open the door for me it
was nice of him to show me out in any case Im extremely sorry Mrs
Bloom believe me with making it too marked the first time after him
being insulted and me being supposed to be his wife I just half
smiled I know my chest was out that way at the door when he said
Im extremely sorry and Im sure you were…

    yes I think he made them a bit firmer sucking them like that
so long he made me thirsty titties he calls them I had to laugh yes
this one anyhow stiff the nipple gets for the least thing Ill get him to
keep that up and Ill take those eggs beaten up with marsala fatten
them out for him what are all those veins and things curious the way
its made 2 the same in case of twins theyre supposed to represent
beauty place up there like those statues in the museum one of them
pretending to hide it with her hand are they so beautiful of course
compared with what a man looks like with his two bags full and his
other thing hanging down out of him or sticking up at you like a
hatrack no wonder they hide it with a cabbageleaf the woman is
beauty of course thats admitted when he said I could pose for a
picture naked to some rich fellow in Holles street when he lost the
job in Helys and I was selling the clothes and strumming in the
coffee palace would I be like that bath of the nymph with my hair
down yes only shes younger or Im a little like that dirty bitch in that
Spanish photo he has the nymphs use they go about like that… theres
the mark of his teeth still where he tried to bite the nipple I had to
scream out arent they fearful trying to hurt you I had a great breast of
milk with Milly enough for two what was the reason of that he said I
could have got a pound a week as a wet nurse all swelled out the
morning that delicate looking student that stopped in No 28 with the

[470]

Citrons Penrose nearly caught me washing through the window only
for I snapped up the towel to my face that was his studenting hurt me
they used to weaning her till he got doctor Brady to give me the
Belladonna prescription I had to get him to suck them they were so
hard he said it was sweeter and thicker than cows then he wanted to
milk me into the tea well hes beyond everything I declare somebody
ought to put him in the budget if I only could remember the one half
of the things and write a book out of it the works of Master Poldy yes
and its so much smoother the skin much and hour he was at them Im
sure by the clock like some kind of a big infant I had at me they want
everything in their mouth all the pleasure those men get out of a
woman I can feel his mouth O Lord I must stretch myself I wished
he was here or somebody to let myself go with and come again like
that I feel all fire inside me or if I could dream it when he made me
spend the 2nd time tickling me behind with his finger I was coming
for about 5 minutes with my legs round him I had to hug him after O
Lord I wanted to shout out all sorts of things fuck or shit or anything
at all only not to look ugly or those lines from the strain who knows
the way hed take it you want to feel your way with a man theyre not
all like him thank God some of them want you to be so nice about it I
noticed the contrast he does it and doesnt talk I gave my eyes that
look with my hair a bit loose from the tumbling and my tongue
between my lips up to him the savage brute Thursday Friday one
Saturday two Sunday three O Lord I cant wait till Monday…

frseeeeeeeefronnnng train somewhere whistling the strength
those engines have in them like big giants and the water rolling all
over and out of them all sides like the end of Loves old sweet
sonnnng the poor men that have to be out all the night from their
wives and families in those roasting engines stifling it was today… I
thought it was going to get like Gibraltar my goodness the heat there
before the levanter came on black night… I think dont you will
always think of the lovely teas we had together scrumptious currant
scones and raspberry wafers I adore… its like all through a mist
makes you feel so old I made the scones of course I had everything
all to myself then a girl Hester we used to compare our hair mine
was thicker than hers she showed me how to settle it at the back
when I put it up and whats this else how to make a knot on a thread
with the one hand we were like cousin what age was I then the night
of the storm I slept in her bed she had her arms round me then we
were fighting in the morning with the pillow what fun he was

[471]

watching me whenever he got an opportunity at the band on the Alameda esplanade when I was with father and Captain Grove I looked up at the church first and then at the windows then down and our eyes me I felt something go through me like all needles my eyes were dancing I remember after when I looked at myself in the glass hardly recognised myself the change I had a splendid skin from the sun and the excitement like a rose I didn't get a wink of sleep it wouldnt have been nice on account of her but I could have stopped it in time she gave me the Moonstone to read… I dont like books with a Molly in them like that one he brought me about the one from Flanders a whore always shoplifting anything she could cloth and stuff and yards of it this blanket is too heavy on me thats better I havent even one decent nightdress this thing gets all rolled up under me besides him and his fooling thats better I used to be weltering then in the heat my shift drenched with the sweat stuck in the cheeks of my bottom on the chair when I stood up they were so fattish and firm when I got up on the sofa cushions to see with my clothes up and the bugs tons of them at night and the mosquito nets I couldnt read a line Lord how long ago it seems centuries… where does their great intelligence come in Id like to know grey matter they have it all in their tail if you ask me those country gougers up in the City Arms intelligence they had a damn sight less than the bulls and cows they were selling the meat and the coalmans bell that noisy bugger trying to swindle me with the wrong bill he took out of his hat what a pair of paws and post and pans and kettle to mend any broken bottles for a poor man today and no visitors or post ever except his cheques or some advertisement like that wonderworker they sent him addressed dear Madam only his letter and the card from Milly this morning see she wrote a letter to him who did I get the last letter from O Mrs Dwenn now whatever possessed her to write after so many years to know the recipe I had for pisto madrileno Floey Dillon since she wrote to say she was married to a very rich architect if Im to believe all I hear with a villa and eight rooms her father was an awfully nice man he was near seventy always good humour… O thanks be to great God I got somebody to give me what I badly wanted to put some heart up into me youve no chances at all in this place like you used long ago I wish somebody would write me a loveletter his wasnt much and I told him he could write what he liked yours ever Hugh Boylan in Old Madrid silly women believe love is sighing I am dying still if he wrote it I suppose thered be some truth in it true or

[472]

no it fills up your whole day and life always something to think
about every moment and see it all around you like a new world I
could write the answer in bed to let him imagine me short just a few
words not those long crossed letters Atty Dillon used to write to the
fellow that was something in the four courts that jilted her after out
of the ladies letterwriter when I told her to say a few simple words he
could twist how he liked not acting with precipit precipitancy with
equal candour the greatest earthly happiness answer to a gentlemans
proposal affirmatively my goodness theres nothing else its all very
fine for them but as for being a woman as soon as youre old they
might as well throw you out in the bottom of the ash pit.

      Mulveys was the first when I was in bed that morning and
Mrs Rubio brought it in with the coffee she stood there standing
when I asked her to hand me and I pointing at them I couldnt think of
the word a hairpin to open it with… for his Majestad an admirer he
signed it I near jumped out of my skin I wanted to pick him up when
I saw him following me along the Calle Real in the shop window
then he tipped me just in passing I never thought hed write making
an appointment I had it inside my petticoat bodice all day reading it
up in every hole and corner while father was up at the drill
instructing to find out by the handwriting or the language of stamps
singing I remember shall I wear a white rose and I wanted to put on
the old stupid clock to near the time he was the first man kissed me
under the Moorish wall my sweetheart when a boy it never entered
my head what kissing meant till he put his tongue in my mouth his
mouth was sweetlike young I put my knee up to him a few times to
learn the way what did I tell him I was engaged for fun to the son of
a Spanish nobleman named Don Miguel de la Flora and he believed
that I was to be married to him in 3 years time theres many a true
word spoken in jest there is a flower that bloometh a few things I
told him true about myself just for him to be imagining the Spanish
girls he didnt like I suppose one of the wouldnt have him I got him
excited he crushed all the flowers on my bosom he brought me he
couldnt count the pesetas and the perragordas till I taught him
Cappoquin he came from he said on the blackwater but it was too
short then the day before he left May yes it was May when the infant
king of Spain was born Im always like that in the spring Id like a
new fellow every year up on the tiptop under the rockgun near
OHaras tower… you could do what you liked lie there for ever he
caressed them outside they love doing that its the roundness there I

was leaning over him with my white ricestraw hat to take the newness out of it the left side of my face the best my blouse open for his last day transparent kind of a shirt he had I could see his chest pink he wanted to touch mine with his for a moment but I wouldnt let him he was awfully put out first for fear you never know consumption or leave me with a child embarazada that old servant Ines told me that one drop even if it got into you at all after I tried with the Banana but I was afraid it might break and get lost up in me somewhere yes because they once took something down out of a woman that was up there for years covered with limesalts theyre all mad to get in there where theyd come out of you think they could never get far enough up and then theyre done with you in a way till the next time yes because theres a wonderful feeling there all the time so tender how did we finish it off yes O yes I pulled him off into my handkerchief pretending not to be too excited but I opened my legs I wouldnt let him touch me inside my petticoat I had a skirt opening up the side I tortured the life out of him first tickling him I loved rousing that dog in the hotel rrrsssst awokwokawok his eyes shut and a bird flying below us he was shy all the same I liked him like that morning I made him blush a little when I got over him that way when I unbuttoned him and took his out and drew back the skin it had a kind of eye in it theyre all Buttons men down the middle on the wrong side of them Molly darling he called me what was his name Jack Joe Harry Mulvey was it yes I think a lieutenant he was rather fair he had a laughing kind of a voice so I went around to the whatyoucallit everything was whatyoucallit moustache had he he said hed come back Lord its just like yesterday to me and if I was married hed do it to me and Id promised him faithfully Id let him block me now flying perhaps hes dead or killed or a Captain or admiral its nearly 20 years… the same way that we went over middle hill round by the old guardhouse and the jews burial place pretending to read out the Hebrew on them I wanted to fire his pistol he said he hadnt one he didnt know what to make of me with his peaked cap on that he always wore crooked as often as I settled it straight H M S Calypso swinging my hat that old Bishop that spoke off the altar his long preach about womans higher functions about girls now riding the bicycle and wearing peak caps and the new woman bloomers God send him sense and me more money I suppose theyre called after him I never thought that would be my name Bloom when I used to write it in print to see how it looked on a visiting card or

[474]

practising for the butcher and oblige M Bloom youre looking
blooming Josie used to say after I married him well its better than
Breen or Briggs does brig or those awful names with bottom in them
Mrs Ramsbottom or some other kind of a bottom Mulvey I wouldnt
go mad about either or suppose I divorced him Mrs Boylan my
mother whoever she was might have given me a nicer name the Lord
knows… I was thinking of him on the sea all the time after at mass
when my petticoat began to slip down at the elevation weeks and
weeks I kept the handkerchief under my pillow for the smell of him
there was no decent perfume to be got in that Gibraltar only that
cheap peau despagne that faded and left a stink on you more than
anything else I wanted to give him a memento he gave me that
clumsy Claddagh ring for luck that I gave Gardiner going to South
Africa where those Boers killed him with their war and fever but
they were well beaten all the same as if it brought its bad luck with it
like an opal or pearl must have been pure 16 carat gold because it
was very heavy I can see his face clean shaven
Frseeeeeeeeeeeeeeeeeeeefrong that train again weeping tone once in
the dear deaead days beyond recall close my eyes breath my lips
forward kiss sad look eyes open piano ere oer the world the mists
began I hate that istsbeg comes loves sweet ssooooooong Ill let that
out full when I get in front of the footlights again Kathleen Kearney
and her lot of squealers Miss This Miss That Miss Theother lot of
sparrowfarts skitting around talking about politics they know as
much about as my backside anything in the world to make
themselves someway interesting Irish homemade beauties soldiers
daughter am I ay and whose are you bootmakers and publicans I beg
your pardon coach I thought you were a wheelbarrow theyd die
down dead off their feet if ever they got a chance of walking down
the Alameda on an officers arm like me on the bandnight my eyes
flash my bust that they havent passion God help their poor head I
knew more about men and life when I was 15 than theyll all know at
50 they dont know how to sing a song like that Gardner said no man
could look at my mouth and teeth smiling like that and not think of it
I was afraid he mightnt like my accent first he so English all father
left me in spite of his stamps Ive my mothers eyes and figure anyhow
he always said theyre so snotty about themselves some of those cads
he wasnt a bit like that he was dead gone on my lips let them get a
husband first that fits to be looked at and a daughter like mine or see
if they can excite a swell with money that can pick and choose

[475]

whoever he wants like Boylan to do it 4 or 5 times locked in each others arms or the voice either I could have been a prima donna only I married him comes looooves old deep down chin back not too much make it double… my hole is itching me always when I think of him I feel I want to I feel some wind in me better go easy not wake him have him at it again slobbering after washing every bit of myself back belly and sides if we had even a bath itself or my own room anyway I wish hed sleep in some bed by himself with his cold feet on me give us room even to let a fart God or do the least thing better yes hold them like that a bit on my side piano quietly sweeeee theres that train far away pianissimo eeeeeeee one more song

          that was a relief wherever you be let your wind go free who knows if that pork chop I took with my cup of tea after was quite good with the heat I couldn't smell anything off it… Goodbye to my sleep for this night anyhow I hope hes not going to get in with those medicals leading him astray to imagine hes young again coming in at 4 in the morning it must be if not more still he had the manners not to wake me what do they find to gabber about all night squandering money and getting drunker and drunker couldnt they drink water then he starts giving us his orders for eggs and tea Findon haddy and hot buttered toast… Whit Monday is a cursed day too no wonder that bee bit him better the seaside but Id never again in this life get into a boat with him after him at Bray telling the boatmen he knew how to row if anyone asked could he ride the steeplechase for the gold cup hed say yes then it came on to get rough the old thing crookeding about and the weight all down my side telling me to pull the right reins now pull the left and the tide all swamping in floods in through the bottom and his oar slipping out of the stirrup its a mercy we werent all drowned he can swim of course me not theres no danger whatsoever keep yourself calm in his flannel trousers Id like to have tattered them down off him before all the people and give him what that one calls flagellate till he was black and blue do him all the good in the world… I wonder what kind is that book he brought me Sweets of Sin by a gentleman of fashion some other Mr de Kock I suppose the people gave him that nickname going about with his tube from one woman to another I couldnt even change my new white shoes all ruined with the saltwater and the hat I had with that feather all blowy and tossed on me how annoying and provoking because the smell of the sea excited me… he was going to make on the first floor drawingroom with a brassplate or Blooms private hotel

[476]

he suggested go and ruin himself altogether the way his father did down in Ennis like all the things he told father he was going to do and me but I saw through him telling me all the lovely places we could go for the honeymoon Venice by moonlight with the gondolas and the lake of Como he had a picture cut out of some paper of and mandolines and lanterns O how nice I said whatever I liked he was going to do immediately if not sooner will you be my man will you carry my can he ought to get a leather medal with a putty rim for all the plans he invents then leaving us here all day you never know what old beggar at the door for a crust with his long story might be a tramp and put his foot in the way to prevent me shutting it like that picture of that hardened criminal... not that hed be much use still better than nothing the night I was sure I heard burglars in the kitchen and he went down in his shirt with a candle and a poker as if he was looking for a mouse as white as a sheet frightened out of his wits making as much noise as he possibly could for the burglars benefit there isnt much to steal indeed the Lord knows still its the feeling especially now with Milly away such an idea for him to send the girl down there to learn to take photographs on account of his grandfather instead of sending her to Skerrys academy where shed have to learn not like me getting all at school only hed do a thing like that all the same on account of me and Boylan thats why he did it Im certain the way he plots and plans everything out... he cant say I pretend things can he Im too honest as a matter of fact I suppose he thinks Im finished out and laid on the shelf well Im not no nor anything like it well see well see now shes well on for flirting too with Tom Devans two sons imitating me whistling with those romps of Murray girls calling for her can Milly come out please shes in great demand to pick what they can out of her round in Nelson street riding Harry Devans bicycle at night its as well he sent her where she is she was just getting out of bounds wanting to go on the skatingrink and smoking their cigarettes through their nose I smelt it off her dress... and she didnt even want me to kiss her at the Broadstone going away well I hope shell get someone to dance attendance on her the way I did when she was down with the mumps her glands swollen wheres this and wheres that of course she cant feel anything deep yet I never came properly till I was what 22 or so it went into the wrong place always only the usual girls nonsense and giggling that Conny Connolly writing to her in white ink on black paper sealed with sealingwax though she clapped when the curtain came

down because he looked so handsome then we had Martin Harvey
for breakfast dinner and supper I thought to myself afterwards it
must be real love if a man gives up his life for her that way for
nothing I suppor there are few men like that left its hard to believe in
it though unless it really happened to me the majority of them with
not a particle of love in their natures to find two people like that
nowadays full up of each other that would feel the same way as you
do theyre usually a bit foolish in the head his father must have been a
bit queer to go and poison himself after her still poor old man I
suppose he felt lost always making love to my things too the few old
rags I have wanting to put her hair up at 15 my powder too only ruin
her skin on her shes time enough for that all her life after of couse
shes restless knowing shes pretty with her lips so red a pity they
wont stay that way I was too… she had me that exasperated of
course contradicting I was badtempered too because how was it there
was a weed in the tea or I didnt sleep the night before cheese I ate
was it and I told her over and over again not to leave knives crossed
like that because she has nobody to command her as she said herself
well if he doesnt correct her faith I will that was the last time she
turned on the teartap I was just like that myself they darent order me
about the place its his fault of course having the two of us slaving
here instead of getting in a woman long ago am I ever going to have
a proper servant again of course then shed see him coming…
bringing in his friends to entertain them like the night he walked
home with a dog if you please that might have been mad especially
Simon Dedalus son his father such a criticiser with his glasses up
with his tall hat on him at the cricket match and a great big hole in
his sock one thing laughing at the other and his son that got all those
prizes for whatever he won them in the intermediate imagine
climbing over the railings if anybody saw him that knew us wonder
he didnt tear a big hole in his grand funeral trousers as if the one
nature gave wasn't enough for anybody hawking him down into the
dirty old kitchen now is he right in his head I ask pity it wasn't
washing day my old pair of drawers might have been hanging up too
on the line on exhibition for all hed ever care… every day I get up
theres some new thing on sweet God sweet God well when Im
stretched out dead in my grave I suppose Ill have some peace I want
to get up a minute if Im let wait O Jesus wait yes that thing has come
on me yes now wouldnt that afflict you of course all the poking and
rooting and ploughing he had up in me now what am I to do Friday

[478]

Saturday Sunday wouldnt that pester the soul out of a body unless he likes it some men do God knows theres always something wrong with us 5 days every 3 or 4 weeks usual monthly auction isnt it simply sickening that night it came on me like that the one and only time we were in a box that Michael Gunn gave him to see Mrs Kendal and her husband at the Gaiety… I smiled the best I could all in a swamp leaning forward as if I was interested having to sit it out then to the last tag I wont forget that wife of Scarli in a hurry supposed to be a fast play about adultery that idiot in the gallery hissing the woman adulteress he shouted I suppose he went and had a woman in the next lane running round all the back ways after to make up for it I wish he had what I had then hed boo I bet the cat itself is better off than us have we too much blood up in us or what O patience above its pouring out of me like the sea anyhow he didn't make me pregnant as big as he is I dont want to ruin the clean sheets the clean linen I wore brought it on too damn it damn it and they always want to see a stain on the bed to know youre a virgin for them all thats troubling them theyre such fools too you could be a widow or divorced 40 times over a daub of red ink would do or blackberry juice no thats too purply O Jamesy let me up out of this pooh sweets of sin whoever suggested that business for women what between clothes and cooking and children this damned old bed too jingling like the dickens I suppose they could hear us away over the other side of the park till I suggested to put the quilt on the floor with the pillow under my bottom I wonder is it nicer in the day I think it is easy I think Ill cut all this hair off me there scalding me I might look like a young girl wouldnt he get the great suckin the next time he turned up my clothes on me Id give anything to see his face wheres the chamber gone easy Ive a holy horror of its breaking under me after that old commode I wonder was I too heavy sitting on his knee I made him sit on the easychair purposely when I took off only my blouse and skirt first in the other room he was so busy where he oughtnt to be he never felt me I hope my breath was sweet after those kissing comfits easy God I remember one time I could scout it out straight whistling like a man almost easy O Lord how noisy I hope theyre bubbles on it for a wad of money from some fellow Ill have to perfume it in the morning dont forget I bet he never saw a better pair of thighs than that look how white they are the smoothest place is right there between this bit here how soft like a peach easy God I wouldnt mind being a man and get up on a lovely woman O

[479]

Lord what a row youre making like the jersey lily easy O how the waters come down at Lahore

who knows is there anything the matter with my insides or have I something growing in me getting that thing like that every week when was it last I Whit Monday yes its only about 3 weeks I ought to go to the doctor only it would be like before I married him when I had that white thing coming from me and Floey made me go to that dry old stick Dr Collins for womens diseases on Pembroke road your vagina he called it… O anything no matter how except an idiot he was clever enough to spot that of course that was all thinking of him and his mad crazy letters my Precious one everything connected with your glorious Body everything underlined that comes from it is a thing of beauty and of joy for ever something he got out of some nonsensical book that he had me always at myself 4 or 5 times a day sometimes and I said I hadnt are you sure O yes I said I am quite sure in a way that shut him up I knew what was coming next only natural weakness it was he excited me I dont know how the first night ever we met when I was living in Rehoboth terrace we stood staring at one another for about 10 minutes as if we met somewhere I suppose on account of my being jewess looking after my mother he used to amuse me the things he said with the half sloothering smile on him and all the Doyles said he was going to stand for a member of Parliament O wasnt I the born fool to believe all his blathers about home rule and the land league sending me that long strool of a song out of the Huguenots to sing in French to be more classy O beau pays de la Touraine… O I laughed myself sick at him that day Id better not make an all night sitting on this affair they ought to make chambers a natural size so that a woman could sit on it properly he kneels down to do it I suppose there isnt in all creation another man with the habits he has look at the way hes sleeping at the foot of the bed how can he without a hard bolster its well he doesnt kick or he might knock out all my teeth breathing with his hand on his nose like that Indian god he took me to show one wet Sunday in the museum in Kildare street all yellow in a pinafore lying on his side on his hand with his ten toes sticking out that he said was a bigger religion than the jews and Our Lords both put together all over Asia imitating him as hes always imitating everybody I suppose he used to sleep at the foot of the bed too with his big square feet up in his wifes mouth damn this stinking thing anyway wheres this those napkins are ah yes I know I hope the old press doesnt creak ah

[480]

I knew it would hes sleeping hard had a good time somewhere still
she must have given him great value for his money of course he has
to pay for it from her O this nuisance of a thing I hope theyll have
something better for us in the other world tying ourselves up God
help us that all right for tonight… wait theres Georges church bells
wait 3 quarters the hour wait 2 oclock well thats a nice hour of the
night for him to be coming home at to anybody climbing down into
the area if anybody saw him Ill knock him off that little habit
tomorrow first Ill look at his shirt to see or Ill see if he has that
French letter still in his pocketbook I suppose he thinks I dont know
deceitful men all their 20 pockets arent enough for their lies then
why should we tell them even if its the truth they dont believe you
then tucked up in bed like those babies in the Aristocrats Masterpiece
he brought me… I suppose Im nothing any more when I wouldnt let
him lick me in Holles street one night man man tyrant as ever for the
one thing he slept on the floor half the night naked the way the jews
used when somebody dies belonged to them and wouldnt eat any
breakfast or speak a word wanting to be petted so I thought I stood
out enough for one time and let him he does it all wrong too thinking
only of his own pleasure his tongue is too flat or I dont know what he
forgets that we then I dont Ill make him do it again if he doesnt mind
himself and lock him down to sleep in the coalcellar with the
blackbeetles I wonder was it her Josie off her head with my castoffs
hes such a born liar too no hed never have the courage with a
married woman thats why he wants me and Boylan though as for her
Denis as she calls him that forlornlooking spectacle you couldnt call
him a husband yes its some little bitch hes got in with even when I
was with him with Milly at the College races that Hornblower with
the childs bonnet on the top on his nob let us into by the back way he
was throwing his sheeps eyes at those two doing skirt duty up and
down I tried to wink at him first no use of course and thats the way
his money goes this is the fruits of Mr Paddy Dignam yes they were
all in great style at the grand funeral in the paper Boylan brought in
if they saw a real officers funeral thatd be something reversed arms
muffled drums the poor horse walking behind in black L Bloom and
Tom Kernan that drunken little barrelly man that bit his tongue off
falling down the mens W C drunk in some place or other and Martin
Cunningham and the two Dedaluses and Fanny McCoys husband…
theyre a nice lot all of them well theyre not going to get my husband
again into their clutches if I can help it making fun of him then

[481]

behind his back I know well enough not to squander every penny piece he earns down their gullets and looks after his wife and family goodfornothings poor Paddy Dignam all the same Im sorry in a way for him what are his wife and 5 children going to do unless he was insured comical little teetotum always stuck up in some pub corner and her or her son waiting Bill Bailey wont you please come home… and Simon Dedalus too he was always turning up half screwed singing the second verse first the old love is the new was one of his so sweetly sang the maiden on the hawthorn bough he was always on for flirtyfying too… hes a widower now I wonder what sort is his son he says hes an author and going to be a university professor of Italian and Im to take lessons what is he driving at now showing him my photo its not good of me I ought to have got it taken in drapery that never looks out of fashion still I look young it it I wonder he didnt make him a present of it altogether and me too after all why not I saw him driving down to Kingsbridge station with his father and mother I was in mourning that 11 years ago now yes hed be 11 though what was the good in going to into mourning for what was neither one thing nor the other of course he insisted hed go into mourning for the cat I suppose hes a man now by this time he was an innocent boy then and a darling little fellow in his lord Fauntleroy suit and curly hair like a prince on the stage when I saw him at Mat Dillons he liked me too I remember they all do wait by God yes wait yes hold on he was on the cards this morning when I laid out the deck union with a younger stranger neither dark nor fair you met before I thought it meant him but hes no chicken nor a stranger either besides my face was turned the other way what was the 7th card after that the 10 of spades for a Journey by land then there was a letter on its way and scandals too the 3 queens and the 8 of diamonds for a rise in society yes wait it all came out and 2 red 8s for new garments look at that and didnt I dream something too yes there was something about poetry in it I hope he hasnt long greasy hair hanging into his eyes or standing up like a red Indian what do they go about like that for only getting themselves and their poetry laughed at I always liked poetry when I was a girl first I thought he was a poet like Byron and not an ounce of it in his composition I thought he was quite different I wonder is he too young hes about wait 88 I was married 88 Milly is 15 yesterday 89 what what age was he then at Dillons 5 or 6 about 88 I suppose hes 20 or more Im not too old for him if hes 23 or 24 I hope hes not that stuck up university student

[482]

sort no otherwise he wouldnt go sitting down in the old kitchen with him taking Eppss cocoa and taking of course he pretended to understand it all probably he told him he was out of Trinity college hes very young to be a professor I hope hes not a professor like Goodwin was he was a patent professor of John Jameson they all write about some woman in their poetry well I suppose he wont find many like me… the Lord knows to have an intelligent person to talk to about yourself not always listening to him and Billy Prescotts and Keyess ad and Tom the Devils ad then if anything goes wrong in their business we have to suffer Im sure hes very distinguished Id like to meet a man like that… I often felt I wanted to kiss him all over also his lovely cock there so simply I wouldnt mind taking him in my mouth if nobody was looking as if it was asking you to suck it so clean and white he looked with his boyish face I would too in ½ a minute even if some of it went down what its only like gruel or the dew theres no danger besides hed be so clean compared with those pigs of men… O but then what am I going to do about him though

no thats no way for him has he no manners nor no refinement nor no nothing in his nature slapping us behind like that on my bottom because I didn't call him Hugh the ignoramus that doesnt know poetry from a cabbage thats what you get for not keeping them in their proper place pulling off his shoes and trousers there on the chair before me so barefaced without even asking permission and standing out that vulgar way in the half of a shirt they wear to be admired like a priest or a butcher or those old hypocrites in the time of Julius Caesar of course hes right enough in his way to pass the time as a joke sure you might as well be in bed with what with a lion God Im sure he have something better to say for himself plump and tempting in my short petticoat he couldnt resist they excite myself sometimes its well for men all the amount of pleasure they get off a womans body were so round and white for them always I wished I was one myself for a change just to try with that thing they have swelling upon you so hard and at the same time so soft when you touch it… what else were we given all those desires for Id like to know I cant help it if Im young still can I its a wonder Im not an old shrivelled hag before my time living with him so cold never embracing me except sometimes when hes asleep the wrong end of me not knowing I suppose who he has any man thatd kiss a womans bottom Id throw my hat at him after that hed kiss anything unnatural where we havent 1 atom of any kind of expression in us all of us the same 2 lumps of lard before ever I do that to a man pfooh the dirty brutes the mere thought is enough I kiss the feet of you senorita theres some sense in that didnt he kiss our halldoor yes he did what a madman nobody understands his cracked ideas but me still of course a woman wants to be embraced 20 times a day almost to make her look young no matter by who so long as to be in love or loved by somebody if the fellow you want isnt there sometimes by the Lord God I was thinking would I go around by the quays there some dark evening where nobodyd know me and pick up a sailor off the sea thatd be hot on for it and not care a pin whose I was only to do it off up in a gate somethwer or one of those wildlooking gipsies in Rathfarnham… only I suppose the half of those sailors are rotten again with disease O move over your big carcass out of that for the love of Mike listen to him the winds that waft my sighs to thee so well he may sleep and sigh the great Suggester Don Poldo de la Flora if he knew how he came out on the cards this morning hed have something to sigh for a dark man in some perplexity between 2 7s too in prison for Lord knows what he does that I dont know and Im to be slooching around down in the kitchen to get his lordship his breakfast while hes rolled up like a mummy will I indeed did you ever see me running Id just like to see myself at it show them attention and they treat you like dirt I dont care what anybody says itd be much better for the world to be governed by the women in it you wouldnt see women going and killing one another and slaughtering when do you ever see women rolling around drunk like they do or gambling every penny they have and losing it on horses yes because a woman whatever she does she knows where to stop sure they wouldn't be in the world at all only for us they dont know what it is to be a woman and a mother how could they where would they all of them be if they hadnt a mother to look after them what I never had thats why I suppose hes running wild now out at night away from his books and studies and not living at home on account of the usual rowy house I suppose well its a poor case that those that have a fine son like that theyre not satisfied and I none was he not able to make one it wasnt my fault we came together when I was watching the two dogs up in her behind in the middle of the naked street that disheartened me altogether I suppose I oughtnt to have buried him in that woolly jacket I knitted crying as I was but give it to some poor child but I knew well Id never have another our 1st death too it was we were never the same since O Im not going to

[484]

think myself into the glooms about that any more I wonder why he
wouldnt stay the night I felt all the time it was somebody strange he
brought in instead of roving around the city meeting God knows who
nightwalkers and pickpockets his poor mother wouldnt like that if
she was alive ruining himself for life perhaps still its a lovely hour so
silent I used to love coming home after dances the air of the night
they have friends they can talk to weve none either he wants what he
wont get or its some woman ready to stick her knife in you I hate that
in women no wonder they treat us the way they do we are a dreadful
lot of bitches I suppose its all the troubles we have makes us so
snappy Im not like that he could easy have slept in there on the sofa
in the other room I suppose he was as shy as a boy he being so young
hardly 20 of me in the next room hed have heard me on the chamber
arrah what harm… Id have to introduce myself not knowing me from
Adam very funny wouldnt it Im his wife or pretend we were in Spain
with him half awake without a Gods notion where he is dos huevos
estrellados señor Lord the cracked things come into my head
sometimes itd be great fun supposing he stayed with us why not
theres the room upstairs empty and Millys bed in the back room he
could do his writing and studies at the table in there for all the
scribbling he does at it and if he wants to read in bed in the morning
like me as hes making the breakfast for 1 he can make it for 2… I
know what Ill do Ill go about rather gay not too much singing a bit
now and then mi pietà Masetto then Ill start dressing myself to go out
presto non son piú forte Ill put on my best shift and drawers let him
have a good eyeful out of that to make his micky stand for him Ill let
him know if thats what he wanted that his wife is fucked yes and
damn well fucked too up to my neck nearly not by him 5 or 6 times
handrunning theres the mark of his spunk on the clean sheet I
wouldnt bother to even iron it out that ought to satisfy him if you
dont believe me feel my belly unless I made him stand there and put
him into me Ive a mind to tell him every scrap and make him do it in
front of me serve him right its all his own fault if I am an adulteress
as the thing in the gallery said O much about it if thats all the harm
ever we did in this vale of tears God knows its not much doesnt
everybody only they hide it I suppose thats what a woman is
supposed to be there for or He wouldnt have made us the way He did
so attractive to men then if he wants to kiss my bottom Ill drag open
my drawers and bulge it right out in his face as large as life he can
stick his tongue 7 miles up my hole… then Ill suggest about yes O

wait now sonny my turn is coming Ill be quite gay and friendly over it O but I was forgetting this bloody pest of a thing pfooh you wouldn't know which to laugh or cry were such a mixture of plum and apple no Ill have to wear the old things so much the better itll be more pointed hell never know whether he did it nor not there thats good enough for you any old thing at all then Ill wipe him off me just like a business his omission then Ill go out Ill have him eyeing up at the ceiling where is she gone now make him want me… I can get up early Ill go to Lambes there beside Findlaters and get them to send us some flowers to put about the place in case he brings him home tomorrow today I mean no Fridays an unlucky day first I want to do the place up… Id love to have the whole place swimming in roses God of heaven there's nothing like nature the wild mountains then the sea and the waves rushing then the beautiful country with fields of oats and wheat and all kinds of things and all the fine cattle going about that would do your heart good to see rivers and lakes and flowers all sorts of shapes and smells and colours springing up even out of the ditches primroses and violets nature it is as for them saying theres no God I wouldnt give a snap of my two fingers for all their learning why dont they go and create something I often asked him atheists or whatever they call themselves go and wash the cobbles off themselves first then they go howling for the priest and they dying and why why because theyre afraid of hell on account of their bad conscience ah yes I know them well who was the first person in the universe before there was anybody that made it all who ah that they dont know neither do I so there you are they might as well try to stop the sun from rising tomorrow the sun shines for you he said the day we were lying among the rhododendrons on Howth head in the grey tweed suit and his straw hat the day I got him to propose to me yes first I gave him the bit of seedcake out of my mouth and it was leapyear like now yes 16 years ago my God after that long kiss I near lost my breath yes he said I was a flower of the mountain yes so we are flowers all a womans body yes that was one true thing he said in his life and the sun shines for you today yes that was why I liked him because I saw he understood or felt what a woman is and I knew I could always get round him and I gave him all the pleasure I could leading him on till he asked me to say yes and I wouldnt answer first only looked out over the sea and the sky I was thinking of so many things he didnt know… and I thought well as well him as another and then I asked him with my eyes to ask again yes and then he

[486]

asked me would I yes to say yes my mountain flower and first I put my arms around him yes and drew him down to me so he could feel my breasts all perfume yes and his heart was going like mad and yes I said yes I will Yes.

Trieste-Zurich-Paris, 1914-1921

ACKNOWLEDGEMENTS

Michael acknowledges his grandfather for instilling in the family the reading of great books, and for his grandfather's inheritance gift of one of the first U.S. publications of the novel. He resonates with his father's pride for their Irish heritage and his companionship on two trips to Ireland. He appreciates the encouragement of Matthew Spangler, Paul McNamara, Ken Kelly, Tony Becker, Jeff Paul and our Zen Meditation Sangha. Moreover, this editor was motivated by those persons who, daunted to read Joyce's tome, welcomed an abbreviated version to take up. Ms. Patricia Nguyen deserves special recognition as Patricia hosted her professor at All Hollows College and helped guide this Joyce celebrant around Dublin town for Bloomsday week 2013. Advice, publishing and technical assistance was provided extensively by high school classmates reunited by Zoom during Covid, friends Gary Eberle and Ron Nicholas. Spouse Rita is commended for her patience through this long process. Finally, O'Flaherty's Irish Pub, San Jose, also merits mention! Sláinte, all!

Michael James Fallon
Santa Clara CA 95051
michael.fallon@sjsu.edu